BISON
BOOKS

DG885771

Swords from the East

Harold Lamb

Edited by Howard Andrew Jones

Introduction by James Enge

UNIVERSITY OF NEBRASKA PRESS
LINCOLN AND LONDON

∞

Library of Congress Cataloging-in-Publication Data
Lamb, Harold, 1892–1962.
Swords from the east / Harold Lamb;
edited by Howard Andrew Jones;
introduction by James Enge.
p. cm.
Includes bibliographical references.
ISBN 978-0-8032-1949-6 (pbk.: alk. paper)
I. Jones, Howard A. II. Title.
PS3523.A4235S944 2009
813'.52—dc22
2009039689

Set in Trump Mediaeval by Kim Essman.
Designed by Ray Boeche.

Contents

Foreword

Harold Lamb wrote that he'd found something "gorgeous and new" when he discovered chronicles of Asian history in the libraries of Columbia University. He remained fascinated with the East thereafter, which is evident from his first stories of western adventurers in Asia to the last book published before his death in 1962, *Babur the Tiger*. All of his popular fiction is anchored in Asia, whether it be the cycle of Khlit the Cossack, descended from the Tatar hero Kaidu, or Durandal's Sir Hugh of Taranto, who travels into Asia during the conquests of Genghis Khan, or even the adventures of Genghis Khan himself, as related in "The Three Palladins" in this volume.

Lamb tried his hand at contemporary fiction and was published in a number of top-flight magazines; these stories, though, do not hold up very well today. The characters, even when adventuring in Lamb's favorite stomping grounds, come across as wooden and dated.* In this age, both the 1920s and the 1120s are remote to us. It might seem odd that a story set in one time can sound old-fashioned and quaint while one set in the other does not, especially when they were crafted by the same writer, but looking over the whole of Lamb's work, one reaches an inescapable conclusion: it is when Lamb looked backward that his prose sprang to life. His historical characters are far better realized than his modern heroes. Passion for his subject was writ large in every historical story. Lamb loved what he was writing, and it shows, most especially in the tales crafted for *Adventure* magazine, where editor Arthur Sullivan Hoffman gave him free rein to write what he wished. Even today, some eighty or ninety years

*The best of Lamb's contemporary fiction is probably his short novel *Marching Sands*, which has been reprinted several times.

after their creation, no matter changed literary trends and conventions, these stories beguile with the siren song of adventure. Lamb's polished and surprisingly modern sense of plotting and pacing is in full evidence in every story in this volume.

Lamb's first real writing success came from sending characters into Asia to adventure, but before too long he tried his hand at writing of adventurers who *were* Asian. (Khlit, of course, is of Asian descent, but he would have been more "western" and familiar to his first readers than those characters he encounters through his wanderings.) Lamb tried his hand at several shorter tales with Mongolian protagonists, including "The Wolf-Chaser," a story of a last stand in Mongolia that proved so inspiring to a young Robert E. Howard that Howard outlined it and took a crack at drafting a version of the story himself.*

Lamb then tackled a novel of a Mongol tribe's perilous migration east, with a westerner as one of the main—though not the only—protagonists. Before too much longer, though, he drafted what he might always have longed to do, given his abiding fascination with Genghis Khan. The result was "The Three Palladins," which explores the early days of Temujin through the eyes of his confidant, a Cathayan prince. On first reading it as a younger man, I was for some reason disappointed that it had nothing to do with Khlit the Cossack, and I failed to perceive its worth. Like almost all of Lamb's *Adventure*-era fiction, it is swashbuckling fare seasoned with exotic locale. There is tension and duplicitous scheming on every hand. The author seems to have had almost as much fun with the characters as the reader, for some of them turn up in other stories—the mighty Subotai, and the clever minstrel Chepe Noyon in the Durandal cycle and "The Making of the Morning Star," which is included in *Swords from the West* (Bison Books, 2009). And Genghis Khan, of course, as a shaper of events and mythic figure, haunts much of Lamb's fiction, affecting even the Khlit cycle set hundreds of years later, most famously in one of the best of all the Khlit the Cossack stories, "The Mighty Manslayer," which appears in *Wolf of the Steppes* (Bison Books, 2006).

Lamb was fortunate to have become established as a writer of both screenplays and history books by the time the Great Depression hit. *Adventure*, his mainstay, was no longer published as frequently or capable of

*His outline and the aborted draft of the story can be found in *Lord of Samarcand and Other Adventure Tales of the Old Orient* (Bison Books, 2005).

paying as well. Lamb's fiction began to be printed in the slicks—*Collier's* and, a little later, the *Saturday Evening Post* (among a handful of similar magazines)—where he still wrote short historicals as well as contemporary pieces. Among the later work included in this volume is a deft little mystery adventure titled "Sleeping Lion," with none other than Marco Polo as one of the primary characters, the other being a Tatar serving girl. Unfortunately, *Collier's* printed this story without its middle third. What remains is included. Sadly, the original is long since lost.

There also exist two curious pieces from Lamb's *Adventure* days: "The Book of the Tiger: The Warrior" and "The Book of the Tiger: The Emperor." Together they tell the story of Babur, the Tiger, first Moghul emperor, mostly transcribed and condensed from Babur's fascinating autobiography. They presage Lamb's later books like *Alexander the Great* and *Theodora and the Emperor,* where the narrative is a history that occasionally drifts into fiction. Those volumes have never been among my favorites (*Hannibal,* both volumes of *The Crusades,* and *March of the Barbarians* top my list), but I'm fond of these Babur pieces even if they sometimes sound more like summaries than fully realized stories. Lamb captured the tone of a truthful and engaging historical character. The amount of luck (and the stupidity of his fellow man) involved in Babur's survival through adversity is difficult to believe. Were I to invent such a story and submit it to a publisher, it would be dismissed out of hand as preposterous, but this one seems to be true! Lamb later turned to other Asian characters as protagonists and narrators, and you can find many of those tales in *Swords from the Desert* (Bison Books, 2009).

Much of Lamb's fiction output revolved around conflicts generated by the colliding motivations of his characters and their cultures. Through most of the stories in this book, the physical environment takes on an antagonistic role as well, for the people in these tales of high Asia must contend with steep mountain passes, blinding snows, searing deserts, and ice-choked rivers. While justice may win out or protagonist triumph, the victories seem transitory, to be celebrated briefly before the candles are extinguished and the central characters shuffle off the stage. Kings, kingdoms, and heroes fall and fade to memory; nothing is eternal but the uncaring miles of mountain and steppe and the shifting northern lights that shine above them.

That life is sweet and Lady Death ever eager for the embrace of heroes is a theme that can be found in Lamb's fiction from the very beginning, but readers may note that all of these tales—even the relatively light "Azadi's Jest"—are infused with a certain bleakness more marked than usual. We can exult in the adventure, but we are reminded to savor our sand castles before time and tide sweep them away.

If you enjoy these stories of Mongolia, you have not far to look for more of Lamb's writing on the subject; his history and biography books are still held in many public libraries. Harold Lamb's first book, a biography of Genghis Khan, has fared better than any of his other works, remaining in print since 1927. Lamb himself thought this was peculiar because he believed his later books were better written. While *Genghis Khan* is a good read, I tend to agree: *Tamerlane* is a strong book, and *March of the Barbarians* is riveting. The latter title does little to reveal the quality within, for *March* is an in-depth history of the complex inner workings of the Mongol empire, written when Lamb was more experienced and had the financial wherewithal—as well as the clout with publishers—to take the time for extensive research. His Genghis Khan proposal had been approved by the publisher only so long as he could write the book in two weeks, a demanding request even for someone intimately familiar with the subject matter. *March of the Barbarians* covers the same material as *Genghis Khan* in richer detail, and then goes on to describe the great Khan's successors with the same care. Frederick Lamb, Harold's son, named it the favorite of all his father's writing.

Lamb always had the gift of taking facts and infusing them with fascinating vitality, be it in fiction or history or a combination thereof. It is my privilege now to step aside so that you can acquaint yourselves with some of the most extraordinary people and events he ever brought to life on the printed page.

Enjoy!

Acknowledgments

I would like to thank Bill Prather of the Thacher School for his continued support. This volume would not have been possible without the aid of Bruce Nordstrom, who long ago provided Lamb's *Collier's* texts and other research notes, and Alfred Lybeck, who provided "Camp-Fire" letters and additional information. I am grateful to Kevin Cook, who loaned me the *Adventure* text of "The Three Palladins"; to Sara E. F. Edwards for manuscript assistance; and to Simon Elliott of the Charles E. Young Research Library, Department of Special Collections at UCLA, who searched through the library's Harold Lamb collection for the original manuscript of "Sleeping Lion," unfortunately without success. The staff at Bison Books was, as always, a pleasure to work with, and I must give a special tip of the hat to Sabrina Stellrecht, Alicia Christensen, Jonathan Lawrence, and Alison Rold for their excellent work. I would also like to express my appreciation for the advice of Victor Dreger, Jan van Heinegen, and James Pfundstein, gentlemen and scholars. Lastly, I wish again to thank my father, the late Victor Jones, who helped me locate various *Adventure* magazines, and Dr. John Drury Clark, whose lovingly preserved collection of Lamb stories is the chief source of 75 percent of my *Adventure* manuscripts.

Introduction

JAMES ENGE

It was all Harold Lamb's fault. I had just asked my mother another one of Those Questions. Most questions we asked her got answers, but Those Questions got very serious, lengthy discussion-type answers. My first one of Those Questions, I distinctly remember, was when I asked my mother the meaning of a word which, as far as I was concerned, was just something that rhymed with "truck." The answer turned out to be quite complex, linguistically and biologically. The current question got almost as unexpected and serious an answer: I had asked my mother if "Mongol" meant the same thing as "Mongoloid."

The question was important to me, because I had been reading Harold Lamb's *Genghis Khan: Emperor of All Men* and, as far as I was concerned, the Mongols were pretty damn cool, and it was also fairly clear what they were: a confederation of tribes from the Gobi Desert who swept out under the leadership of Genghis Khan to establish the greatest empire in the history of the world. (It was like *Dune*, except real. Also, they weren't religious fanatics or spice addicts.) But I had been reading some other stuff (Heinlein's *Sixth Column*, I think) where "Mongoloid" was used as a racial designation, along with "Caucasoid" and "Negroid" and other ugly but impressive-sounding words. (Everything becomes more manageable if you slap the "-oid" suffix on it. A complex human individual turns out to be merely one sample of a type of humanoid, and even a hemorrhage is demoted to a mere hemorrhoid. Apply the right medicine to any "-oid" and it will shrink until you hardly notice it anymore.) And I had been hearing "Mongoloid" used as a slur on the school playground. I consulted a map and found the Caucasus Mountains and, as it happened, an Outer Mongolia but no Inner Mongolia, which struck me as very suspicious, very suspicious indeed. The Internet not having been invented yet (it was *that* long ago), I finally decided to ask Mom.

My mother, it seems to me now, was not a naturally patient woman, and the patience she was born with had lots of work to do, but she took a lot of trouble answering Those Questions from any of her kids. This was not one of her more satisfying answers, but that wasn't her fault: it's what she had to work with. By the end of it I had a lot of information about Down syndrome and abusive terms that one could but *should not* use in a variety of social environments, but the big (if unspoken) takeaway was how stupid people could be about race (a lesson worth learning early and often, unfortunately).

Never mind. Certain things became clear: people with Down syndrome were people with Down syndrome. People who used "Mongoloid" as a slur in any context were losers. And Genghis Khan was the emperor of all men.

I soon tracked down Lamb's historical narrative of the Mongol conquests, *March of the Barbarians*, and his last book, *Babur the Tiger* (based on Babur's autobiography, which Lamb also adapted for two stories that appear in this volume), and I even branched out to his other biographies, like *Hannibal* (although nowadays I think the good guys won that particular world war) and his two-volume history of the Crusades. One book I was especially eager to lay my hands on was his biography of Tamerlane "the Iron Limper." I never did find it (though I did file away that image of a tough guy who limped; seemed like it might be useful one day). Looking for Lamb's *Tamerlane*, I found Marlowe's *Tamburlaine the Great*, and whole new worlds opened up.

New worlds: that is probably Lamb's greatest gift to most people who discover him. There are some who have the history of the Moghuls in India or the migration of the Torgut Mongols at their fingertips: they won't have this experience from Lamb. For the rest of us, and I think it's most of us, no matter what our heritage, Lamb takes us places that are new, even though they have always been there—places that are richly imagined, even though they are real.

As a westerner writing about Asia, Lamb is often concerned about the clash between East and West, but his fiction is not polluted by the Yellow Peril hysteria so common in his generation (and later ones). As has often been observed, Fu Manchu and his villainous ilk can only exist as aliens in someone else's culture; in these stories, the westerners (if any) are the outsiders. Western characters play the villain as often as the hero, and in the longest story in this book there are no European characters at all. Lamb is confronting Genghis Khan, Subotai Bahadur, Ye Liu Chutsai, and others on their own ground, and he does so by taking the radical position that they are human beings—of various cultures, to be sure, but no more or less inherently inscrutable than someone from Brooklyn or Chicago. In fact, Lamb's stories are unusually free from racism of any sort, so that it is startling to read in one a casual reference to "thieving blacks." (Even that might be the attitude of the viewpoint character rather than the narrator.)

Buddhists are not so lucky: Buddhism and the allied (or at least entangled) tradition of Bon are normally painted in hostile colors in Lamb's fiction. I don't mean to minimize this; I would just say that this represents a historical attitude that Lamb probably found in his sources, rather than importing it there. Howard Jones, the editor to whose tireless labor we owe these splendid new editions of Lamb's fiction, has wisely decided against meddling with Lamb's text for political reasons or any other reason. Even the rather Victorian dashes that mask the characters' mild and infrequent profanity survive in these editions unaltered.

In these adventures in a patriarchal world, most of the characters are men, but when women appear, they are not mere plot-coupons or MacGuffins. Nadesha (from "The Road of the Giants"), in particular, is a dashing, heroic figure, and the bitter Cherla ("The House of the Strongest") and the tragic Aina ("The Net") are, in their ways, equally memorable. Lamb often draws his characters in broad strokes, but they are never mere caricatures, and if he is intent on portraying historical realities that test the limits of our sympathy, he never forgets to make his characters sympathetic.

Lamb was also a gifted stylist of plain, eloquent English. That may be surprising: most of the stories in this volume originally appeared in a pulp magazine, not a medium famous for its literary sophistication. But *Adventure* was an unusual pulp, deliberately pitched at readers looking for more intelligent fare. (The young Sinclair Lewis worked there as an editor.) And, even when he was being paid by the word, Lamb just wasn't the type to lard his sentences with excess verbiage. He almost invariably (as Twain puts it) picks "the right word, not its second cousin."

I like, for instance, the ambiguous threat the hero makes to the opposing general in "The Wolf-Chaser": "'Tell Galdan Khan what you have seen,' smiled Hugo. 'Say that he will never see his mirzas again. On the first clear night I will come into his lines and speak with him.'" His characters don't all sound the same, but he likes to craft ones that speak with a certain snap. An exchange from "Sleeping Lion" (a tale of Marco Polo at the court off Kublai Khan):

> *"Can you make me invisible so that I may pass through gates unseen?"*
>
> *"I can make a mountain invisible," he croaked.*
>
> *"How?"*
>
> *"By looking the other way," he snarled.*

Lamb doesn't bother to strain for unusual verbal effects. He picks subjects worth talking about, then describes with searing directness what his mind's eye sees. Here are the Torguts on the move (from "The Road of the Giants"): "With steady eyes he was looking into a sunrise that, seen through the smoke, was the hue of blood. This ruddy glow tinged the brown faces that passed the Khan; it dyed red the tossing horns of the cattle. Two hundred thousand humans had burned their homes and were mustering for a march in the dead of winter over one of the most barren regions of the earth."

Lamb writes a good deal about war, and he doesn't write about it, as someone once said of Vergil, "with eyes averted." These are ripping yarns in the finest tradition. Out of many examples, here's part of a scene from "The Three Palladins" where the Mongols are fighting over the ruins of their leader's tent. It was attacked during the night by assassins, shot full of arrows, and finally set afire. Temujin (later Genghis Khan) is feared dead, but then "the sand [was] stirring at the edge of Temujin's crumpled and blazing tent. The sand heaved and fell aside as if an enormous mole were rising to the surface, but instead of a mole a blackened face was revealed by the glow of the fire. Presently the body of a man followed the face, and Temujin climbed out of the hole he had dug in the loose sand while the arrows slashed through his yurt." He tunneled his way out of the assassination scene and lived to make his would-be assassins sorry that they'd missed. All in a day's work—if you're Genghis Khan.

But Lamb, in his interest in heroism, doesn't shy away from war's essential ugliness. Here (from "The Wolf-Chaser") a French nobleman takes a stroll through a Tatar village as it is being sacked by its enemies: "Captives were being roped together by the necks. Children were lifted on lances, to guttural shouts. Almost within reach, Hugo saw a Tatar's eyes torn out by a soldier's fingers." It's all quite repellent, and Hugo is repelled—but, with equal realism, he does not get involved. It simply did not occur to Hugo to draw his sword in a quarrel between peasants and common soldiers. "'*Peste!* What is it to me?' he grumbled."

Hugo will eventually become involved, and thereby hangs the rest of the tale, which I won't spoil for you. But this is a good example of Lamb's historical imagination at work. Hugo is all wrong by our standards, and Lamb doesn't attempt to justify him. But Hugo's attitude makes perfect sense in the world through which he moves.

Lamb's greatest talent (as a biographer, popular historian, or writer of fiction) is sheer storytelling. Whether his hero is a reindeer herder trying to keep his herd safe from interlopers who view the animals as mere commodities ("The Gate in the Sky"), or a French adventurer, looking for his missionary brother, who fights in a Mongolian Thermopylae ("The Wolf-Chaser"), or a Chinese nobleman who flees a murderous intrigue to become an adviser and court-champion to the young Genghis Khan ("The Three Palladins"), or a Siberian girl whose encounter with outsiders has tragic consequences for both sides ("The Net"), Lamb tells a tale where things happen that have an emotional impact, and where a surprise often lurks on the story's last page.

These pieces of historical fiction have a certain importance for literary history. Lamb's fiction, almost forgotten now, was an enormous influence over later writers of popular fiction such as Robert E. Howard, Norvell Page, and Harry Harrison, to name just three.

But that's not the reason to read these stories now, or at least it's not the most important reason. They are worth reading because they are *worth reading*: fascinating stories of heroism from a skilled storyteller who breathed life into his characters and the world they inhabit.

It's been a long generation since I discovered Lamb. My mother has since passed through the gate in the sky, and now, instead of asking Those Questions, I am occasionally tasked with answering them. I'm no longer sure that Genghis Khan is the emperor of all men, or that empires are really such great things after all. But I'm more sure than ever that Harold Lamb is one of the great storytellers in the eternal republic of letters. For proof, I offer the book you hold in your hands.

The Gate in the Sky

The long night of winter had begun. Snow flurries swept the heights of the Syansk Range that separates Mongolia from Siberia proper. In that year early in the eighteenth century under the heights a great quiet had fallen.

Ice formed along the banks of the streams. Another week and the passes into the northern plain, with its scattered settlements, would be closed. The few traders who still lingered in the Syansk were hurrying down to the towns, several hundred miles away.

More and more the play of the northern lights obscured the brightness of *Upener*, the polar star.

As he had done for a score of years, Maak, the Buriat reindeer keeper, led his herd from the upland pastures down to the valleys where the streams were still open and the larches had a thin garment of foliage.

His beasts were sleek from a season's cropping of lichen and Pamir grass. Their coats were growing heavier against the frost that was sending to cover all animal life on the heights. Two hundred or more, they followed obediently the white reindeer that was Maak's mount.

Maak's broad face was raised to the sky of evenings. His keen, black eyes followed the flicker of elusive lights above and behind the mountain summits. A gate, he knew, was ready to open in the sky, and through it the spirits—the *tengeri*—would look down on the earth.

This happened only occasionally, when the magic lights were very bright in the autumn—as now. For those who saw the open gate in the sky it was an omen. An omen of death or great achievement—one would not know which until time brought fulfillment.

"Someday the gate in the sky will open," he repeated to himself quietly as he watched of nights.

It might well mean death when he would be drawn up by the *Qoren Vairgin*, the king-spirit of the reindeer. Then he would make brave sport among the flaming lights and perhaps look forth in his turn from the spirit gate upon the whole world—upon the Mongolian plain whence the Chinese merchants sometimes came to barter for the soft horns of a young reindeer, to the towns from which the Russian colonist traders arrived every other year or so. Maak knew of no world other than this.

At times he wondered whether the gate would ever open.

Maak had seen no living being but his clansmen, the Buriats—and had seen them only in the spring and fall changes of pasture. He belonged to the wandering ones of the clan, the reindeer keepers. He had been told that the traders were superior fellows indeed.

Never did Maak leave his reindeer. The herd furnished him milk and fat. His long coat, soft boots, and cap were of their skins. His bowstring was reindeer gut; the skinning knife he inherited from his father, who had been a herder.

No one had ever seen Maak kill one of his herd. When he wanted meat he shot down other game with his bow. He was as lean as the reindeer—with long, supple muscles that hid his strength. His slant eyes were mild.

This shyness of Maak came from long isolation. Barely did he remember the chants of a dead grandfather—chants of Mongol warriors who had taught the meaning of fear to their enemies.

Traders who learned that Maak—like the other wandering ones—did not kill his reindeer or sell them—the traders laughed, saying that he was mad, a *khada-ulan-obokhod*, an old man of the mountain—a spiritless coward.

"He has turned into a deer," they said, "with only enough wit to run away. Pah. He would not fight even for his own life!"

Nevertheless the other Buriats were superstitious about *khada-ulan-obokhod* and did not molest them.

As they came to a bend in the upper valley, Maak's mount, an old white buck, halted with lifted muzzle. The herd, following the example of their leader, stopped and bunched together, eyes and ears pointed in the same direction.

They were in sight of a large stream that gave into the Irkut. Beside the river were three canvas tents and a knot of packhorses. Smoke rose into the chill evening air. Three men came from the fire and looked at them.

Maak would have turned when one of the travelers, a stocky, bearded man in a fine mink coat, waved to him.

Now Maak had been seeking that very spot to camp for the night. When the men invited him by gestures to join them he hesitated. Finally he edged the reindeer up to the tents and dismounted.

They were traders; the bearded man a Siberian colonist; a handsome, brisk young fellow was Orani, a Yakut half-breed; the third a silent Mongol.

"Greetings, *nim tungit*—tent companion," Orani, who acted as interpreter, proclaimed.

Maak nodded and accepted their hospitality shyly. His herd he let to graze on the moss in a birch grove, out of sight of the tents.

They gave him a luxurious brick of tea, and all four quaffed numberless bowls of the potent liquid as they sat around the fire.

"We have no meat, —— take the luck!" explained Orani. "Game is bewitched around here and our bullets all miss. Sell us one of your fine, plump beasts and we'll have a feast; eh, Maak?"

The reindeer keeper shook his head. The men exchanged glances, and the Siberian, Petrovan, looked angry.

The traders had had ill luck with more than game for the pot. The fur they were taking back from the Syansk was a poor lot—some fair mink, but only a few ermine and no black foxes at all. The Mongol hunters were harder than ever to deal with. Petrovan considered it a personal grievance. Until now his summer trading had been good.

"The gentleman," informed Orani, "will give you a powder-flask and a handful of bullets for a brace of deer. Come, Maak; strike a bargain, man!"

Absently the Buriat shook his head. He had no musket, and he was admiring the businesslike hunting-piece of the trader and Orani's silver-mounted flintlock. He offered them some of his reindeer milk; they declined with a grimace, but the ever-hungry Mongol emptied all portions down his gullet.

Orani was surprised that Maak had no gun. How did he deal with bear and moose?

"They do not trouble me," said Maak after he had thought it over.

He was slow to think things out.

"Well, you're a fine fellow all right," agreed the half-breed. "Look here, we're on the trail to the Irkut, going to Irkutsk. Come along with your herd; sell them in Irkutsk, and I'll wager they fetch a good price. Then you'll be rich like this gentleman here, and have tobacco enough to smoke every minute until you die, and a horse and sleigh."

He gulped the heavy smoke of his pipe down into his lungs, and glanced keenly at the Buriat.

The creases in Maak's leathern face changed as he rubbed some more tobacco into the bowl of his pipe. His black eyes twinkled. Maak had come as near as possible to a smile.

"No," he grunted. "What would I do without *them*?"

He pointed at the white buck that lingered near his tent.

When the Siberian retired to the big tent with a rug on the earth and a cot and lantern, Maak examined it from the opening with great appreciation. He was the last to retire to shelter from the cold.

The evening had been an eventful one. Maak would have enough to think about all winter. He had been entertained by a trader.

It was long after Maak had disappeared that Orani came out of his tent and moved silently off into the dark. An hour later the half-breed returned, and sought his blankets.

The camp by the stream was motionless except for the anxious movements of a big reindeer and the illusion of motion produced by the play of the northern fires in the sky.

The next morning they had no glimpse of *Qoren Vairgin*, the king of the spirit world who drives the sun across the sky behind flying white reindeer. Heavy clouds, settling athwart the snow peaks of the Syansk, hid the sun.

"Snow is coming in the valley," muttered the Mongol servant to Orani.

Thoughtfully the half-breed nodded but made no move to rise from his blankets by the fire.

The reindeer keeper also had noted the signs in the sky. He lingered for awhile hoping to see the departure of the trader; he even ventured to offer Petrovan some tobacco.

"Pah!" the trader grunted to Orani. "I would rather smoke dried horse-droppings. These mountain men are mongrels."

Orani's slant eyes narrowed and his hand went instinctively to his knife. When Petrovan had traded or gambled in a bad streak of luck, the Siberian was accustomed to slur Orani's mixed parentage.

"They are no better, excellency," he retorted, "than the overfed hounds that lie in the ditches of Irkutsk."

More than once Petrovan had been carried out of these same ditches when drunk.

Orani did not touch his knife, for he saw the other's eyes on him sidewise and knew that Petrovan's heavy pistol was in his belt. The Siberian shrugged and fell to watching Maak, who had mounted the white buck and was mustering his herd.

Two beasts were missing—young bucks that often strayed. Maak was anxious to work down into the larch and beech forests before the snow came, and he set out in search of the two reindeer.

He cast up the mountainside to the edge of the snow line without finding reindeer or tracks. Then he circled down, looking into the gullies where moss beds might have tempted his pets. Maak knew his charges as a shepherd knows his sheep. Reindeer were in fact very much like sheep.

When he had searched vainly for two hours, Maak headed back to camp expecting that the missing animals would have returned to the herd. Glancing into a ravine giving into the river, he stiffened in his saddle.

Below him lay the young reindeer, their throats cut. Maak bent over them and saw that they had been dead for many hours. He looked for the place where steaks might have been cut from the haunches. A puzzled glare came into his black eyes.

His first thought had been that the Mongol servant or Orani had butchered the half-tame animals, to get the meat he had refused to sell. But no meat had been taken from the carcasses. Only the throats had been cut.

Suddenly Maak grunted and climbed into the small saddle on the shoulders of the stalwart white buck. He raced the short distance into camp, and found that there was no longer a camp. Even his skin tent had been kicked down and thrown on the fire.

Men, horses, and reindeer herd had disappeared. Maak was a figure turned to stone. He was thinking out the thing slowly. Someone had killed his two animals—someone who knew that he would search for them, perhaps for hours, and leave the herd unwatched.

He trotted around the ashes of the fire, found the trail that led north along the stream. The ground was frozen, but here and there patches of fern and bracken told him what he wanted to know. His herd had been driven off, bunched, followed by horses.

Petrovan had taken his reindeer.

The thought stung Maak into action. The vacant stare hardened in his eyes, and his hands clenched. With worried, anxious movements he urged the white reindeer after the herd. He was angry, puzzled.

Why had the trader tried to steal his herd? The Siberian had more than an hour's start, yet Maak knew that he would be up with the fugitives before noon, so swiftly did his white beast eat up distance. Then, of course, Petrovan must give him back his reindeer. What else could be done?

Three hours later, rounding a turn in the ravine, Maak heard the *whang* of gun in his face and the shrill flight of a bullet close overhead.

He did not stop. A second report, and dirt flew up under the nose of the white buck. Then Maak knew that this was no strange jest of the gentleman's—no attempt to beguile him to the Siberian towns with his herd. He, Maak, had been robbed of the herd that had been his father's and his grandfather's. If he tried to follow the thieves they would kill him as speedily as they had butchered the two young deer.

With a wild cry the Buriat turned his steed aside and scrambled headlong away up the mountain slope, pursued by shots from Petrovan's gun and a shout of laughter from where Orani hid behind the rocks.

Maak passed from sight swiftly, for the heavy flakes of snow began to screen the mountain from the river and to cover all traces of the vanished herd.

Only one thing troubled Orani; they had let Maak know, before they decided on the rape of the herd, that they were headed for Irkutsk.

"Do you think the old man of the mountain would sneak after us to the settlement?"

Petrovan laughed until his beard bristled at the thought.

"I'd like to see him before a magistrate!"

Orani spat and closed one eye.

"This snow," he muttered. "Two days it has snowed and the —— himself could not smell out hoof marks under a foot of this. But, you see, excellency, we have had to go slowly, driving this accursed herd, and Maak knows that we must have gone through the northern pass to Irkutsk. It would be better if we had not told him."

They both looked back at the ragged rock summits of the Syansk, now coated from river to summit with unbroken white save where the gray network of forest showed.

No living thing was to be seen. Their spirits had mounted since leaving the pass unmolested, although they knew that the heavy snow—just now ceased—had covered their flight.

Petrovan shrugged.

"A rabbit couldn't come near us out here without being seen, you fool! That rascal of a Maak was frightened out of his senses by my shots. He is as timid as that white mongrel stag he rides. Come now; tonight we camp on this bank of the river."

Petrovan was indolent about crossing streams before making camp.

"Tomorrow, by the holy relics, we'll be across the Irkut and on the Siberian steppe."

Somewhat to their surprise, the silent Mongol slave broke into tongue as they rode down to the river—now wide and swift and to be forded only here for many miles. He wanted to cross the water before making camp.

"He is afraid that that dog of a Maak will make magic back yonder on the mountains," leered Orani.

The half-breed swore at the Mongol, and they made camp where they were. Orani rather wished Maak had shown up again. He wanted a shot at the Buriat—Petrovan had made a mess of the shooting.

While Petrovan snored through the night the half-breed sat with his back to a broad tree, watching, by the intermittent flickering in the sky, lest a thin, black figure try to approach the herd over the snow.

No one came. The herd edged about restlessly, seeking moss under the snow. Their flanks were beginning to fall lean. They had been driven hard. All their instincts led them to follow blindly after the one who happened to be the leader.

"Well, they will carry their skins a good way for us yet," remarked Petrovan the next morning as the men were preparing to mount. "We can get a good price for the skins."

"We might have had the white buck," grumbled Orani, "if you had attended to the old man of the mountain that night in his yurt."

He had had his vigil for nothing. Even Orani—who had attended to more than one man who was in his way—would not try to ambush three riders in daylight. And Maak, who had only a bow, could never attempt it now. Moreover, on the snowbound steppe not a rabbit could hide.

"Gr-rh!" hissed Petrovan. "The river will be cold—look at the ice on the bank!"

He was glad that they would not have to swim their horses more than halfway over the ford. Even the shaggy steppe ponies did not relish the embrace of the black Irkut; but the reindeer scarce heeded it as Orani drove the herd down, crashing through the border of thin ice, out on the ford.

Petrovan hitched up his knees and yelled for the Mongol to wait with the pack animals until the reindeer had crossed. He had fortified himself with black tea and brandy, and the blood raced through his stout body, well protected by the mink coat.

"Hey," he shouted to the servant, "take care of those packs or I'll send you to trim the ——'s corns!"

Now that he was leaving the Syansk behind his mood was pleasant. Not that he had been alarmed by the Mongol's remark that Maak was perhaps making magic, sitting on one of the peaks of his hills, talking to his *tengeri*. But Petrovan had feared that even in the snowstorm the reindeer keeper might find his herd and cut it out.

"He is like the reindeer after all," Petrovan thought. "He is a *khada-ulan-obokhod*, an old man of the mountain. Where he is driven, he will go."

Then the Siberian scowled. His horse was swimming, and in spite of his efforts to keep dry, the man was wet to his waist. An icy chill shot through his nerves.

"What in the fiend's name are you about?" he roared at Orani.

The half-breed, almost across the Irkut, had let the reindeer get out of hand. The leaders of the herd had no sooner gained footing on the farther bank than they about-faced, throwing the great mass of animals into confusion.

Orani bellowed and waved his arms to no avail. The herd churned the water, tossing their horns. Then they started back toward the Mongol and Petrovan.

At the same instant, Petrovan stopped cursing and Orani ceased his unavailing shouts. A white buck paced down the farther bank to the river edge, and on the white buck was Maak.

They had heard the reindeer keeper give no command, but the herd went before him as he splashed into the water. They could see that his face had changed. Fasting had thinned it, and it wore a fixed smile.

Orani's musket cracked. He had pulled it forward from his back where it had been slung. His pony, however, was flustered by the reindeer, and the bullet carried wide.

Hastily the half-breed reloaded and settled himself in the saddle. Maak's white buck was swimming toward him steadily, not twenty paces away. Ten paces. Orani held his shot, sure of his aim this time.

Maak was leaning forward, one hand on the antlers of his beast. The water was up to his belly.

"Ho!" he shouted.

His free right hand went back to his shoulder. An arrow flashed in it; the bow held on his other hand twanged, and as the musket of Orani flashed the reindeer keeper threw himself sidewise into the water.

"Hide of the ——!" muttered Petrovan.

He could see the arrow sticking in Orani's throat. The half-breed slumped into the black surface of the Irkut.

"They are both dead," thought the trader. "Well, that is not so bad."

Nevertheless his nerves were running chill, and he turned his horse's head back to the Syansk shore, in the midst of the herd. The reindeer could be brought under control, and Orani's wages were clear profit.

These calculations were ended by a glance over his shoulder. Close behind him the antlers of the white buck were gaining on his tired horse. Beside the black muzzle of the reindeer was Maak's fur-tipped head.

The eyes of the reindeer keeper were fixed on the trader. One hand gripped the antlers of the white buck. His bow had disappeared, rendered useless in any event by submergence in the river.

The teeth of Petrovan clinked together and his jaw quivered as he reached vainly for the musket slung to his back. He was a bulky man, and the sling was tight. Moreover, the pony under him, nearly exhausted, was unsteady.

Petrovan was up to his chest in water. Cold fingers gripped at his groin, and his teeth chattered harder than ever.

"Keep away!" he shrieked. "I swear I will pay—pay for your herd."

Still Maak smiled.

"By the mercy of God," the trader's cry went on, "I swear I will pay twice over. The herd is yours—you hear? Yours!"

It did not occur to him in his fright that Maak did not understand Russian and knew not what he was saying. The other's silence wrought on Petrovan's mounting fear, and he snatched out his pistol from his belt, which was now under water.

Maak's head was only a man's length away, and the trader twisted in his unstable seat to pull the trigger as swiftly as his chilled fingers permitted. The flint clicked harmlessly on the steel that could not ignite the wet powder.

Shifting the man's weight caused the pony to sink and lurch. Petrovan was in the water where sharp hoofs struck and darted on every side. One split his cheek open. The heavy coat, water-soaked, and the musket weighed him down. An icy cold strangled the breath in his throat and numbed his heart.

But the panic that gripped him was from the man who floated after him, the man who walked forward against gunshots, who smiled at the weapon in Petrovan's hand and whom the deadly cold of the river could not hurt.

Petrovan clutched wildly at the antlers of a reindeer swimming by, missed, and was struck again by a hoof. His arms moved weakly now, and his head went under.

Maak, numbed and helpless from submergence in the water, could only cling to the antlers of the white buck. As impotent to aid Petrovan as to harm him, the reindeer keeper was drawn into shoal water and to the shore.

Turning here, he saw Petrovan's bare head an instant at the edge of the shore ice. Then the trader went down. Maak grunted and glanced at the Mongol, his hand moving toward the knife in his belt.

But the erstwhile servant of Petrovan was building a fire on the ashes of the old campfire. The Mongol, who was trembling a little, motioned for Maak to draw near and warm himself. Then he pointed out the pack animals, saying that they were Maak's and that he—the Mongol—had never had aught but peace in his heart toward a *khada-ulan-obokhod*.

Not until Maak had dried himself and eaten a little of the bread and tea of the other did he respond. Then he said that the packs and the ponies could go with the Mongol. Maak did not want them. He had his herd again.

"It was a strong *ijin*—magic spell—that you made on the mountain heights. It bewitched the guns and slew the Russian pig without a blow. Is not that the truth?"

So spoke the Mongol.

"Nay."

Maak shook his head.

"I went to the mountain top to see the camp of the thieves when the snow ceased. Otherwise I could not have seen it."

The Mongol was silent. He was in no mood to contradict his guest. But later among the Buriats he voiced the thought in his mind.

"Maak has looked into the spirit gate. When he sat on the mountain looking for his enemies the gate in the sky was open. He talked with the *Qoren Vairgin* and his spirit ancestors."

And the Mongol spoke truth, though not in the way he thought. The urge to do battle for the herd that was dearer to Maak than his own life was a heritage of forgotten ancestors.

Maak had looked through the gate in the sky.

The Wolf-Chaser

Chapter I
Aruk and the Krit

Bouragut, the great golden eagle, was flying high over the snows and rocks of the Altai Mountains. It was a brisk day in spring, that year 1660—an eventful year for Central Asia. Six feet from wing to wing, the golden eagle soared, alone and calmly bent on his own business.

Rarely indeed was Bouragut to be tamed, to be hooded and shackled into a falcon, used by men to strike down prey. He went as he pleased, for he feared no one. Alone of the feathered folk he would sweep down, to attack with talons and curved beak foxes and even wolves. For that he was called the Wolf-Chaser, and men were proud to have him at their call.

Unlike the vulture, the golden eagle did not wait for others to make his kill. His telescope-like eyes sought for game on the mountain slope, peering down between the cloud-flocks.

He was Bouragut, the Wolf-Chaser; his brown, black-and-white-flecked coat of feathers glistened; his wings, moving lazily, supported him in the vastness where he had his kingdom by right.

Yet it was not a king but an old falconer, a native Mongol and Christian, who had made himself master of Bouragut.

From a thicket by the snow of the Urkhogaitu Pass, Aruk the hunter looked up, recognized the golden eagle, and waved cheerfully. He was a young Tatar with alert eyes. His hut was in the thicket, nearly two miles above the verdant plains of Tartary, to the north, because he was the keeper of the gate. It was his duty to watch for enemies coming over the pass from the south, where was the land of the Kalmuck and the Turk.

Just now he was stringing his bow with fresh gut, in an excellent humor. That morning the omens on the mountainside had been good. A rainbow had come after dawn. Now the eagles were on the wing, and—yes; he cocked his head attentively—his horse neighed.

All at once Aruk was on his feet, his bow strung. Up the pass another horse had neighed. Now the snow in the pass was still unbroken, for no riders had come over the Urkhogaitu—the Gate of the Winds—that winter, owing to the severe cold and the storms that swept the gorge between the rocky peaks of the Altai.

Still, a horse had neighed, and where there was a horse in the Urkhogaitu, there was a rider. In a moment Aruk had mounted his shaggy pony—a Mongol of the plains will not move afoot if he can ride—and had drawn an arrow from the quiver at his saddle-peak.

When he broke from a fringe of firs into the trail Aruk found himself facing a tall horseman. In fact, the horse—the Tatar's eye made swift note of this—was massive and long-bodied—a bay stallion. Aruk had never seen such a beast nor such a rider.

The man who came down the pass had deep-set eyes under shaggy brows, eyes that held a fire of their own. Aruk's bow was lifted, the shaft taut on the string. A slight easing of the fingers would have sent the arrow into the throat of the stranger, above the fur-tipped cloak that covered his long body.

The rider halted when he reached Aruk, but apparently for the purpose of looking out from the pass over the wide plain of Tartary, visible here for the first time from the pass—the plain speckled with brown herds and adorned with the deep blue of lakes, like jewels upon green cloth.

Here and there below him were the tiny lines of animals that barely seemed to move, camels of the caravans that came from China to Muscovy.

Under a close-trimmed mustache the thin lips of the stranger smiled, as if he made out a curious jest in the aspect of the sparkling plain.

He looked at Aruk, and the hunter lowered his bow.

"This one is a falcon," thought Aruk, taking counsel with himself. "May the —— eat me though if he isn't a Frank."*

In the minute just passed Aruk had seen that another Frank, one of the two servants who rode after the leader, had drawn a long pistol and pointed it at him. The hunter had no great respect for Turkish pistols, but it oc-

*A European.

curred to him that the rider in front of him must be a personage of importance if others would fight to see that his path was cleared.

Surely the Frank was a chieftain from the west, from the lands of the Christians that lay beyond Muscovy—so Aruk had heard. Being keeper of the pass, many tales came to his ears.

"Are you a khan—a chief?" he growled.

The tall stranger seemed to find food for mirth in this. He half-smiled, and when he did so his thin, dark face with its down-curving nose was likable.

"I am not a khan," he made response tolerantly, and—to Aruk's surprise—in fair Tatar speech.

Yet his manner was that of one who was accustomed to pass sentries without being challenged, even to having honor shown him.

The stranger was a man in ripe middle age. His heavy boots were of finest morocco and well cleaned. The doublet under the torn cloak was rich blue velvet, and, above all, the hilt of the curiously thin, straight sword was chased with gold.

"Then you are an envoy from God."

"I?" The Frank raised his brows. "No!"

Now the last traveler from the lands of the Franks, the only one who, to Aruk's knowledge, had come over the Urkhogaitu Pass, had been a priest. Those few among the Tatars that had been baptized by the priest called him an envoy from God. The lives of envoys were inviolate. So the priest had not been slain. Something in the face of the tall Frank reminded Aruk of the priest.

"If you are not an envoy or a chief, what is your business in Tartary, Sir Frank?"

"'Tis the Devil's affair, not yours."

Aruk blinked reflectively. The stranger might be speaking the truth. There was an eagle's feather in his hunting-cap. And the lords of Galdan Khan, chief of the Kalmucks, who were deadly enemies of the Tatars, wore such feathers. Moreover, there were Franks among the Turks and Kalmucks of Galdan Khan, mercenaries from Genoa and Greece. This might be one of them, sent as a spy to gather news before a raid on the part of Galdan Khan.

That would be the Devil's business, surely. And that was why Aruk had all but shot down the stranger with his bow.

Yet Aruk, whose life hung on his wit, could read the faces of men. He knew that no spy from the Turks would come to the fair fields of Tartary wearing one of the feathers of Galdan Khan. Nor would he come boldly in daylight with blunt words on his lips and a contempt for the keeper of the pass.

Seeing that the stranger was paying no further attention to him, Aruk drew aside and spoke under his breath to the dog-faced Mongol who was the second servant.

The Mongol, a scowling, sheepskin-clad Dungan, answered Aruk's questions briefly: "He was a paladin of the Franks. But now he has no tribe to follow him. Still, there is gold in his girdle and costly garments in the packs on the horses. I will tell Cheke Noyon, the khan of the Altai, in the city of Kob, to let out his life, so I will have some of the gold—"

"*Hai*," Aruk grunted, "where are you from, dog-face?"

The Mongol's eyes shifted.

"I was a captive of the Christian Poles. This warrior was fighting under their banner. He freed me, telling me to guide him to Tartary. When I first saw him he lived in a castle with servants. Now he has only one dog to follow him. As he makes his bed, he shall lie in it."

Aruk's lined face twisted reflectively.

"You are a jackal, and the skies will spew out your soul when it leaves your body. *Kai*. It is so."

"Nay," the servant grinned surlily, "I will tell my tale to the *baksa*, the witch-doctors, and they will make a sacrifice for me to the spirits. They have no love for the Krits* who come here and say that they can work wonders. It is so."

"What is the name of the Frank?"

"He calls himself Hu-go."

Impatiently the archer moved to the side of the Frank as the latter gathered up his reins.

"An hour's ride, Sir Hu-go, will bring you to the hut of Ostrim, the falconer. He is a Krit, like you, and he will not steal. Beware of the *baksa*, for they will strip you of wealth and skin."

When the three riders had vanished around a bend in the gorge, Aruk settled himself in his saddle to watch the Urkhogaitu. He wanted to be very sure that no Kalmucks were coming, behind the stranger called Hugo.

Although the spot was exposed to the icy winds that made a channel

*Christians.

of the pass, the archer did not move for hours. He watched the golden eagle circling over the network of forest, muttering the while a song that was half a prayer chant:

"Oh, bright falcon,
My own brother,
Thou soarest high.
Thou seest far—"

A slight sound on the mountainside behind him caused Aruk at length to wheel and ride swiftly down in the trail left by the three travelers. Other ears might have caught it, as an echo, but Aruk was sure that a shot had been fired near the hut of Ostrim the falconer.

The reason for his haste was soon apparent. Halfway down the mountainside, where the snow lay only in patches in the gullies and the larch thickets, Aruk came upon a brown-faced maiden no larger than he.

From a clump of larches she was peering, bow in hand, her slant eyes intent on the trail, teeth gleaming between full, red lips.

"*Ohai*, Yulga, daughter of Ostrim," he hailed her, slowing his pony at once in an effort to appear unconcerned, "was the Devil firing off his popgun down here, or did a boulder crash from the cliff? I heard—"

"A splendid protector, you," the girl mocked him, unstringing her bow.

The sight of the hunter had relieved her fear, and now she teased him.

"You come nimbly after the fight is finished, like a jackal instead of a wolf. Our heads might have been hanging to the saddle-peak of the robber band who just passed this way, for all the aid we had from you!"

Aruk grew red and muttered beneath his breath. Under Yulga's laughter the hunter always waxed clumsy as a bear cub. He despaired of ever gathering together the horses and furs necessary to buy Yulga for his wife from the old Ostrim. In like degree he had small hope that the fair child of the falconer would ever look upon him and smile without mockery.

"Perhaps," pursued Yulga, tossing her long black hair back from her eyes, "it is because you are so tiny that you dare sit up yonder to watch the pass. You think that anybody will take you for a ferret, or a fox looking out of its hole—"

"Peace little woodpecker," growled the hunter.

His lined cheeks grew red, for he was acutely conscious of his small figure. Although no man might belie Aruk's boldness, or hope to outdo his ready tongue, he was at a loss for words before Yulga.

"Did the Frank draw sword on Ostrim?" he demanded. "I will let the life out of him for that—"

"Ohai!"

Yulga threw back her head and laughed delightedly.

"The big Frank would swallow you, pony and arrows, and only swear that his gullet tickled him," she cried. "Nay, the robbers were black-boned Mongols with faces like dogs. Here they are—"

They had come to a clearing where a thatched hut stood among the larches. At the door sat a white-haired Tatar, a small *bouragut* perched on his shoulder. On the rooftree of the dwelling a hawk screamed gutturally, flapping its wings so that the bells on its throat jangled.

On the grass of the clearing lay five bodies, distorted and sprawling. Aruk went from one to another, turning them over with his foot.

"Dead," he commented. *"Hai*—here is that dog-brother who led the Frank. Well, the evil spirits from below will be the gainer by a dung-picker. No one need kill a horse for him to ride in the other world. He turned his back to the scimitar, it is clear. Hum—this black beetle was shot in the face."

"By the servant of the Frank."

Ostrim lifted his venerable head and spoke quietly.

"The robbers were four. They sought to pick my poor hearth. As they came up the party of the Frank rode into the clearing. So the black-souled ones scented gold and attacked with their swords, slaying the follower and striking down the old servant who had no more strength than a sick woman."

"And the Frank—he let out the lives of three?"

"With the point of his sword that is long as a spear. He warded their cuts and thrust, once each time. The Frank wiped his sword in the grass and picked up the servant, who was cut in the belly, and rode off, saying that he sought a hut for the sick man and a doctor to close up his wound."

"He is an old buck, that one," admitted Aruk grimly. "He has a horned soul in him. Three dead with three thrusts! I could do no more with my arrows."

"Aye," responded Yulga, hanging up her bow; "you might do that, Aruk, among the suckling litter of boars up in the larches—if the old sow were away."

"By the mane of my sire!"

Aruk bared his white teeth. He caught the girl by the luxuriant coils of hair that hung down her breast. Her round face he held close to his, while his anger melted.

"Ho, I will bind your tongue for you yet. Now bring me *kumiss* to drink, for I ride to Kob with news. This dawn there were beneficent omens in the pass."

Curiously enough, his sudden act quieted the girl, who looked at him long and withdrew for the mare's milk he sought.

Aruk emptied the bowl Yulga brought him at a gulp and wiped his mustaches.

"Ho, it would have been better for the tall warrior if he had left his body and that of his servant in your keeping. The *baksa* will make short work of him in Kobdo. They like not these Krits who come from the other end of the earth and oppose the *baksa*."

"The other Krit was a holy man."

A light came into the mild eyes of the Christian falconer.

"He was an envoy from God. And this one is like him, in face."

"The other had dove's eyes; this one is a falcon," Aruk retorted.

Aruk jumped into his saddle, pretending not to look at Yulga.

"He has a horned soul in him. *Tfu!* The killing of him would be worth seeing."

Chapter II
The Candles on the Altar

The man called Hugo did not ride far with his wounded servant. The shattered body he supported easily in his arms, for he had a strength that matched his great stature. The bay horse bore them both easily.

But the life of the old servant was flickering out. Too many times had Hugo witnessed this passing of nature on the battlefield to mistake it now. So he turned the bay aside from the road into a faint path that ran among the pines.

It brought him to a hut of logs. Hugo carried the servant to the door, kicking it open with his heavy boot. As the windows were only slits in the logs, Hugo could make out the interior of the cabin only vaguely. Noticing that it was empty, he laid the old man on what appeared to be a long bench and covered his limbs with his own cloak.

He went out and presently returned with his leather cap full of fresh, cold water, taken from a nearby stream.

"A sorry bed, Pierre," he observed in French, "and a poor drink to speed you on your way. Now a goblet of good Burgundy—"

"Ah, *monsieur le comte,* no."

Pierre lifted his thin head wistfully.

"If there were but a priest in this wilderness! Or—or a holy spot where the sign of the cross is to be seen."

Hugo Arnauld, Count of Hainault, castellan of Grav, once captain of musketeers at the court of Paris, then colonel in the border armies of the King of France—the man who now called himself Hugo—tugged at the small tuft of his beard and raised one shaggy eyebrow without answering.

Having no good to say of priests or the houses of priests, he held his peace before the dying man. Seldom indeed had he failed to speak boldly to priest or minister, wherefore was he now an exile from France, publicly proclaimed an intriguer.

It did not make much difference to Hugo. It rather amused him that the worthy ministers should now be hoarding the revenues from Hainault which he had squandered so royally when he was young. Doubtless, he reflected, the very intelligent courtesans who were great ladies were drawing their tithes from the ministers.

"Ali, monsieur," breathed Pierre again, his thought returning with the habit of a lifetime to his master, "there will now be no one to—to brush your cloaks, to set out your linen and clean your swords."

Hugo laughed. Facing the gleam of sunlight in the door, now that his hunting-cap was off, gray was to be seen in his black hair. His dark countenance, on which the skin stretched taut over the bones, bore the stamp of pride; his wide mouth under the trim mustache was hard, his long chin stubborn. Women in other days had looked twice at the man who was Count of Hainault.

"One forgets, my Pierre," he remarked gruffly, "that here there exists no need to wear fresh linen or draped cloak over a scabbard. Judging by the manners of the *habitants,* we have arrived at last in the land of Gog and Magog, so inscribed in the charts of the geographers. My faith, the end of the world—Tartaria. I have made good my promise."

Pierre coughed and lay back weakly. *Monsieur le comte* had always been such a stickler for the niceties of dress. Even now, with the habit of a soldier, his coat and shirt were clean. The promises of *monsieur le comte* were always kept.

It had been at Zbaraj. They had wandered, exiled, from France to the court of the Commonwealth of Poland. Here honest Pierre had taken heart again, seeing cathedrals and the retinue of great nobles. But his master had declared that the nobles reeked of fish, and the mead soiled his mouth after the red wine of Burgundy.

So, hearing that the Cossacks and Crimea Tatars were making war on Prince Yeremi, the champion of the Commonwealth, on the southern marches of Poland, they had enlisted under the banner of the prince, had marched for years through blazing forests and over the steppe that was like a sea of grass.

When Zbaraj, the stronghold of the Poles, had been besieged, Hainault, as castellan, had been called the lion of Zbaraj. Pierre remembered that one night when they had been eating horseflesh, the warrior-priest, Yaskolski, had made the round of the walls in the procession of the holy sacrament.

Candles borne before the tall figure of the priest had shone upon gilded monstrance and swinging censers, even while cannonballs plunged through the air overhead.

Pierre had fallen to his knees as the procession passed, and bared his head. Hugo, the doubter, rose from his seat in a trench, but kept his steel cap in place. Yaskolski had looked at him just as a flight of balls drove overhead with the scream of a thousand hawks.

"Those cannoneers should be herding cattle," the burly priest had said to Hugo. "They cannot aim."

Hugo had looked after the calm figure of the priest curiously.

"That priest is a man: He has smelled powder before."

When the war was over Hugo had waxed restless, as always. He had been offered a county by Yeremi himself, with an income sufficient to support a noble of his rank, if he would swear allegiance to the Diet.

"Be under the orders of swine who stink of ale? Pfagh!"

In view of his services, Hugo's insolence was overlooked, but thereafter he drank alone in Zbaraj, until Pierre brought to his chamber the warrior-priest, Yaskolski, who offered the exile the colonelcy of a regiment of armored cavalry.

Hugo had hesitated. He respected Yaskolski. Unfortunately, he had been in his cups.

"So, you would buy a man's sword—the sword of a Hainault. Well, you are another breed from the shaven polls who prune their souls and nourish their bellies with tithes from the peasantry. But—death of my life—I will not do business with you."

Then he smiled.

"Your words, Sir Monk, are an echo of my brother, who is likewise a priest. Doubtless he is still praying for my soul. I have not seen him for a dozen years. They tell me he has gone, probably with others of his cloth, to the particular demesne of the Devil on earth. That is Tartary. Well, I have a whim to go and see how Paul and his brethren relish the Devil's demesne."

These words had been like wine to the faithful Pierre, who had yearned for a sight of the young son of Hugo's brother. Paul had promised Pierre that he and Hugo would yet sleep in the same bed. And Hugo's cynicism hid anxiety for the welfare of the priest, Paul.

Yaskolski raised his great hands.

"What, Sir Count? In Tartary are hordes of savages, and werewolves. That is a land beyond the domain of God. No man would go there, for he would be skinned alive and roasted by pagans."

"Permit me to correct you. I would go there. These burghers and butchers are but tedious society. The domain of the Devil would at least be entertaining."

In these words, Pierre knew, *monsieur le comte* had declined a colonelcy to go to search for his brother. And from place to place as far as the Urkhogaitu they had had news of Paul, for few Franks passed over the caravan route that led from Moscow to Tartary.

Pierre came out of his stupor with a rattle in his throat. He caught his master's hand.

"You will be—alone, *monsieur le comte*," he whispered. "There will be no one to laugh at your jests. If Monsieur Paul, your brother, had not left you—"

"The conversation of Monsieur Paul ceased to interest me years ago. These savages are, at the worst, originals. I learned somewhat of their speech in the Polish campaigns, and more from the dog who led us on our way."

On their way hither! Pierre groaned at memory of the endless steppe where wild Cossack bands attacked them, cutting down the rest of their followers, of the gaunt mountains that led to a desert of sand and clay, and then the snow of the Altai. All at once his eyes started, and he pointed toward the interior of the hut.

"A cross! I see the cross of the Redeemer hanging on yonder wall."

He closed his eyes and clasped his frail hands.

"*Monsieur*—a holy spot to which we—have come."

As his master continued to stare idly at the sunlight in the door at Pierre's back, a sudden anxiety clouded the pallid face of the old servant.

"Look, *monsieur*, and tell me if it is not true—what I see. There, in the shadows, over your shoulder. It is so dark I did not see the blessed cross before. And, look, Monsieur Hugo, there is the figure of the Mother of Christ and the silver candlesticks—on the altar. See—"

The count turned his head casually. He felt that the fever-ridden old man must be the victim of a hallucination.

And actually his eyes, dimmed by the sunlight at which he had been staring, saw nothing in the shadows.

"There is—"

He was on the point of saying there was nothing to be seen. But the cold hand of the dying man was on his wrist. Again Hugo shrugged and made up his mind anew.

"There is the cross indeed," he responded. "And the altar, as you have said."

So Hugo, to his own mind, deceived Pierre. It would make the dying man rest easier.

"Ah, *monsieur*, you have never lied," the servant muttered. "Now I can believe the miracle."

He began a litany under his breath. When his voice ceased his lips moved. Presently Hugo glanced at him, reached over, and closed the eyes of the dead man. He freed his wrist from the grip of the clay that had been Pierre.

After drawing the cloak over the other's face he rose to seek some tool with which to dig a grave. A gleam of metal came from the interior of the cabin, and he strode toward it. He saw for the first time two silver candlesticks standing on a rude altar of wood.

"*Peste!*" was his thought. "Pierre has cast a spell over me, that is all."

Still, a closer inspection disclosed the wooden effigy of Mary beside the skillfully carved cross on which hung the figure of Christ. Untold labor must have gone into the making of it.

Hugo glanced from it to the body of his servant, to the cabin of logs with the thatched roof, made after the fashion of peasants on his old estate. The floor was earth, strewn with pine needles.

He was glad that he had said what he did to the dying man. Probably, he reflected, there were some Christians among the Tatars here. Yes, that old Ostrim, the falconer up the mountain, was one. Well, this was their chapel.

And Aruk had said something about another Frank! That might well have been Paul. What had the Tatar hunter said? An ambassador from God? There was no one here, and the place bore no traces of occupancy.

Suddenly Hugo raised his head and adjusted the pistols in his belt, looked briefly to the priming, and went to the door. He had heard the tread of horses without.

The pine grove was filled with riders. Some wore the skins of beasts over armor. All bore weapons. They sat in their saddles gazing at him curiously. One held the rein of his horse.

"A strange congregation," thought Hugo, freeing his sword in its scabbard, "has come to mass."

For the first time *monsieur le comte* was face to face with inhabitants of the land in a body. His quick eye ran over the throng, noting the ease with which they sat their ponies, their garments of leather and coarse wool and furs, their wild faces and direct eyes. He picked out two that appeared to have authority—a huge, gray rider with but one eye, and a scrawny figure in a long purple tunic and square, yellow cap. Hugo suspected this last was one of the *baksa*, the witch-doctors.

This was the one who spoke first.

"I am Gorun," he chanted, "of the *baksa* of the Altai. I know when a tongue speaks a lie. I can, without touching you, place a serpent in your mouth and summon it forth. If I do not take it out it will sting you to death. Have a care, Frank—" his eyes gleamed shrewdly—"for you have come to the place of the other Frank!"

Hugo did not see fit to answer.

"You are a spy of Galdan Khan," growled Gorun resentfully. "You wear an eagle feather, like his officers."

A smile crossed Hugo's lips. It was like child's play. But, much in this manner, he had heard himself accused by a great cardinal at the court of France. So, he was an exile. What next?

"You came to learn the secrets of the other Frank, who came to spy upon us—and tell them to Galdan Khan," muttered the *baksa*. "I saw omens in the sky this dawn and said that evil was afoot. It is so. You shall have your skin pulled off and the noble khan of the Altai will take your weapons."

For the first time the one-eyed warrior seemed to take an interest in the words of the *baksa*. He glanced with interest at the silver-chased pistols and the long sword with its heavy hilt.

Just then a horse pushed forward into the cleared space between Hugo and the khan. Aruk bent down and touched his forehead.

"Grant me speech," he chattered. "May the fires of Yulgen burn me, but this is no spy. He is a falcon, or I am a toad. He is a chief of warriors."

"Proof!" screamed the witch-doctor.

"It is lying in front of Ostrim's yurt, feeding the crows. Aye, with four thrusts of his sword this falcon slew four robbers."

Aruk bethought him of something else.

"Before his coming the omens in the sky were good."

Hugo was surprised that the little hunter seemed to be speaking in his behalf—much of the meaning he lost, being rudely schooled in the chuckling speech of the Tatars. The exile did not know that a few hours ago he had unwittingly saved the life of Yulga, the beloved of Aruk.

At this Cheke Noyon, khan of the Tatars, raised his head and spoke for the first time.

"To the dogs with this squabbling. If this Frank is a chief of warriors, he is not a spy. Then let him use his sword so that we may see the truth with our own eyes. So, let him fight with all his strength. If he conquers our strongest, then he is a falcon and a chief, and no man of mine will raise hand against him."

Ere the last words had left his lips, Cheke Noyon was off his horse. Stalking toward the French noble, Cheke Noyon drew a heavy, curving sword as wide at the head as two hands joined together.

Hugo, hand on hilt, bit at his mustache. This was something of a Gordian knot. If Hugo should by chance strike down the chief of these barbarians, his own life, he thought, would not be worth a broken ducat.

So he reasoned, not knowing the absolute obedience of these men to the word of a chief, living or dead. Cheke Noyon made no salute with his weapon, or any feint. His first stroke was a swishing lunge that would have cut Hugo to the backbone if that gentleman had not stepped aside.

In so doing he felt the logs of the cabin against his back.

"Horns of Panurge!" he grimaced. "What a *duello*!"

Well tempered as was his long campaign blade, he could not oppose it squarely to one of the Noyon's cuts without having it break in his hands, so great was the bull-like strength of the old warrior and the weight of his huge sword, which seemed to be designed for two hands rather than one.

Nor could Hugo step back any farther. True, a swift thrust and he could pierce the cordlike throat of the other. But the mail on the chieftain's body made impossible any disabling thrust.

Quickly, as the Tatar lifted his weapon for a second cut, Hugo's blade darted forward and its edge touched the Noyon on the brow over his good eye. Blood ran down into the eye, but Cheke Noyon merely grunted with rage and lashed out again, blindly.

Cleverly the tall Frenchman warded the other's weapon, before the blow had gained force. For all his strength the Tatar was a child before the master of a dozen duels who had learned the tricks of fence as a boy. Hugo's skill was the more in that he never seemed perturbed.

His long blade flashed here and there, and the Tatar's rushes were staved off. The blood in his eye maddened Cheke Noyon. He seized the hilt of his sword in both hands, raised it above his helmet with a roar—and stared about him, dazed, with empty hands.

Hugo had stepped forward and engaged his blade in the other's hilt. The curved weapon of the Tatar lay a dozen feet away on the ground.

"Hai!"

A yell burst from the onlookers.

Cheke Noyon peered at his foe. Then, shaking his brow clear of blood, he caught up his weapon, tossed it in air, snatched it in his left hand, and struck as a wolf leaps.

But the gray eyes of the other had followed his movement, and the blow was parried. There came a clash of steel, a grunt from the Tatar, and his sword lay at his feet again.

Gorun spurred his horse forward with a shrill shout, seeing his opportunity.

"Sorcery!" he asserted. "O khan, no living man could do this thing to the greatest of the Tatars. A hand from the spirit world has helped him. He has bewitched your sword. How otherwise could he overcome the lion of Tartary? Let him die!"

Hugo stiffened, realizing the danger that lay in the appeal of the wily *baksa* to the vanity of the old chief. By agreeing with Gorun, the khan could wipe out the stigma of his defeat in the eyes of his followers.

Cheke Noyon puffed out his cheeks, and his bleared eye flamed.

"Dogs!" he bellowed. "Is my word naught but smoke? You heard my pledge. This khan goes free."

He glared at Gorun.

"Liar and toad. That was no witchery. It was the blow of a man who can use a sword."

As the chief mounted, Hugo stepped forward, drawing the Turkish pistols from his belt. He held them out in the palm of his hand to the khan.

"A gift," he said, "to a brave man. In a battle you could strike down four to my one. I know, for I have seen the Cossack fight, and the Ottoman, the janissary, and the Russian hussar."

With a nod the khan took the weapons, looked at them, pleased, and stared at the stranger. He observed the dark face of the Frank, the keen eyes, and the long, muscular arms.

"By the mane of my sire, I will take you to serve under me. You are no nursling in war. Is it done?"

Hugo shook his head with a laugh. To serve under such as that!

The broad face of Cheke Noyon grew black with anger.

"Go your way, Frank, in peace," he growled, "but keep out of my sight. You have made me angry."

Hugo watched the riders trot out of the grove.

"*Canaille*—dogs," he thought. "Cerberus, it seems, has left offspring on the world. Ah, well, the old chief has good stuff in him."

He looked around.

"Ho. Aruk, you are still here. Tell me, where lives the other Frank who came before me?"

Aruk wiggled his mustache and pointed to the chapel.

"'Tis a queer world," Hugo ruminated, leaning on his sword and looking at the wide vista of the mountain slope that already cast its shadow on the grove. "Here in the place of the giants—or dwarfs—ruled by a bloodlusting Oedipus—why, he must have been a Mongol, a misanthrope, or a madman to come here. Paul—would he have come here?"

To Aruk he added—

"Did the Frank wear a long, black robe, and have a shaven poll?"

"Aye, my falcon! He was an envoy from God."

"His name?"

"Paul, it was," said the hunter carelessly, "and something else I cannot remember."

"Paul!"

Hugo lifted his head.

"Paul—of Hainault. Of Grav?"

Aruk rubbed his chin and yawned.

"Perhaps. How do I know? Yulga said it is written in the book of the Frank, under the altar."

Hugo disappeared into the chapel. Feeling in the darkness under the rude altar, his hand came upon crisp parchment. Drawing the sheaf from its resting-place, he shook off the dust and opened the goatskin cover.

On the parchment fly-leaf was the seal of a Carmelite and the name, neatly written in Latin—

Brother Paul of Hainault.

Well did Hugo know that writing.

Paul, who had spent his youth shut up with books of the Latins and Greeks; who had pored over the journals of the Fras Rubruquis, Carpini, and the Nestorians who carried the torch of Christianity into Asia six hundred years before. He had come hither alone.

While Hugo had become notorious among the gallants of the court, Paul had given his life to priesthood. Paul had never been as strong as his brother, but he had the great stubbornness of the Hainaults. They had quarreled. Hugo remembered how the pale cheeks of his brother had flushed.

"So," Hugo had said bitterly, "you go the way of the coward to pray for your soul. I go the way of the damned. The world is wide; one road to you, another to me."

"Our roads will meet. Until then, I shall pray for you, Hugo."

And now, Hugo reflected, they had come to the same spot on the earth; and such a place. It seemed, then, that he had wronged Paul. The youngster—Hugo always thought of him as that—had courage. If he had come here alone he was no coward.

All at once he was filled with a longing to see the yellow hair of his brother, to hear his low voice. They would talk of the wide, sweet fields of southern France, and the high castle from which one could see the river—

And then Hugo remembered that there had been dust on the Bible.

"Where is the other Frank?" he asked Aruk, who was watching curiously.

"Under your feet, my falcon. Ostrim buried him beneath this yurt when the snow came last."

Hugo's mustache twitched and an ache came into his throat. He questioned the hunter and learned that Paul had died of sickness; his body was not strong. Yes, he had made only a few Krits out of the people of the Altai—Ostrim, Yulga, and two or three more.

"Leave me now," said Hugo after a while. "I have something to think upon."

"Will you stay here?" Aruk asked. "I like you, my falcon. But you have made old Cheke Noyon angry, and he is like a bear with a thorn in its paw. Come, and share my yurt; then he will not see you and bite you because of his anger."

Hugo waved his hand impatiently.

"I stay here."

During that afternoon, when they had buried Pierre, Hugo walked moodily among the pines, twisting his hands behind his back. The words of Paul had come true. Their paths had met. But now Hugo could not say to Paul that he had wronged him—could not delight again in the gentle companionship of the boy with whom he had played in what seemed a far-off age.

"I am an exile," he thought. "There was no roof where I might lay my head. So, I came here, where no one knows my name. But Paul, why must he come to this place of desolation?"

From the log hut came the murmur of a low voice. Hugo moved to one side and saw, through the door, that the candles were lighted on the altar. With a sudden leap to his blood, he made out a figure covered by what seemed a white veil, kneeling, between the candles.

Straining his ears to catch the words that were neither French nor Tatar, he at last made them out—for the murmur was only two or three sentences repeated over and over: "*Requiem aeternam dona ei Domine*—grant him the peace everlasting, O Lord," he repeated.

Now the figure stood up to leave the chapel, and he saw it was Yulga, a clean white hood over her long hair. She left the grove without seeing him. Hugo reflected that she must be repeating the ritual she had heard Paul say many times, without understanding its full meaning.

So, he wondered, had Paul's life been taken that the souls of two or three barbarians might be saved?

Hugo's head dropped on to his chest as he sat on a bench in the hut. Weary, exhausted by hunger, he slept.

For a while the candles flickered. Then one went out and the other. The cabin was in darkness. Outside the night sounds of the Altai began—the howl of a wolf, the whir of a flying owl.

Chapter III
The Storm

One night in early summer, from the fastness of the Altai, Aruk the hunter heard a whirring in the air, a rustle in the underbrush. Against the stars he made out the flight of birds, going north, down the mountain. Against a patch of snow—for in the Urkhogaitu Pass, the snow never quite melts—he saw black forms leap and pass.

Aruk knew that those leaps were made by mountain sheep. They were running down the rocks from the pass. Near at hand several deer crackled through the saxual bushes. A soft *pad-pad* slipped past him.

That was a snow leopard, leaving his fastness in the bare rocks of the heights.

Aruk was on foot in a trice, and slapped the halter on his pony without waiting for the saddle. Snatching up his bow, he was off on the trail to Kob.

Behind him black masses moved against the snow, and horses' hoofs struck on stone. An arrow whizzed past his head. Another. The nimble feet of his pony carried him out of range, and presently to the yurt of Ostrim, the falconer.

Reining up at the door, he struck it with his foot and shouted: "Up and ride! 'Tis Aruk that calls."

Too wise to ask questions, the old man got together his several ponies and sprang upon one, the great Bouragut, the golden eagle, on his wrist. Yulga carried the hawk.

"The Kalmucks are in the pass," Aruk called to Yulga. "They are stealing through like ferrets, hundreds of them. Galdan Khan has loosed the vanguard of his dog brothers on our Tatar land."

Yulga, at this, urged her pony the faster with voice and heel. Like three ghosts they sped down to the rolling slopes of the foothills.

"The Krit warrior said," observed Ostrim after a space, "that ten could hold the summit of the pass against a thousand. Why did not Cheke Noyon post a guard in the Urkhogaitu?"

"Because the ten would be food for the crows by now," grunted Aruk. "When did our Tatar folk ever post a guard—"

"The Krit!" cried Yulga suddenly. "We are passing his yurt, and he will be slain in his sleep if he is not warned."

Swearing under his breath, Aruk reined in, calling to the others to ride on and take the news to Kob. He would go for the Krit.

"Be quick!" Yulga was alarmed. "Do not let them take you—"

But Aruk was a fox in the night. The chapel in the grove proved to be deserted, Hugo having gone far afield on his horse that night; and the hunter edged down to the steppe by paths that did not meet the main trail on which the Kalmucks had already passed him in force. He did not fear for Yulga or her father.

"The hut of the Krit will soon be ashes," he muttered, for fires were already making the night ruddy behind him.

The Kalmucks, seeing that their approach was observed, were slaying the people of the countryside and setting fire to their yurts.

Once, crossing a clearing in the gray of the false dawn, Aruk saw a patrol of the Kalmuck Turks surround a nest of tents. He could make out the black, quilted coats of the dreaded riders, could see their round, sheepskin hats and the points of their long lances.

They were driving the flocks of sheep in the clearing, and harrying out the tents whence men and boys ran, half-clothed, to be spitted on lances or hewn down with scimitars.

The wailing of women rose on the air, to subside into moans. Aruk made out the small form of a young girl fleeing toward the trees. Three of the Kalmuck horde ran after her, on foot. The squat men of the Turks dragged her down as dogs pull down a hare.

Only a black blotch showed on the grass of the clearing. Safe within the screen of the poplars, Aruk hesitated, fingering his bow.

"Dogs and sons of dogs!"

From his pony the hunter fitted shaft to string and discharged his arrows swiftly, heeding not whom he struck; for he knew the sheep-herder's child was as good as dead already.

The unexpected flight of arrows from nowhere set the Kalmucks to yelling. Two fell writhing in the grass. Another began to run back toward the yurt. The girl lay quite still on the grass, a shaft through her body.

A last arrow whistled from Aruk's bow, and the fleeing man dropped to his knees.

"Yah allah—il'allah!"

Aruk heard his groan. Others in steel helmets were running out to the sound of conflict. The hunter turned his pony and was off again, changing his course to strike for Kob, leaving the sounds of pursuit behind him.

"I was a fool," he assured his pony's ears, "since the —— only knows where I will get more arrows. There is small store of weapons in Kob, and Galdan Khan has mustered the hordes from the Kalmuck steppe and the Moslem hills to his aid. A Moslem cried out back there. This is not at all like a joke."

Indeed, the dawn disclosed a forest of spear-tips streaming out from the shadows of the foothills toward Kob. The black coats of the Kalmucks were mingled with the green and red of the Turks. Fur-clad archers from Sungaria rubbed stirrups with the fierce, mailed riders of the Thian Shan.

Behind these, down the broad, grassy trail, sheepskin-clad footmen escorted the creaking carts of the Kalmucks. A camel-train appeared when the sun was high, dragging small cannon.

Above the tramp of the horses, the squeaking of the wagons, the shouts of the drivers, rose the mutter of kettle-drums, the shrill clamor of the pipes, and the hoarse song of disciplined Moslem soldiery.

Like pillars along the line of march ascended shafts of smoke into the transparent air of a mild June day.

On each flank dust rose where the masses of cattle were driven in and turned over in a bedlam of bellowing and trampling, to the butchers who rode among the wagons. Here and there prisoners were dragged in by groups of horsemen, to be questioned briefly by the mirzas and beys of the horde, then to be slain and tossed into ditches.

In this manner came the Kalmucks to the old mud walls of Kob and the moat that had been dry for an age. Before sunset the cannon were set in place, and a roaring, flashing tumult spread around the beleaguered side of the doomed city.

Before darkness served to reveal the flashes of the guns, the walls of mud bricks were caved in here and there. Like disciplined bees, the spearmen and horse of the Kalmucks swarmed forward into the openings.

A half-hour's dust and flashing of weapons where one-eyed Cheke Noyon struggled in fury with his groups of Tatar swordsmen, and the yelling mass pressed in among the houses.

Surprised, ill-prepared for defense, beset by a trained army of relentless fighters, Kob changed masters in the dusk of the June day. The standards of Galdan Khan were carried, through the alleys, into the marketplace.

Galdan Khan was preparing to write his name large upon the annals of inner Asia. Chief of the Kalmucks, ally of the Turkish Kirei and the "wolf" Kazaks of Lake Balkash, as well as the Moslem Sungars of the Thian Shan, the Celestial Mountains, he was reaching out from his homeland in the great Sungarian valley.

This Sungaria lay between the Altai on the north and the Thian Shan on the south. Galdan Khan vowed that he would seize for himself the fertile grasslands of the Tatars in the north before turning his sword upon the richer temples and caravan routes of the south.

"I will take to myself the lands of high grass. I will take in my hand the herds, the cattle, the sheep, the furs, and the weapons of the men of the North," he proclaimed in the council of chieftains assembled. "Thousands of captives I will keep to serve my army and do siege work. The rest my men will slay, for a dead enemy cannot strike again."

Years after the events narrated here, Galdan Khan had carved for himself an empire out of the heart of Asia. He had driven the Chinese back across the Gobi; he held the northern Himalayas, Samarkand, Varkand. His men had looted the lamaseries of Thibet. His "wolves" pushed the Russians back from Turkestan.

But his first step was toward the pastures and villages of the nomad Tatar tribes beyond the snow wall of the Altai. And in Tartary a strange thing happened.

"The van of my army," he had explained to the mirzas of the Kalmuck and Kazak hordes, who sat picking their teeth and chewing dates, "will be under your standards. Your scimitars will be resistless as the sword of Mohammed—upon whose name be praise."

Galdan was not a Moslem, but saw fit to cater to his savage allies.

"I will supply you with siege cannon and mailed footmen. You will sweep through the Gate of the Winds like a storm and gobble up Kob. The clay walls of the city of the herdsmen will melt before you like butter. The sack of the city will fill your girdles. Your swords will exterminate the unbelievers, their wives and children. Then you wilt set the captives to rebuilding the walls, this time with stone."

Nothing could have been more to the liking of the chiefs of the wolves.

"By holding the Urkhogaitu Pass, which is the only path into Tartary, and the nearby city of Kob," Galdan had pointed out, "you will make clear the way for the main army which I shall lead to join you, and together we will rub off the face of the earth two hundred thousand Tatars; for, like the plague, we will spread over the valleys of the North, through the lands of the Torguts and Chakars to the far Buriats before they can unite to defend themselves."

By this it might be seen that Galdan was a shrewd schemer, that he arranged to make his allies bear the brunt of the fighting, and that he knew how to appeal to the religious zeal and the lust of men.

Perhaps because of this, the first part of his plan was carried out to a word.

At the first rumble of cannon the wise bay horse of Hugo of Hainault pricked up its ears. Long before dawn that day, Hugo, unable to sleep, had mounted and galloped to the shore of Kobdo Lake, beyond the city.

Returning after sleep for the man and rest for the horse, they met lines of riders, silent women and tired children, bellowing cattle and disordered sheep. Often he had to turn aside into a grove to let a flock of the fleeing pass. There was no outcry.

Pressing on with some difficulty and making his way toward the north wall, by avoiding the main highways that were choked with humanity, he caught the unmistakable rattle of musketry.

Mounting a rise in the plain, his experienced eye could discern the lines of the besiegers on the far side of the city. He traced the cannon by puffs of smoke and the breaches in the clay rampart by clouds of dust. It meant to him merely that it would be difficult to retrace his way to the cabin in the grove.

This had been but a rude *hôtel* for *monsieur le comte,* and he had fared haphazard on game brought there by Aruk, and grain and fruits bought from Yulga. Still, he found that he was unwilling to leave it. It held him. It was, he reflected, the grave of his brother.

Forcing his way through one of the gates, he beheld the scrawny figure of Gorun, the *baksa,* his cap gone, his eyes starting from his head. The priest, followed by a cavalcade of his kind, struck and kicked children and animals in a mad endeavor to clear the city.

"My faith," thought Hugo, "he seems as anxious to leave as I am to arrive."

On the heels of the priest came a sheepskin-clad rider, blood flowing from his forehead and his shield broken in two.

"Wo! The wolves of Galdan Khan are in the marketplace!" the man was crying, over and over. "Fly, all who would save their lives. The wolves are here."

Accustomed to tight places, Hugo twisted his mustache and shrugged. Ahead of him in the narrow streets of Kob, between the flat-roofed clay houses, he heard the clash of weapons, saw smoke uprise, to make of the sun a red ball. Behind him, the flood of the flying.

He had no wish to thrust himself into the crowd pressing out of the city. So he drew the bay into an archway and pondered. Soon the alleys around him were deserted.

A last bevy of Tatar riders galloped past—archers without bows, old men, wounded and silent. A man who carried a musket turned and flung his weapon at a group of helmeted, black-coated horsemen.

Hugo saw several Tatars struck down in the doors of the houses they tried to defend.

"The cattle!" he thought. "They are driven like animals. No discipline, no powder for their muskets, no leaders. *Pfagh!* The Turks at least know what they are about."

A sharp-featured bey of a Kazak regiment led his men up to the alley, stared long at the quiet Frenchman, lifted his hand in a salute.

"Salamet, effendi!"

He called out to his men, who began to run into the deserted houses, laughing and jesting. Hugo, palpably not of the Tatars, remembered that there were Europeans with Galdan Khan, and that the feather in his cap was some kind of a symbol of rank. The bey must have thought him a man of Galdan Khan. Seeking to leave the alleys, he turned back through the arch, into a small square.

Here he reined in sharply with an oath. This was the quarter of the Chinese merchants. In the teakwood doorway of a cedar house sat a fat man in embroidered silk, a knife in his hand. Through the opened door Hugo could see the bodies of several women, some still stirring feebly. There was blood on the knife in the merchant's hand. His broad, olive face was expressionless. Having killed his women, according to the code of his caste, the Oriental was awaiting his own fate.

Hugo could go no farther in that direction. A group of Kalmucks were harrying a small pagoda. Others were intent on seeking out the unfortunates who still lived in nearby dwellings. Captives were being roped together by the necks. Children were lifted on lances, to guttural shouts.

Almost within reach, Hugo saw a Tatar's eyes torn out by a soldier's fingers.

A sound caused him to turn. From a post by the gate of the merchant's house the Kalmucks had cut a stake. Upon this they had drawn the passive Chinese. While Hugo looked he wriggled convulsively, his eyes standing from his sweating face.

Never before in the wars had Hugo seen the deliberate slaughter of a people. It sickened him, and he was beating his way through the square when a song arrested him.

"Oh, bright falcon,
My own brother!
Thou soarest high,
Thou seest far—"

It was dusk now in Kob, a dusk thickened by a pall of smoke and reddened by mounting fires. The song had come from the entrance of the pagoda. Aruk was the singer. Hugo could see the little hunter clearly in the glow from a burning house across the square. Beside Aruk were clustered a handful of Tatars, women among them.

With spears and swords they were defending themselves, for they had used up all their arrows. Aruk, half-naked, was fighting desperately, swinging a scimitar too large for his short arms. His broken body was streaked with sweat and shining blood; his teeth bared in a grin of rage.

Suddenly he caught sight of the tall form of the Krit.

"Aid!" called Aruk. "Aid, my falcon."

For a space the clash of weapons had stopped. The Kalmucks, ringed around the pagoda steps, were waiting the coming of more men.

"Aid, my Krit," urged the hunter. "Chase these wolves away before others come."

It simply did not occur to Hugo to draw his sword in a quarrel between peasants and common soldiers. He was already gathering up his reins when his eye caught the anxious face of Yulga. She did not call to him, but her clasped hands were eloquent of appeal.

This made him ill at ease. Yulga had come daily to say her garbled prayer at the grave of his brother. She was a handsome little thing, and her eyes were tragic.

"*Peste!* What is it to me?" he grumbled.

Then he growled at the watching Kalmucks: "Back, dogs! Back, I say. These Tatars are my prisoners."

The soldiers hesitated at the ring of command in the voice of the tall Krit. They eyed the feather in his cap, the accouterments of his horse, sullenly. Were not the Tatars their legitimate prey? Who was this tall bey they had not seen before?

Aruk, Ostrim and his daughter, and the other Tatars gathered about the horse of Hugo, fingering their weapons defiantly.

"These are prisoners, to be questioned by the chiefs," Hugo asserted, watching the Kalmucks. "Would you taste a stake, that you disobey the command of a bey? Be off, before I am angry. Loot the temple yonder."

Sight of the deserted doorway of the pagoda decided the Kalmucks. Here was easy spoil. The Tatars could still bite. Let the bey have them if he wished. They made off.

At a sign from Aruk, Hugo urged his horse toward the archway through which he had come. The fires had not yet reached that quarter, and once in the darkness they would be reasonably safe from discovery.

Abreast of the burning house he reined in with a muttered oath. Several riders paced out of the alley to confront him. He saw a stout officer in a fur kaftan and the round, white hat of a Turkish janissary.

In response to the man's question, Hugo answered that he was escorting prisoners to be questioned. But the other stared evilly and shook his head. Prisoners with arms! They should be bound by the necks.

He peered closely into Hugo's bearded face and drew back with an angry hiss.

"You are a Christian. I have seen you before. What are you doing here?"

Without replying, Hugo edged his horse nearer the other. Suddenly the Turk snatched at a pistol in his belt.

"*Caphar*—dog!" he screamed. "You have fought against the believers. You were at Zbaraj. I was there—"

Before the long pistol was fairly in his hand his words ended in a groan. Drawing his sword, Hugo had caught the Turk under the chin with the hilt while the point was still in the scabbard. The janissary swayed, choking and clutching his throat.

Putting spurs to his mount, Hugo rode down another rider, his big bay knocking the small Arab off its feet.

"Kill, kill!" cried the other Turks.

Before they could put their weapons in play, the Tatars were dragging them from their horses, slipping under their scimitars.

One or two of the Tatars fell in the short struggle, but the rest were now mounted. The feel of horseflesh between their legs put new heart into them, for a Tatar is at sea without his horse.

Under the guidance of Aruk, who knew every alley of Kob, they made their way unmolested to one of the gates. The sack of the city was beginning in earnest, and no guards had been posted as yet by the Kalmucks. A drunken cavalry patrol fired shots after them as they sped away in the darkness.

Some distance out on the quiet plain toward the lake, Aruk dismounted and came to Hugo. He seized the stirrup of the Frank and bent his head.

"Our lives are yours, my lord. Have I not said to these other jackals that you were a falcon and a wolf-chaser? *Hai*—they will believe me now."

Out of the darkness came the guttural answer of the other men.

"Our lives are yours. We have seen you strike a good blow against the wolves."

Hugo moved impatiently, wishing to be gone.

"Because of that blow," went on Aruk slowly, "you cannot go back to your yurt on the mountain. The Turks would skin you alive and set you on an ant-hill. Besides, they have set fire to the yurt where you slept, and plundered your goods. Come then with us, with the men of the Altai."

"Come," echoed the others.

Chapter IV
The Gate of the Winds

The water of Kobdo Nor was like a mirror under the stars, a mirror that reflected as well the scattered glow of fires about the shore of the lake. Water-fowl, roused by the presence of men in the unwonted hours of darkness, flew about with a dull screaming.

Cattle lowed from the plain, whence riders came in on sweating horses, from the steppe, from the more distant tribes of Tartary, to learn what had befallen at Kob.

They saw the crimson spot in the sky that showed where the city still burned on the second night of the sack.

On his back near the reeds where the women and children from Kob had taken refuge, Hugo of Hainault lay, his head on his hands, his eyes closed. He was rather more than hungry. Never having accustomed himself to the *kumiss* of the Tatars, or the poorly cooked meat they ate, his one meal of the day had been black bread and fruit, washed down by cold water from a spring near the lake.

Above the whistle of the wind in the reeds and the murmur of a woman quieting her child, his quick ear caught a light step. Opening his eyes, he saw a slim figure standing over him.

"It is Yulga, my lord, and I scarce could find you. I have some cold lamb's flesh and a bowl of wine. Aruk said that you have a throat for the wine of China, so I had this from a merchant whose caravan has wandered here."

"Wine!"

Hugo sat up and brushed his mustache. "You are a good child."

"The girl has manners of a sort," he reflected, "and it is necessary to remember that here is not *monsieur le comte*, but a vagabond of the highways. Even the remnant of my clothing and money is gone with my forest chateau."

"My lord," Yulga's low voice broke in, "the *kurultai*—the council of the clans—has been assembled since the setting of the sun. The wise ones among the *noyons* are trying to discover the road we must follow. They have heard that Galdan Khan has ordered the death of all the souls in Tartary. His main army is on the road leading to the Urkhogaitu Pass. Soon he will arrive with his banners in Tartary, and with him will be five times ten thousand riders."

Yulga spoke quickly, almost breathlessly.

"My lord, we will not flee, for where would we go? Cheke Noyon yielded his breath in Kob, and others of our bravest are licking their wounds here. More horsemen are coming in from the Torgut and Buriat clans, and before long others will ride hither from the north.

"We have no khan like Galdan," went on Yulga sadly, "for the *kelets*—the evil demons of the air—bring him news, and he is invulnerable. Gorun shivers in his tent and says that Galdan Khan has made magic. The priest can make no magic for us."

She paused and then lifted her head.

"My lord, there is a magic that can help us. I heard of it from the Christian priest who is dead."

"The one for whom you pray?"

"Aye, my lord. He told us that God opened a path through a sea, so an army of Christians could pass with dry feet."

Hugo was silent. Once at a banquet at the Palais Royal he had made a jest of this, remarking that if the Israelites of Egypt had been monks and the Red Sea a sea of wine, they would not have passed unwet.

"And an evil horde," pointed out Yulga eagerly, "that pursued the Christian khans was swallowed up in the sea. Is not that the truth?"

Thought of Paul stayed the gibe that rose to Hugo's lips.

"If the Christian priest said it," he responded grimly, "it is true. He was my brother."

Yulga pondered this.

"Then you must be a Christian from God, because he was an envoy, and you are a khan, a leader of men. And you came to help us in our need. If we do not have a miracle we will all die."

Breathlessly she kneeled beside the wanderer. He could hear her heart beating. So, he thought with a wry smile, a price must be paid for one's supper even in the wilderness.

"Then you will die," he said gruffly.

Yulga laughed patiently.

"My lord jests. How else could the priest who was your brother live after death came to him?"

"Live? How?"

"In the yurt where we pray. When we are there we hear again the words he spoke to us. And how did you, my lord, find his yurt if you did not know where it was?"

Emboldened by the silence of the man, she went on swiftly,

"Tell us how we can overthrow Galdan Khan. In two days he will be at the pass. He has ten times the numbers of the riders that are here. Soon we will have as many as he perhaps, but then it will be too late. And he has powder and cannon and muskets."

She pointed at the glow in the sky that was Kob.

"See, yonder the mirzas of Galdan Khan are building new walls. They are putting their cannon on the walls. Our horses cannot ride over stone ramparts.

"Do you tell us what we must do, my lord," she sighed. "And I will bear the counsel to Aruk, who is sitting in the *kurultai*."

"My faith!" thought the Frenchman. "I would not care to go myself. They smell too rank of horse and mutton."

He glanced at the nearby campfires, noting the anxious men who stood weapons in hand beside their sleeping women. Again he heard the plaint of the sick child and the murmur of its mother.

A blind man sat patiently, the nose-rope of a solitary cow in his hand. More distant from the fire, herders slept on their horses; fishers and skin-clad peasants armed only with sticks stood staring numbly at the crimson spot in the sky.

"What an army!" he thought. "What animals, that Paul should waste his life among them! Pfagh!"

Touching Yulga on the shoulder, he said: "You have wit. How many Kalmucks and Turks are in Kob?"

"Aruk says four times a thousand. There were more, but many died in the battle."

"Well, tell Aruk this. Say that your horsemen are useless except as horsemen, skirmishers, and archers. Still, you can win back Kob. Spread a circle of riders about the place. Cut off all food. If the Kalmucks sally out, draw them off to the hills, or the marshes by the lake. Tire out their horses, then attack them if you will. It does not matter, so food is kept from their hands. They have but little."

"Aye, my lord. But Galdan Khan will be at Kob in three days."

With his hand Hugo turned the head of the girl toward the black mass of the Altai Mountains.

"There is the barrier that will keep out Galdan Khan. Through one gate only can he come. You have heard the tale of the army that passed through a gate in the sea. Well, it is easier to close a mountain than to open it. Your khans cannot spare many men, for a space until others come in from the north. But two hundred can hold the Urkhogaitu Pass, among the rocks. Let them hold it then until your allies are here."

Yulga sped back with her tidings, and whispered long into the attentive ear of Aruk, while the assembled khans talked and stared into the fire. When the hunter rose to speak he was listened to, for as the keeper of the pass he was well known.

When he had finished repeating the advice of Hugo, the khans gazed at each other grimly.

"Who will hold the pass?" One voiced the thought of all. "There is no man who does not fear Galdan Khan, who fights with the Devil at his back."

"I will try, good sirs," spoke up Aruk.

"A pigmy to match blows with a hero?" The Buriat spat. "You are bold enough, but the warriors will not take you as leader."

"What leader," countered another, "could hold the bare rocks of the Urkhogaitu against fifty thousand with artillery and—Galdan Khan?"

They were silent, uneasy, while the khan of the Buriats, who had ridden far that day, traced figures in the sand by the fire with his gnarled finger.

"It is a good plan," he ruminated, "a wise plan, that of the hunter. For we could cut communication between Galdan Khan and his wolves in Kob."

"But if the mirzas who hold Kob sallied back to the pass—"

"Fool, they will not do that. They have orders to roost where they are. They will expect Galdan Khan to appear every day. When he does not come, they will be suspicious—likewise hungry. Then will they sally out, not before. Yet then our allies will be here; aye, we will be stronger than they, if Galdan Khan is held at the pass."

At this, silence fell again. The chiefs who squatted, looking into the fire, were leaders of tribes but not of nations. There was no one to give commands in the place of Cheke Noyon.

They were not afraid. They knew not how to build a fort to oppose Galdan Khan, even if they all went to hold the Urkhogaitu. And if they did that, there would be no one to keep the mirzas hemmed in Kob.

So each one avoided the glance of the others, and the Buriat who was a famous sword slayer snarled in his throat as he drew lines in the sand.

At length Yulga, who had left the council-ring, reappeared at Aruk's side and whispered to the hunter.

Aruk looked surprised; but his eyes gleamed, and he rose.

"Good sirs," he said, "Hu-go, the Krit lord, will hold the Urkhogaitu Pass."

The khan of the Buriats grunted and smoothed the lines in the sand with his sword.

"He is mad!"

"Not so. For the plan you have just heard, the plan I bespoke, was his. Yulga brought me the word."

"With what will he hold the pass?"

"Noble khan, with twice a hundred picked men, bold men—he asks that they be from your clan."

Pleased, the Buriat grunted and looked around.

"He must have likewise," went on Aruk, "all the powder in our bags, and steel shirts for the warriors, and we must seize him cannon from the broken walls of Kob—"

"This is a wise khan," barked the Buriat. "He is no madman."

"But," pointed out Gorun, who squatted behind the council-ring, "he cannot work wonders."

To this old Ostrim from the outer ranks made rejoinder: "Once, when the horde of the Krits in another land were being slain in battle by a powerful foe, the prophet of the Krits went to a mountain, and talked to God, holding up his hands the while. So long as his hands were held up, the Krits conquered; and before very long they had cut off the heads of their enemy and taken many horses. *Kai!* It is true."

"But why," asked the khan of the Buriats, "will Hugo Khan go against Galdan?"

At this Yulga broke the custom of ages, and a woman spoke in the council.

"To me he said it. My lord Hugo would sleep in comfort in his own yurt. Galdan Khan is like a buzzing fly that keeps him from sleep. He said that he was tired of the buzzing and would drive away the fly."

For a space the flippant answer of Monsieur le Comte d'Hainault sorely puzzled the councilors. Then the khan of the Buriats struck the sand before him with the flat of his sword, roaring: "That lord is a great lord. He is a hero. The men will follow him. He thinks of Galdan Khan as an insect. No fear of Galdan Khan has he!"

"No fear has he," echoed others.

"I will go!" cried Aruk, and his voice was followed by many others.

In this way did Hugo offer to defend the mountain pass. The thought had come to him that these people were after all the people to whom his brother had ministered, and if they were slain the work that Paul had done would be lost.

Chapter V
The Bed of Monsieur le Comte

Galdan Khan, general of the Turco-Kalmuck army, was not disturbed when for three days he received no couriers from the mirzas who had captured Kob. The mirzas were officers who would rather fight battles than report them.

With pardonable pride he watched the van of his well-trained army surmount the slope of the Altai, cutting away trees on either side of the trail through the timber belt to make room for his wagon-train, and bridging over the freshets. He planned to make the passage of the Urkhogaitu in one day, so as not to pitch camp in the snow at an altitude where sleep was hard to come by and horses bled at the nostrils.

The approach to the pass was a wide rock plateau, something like a vast Greek theater, from which the glaciers rose on either side to the white peaks that stood against the sky like the banners of Galdan Khan.

From the plateau the advance of his army—irregulars, supported by a regiment of Black Kalmucks—filed into the ravine that ascended to the Urkhogaitu. One curve in the ravine, and they would be at the summit of the pass.

Galdan Khan announced that the plateau was an auspicious spot—he would break his fast there while his men crossed the pass. It was a clear day, the sky as blue as the kaftan of a dandy of Samarkand. Pleased with himself, Galdan drank spirits and chewed dates.

Came one of the stunted, skin-clad irregulars who prostrated himself.

"O lord of the mountains, there is a great crevice in the pass that we cannot surmount."

"Bridge it," growled the khan, "with rocks and the bodies of wagons from the rear."

The man hurried off, but presently there was a stir among the officers under the standards, a murmur of whispering, and a helmeted bey of the Kalmuck regiment approached his leader. Men, hostile to Galdan, held the other side of the crevice. They would not be dislodged by arrows; horsemen could not get at them.

Angrily Galdan spat dates from between his sharpened teeth.

"Let a company of janissaries climb into and over the ditch; let the horsemen cover them with arrow-flights. Begone, dog, and if you value your head do not delay the march!"

But the march was very much delayed that day. The Kalmuck bey died at the ravine with many scores before Galdan decided to ride up and see for himself what was holding up his advance.

When he rounded the turn in the ravine he growled under his breath. Here the glacier sides rose steeply, and the footing—the bottom of the pass was the dry bed of a watercourse—was treacherous. Snow was everywhere save on a massive rampart of rocks built on the far side of the broad ditch, rising to the height of three spears.

Both flanks of the rampart were protected by rough towers of stones fitted together, as broad as they were high. Flanking the towers were the moraines, where no man could stand on the ice.

When Galdan saw that the ditch had been blown out of the frozen earth with gunpowder, he was puzzled. An organized force of his enemies stood against him. Yet there should be no enemies between him and the victorious mirzas.

He ordered a storm, by Turkish spearmen, and withdrew behind the bend in the ravine. It was well he did so. Cannon roared in the pass, and the groans of wounded rose into the air.

At noon the mirza of the Turks came to Galdan wrathfully.

"Lord," he cried, "send your own men against the wall of rocks. Mine are lying in the pass, slain by arrow and cannon while they climbed the ravine. The river of the pass runs again—with blood!"

Galdan snarled and laid hand on sword. Remembering that he must have the aid of the Turks, he stifled his rage. He learned for the first time that two pieces of artillery were in the hands of his foes—one in each tower, so that they cross-raked the narrow chute leading up to the ditch.

"Send men to climb the slopes above the rampart," he ordered.

The Turk sneered.

"By Allah, the all-wise, do you think my soldiers are birds, to fly up a slope of ice!"

"Then stand aside," growled the Kalmuck. "Tomorrow I will pitch my tent beyond the pass."

After thinking for a while, he ordered scouts to be sent out on either flank to explore the nearby slopes of the Altai for another way into the plain of Tartary.

It was dusk when they returned, wearied, and reported that single men might perchance climb the snow summits here and there, but the army with its horses, its wagon-train, and cannon must go through the Urkhogaitu or not at all.

The lips of Galdan Khan smiled, but he did not touch the food that was brought to his pavilion on the plateau. He had learned that there were but twice a hundred defenders in the pass. Well, he would crush them like ants upon a stone.

He wondered how the stone fort had come to be built. It was contrary to the custom of the haphazard Tatars.

He did not know that for three days and nights before his coming, two hundred men had grappled with the stones of the ravine, mortaring them together with moist dirt, thrown up by the explosion of mines in the bed of the ravine, and fixing between the stones the pointed trunks of trees, under the orders of a man who knew more about fortification than Galdan Khan.

For three days the big Buriats had labored, trembling with fatigue in the thin air, bleeding at the hands and ears, sleeping only fitfully and chilled by the cutting wind that swept the pass, scarce warmed by fires of pine branches. They had been cursed by their commander, beaten by the flat of his sword.

When the hundred paces of massive rampart had been built, and the wide ditch excavated, they murmured when he commanded the erection of towers for the cannon that, plundered from Kob, had just been brought up.

Whereupon the blue-faced commander ordered them to flog each other until they were exhausted. Under the lash of his tongue the bartizans had been erected laboriously. And in the evening of the third day the Frankish commander had approved the work.

"Our bellies are empty, father," they said. "We cannot fight with empty bellies."

The Frank had foreseen this, and ordered them—all except a half-dozen sentries that he kept by him at the rampart—to repair to the abode of Aruk down the mountain where there was mutton and huge fires and liquor and a place to sleep in comfort. He wondered when they staggered off whether they would come back.

Before dawn they did come back, and he heard them from quite far away. They were quarreling among themselves, and staggering, though not from weariness this time. They sang guttural songs and roared a demand to be shown their enemy. They clutched their bows and heavy swords and surged round him.

Monsieur le comte drew back his soiled cloak from their touch and snarled at them. And then came Galdan Khan and the first day of the attack.

The dawn of the second day showed a change in the aspect of the ravine. During the night, patrols from the Kalmuck camp had almost filled in the ditch with stones, small trees, and bodies of the dead. This the Tatars had been unable to prevent.

It was just after sunrise had made clear the outlines of the rampart that the attackers came up the ravine, silently at first, then with a clamor of kettle-drums and wailing of pipes as if to frighten the defenders by the very noise.

They ran full into arrow-flights that splintered shields and tore through chain armor. Notwithstanding this they pressed forward until there was a yellow flash from each tower and a rain of small shot cut up the ranks in the rear. Now the Kalmucks were accustomed only to round shot, and they gave way with cries and oaths.

But they were re-formed by the beys and advanced again, this time with picked men in the front ranks. These crossed the ditch and began to climb the steep slope of the rampart, despite the slow discharges of the cannon.

They were met with battle-ax and sword from above, and, clinging to the sharp rocks, could use their spears only at a disadvantage. Those who gained the top of the rocks were hurled back on their comrades.

It was, for a time, a hand-to-hand affair in which the steel helmets and mail shirts of the struggling defenders saved them from being cut to pieces by the spears and scimitars of the Kalmucks and Turks.

The sun was high enough to cast its light full into the ravine, and Galdan Khan, seeing that the fort was on the verge of falling, had ordered up fresh clans from the plateau, when the explosion came.

The rock walls of the gorge echoed thunderously, and a pall of smoke rose from the center of the Kalmuck ranks. Stones hurled into the air fell back upon the bodies of dazed men.

As he had done more than once before, Hugo had constructed a mine midway down the ravine, bringing a powder-train, deep in the frozen earth where the moisture of the snows could not penetrate, back to the rampart. He did not know, of course, whether the powder-train would burn.

But the mine had gone off. Probably Hugo himself had not foreseen the full consequences of this. The shock of the explosion displaced masses of ice and rock on the morains at either side. Single stones falling from the buttresses that led to the peaks carried others along with them.

The echoes were still in the air when the crashing of the boulders began. One of the towers of the Tatar fort was wrecked. The Tatars themselves, protected by the stone mound, did not suffer greatly; but the havoc among the Kalmucks was a grim thing. Bodies lay where men had stood a moment before. Then the bodies were covered with glacier ice. Stones still muttered and rolled down the length of the ravine.

The thinned groups of Kalmucks that made their way back down the gorge looked like men fording a river of snow. They had no thought but to escape from the rocks before a second blast went off.

Never having experienced a mine before, it was a blow to their morale; and the avalanches seemed to them to be the work of demons.

Galdan Khan knew otherwise. After midday prayers that day, he sent a Kalmuck officer with a white flag up to the gorge and the rampart. For the first time it had come to the ears of the khan that a Frankish lord commanded the fort on the heights.

The message the Kalmuck bore was for the ears of the Frankish lord alone, and it was brief:

> *The prayers and greetings of Galdan, Khan of the Kalmucks, of the Thian Shan, of Sungaria, to the lord commander of the fort. You, lord, have a hundred unwounded men; I have fifty times a thousand. If you keep on fighting beside the Tatar dogs, your bones will never leave the Urkhogaitu; if you surrender to me, I will give you ten thousand thalers and five regiments for your command. You are a brave man; I think you are also wise.* Salamet!

The Kalmuck added under his breath: "Lord, there are Greeks and Wallachian officers with Galdan Khan. He will keep his word with you, and will cut off the faces of these, your men, so that no one will know what has passed. Otherwise he will bring up the cannon and make dust of the stones you hide behind."

Hugo twirled his beard and raised one eyebrow. It was a fair offer, all things considered, and the cold of the Urkhogaitu had eaten into his bones. He had not slept for three days, and his eyes were burning in his head.

Taking the Kalmuck away from the staring Tatars, Hugo led him a little down the ravine to the point where they could see the northern plain. Some herds of Tatar cattle were visible; but no smoke rose from the villages, and the quiet was ominous to the eyes of the invader.

"Tell Galdan Khan what you have seen," smiled Hugo. "Say that he will never see his mirzas again. On the first clear night I will come into his lines and speak with him."

But on that night, and for three days, no men crossed the rampart of the stone fort. Clouds gathered, above and below the pass. Snow came, and hail.

The loose snow in the pass was covered with an icy coating at the touch of the wind that screamed through the walls of the Urkhogaitu. The temperature dropped many degrees; and the few sentries on either side were changed often, or they would have frozen to death.

Truly was the pass the Gate of the Winds—the winds that brought with them the cold of outer space, and snow. Attackers and defenders alike retreated down below the snow line and camped under the canopy of the forest, Galdan Khan going down to the main body of his troops among the foothills, and Hugo to the camp of Aruk, where his men slept, allowing their wounds to heal.

On the sixth night of the siege the stars were clearly to be seen. The snow flurries passed from the peaks of the Altai, leaving the white pinnacles framed against the sky in the light of a three-quarters moon.

Promptly Hugo returned to his battlement with his Tatars and some others who had come up to the pass for news.

Hugo, his tattered cloak wound around his tall figure, stood in the snow of a towertop and stared reflectively into the gleams and shadows of the ravine. In the half-light he could see no bodies; for the storm had blanketed the slain, and the dark outline of a frozen limb or a rusted weapon was softened by the moon.

The wind, gentle now, stirred in the ragged beard of *monsieur le comte* and caressed his hot eyes. He lifted his eyes to the stars, picking out the ones he knew.

It reminded him of a night when he had made the rounds of the guard on the wall of a mountain fort in the Pyrenees. There had been snow on the ground, and he remembered a chapel bell that tolled during an all-night mass. But he had listened, then, to the song of a woman in the château of the town—a fair woman, that.

He hummed to himself the air of the *chanson,* twirling his mustache with a hand that trembled from the cold—

"O mon amante—sachons cueillir—"

Well, the woman, whose slipper he had kissed, was no doubt dead—as dead as the soft-hearted Paul who had prayed for her soul.

"Paul," murmured Hugo, making a sweeping bow with his hat—on which the plumes were quite bedraggled—"I commend her to you, a beautiful and a virtuous woman. There were few like her, my brother. Paul, will you tell me why in the name of the —— I should waste my life on these brats of yours back yonder, these Tatars who make but sorry Christians at best? That would be but a foolish end to a career that at least has had its distinctions."

Replacing his hat, for he was cold, Hugo reasoned tranquilly, although the rarefied air, as always, made him a little dizzy. Galdan Khan would bring up his cannon. A slow and difficult matter that, and not much gain in the end. But another assault over the ravine floor, leveled by the snow, and over the broken rampart—Galdan Khan would take the fort, such as it was, on the morrow.

Well and good. Then why should Hugo stay where he was, like a cow in the butcher's pen?

"That is not how I would choose to be remembered at court," he reflected. "*Monseigneur* the cardinal—if he is still *monseigneur* the cardinal—would laugh over his cards at such a droll thing. And then everyone else would smile because, forsooth, *monseigneur* made a jest. That would be droll. Perhaps they have forgotten Hainault. By the horns of Panurge, if I should return—"

Hugo laughed, reflecting that the soul of Pierre would be offended, up among the stars; for Pierre, the valet, had always believed that *monsieur le comte* would never break his word, even to a Tatar.

Well, it was too cold to stand there any longer. So Hugo, his long sword clanking at his side, strode down to where his men had gathered in a black bulk behind the rampart. For the first time they had horses in the pass, one to each man.

They numbered a hundred and twenty, Hugo counted. Respectfully they waited for him to speak.

"Eh, my dogs," he cried, "have you your weapons? Have you eaten well?"

"Father, we have."

"And each warrior has a horse? Good. It is time—time. Will you come with me, my dogs?"

A guttural murmur answered him.

"Aye, father. We will go with the Wolf-Chaser."

Tugging at his mustache, Hugo slapped Aruk on the back, a twinkle in his eye. He no longer minded the smell of sheep that exuded from the Tatars.

"You will do better in the saddle than behind a wall—eat me if you won't. You have called me Wolf-Chaser. Eh, we will look for the wolf."

So saying, Hugo mounted a shaggy pony that made its way with some difficulty over the rocks of the rampart on the hard-packed snow. The others followed irregularly.

They headed down the ravine toward the Kalmucks. Keeping close to one side of the ravine, they were within the shadow, and the snow dulled the sound of the horses' hoofs. So it was some time before a shape rose in the shadow to challenge them.

Two Tatars spurred past Hugo and cut down the Kalmuck sentry, with only a dull *clink* of steel on mail.

Other figures were stirring, though, down the ravine, which was broader here where they neared the bend in the gorge. Hugo quickened to a trot.

A pistol flashed and roared, echoing from the rocks.

The Kalmuck patrol shouted and turned to run; but they were afoot, and the rider from the upper gorge caught them up at the curve in the ravine. A few blows, and the bodies of the Kalmucks sprawled in the snow.

"Swiftly now," instructed Hugo.

The Kalmuck camp in the plateau into which the ravine gave was occupied only by two regiments of foot. These ran from their tents, snatching up the first weapon to hand as the Tatar horsemen reached the lines of the encampment. A few muskets barked, and arrows flickered in the moonlight.

The Tatars shot their arrows as they galloped, for here the snow surface was level. Their beasts crashed in among the tents, trampling belated sleepers—for an attack from above had not been thought of.

Over the horses' heads sabers flashed and rose again. Men leaped to grapple with the riders. The fight was silent except for the scream of an injured horse and the wild shout of a Tatar who felt death.

More slowly now, the horses pressed forward. Old Ostrim, shooting the last of his arrows, drew an iron war-club and laid about him.

"Hai!" he muttered. "Taste this, wolves."

His arm was caught, and a tall Sungar warrior buried a knife in the chest of the falconer. Ostrim was pulled from his horse and disappeared.

Many had fled from the camp, believing themselves lost. But when the struggle had spread to the center of the tents, other warriors began to appear, running up from below where the main body of the Kalmucks had taken alarm. The tangled knots of men had been pushed almost to the edge of the plateau, and more than once a horse or man crashed off to fall on the rocks below.

The cries of *"Hai!"* grew fainter, and fewer horsemen were to be seen. Reinforcements came up to the Kalmucks, but the Tatars did not give ground, choosing instead to die where they were.

Galdan Khan, riding up with his officers, heard from fugitives what had happened.

"It is the Frankish lord," they cried. "He has come to seek you."

Starting, the khan clenched his fist. For three days he had pondered the message sent back by Hugo, wondering whether the Frank meant to come over to him.

"He has slain a score," reported those who approached the khan. "His sword is like a spear, and we cannot slay him. He looks for you, and shouts that he has kept his word to you."

But, being a prudent man, Galdan Khan did not desire to face Hugo. So the chief of the Turks remained below the plateau until the fighting was at an end. Meanwhile it was only too clearly to be seen that the courage of his men was shaken, that they stared uneasily into the pass where they had encountered once too often the grim visage of death.

It was late the next day when a crowd of Tatars rode up the trail toward the pass, from Kob. They found the debris of the fort, on which perched Aruk, the keeper of the gate, his shoulder slashed in two, his armor cut and bloodied.

Beside him stood a single Tatar, a Buriat, looking down the gorge to the south. By the fire the two had kindled, a badly wounded man lay, moving restlessly. Yet the snow around them was unstained and marked only by the hoofs of scores of horses.

The khan of the Buriats strode to Aruk.

"The work at Kob is finished—the wolves scattered," he said. "What of the pass, O keeper of the gate?"

"Galdan Khan has gone back to his own land."

Galdan Khan was a shrewd man. News leaked in to him, brought by stragglers over the Altai, that the mirzas were cut up and their followers scattered. Including the affair at the plateau, he had lost two thousand warriors at the pass. Meanwhile he knew the Tatar clans had gathered in the northern plain, heartened by victory. His men, disheartened by the night attack, were murmuring.

So Galdan Khan knew that the hour for the conquest of Tartary had passed.

"What of Hugo, the Krit?" asked the Buriat khan, when he had heard the details of the defense of the pass.

Aruk pointed to the single sentry who stood over a figure covered by a cloak that had once been elegant with bows and satin lining. The khan of the Buriats drew back the cloak and looked into the dead face of Hugo. He lifted his hand toward the rocks of the gorge.

"He kept his word," he said.

Aruk nodded.

"Aye, did I not say he was a falcon, a wolf-chaser? *Kai*. It is so."

"It is so," echoed the Tatars.

After consulting together they buried the body of Hugo beside that of his brother the priest, in the flame-blackened hut where the crucifix was still to be seen over the altar. In this fashion did Hugo and Paul come to sleep in the same bed.

In time the name of Hugo of Hainault, and that of Paul his brother, were forgotten in the stirring of the troubled land of their birth. But the children of Aruk and Yulga and their children after them came to the hut, repeating prayers that grew more indistinct with time because they did not know the meaning of the words.

The Three Palladins

I
The Shadow

The gong in the palace courtyard struck the third hour of the morning, awakening Mingan, prince of Cathay, from what would otherwise have been his last sleep.

He was a boy of fifteen, and the echoes of the gong had not died in the upper corridors of the slumbering palace before he was wide awake, before he had slipped from his teak pallet and opened the lid of the ebony chest beside it.

The day was the fifth of the fifth moon, and it was to be a feast day—the feast of Hao, in midsummer of that year of the Ape, by the Chinese calendar, otherwise the year of Our Lord 1100. But what had aroused Mingan was the recollection that at dawn the old emperor would assemble the court and ride forth on the customary hunt of the festival of Hao.

The hunters would go from the palace, out of Taitung—the Western City—to the Western Gate of the Great Wall, and beyond, to where Cathay ended and the wide desert began. Mingan wished to be ready in plenty of time. He was quivering a little with excitement—and the damp air that swept through the open arches of the sleeping chambers—as he took out from the chest the new garments he was to put on.

And then he saw the shadow.

Inside the entrance to his room stood a screen, placed there so that evil spirits might not have easy access, because demons must walk in a straight line and cannot turn corners. In the corridor outside the screen a lantern was hung. Athwart the embroidered silk of the screen was now the black figure of a tall man whose head was bent a little forward.

Mingan smiled—he hardly ever laughed—thinking that it was one of the men-at-arms on guard in the upper halls, who had fallen asleep. The figure, however, held no spear, nor did it wear the helmet with the dragon crest of the Liao-tung guardsmen, who came from Mingan's province on the northern coast and were the picked men of the emperor's host. As he watched, the figure advanced a step, and Mingan knew that it was a man standing against his screen, listening. A cup-bearer or slave might, perhaps, do that. Many such were paid to listen at doors in the imperial palace—Mingan had surprised them more than once, because the boy had been bred in the northern forests and could move as quietly as a panther when he chose. He wondered who paid them to do it.

Mingan put on the new garments—the soft boots, the silk tunic and wide, nankeen trousers, the over-robe of yellow and cloth-of-gold, and lastly the black velvet hat with its peacock feather—the insignia of manhood and nobility that he was to wear for the first time that day.

By now the man at the screen had come into view around the end, and proved to be a Cathayan of unusual stature, clad altogether in white, his head shaven.

"The Servant of Mercy," breathed Mingan, and no imaginable devil could have been a less welcome visitor in that place and hour.

Because the Servant of Mercy was the executioner of the court, serving the emperor by strangling culprits whose rank made them immune from beheading, Mingan's heart leaped and struck up a quick beat, akin to the roll of the kettle-drums of the mailed cavalry of Liao-tung whose regimental emblem the prince wore and whom he should command in a few years.

Without a sound Mingan moved backward and out of the tall window that gave access to the balcony of the tower where he was quartered. There was only the one door to his room, and there was no other entrance or exit to the balcony than the window. Leaning against a carved pillar, Mingan observed the Servant of Mercy advance soundlessly to the bed, feel of it, and peer around the ill-lighted chamber. The quilts in which the boy had slept were still warm.

"*Wan sui*—live for a thousand years!" the executioner whispered. "Ye Lui Kutsai Mingan, Bright One of the North, Prince of Liao-tung, it has been decided that you must go in this hour to the guests on high, to face the honorable ones, your exemplary ancestors. Are you afraid?"

Mingan had seen two of his kindred take the happy dispatch by poison put into their wine cups, and he was afraid. The tall man was listening again, his head on one side. And then he was moving toward the balcony, where he had heard the prince breathing. From his right hand hung the loop of a silk cord.

The boy's body did not move, but his mind probed for the reason of his death—secret, and bloodless, by token of the strangler's cord.

His uncle, the emperor, had never noticed him; his father and his Liaotung mother were dead: Chung-hi, the heir and son of the emperor, was his classmate—a powerful youth, given to brooding and superstition.

Chung-hi had been good-natured with Mingan, had gone on escapades with him, when the two princes went out incognito and joined the ranks of the court troupe of actors, or played on the ten-stringed lute in the gardens of the courtesans.

Now Mingan's studies were at an end, and his tutors had announced to the emperor that Mingan was a little inclined to shirk his books for the hunting chariot, at night, when he climbed down from his room, and drove his matched horses out of the walls of Taitung. He was expert in swordplay, well versed in the wisdom of the sages, and in history.

An old proverb came into his mind as he pondered. "A hunted tiger jumps the wall," he said in a low voice.

The Servant of Mercy stepped through the window, made the triple obeisance of respect, and paused.

"An intelligent man recognizes the will of the heavens," said he.

"Panthers," rejoined Mingan steadily, "eat men in the northern mountains, and," he added reflectively, "panthers eat men in the southern mountains too. Yet it is written in the books that for everything there is a reason."

He perched himself on the railing by the pillar.

"Tell me who gave the order for my death. I will never speak of what you say."

The Servant of Mercy moved a little nearer, and the ghost of a smile touched his thin lips. No, Mingan would not speak hereafter. Yet now!

"Pledge your slave," said he, "that you will make no outcry, and I will relate the cause of my coming."

"I pledge it you."

"Then, O prince of Cathay, look into the sky behind you and see the cause."

Mingan turned a little, so that he could still watch the man in white.

Hovering at the horizon was a red moon, as if a film of blood had been drawn over a giant eye of the sky.

Miles distant, outlined against the moon, Mingan could trace the line of the Great Wall. That night he had dreamed of the wall. Standing alone on the summit, he had labored at casting down rocks at a mass of beasts that had run in from the vast spaces of the steppe and the desert of Gobi, to leap and snarl at him—the beasts changed to a pack of horsemen clad in furs, figures that grinned at him and rode their shaggy ponies up the sheer side of the wall—

Mingan knew now that he had been thinking of the men from the country of the Horde that lay even beyond the hunting-preserves of the emperor. He had often been tempted to drive his chariot out to the steppe to catch sight of these barbarians, who—his tutors said—were no better than beasts. Perhaps—

"What mean you?"

He slid his boots from his feet and braced his toes in the lacquer work of the balcony.

"Your birth-star, ill-fated one, shines in the favorable constellation of the Lion, betokening power and success to you. The star of the dynasty of Cathay has entered into the region of ill-omen, foretelling disaster. So that the prophecy of the stars may not be fulfilled, your death has been decreed."

"By whom?"

Instead of answering, the executioner cast the loop of his cord at the boy's head. But Mingan gripped the pillar with both hands and swung himself out, over the railing. His feet found holds in the lacquer work on the tower's side, and he let himself down swiftly, escaping the clutch of the executioner's hand.

Often in this way he had escaped his tutors, to snatch the forbidden joy of the stables and a ride under the stars.

For the nonce he was free; if the emperor was his foe, he would not be safe, even beyond the wall; if, however, some favorite in the court had sought his removal, now that he was about to assume his rank and ride with the armies, there was hope. Mingan had been taught to obey implicitly the will of the Dynasty, yet he had in him a wild streak that would not let him be taken easily. He shivered a little, as he felt a surging impulse to turn and flee. To run would be to reveal his movements; to stay where he was would be impossible.

Mingan folded his cold hands in his sleeves and walked slowly to the stables, beyond the gardens of the palace enclosure. Here a Manchu slave nodding beside the glow of a horn lantern started up at sight of a young noble, clad in the dragon robe.

"I will ride," said Mingan composedly, "in a small hunting-chariot. Harness two horses to the shaft. Make no noise, for the Court sleeps."

The Manchu held up the lantern to look keenly into his face. Recognizing the prince, he hastened away. Often in the last months he had obeyed similar commands from Mingan, yet this time he was prompter than usual and the prince saw that the two matched horses were of the best.

"*Wan sui!*" breathed the slave, making his obeisance. "Live for a thousand years."

As Mingan stepped into the chariot—a low, two-wheeled affair of light, gilded cedar—the man's glance fell upon his bootless feet. The slave hesitated, and put the lantern behind him.

"The gate of the palace enclosure is barred and guarded, by the order of Chung-hi, the Discerning, the elder prince. Your servant dares to mention that the lane to the horse pastures behind the stable is not guarded. Drive with a loose rein and—forget not that the night air is not healthy for a Northerner."

Understanding the covert warning, Mingan nodded and turned his chariot slowly in the stable yard, until he reached the grass lane. Here he tossed the reins on the horses' backs and let them graze, while he slipped to the ground and walked back through the gardens, starting at glimpses of stone pillars and evergreens trimmed to the height of a man. He knew well the bypaths of the gardens and presently crossed a bridge over a miniature lake, entering a grove of plane trees where the shadow was like a heavy cloak over his head.

Feeling the tiles with his bare feet, he made his way to a wall illumined by the glow from an incense brazier. Taking fresh powder from the bowl under his hand, he dropped it on the smoking incense and kneeled in front of the tablet of his ancestors that hung in the shrine.

"Honored Ones of the North," he whispered, bending his forehead to the tiles, "I, unworthy, have put upon my person the insignia of a warrior prince, casting aside the garments of childhood. In this hour I, inexperienced, will set my feet on the highway leading from the palace where my elders have taught me wisdom. It is my prayer that no act of mine will make it impossible for me to look into the faces of my illustrious sires with clear honor."

Nine times he made the *ko-tow*, and withdrew, satisfied. The bronze tablets hung in their places as always, the smoke from the brazier curled upward; no sign was vouchsafed Mingan that what he was doing was dishonorable. His senses were keyed to perceive any omen. All he saw was a gleam in the upper corridors of one of the residence palaces of the enclosure.

It was the only light visible, and he stopped to puzzle over it, realizing that it must come from the palace of Benevolent Youth, the quarters of Chung-hi, the heir-apparent. Chung-hi, then, like himself, was awake. Mingan wondered if Chung-hi had sent the Servant of Mercy.

Then, as he passed the stables again, he caught the glow of the Manchu's lantern, and drew closer. The slave seemed to be asleep, but Mingan knew that he could not have dozed so quickly. The face of the slave was composed, but from the breast of the man who had warned him the hilt of a knife projected.

The Servant of Mercy had traced him to the stables, had discovered that horses were missing, and slain the attendant, and then—what? Although nothing was to be heard, Mingan caught the reflected glimmer of lanterns moving toward the gate of the palace enclosure. Guards were already searching for him in that direction; there would have been just time for the executioner to arouse them and order them to the gate to stop him. Then it was probable that his chariot, in the back lane, had not been discovered. Listening intently, he could make out the crunching of the horses as they moved over the grass, and the faint *slap* of the traces.

Seconds were precious, and he ran to the vehicle, caught up the reins, and urged on the horses. They were fresh, and he passed out of the lane to the pastures swiftly, turning here into a path that led to the highway running out of Taitung to the northwest. Once on the road, smoothed and beaten for the passage of the emperor that day, he gave the horses their heads and sped on through the darkness.

The moon had set and the brightest of the stars over his head was the planet of his birth. Mingan, feeling the damp of the dew on his face and the chill of the wind on his skin, wondered that men should so believe in the stars that they should be impelled to slay him because of this omen. It seemed ridiculous that he, cold, shivering, fleeing with throbbing pulse, should be destined to a higher fortune than the Dynasty.

And yet—he had been taught the stars never lied.

The dawn had flooded the sky behind him when Mingan reached the Western Gate of the Wall of China, and found a hundred men-at-arms drawn up beside the barred portal. The captain in command informed him respectfully that orders had been issued from the Court that no one was to pass through the gate before the emperor, who was on the way to the hunt.

Mingan decided to wait where he was. If he went back, he would meet the cavalcade from Taitung; if he turned aside from the highway into one of the earth lanes, his chariot would be bogged down in the mud before he had passed beyond view. So he stood in the miniature chariot, to hide his bare feet, and let his horses breathe.

By the eighth hour of the morning, the gong on one of the gate towers was sounded and the hundred soldiers lifted down the massive bar, swinging open the iron-studded gates. Then they threw themselves down on their faces. A troop of horsemen bearing wands appeared around the first bend in the highway.

Mingan, being of royal blood, and in robes, kept his feet while the horsemen passed, saluting him. He watched a company of the palace guards march past with drawn swords on their shoulders, followed by the dignitaries of the Court, under canopies carried by slaves. Then, at the head of the princes of the blood, and the palanquins of courtesans, appeared the sedan chair of the emperor.

The prince left his chariot and kneeled by the road, feeling his heart quicken as the sedan halted, and the side lattice was lowered at a command from within. The thin face and shrewd eyes of the Son of Heaven peered out at him. He heard the emperor ask his name, and the attendants answer.

"Young nephew," the modulated voice spoke from the opening in the yellow lacquer, "it was said to us that you had left our presence during a revel of the night, thus showing us disrespect, inappropriate in the young in years."

Mingan bent his head nine times.

"Live for a thousand years! I, presuming beyond my merit, ventured to await your passing, to pay my respects for the first time in the robe of a man."

"You are young to be a warrior and a councilor? Have you passed your examinations?"

Before Mingan could answer, a sedan approached and was set down a few paces in the rear of the yellow chair that bore the monarch. From it dismounted Chung-hi, the heir-apparent, a thick-set youth of twenty years with a broad, stubborn face. He bowed three times to his girdle and folded his hands in his sleeves.

"Live forever, O my father. Know that Mingan, cousin of the northern forests, has been lacking in his studies, and has given himself overmuch to driving his chariot of nights, and to making melody with his lute."

The old emperor tapped gently with his fan against the opened lattice, and the lines about his mouth deepened. The devils of sickness had been plaguing him of late and he felt that his years were numbered. Also, the astrologers had dared to point out that the star of his Dynasty was sinking, which troubled him.

"Why do you tell me this, Chung-hi?"

"Be it forgiven me, O beloved of the Dragon! Those who are enemies of Mingan would be affronted at sight of the boy, who is yet a student, appearing in robes; they might think him exalted by the ascendancy of his star, and do him harm."

"Who are his enemies?"

The Cathayan turned to Mingan.

"I know not."

The emperor sighed. As his sight failed, he perceived nevertheless a growth of arrogance in Chung-hi, his son. Presently he looked up and began to question the heir-apparent as to what lay beyond the Great Wall. Taken by surprise, Chung-hi answered haltingly, proving ignorant of more than a smattering of geography and history, although he had just been appointed Warden of the Western Marches.

Realizing this, the emperor nodded to Mingan. "I will test your knowledge and so decide whether you are fitted to assume the duties of a warrior prince at our court. When was this wall built?"

Today Mingan was to have been examined by the old monarch on his studies. Now, however, he was caught leaving the palace before dawn, and he was forced to speak under the stolid stare of the elder prince.

"Thirteen hundreds of years ago, your majesty," he responded quietly. "It was built to keep out of Cathay the marauding tribes of the steppe and the desert of Gobi."

"What tribes?"

"In the steppes are the Taidjuts, who live by raising and stealing cattle and by largesse from your majesty's hand. They provide huntsmen for the time when the peoples of the world watch the Son of Heaven ride to the hunt."

In Mingan's thoughts was the question: Had the emperor ordered his death, or was it Chung-hi, or another?

"Beyond the Taidjuts?"

"Begins, O most wise of the sages, the desert and the people of the desert—Tatars, Mongols, the Jelairs of Turkish race, and the Gipsies. The strongest of these are the Mongols, whose chief is Yesukai, and who are called the Brave. Of their homeland we know only that it is in the high prairies, by the Three Rivers. From there to the south they move their tents, which are their houses, thus giving their herds seasonal pasture. They number forty thousands of tents, and they are hostile to us—"

"Wherefore? Of what are you prating?" demanded the emperor testily.

"In your memory, O beloved of the Dragon, Kabul, khan of the desert tribes, was bidden to the court of Cathay, where he behaved like a wild boar. On his return he was given poison by servants of Cathay, and—"

"Enough!"

The man in the sedan waved his fan impatiently.

"The Prince of Liao-tung," spoke up Chung-hi, "comes from the land next to the Tatars on the north and speaks their language. Surely he shows knowledge of them, when he is close to their counsels."

The emperor frowned slightly. The Mongols were a thorn in his side. He questioned Mingan on strategy and the art of war, and was answered readily.

A gleam of pleasure penetrated the faded eyes of the emperor.

"We," he said, "sitting as judge, decide that the youth Mingan is qualified for the decree of master of scholars, and councilor. Would there were more of his merit to defend our western marches against the raids of the people of the Horde. He has put to shame your learning, O my son, and you are appointed Warden of the Western Marches."

His glance was an accusation, and the elder prince paled a little with anger.

"Lord of Ten Thousand Years," he responded, "while Mingan has spent his days in pondering books and shooting mock arrows, I have taken measures to safeguard your hunting, and the shaft sent from my bow will strike in the heart of Yesukai, khan of the Mongols, your enemy."

He hesitated, looking around at the bowed heads of the attendants, and lowered his voice so that Mingan could catch only snatches of what he said.

"By giving some gold to the Taidjuts—like Kabul, foe of your grandsire—nothing failed, and no one suspects—will not trouble your hours of pleasure."

Mingan thought only that Chung-hi had arranged for the Taidjut tribesmen to protect the wide area of the Ming hunt, and that a blow against the Mongols was in prospect. He drew a deep breath, knowing that he had had narrow escape, for if he had failed to satisfy the emperor, he would have been sent back to the Taitung palace and warded closely, and before many hours had passed he would have received a second visit from the Servant of Mercy.

He suspected now that Chung-hi, not the emperor, had plotted his death, and now it would not do to return to Taitung. The heir-apparent had lost face in the examination before the monarch of Cathay, and he would allow Mingan little time to enjoy his success. Within the Great Wall, there would be no safety for the Manchu.

The emperor turned to him, after dismissing Chung-hi, satisfied with the tidings the prince had whispered.

"It is the feast of Hao, of the fifth day of the fifth month. Speak then, and say if there is any award we can make in honor of your new rank as prince-warrior."

Mingan thought quickly, aware of the covert scrutiny of Chung-hi and the ministers of the elder prince.

"If the Son of the Dragon is pleased, my reward is more than enough," he said slowly. "Yet I crave one thing, to drive my chariot in advance of the imperial guard, to be courier this day for the coming of your benevolent presence."

"It is granted."

The emperor shook his sleeve and signed to the bearers to lower the side of the sedan and take up the poles. Chung-hi seemed satisfied with the request, and Mingan reflected that his enemy was in command of the imperial huntsmen, by virtue of his office as Warden, and that an arrow, loosed in the turmoil of the drive, would end his days as surely as the hand of the Servant of Mercy.

The voice of the old man reached him from behind the lattice.

"Swear to me, Mingan, that you will be faithful to the Dynasty and seek to build up by every act the greatness of Cathay, as the stone layers built up this Wall."

A rush of feeling swept over the Manchu at the faint words of the oath administered to everyone of blood kin to the emperor on arriving at manhood. The splendors of Pekin, the halls of the philosophers, the massive walls of a hundred cities, the never-ending lines of junks on the rivers, and the laden camels on the caravan routes—the myriad warriors he had watched at maneuvers during his childhood—these were some of the pictures that flashed through his mind. Cathay!

"I swear!" he cried, his voice unsteady, his heart thumping.

Chung-hi raised his fan to hide a smile.

So Mingan had the wish of his boyhood when he drove his chariot through the Western Gate, in advance of the wand-men and the court.

Not until the emperor's chair had passed did the guards of the gate venture to raise their faces from the dust.

"Live for ten thousand times ten thousand years!" they cried, holding up their spears.

A group of aged men in long robes, mounted on fat, ambling mares, looked up at the shout and fell to talking together, disputing with much head-wagging. The astrologers were debating hotly the honor shown Mingan, wondering how the youth was to win to greater dignity and the Dynasty fall into decay at the same time, when Mingan had sworn fidelity, and Mingan was known ever to keep an oath.

The highway was broad and its surface level as a stone-paved courtyard. The horses were rested and drew the youth swiftly onward. They passed the villages of farmers that became more scattered as they began to ascend the foothills of the Kinghan Mountains.

Watch-towers, wherein beacons were placed ready for the torch, sped past them. When the horses tired, Mingan changed at a post-station: at midday he changed to fresh beasts again, pausing only to drink a bowl of tea.

By nightfall he had put eighty miles behind him and had outdistanced the cortege of the emperor. He slept at an inn. He was a light sleeper, and in the early hours of the morning he heard a clatter of hoofs on the highway. Listening, he made out that the rider halted only a minute at the post-station near the inn; then the crescendo of hoofbeats again, dwindling out on the road. Only a courier from a high official, on business of the emperor, would be given a horse at the relay station.

A messenger from the court had passed him. And the odds were that the message was sent by Chung-hi, Warden of the Western Marches. Was it merely routine business that sped a rider through the small hours of darkness?

Mingan thought not.

He knew that Chung-hi, superstitious to the core, feared the omen of the stars. Besides, he was jealous of the Northerner, who might, under favor of the old emperor, rise to an important post in the army—perhaps to the command of the Liao-tung swordsmen, the elite of the Cathayan warriors. So Chung-hi sought to remove Mingan from his path, as a man might pluck a thorn from his foot. And Chung-hi, failing to find him at the stopping-place of the courtiers, fifty miles back, had sent a courier ahead—perhaps to the hunting pavilion that was to be the headquarters of the court the week of the great hunt, at the edge of the Taidjut lands—some sixty miles beyond the inn.

At daybreak Mingan was on the road again. Here he circled the shoulders of massive hills, rising into the region of evergreens, where the cool air struck his face pleasantly. His chariot rumbled lightly over gorges, spanned by arched stone bridges.

Mingan changed horses frequently, and sang as he sniffed the odor of the damp forest. He was too glad to be at liberty on the open highway to ponder the future.

Before he was aware of it, he had passed the road leading to the hunting pavilion. So he turned aside into a lane that would take him, as he fancied, to his destination. There were no houses to be seen, and the rolling country cut off his view of landmarks. He let the horses slow down to a foot pace. Presently he reined in and listened.

Faintly, he heard hoofs in the grassy lane behind him. After a moment the sound ceased. Mingan went on, around a bend in the trail, and listened again. The rider—only one horse was to be heard—was following him, because when the chariot moved, its axles creaking, the horse advanced, and when Mingan halted the rider proceeded with caution.

Mingan took up the short hunting-bow from the side wall of the chariot, and fitted to it an arrow from the sheath under his hand. Around the bend in the trail came a rider, but not the spy Mingan looked for.

Instead he beheld a youth of his own age in a ragged woolen cloak and leather tunic—a boy whose keen, black eyes went from the Cathayan prince to the horses of the chariot. The shaggy pony he bestrode was dark with sweat and all but spent.

"Your horse," the stranger said promptly. "Give me it—one of them."

Mingan was surprised to hear the guttural speech of a Mongol, and more surprised at the request, which was little to his liking. He saw that the other was armed like himself—a bow of tough wood, a sheath of arrows behind him at the saddle, a knife in his girdle. But the Mongol's bow was unstrung, his hands empty.

"Who are you and whence come you?" he asked quietly.

The Mongol heeded Mingan not. His head, browned by the sun, projected forward from high, square shoulders; the skin was stretched tight over the bones, and his dark eyes glowed as if from fever.

"Your horses are fresh," he responded curtly, "and I have need of a fresh horse. Loosen one from the shaft if you would live."

"If you return not whence you came," Mingan warned in his fair Mongol, "I will give you this shaft in your heart—"

As he spoke the stranger flung himself bodily from the saddle of the gray pony, striking the ground on hands and knees. Involuntarily, Mingan loosed his arrow, but it glanced harmlessly from an empty saddle. Before he could fit another shaft to string the Mongol leaped into the chariot, seized his shoulders, and bent him back over the front wall of the vehicle.

Mingan writhed and twisted in vain. He felt the bones of his shoulders click together, and a sharp pain shot through his back. Realizing that the Mongol was stronger than he had thought and would break his back in another moment, he groped for the hunting knife in his girdle, pulled it free, and thrust the point through the leather shirt of his adversary, below the ribs.

When the Mongol felt the steel tip in his flesh, his eyes, not a foot from Mingan's twisted face, glowed and his wide mouth set in a straight line.

"I am Temujin," he panted, "son of Yesukai, the Mongol khan, and I am stronger than you. Bear in with your steel, but I will slay you!"

The two boys glared at each other, until a red mist floated before Mingan's sight. He knew that if he thrust home the knife, the iron fingers of the Mongol would snap his spine. Each held the other's life in his hand, and Temujin seemed to exult in the conflict.

Suddenly the Mongol released his hold and stepped back, freeing himself from Mingan's knife.

"You are not a coward, like most Cathayans. Why should I slay you? Abide here and your horse will be brought back to you in the third hour of the night."

Mingan got back his breath slowly, and stood erect with an effort. He could have struck at Temujin with the dagger, but he had an idea that to try to do so would be a mistake. Temujin had judged correctly the intelligence and the honesty of his foe. Mingan noticed the poise of the other's lithe body, the rippling muscles of the wide shoulders under the sleeveless tunic, and the polished, iron armlets that bound each powerful forearm of the Mongol. These, he fancied, had given the boy his name—Man of Iron.

Mingan put away his knife, stealing a glance at the dark stain that appeared on the other's tunic, and folded his arms in his sleeves. By heritage and training, Mingan kept both his dignity and presence of mind.

"We are going in the same direction, O Mongol," he said reasonably. "I may not abide here, so you shall ride in my chariot to the place you seek. Meanwhile, shall there be fellowship between us?"

In silence Temujin eyed him. Friendship, to a Mongol, had a deep significance. He made decisions quickly. "*Tahil tebihou*, the bargain is struck. Drive!"

Mingan would have liked to parley awhile—to know what the son of Yesukai was doing three hundred miles from the Three Rivers, his homeland.

"Your horse," he began—

Temujin stirred impatiently.

"The gray pony will follow, in time. The shadows are turning to the east: we have far to go. Take the reins!"

Although Mingan put the horses to a sharp trot, Temujin was not satisfied until they were whipped into a headlong gallop that set the chariot to plunging dangerously. He watched the road ahead steadfastly. Mingan studied him, when opportunity offered, from the tail of his eye.

"In the ebony box behind you," he ventured, "you will find rice, and fruit and quail meat. You are hungry—"

Promptly Temujin reached down, without shifting his scrutiny. He emptied the box by fistfuls, gulping down the food avidly, as if he had been without a meal for several days. Then he gripped the side of the chariot and planted his legs wide. Presently Mingan saw that he slept, on his feet. It was a cloudy day and the mountain slopes were swept by a chill wind, while a light rain drove in their faces. But Temujin slept on.

After awhile Mingan allowed the horses to slow down to breathe and the boy opened his eyes at once.

"This is not the place. We draw rein to a ravine. The road from the Taidjut steppe runs through it to these hills. In the time milk takes to boil we will be there."

"What seek you in the ravine? If we are to ride together as comrades it is fitting that you should tell me."

Temujin, always sparing of words, explained swiftly, his voice falling into the deeper notes of a Mongol who speaks of vital things.

"Four suns ago a party of Taidjuts came to the tents of Yesukai while most of our warriors were out on the plains hunting. Yesukai, my father, gave them seats at the fire on the guests' side, and milk and mutton and drank with them in fellowship. When they rode off, at dawn, they slew the boys who were guarding the horse herd at the tents and drove off the herd. Yesukai swore by Erlik, but he is old and the chill gets into his bones, so he called for one to pursue the thieves, and slay them."

As Temujin seemed to think this enough said, Mingan prompted him.

"How many were the Taidjuts?"

"Eight or nine."

"Where are your men?"

"I am alone."

"Why did you not rouse up the leaders of your tribes? You cannot cope with so many warriors alone."

Temujin made no answer, and Mingan reflected that the Mongols would have thought it strange if the khan called for others to win back horses stolen from him, or if he had called back the *orkhons*, the heroes, from the hunt.

"There is peace between us and your emperor, O Cathayan," said the boy slowly. "If I had sent the boors from my household to pull down the Taidjuts, they would have become drunk and fallen upon some of your hunting parties. For this is the moon of the emperor's hunt. So said Yesukai, who is old, and wise."

Mingan hid a smile, but presently fell serious. If it became known that he had aided a prince of the Mongols against the Taidjuts, Chung-hi would accuse him of a crime. What was it that the Warden of the Western Marches had said of the Taidjuts? He had prepared some intrigue against Yesukai, with their aid.

"Here is the ravine," quoth Temujin, signing for the Cathayan to draw rein.

The trail they were following dipped sharply down into a wooded glade where it joined another road, marked by many hoofs, running east and west. This, Mingan knew, was the main trail from the Taidjut pastures to the Kinghan Mountains, whither many of the tribesmen had come to aid in the great hunt of the emperor.

The wind had ceased, and with it the mist of rain. Far out on the brown prairie the setting sun cast its rays in among the trees. Mingan saw, about a mile out on the Taidjut road, a mass of moving beasts, and the tiny glints that were the sun's reflection on spear tips.

"We have come in time," he said, and Temujin nodded silently.

II

A Hobgoblin and a Woman

It was the part of wisdom for Mingan to withdraw now, especially as the Mongol youth did not want the chariot to descend into the ravine, where its wheel tracks would be visible to the approaching horse thieves. Especially, too, when after a few moments he heard a neigh, and saw the gray pony trotting up.

It would not do for the Taidjuts to see him with Temujin, to bring word of what they had witnessed to the Cathayan Court. That they would reach the hunting pavilion safely, he had no doubt. They must be bound thither with the captured horses, to sell to the Cathayans. And how could one boy—or two for that matter—armed only with a bow and knife overcome eight men full grown, well mounted and armed?

Temujin guessed what was in his mind.

"Blood will be spilled here," he said, "and Erlik, the lord of the underworld, will welcome new souls to his court of darkness before night falls on the ravine. Turn to the left, and seek the road below you when you have gone three arrow shots, and you will reach the assembling place of the Taidjuts at the pavilion, if that is your wish."

As Mingan made no move to go, he added shortly—

"No man will know you have been with me."

But Mingan found that he did not wish to go. He was curious, and desired to see how Temujin would strive against the tribesmen. The boy's eyes were sunk in his head from weariness, yet the mist of sleep had cleared from them. He was not mad; still single-handed he was preparing to attack his enemies. Mingan's pulse began to throb, and he felt a thrill stealing through his veins that was more than the exhilaration of driving a racing-chariot or the excitement of the chase. For the first time he stood where men would slay each other.

To Temujin, he knew, this feeling was an old experience. Born in the heart of the feuds of the great plain of the Gobi, the Mongol was older in experience than he, who had been weaned on books. And Temujin's quarrel was just.

"I will stay," Mingan said, under his breath.

And in a moment he was glad he had chosen so; he felt a great liking for the Mongol boy; at the same time his hands quivered, and his lips twitched.

Temujin looked at him sharply, grunted, and swiftly set to work tearing strips from his girdle to bind the muzzles of the chariot horses so that they would not neigh at the approach of the Taidjut beasts.

"What is your plan?" Mingan spoke in a whisper, involuntarily.

Temujin shook his head impatiently and signed for him to follow. Making sure that the three horses were screened by bushes from the trail below, the two boys scrambled down the bank and sought among the willows until Temujin found what he was looking for—a clear spring, about which were the ashes of former campfires. He glanced out at the sun, now close to the horizon.

"Can you write words, O Cathayan?" His eyes were on the miniature silver jar of India ink, and the brush tied, as always, to the girdle on the prince.

As Mingan nodded, he continued.

"Then write these words: *Under this tree*"—hastily he ripped the bark from the hole of an aged chestnut with his knife, exposing the gray under-surface—"*will die the khan of the Taidjuts, a thief.*"

Swiftly Mingan dipped brush and ink fragment in the spring and traced the six Mongol characters, a hand's length high on the bare bole of the tree. As he did so the last rays of the sun passed from the branches over their heads, leaving the ravine in obscurity.

Temujin raised his head, hearing the hoofs of many horses drawing nearer, and pulled Mingan back through the willow clumps until they were hidden from the spring and the message on the tree. Then he strung his bow, tested the gut, and squatted down, placing between his knees the quiver he had taken from the saddle of his pony. Mingan had to make two attempts to fit the silk string of his bow into the notch.

Then he found that he had no arrows. Temujin gave him two and whispered: "Some of the dogs will be out of sight, at the rear of the herd. We must not suffer them to escape, or the whole tribe will be raised against us, and our graves will be dug not far from here."

Mingan saw a rider trot up to the spring, dismount, ward off his pony from the water with a blow, and kneel to drink. He was a broad man with massive shoulders; a sword as long as his leg, and wide at the head as a battle ax, hung from his belt.

Five others came up in a group, and four of them followed the example of the leader. The fifth, who carried a bow ready strung and wore the eagle feather of a chief in his fur cap, glanced around keenly as if he had seen or heard something suspicious. He sighted the writing on the tree, moved closer to peer at it, and called for a torch.

Mingan felt Temujin touch his shoulder restrainingly. The boys held their breath while one of the Taidjuts kindled a light leisurely and ignited a torch taken from his saddle. When he had waved it around his head and the flames spluttered up brightly, he handed it to the chief of the Taidjuts.

Still Temujin did not move, and Mingan studied the brown, seamed faces and the evil, glittering eyes that peered around under bronze helmets and sable hats. Suddenly the khan gave a shout of rage, as he grasped the meaning of the writing. At the same instant Temujin stirred, and an arrow sped between the willow stems, thudding into the neck of the chieftain.

The stricken man rose in his stirrups, the torch still gripped in a rigid hand. Twice more Temujin loosed shafts, while Mingan fumbling with cold fingers missed his first shot. His second shaft, better directed, pierced the chest of one of the warriors. Then the torch fell to earth, and the body of the khan slumped down on it, casting the glade into deep shadow.

Two of the Taidjuts were dead and two sorely hurt. Temujin began to creep away on hands and knees. Mingan had stood up, to loose his arrows, and now a shaft whizzed past his ear. He saw the first comer, the Taidjut warrior who had drunk from the spring, advancing toward him, gripping with both hands the hilt of the sword—the weapon that now seemed to Mingan to loom large as the warrior himself.

Tapering to a hand's breadth at the hilt, it widened to the length of a man's forearm at the tip. It rested on the Taidjut's right shoulder, curving down over his back. Mingan could see the small, black eyes of his foe fixed on him, and hear the grating of his pointed teeth as he snarled in rage. His two arrows being sped, the boy cast aside his bow and drew his knife, standing his ground.

The skin of his back prickled ominously and his muscles were rigid for action, yet what to do he knew not. The Taidjut leaped forward, letting the ponderous blade slide down behind him, while both fists raised the hilt over his head. Up came the blade and down at Mingan, who leaped aside.

His heels caught in the roots of the underbrush and he fell, while the warrior raised his weapon for a second stroke, grunting in triumph.

Then was heard the whistle of an arrow—a shaft that thudded into the knotted chest of the man as if into a wooden drum. A wheezing of air from pierced lungs, a bubbling of blood in the throat; the Taidjut staggered, yet took another step forward grinning in a ghastly fashion at Mingan.

"Dog—Cathayan!"

A second arrow from the underbrush buried itself in the side of his head and he went down in his tracks. Mingan had not thought that a bow could be as powerful as that of his Mongol ally. He took up the sword of the dead man and looked around. The last of the six Taidjuts had mounted his pony and was riding off toward the horse herd.

Temujin left his cover and jumped on one of the best of the horses moving restlessly beside the spring. Leaning down in the saddle, he caught up from the earth a lasso dropped by one of his enemies—a stout bamboo pole to the end of which was attached a cord terminating in a running noose. Wheeling his pony, he started after the fugitive, leaving Mingan breathless, with the great sword in his hand, but not a man on foot to face him.

He watched the two riders disappear into the gathering twilight. Then, half-disbelieving the reality of all that had passed in the last two or three minutes, went to the Taidjut khan, whom he found to be stone dead. So little time had elapsed in the fight that Mingan was able to light a fresh torch from the smoldering one on the ground.

Trailing the sword, he stooped over one of the wounded riders, and found him mortally hurt. Turning to the other, who still breathed, he started. In the dim light he had not seen that this was not a Taidjut warrior, but a Cathayan, and, by the feathers in his square cap, an imperial courier.

The man's sight was failing, but he made out the glitter of the yellow robe of the prince, and the peacock feather.

"Lord," he panted, striving to grip the edge of Mingan's dress, "you are of Cathay, not of the Horde. Know that I, an unworthy servant of the planets around the sun, have fulfilled my mission."

"What mission?"

The man peered at Mingan vainly, passed his hand over his eyes.

"I cannot see your face, lord of the Dragon brood. But you wear the robe of the Dynasty and bear a warrior's sword—I was sent by him who stands behind the Dragon Seat—Chung-hi—who bade me give order to the Taidjut khan to see that Ye Lui Kutsai Mingan, a young prince of the north, was slain if he came alone to the hunting pavilion. Make it known, honorable sir, to Chung-hi that I—"

He coughed and fell back on his side.

"It shall be known that you delivered the message."

Mingan spoke mechanically, while he wondered if this were the rider that passed him last night. A swift courier, and faithful to Chung-hi. So the prince who stood behind the Dragon Seat was seizing already his heritage—issuing commands that should come only from his father! The aged emperor could not protect the youths of royal blood who came to his court from the outlying provinces.

Even the hunt was a scene set for intrigue. Mingan felt as if he stood on a quicksand, not knowing in what direction to take the next step.

His torch died out, and the darkness seemed to close in threefold. Wraiths of gray mist were forming in the hollows—smoke, the Mongols said, that rose up to the surface of the earth from the halls of Erlik, the lord of the lower regions.

In fact the mist veiled the rider that Mingan heard coming toward him from the plain. Not until horse and man were within arm's reach did he recognize Temujin.

The Mongol for once moved slowly. He was dragging at the bamboo pole of the lasso, and at the other end of the rope the body of the sixth Taidjut slid over the grass.

"Leave the chariot," said Temujin quickly. "It will avail not where we are going."

"Where?" asked Mingan.

"Not far; to the forest line of the highest of these hills. The three Taidjuts guarding the rear fled when they heard the music of weapons. They saw this one die. They will spread the word in our rear that Mongols are raiding. We cannot go back through the Taidjut country to the Gobi; we must seek a safe place and spy out where our enemies gather."

"On your right hand, high on the slope of the mountain Pisgah, overlooking the Kinghan Range is the shrine of Kwan-ti, the god of war," Mingan observed. "In the week of the great hunt no one makes the pilgrimage to the place of Kwan-ti. Are you afraid to go there?"

"Why?" Temujin leaned down to study the face of his comrade.

Satisfied, he took the saddles from four of the riderless horses and left them on the ground. Leading up a pony for Mingan to ride, he instructed the Cathayan to go ahead to point out the way, while he gathered up all his arrows and rounded up the scattered ponies—no easy task in the darkness.

"Keep the Cathayan sword: you cannot use a bow," he ordered. "Light no more torches to guide our enemies to us. In whose tent have you passed your days that you know no more than that?"

"In the palace of the emperor," said Mingan frankly. "My name is Ye Lui Kutsai Mingan."

"Min-gan, the Bright One," Temujin grunted. "You cannot drive horses; can you ride one?"

"Yes," declared the prince.

As a matter of fact he had not sat in a saddle since childhood, but he would have been ashamed to admit that to Temujin.

Under the tall firs of the higher slope of Pisgah the lane of Kwan-ti overlooked the brown plain of the Gobi, behind the green hill country that formed the heart of the Taidjut lands. As Mingan said, the shrine was deserted, for no one would have presumed to enter the lines of the beaters that drove game from the plain and the ravines, to be killed by the courtiers.

It was a clear day, and the two boys sat comfortably on the stone steps leading up to the pagoda, watching the panorama of the hunt. So vast was its extent that they could observe only the lines of riders out toward the plain and the cavalcades of bright-robed Cathayans who, with their slaves, rode out to the rendezvous of the kill each day. Temujin's ponies grazed and rested in the open glades of the forest, and Temujin himself shot down quail and hares for the pot, and kindled the cooking fire in among the trees after darkness when the smoke would not disclose their presence. He never asked Mingan's help, although he always shared what food they had fairly.

"How long will your emperor hunt?" he asked.

"For three days more." Mingan thought this would impress his companion. "Each day they will kill twenty stags, thrice as many boar, and hundreds of antelopes."

Temujin looked up impassively.

"When the *orkhons* of the Horde hunt in the Gobi, they slay each day a thousand deer, and load a hundred camels with the skins. When the hunt is ended the prairie cannot be seen for the wolves that gather about, nor the sun in the sky for the vultures that flock to our trail."

This was hard for the Cathayan to believe. He had seen the gray wolves of the northern forests harry villages in Liao-tung unhindered. He had heard that the Mongols of the Three Rivers lived by hunting and raiding—by eating the horses of their herds and wearing the skins of animals, and he thought that must be a miserable existence.

"Some of the Horde," went on the chief's son, "ride deer—reindeer, and wear their hoofs for heels on their boots. They are the Tungusi who dwell in the frozen prairies of the north. They have red hair and are good fighters."

Now Mingan smiled, believing that Temujin jested, but the Mongol was occupied with his own thoughts.

"Could a horse jump your Great Wall?" he asked abruptly.

"Can a horse jump five times the height of a man?"

"When I am Khan of the Horde I will send my warriors to break through it."

Looking at the restless boy whose ragged sheepskin barely covered his brown limbs, Mingan did not take his words seriously. Later, he had cause to remember the boast of the chief's son.

"You have no siege engines," he pointed out, "and we have many stone- and arrow-throwers on the Wall. Besides, you have not men enough."

"*Kai*—it is true. The tribes fight among themselves, and turn not upon their enemies." Temujin nodded, rubbing his iron sleevelets thoughtfully. "The Cathayans slew my grandsire's sire foully. It is also true that the strength of a wall is not in the stones that built it."

"In what, then?" Mingan was a little proud of his learning, and was not minded to be corrected by a herd boy—as he considered Temujin to be.

"In the men on top of it. If they are weak, the wall is useless, though high as a hundred spears." He pointed down at the plain. "Look—who is that Khan, riding on the shoulders of his men?"

Temujin had the eyes of a hawk. Only after a long peering did the prince make out a yellow speck among other dots moving out toward the beaters.

"It must be Chung-hi, who someday will be emperor. He is sitting on the hunting platform, carried by slaves, so that no beast can harm him when he casts his spear."

The Mongol grunted.

"The jackal! He kills when others drive in his game—" He yawned and lay back. "I could take a wall that Chung-hi defended."

"How?" Mingan was interested, for the heir-apparent was Keeper of the Great Wall.

"By making the jackal afraid. Then he would run away. That is a jackal's nature."

Now, because it troubled him and because he fancied that after a day or so he would see no more of the chief's son, Mingan told Temujin of the plot against him, the deaths of his cousins, and the peril that stood in wait for him if he should return to the court. The memory of the overthrow of the Taidjuts in the ravine was strong upon him, and perhaps he wished to show the Mongol that he, also, was not without enemies.

But Temujin, watching the Cathayans on the plain, seemed not to heed his words. As a matter of fact he listened carefully, as Mingan discovered on the morrow.

"I could escape from you, O Temujin," he pointed out, annoyed by the other's silence, "and disclose your hiding-place to the emperor, thus winning his favor."

"You are free to go."

Two things restrained Mingan. After all, the Mongol had saved his life, and there was truce between the Horde and Cathay. Besides, he had a suspicion that if he led a pony to the shrine of Kwan-ti, the boy and his herd would be found there, for Temujin would take a chance with his enemies on the plain rather than be cornered by the Cathayans.

Temujin observed him, and looked away, satisfied. If Mingan meant to betray him, the prince would not have spoken his mind.

"You are a *usenin*—a teller of tales. Is that how you pass the time when you are shut up in the houses of Yen-king?"*

To the Mongol it seemed strange that the Cathayans chose to dwell under a roof. Mingan, falling in with his mood, told of the tens of thousands of mailed warriors that drilled under the generals' eyes in the fields within the walls of the city—walls that a rider on a swift horse could not circle

*The great court, Peking.

between sunrise and sunset—and of the myriad junks that came up the river from Zipangu, the island of savages, and other places of the sea.

"It is time for me to go forth with my bow," Temujin observed, "and seek out meat for our eating. Will you watch the horses?"

This was the first time he had asked Mingan to do anything for him, and the prince was surprised. He waited a long time after the other had disappeared into the forest, but Temujin did not return. The sun went down—a red ball that sank into the golden prairie out of the purple vault of the sky. A whippoorwill began its evening plaint, and somewhere behind the bulwark of the mountains the moon rose. Mingan could make out the dark blur of the ponies that clustered together with the coming of night.

He felt the chill touch of damp air and turned toward the pagoda of Kwan-ti, god of war, drawing in his breath sharply upon beholding the dark form of the god outlined against the pallid sky in the east—for the temple was no more than a roof, set upon bamboo pillars.

"What shall I do?" he thought. "Harm may have befallen Temujin. If I am absent from the hunting pavilion another night, they will search for me, and when I return the emperor will look at me with a darkened face. O Kwan-ti, to whom all things are known, send me a sign to show the path that I must follow."

No sooner had he said that than he was frightened. Here were no priests to frighten away the evil spirits that dwelt on the mountain summit, and the deserted shrine seemed to be peopled with shadowy forms. If he had not promised his companion to watch the horses, Mingan would have fled.

The whippoorwill ceased its song abruptly, and the boy sprang up, grasping his heavy sword. From the edge of the forest a rider was moving toward him soundlessly. Mingan knew that no Cathayan noble would seek the shrine of Kwan-ti without attendants with lights and cymbals to drive away the mountain devils, and no one but a noble would possess a horse.

The newcomer halted at the foot of the steps, almost within reach of the boy, who, feeling the hot breath of the horse's nostrils, knew that it was no apparition but a living being.

He lifted the long blade, and the rider moved. "Stand and stir not. I have an arrow fitted to bow, and if you bring down your big sword I will loose my shaft." The words were Mongol, and Mingan, straining his eyes, could make out in the treacherous light what seemed to be a child, muffled in a fur cloak, a child with tresses of dark hair bound by a silver fillet. Surely the voice was a girl's.

"Do you understand, Cathayan? Where is Temujin?"

Mingan lowered his sword.

"I do not know."

"Ahai! Does the kite not know where the dead hare lies? Here are his ponies—I have felt of the *tanga,* the brand on their flanks. Have you slain him, Cathayan, for a sacrifice to your god?"

Mingan explained that the chief's son had gone in search of game and had not returned. By now he could see the delicate features and dark eyes of the girl, and the arrow that she still held on her bow.

"What man are you? What are you doing here?" Her voice, soft, with a quick lisp that Mingan found hard to understand, made the harsh gutturals musical.

He told her, not without some pride, his name and how he had met with Temujin; and she was not satisfied until she had heard the story of the fight in the ravine. Then she laughed, under her breath.

"Kai—it is true. You are the fool."

"How?"

"So your Cathayan warriors said—they who are camped in the ravine of the Taidjut road. They said that you were witless and blind with pride in your new finery."

She stopped to gaze, wide-eyed, at the yellow robe and the peacock feather, then continued: *"Kai*—it is true that you are like a wood-pheasant, fair to look at. But the talk at the Cathayan fire was that your enemies would put out your life like a candle in the wind."

"How did you understand our speech? Are you a Mongol?"

"Nay, I know many things. The night speaks to me, and the raven sits on the ridge-pole of my tent—"

"Daughter of Podu, the Gipsy—" Temujin's deep voice came from beside them although neither had heard him approach—"you have the tongue of the cat-bird that is never still. Peace!"

The girl unstrung her bow and perched sidewise in her saddle with a little sigh of relief.

"Son of Yesukai, have you become a Cathayan house dog, to think only of food, while the wolves gather around you, sitting on their haunches—"

"Peace, I said." The Gipsy fell silent. "Little Burta, has the smoke of Podu's tent fire died away, that you seek me in such a spot?"

At this the corners of her small mouth drooped and she lowered her eyes.

"Nay, Temujin, it is your tent fire that grows cold. Yesukai, your father, is dying, and asks for you."

The Mongol threw down the brace of quail he was carrying and his eyes went out over the moonlit plain.

"He has been poisoned," she went on. "The Taidjuts who came to his yurt as guests put poison in his drinking-cup. May they be torn by the dogs of Erlik! Because you had passed our camp, when you pursued them, the Mongols who went in search of you took me with them to point out your trail. When we came to the lines of the Cathayan hunters, they could approach no nearer, but I went among the Taidjut fires at night and heard of the death of their khan at your hand in the ravine. I was glad, and from the place of the slaying I followed your trail to this mountain, and at sunset saw the horses."

"The slayers of Yesukai have already gone to give greeting to Erlik," the Mongol said slowly.

Burta's teeth flashed in a smile, then she glanced at Mingan coldly.

"Why do you suffer him near you?"

Temujin, sunk in thought, seemed not to heed her.

But Mingan started, remembering the words of Chung-hi spoken several days ago at the Western Gate:

"By giving gold to the Taidjuts—nothing failed and no one suspects—will not trouble your hours of pleasure."

The party of the horse thieves had returned from the Mongol prairie to the road to the hunting pavilion: Chung-hi had sent a messenger to them. Surely the Taidjut khan had been acting under orders from the Warden of the Western Marches.

And this messenger had given the Taidjuts the command to slay him—Mingan—if they found him alone.

"Mingan—" the chief's son roused himself—"is my comrade. Do him no mischief!"

The Gipsy child pouted and, from the corners of her eyes, peered at the tall prince with distrust, even with jealousy. Leaning toward the Mongol she whispered anxiously, until Temujin silenced her by taking the two heavy braids of hair, crossing them over her lips, and knotting them forcibly behind her head. Mingan gathered from her gestures that she wanted Temujin to kill him, strip him of his clothes, and use them as a disguise in penetrating the Cathayan lines.

"We must mount and ride swiftly to the country of the Three Rivers of my father, Yesukai," Temujin declared. "You must come to clear the way for us if we fall in with a strong band of your Cathayan hunters."

At this Mingan would have protested, when he thought of the plot of Chung-hi against the boy's father. If Temujin should be caught by the soldiers of the warden, he would be tortured, if not killed; if the Taidjuts captured him, his fate would be no better. As for Burta—

A proverb of the Master K'ung occurred to him: "A man who slays an enemy with his own hand is better than one who stirs up others to kill."

"I will go," he agreed thoughtfully, "as far as the last cordon of my people."

But Temujin had left him and was already rounding up the ponies, assisted by Burta.

It seemed to the prince that it would be fatal to attempt to take the horses with them through the encampments of the Taidjuts.

Temujin, however, would not think of leaving them behind. That evening he had descended the mountain slope to scout around the nearest fires of his foes—this had delayed his return—and had discovered a trail leading down among the gullies on the left flank of the hunters' lines. Mounting a big, roan stallion, the leader of the herd, he led the way thither, followed by the other ponies, with Burta and Mingan bringing up the rear.

The night was young enough for them to make out the ruddy glow of the fires, where men had settled down for the night, and to avoid them. And the clear moonlight enabled Temujin to pick out the trail easily.

Without being challenged they descended the forested slope of the mountain, wound among the gullies of the foothills, and felt themselves in the warmer air of the wide plain. Heading from copse to thicket, and keeping clear of the skyline on the ridges, the Mongol finally left the last of the cover and struck out into the sweep of high grass, going slowly to make it seem as if he were leading the ponies from one camp to another.

Often he stopped, taking warning from sights or sounds unperceived by Mingan. They came presently upon a stream, lined with gnarled willows through which the moonlight filtered sparingly, and here Temujin led the ponies down to water, and to let them breathe.

Mingan presently heard him grunt warningly at Burta and stride up the bank to look out. Voices approached, and Mingan stepped back into the deep shadow of the trees.

Four riders descended the bank and, halting to let their horses drink, noticed the other ponies.

"What herd is this?" one called out in the western dialect of Cathay. Mingan could see that it was one of the palladins of the court, a stout warrior encased in a mass of quilted armor, a ten-foot spear hanging at his back.

"Mine, if it please you, uncle," responded Burta, advancing to his stirrup.

"And whose are you?" ejaculated the warrior, somewhat vaguely, being a little the worse for wine at the festival. "A star-eyed, lissome maid, by all the *rakchas* of the air!

"A pavilion of trees,
And a goblet of wine.
Alas, what are these,
No companion is mine!"

He stooped to kiss the face of the girl, but she bent her head under pretense of stroking the silver-inlaid breast-strap of the charger. Recovering his balance with some difficulty, the hero seemed inclined to continue his song, when one of the men-at-arms pointed out the figure of Temujin, advancing toward them in the gloom under the trees.

"You have your shadow, O Commander of a Thousand! Is not that companion enough?"

The mirthful rider bent his head cautiously, stared at his image in the pool and smiled. Whereat the others urged their horses on, and the charger splashed across the stream after them, bearing with it the palladin whose thoughts seemed to have turned from women to wine, for the last heard of him was the announcement in a hearty voice:

"The moon cannot swallow
Her share of the grog,
And my shadow must follow
Wherever I jog!"

Mingan drew a long breath of relief, for he had expected that any second the Mongol's arrows might begin to fly through the air, and Burta was silent as they changed their saddles to fresh beasts and started forward again.

Cre-ak—*cree-eek*: the leather of Mingan's saddle squeaked louder and louder. *Slap—flap, slap,* went the breast-strap and reins. He started out of a doze, aware that he was shivering in the early morning chill, and that his legs ached.

The herd had struck up a smart pace and was passing over a stretch of rolling country, dotted with thickets. The rising sun warmed his back, and he felt refreshed.

"Are we out of the cordons?" he asked Burta, seeing no sign of other riders.

The girl made a face at him and shook her head. Temujin, too, was uneasy. Mingan sighed, for he would have liked to halt and rest—though not to sit down, as yet. His glance was caught by several antelope, breaking from cover before them. A fox appeared out of a clump of sage, and turned in its tracks at sight of them, vanishing before it was fairly seen.

Then Mingan was aware of a clamor behind them, a medley of cymbals, drums, and hand-gongs, and knew that the beaters of the royal hunt had started forth to the plain, evidently driving west.

Temujin turned his horse's head more to the left, and quickened his pace. For some time they made rapid progress, leaving behind them the tumult of the beaters.

Then, topping a rise, they saw along all the left flank a long line of Taidjuts bearing in toward them.

Reining in sharply, Temujin scanned the line in vain for a break, and then started forward to the right, away from the riders. Now the ponies bunched close together, heads up, snorting with sudden fear. Here and there more deer came into view, racing away from the Taidjuts, and a leopard turned up almost under the horses' noses, streaking away like a shaft loosed from a crossbow.

A fine wapiti stamped up to the summit of a knoll, and wheeled about, laying its antlers low on its back. The sight and smell of the plains animals made the ponies frantic, and Mingan had all he could do for awhile to manage his horse. He thought that they must surely out-distance the hunt, at such a pace. But Temujin pointed out that many of the animals appeared from in front, running toward them. They swept down into a long, grassy gully, among groups of darting antelope, and rounding a bend in the declivity, came full into a confusion of beasts.

Across the ravine in front of them a squadron of mailed cavalry was deployed, shouting and waving mantles at the game.

The headlong rush of the ponies carried the three fugitives up to within arrow-shot of the Cathayan horsemen before Temujin worked his horse out of the press and halted, his bow strung and an arrow on the string.

Burta forced her pony to his side. The Cathayans promptly took up javelins and bows and slowly drew nearer.

Mingan, seeing that they were nearly hemmed in, called to his companions in Mongol not to resist, and searched for the leader of the mailed archers. At sight of the young prince in court dress the captain in command dismounted and came forward to hold Mingan's rein and hear what he had to say.

"Leader of a Hundred," the boy ordered clearly, "I am Ye Lui Kutsai Mingan, and I have rank in your country, Liao-tung. For the first time since coming of age I see the warriors of Liao-tung—" with pride his glance went around the circle of watching men—"when, by command of the Son of Heaven, I am to ride before all others of the hunt. With these two barbarians I would pass your line, taking with me their ponies."

He indicated the emblem of the Northern banners on his shoulder, in which command the mounted archers were included.

The captain bowed several times, then made pretense of adjusting a buckle on the pony's halter. Mingan noticed that his fingers trembled.

"Your servant is honored by your discerning order. O son of illustrious fathers, when you have passed beyond the sight of the Cathayans, heed these words. Evil awaits you in the Dragon Court. Do not return, but ride with your companions to your people of Liao-tung who impatiently desire sight of their prince. Favored of the stars, has your servant leave to withdraw?"

Mingan nodded, shaking his sleeve slightly. The Cathayans drew off, staring awhile at Temujin and Burta, then set about the business of the hunt. Beyond their ranks the nearest Taidjuts were coming into view and Mingan and Temujin lost no time in trotting out of sight down the ravine.

When they came to the open prairie again, Mingan reined in.

"Here you are safe, son of Yesukai. You are in the land of the Horde. Now will I say farewell and go to the emperor."

Temujin brought his pony up and stretched out his right hand, clasping both the prince's wrists between his fingers with a sudden motion.

For a moment Mingan strained to free himself, and realized that the grip of the stronger one could not be broken. Temujin, still holding Mingan helpless, dismounted, drew with his free hand the Cathayan's long girdle from his waist, and bound his wrists; then, taking a rope from his own saddle, tied the boy's feet together under the horse's belly.

"Fool," he grunted, looking up quizzically. "Would you turn back into a snare set for your feet? Have you forgotten the ill-will of the son of the emperor? Burta whispered to me the words of the commander of the archers. Would you escape to Liao-tung?"

Mingan shook his head. It would be useless—he would be sent for, and, failing to appear, would be proclaimed a rebel at the court of Yen-king, and the tablets of his fathers would be taken down and broken—which was not to be thought of.

"Then," said Temujin gravely, "you will be my friend, and my *usenin*—teller of tales. Come, we will take the trail that leads to the desert."

Meanwhile the feast of Hao was nearly at an end, and the aged emperor of Cathay declared he had seen enough of hunting and summoned his councilors and astrologers to hear the evidence of the disappearance of the Prince of Liao-tung, and to decide what had become of him.

The Taidjuts who had escaped from the fight in the ravine gave their testimony, and, to justify their flight, stated emphatically that a hundred hobgoblins of the steppe, armed with thunderbolts, had attacked them and had slain their chief after writing the mysterious prophecy on the tree-trunk.

They had not seen Mingan, and they said that if Temujin had been in the ravine, he must have been in league with the spirits of the waste-places, because the chief's son could not write, and there was the inscription on the tree for all to see.

Cathayan priests who had gone to offer belated sacrifices at the shrine of Kwan-ti reported hoof marks all about the pagoda, and heaps of ashes where spirit fires had been kindled—surely supernatural, because they had been seen by no man.

Mingan's abandoned hunting-chariot and horses were shown to the emperor, and those who found it reported that there were no boot tracks visible around it in the moist earth by the stream—only the prints of bare feet, which surely could not belong to the prince.

Lastly, rumors came from the Liao-tung banner-men that Mingan had been seen riding in company with a hobgoblin and a woman like no other in Cathay, beautiful beyond words, and clad in ermine skins.

This jogged the memory—a trifle wine-tinted—of a certain fat under-officer, who proclaimed loudly that he had spoken to the woman herder of the horses and without doubt she was a *rakcha*, a female vampire, who had tried to fasten herself on him.

So it was decided that Mingan had been carried off by devils.

Perhaps he had been turned into a horse or wolf by the woman-spirit of the steppe; perhaps he wandered through the wastes of the Gobi in human form, but a devil incarnate. In any event, if he reappeared in Cathay, he was to be bound and turned over to the priests.

The old emperor sighed and said in a solemn voice: "The spirits of the steppe are very powerful and this place is ill-omened. Let us return to the wall, and to our palace at Taitung where our actors will devise a new play portraying the virtues of the Cathayans and the evils of the demons of the sandy steppes. Let gongs be beaten, and paper-prayers burned; let paper also be scattered across the path behind us, so that any devils who follow will be led astray. I grieve for the evil fate of Mingan, who was my second son."

Thereafter no men of Cathay ventured in the ravine where the dead bodies lay under the tree, and the Taidjuts made a new road around the place. Only Chung-hi, struggling against his deep superstition, passed that way to make sure that his messenger and his hired slayers, the Taidjuts, were beyond all doubt powerless to reveal his plot.

He was well content: those who could have betrayed him were dead, Mingan was powerless, even though living, and the prestige of Chung-hi was greater than ever. Only one thing troubled him.

In the heavens Mingan's birth star glowed in a favorable constellation, and the northern warriors whispered among themselves that the time would come when the Prince of Liao-tung would return to dwell among them again, and take his place as leader. Chung-hi shifted uneasily when he thought of it.

III
The Master of the Horde

For several days Temujin and his two companions passed swiftly over wide prairies where the dry grass rose high as the horses' noses.

Here were no villages, but only clusters of gray, Tatar tents visible at times on the horizon, and scattered herds of ponies and cattle. Temujin avoided these and pressed on without halting, except to rest the horses. He and Burta slept in the saddle, and Mingan from very weariness learned to do likewise.

The son of Yesukai touched no food for four days, and Mingan would have fared badly if the Mongol boy had not ordered Burta to share her dried mutton and raisins—with which her saddle bags were filled—with him. This, seeing that the prisoner was suffering, she did willingly enough, and even prevailed on Temujin to take off his bonds on the morning of the second day.

Mingan was too tired to think of trying to escape from the Mongol that night even if he could have stolen away from the keen eyes of the children of the plains.

The third day, Mingan judged that they covered four hundred *li** by the late afternoon. Temujin's will to go on would suffer no hindrance; his eyes were smoldering, as if he were faced by a visible foeman. It was a hard race, that ride over the plateau of the northern Gobi; to Mingan it was torment. But Temujin was racing against time, and the hand of death.

"Look toward the sun," said Burta to Mingan.

The chief's son already had seen what she noticed—a long line of dust ahead of them. They were on a small knoll in the prairie, and the wind from the west whipped at the girl's dark tresses, and dried the sweat on Temujin's hollow cheeks. Mingan watched the dust draw nearer, revealing dark specks that proved to be horsemen, riding along a front of a half-mile.

As the gap between the strangers and Temujin closed, Mingan saw that there were other lines, evenly spaced, behind the first—several thousand riders in all. In the center of the moving square above the film of dust that rose from the dry soil appeared a long pole, topped by the antlers of a wapiti—a rude enough standard.

"Tatars," said Burta briefly.

They rode not close together with the slow pace of the chargers of the mailed Cathayan cavalry but in squadrons of a hundred, each with its leader in front. They were thick-set men, brown of skin and clad in black, rawhide armor, coated with dust, and Mingan looked in vain for supply train or pack-animals. The Tatars had goatskin saddle bags tied to the peaks of the high saddles, and two bows slung at their shoulders, with a sword or ax in their belts, and every warrior had a spare pony.

As if the three wanderers on the knoll had been an islet and the riders a succession of swells, the Tatars dashed up and divided to pass them. Mingan caught glimpses of scarred faces, and occasionally steel ring mail gleaming under flying fur cloaks.

"*Hai, ahatou! Koke Mongku, hai!* (Ho brothers, warrior Mongols, ho!)"

The lines took up the shout as they came abreast, and echoed the war

*About a hundred and forty miles.

cry of the Horde. Mingan stared at them, aware of power in the steady gait of the ordered ranks, in the deep voices of the riders. It was his first glimpse of the fighting men of the Horde that was made up of Tatars, Mongols, Merkets, and even the strong Keraits* of the west, the desert tribes of the south, and the reindeer folk of the white regions in the north—but of which the Khan of the Mongols had always been the leader.

As the standard passed close to them, a burly rider, hatless and white-haired, galloped up, and reined in sharply by Temujin.

"Are you hale and well?" asked the boy quietly, raising his hand in greeting. "O Mukuli, Khan of the Tatars, are your cattle fat, and your herds numerous? Have your sheep fat tails, and is the grazing good in your land?"

"Hale and well," growled the old chieftain, responding to the customary salutation, while his black eyes scanned the three keenly, thereafter shifting to the mist on the horizon through which the sun flamed dully. "Why are you in my land, far from the Three Rivers?"

"I have slain the Taidjut khan who put poison in Yesukai's cup."

Mukuli considered this, with approval.

"Good! A snake has been trodden down." He pulled at his mustache thoughtfully. "It is well that you did this. You are a slender arrow, but you are Khan of the Mongols and Master of the Horde. Yesukai died last night. The women are wailing in the death tent."

The corners of Temujin's lips drew down, and his shoulders stiffened. Beyond this he displayed no emotion. Mukuli, squinting at the setting sun, fingered his reins.

"Do not stop to pull thorns from your feet, or stones from the hoofs of your ponies. Go swiftly to your *ordu*, your encampment."

When Temujin made no response the Tatar explained that the *orkhons*, the chieftains, who had assembled at Yesukai's side on learning of his illness, were talking now of dispersing to their various tribes. They had acknowledged the leadership of Temujin's father, not without some discontent—for Yesukai had been more of a leader in the field than a chief of a confederacy.

Now that the mastery of the Horde had fallen to Temujin, most of the khans declared that they would not be ruled by a boy.

"What said you, Mukuli?"

---

*Kerait or Krit is the Mongol version of the word Christian.

"When Yesukai sat on the white mare's skin at the head of the *kurultai*, the council, I was his sworn brother, as was Wang Khan, master of the Keraits."

"He who is called by some Prester John of Asia," nodded Temujin. "And now?"

"Can a nursling carry the yak-tail standard?" asked the Tatar dryly. "Nay, it is heavy. It was for this talk that I left the *kurultai* to seek you, hearing that you had crossed the Tatar grazing lands to follow the path of vengeance into Cathay. It is one thing to slay a thieving Taidjut; it is another to lead a million warriors."

"What is your mind?" observed the boy again, quietly.

"True, the Tatars are knitted to Mongols as flesh is to bone. As a friend, the tents of my people are open to you—we will give horses and food without stint. But if you seek to be verily Master of the Horde, and my overlord, then first you must prove your worth, as good metal is tested. Then will I place my standard behind yours. That is my word, and by the white horse Kotwan I will not unsay it."

"Am I a dog, to come to your heel?" Temujin's lips drew back a little from his teeth.

Mukuli nodded, as if he had expected such an answer, and watched with interest the sun disappear behind a pall of gray.

"Yesukai, who was my comrade, gave me a message for your hearing. 'Go,' he said, 'to Wang Khan, in the south and west of the Horde, who holds the castle above the sands. He is the king called Prester John and he will aid you, being wise in all things, and my friend.'"

Temujin shook his head.

"Was Prester John at the council?"

"Nay, for he goes not beyond the walls of his castle, wherein you must seek him."

Mukuli gathered up his reins. "The wild goose, Temujin, takes flight in the face of the storm, but the snow pigeon seeks safety in the earth, when the winter is hard, among its kind. Turn not aside from Prester John, who is shrewder even than Jamuka, our Master of Plotting. You and he and I could conquer the world."

"I have heard your word. May the rain make your pastures green; may the way be open before you."

He lifted his hand to his head and dropped it to his lips, in farewell. Mukuli, ill-pleased at this sign of authority, glanced at him briefly, hesitated as if he would urge him further to make the alliance he suggested, and then wheeled his horse away.

"May you come in peace to the end of your journey," he growled over his shoulder.

The standard-bearer and the group of officers who had awaited him at a little distance put their horses in motion. The last line of the horsemen, which had halted behind their khan, swept past with a shout.

"Hai, ahatou! Koke Mongku hai!"

A drumming of hoofs on the baked earth, a taste of dust in the air, and the array of the Tatars left them.

Mingan had thought of the Gobi as a waste of sand. In the last day's ride they galloped over a level sward, sparkling with daisies, where the rarefied air was like wine. They crossed a river near a range of blue mountains, and in the early afternoon came to the *ordu* of the dead Yesukai—a city of tents in a shallow valley, where large herds of horses were grazing under guard of boys little younger than Temujin.

At the crest of the valley Burta dismounted and picked out her pony from the small group that had survived the journey.

"It is better that I should depart to Podu's lands," she said to the Mongol. "My father would be angry, if he has been drinking *kumiss* and sees me come to the *kurultai* at your side. Are you—" she lowered her eyes—"pleased with me, or angry?"

Temujin had been silent all day, and now he frowned. "*Kai,* so you fear to be seen at my side!"

Burta flushed and tossed her head, the silver earrings jingling.

"I go where I will and now, because I am weary, seek the path to my home."

As Temujin watched her without comment, her flush deepened.

"Because you are Master of the Horde you cannot summon or dismiss me at pleasure. You can be angry, if you like—it is all one to me!"

The boy suddenly drew his horse close to her and placed his hand under her chin so that he could see into her eyes.

"Little Burta, I am pleased with you."

"Verily! The king is kind!"

She tried to free herself, and, failing, fell to whimpering. Temujin released her.

"I will come to your father's tents before another summer has passed."

Burta glanced at him fleetingly, and turned away. Yet Mingan noticed that she rode slowly, and presently she called over her shoulder softly—"I will pray that the spirit of Yesukai finds peace in the sky-world."

Nearing the tent village, Temujin waited until the girl was lost to sight and then turned his ponies loose into a herd belonging to the Mongols. Mingan noticed that his hands trembled a little and the pulse in his brown throat beat furiously as they rode in among the tents, prepared to face the council that sat by the death tent of Yesukai.

Word of their coming had preceded them, for men lined the path they took—squat warriors, bow-legged but massive of shoulder, with the skin of their faces wrinkled like dried grapes. They wore high boots and walked with the short, clumsy step of those more at home in the saddle than on foot. They were armed with bows, javelins, and short iron maces. As Temujin passed, paying no attention to them, they grunted in pleasure and tried to touch his horse or stirrup. These, Mingan learned later, were the warriors of Yesukai's clan, the backbone of the Mongols.

But as the young chief neared the largest tent, a cavalcade of riders, hemmed in by the assembled throngs, barred his way.

The leader of the horsemen, an old desert man brilliantly clad in a crimson Turkish *khalat* and a purple, plush cap, seemed ill at ease at seeing the pair.

"Greetings, Podu," observed Temujin. "Has the fire of the council died out, and is the cask of liquor empty that you mount to leave the *ordu* before the new khan comes to take his seat?"

Podu's fine brown eyes were moist with the warmth of wine, and his white teeth bared in a smile.

"Nay. Temujin, I have paid honor to the dead hero Yesukai, your sire. I have left a fine white horse to be slain on his grave, so that he can ride fittingly in his journey through the sky-world to the banquet hall of the dead palladins. As for the *kurultai*—" he fingered his gold earrings slyly—"that is quite broken up, quite."

"How, Khan of the Gipsies?" Temujin's eyes narrowed.

"Why, like a raven's nest when the black sandstorm sweeps it away. *Kai*, it is so! Mukuli has turned his back, and the khan of the spear-bearing Merkets, and the chief of the reindeer folk have ridden off on their horned beasts. They bayed like dogs—" old Podu swayed in his saddle and his words were twisted—"and slunk off like foxes. May their heads be cut off and salted down—"

"But the ten Mongol khans abide my coming?"

Podu shook his head mysteriously.

"The half of them have gone back to their clans saying that they will not follow in battle a nursling yet smeared with milk."

The veins in the boy's forehead stood out, and the muscles of his arms tightened. Podu started and, eyeing the motionless throng of warriors, sobered visibly.

"Nay, Temujin. It is only that your khans grumble like camels when the load is bound on. I would not leave your side, but I must assemble my trade caravans before the autumn storms."

Temujin's fingers caught at the arrows in the quiver at his saddle-peak, and his men surged forward, waiting for his word. But his glance went to the valley's side where Burta had said farewell, and he sat silent a moment, thinking.

"Pass, Podu, and seek your tents. Yet give up to me the gold tablet that marks you for an *orkhon*, a palladin of Yesukai. When you have left this camp you will be no longer a khan of the Horde."

Slowly Podu obeyed, his eyes watchful. With a sigh he handed over a small square of gold, inscribed with writing, hefting it reluctantly as he did so. Temujin put it into his girdle and waited until the nomads had ridden off before he sought the council tent, and dismounted.

A tall chieftain, clad in rich nankeen, with a sapphire-studded scabbard and a sable hat, came out of the tent and held his horse, smiling a welcome.

"Successful as always, you return O Temujin, my khan," he said. "This time with a Cathayan captive."

Temujin greeted the newcomer by name, Jamuka. This was the Khan of the Jelairs, of Turkish descent, called in the Horde the Master of Plotting. By his proud bearing and quick, intelligent eyes Mingan judged him to be wiser than the Mongols—a judgment that afterward proved most true. He saw, too, that Temujin was pleased to see his cousin.

The more so, because, drawing back the entrance flap of the council tent, the young khan beheld no more than five elderly Mongols awaiting him—some sleeping and some the worse for wine. In truth the leaders of the Horde had forsaken him.

He let fall the flap and put his hand on Jamuka's shoulder, his eyes blazing from his gaunt face.

"O my cousin, the *orkhons* have scattered to the far corners of the earth, and you alone, save these five, stand to await me. I will not seek them."

He raised his hand toward the high standard before the tent—a pole bearing a yak's horns and cross-piece from which hung the long yak-tails. "I will find new palladins to take the seats of the old. This is my word and it will not change."

Jamuka shook his head reflectively.

"Where will you seek for new heroes? You are lean with hunger, and consumed by the fires of anger." His glance shifted to Mingan. "It is well you have brought this Cathayan, to be slain at Yesukai's grave."

Temujin's eyes narrowed.

"I have gone among the riders who went to the edge of the emperor's hunt to seek you," went on Jamuka gravely, "and I have learned what they heard whispered among the followers of the Dragon around the fires at night. The Taidjuts who slew Yesukai had gold upon them, and it was coin of Cathay. Two of them escaped your arrows and went back to rob the bodies of their comrades; having great wealth, their tongues wagged.

"This thing is true."

A murmur of assent came from Jamuka's retinue of nobles, and an answering growl from the Mongol warriors massed around them. Those who could not see Mingan pressed forward upon their fellows; those who stood nearest laid hands upon weapons.

The prince folded his arms and looked at them calmly; he had been schooled to keep from betraying emotion, nor did he lack dignity. Those who saw him so did not realize that cold shivers were chasing up and down his back, or that utter fatigue gripped mind and body.

He, too, knew that Jamuka spoke the truth.

"Yesukai," Chung-hi had whispered to the emperor within Mingan's hearing, "will not trouble your hours of pleasure."

From the death tent near at hand sounded the subdued beating of a drum, mingled with the shrill lament of women.

Chung-hi, Mingan reflected, could not have planned more shrewdly if he had schemed for the Prince of Liao-tung to be slain beside Yesukai. Temujin, grieving for his father, and sorrowing over the loss of his heroes, could hardly fail to give him up to the throngs that thirsted for his death. For one thing, the young khan could not afford to deny the wishes of his men.

"Why do you hesitate, Temujin?" questioned the Jelair chief carelessly. "Let your followers take life from the Cathayan."

"Aye," said another. "Surely this thing must be!"

"Kabul also died of poison from the Dragon's claw."

"Twenty pieces of gold, it was—"

"We will throw this youth's head over the wall—"

"Nay, Temujin will make of it a silver drinking-cup."

All the whispers that reached Mingan's ears were hostile. Only one voice was lifted in his favor: "He bears himself well; he is no black-boned knave," a Mongol warrior said judiciously.

All at once Temujin flung up his head.

"Peace, dogs! I am the khan. No man speaks before me."

At this Jamuka, who was the boy's elder by ten years or more, started angrily, and would have spoken, but Temujin was before him.

"Abide in this place, Jamuka. I go to the tent of Yesukai. When I come forth the lot of this Cathayan will be decided."

He instructed several Mongols to take Mingan to his own tent and to keep him there until other orders were issued.

Mingan was led out of the gathering to the leather yurt of the khan, which his guards did not enter, contenting themselves with squatting in the entrance where they could watch him. He sat down on a pile of leopard skins, paying no attention to them. Presently others came with a bowl of fermented milk thickened with rice, and cheese, and offered it to him.

His hunger was acute and, finishing off the food, he asked for more. The men glanced at each other in surprise at being addressed in the Mongol tongue, and when Mingan had emptied a second bowl, one—the officer who had commented on his bearing heretofore—muttered that he ate like a noble.

The truth was that Mingan's exhaustion was so great that the peril of death was no more than a new, numbing pain.

After awhile Temujin appeared and sat down by him.

"I have said to my men that you are my comrade. Speak openly and tell me what you know of the death of my father."

Mingan hesitated but, aware that the Mongols already knew the truth, explained that it had been a plot of one of the favorites of the court, and that the emperor had had no hand in it.

"Chung-hi!" said Temujin.

Mingan remained silent, and the young khan went on to say he had thought, from his talk with Mingan at the shrine of Kwan-ti, that the Prince of Liao-tung had not been concerned in the plot against Yesukai. Under the circumstances, he said, he—Temujin—would be a dog and the son of a dog if he let Mingan die.

"You must pass between the fires, O my first friend," he concluded. "That is our test of all strangers. If you are brave you will not be harmed; if you are a coward, you will be burnt by the fire and we will break your limbs and throw you to the dogs."

Mingan could smile a little, thinking that it made little difference if a man were innocent or not, so long as he was bold enough to satisfy the Mongols.

"Heed what I say," went on Temujin earnestly, "and you will not be marked by the flames. You are brave and hardy, I know. First, strip off these long garments and put on no others. The heat is such that clothing will catch fire, and the man who wraps himself up will be marked."

When Mingan had rid himself of all garments, Temujin rose and added a low-voiced warning.

It would seem, when he was led to the fires, as if they were a solid mass of flames without interval of any kind. As a matter of fact they would consist of two lines of fires, some ten feet apart, but with the end of this lane nearest the victim closed by a heap of blazing brush.

If he leaped over this, he could then run swiftly through the narrow lane and come out unharmed. There was no wind, and the flames rose straight into the air. If he did not jump with all his strength, his feet would be caught in the brush and he would fall. To hesitate after he was once in the lane would be equally fatal.

"And do not hang back when you are led up to the fires or twenty arrows will seek you out. Fear not, for only a weakling dies in this test."

Mingan nodded, and was surprised when the Mongol officer who had brought him food, asking consent of his chief, knelt in front of him and fell to chafing his legs vigorously, starting up the circulation in the stiffened limbs. Then he was led from the tent, through the gathering to where, in a cleared space between the tent-lines, flames crackled and smoke poured from small heaps of rushes and brush for a length of some fifty feet.

It looked, as Temujin said, as if the fires were in a solid mass, for the biggest pile in front of him gave forth a dense smoke that hid the lane of which his friend had spoken. For a second Mingan wondered if Temujin had tricked him.

But he was allowed no time for reflection. At one side of him he noticed the Jelairs, mounted on fine-looking horses, watching him as he was conducted to the end of the fires. Someone gave him a push, and he sprang forward.

Taking off at the edge of the flames he leaped, drawing in his breath and holding it as he did so. A hot wave seemed to engulf him and his knees smarted. Then his feet came down upon cool earth, although the heat around him was unbearable.

Mingan stumbled, caught himself up, and ran on, his eyes stinging with the effort to keep them open in the smoke. In spite of himself, he was forced to close his eyes, while his legs still urged him forward.

He ran into something solid, felt himself clasped by mighty arms, and opened his eyes to gaze with blurred vision into the seamed face of a Mongol warrior at the edge of the crowd. The fires were a dozen paces behind him. Other men crowded about to inspect his skin for burns.

A shout announced that he had passed through the fire safely, and he was brought to where Jamuka was bidding farewell to Temujin.

"You are a fool, my cousin," he heard the thin Turk say, "to keep this Cathayan alive. He will work you harm. The spies of Chung-hi are thick as jackals in the trail of a hunt. I go to my lands, beside Tangut, the city of Prester John, whom you call Wang Khan."

"Will you go to the castle that is guarded by beasts?"

Laughing, Jamuka shook his head.

"Not I! A word of warning, stripling. Prester John is your foe, because he desires the mastery of the Horde. May the way be open before you!"

Temujin raised his hand silently and the Jelairs cantered off.

Mingan was taken to the khan's tent, where he was clad in the rough Mongol garments, and more food was brought him by the warrior who had befriended him and who seemed anxious to observe how much he could eat.

Being hungry again, Mingan did justice to the milk and cheese, and the Mongol growled approvingly—"He eats like a king of a great people."

Temujin, brooding beside him, glanced at him with keen surprise. But Mingan's head sank on his shoulder and drowsiness overcame him.

It was night when he was awakened by the sound of a groan near at hand. Temujin was sitting over a fire in the hearth of the small tent that reeked of leather and horses, his chin propped on his iron-bound arms, tears running down his cheeks.

When Mingan stirred, the Mongol bent his head to hide his emotion.

"Except for a few, my palladins have left me. Will you abide with me, my first friend, and become my teller of tales? Unwillingly you came to my place, the country of the Three Rivers, yet your voice comforts me and your fellowship strengthens me."

For a long time Mingan stared into the embers, and then answered gravely—"Aye, Temujin, for so long as the gods permit, I will remain at your side."

Fate, he thought, and the hand of Temujin, had brought him into the Horde, so that he could learn its secrets, and return to Cathay to place the knowledge he had gained on the step of the Dragon Seat, thus lending aid to the Dynasty of his father.

So the Cathayan youth reasoned, not knowing that it would be his lot to make out of his adventures in the Horde a song to which kings would listen with bowed heads.

IV

The Race

Two years passed, and Mingan found he was faced with a riddle that neither the wisdom of the sages nor the reading of the stars would help him unravel.

Of the five Mongol khans who had been faithful to Temujin, two died, and one fell sick of a wasting illness. Temujin's herds were thinned, and of the best horses kept near the yurt of the young chief, many disappeared in the night in spite of the most vigilant watch. True, the last winter had been a hard one, the prairie swept by blizzards, and the rivers frozen over. The horse thieves had left traces of boots with heels fashioned of deers' hoofs, but none of the reindeer people had been in the Three Rivers country.

Temujin himself was tireless in his efforts, riding in snow or wind storm, from clan to clan of his tribe, leading his fighters in pursuit of the raiders who seemed to descend upon him from every quarter. He recruited supplies from raiding, in turn, caravans that crossed the southern edge of his pasture lands bound to Cathay from India, gaining wine, weapons, cloth, and camels that he sorely needed.

Once he was taken prisoner by riders who attacked his camp at night, but escaped, with the wooden yoke that was used by Tatars to confine their prisoners still on his shoulders. When his men had chopped off the *kang*, he sent it by an envoy to Mukuli, saying that he would not keep the property of one who had been his ally.

It amused Mingan that old Mukuli gave the envoy a feast and sent back the message that he had nothing to do with the *kang*.

But from an unknown source, Temujin was still harassed and Mingan knew now that it could not be by the horse thieves who had taken gold from Chung-hi.

And then came a messenger from Podu's camp, in the southern Gobi, to invite Temujin to a feast that would be shared by the other khans of the Horde.

More than once had Temujin disappeared from the Mongol pastures when his herds were nearest the Gipsy lands, and Mingan knew that he had taken the gray pony and gone to have speech with Burta. The last time he returned from his long ride he was moodier than usual. Podu, he said to Mingan, intended to give his daughter in marriage to a khan of the Horde within a few months, at the frost of the autumn hunting season.

"The number of the Mongol *orkhons* is growing smaller," he meditated aloud. "The sword of an enemy is thinning our fellowship. Podu sees this—he is a great trafficker and trader."

It was the first time Temujin had mentioned the girl to his comrade, and Mingan asked a question—"Do you wish for Burta to be your wife?"

Temujin's keen eyes darkened.

"I will take her."

"Not at the feast of Podu, in the next moon. You must not be among the assemblage at the feast. Your warriors are too few to protect you against your enemy, who will be there."

"What enemy? I have as many as a litter of dogs." The khan laid down the arrow he was whittling into shape and frowned. "What is your thought? No hidden thing must come like a snake between us."

Mingan, however, had not solved the riddle that perplexed him; so far, he could not put a name to the foeman who worked under cover of darkness, striking at Temujin each time with more deadly aim. Who were the riders who, purporting to be Tatars, had taken the Man of Iron captive to bear him alive to their master? Mukuli, the Tatar, would have slain the Mongol rather than take him prisoner.

And who were the raiders that left, instead of the tracks of men, the print of deers' hoofs in the snow?

"This is my thought," he explained frankly, knowing better than to conceal anything from Temujin, who was intolerant of secrecy. "Instead of many foes, as you say, you have but one. His messengers of evil have taken the guise of other tribesmen. The *kang* was placed on your shoulders so that you would muster your standards against Mukuli, and so destroy yourself. The deers' hoofs were donned by the men of this enemy so that you would bear hatred against the reindeer people of the north, who had not come from their fastness in a month of moons."

He swept his hand before his eyes as if brushing away a veil.

"This foeman is wiser than you, and stronger. Who can tell his name?"

"If we go to the feast of the desert men, then we can make him uncover his face."

Thoughtfully, Mingan shook his head. Although, in the Gobi, he had been deprived of books and his astronomical instruments, he had not lacked of knowledge. He had learned to train falcons and fly them at game, even the *bouragut*, the golden eagle that would pull down a deer. He was able to keep to the saddle for days, and he knew the prairies almost as well as Temujin, who—perhaps because he could not read—never forgot what once he saw or heard. Hardship and constant suspense, holding himself ready to rouse up by night and take to the saddle and flee, had sharpened Mingan's keen wits.

"Like a play actor in Cathay, this foeman has a mask over his face, and he would strike you before you could guard against him."

Temujin took up his arrow and fell to sharpening it. "Jamuka bade me beware of Wang Khan, Prester John, who is a Christian and strongest of the lords of the west. Sixty times a thousand tents are on his lands. But he alone of the chiefs of the Horde dwells in a castle. He gives no feasts, nor does he ride forth from his hold; perhaps because he has under his hand treasure of gold, of silver, of carved ivory and sable furs, of jeweled saddles and fine, red leather. Yesukai, my sire, visited his castle, and at that time the beasts that guard it were chained—he could hear their snarling.

"Nevertheless, many of his men died from the *burans*, the black sandstorms of the southern Gobi. He said that as they drew near to Tangut—the castle of Prester John—he saw it first on one hand, then on another, and oft-times in the air before his horse. He saw a rich land, with wide rivers and trees, though no trees stand in that quarter of the earth."

Neither Temujin nor Mingan had seen a mirage. Yet the Cathayan did not doubt Yesukai's words—he had learned the bluntness of the Mongols.

It was said that the master of the Keraits had been alive for many generations. Also that, since Prester John did not go forth from his castle, he sent a trusted leader in command of his horsemen, who—so that enemies might not know the faces of his lieutenants—wore the skin of an animal's head over his own.

"Did Yesukai see the god that Prester John worshiped?" Mingan asked.

It was said too, that the power of Prester John, the friend of Yesukai, had been due to a talisman that was closely guarded in his castle, but to Mingan this meant a god.

"Nay, my first friend, he saw gold cups, and a white cloth under them, and a bird with feathers of every color that talked like a man. That, to my mind is enough. When we go to Tangut we must be wary and look on every side, for Prester John has sent me no word, and I know not what is in his heart toward us."

Temujin lifted his head, and Mingan put behind him the lute that he was fingering.

A rider was passing between the rows of tents of the Mongol camp, glancing carelessly about. Seeing the yak-tail standard planted at Temujin's side, he wheeled toward it, and drew up sharply, the forefeet of his pony not a yard from the Mongol's knees. Temujin did not put his hand to a weapon, not liking to make a threatening gesture without intending to strike, or, for that matter, to give warning when he meant to use a weapon. He had noticed that the newcomer rode the pony that was Burta's special property—a sorrel mare.

"O Khan," said the messenger without dismounting, "I bear word to you from the daughter of Podu. Grant me freedom from harm, and I will dismount and speak; otherwise, the saddle suits me best and you will burn in the entrails of Erlik before you will catch this mare. Speak your mind."

He was a youngling, neat as a fawn from red morocco boot-tips to silver-adorned sable-cap. His brown eyes danced in a round face and, as Temujin observed, the scabbard of his long scimitar was set with sapphires.

"What name bear you, O sharp of tongue?"

"Chepe Noyon, O long of face."

"The Tiger Chief," Temujin repeated, grimly. "Sit, and drink, and speak, and fear not for your swaddling-clothes or the limbs in them. Whence had you that mare?"

"From the hand of Burta, who is like the moon in the sky at night," quoth the stranger, following out Temujin's suggestion without further reluctance.

Mingan judged from his attire that he might be Jelair or Gipsy; at any rate his restlessness and his smooth, olive skin might well have earned him the surname of Tiger.

"Burta sends this warning," the stranger continued. "Do not come to the feast of Podu, or the feasters will sprinkle your blood as a libation on the sand, and hang your skin on the tent ropes. At least that was her meaning, the words are of my fashioning."

Hereat the Tiger Lord paused to quaff deep of the mare's milk that Temujin's mother brought from the yurt. Catching sight of Mingan's lute, he brightened.

"You are no Gipsy," said Temujin bluntly. "What are you?"

"O Khan, a Kerait, and a better man than your minstrel. I have a gold lute. Harken, lutist, come not to the sands of the Gobi, to the feast, to sing *ting-tang*, like the thrush, before the hawk swooped and the songbird squawked by way of a last note. Get drunk and sleep in a wolves-lair if you will, but drink no wine of Podu's making."

"Wise counsel from a beardless mouth," smiled Mingan, and the Tiger—as they came subsequently to call him—looked up in surprise at the pleasant accent of the Cathayan. "Did the beauty of Burta bring you from the sands of Tangut—alone?"

"Alone as a lame fox, O minstrel. Nay, I set forth to find adventure, and heard before long of the great feast of Podu. When I rode thither the daughter of the chief smiled at me, and I was her slave. Would I might be among the suitors that Podu sorts out in his shrewd brain! But she gave me a quest, and I am here."

Mingan nodded politely, thinking that the Tiger, young as he was, could play a part as well as the Cathayans. Certainly the western chief was no fool, for as he spoke his eyes took in the camp shrewdly, sizing up the horses, the raw-hide armor of the Mongols, the weapons in Temujin's tent.

"Why alone," murmured Mingan, "if Prester John, your master, rides to the feast?"

"Not he. Nor his men. I tired of watching horses in our lands. Nay, give me the nomad's tents. O Khan, if my words are clear, I mount to retrace my journey at sun-up. Have you a message?"

"Your words are clear," acknowledged Temujin promptly, "yet you will bear no message from me, for I will draw my reins to Podu's tents and speak for myself. If any fox sent you to turn me aside with your threats, I will give you your fill of adventuring."

The same thought had crossed Mingan's mind—that Chepe Noyon might have lied. As warranty of the boy's faith there was the sorrel mare and the Tiger himself. For certainly no spy could be so careless of events, or could chuckle so heartily as the Tiger at Temujin's warning.

"You pledged me freedom from harm," he pointed out, "and I have heard that Temujin forgets not, nor fails to keep a promise." The mirth faded from his clear brown eyes, and he glanced at Temujin as if seeing him for the first time. "I have caught rumors in the Gipsy tents, the black tents, that there will be a new khan over the Horde before the snow comes."

Mingan, too, added his remonstrance, aware that Temujin had not men enough to ensure his safety, nor—which was more to the point—to make an impressive display among the other chieftains. It struck him suddenly, comparing the young Kerait and the powerful Mongol, that Temujin was no longer a boy. Mingan did not know that he himself had grown in stature and wisdom to manhood.

"If I lurk in my tent like a dog," snarled the khan, "my enemies will take counsel together and elect a leader. Nay, I have a mind to the feast." He caught the Kerait suddenly by the wrist. "Tiger, you are bold and open in speech. Will you stand with me? When the snow comes, I will still be Master of the Horde, and Burta will be in my tent. She waits until I take her from her father's yurt, and this shall be at the feast. Before the feast is ended," added Temujin dryly, "you may be in your grave, and Mingan too. Otherwise, you shall have honor rare in one of your years. Of my *orkhons* two are gone from the earth and one is ailing. The remaining two are needed to guard the herds at the Three Rivers and to watch the Tatars. That leaves no more than two or three *gurans** of riders to attend me, and no palladins. That is too few and too many—too few to guard me at the feast, too many Mongols to die. So we take three hundred picked men, a hundred to each of us."

Chepe Noyon flushed with pleasure, while Mingan nodded assent.

"As for *orkhons* to attend me, I will take two even though they be but sham heroes."

Temujin rose and went into his yurt, reappearing with two gold tablets in his hand, each engraved with an inscription. He gave the first to Mingan, the second to Chepe Noyon.

---

*Thousand.

The Cathayan and the Kerait, surprised, bent their heads and lifted their hands. Temujin's eyes were cold.

"I mean this as a truth. At the last *kurultai* of the Horde I swore that I would choose new heroes, rather than take back those who left me. Now, each of you is raised above other men; you are immune from punishment; you are inviolate from the death penalty nine times. Wherever you go in the country of the Horde, you will be honored; you are to command, each one, a *tuman* of ten thousand chosen warriors."

Mingan looked down at his tablet and read the words—

PALLADIN OF THE MONGOL FELLOWSHIP

"Are you content?" Temujin's keen glance searched them. "Good. Guide and support each other, steal not, and remember that a lie earns for others than the *orkhons* the death penalty. Be falcons, going before my coming, spying out what is hidden and the place of danger; be the harbingers of war—aye, of death. Never spare a foe who still has a sword in hand, waste no thought on the weak; learn to care for your men and their ponies, for a brave man is useless if he aids not those under him."

He considered a moment.

"Take Chepe Noyon to your tent, Mingan, and share it with him. Then do you both choose a hundred to follow you, also the swiftest of our racing horses and the strongest wrestlers among our warriors for Podu's games."

Podu, seated under a pavilion at the finish line of the racing field on the hard, sun-baked clay of the Gobi, fingered his gold earrings and sipped pleasantly the red Cathayan wine, spoil of an excursion before the moon of his feast. For several reasons he was well content with life.

As far as the eye could reach, on one side of the race course stretched his wagon yurts—black, felt tents mounted on the framework of carts—and the herds of cattle that drew his clans from place to place as his whims elected. His horse herds had never been fatter or more numerous, because the Gipsy wasted no opportunity to trade beasts at the festival, and his trades were good ones—for him. Wagers upon the games, too, had gone his way.

That was one reason for his content. Another was Burta, who sat on a fine carpet behind him. Youths from the distant tribes of the Horde had come to woo the daughter of Podu, and lay gifts before her father, whose choice would decide the matter. Jamuka especially had given freely rare, river-sable skins, gold-inlaid weapons, Cathayan crossbows, white camel-skins, and jewels from the mountain mines of the west.

Podu liked the gleam of pearls and the fire of rubies, and he liked an open-handed suitor, who gave whenever he drank Podu's wine, and drank the more he gave. The Gipsy had just sent a cask to the Jelair's tents that stood opposite, blue and purple pavilions, heavy with silk and topped with long banners. That was another reason Podu found life good. All the khans of the Horde were guests at his board, save Temujin, who, Podu knew, was hard pressed guarding the country of the Three Rivers, to the north.

As soon as it was clear that Temujin would not attend the feast, Podu had heard whispers that if Mukuli, the veteran Tatar, would call together a council, a new Master of the Horde would be chosen. Podu did not greatly care who was elected by the voice of the council—he would see to it that Burta married the fortunate man, and his own life would be one of ease henceforth.

"Little squirrel," he addressed his daughter, "I see you wear the cloth-of-silver cap, the gift of Jamuka. He looks long upon you; he is a clever soul."

"Aye, that is why you cheat him so easily. Is he not the Master of Plotting?"

Burta went on sampling the sugared fruits in a bowl under her hand; she always gained something from the spoil of a caravan.

Podu looked at her uncertainly. Of late her temper had been like the clear sun of a fair day, and when his daughter was tractable it meant she had a secret that she did not wish him to know.

"If the young Temujin rides hither alone, as he has done in the past," he ventured, "he would be like a lone raven in the company of vultures; he would be a thing made for mockery by these palladins who have each one a thousand tents behind their standards. If he brings the remnants of his dark-faced Mongols, his herds on the Three Rivers would be plundered, and his pastures taken. Temujin is like an arrow that has sped."

"True," nodded Burta, selecting another dainty. "And yet, O my father, Temujin would provide horses for more races, while now none will match their beasts against yours, so often have you been the victor."

Podu nodded regretfully. He was just about to declare the races at an end, and call for the wrestlers' carpet and the archers' staves. Temujin always matched him closely with horseflesh, especially with the gray pony, and Podu, always provident against possibilities, had a card up his sleeve as it were, that he would have liked to play against the Mongol.

"There will be another race," observed Burta. "Harken to the dogs!"

A clamor of yapping hunting dogs resounded from behind Podu's pavilion, and presently he heard the muttering of kettle-drums drawing nearer on horses, and the clangor of cymbals. He rose and peered out.

Dust was rising behind a cavalcade of riders at the head of whom advanced the yak-tail standard of the Horde, escorted by two youths in brave attire, one very tall, the other slender and small. Behind the standard rose Temujin, in hunting dress, carrying only a light spear beside the sword at his girdle. Podu concealed his surprise and pushed through the throng that gathered to stare at the small body of Mongols, who had announced their arrival by the drums and cymbals.

"Dismount," said the Gipsy heartily, taking the reins of the gray pony himself, "and sit at ease in the shadow."

He called for attendants to bring more wine, fruit, and meat, and others to care for the horses of the heroes, and more to set up three-score tents near the Gipsy camp. "Are your herds fat? Is your health good, O my Khan?"

"Fat—and good," nodded Temujin, stooping under the pavilion, and, after a quick glance, taking no heed of Burta. "Have cushions brought for these two *orkhons*, O Khan of the black tents, and take your place behind them. They have each the rank of commander of a *tuman*, and you are no more than leader of four thousand."

Podu quivered at the reminder, but after a moment's hesitation obeyed. His complacency was ruffled. With Temujin in the camp and in no conciliatory mood, trouble was a certainty between him and the other khans, and Podu fared best when he hitched his wagon to one of the brighter stars. Now his position of host would make it necessary to struggle to keep peace, and, in any event, he would suffer from a quarrel in the Horde. And there was Burta.

He writhed as Mukuli and others drifted in to share the refreshments and pay their respects, in duty bound, to the chief of the Horde. Only Jamuka was absent. And Temujin calmly allotted all who came places behind his two heroes.

Stimulated by several cups of hot liquor, Podu addressed Mingan, whom he failed to recognize as the Cathayan prince who had come with Temujin to the death tent of Yesukai, owing to the *orkhon*'s beard and long hair worn Mongol fashion, coupled with his rawhide armor, faced with silver trimmings.

"Where is your *tuman*, O hero?"

"Where it can be summoned at need."

Mukuli was regarding Chepe Noyon with disfavor as the Tiger sat in the place formerly occupied by the Tatar, at Temujin's left hand.

"And where is yours, O maiden cheeks?" he growled.

"I left it at Tangut, by the palace over the sands, O bear's paws," smiled the youth, who was not at all slow-witted.

The feasters looked up with interest, and Podu fingered his earrings thoughtfully. He knew Chepe Noyon for a Kerait; the sudden honor shown the youth by Temujin must mean that the Mongols were allied in some fashion to Prester John, and Tangut held the balance of power in the Horde.

"Verily," he asked, "do you draw rein toward Tangut, my Khan—with how many warriors?"

"You have already counted them," responded Temujin quietly, and Podu turned the talk to the absorbing topic of racing. He suggested that Temujin match his beasts, and the Mongol assented.

"Yet, my Khan," the Gipsy pointed out craftily, "your animals are tired from a half-day's travel. So we will shorten the course to the length of six *li*."

This was about two miles. The usual race of the Mongols covered twenty miles, being a test of stamina, both of rider and horse; three ponies started for each contestant, matched in pairs, and the ride took several hours before the winner of each pair crossed the line in front of the khan's tent. It was customary to allow a few minutes between each pair, to prevent any confusion as to the order in which they were matched.

"As you will. My ponies are strong and fresh."

Temujin called for three boys to lead from the horse lines the gray pony, the sorrel mare that now bore his *tanga*—branding mark—and a piebald horse of unusual endurance that had won many events in the past.

Podu on his part entered two black ponies, and a small gelding that had not appeared on the course as yet. The khans scanned this curiously, struck by its unfamiliar marking—white with blackish streaks rising from the fetlocks. It had dainty, small-boned legs, and carried its intelligent head high; its tail was sweeping.

The horse was an Arab, secured by Podu on one of his trading ventures into India, and the Mongols had never seen its like.

Temujin instructed his boys to start the piebald first—it being the worst of the three—the mare second, and the gray pony last, in the customary order, reserving the fleetest for the last. Podu arrayed his beasts and sent one of his gur-khans off with them to the starting point, a rocky knoll barely visible on the plain. While the visiting warriors, hearing that a race was on, flocked to kneel by the course, the Gipsy turned to Temujin after sizing up the opened loads of the Mongol's pack-camels.

"You are the Master of the Horde and bring no gifts to me. It is fitting that we wager worthily on this race. Do you place two camel loads of musk on the first race, a dozen *tarkaul*, white camel's skins, on the second, and on the third—" he pondered a moment—"enough weapons, gold-inlaid, and of good steel, to cover this carpet."

It was a valuable stake, and about covered all the riches Temujin had brought with him.

"I will place against your goods," Podu concluded, "silver bars and gold ornaments enough to equal your stakes."

"So be it." Temujin was no quibbler.

A ball of dust out on the clay flat showed that the first pair of ponies were off. The khans crowded forward to see the better, and Burta clapped her hands. The dust rolled nearer and two black specks grew into the forms of ponies, saddle-less, two boys urging them on with heel and whip.

When they reached the lines of spectators it was seen that Podu's black horse had the lead easily. It finished a half-dozen lengths in front of the piebald, which coming on in a long stride seemed to be hardly in the race as yet, while the black was sweating.

Chepe Noyon grimaced and turned to Mukuli.

"My scabbard against your sable cloak that the mare finishes first in the coming pair." They were still distant, in the dust.

"Agreed!"

Podu smiled and suggested to Mingan that they also make a wager. The Cathayan's eyes twinkled and he shook his head. Barely had he done so than the black pony of the Gipsy crossed the line of the tent a length ahead of the sorrel mare, which was closing the gap at each stride. It was clear to Mingan that Podu had trained his beasts over the shorter course, while the Mongol horses were unable to strike a pace that would win in two miles. There was, however, the gray pony, coming between the two lines of men.

Podu shaded his eyes and called to Mukuli—"My jeweled hunting-saddle against the gemmed scabbard you have just won, that my white horse conquers the gray."

The Tatar nodded eagerly. More than once he had seen the pace of the swift little pony that Temujin prized, and he had observed that the two beasts, for the first time, were reaching the finish abreast. Even the cup-bearers crowded the khans to see the end of the last race.

Temujin's boy was stroking his whip against the mane of the gray, for the pony was trained to do its best without the lash; and Podu's rider leaned low over the arched neck of the Arab. An arrow's flight from the finish, the white pony seemed to take wings—at least it pressed low over the ground and fairly skimmed across the line ahead of the gray.

Temujin clapped his hands.

"Bear the goods to Podu," he ordered his few attendants.

The Gipsy smiled. He liked a good loser almost as well as a liberal giver, and he bowed acknowledgment of Chepe Noyon's tender of his scabbard.

"In your camp," said the Tiger, "I will need no sheath for my sword."

After the feasting was over that night, Temujin came to the *orkhons'* tent, chagrined by the defeat of his best ponies.

"It was an ill thing to make a remark such as yours," he told the Kerait, "to stir up ill-will before the time of sword blows is at hand."

"O my Khan, that is true; yet in my country we strike a thicket with a stick before lying down to sleep near it, to rout out snakes. Yet Podu is not the enemy whose face you seek to uncover."

"Why is that?" Mingan was interested.

"He who thinks of slaying will not have his blood stirred to fever by the racing of swift horses."

Mingan assented to this. He was beginning to realize that the brain which directed the attacks on Temujin was of a higher order than the intelligence of Podu or Mukuli. And he suspected the unknown king, Prester John.

"If you will have Podu race again on the morrow, I can win for you two of the three races," he offered, noticing his friend's moodiness.

Both Temujin and the Tiger were lovers of horseflesh, while Mingan had not this leaning, and they grunted incredulity.

"Have you better horses than mine, O my *orkhon*?"

"Nay, I will race your three ponies and win twice. Ask of Podu naught save that I be allowed to start your horses as I please."

On the morrow, after the dawn trumpet had sounded and the khans of the Horde had assembled, Podu acceded willingly enough to this request, but asked again for a good wager. It was unexpected luck, as he saw it, that Temujin should want a return match—although it was like the Mongol not to sit at ease under a defeat.

In fact the young Khan did not change countenance under the prospect of a second heavy loss.

"So be it," he nodded. "I will stake my three ponies against yours, that the Mongols win two of the three starts."

"The distance must be the same."

"Aye, the same."

Podu hesitated only a moment. His racers were trained in the shorter dash, and each one was swifter than its Mongol adversary. He would send along his official to the starting point to see that the ponies were given a fair break—how could he lose?

"The bargain is struck!"

So Mingan led off his cavalcade to the point of rocks, where they dwindled to specks in the plain. This time the khans who were watching made no bets among themselves, believing that Temujin's ponies could do no better than before. The Master of the Horde himself had no great hopes, but he had never known Mingan to make a promise that he did not redeem.

It was hard for him, however, to sit on the carpet and watch the first pair draw nearer on the course without shading his eyes and peering to see which was ahead. He would rather have lost an arm than the gray pony that he had broken in with his own hand. Harder still, when Mukuli swore vehemently, and Podu chuckled—"I have drawn the first blood, O Mongol."

In truth it was not so much a race as a pursuit, Podu's pony being a hundred yards in front of the laboring Mongol horse. Chepe Noyon leaned forward and shaded his eyes against the level rays of the rising sun.

"My saddle and cloak against the jeweled scabbard you won from me yesterday that we win two races," he offered quickly. "I may need the sheath—after I have left the dust of this camp behind me."

"The bargain is struck," nodded Podu eagerly. Then, as the ponies came into full view at the finish line he looked puzzled, perceiving what the sharp-witted Kerait had seen before, that the winner was his prized Arab, and the loser Temujin's plugging piebald that could encompass no faster pace than a loose canter.

Still, he reasoned, his second entry had scored over Temujin's new mare, and—Podu was a race in hand.

All at once he sprang up with an exclamation, and subsided into a tense silence. The second pair were entering the stretch close together, but Podu, alert now, saw that Temujin's swift gray was matched against the better of his pair of blacks. He watched the shaggy pony of the Mongol drive forward with drumming hoofs under the touch of the stick its rider carried and sweep past him two lengths ahead of his second entry.

Temujin's face revealed no emotion, but he took up a cup of wine and emptied it with relish. He could not have been better pleased if his heroes had conquered in all the coming games that were so vital a part of the life of the Horde.

A few moments later the sorrel mare won the third race, finding her speed in the last quarter and getting her neck ahead of the tiring black pony. Podu snarled and his hand crept toward his belt, but fell to his side, feeling an empty scabbard—the weapons of the khans were stacked outside the pavilion carpet.

"Trickery!" the Gipsy raged. "You matched your poorest horse against my Arab, and so, undeserving, won the last races."

Temujin had not been unobserving of Podu. He signed to Chepe Noyon to answer, which that youth did right willingly by ripping the scabbard out of the Gipsy's girdle.

"O small of wit," he mocked, "yours was the trick, for you persuaded the Khan to race over a course on which your horses were swifter. Did I hear you grant him the privilege of starting the ponies as he pleased?"

Being wise, Podu swallowed his anger, or rather took it out on the skin of the hapless officer he had sent to the starting point, beating the man with a stick until he howled. Mingan would have dismounted and taken his seat unobserved. The trick of the ponies was a small matter to one who had played at chess with the sages of Cathay; but Temujin signed to him as the racers were led up to be delivered.

"Henceforth," said the Khan, "you are the master of the gray pony. Cherish him, and strike him not with the whip. It serves to stroke his mane to gain his best speed. Mounted and afield, you can overtake any man; no man can overtake you."

Mingan bowed respectfully as Temujin with his own hand placed the reins of his steed in the grasp of the Cathayan. To Chepe Noyon, the Khan gave the mare, saying that the youth had ridden her in a good cause once, and was privileged to do so again. The Arab he kept, being a judge of horseflesh.

Of those who watched enviously, perhaps only Temujin guessed how important it would prove to the Mongols to have at hand the four best horses in the Gobi.

V

The Masked Face

Mingan was accustomed to use his ears as well as his eyes, and was gifted with a sense of undying curiosity. He made a point of going about in the crowds that looked on at the games, and so became aware of a whisper.

It was no more than a whisper, although its purport was plain enough.

"The Mongols are no longer heroes, their leaders are unskilled boys who are mock-heroes; they cannot prevail in the test of the strength of men."

The source of the rumor was not to be traced, but Mingan suspected that warriors were passing through the ranks of the Horde, scattering the words as they might live coals in the dry grass of the prairies, hoping to fan into being a devastating fire.

But this did not alter the fact that honors in the games went to tribes of the Horde other than the khan-tribe, the Mongols. The Merkets, a branch of the Tatars now aloof from the Horde, won the javelin cast; the Jelairs—fine riders, they—were first in the arrow test; the men of old Mukuli overcame the others in wrestling.

Temujin, if he could have competed, would have been unmatched in archery or wrestling; but the khan could not take part in the sports of the warriors, custom decreed.

Mingan, while a skilled bowman, found the test too severe for him—to ride at the full gallop of a horse, discharge three arrows from the right side, unstring his bow, use it as a whip, and, stringing it again, shoot three more shafts from the left side. This he could manage, but the winning Jelair planted five out of six arrows in a mark placed on a stake as he galloped past; Mingan scored but three hits. Nor could he wheel, on a pony, around a great tree, lopped of its branches, and hit, with three shafts out of three, a large crane tied to the summit of the tree.

As for Chepe Noyon, he earned not a single hit, being careless of bow work, loving best his swordplay. Temujin knew that he was a skilled swordsman, but Podu, master of the sports, had forbidden contests with bare steel, knowing that they would lead to a killing and fan the old feuds into life.

"Temujin no longer is the victor at the tests," the whisper went on. "He fears to compete now as he did aforetime. His heroes are dead, or have left him. Nothing is left him but his shadow."

The fiery Tiger heard the whisper and lifted his voice in prompt rebuttal. Hands were put to sword hilts, and it needed all Mingan's diplomacy to prevent bloodshed. He sent a warrior with word to Temujin, but the man returned saying that the Master of the Horde was drinking heavily in his tent and would not come forth. By this Mingan knew that one of his black moods was on the Khan, and that he strove to hold his temper in leash. The whisper had come to Temujin's ears.

"Go among our men," he murmured to the Tiger, "and warn them to say no angry word or to draw weapon. The one who is our enemy is starting this talk, to breed trouble. Temujin knows that he must not show his anger."

"Temujin broods because the Mongol wrestlers have been vanquished, with aching limbs and broken ribs. Go among the men yourself, minstrel, and prate of gentleness. I came not here to anoint wounds but to open them up."

Chepe Noyon checked his words, and pointed to where a crowd gathered about the empty wrestling mats: "Now here is a moil to my mind."

Unwillingly, Mingan followed the youth, and the two *orkhons* shoved through the spectators until they paused in surprise.

In the center of a ring of warriors stood a strange figure—a man as tall as Mingan, who stood well over six feet, but as broad across the shoulders as Temujin, and as heavy as the two combined, almost. His body was bare save for a white reindeer skin that served as a cloak; his naked arms were scratched and scarred—massive as a bear's; the low boots were tipped at the heel with a deer's hoof; his long, fiery-red hair was plaited instead of falling back, Mongol-fashion, in a scalp lock. Gray eyes, greenish-tinted, gazed at the crowd with no more expression than an animal.

"It is a khan of the reindeer folk," said a Mongol captain of ten to Mingan, after saluting. "He left his beasts and came hither on a camel to attend the feast from afar, and because of the sun of the Gobi he has ripped off his garments."

The man bore no weapon of any kind. Seeing this, some of the Gipsies were plaguing him.

"He will not wrestle or hurl a spear. He is afraid," they said.

As the stolid visitor from the frozen tundras of the north made no objection to this statement, the warriors grew bolder. A Tatar champion, almost of a size with the giant, challenged him to a bout at grappling, but the reindeer man shook his head.

"Ahai," growled the Tatar, "he is *subotai,* the buffalo. He stands his ground and lowers his head, yet will not fight."

In derision he pointed out the small pair of antlers that formed the crest of the hood the man wore. "Subotai!" the others chuckled.

Mingan would have passed on, but just then he saw Mukuli approach with Temujin and lingered. The old Tatar khan was looking about for trouble, having looked well on the wine cup, and pushed forward, perceiving the towering body of the Tungusi, the reindeer tribesman. He knocked off the cape the other wore, and pointed to his hair, gleaming red in the sunlight.

"Mao tze! A red man. Ho, cousin of the tundras, why will you not wrestle my champion, hey?"

"I fear," said Subotai earnestly.

At this a sudden silence fell on the watching throng. For a man in the Horde to confess to cowardice was an unheard-of thing; to plead with Mukuli was madness. Yet the red-haired man had acted like a fear-ridden clown—and assuredly he was not mad. Mukuli swept away with his arms those nearest him and strode to a great fire close at hand over which boiled and sizzled in a cauldron the sliced flesh of a horse, cooking against the feast of the evening an hour hence.

Jerking the pot from its supporting stakes, the Tatar wheeled and in the one motion cast it—meat, water, and cauldron—at the giant. It struck full against Subotai's chest, and he roared with pain, while the skin of his body turned red with the sting of the scalding water. Pawing at his face, he staggered, shook his head.

"A little sting makes the Buffalo bellow," chuckled Mukuli, and the crowd shouted approval of his words.

Even as he spoke, the Tatar chewed at his mustache, and with all haste drew his sword—a wide-bladed affair a hundred pounds in weight.

Subotai's eyes had turned red. He snatched at the weapon nearest him, which happened to be the scimitar of Chepe Noyon. Yet, measuring the slender length of blue steel in his fist, Subotai cast it down on the sand and probed the throng with gleaming eyes until he spied a Mongol gur-khan leaning on the handle of a battle-ax as massive as Mukuli's sword.

Striding forward, Subotai put his hand on the ax, and, although the surprised captain clung to it with both fists, drew it free of the other's grasp as easily as he might have pulled a knife from a piece of meat.

At this the crowd gave back discreetly with huge relish and Mukuli's eyes gleamed with pleasure. It looked as if there was fight in the Buffalo after all. Instead of swinging the ax over his head in both hands, he gripped it halfway up the handle with his right and extended his left in front of him, meanwhile striding toward the Tatar.

Mukuli waited until one of Subotai's feet was midway in a step, and—sure that the giant could not sidestep or leap away—whirled his sword up and down at the outstretched arm. The blow would have sliced Subotai's limb from the shoulder, even as it would have shorn through the back of an ox. It would have done so, that is, if the Buffalo had not checked his stride and let his arm fall to his side.

The sword of Mukuli whistled through the air, grazing his chest, and the blade was buried deep in the sand a yard in front of the man of the reindeer folk. Seeing this, Subotai completed his step forward, but placed his booted foot on the sword of his adversary and gripped Mukuli's right wrist with his left hand. Instinctively, the Tatar tried to pull free.

While he tugged, Subotai's ax chopped down sharply. Mukuli thrust his head forward and the blade of the ax rang on his bronze cap, glanced down, sliced a segment of the rawhide armor off his shoulder, along with a goodly bit of skin.

"Hey," chuckled Chepe Noyon, "the Buffalo can gore."

It was Mukuli's turn to roar with anger, and, dropping his sword hilt, to spring at his foe. Subotai let fall the ax and planted his legs firmly in the sand, meeting the rush of his foe with the weight of his body. The two warriors grappled, and the gray eyes of the Buffalo glinted with pleasure.

He let the veteran maul him for a moment, while he worked his arms free and encircled the other's body. His arms tightened and presently Mukuli's writhing ceased. A bone in the Tatar's body cracked.

And then Temujin put an end to the fight. He had gone to the fire and pulled out the blazing branch of a tree. With this he smote the taller man over the eyes, knocking his head back and searing his flesh.

Subotai slid to the sand, and Mukuli, dazed by the blow on his helmet, got back his breath with difficulty, investigating the while the damage done to his ribs. Then he recovered his sword, wincing at the motion, and surveyed Subotai in mild amazement.

"If you have let out his life, it was ill-done, Temujin," he observed sullenly. "Another moment and I would have strangled him."

"Another moment, Mukuli, and you would have been quaffing the cup of greeting with your ancestors in the sky-world."

Temujin ordered his gur-khan to see that the unconscious fighter was brought to his tent on a litter and set down by the fire.

When the man recovered consciousness, the Mongol khan, the Tiger, and Mingan were sitting beside him.

"What brings you from the snow circle, O head of fire?" Temujin asked.

"Enough of fire," smiled Chepe Noyon, "has he had on his head to suffice for the rest of his life, which will be short if Mukuli gets a second chance at him."

Subotai, however, seemed to take all that happened as a matter of course.

"I know not the customs of your Horde, O Khan!" he vouchsafed. "If you feed a guest with the pot itself, and put him to sleep with the fire, it is all one to me. But if I ask for a drink and you ram the cup down my throat, I will not stay any longer."

Chepe Noyon chuckled, but Temujin scanned the injured man seriously. He watched Subotai shake his head, brush the ashes out of his eyelids, and empty the goblet of wine Mingan gave him.

"Another," instructed Temujin.

But as Mingan was about to refill the goblet, Subotai climbed to his feet, apparently little the worse for his harsh treatment.

"If you are giving me wine, do not trouble yourself with that child's cup. I will take the cask."

"Give him the cask," nodded Temujin.

It was a gift of Podu, half-empty, true enough, but when Subotai had taken it up and poured liberal libations to the four quarters of the sky, there still remained enough to fill a half-dozen goblets. However, the big man raised the edge of it to his lips and began to tip it higher.

Chepe Noyon listened to his swallows.

"He drinks like a captain—like a colonel of a thousand—nay, like a hero. By the hide of Afrasiab, the keg is empty! We must go to Podu's tent or eat with dry gullets this night."

"Good!" said Subotai with a hearty sigh. "Let us go to the tent of this Podu."

"Only the khans sit at the feast," remarked Mingan, "and you have neither rank, nor weapon, nor horse, nor standing in any tribe here."

"I came, O Khan—" the Buffalo bethought him of Temujin's question—"from the reindeer country because word came to me that riders who left the tracks of our boot were in the southland and I meant to herd them back, because we are at peace with your Horde, which is well for you."

"Have you found your riders?"

"Not a hair of their hide, O Khan. I turned my steps to this place, but no men of mine are here."

There was no doubting the truth of the man's statement, voiced slowly as if he thought over every word. Mingan reflected that others than the reindeer people had left the tracks of hoofs in the snow when the Mongol ponies were stolen.

"What rank have you with your own people?" demanded Temujin.

"A smith, O my host, and the son of a smith. I can beat out on the anvil and weld the strongest axes."

"Yet you do not carry one."

"I feared to do that, coming into the Horde."

"And you feared to wrestle," assented Temujin, puzzled. "Why? You were not afraid of Mukuli, whom no man of the throng—save myself—would have faced when he was minded to kill, as then."

Subotai cracked his thumbs uneasily.

"O Khan, my nature is weak. It is my nature when a warrior wrestles with me or we play with swords to grow angry. Then the red comes into my eyes, and I kill the other. I cannot take part in the games of the khans; it is better to make weapons."

After pondering this, Temujin looked up.

"If I name you, O Buffalo, my sword-bearer, and give you a weapon like Mukuli's brand, will you serve me in all things and be faithful? Mine is no easy service, and there will be more blows than gold pieces."

"I see that." Subotai, in his turn, thought the matter over. "The wine is good, the meat is plentiful. Your men obey when you speak. All that is as it should be. I will take you for my khan. But I do not want a sword. Give me the ax I took up and I am your man."

"Granted, and the big piebald horse shall be yours—Mingan, see to it this hour. We will need horses before this moon is older. Chepe Noyon, and you, Subotai, come with me to Podu's feasting pavilion."

Subotai grunted with pleasure. Although they had not seen him before that hour, the Mongols felt that, his assurance given, Subotai would be faithful to Temujin. Mingan, knowing the khan's ability to judge men and attach them to him, suspected shrewdly that Temujin meant to form an alliance with the reindeer folk through Subotai. He was only sorry that they would attend the feast that night. Temujin, however, had not seen Burta in the camp for the last two days, and Mingan knew that although he did not speak of it, the girl's absence troubled his master.

The moonlight cut clearly through the dry air of the desert, and a warm breeze stirred the tent sides as Mingan left Subotai's new horse at the entrance of a small yurt between his own tent and Temujin's, and turned his steps toward the high pavilion where the warriors were feasting on this the last night of the concourse.

Yet, as he went with bowed head, the Cathayan heard a whisper other than the note of the wind—an almost inaudible murmur that came from the shadows where men sat unseen, and followed after him. So, coming into a darkened lane between lines of the Gipsy wagon yurts, Mingan stopped and waited, his eyes alert, his hand on the ivory hilt of the hunting knife he always carried concealed in the folds of his girdle.

Standing so, he sniffed at the smoke that drifted from the fires, scenting the faint odor of the sun-warmed sand, listened to the movements of the horse herds—sampling the sounds and smells of the night, for he little expected to see that which followed him. He was being followed, he knew. But, after resuming his course and twisting among the carts, he felt that he had shaken off whoever might be on his track.

After convincing himself of this, he sought out the wagon where Podu's women slept, keeping still to the lane of the shadows. He was now directly behind the feasting pavilion, where all the khans of the Horde were gathered. Mingan wanted very much to know what had happened to Burta, and he meant to find out. The girl had warned Temujin of danger, in the black tents, and now the daughter of Podu had disappeared.

By pressing his ear close to the silk wall of the yurt, he could hear the lisping of Gipsy women's voices, but could not make out words. Mingan had unlimited patience, but his time was short. Presently he might be missed if anyone in the pavilion should happen to call for a song or story.

So, taking out his knife, he slit the silk noiselessly and pried open the slit with two fingers. Darkness. Mingan sighed and felt upon the ground with an exploring foot. Turning over a stone, he picked it up and tossed it over the wagon, hearings its impact on the earth on the far side.

Mingan saw several old women, all looking warily toward the yurt entrance. He saw, too, Burta almost under him, propped up on cushions, her limbs bound tight to her slender body by veils, a fan thrust in her teeth and bound fast to gag her.

"A dog," muttered one woman, "made the noise. Are not Podu's men all about us, on this night? No one would come to that side of the wagon."

"Wine flows," observed another, shaking her head, "and when it does who can trust the guards? I shall be glad when the night is past and Burta is still here under our charge. Otherwise—for us the whipping-post."

Burta turned her eyes toward them and twisted angrily in her bonds. Mingan dared not speak to her. Besides, he had learned something. Podu expected fighting that night. It could be no trouble of Podu's making, or he would have sent his women away into hiding in the desert.

He was waiting to hear more, when he released the tent wall and dropped to the sand, rolling under the wagon. Near him—he did not wait to discover where—sounded the muffled footsteps of men. Against the tent his form would have been outlined clearly.

The men, two of them, drew close and stopped, their boots within reach of Mingan's hand. Lying so, he could make out against the luminous sky that one was as tall and broad as Subotai. In fact this one seemed to have a head the size of a wine cask—a roundish head, gleaming at the top with jewels. The other, too, had something queer about his face. It did not look like a man's face, yet the voice that came from it was undeniably a man's.

Mingan listened attentively, but the two were speaking in a dialect he did not know. Round Head had a shrill voice; Mis-shapen Head whispered. Everyone in the camp was whispering, it seemed, that evening. Presently they moved away a little and Mingan started to roll out from under the wagon to follow.

Then the smaller of the two said distinctly: "If Temujin leaves the pavilion alive, he will not leave his tent so. Go to the riders; bid them see to their horses and await my command."

Whereupon the speaker glanced at the lighted tent, made a sign of caution to his companion, and drew away.

Rising, Mingan went after them, out into a space bright with moonlight. Still in shadow himself, he coughed deliberately. The pair turned to stare behind them, and he saw that the bigger man had a round, black face, surmounted by a wide roll of white cloth; the other had no face at all.

That is, no human face. Over head and shoulders was drawn the skin of a bear, the jaws propped wide, the teeth gleaming. His eyes seemed to penetrate the darkness in which Mingan stood. He clapped his hands softly, and Mingan heard the rush of feet behind him.

A second time he threw himself on the sand as a man's legs crashed against him, and their owner tumbled headlong.

Waiting for no more, the Cathayan leaped up and fled among the darkened wagons, fleetly for all his height, and presently found himself in among the fires where warriors sat eating. Here he fell into a walk, and, making sure that he was not followed, circled the tents to approach the feasting pavilion by the main entrance.

Once inside, he ran his eye over the ranks of the revelers, seeking if any were missing. If one were absent, he would know the name of him who had worn the bear's head. They were all present, the khans of the Horde, seated about the dais on which Temujin sat cross-legged on a leopard skin. In the outer circle, near the wall of the tent, Subotai's red head reared up from the caps of the lesser officers.

Following the direction of his new friend's gaze, Mingan beheld first a wide carpet running from the massive teak pole of the pavilion to the foot of Temujin's throne-seat; second, prostrated on the carpet with his white turban pressing against it, the big man who had been with Bear's Face, half an hour ago. Mingan, as he went to his accustomed place in the gathering by Chepe Noyon, felt quietly in his girdle to make sure that his dagger was secure—then remembered that it had fallen from his hand in the scuffle behind the tent.

"What man is this one?" he questioned the Tiger in a whisper.

"A Turk, captured by Podu, 'tis said, in a caravan from India way. A mighty wrestler, he boasts himself. Just before your coming he walked in and challenged any of the Horde, asking that if he conquered he be given life and freedom."

"Did he come in alone?"

"As I said. No one is eager to step on the carpet, for the Turk is big enough to break a foe in twain."

Now Mingan was aware of the stir of excitement in the revelers, and knew why his entrance passed almost unnoticed. Podu was fingering his thin mustaches in chagrin.

"O my Khan," the Gipsy observed, "this wrestler of the Turks is a mighty wrestler. He has thrown the best of my champions, breaking of one the back, of another the leg, until my followers will not go up against him. The Jelairs of Jamuka have seen him at work and they likewise sit still in their places. The Tatars are licking their sore joints from the contests of the day. Yet we cannot let the challenge of the stranger pass."

As if guessing the meaning of the chieftain, the swarthy Turk lifted his head and smiled contemptuously. The khans began to mutter, because it was without precedent that a champion came to the games of the Horde and held the carpet unchallenged. The muttering rose to a demand that Temujin call out a contender.

"O my cousin," spoke up Jamuka coldly, "have you sat so long on the carpet of the council that you fear to set your feet on the wrestling rug? It was not so with Yesukai, your father. Show us, as aforetime, your strength and skill."

Mingan could not speak to Temujin without being overheard, but, catching his chief's eye, he shook his head slightly in warning. Whatever the Turk and the man in the mask had planned, it meant no good to the Mongol.

In the past Temujin had found that Mingan did everything for a good reason, and he glanced to where Subotai sat, looking on eagerly. A match between the Turk and the Buffalo would be worth watching.

"So the Khan is afraid?" the soft voice of Jamuka broke in on his thoughts. "Was Yesukai the last of the Mongol heroes?"

Hereupon men set down their cups, gently, so as to hear the better what would follow; the cup-bearers ceased moving about, and there was heard the rustling of the long silk banners suspended over the head of Temujin. Podu twisted the turquoise rings on his thumbs, biting his mustache uneasily.

Old Mukuli chuckled with heavy amusement.

"Aye, Temujin, in the days aforetime the Mongols would start up at the trumpet heralding the day's march, but now you and your men love well the lute that summons to a feast. If you sit too long under the banners someone will roll you up, with one for a shroud—by Natagai, so it will happen."

Memory of his discomfiture at the hand of Temujin's new sword-bearer that day rankled.

Very promptly at this Temujin stepped down from his high seat and threw off feast robe and mantle. Naked to the waist he advanced toward the Turk, who had stripped himself of turban, vest and shirt. A murmur came from the lips of the assemblage at sight of the Turk's solid chest over which rippled muscles, of the round arms and the white teeth agleam under a black mustache. For all his weight, he was quick on his feet as he circled his adversary warily.

Temujin was short in the leg, but long of body; his back was straight, his arms knitted to high shoulders by massive sinews—muscles better adapted to swinging a weapon than to quick and cunning hand grips. Mingan noticed that his chin came no higher than the Turk's shoulder, and that his skin was scarred by old wounds, and the flesh of his neck by the wooden *kang* he had worn when a prisoner.

The Khan followed the motions of the experienced Turk with expressionless eyes, but slipped aside as the big wrestler sprang forward to butt him in the chest, and strived to trip him. No whit disconcerted, the big man reached out, caught one of Temujin's wrists, and sent the Mongol flying over his shoulder by wheeling his body and pulling down on the wrist he held.

Before Temujin could roll clear, the wrestler fell on him heavily, driving both knees into the Mongol's stomach. He sought for a grip on the chief's head, but Temujin broke his hold and kicked loose, springing to his feet. Mingan saw that blood was dripping from the mouth of his friend.

"A goblet full of gold pieces," cried Podu, beside himself with excitement, "that the Turk pins the Khan to the carpet!"

No one took his wager, and it dawned on the Gipsy that here was no friendly bout, but a struggle out of which one man might come crippled for life. If it should be Temujin—

"Let us stop the match," he exclaimed to Mukuli.

The Tatar wiped his mustache mechanically, but before he could answer an outcry filled the pavilion.

The Turk had thrown Temujin again, with one of his panther-like tricks of hand and body. Leaping down at the chief a second time, his knees met only the carpet. Temujin had rolled out from under in time. But what brought the spectators to their feet was the sight of a dagger that fell from the girdle of the big wrestler, shaken loose by the heavy impact.

"*Hai*—the man had steel upon him! Slay him!"

Chepe Noyon's hand went to his empty scabbard. Then, remembering that all their weapons had been left at the threshold of the pavilion, he was starting toward the entrance when Mingan pulled him down.

"Wait, and watch!" whispered the Cathayan.

The gleaming steel had caught Temujin's eyes, and he had kicked the dagger away from the wrestler to the carpet's edge where Subotai, surging through the onlookers at Chepe Noyon's shout, set his foot upon it and glared around, as if daring anyone to try to pick it up.

Gaining his feet, the Khan rushed his adversary, and now his head was down, his deep eyes glowing with the fire of conflict. The two locked grips, chin pressing shoulders, fingers digging into flesh, and this time it was the Turk who strove to break free. He tried trickery, leaning his weight on the Mongol, then, all at once he began to squeal with rage; he was being hurt.

"By the beard of my sire," grunted Mukuli, licking his lips, and—finding them dry—handing up his goblet to a staring cup-bearer who was quite oblivious of the act. "By Natagai, by —— one will break the other's back. Ha! For all the gold in Cathay I would not set hand between the Khan and his foeman now."

For Temujin's narrowed eyes gleamed red under the beads of perspiration.

"Make an end!" a voice cried somewhere in the crowd.

Exerting all the remaining power of his big limbs, the Turk broke free. Wise in the way of his profession, he knew that Temujin was seeking his life, and he cast himself at the Mongol, forgetful of everything but the need of pinning the other's arms to his body.

Stooping, Temujin caught the man around the knees and raised himself erect, shifting his grip swiftly, so that the Turk balanced on one shoulder. A shrill sound came from the mouth of the wrestler as he felt himself helpless. Then Temujin caught his legs and whirled him through the air with all the strength of mighty sinews and straining back.

The head of the Turk thudded against the teak pole of the pavilion, and he dropped to the carpet, silent now, his skull shattered.

"A good match!" roared Mukuli. "Now—"

Temujin, staggering and gasping for breath, made his way toward Subotai, thrust the giant aside, and picked up the dagger.

"A viper was sent to sting me: now the viper is crushed but his sting remains. Who sent it—who?"

"Cousin," said Jamuka's quiet voice, "I know not, save that the dagger is Mingan's—your *orkhon*'s."

Mingan started as Temujin, his face a mask of anger, strode toward him.

"Though he has changed his skin," cried the Jelair, "I know him for the Cathayan who came to you through the Wall. I bade you slay him once, but there is still time, before he deprives the Horde of its master."

"He is a snake!" added Podu vindictively, thinking of his lost ponies, and thankful that Temujin's anger had been centered on one whose death would not promote a new feud in the Gobi.

Standing up, Mingan started to speak, but—aware of the blind rage in the heart of his friend—folded his arms and kept silence. No words would serve to turn aside the torrent that was ready to engulf him.

His calmness, however, did not stay Temujin, who caught his beard in one hand and raised the knife with the other.

A tensing of iron muscles, and the dagger flashed downward, but its course was checked abruptly by a more powerful arm. A hand gripped Temujin's wrist, and a voice spoke in his ear: "Your nature is likewise weak. Because," went on the Buffalo, "you, O Khan, like myself, cannot take part in the games without lusting for blood."

A simpleton, thought the watchers—nay, a madman—to curb Temujin when he was angry. But the man of the reindeer people kept his grip on his master until, perforce, Temujin relaxed his arm.

"The knife is yours!" he snarled at Mingan.

And Mingan saw that it was the one he had lost when he fell outside the tent. The Turk must have picked it up or it had been given to the wrestler to use on Temujin.

"Aye," he admitted. "I dropped it within the hour, but the wrestler was no man of mine."

"For all of that," put in Subotai, who seemed to have no sense of ceremony in the presence of his superiors, "there is a fine pile of weapons outside, and the fat brown man could have taken his pick. Wait until the sun rises on the morrow, O Khan, and then slice up your palladin if you want to—it is all one to me. But now your eyes are red, and if you slay him, you will grieve—like me."

Sheer surprise had kept Temujin passive. Now, thoughtfully, he put the knife in his belt, stirred the dead body of the Turk with his foot to see if the man were beyond telling the secret that had been his, and signed to Chepe Noyon to bring his mantle and robe.

"Master," whispered the young Tiger, as he put the garments over Temujin, "Mingan is not a traitor—a man's eyes cannot lie, though his tongue be crooked as a ram's horn. The Cathayan was right. There is one in this assemblage who is wiser than you, and all but contrived that you should slay your friend. Wait until the morrow."

"Aye, be it so." Temujin nodded. "Subotai, guard Mingan, the *orkhon* —keep him ever under your eyes. Podu, the feast is at an end. Let no man leave the pavilion until the Mongols pass out."

His glance swept the lines of the watchers, probing and warning. Then, followed by the three palladins, he strode out, leaving the khans staring at the broken body of the giant wrestler.

In this fashion did the friendship of the three heroes begin, for that night they were together in the same tent, and that night was a memorable one in the annals of the Gobi.

VI

The Tiger Goes A-wooing

"Quick," said Mingan, when Chepe Noyon came in from mounting the guard, and the tent flap fell behind him, leaving the three alone, "go to Temujin, tell him to rouse his captains and arm his men. Danger stands near us and there is little time."

"Little time, indeed, Mingan for you to abide among the living—if I disturb the khan now and bring you into his thoughts again. He is like a bear with a thorn in his paw. Let him sleep." He threw himself down on his sleeping furs. "Is danger something new, that you mew about it like a cat with a cup of sour milk?"

Mingan sighed and related his experience among the Gipsy wagon yurts. He repeated the words of the man in the mask, that Temujin, if he left the pavilion in safety, was to be attacked in his tent.

"A bearskin?" Chepe Noyon frowned. "That is the mask worn by the leader of the Kerait warriors—Wang Khan's commander." He yawned. "You are always dreaming about something or other, Mingan. Now you should be thinking of your plight. It is said Temujin never forgets a friend, but, by Kotwan, he never fails to remember an enemy. As for the Keraits, they are all in Tangut."

Mingan stepped to the tent entrance to look out, but felt the hand of the Buffalo on his shoulder.

"'Bide where I can see you, Cathayan. The story-tellers relate that all your folk are magicians, and I do not wish you to vanish."

Without turning, Mingan said softly: "Burta lies bound and gagged in the tent of Podu's women, beside the wagon of the Gipsy chief. Does that mean nothing to you, O Tiger?"

"Now—the —— take me—how can you see that from where you stand?"

"My eyes can see at night—if the moon is bright enough. But do you go quietly, Chepe Noyon, and seek word with her, prevail on Podu's sentries to let you pass. But first visit the picket lines and have the three best ponies saddled and brought here."

Hereat the Tiger grumbled, but yawned no more. Presently his eye fell upon Mingan's lute and he brightened. Unobserved by his two companions he picked up the instrument and put it under his cloak, and went out, with a word of assent. He noticed that the light was still burning in Temujin's tent and pondered whether he should tell the Khan of Mingan's fears. Remembering the lute he was carrying, he decided to go to the horse lines instead.

He took his time about ordering the three ponies from the horse tenders and carefully tested saddle-girths and stirrups of the gray pony, the Arab, and his mare. When he was satisfied that the camp had quieted down to sleep, he swung into the saddle of the mare and took the reins of the two others, leading them after him at a foot pace. Their hoofs made no sound in the sand, and Chepe Noyon passed unchallenged into the dark lanes of the Gipsy wagons. From time to time men looked out at him, but the sight of a rider leading his ponies about at all hours in the camp was common enough, when the day's gaming had ended and wagers won and lost made new masters of horses.

Sighting the lofty summit of the feasting pavilion, the Tiger counted the tents behind it. Nearing the third one in the line, he tethered the ponies to a cart wheel, unshipped his lute, and advanced, keeping to the shadow, a little surprised that he had not been stopped. But the guards of Podu seemed to be slumbering with the rest of the camp and Chepe Noyon squatted down under the side of the women's yurt.

He cleared his throat and touched the lute's strings with a gentle finger.

As nothing happened to disturb him he began to sing, under his breath, his favorite chant, the "Lament of the Doleful Hero."

"My way leads forth by the gate on the north;
My heart is full of woe.
I hav'n't a cent, begged, stolen or lent,
And friends forget me so.
So let it be! 'Tis heaven's decree.
What can I say—a poor fellow like me?"

Cocking his head, the Tiger listened for stealthy footsteps, for the scrape of an arrow shaft against the wood of the bow, for the *slick* of steel-sword drawn from scabbard. Almost beside his head the silk wall of the tent quivered and was still. Emboldened, he sang on, more softly:

"The pigeon is petted, the wild goose is netted,
the squirrel amasses a store.
When I enter your camp, they call me a scamp,
And thrust me from the door.
So let it be! 'Tis heaven's decree.
What can I say? A poor fel—"

The Tiger stilled his song and listened with all his ears. Near at hand he was aware of a tiny sound, monotonous as the drip-drip of water from a leaking bucket. He peered around him and noticed that from the wagon shaft of the yurt opposite something was dropping regularly into the sand.

This wagon should be Podu's, and Chepe Noyon was not minded to risk an arrow sent in his direction if anyone were astir. Squinting into the shadow that covered the front of the yurt, he fancied that a man was crouching over the wagon-tongue. After a quarter of an hour he was sure of it. But the man did not move.

Instead, the silk near his ear shook again, violently as if to convey to his understanding an urgent message. He heard the drowsy voice of an old woman mutter within the tent.

"Be still, Burta. After dawn you will be released, so Podu said. Are we to have no sleep, because of your fidgets?"

Still the figure opposite him did not stir, and the Tiger was puzzled, also his patience was exhausted. He could hear the ponies beginning to toss their heads and paw at the sand. So he rose, his hand on his sword hilt. As he did so he flung a handful of sand into the face of the watcher.

Now that he was erect, he could make out a wide, dark stain in the ground where the moonlight touched the tip of the wagon-shaft. With a glance around, he strode across to the silent yurt and stooped to feel of the figure, finding it to be the body of a man, warm to his touch. But in the throat of the man was a hunting knife, and from this trickled a sluggish current that moistened the wooden shaft and dripped into the sand.

No longer wondering that the rear of the tent was unguarded, Chepe Noyon was about to withdraw as swiftly as might be when he glanced into Podu's tent. The moonlight on the thin, silk wall of the back cast a faint glow over the floor of the wagon, and here, too, was a form prone on the sleeping skins. The Tiger entered and felt of it.

By the heavy earrings and the jeweled belt, he knew it to be Podu, but a dead Podu, slain by an arrow that had pierced his brain.

Now Chepe Noyon cursed under his breath, and fell silent, harkening to a new sound some distance away, like the buzzing of bees. He had heard its like before, and knew that the buzzing was made up of the trampling of hoofs, the creaking of saddle leather, the low voices of men.

Whereupon, abandoning Mingan's lute, the Tiger leaped to the ground, circled the yurt, and gained the spot where he had left his horses, hardly checking his stride as he jerked the reins free and mounted the mare.

Drawing the others with him he sped like a drifting shadow past the dark pavilion, out into the central lane of the camp at the end of the race course, and shouted aloud in anger and surprise.

Torches flickered and smoked down the race course; groups of horsemen cantered up, to disappear among the tents of the Mongols. Here and there steel flashed, as Temujin's men ran out of their shelters to stand against the riders. The twanging of bowstrings and the groans of the injured mingled with the screams of wounded ponies and the splintering of tent poles.

The Mongols had been surprised. Chepe Noyon cursed his folly in going to the camp of Podu, who was dead and could in no wise come to the defense of his erstwhile guests.

He saw the captain of the Mongol guard struck down by a raider in front of the yak-tail standard; a young brother of Temujin, a boy armed with a toy bow, stepped out of his tent and discharged a shaft pluckily. As a horseman sighted him and flourished a javelin, the youngster cast down his shield and bow, knowing the uselessness of flight. As the Tiger watched, the raider passed a spear-point into the youth's chest and cantered on.

Temujin's tent was surrounded by attackers, so that a ring of torches was formed, and in the bright glow Chepe Noyon made out that the riders were riddling the tent with arrows, piercing it in a hundred places so that nothing above ground might survive. The light still burned in the tent.

All this the Tiger perceived in the minute it took him to gallop up to his tent before which stood Subotai, wielding his ax, and Mingan a sword, back to back. A half-dozen men circled around them, warily, for two of the raiders lay outstretched in the sand.

Through this ring of horsemen Chepe Noyon dashed, striking a man from his saddle as he passed by, the two ponies rearing and kicking under his hand what with the lights and clamor that filled the night.

"Mount!" cried the Tiger to his friends.

The rush of the three ponies afforded the hard-pressed warriors a half-moment's respite, which Chepe Noyon used to advantage. Wheeling the quick-footed mare, he faced one of the assailants and feinted at the strange warrior's head. With a turn of the wrist he altered the direction of the blow, slicing the leather buckler from his foeman's arm.

"Jackal!" he snarled, his teeth flashing in his dark face. "Who is your master?"

It struck him suddenly that the raiders were fighting in silence, uttering no war cry, and apparently leaderless. The man in front of him responded by striking at the Tiger's throat—a blow that slid off the agile scimitar of the swordsman harmlessly, while Chepe Noyon's return stroke severed the warrior's right wrist and set him swaying in the saddle. By now, Subotai and Mingan reined up on either side of him, and the four remaining horsemen hung back.

In the pause that followed, Chepe Noyon was aware of two things: first, that the riders had finished their shooting to pieces of Temujin's tent, and, flinging their torches at it, had galloped off, not wishing, it seemed, to be seen in the vicinity; second, the leader of the horsemen, with another at his elbow, had sighted the two *orkhons* and Subotai together nearby and had trotted over to their assailants, and it was clearly to be seen that he wore the mask of a bear's head.

"Arrows!" the enemy chief ordered.

And arrows he had, though not from the hands of his own men. Chepe Noyon trotted up with Mingan and the Buffalo guarding his back with drawn weapons, and uttered a question under his breath.

"Dog!" The Tiger said. "You are no Kerait. Take off the mask!"

His left hand shot forward, clutching at the bearskin. The chief swung over in the saddle, whereupon Chepe Noyon raised his scimitar to smite, and urged the mare forward at the same instant. The other's pony, taken unaware and hampered by the weight of its rider hanging on the off-side, stumbled in the soft sand and threw the chief.

"Die then," snarled the Tiger, "as Temujin died—"

A javelin cast by the chief's attendant clashed against his shield, but what stayed his hand was the sight of the sand stirring at the edge of Temujin's crumpled and blazing tent. The sand heaved and fell aside as if an enormous mole were rising to the surface, but instead of a mole a blackened face was revealed by the glow of the fire. Presently the body of a man followed the face, and Temujin climbed out of the hole he had dug in the loose sand while the arrows slashed through his yurt.

He reached behind him and drew out a bow and a fistful of arrows. Kneeling almost in the flames, and half-screened by the whirling smoke, he began to loose shafts at the five enemies who still remained in the saddle.

"Ride him down!" cried the man in the bearskin, warding off Chepe Noyon's belated stroke.

His men started to obey, but one passed too near Subotai and had his skull shattered by a blow of the long ax. Another was knocked out of his saddle by one of Temujin's shafts, and the others cast their torches down and shouted for aid.

Meanwhile, Mingan had availed himself of the moment's respite to free Subotai's piebald pony that was straining at its reins before the Buffalo's tent. He rushed up to the Khan, who climbed into the saddle of the tall horse as reinforcements came up to their assailants.

Chepe Noyon was forced back from his prey and the three warriors formed around Temujin.

"Hai, ahatou, koke Mongku—hai!"

The Khan of the Mongols roared his battle-cry, his voice carrying above the tumult. Here and there a wounded Mongol fought his way toward him. A gur-khan rode up on a sweating horse, followed by a single warrior.

For every one of his men that came, three enemies appeared, and Temujin, rising in his stirrups, saw that the butchery of the Mongols was nearly completed. His eyes glowed with a mad fire, but he saw the folly of making a stand.

"Follow me to Podu's tent!" he ordered, wheeling his horse.

"Podu is slain," Chepe Noyon cried, reining his pony beside his chief, "by one of these jackals of the night." But Temujin did not alter his course. With his handful of followers he reached the wagons of the Gipsies, the foemen close behind, hindered in their pursuit by lack of torches. Before the women's tent a pair of Podu's tribesmen were struggling with a group of the riders.

The rush of the Mongols scattered these, Subotai's ax and Chepe Noyon's sword working havoc. Temujin tossed his reins to Mingan, dismounted, and, thrusting past the exhausted guards, entered the tent. In a moment he appeared, carrying Burta, bound and gagged, in his arms. As he did so, the pursuers rounded the pavilion and loosed a flight of arrows.

The gur-khan and one of the Gipsies fell, pierced by the missiles, and Mingan, as he assisted Temujin with his burden into the saddle of the piebald, rose in his stirrups with a cry. Something seared his breast, and a warm flood rose in his throat. The vista of the tents and the moonlit sky whirled and tossed before his eyes.

He was aware of Subotai's arm that drew him out of his saddle, to the back of another horse. Then the air rushed past his ears. He coughed, and pain wracked him so that everything disappeared in a red mist.

He felt vaguely the motion of a galloping horse, and in the mist beheld Chepe Noyon dismount, run beside a riderless horse, and mount again without stopping. He wondered what it was all about—saw, presently, Burta sitting astride the Arab, her long hair streaming over her back, and on every hand the wide sweep of the desert, shining in the radiance of a crimson moon. And then—nothing.

The red glory of dawn over his head, the chill of dawn on his outer skin, and burning heat in his chest and throat—of these things Mingan became conscious, but chiefly of an all-enveloping thirst. Although he made no movement, his head was being raised by degrees until he looked into the strained, gaunt face of Temujin.

The Khan had Mingan's head on his knee, and was holding to the lips of the wounded man his leather hunting cap filled with water. Mingan drank and straightway coughed, the sweat starting on his forehead. But his thirst was assuaged. The dark eyes of his friend searched his face keenly.

"Burta, my wife-to-be," said Temujin, "the soul of this *orkhon* is near to the spirit world. He has need of your hand and the care of the Gipsies. Abide with him in this place, and leave him not until I come.

Mingan tried to turn his head to see Burta, yet could not. He wondered whither the multitude of the camp had vanished and why. Presently, Temujin and Chepe Noyon alone were working over a long figure stretched on a saddle cloth beside him. This was Subotai, he fancied, and his two companions were pulling into place a bone dislocated in the giant's arm. Subotai watched them at their labor, chewing his lip. His glance wandered to Mingan and he grinned widely, brushing the dust from his eyes.

"Eh, the hard blows were not long in coming. Yet we left a trail of dead foemen along the length of the camp—"

He shut his lips as the bone snapped into place, and Temujin rose.

"I must ride to the Three Rivers where my people await me," said the khan. "My enemies wax stronger, and few stand near me." His dark face lighted with a secret exultation. "Yet have I found three heroes, and now I know the name of my foe—aye, of him who smote my camp."

Burta questioned, and stamped her foot angrily when he shook his head, saying nothing more. Finally, Mingan heard her weeping when the men had left.

"It was the men of Prester John who slew Temujin's Mongols, and now there will be war in the Gobi," she said.

Fever-bred dreams tormented him. He was standing again on the Great Wall of Cathay, looking at the western plain over which hung the red ball of the sun. Against the wall the riders of the Horde were surging. Little by little they were forcing the gate that barred their way into Cathay, and Mingan sought to throw stones down on them. But his hands would not move. They were smiling at him, waving bared swords in the dust-cloud under the wall and—passing through the gate. Mingan was wearing an imperial robe, with the dragon curled on his breast, heavy with yellow gold.

It was the robe worn by members of his dynasty when death's hour was at hand. Scarcely had he perceived this than the sun dropped out of sight and darkness came on the world.

Again Mingan looked out at a campfire over which a cauldron boiled merrily, and near which crouched an old woman, shredding roots and herbs in her hands. The shadow of the woman was thrown against a great rock, and Mingan fancied that she was a witch brewing eternal torment for him over the red fire.

He cried out and perceived Burta standing by him. The girl's hand, cool as a leaf of the forest, was on his forehead, as against his lips she pressed a bowl of something warm and astringent. Mingan coughed and swallowed a little. And presently the welcome darkness came again.

VII

Jamuka Is Amused

A barbed arrow through the lung is one of the worst possible wounds, and only Burta, and the Gipsies who came to serve her in a rock-lined gully of the desert, knew how hard had been the struggle to bring Mingan back to life. When the fever left him, Mingan lay on his side for days before strength came to him and he could talk.

Meanwhile he saw that he was hidden near a well, below the level of the surrounding plain, around which, like inanimate figures, stood pinnacles of red and gray sandstone. That it was midwinter he knew by the cold of the nights, and the stars that circled over his head.

"You are like a man of bones," observed Burta critically, "and not a hero at all, except that you have a fine beard."

There were hollows in her cheeks and shadows under her fine eyes. As she talked she stroked the head of a gyrfalcon chained to its perch near the well. Beside her, on her sleeping furs, was stretched a brown dog with a sharp muzzle and inquisitive eyes.

"When my people dare not come to the well," she explained, "Chepe Noyon and Mukuli hunt with me, and we do not lack for hares or wild geese. This is Chepe Noyon—" she nodded at the hawk—"I call him that because he is so quick and bad-tempered. Mukuli is the dog—he growls just like the old Khan and likes to lie near the fire."

Mingan smiled.

"Why do you stay here, daughter of Podu? I am whole and well."

"You are not. Half a moon will pass before you walk about, and another moon before you ride a horse. But I am glad you can talk. Mukuli is wise, but he agrees to everything I say."

"Being wise," nodded Mingan.

"Hum. Temujin never does what I say and he is wiser than anyone—"

"Except the man in the bear's head."

Burta frowned a little and stood up to look out of their shelter.

"Then you have seen him, too, Mingan? My people gather news for me as squirrels gather acorns, and they say the chief with the bearskin has been seen in the desert near here. They say the omens have been many; vultures have been seen in the sky at dawn, and a raven has made a nest in a dead pine. The tribesmen have wintered close to their *ordus*, their chief's camps; rumors are many that blood will run freely in the Gobi and the bones of men whiten on the battlefield."

She sighed and bit her lip.

"I hate Temujin," she added fiercely. "He has been away for so long, and no message has come from him."

"Yet you abide here, as he ordered, to await his coming."

"Kai!" She poked at the sables resentfully. "You were too ill to be moved."

Mingan noticed, however, that Burta continued to make her home at the well, although dark-skinned men, adorned more often than not with the spoil of the desert caravans, rode up from time to time to urge her to seek a place of greater safety.

One day she returned from a hunt with the falcon and her eyes were shining. She had met, it seemed, the old woman who had helped her nurse Mingan, and had news in plenty. The Mongols had not been idle during the winter. They had been joined by several regiments of the reindeer people, brought by Subotai, and Temujin had won over the famous spearmen, the Merkets, to his standard. Then, during a blizzard, he had marched against the Tatars and surrounded Mukuli in his *ordu*.

There had been a brief fight when Temujin went to the old khan and asked him to give in to his power. Mukuli had growled, and then fell to laughing aloud.

"'My word is not smoke, O Khan,' he said, 'and aforetime I swore that I would join you when you proved yourself good metal. Verily, no man has taken Mukuli unaware before now,' he swore, 'and I will be your man in all things.'"

Burta pondered smilingly.

"I think Mukuli yearned toward Temujin at the feast in my father's camp when he overthrew the Turk."

She patted the muzzle of the brown dog, who was the self-appointed watchman of their covert.

So, at the end of that winter the northern half of the Horde—the Mongols, Tatars, Tungusi, and Merkets—was divided from the southern half, the Keraits and the Jelairs of Jamuka. The Master of Plotting, although Temujin's cousin, had proclaimed that he was sworn to fellowship with Prester John, and must side with the Christians. Temujin sent messengers to Prester John to say that no quarrel was between them, nor should they take up the sword against each other—who had been allies in the past. But the messengers were slain on the way, and the Mongol outposts brought back word of the Kerait's preparations for war. So Temujin held a council to muster his full power.

"He gave Mukuli back the gold tablet of an *orkhon*, and entreated him kindly," Burta added, "and then—"

"Temujin did well—"

"Nay, there is no Temujin, no Man of Iron now. *Ai*, he who raced horses and snared hawks with me when I was a child—is no more."

Mingan started.

"What mean you?"

"His khans at the council gave him a new name because now he has truly earned the leadership of the Horde. They named him the Great Khan, Genghis Khan."

Wrapped in his thoughts, Mingan did not hear the slight sound of a footstep nearby; nor did he notice the sudden uprising of the brown dog, who sniffed the air and whined. Temujin had grown at his side from boy to man and from man to master. Probably this was what had earned him the hatred of Prester John, of the Christians.

In Cathay there was a proverb that there could not be two suns in the sky, nor two emperors in the land. Prester John had sought to slay Temujin, or, as Mingan must think of him now, Genghis Khan; failing that, the Christians had declared war on him—

Mingan sighed. He should have rejoiced at the good fortune that cut the Horde in twain and started a great feud in the Gobi, because the Horde was the enemy of his dynasty—of Cathay itself. Had not Mingan come into the desert with Genghis Khan to study the weakness of this enemy, and profit by it? But it was hard for the Cathayan prince to think of Genghis Khan as aught but Temujin, who had befriended him. He found himself wishing for the Tiger and the Buffalo. He wanted to talk things over with them.

The brown dog barked once, angrily, and looked over his shoulder at his mistress.

"Be quiet, Mukuli—I will not play with you." Burta frowned at the sable furs on which she sat, chin on hand, her brown eyes brooding. "Now that Temujin has become Genghis Khan, he takes no thought of the daughter of Podu. For five moons I have awaited his coming as he bade me at this place, and—I hate Genghis Khan."

She struck at the rich furs contemptuously.

"*Kai*, I will await him no longer, and I will take my people to the Christians, so that he will learn the Gipsies are not to be despised—

She sprang to her feet, hands on her breast, eyes wide with swift alarm. Thus encouraged, the brown dog raced forward, barking.

A man, walking quietly, had entered the gully and stood between two rocks, smiling at her words. It was Jamuka. Mingan noticed that he wore new, silvered, chain mail and a velvet kaftan, and that a few yards away a dozen of his Jelair tribesmen had come into view, fully armed with javelins and bows.

"So, little vixen," observed Jamuka, much amused, "this is where you have run to earth! My men espied you against the skyline an hour ago, when we were following the trail of some of your Gipsies that circled around this well. May Allah cast me down, but I was hoping for a sight of you before we don helmets and mount for battle—"

He broke off, eyeing Mingan thoughtfully.

"Ah, my Cathayan—meseems you have shrunk somewhat, like a dried-up waterskin. It is the fortune of a spy, sometimes, not to eat from gold dishes, nor to ride the horses of a king."

He swept the well and the gully with an appraising glance and spat at the dog who stood, short legs planted wide, menacingly before his mistress. Jamuka's thin, handsome face and down-curving nose revealed more strongly than ever the Turkish blood in him.

"So, Burta, you hate Temujin, or, I should say Genghis?"

Color flooded into the girl's face and she did not respond.

"And you will lead your Gipsies to Prester John? Good. He will have gold for your men and pastures for your horses, within Tangut. You have never seen Tangut, little Burta; it is green and pleasant while the desert is brown and bare. The castle is a pearl set in splendors—gardens and lakes, wherein every kind of beast and bird is to be found. He has a hundred snow-white peregrine falcons, and as many hunting leopards—"

He glanced half-scornfully at the small brown gyrfalcon on the perch by the girl.

"Does the chief hero of Prester John wear a bear's head upon his own?" she asked thoughtfully.

"Why, so he does," Jamuka smiled. "When he goes forth from his castle, so that all his men will know him from afar and his enemies will not see his face."

"Then is he my foe!" Burta tossed her head and her white teeth gleamed between parted lips. "It was a man in a bear's mask that slew Podu, my father, and the guard at his tent. Another Gipsy, too, was surprised and struck down, but lived to tell me the truth afterward."

Jamuka frowned and tapped the jewel-studded hilt of his sword.

"And, if so? You cannot bring life to Podu again, and you must think of yourself. Prester John is wiser than other men; his acts are stones that pave the way to success. You may not stand alone—a woman served by a handful of wanderers."

"And so, Jamuka, must I choose between Prester John and Genghis Khan—aye, choosing the first, you will honor me with your protection and love. Is not that what you would say?"

For the second time in as many minutes the quick-thinking chief was surprised.

"By Allah, you have the right of it! It was for that I sought you out, even though an army waits without a leader in my absence. Prester John has named me his ally—"

"You, the cousin of Genghis Khan!"

Not often was Jamuka put upon the defensive in this manner, and it ruffled him.

"Aye, but your Great Khan and I cannot sleep on the same side of the fire. He is a warrior, true, but a luster after blood. I—though this you may not know—am master of the caravan trade from India to Cathay, and must needs keep open the caravan routes so that the silks, spices, tea, and cotton—aye, the goods of the world—can pass—"

"Under your hand that doubtless keeps much within its grasp. Oh, I have heard many things from my—wanderers—Jamuka. Tales of your wealth and the women of many lands that you have bought. You will never win me to your hand, for your master is Podu's murderer."

She stamped furiously and brushed the hair back from her forehead. Jamuka considered her with glowing eyes, and seemed not ill-pleased at her anger.

"Genghis Khan is a scourge—a man-slayer. Burta, your Gipsies have enriched their tents and increased their herds by taking toll of my caravans. This is ordained, perhaps, and I have no quarrel with you; but Genghis would turn every camel and pony, aye, and cameleer of the caravans into a beast of war, or a warrior. By trade Cathay rose to greatness, aye, and the empire of the Turks, my fathers, in the mountains that are called the Roof of the World; and by trade I would make the empire of the Horde equal to Cathay, while Genghis would make of it a field of white bones."

She held her brown head high, although her chin came only to the shoulder of the tall Turk.

"White bones, you say, Jamuka—ah, tell me what else has Wang Khan made of my father? Is trade a god that demands human life for sacrifice? Nay, you cannot paint a wrong to make it shine like a righteous act, nor ask me to tread softly and speak not of vengeance when I am wronged. Go, Master of Plotting, I abide here until the coming of Genghis Khan, who will listen to my plea."

Jamuka's dark eyes glistened with admiration.

"*B'illah,* little daughter of fury, you will do no such thing. Why do you think I sought you out, at some pains, while your Khan tarried?"

He knew when to make an end of words in dealing with a woman. Calling to his men to bring up their horses, he strode toward Burta, who glanced around swiftly, seeking some means of escape. The Jelairs ringed her in. Mingan started up from his seat, but was stayed by two spearmen, while Jamuka took the reins of a pony and caught Burta's arm.

When he did so the brown dog sprang at the chief. Jamuka kicked it aside, and one of his men launched a javelin at it, knocking Burta's four-legged guardian whimpering to the sand. Meanwhile, the chieftain, not without a deal of trouble, had lifted the girl into the saddle and tied her ankles to the stirrups.

"You have less honor than that dog," said Mingan angrily.

"But more wit," smiled Jamuka. "By the ninety and nine holy names, what is that?"

The hawk, aroused by the scuffle, was screaming and beating its wing, its claws gripping the perch and its hooded head bristling.

"Slay me that squawker," ordered the chief, "or it may break loose and be seen in the air by some of Burta's bands. So!"

An arrow struck the falcon from its stand, whereupon Jamuka was pleased to order his men to dig a grave at one side of the gully, near the rocks, with their swords and axes. The sand yielded to their efforts easily, but they kept on, at a nod from their leader, until they had worked down into the clay bottom, and completed a hole a yard wide and as deep and a little longer.

"You have more wit than the dog, Mingan," observed the chief, frowning. "Too much, I think. I cannot decide whether you are faithful to

Genghis Khan or merely a spy sent by the Cathayans. That being the case I shall leave the issue to destiny, and put you in your grave alive instead of slaying you."

Whereupon the two spearmen seized Mingan and led him to the hole. The Cathayan stifled the compelling impulse to struggle, to throw off the hands that held him. In his weakened condition resistance would have been useless, and he had been trained to submit to ordeals without showing fear. He forced himself to walk to the edge of the hole without compulsion and to look down into it.

Jamuka seemed disappointed in his tranquility, but Burta cried out indignantly that he was a prince of the dynasty of Cathay, and should be treated as a prisoner of rank.

No attention was paid her, and the warriors tied Mingan's feet together with stout leather thongs; then his knees were bound in similar fashion; lastly his wrists were secured together behind his back. The two men at a sign from Jamuka lifted him and sat him down in the hole, placing his legs, stiffened with the bonds, out in front of him. His back was now against one end of the excavation, the soles of his feet against the other, and his wide shoulders pressed upon the sides.

So placed, his chin was on a level with the ground, and he saw that it was not the purpose of the tribesmen to bury him. Instead they began to cast back the clay, sand and stones, first over his legs, then about his waist. Jamuka reined his horse close, to lean down from the saddle and watch his prisoner's face.

"O Cathayan, if it is true that you are a prince," he whispered so that Burta could not hear, "it is not fitting that you suffer the fate of a slave. Nay, by the prophet's beard! Tell me then the plans of Genghis Khan and what he knows of Prester John, and you shall be sent back to the wall with the first caravan that departs from Tangut after we have overthrown the Mongol scourge."

Mingan shook his head gravely.

"*Yah Allah*. As you have chosen your bed you shall lie in it."

Jamuka left him, and the men finished filling in the hole, so that the earth came to Mingan's chin. After stamping it down firmly with a covert kick or two at the helpless face, they went to seek out their horses, well contented with the day's work.

One last thing remained to be done, to complete the ceremony of the burial alive, and Jamuka did it, wheeling his horse in front of Mingan and then driving in his heels so that the pony started directly at the filled-in grave and the man's head, and passed over with a thudding of uneasy hoofs in the soft earth. No horse will tread on a man if he can help it—but this knowledge did not save the Cathayan the agony of sitting tense and powerless while beast and rider passed over him.

Left alone, Mingan's first feeling was one of relief, as he listened to the dwindling sounds of creaking saddles and jangling bits. Forthwith he began to strain upward with his knees, only to discover that his legs, stretched out flat, had no power to push into the three feet of earth. If he could bend them—but he could not.

Then he tried working his body back and forth, and this succeeded a little better. He could press the dirt forward an inch or two. His bound arms he could not move at all, nor was he able to loosen the thongs at his wrists.

In five minutes Mingan, who was a philosophic thinker, was convinced of what the Jelairs who planted him in the earth would have assured him gratis—that he was absolutely helpless. The hard-packed clay at his back and at the soles of his feet wedged him in. The sun, now at its zenith, poured down into the gully on his bare head, and sweat stung his eyes. His legs began to cramp him, then his arms.

An ant crawled up behind his ears and refused to drop off when he shook his head savagely.

The heat from the upper crust of sand and the rocks behind him pierced the skin of his skull, and his throat became dry, even while his eyes sought the cool stones that surrounded the well. From the level of the earth itself, Mingan became aware of many things that lived and moved on its surface. A lizard ran out from between two stones and turned back hastily when he moved his head; from the skins nearby a scorpion crawled toward him slowly. Mingan felt grateful when it altered its course and turned toward the ruffled body of the dead hawk to investigate.

Before an hour passed he had lost control of himself, shouting and struggling to throw off the weight that pressed down his legs, raging aloud at the ants that came more thickly now.

It was the dog that restored his spirits a little. The cut over its head and shoulder had knocked it senseless for a moment, but an animal seldom loses consciousness for long. Mukuli had half-crawled, half-limped after his mistress when the horsemen rode away, but now returned from its fruitless effort, and sighted Mingan. It made no difference to the dog that only the man's head was perceptible. He whined and licked the perspiration from Mingan's cheek, and aroused the man's frantic hopes by digging weakly with his forepaws in the soft earth under his nose.

But when Mukuli had hollowed out enough space to curl himself up in, he slumped down and fell to licking his gashed shoulder, whimpering. When Mingan spoke, Mukuli thumped his tail a little, as evidence of appreciation. Digging had passed out of his canine brain for the time being.

When the sun was halfway down to the horizon Mukuli went to the well and drank thirstily, growling at a jackal that drifted in among the rocks and snatched up the dead hawk savagely, making off with its prey.

Presently the jackal came back and sat down on its haunches. Mukuli retreated to the neighborhood of the man and lay down, too weak to stand on his legs for long. At once the jackal started up, but veered off when Mingan shouted hoarsely. Puzzled, but still hungry, the lean little beast circled the man's head and the snarling dog, darting away, only to draw back a step at a time, until it took up a position for observation and reflection at the spring.

Mukuli looked at Mingan anxiously as if wondering why the man did not get up out of the earth and drive the jackal away. Presently the dog whined and drew closer.

The sun passed behind the rocks, stripping the gully of all color and heat in a moment. But overhead the sky was a brilliant blue, cloudless and clear as space itself. Mingan took a little comfort from the fact that the jackal was no nearer. He had ceased to think of the sky, of Jamuka, or anything except the animal ten paces away.

And then his teeth clicked together spasmodically and the blood roared in his ears. Mukuli lifted his muzzle inquiringly, and the jackal retreated, shadow-like among the rocks, never to be seen again.

Near the well a man was singing and the sound of it was drawing nearer.

"The courtier snores behind locked doors,
Where I keep watch and ward.
The falcon is fed, the slave put to bed,
But I am the palace guard.
So let it be—'tis heaven's decree,
What can I say, a poor fellow like me?"

Two camels loomed over the edge of the gully, and, having made one of the pair kneel, the singer climbed down to the well. He was alone, for the other beast bore only a light pack. Against the shimmering sky of twilight Mingan made out a slender warrior wearing a bronze Mongol helmet, the nose piece and the leather drop all but hiding his face.

It was the Tiger; but, beholding the scattered sleeping furs, the dark stains and many footprints in the sand, and the empty perch of the falcon, his mirth vanished. He picked up and examined some articles left behind by the Gipsy girl and groaned.

"Burta—Mingan!"

"Here, Chepe Noyon!"

The Tiger wheeled and peered into the shadows under the rocks, uncertainly, for Mingan's voice was little more than a hoarse croak. All that was visible was the dog Mukuli standing in front of what seemed to be a round stone. Chepe Noyon took a swift step—backward.

"Abide where you are, devil! Come no nearer but relate to me if indeed you have a human voice what has become of the girl Burta and the hero Mingan."

Mukuli, uncertain whether this were friend or foe, wagged his tail tentatively and sat down, whining. Mingan rasped impatiently—"I am here, buried alive by Jamuka who carried Burta off."

Chepe Noyon's jaw dropped, and, fumbling in the throat opening of his armor, drew out a small ebony cross, holding it high in front of him.

"*In hoc signo vines!*—By this sign conquer! Now, devil, take flight; or if dog you be, show me where my comrade Mingan lies."

Perceiving the friendlier note in the man's voice, the dog barked and crawled to one side, scratching at the earth by the prisoner's chin. Chepe Noyon advanced slowly and peered anxiously into the haggard and distorted features.

"If you are verily Mingan's head—aye, so you are—tell me where lies the rest of you."

"In the sand under your foot—dig me out."

Not until food and drink and the warmth of a fire restored Mingan to something resembling a living being did Chepe Noyon feel fully satisfied that the man at his side was in truth his friend.

"There is evil afoot," he grumbled, relating what had passed in the Three Rivers country.

The failure of the envoys he had sent to Prester John to return had decided Genghis Khan that war with the Keraits was unavoidable, and the Master of the Horde, once his mind was made up, had moved at once toward Tangut, following the northern edge of the sandy desert where his horses would find grazing. Genghis Khan had sent Chepe Noyon to the well to find Burta and bring the Gipsy girl to him.

"He trusts me," said the Tiger moodily, "although I am a Kerait, but it is not fitting that I should command a *tuman* in the coming battle between Prester John and Genghis Khan. I do not understand why my people have taken up the sword. How did the messengers from the Three Rivers perish? Why did Jamuka take his stand beside Prester John?"

Mingan pondered awhile.

"I can see a little both of treachery and trickery. But if Genghis Khan is on the march there is little time to learn the truth. Since you came nearly due south to the well, the Mongols must be as near to Tangut as we. If you are faithful to Temujin, you should ride to Tangut at once—"

"Aye, on Jamuka's trail. I was sent to find Burta and bring her off safely, and that I will do."

"Nay, you would fail. One way is open to us, to seek out the daughter of Podu and at the same time to seek behind the mask of our enemy, who goes about in the skin of a bear—"

"It was not Prester John who raided our tents and who was overthrown by my horse."

"Who wears the mask of a bear," went on Mingan calmly. "And that way leads us to Prester John himself."

Burta had saved Mingan's life, and he knew now that the wayward girl loved Genghis Khan. To venture in the camp of Jamuka's army after her would be to search for one grain of sand in the desert. Their only recourse was to seek an audience with Prester John of the Christians, in the castle of Tangut, and to put their case before him, since he alone had power to overrule Jamuka.

He explained this to Chepe Noyon, who was only half-convinced.

"Yet, in the time of my father, Mingan, and his father, no one of our village has seen the face of Prester John. He has lived for twelve times a hundred years; he is a magician."

Mingan was quite ready to believe this.

"So will he aid us the more."

He was in no condition to set out that evening, so he slept through the night, which was more than the Tiger did. In the morning they made up their packs, gave the camels a drink, and were about to climb into the cloths that served for saddles when the brown dog came lurching after

Mingan, whining anxiously, sensing that they were going to abandon him. Mingan had not the heart to leave Mukuli behind, and placed him on the rump of his camel after bandaging his hurts.

He thought little of it at the time, save that Chepe Noyon grumbled, but thereafter he had reason to be thankful for Mukuli's presence.

For a week they traveled due west.

A sandstorm, sweeping down on the Gobi out of a black sky, and heralded by a devastating wind, obliterated the tracks left by Jamuka and his men before the two palladins had journeyed westward for three days. Chepe Noyon, as the storm cleared away, crawled out from beside his camel and pointed to a series of whirling columns which rose from the earth to the clouds hanging low overhead.

"Yonder are the first of the guardians of Tangut, and it is well for us that *they* passed us by."

Mingan watched the moving pillars of sand circle and vanish into the murk of the tempest, and nodded understandingly. He had become accustomed to the changing moods of the desert and knew that the sand pillars were caused by the suction of the wind. If Chepe Noyon, who was reckless enough, dreaded the approach to the man called Prester John, there must be greater danger than this to be faced.

In fact, coming to one of the last camps of Gipsies on the caravan track they were following, the Tiger halted long enough to trade his camels for two shaggy ponies, a lute, and a suit of beggar's weeds. His own armor and cloak, with his sword, he gave to the headman of the camp with instructions to take them to Genghis Khan and receive goodly guerdon for so doing.

He learned from the Gipsies that Jamuka's cavalcade had passed the day before, and was careful to make sure of the nomad's fidelity by describing the capture of Burta. With the weapon and armor as tokens, the man was to inform the Mongol khan that Mingan and Chepe Noyon would press on to Tangut and search for the girl. He told the Gipsy where to find the Horde—about a week's ride to the north and west. This done, he arrayed himself in the long smock and high-crowned hat of woven reeds and slung the lute over his shoulder.

"We will shave off your beard," he observed, scanning Mingan. "The rest of you looks rarely like a hungry scavenger of the caravan tracks. Lo, I am a minstrel, a singer of songs—you a teller of tales. Whine when you speak and call all men 'Good Sir' and bow when you are kicked. Then no one will know that you are one of the Mongol Horde."

They kept, however, the gold tablets showing their rank in the Horde concealed in their wallets. Other weapons, in their new guise of wandering entertainers, Chepe Noyon said they were better without.

From the Gipsy camp they hurried on through rising ground to a barren waste of rocky plain where Jamuka's trail was lost again, but where Mingan made a discovery. It was after daybreak when the air was clear that he sighted in the plain before them the towers and walls of a city, surrounded by groves of trees rising to majestic height.

"It must be Tangut," he cried.

The Tiger smiled.

"Ride on and enter the gate, if you can."

Sure of what he saw, Mingan hastened forward, yet came no nearer to the city. By afternoon, when he thought to reach the nearest trees, it fell apart while he watched, and vanished, leaving the desert bare and shelterless. With an exclamation, he turned to Chepe Noyon, who was much amused at his discomfiture.

"'Tis part of the magic of Prester John," the Tiger explained. "Those who seek out Tangut see on every hand these cities in the air, and, pursuing them, are completely lost."*

He spoke with satisfaction, for he had witnessed the miracle of the skies more than once, but in Mingan there was a quick stirring of the blood. He had thought he knew the desert, yet now he looked upon the manifestation of forces beyond his knowledge or control. Misgivings crowded upon him, but he set his teeth and took up the reins of his horse again.

As if the vision of the city had been a warning, they suffered much from cold and hunger in a land where the mists crowded in on them, and snow lay in the pockets of the rocks. By the thin air Mingan knew that they must be at the summit of a lofty elevation. Chepe Noyon admitted that he had lost his way, and they fared badly until the dog Mukuli scented out a passing caravan in the mists, and the two warriors joined company with some Arab traders who were hastening on to Tangut, to work south from there out of the Gobi before war should overtake them and their burden of silk, spice, and tea.

---

*The mirages of the western Gobi proved as much of a mystery to other explorers, among them Marco Polo, as to Mingan.

From the cold heights they descended into a broad valley where the sun warmed them. Here Chepe Noyon got his bearings and led the way past bands of warriors riding north, and herds of horses, cattle, and sheep driven south. At night they made their quarters in the village *serais* where by virtue of the lute and the many tales of Mingan, coupled with the tricks he had taught Mukuli, they received food and a sleeping place of sorts.

They were now in the Jelair country, and learned that the army of the Turkish tribesmen and the Keraits was assembling within a day's march toward the setting sun. Jamuka had joined his host, but Chepe Noyon discovered that the men who had been with the khan of the Jelairs had ridden on to the city of Tangut, taking with them a strange woman. Evidently Jamuka had feared to take Burta into the tumult of a mobilization camp.

Nothing had been seen or heard of the Horde which was believed to be still in the Three Rivers country. But Chepe Noyon suspected that it was nearer than that.

Three days more of riding and they reached a fairer land, where the camps of the nomads ceased and villages appeared, where fields of grain, newly sown, lined the highways, and white-kerchiefed women greeted them pleasantly, inquiring for news of the armies. To the south and west a line of forested mountains arose,* and this time Mingan found that they remained in view. Chepe Noyon smiled as they drew in among the foothills, skirting groves of fruit trees in blossom.

"You are within ten arrow flights of Tangut, the chief city of Prester John. Can you tell me where it lies?"

Mingan searched the mountain peaks that rose overhead and shook his head.

"Verily," he admitted, "there is magic in this place for I see naught save some hamlets of shepherds and many roads that twine and twist about."

By way of answer, Chepe Noyon turned aside, to follow a brisk stream that led them to a bridge. Crossing this, the Tiger swerved again into a great white road, wide as any in Cathay. Mingan saw that the road ran into a long, narrow valley almost concealed by two shoulders of the hills—a valley whose middle was a canal from which the stream ran and whose sides were row upon row of clay houses.

Mirrored in the canal, or lake, was the upper end of the gorge, and here

*The range now called the *Thian Shan*—a spur of the Himalayas.

were no dwellings, but a steep slope of the mountain, heavily wooded. At the summit of this height were the black walls of a castle. It was quite unlike the pavilions and pagodas of Cathay, for the high walls shut in a space over which showed the tops of the trees, barely visible at that distance, and in the center reared up a single tower.

At the head of the lake was an open plaza from which steps of black granite began, disappearing in the forested slope, through which zig-zagged a roadway up to the castle, judging from the gaps in the trees.

"There is the abode of Prester John," said Chepe Noyon.

"Where we must go," nodded Mingan.

But evening was at hand, and Chepe Noyon said that now a guard of Jelair bowmen was drawn across the plaza at the head of the lake where the granite stairway began. Orders had been issued that not even the bringers of food were to be admitted to the stair after dark.

"Besides," added the Tiger thoughtfully, "if we go not up by the stair, we must climb the forested height to the wall, where the guardians are not men but beasts of the wilds. If we must face the four-footed sentinels, it were best we did not do so at night."

Mingan finished his scrutiny of the castle approaches and pointed to a pigeon that circled over the valley on the northern side, descending to the houses.

"Aye, now is the hour of rest."

They led their tired ponies back to one of the *serais* at the entrance of the valley, placed there for the Moslem merchants and the caravans that passed through Tangut. That night, however, they were the only occupants of the place who claimed meat and fruit for themselves, and grass for their ponies, from the attendants who ministered to the wants of travelers. Although they dined well and the shelter offered them was clean and comfortable, they were able to sleep little.

Above them the streets of the city buzzed with talk and movement; horses clattered in and out of the roadways, and the Tiger, venturing out to inquire the meaning of the commotion, came back with gleaming eyes.

"The merchants who left the city made no mistake. Ho, the rats are running from the tents when the smoke of fire comes down the wind. A carrier pigeon has come in from the camp of the Keraits and Jelairs in the north. The Mongols have reached Jamuka already and have struck their blow. So the word of the pigeon said."

Mingan smiled.

"Yesukai, who came to this place, said that the birds of Tangut talked, but has a pigeon a tongue? Not three days have gone by since we passed the camp of Jamuka, and none have overtaken us on the road."

"These are carrier pigeons—taken from their home to a distance. A message is written and tied to their claw and, released, they fly between sunrise and sunset the space that a horse covers in thrice that time."

Chepe Noyon sighed and shook his head. "The Horde, to the number of a hundred times a thousand, fell upon Jamuka's array before the main forces of the Keraits came up from the cities yonder in the mountains. All the wiles of the Master of Plotting could not serve to overcome the advantage of the sudden attack. That is always the way of Genghis Khan."

Later messages admitted that Jamuka was retreating rapidly to Tangut.

Knowing the tactics of Genghis Khan, Mingan felt that the Mongols would press the pursuit, hoping to overtake the leaders of the enemy and break up resistance in the city before it could come to a head. The battle had been fought and won by dawn of that day, and before the second sunrise the victors or the vanquished would be within the foothills of the mountains.

What was Prester John doing? No one outside the castle knew.

"One other thing have I learned," said the Tiger. "This morning a woman captive was led through Tangut under escort of some officers of Jamuka's guard, passing through the sentries and into the castle. Those who saw her relate that she is dark of skin and beautiful as twilight itself or the stars at evening, but that she railed at her guards, and maneuvered her horse so that one, a fat Turk, fell into the lake from the plaza."

Mingan smiled, the description fitting Burta well. But for once the gay Chepe Noyon had no mind for mirth. On his knees near the wall of the *serai* he prayed, the palms of his hands pressed together, the ebony cross placed on a stone before his eyes—prayed to his God, Jehovah, to deliver the girl Burta safe from harm, and his people from the sword of the Mongols.

Aware of the Tiger's loyalty to Genghis Khan, Mingan wondered how Chepe Noyon could hope to see all of his wishes fulfilled. But then, Mingan reflected, they were in the domain of a magician.

VIII
The Magi

"Who are ye to attempt the forbidden? Nay, by Allah, stand back! It was said to us that this should not be, and on our heads is the care of the black stair! Dogs! *Caphars*—unbelievers, children of evil impulses—stand back!"

The company of Jelairs had been forced to line up on the lowest steps of the granite stairway leading up to the castle, because as soon as dawn lightened the sky the women and children of Tangut thronged to the plaza at the head of the lake as if by a common impulse. They pressed against the archers, pleading with outstretched hands for word to be sent up to Prester John in the castle of the peril that was closing in on them.

"King John!" they cried. "Let the anointed of God comfort us! Let us see his face that has been hidden from us for years—let us see his armor and his sword that we may be comforted."

The archers drew their short falchions and thrust back the people vigorously, using the hilt at first, then the flat of the blades. A Kerait captain remonstrated with the Jelairs when more than one of their blows drew blood from the women, asking if word of the latest tidings had been sent up to the castle, and offering to go himself to see that this were done.

"Is not Jamuka Khan the leader of your army?" retorted the archers. "Does he not wear the bear's head? It was his command that no one be admitted to the stair until he came. Stand back!"

Mingan, standing near the edge of the lake within ear-shot of the plaza, caught Chepe Noyon by the arm.

"Did I not say there was treachery and trickery to be dealt with?" he whispered. "We must lose no time in gaining the castle. If you make known your name, would the Keraits support you in an attempt to overthrow these Jelairs?"

By way of answer Chepe Noyon shook his head and pointed to the throngs in the streets facing the plaza. Most of the armed men were Turkish tribesmen; the Christians of Tangut had been sent out to meet Jamuka. The older citizens were without arms; in fact they seemed to be a peaceable folk. When all efforts to penetrate the line of archers failed, they drew back and fell to gazing up at the castle and talking among themselves.

The Christians were taller than the average of the desert tribesmen, and lighter of skin.

Mingan looked up at the tiers of white houses set in green gardens—a fair city, mistress of sunshine and fertile fields. The water of the blue lake was fresh and clear. The sky overhead was smiling—white flecks of clouds passing over the forested summits of the hills. But on either hand the heights fell away when they reached the end of the valley, so that the hill of the castle was in reality a separate mountain and the only feasible ascent was by the stair.

"Then will we play a trick," observed the Cathayan. "Come!"

He turned back to the *serai*, the Tiger following, and led out the ponies without saddling them. Making sure that no one from the streets of the city was watching, he crossed the road and sought the stream by the bridge. There he urged his pony into the water until the animal was dripping from head to tail; Chepe Noyon did likewise. Once out of the water the ponies were permitted to roll in the dust by the road, whereupon Mingan sprang to the back of his animal and forced it into a gallop. The Tiger followed, and the dog Mukuli brought up the rear, barking.

They swept past the *serai* and up into the streets where Mingan continued to flog his horse with the whip.

"Way for the messengers from the north!" he cried as he encountered the throng by the lake.

People turned to look, and a lane was opened to the steps of the plaza. Here the two riders dismounted and hurried to the line of archers where the captain of the company barred their way insolently.

"What tidings bring you?" he demanded.

"Our word is for the castle," said Mingan curtly. "Will you halt a courier from Jamuka Khan, and taste the bastinado?"

The leader of the archers scowled, glanced at the wet and dusty ponies, at the bedraggled attire of the two strangers, and fingering his beard, said: "Scant time have you had to ride to Tangut from battle. I am in command of the Jelairs in the city. Speak therefore to me, but softly, so that these dogs shall not hear."

Chepe Noyon thrust forward, having heard one or two of the watchers in the throng saying dubiously that the two riders had been seen about the *serais* the last evening. But the Turk had no ears for the townspeople after the Tiger spoke a few words.

"Fool and son of a fool! We come from Jamuka, not from the army." He took his cue from Mingan and lowered his voice. "We have orders for those who guard Jamuka's woman within the castle—she who was taken from the Gipsy camp and brought hither for the khan himself."

The captain's face changed. He had heard of Burta and knew that this was a matter where meddling might lose him his head.

"A token?" he grumbled. "Surely you were given a token, minstrel."

Chepe Noyon nodded and drew from his wallet the gold tablet given him by Genghis Khan. The Turk made a pretense of reading the Mongol script that was strange to his eyes, but the sheen and heft of the gold spoke volumes. He returned it with a bow and ordered his men to make passage for the messengers.

"But, good sir," he added thoughtfully, "take heed of the watchers at the gate of the castle, for they are not as polite as I."

He turned to beat back some young girls who would have run to the steps after Mingan and Chepe Noyon.

The dog Mukuli, however, writhed and scampered through the array of the archers' legs and made after his master. Thousands of eyes watched the two strangers ascend the stair to the first turn, where they were lost to sight behind the screen of the forest.

For a thousand feet the granite steps led up, zig-zagging across the face of the hill where the ascent was steep, so that the two *orkhons* were unable to glimpse the castle even when they had climbed to the level of the sides of the valley. But presently they came to a landing of black marble, guarded on either hand by a jade lion, one clutching a shepherd's crook, the other a cross.

From here the stair ran up almost sheer, and Mingan saw at its summit the dark line of the castle wall. Against the wall a figure moved and the sun glinted upon an object that darted down, whistling past his head. A javelin, hurled from above, splintered to fragments on the marble.

Chepe Noyon held up his hand with a warning cry.

"A truce. We are—"

He leaped aside just in time to escape being impaled by a second dart and threw himself over the railing of the stair into the brush. Mingan followed him. Another missile hurtled through the growth over their heads, and they crawled, perforce, into the shelter of the nearest fig trees that screened them effectively.

"Now, by the horses of ——," swore the Tiger, "that was a wanton act!"

Manifestly, they could not ascend the last, almost vertical flight of the black stair in the face of such opposition. Nor would it be feasible to descend for help to the archers of the plaza. By now the men-at-arms would have had time to talk things over with the townspeople who had seen them the evening before, and would know that they had not arrived in Tangut that evening as they claimed.

"We will climb through the forest growth," decided Mingan, "and have a look at these custodians of the gate."

It was not easy. The hillside here was almost a precipice and often they were obliged to help each other up over rock ridges and to crawl upon masses of boulders beset by thorns. The earth mold under the stunted trees that clung to the slope was treacherous, and more than once they slid back, starting a miniature avalanche of stones down the heights. Thereafter they circled such danger spots and braced themselves against the boles of the trees.

By necessity, they gave the watchers at the gate a good inkling of what they were about, and when—Mukuli being ordered to sit passive behind them—they crawled into the network of juniper and flowering jasmine at the summit, they beheld two men armed each with a sheaf of javelins standing at the gate of the wall that opened out upon a small landing at the stairhead. And all thought of overtures vanished.

The two guards were negroes, massive of build, wearing the broad turbans of the southern Turks. Moreover, after watching for awhile, Mingan was satisfied that they were mutes. Although he and the Tiger lay passive until they ached, the guards did not cease to peer in their direction. Signing to his companion, he crawled back cautiously to where the dog awaited them, out of sight of the gate.

"They are Jamuka's men," snarled Chepe Noyon, little pleased with the part he was compelled to play. "Has Jamuka made a captive of the king of the Keraits? If we had between us a weapon—"

"We have not," Mingan pointed out.

"If we may not enter the gate, we must climb the wall if we are to have an audience with this king."

With a nod of assent the Tiger led the way to the base of the wall and began to circle it, heading away from the entrance. Here there were no tall trees, and passage through the brush was difficult. The wall was some fifteen feet, and at no place did they come upon an opening or postern door. So at length the Tiger halted, to rub at the scars left on his face and hands by the brambles, and to stare up hopelessly at a clump of slender birches. Spanning the space to the wall, although growing within a dozen feet of it, they offered no convenient limb to the pair.

"This is a river I cannot cross," he muttered. "See, the sun is near its zenith and we are no closer to the castle. Nay, stare not at that wand of a tree. We have no ax to fell it, to make it serve as a ladder."

"Nevertheless, it will serve us."

Mingan surveyed the clump of birches and selected one of the largest—one that tapered up some thirty feet and leaned a little toward the wall.

"But it will not help us back, once we are over. If you are not afraid—"

"Act," grunted Chepe Noyon.

So Mingan began to climb, pulling himself up the bole, rather than trusting to the slender branches of the white birch. For some distance the tree was large enough to support his weight without bending. As he worked higher it commenced to teeter. Mingan paused, gathered himself together, and went swiftly up the tapering stem—clutched it as high as he could reach, and, as it bent, swung his feet clear.

The tip of the birch swung down with a rush, bearing Mingan with it, and as it leaned toward the wall, descended in that direction. There was a rustle of leaves, a crackling of wood, and Chepe Noyon watched him disappear over the wall, releasing his hold as he did so.

The birch whipped back, although now it leaned more toward the wall. Chepe Noyon lost no time in following his companion's example; but he took Mukuli under one arm, and, encumbered by the dog, descended heavily on the wall, let go the birch-tip, and rolled off. Mingan, standing in the soft earth underneath, held out his arms instinctively, and the two men, the dog, and the lute thumped on the ground in a heap.

Mukuli began to growl at once, and Chepe Noyon rolled off Mingan, propped himself up on an elbow, gulped air back into his lungs, and froze into immobility. Mingan started to rise, and thought better of it.

A spear's length away crouched a full-grown leopard, its tawny eyes malevolent, its tail twitching.

Mukuli, between the two men, bristled defiance, and the more the dog growled the louder the leopard snarled.

Slowly Chepe Noyon reached out and took up the lute, the only available weapon, and more slowly he rose to his feet. The leopard ceased to breathe defiance at the dog and centered its attention on the man.

"A wise man," observed Mingan, "will strike the strings of a lute before he hits out with the butt."

Chepe Noyon considered the crouching animal and decided that it was more startled than angry. They could not, however, go forward without arriving at a better understanding with this four-footed guardian of the wall. Smiling skeptically, he placed the cord of the hand-violin over his neck and ran his fingers over the strings. Whereat the leopard gave a hideous snarl.

"He likes not the instrument, perhaps the voice is more pleasing," commented Mingan judiciously.

And the Tiger began to sing in his pleasant, guttural voice, an ode of the land of the Tang. They saw that now the great cat had relaxed its muscles. It stood up, drawing its claws back into sheaths. And then out from the cypresses that hemmed them in walked a small bear, limping with one leg.

The bear considered them awhile, sniffed at Mukuli, and began to nose about indifferently in the lush grass. Chepe Noyon went on singing and along a path through the brush trotted a powerful mastiff with a scar running from jowls to belly.

"A potent minstrel, you," remarked Mingan, picking up Mukuli, who was trembling with excitement, "for here are three surly beasts who yet offer us no harm. Sing on, but let us go forward to the castle."

The path led to their right to a pond where among water lilies swans floated about a stone island and a wooden kiosk. A bridge ran to the islet, but they could see no one moving in the garden house, so turned to the left. Mingan noticed that the mastiff and the bear fell in behind them, while the leopard was to be seen flitting among the cypresses, first on one side, then on the other.

They passed through the wood to a series of grassy terraces where a flock of sheep grazed, and flowerbeds set with iris and thyme ringed round the black bulk of the castle. Suddenly Mingan looked up.

"Strangers! Who are ye? Whence come ye? What do ye seek?"

It was a shrill cry from directly over their heads. Brilliant in the clear sunshine of the mountaintop, a bird with green and blue and red feathers fluttered.

Chepe Noyon stayed his song.

"We are two wanderers from the desert with tidings, O Winged Talker. In peace we seek Prester John."

"Who are ye? Whence come ye?"

The bird circled their heads and there was no doubt that it uttered the words. Then, rising, it flew toward the tower of the castle, and its cry became fainter—

"Strangers—in the garden of Prester John."

The two warriors looked at each other in silence. They had not the least doubt that they were in the abode of a magician. Birds that talked—wild beasts as tame as fireside cats—doubtless the castle sheltered greater wonders. They went over the sheep meadows more slowly, and looked back. Mingan saw that the bear passed the flock with only a casual glance and, more remarkable, the sheep took no heed of the bear.

Chepe Noyon had said that in the place of Prester John was peace, and here, surely, was evidence of it—among the animals. There was something in the garden that was not to be found in all Cathay and the Gobi, so Mingan reasoned. What of Burta? No human being was visible, even the mutes at the gate being hidden by the line of cypresses that stretched from the castle to the wall.

"Come," said the Tiger, shouldering his lute.

The hall of the castle was empty, although two candles burned at the table set below the dais at the upper end. From the walls hung tapestries wherein were worked stories unfamiliar to Mingan—an army on the march, and one that puzzled him, a stable over which a rayed star pictured above a woman with a child who sat in the midst of cattle and sheep.

On the table between the candles were gold vessels bearing food and covers for three.

As the two warriors entered the hall, Mingan fancied that a figure slipped out of sight at one side of the dais. Here a curtain of heavy silk stained with age covered the wall at the end of the hall, and near the curtain a door led them into a side corridor from which stairs ran up the castle tower.

They climbed the steps, seeing dusty armor and spears here and there by embrasures, but no sign of the man who had vanished from their sight. On the tower summit they were able to overlook all the gardens of Tangut, the wall, and the valley of the city. They saw the two mutes standing in the open gate at the head of the stair and the tiny forms of the bear and the leopard moving about on the terrace.

But no other living object. While Chepe Noyon gazed at the dust wreaths on the plain that were horsemen moving in toward the city, Mingan was intent on the panorama of mountain peaks rising to the west, to far snow summits.

"The Roof of the World,"* explained the Tiger, "whence it is said that Prester John came to this land. See yonder, in the east, riders draw in to

*The Himalayas.

Tangut—messengers from the armies, or perhaps the first of the fleeing. Our time is short; before nightfall must we find the daughter of Podu and speak with the master of the castle. Tangut will be ringed in iron and flame."

Chepe Noyon spoke under his breath. True, he could see no sign of the lord of the castle. Yet the table was set and—a magician who could talk through birds might well be invisible to mortal eyes.

"O minstrels, Prester John of Asia gives you greeting and would welcome you at his table."

The warriors beheld a boy at the head of the stairs, who bowed and motioned for them to follow him. Chepe Noyon's teeth clinked spasmodically, but Mingan, who seldom lost his presence of mind, followed the page down to the corridor and into the hall.

A glance showed him that incense was burning now in front of the curtain. At the table, attended by another youth, and by the great mastiff, sat a tall man who did not look up at their coming. He lifted a hand in greeting and Chepe Noyon knelt, while Mingan, harking back to his days at the court of Cathay, made the triple obeisance of respect.

Respect, assuredly, was due the alert brown face, the white beard of the aged king, who wore instead of a crown a cap of cloth-of-gold peaked in the front and the back, and a wide-sleeved robe with a red cape across the shoulders. A shepherd's crook stood beside his chair.

On one shoulder perched the parrot which straightway began its warning—

"Strangers in the garden—"

"Peace, chatterer—" Prester John signed to two chairs at the table—"it is long since men have come to my hall with tidings of the valley and the plain. This is the day the star will be over Tangut. So doubly welcome are ye who come from the desert. Eat, therefore, and rest."

He nodded to the attendants, who brought basins and towels and washed the hands of the wanderers, thereafter setting food before them.

"Few abide in the castle," went on the king, "for those who served me aforetime have been called down into the city, and the warders at the wall are men-at-arms unknown to me." He stretched out a hand and placed it on the broad head of the mastiff. "Yet have I warders three who sleep not, and leave me not. My pages say that you wear the garb of minstrels, O my guests. How come you into the castle?"

Chepe Noyon for once was silent, so Mingan related how they climbed the wall and appeased the leopard. He studied the thin face of the old man, who never looked up or moved in his seat. Prester John's words were those of one who was accustomed to command, and despite his courtesy he seemed troubled. Now, however, he smiled a little and lifted his eyes.

"Well did you, minstrel, when you turned your hand to music, not to a blow. The leopard is restless, and is pleased with my harp and voice when I beguile him so. The bear and this warrior—" he touched the dog again—"are gentle. Aforetime I healed a wound in his chest made by a boar's tusk, and made whole the broken leg of the bear that was caught in a trap near the castle. They have grown up under my hand."

Mingan knew now what he had suspected at first, that Prester John was blind.

He finished a light meal in silence, sharing the suspense that held Chepe Noyon voiceless. The king ate a little fruit and drank some wine, feeding the while pieces of bread to the mastiff.

"Where is the maiden who sought sanctuary in the castle yesterday?" he asked one of the youths.

"O sire, it is not known to us."

A frown crossed the forehead of the blind man.

"In the night I heard her voice at a distance. By old usage she should have shelter in the castle, for that was the law of the first Presbyter—sanctuary, even to the beasts of the field. Of late, however, my people have not come up from the city that I should sit in judgment." He turned to the warriors. "Some men of Jamuka, who is absent on the border, brought into the gate yesterday a woman from the desert who awaits the return of Jamuka near the castle. Have you seen her?"

"Nay," said Chepe Noyon, uneasily.

"She was brought hither against her will," added Mingan quietly. "A captive."

Prester John turned sightless eyes on the Cathayan, as if to probe into the truth of his words.

"The maiden herself can tell us her case, O minstrel." Signing to one of the boys, he ordered them to search for Burta, the Gipsy, and bring her to him.

"Until then I would hear a song, or a tale. Yet first I would know the names of my guests."

"O my king," said the Tiger, "I am Chepe Noyon, of Tangut."

"Who wandered from our land seeking adventure." Prester John smiled a little. "Did you find it, O youthful Tiger?"

"Aye," put in Mingan steadily, "in the camp of Genghis Khan, the master of the desert. And I, too, am a companion of the khan, Mingan, once Prince of Liao-tung in Cathay. Now, sire, a wanderer, seeking justice for—a maid. I have the gift of reading men's faces and I know that here at your hand will I find justice for Burta, and the unveiling of treachery."

The Christian king lifted his hand.

"You speak boldly, O prince of Cathay. What treachery?"

"Among my people it is said that a crooked trumpet will not make harmony, and a lie rings falsely in the ear. There is time—" he glanced up at the sunbeams that came in through the embrasures high overhead—"for naught but truth between us, and our lives—mine and the Tiger's—are pledges of this truth. I will tell you a tale, as you in your bounty gave permission. Then will it be for you to judge what the treachery is."

Prester John considered.

"Begin, and omit naught, my guest."

So it happened that Mingan related to the king of the Christians how he had joined the Horde of the desert, and how Genghis Khan had made himself Master of the Horde, and had come to war with Jamuka. He told of the death of Podu and the capture of Burta. Earnestly and swiftly he spoke, ending his tale with the arrival in the city, and sparing mention of the battle.

When he had done, Chepe Noyon, encouraged by the silence of the blind man, added excitedly: "O sire, deal with me as you will, but know that you have enemies in Tangut. Turks guard the stair leading to the castle, and others the gate. Tidings are kept from your ears—the messengers from Genghis Khan to you were slain. The people call to you from below and are struck down by Jamuka's men—"

Mingan laid a hand on his arm, but the young warrior shook him off.

"O my king, it is said in Tangut that you are able to cast a spell on your foes. Arise, don the armor that in the time of my father's father you were wont to wear among your people, the Christians of Asia! Slay, with your art of magic, the false Turks who hold your gate, and go down to those who cry to you for aid—"

"My son," Prester John stood up and the two warriors rose, "I am blind, and so was I born."

"But you have lived for twelve times a hundred years!"

The old king shook his head.

"My son, you have lived afar from the castle and have listened to idle tales. I have no more than three score years and ten, nor am I a worker of magic, save that beasts are gentle under my hand, and that I seek to serve the Cross."

With the assured step of one who knows his surroundings, he moved to the curtain and drew it aside, disclosing an altar of white marble where, on a spotless cloth, stood a gold cross.

Letting fall the curtain, the blind man knelt a moment on the step of the dais in prayer. When he rose it was with new decision.

"By the voices of men, O Cathayan, I know the speakers of truth, as you read their faces. Harken, therefore, ye two, to the tale of glory of the first of my line, and the shame that is mine.

"Twelve hundred years ago, the king of a tribe in the Roof of the World sought a secret adventure to the south. In early winter, near the city of Damascus, he was attracted by a strange star of surpassing brilliancy. He followed this sign and fell in with two other monarchs of men who had also seen the star.

"It led them to the land of Judea, of the king Herod, where a king was born. The three, out of their wisdom, were called Magi by those who watched them tender gifts and then return to their own lands.

"The one who went back into the mountains of Asia ruled with a strong hand and did not forget. In time, he took on himself a new faith and assumed a new name, John. By some he was called Presbyter or priest, as were the eldest sons of his line—my sires," concluded Prester John. "Aye, they lived their allotted time rejoicing, for they were strong men and very palladins; they feared not the sword of any man, but guarded their people with the sword. Yet I, the last of the line, am otherwise, for I am blind and may not put on the shining armor or take up the brand. That is my shame.

"Since the time of my grandsire, tales have come to us through the Moslem caravans that Christian palladins of the west have conquered Jerusalem, but their armies have not come beyond the Euphrates, and the missives I have sent to them have had no answer."*

So Prester John spoke, and when he ceased one of the pages who had

*The first crusade reached Jerusalem in 1099, and in the time of the last Prester John, Richard of England, called the Lion Heart, had failed, through no fault of his own, in his long conflict with Saladin, the Turkish sultan. The letters of Prester John were forwarded to the Pope, and resulted in the journey of various priests into Cathay, but by then Prester John and his kingdom of Tangut were no more than a legend in the Mongol empire.

returned to the hall cried out—"Sire, there is no woman within the wall of the garden, but out on the plain a myriad horsemen draw in toward the city."

"Come with me to the tower," said the king, "and serve me with your eyes."

Without guidance from the warriors the blind man felt his way up to the summit of the tower. A brisk wind whipped at his long locks, and the level light of the hour before sunset struck through the garden, revealing black specks on the brown plain entering the wooded districts about the river among the foothills. Mingan's keen sight identified the first comers as Jelairs and Keraits, several thousand of them, and behind, in a wide arc, the dark blotches of pursuing cavalry.

"The Horde!" cried Chepe Noyon. "At Jamuka's heels."

Swiftly he told Prester John of Jamuka's attempt to withstand Genghis Khan, his defeat, and flight to the city.

The lines in the blind man's face deepened, but his voice was unhurried as ever as he explained how Jamuka had come to Tangut, professing to be a convert to Christianity; how—in the king's inability to leave the castle—he had allowed Jamuka first to guard his frontier, then to wear the bear's head that was the token of the leader of the Tangut horsemen; how Jamuka had warned him of the arrogance and hostility of Genghis Khan, whom he called the man-slayer.

At first Prester John had waited for the son of Yesukai, who had been his friend, to come to the castle. But Genghis Khan did not appear, and the tale was spread in Tangut that the Mongol had slain old Podu, the Gipsy chief, and had threatened the death of Prester John. Then the Horde had come.

"The Master of Plotting," responded Mingan promptly, "is also a master of lies. Pretending to be the friend of Genghis Khan, he planned to make himself Master of the Horde. Aye, King of the Keraits, he misused the power you gave him, seeking to use the Keraits against the Mongols. Jamuka is a Moslem, and his was the treachery of which I spoke. He is the real gainer from the caravan trade—"

"Yet he trusted me with the maiden whom he will make his wife—"

"See you not," Mingan said fiercely, "his trickery? He has taken away your men from the castle, placing here his own instead—his cavalry patrols control the city, until his coming. He will hold Tangut, at the river, until the full power of the Keraits can join him, coming through the mountain passes to the castle. The daughter of Podu is to be the bride of Genghis

Khan, and Jamuka, aware of her worth as a hostage, has hidden her somewhere within the wall, knowing that none will come to seek her here."

As he spoke the sun left the valley and passed from the great plain, so that the oncoming horsemen and their pursuers were blotted out in the shadow of the mountain. And, plainly to be heard, the bells of the city sounded the alarm, while from the lower valley came the faint fanfare of trumpets.

Prester John faced the city as if striving to behold the truth of what was happening with his blind eyes. Mingan and the Kerait warrior were no more than two voices to him, and their words were the knell of his hopes. Yet his hand did not tremble and his lean, brown face was impassive.

"My people are in danger. I will go down to them."

To go down into the city, a blind man in the center of pandemonium, would be to reveal his affliction to the multitude. His world was, in very truth, falling about his ears. There was stern stuff in the old king, and briefly he explained what must be done.

With Chepe Noyon he would descend the stair and summon Jamuka to him, to judge whether the Master of Plotting had deceived him. If so, Prester John would take over the command of the warriors in Tangut and hold the defenses at the Turkish end of the city by the river long enough to arrange a truce with Genghis Khan. The war must be stopped and the slaying of the Keraits ended before the city fell and was given up to sack by the Horde.

To Mingan, who knew that Jamuka must keep the Keraits in the fight to save his own skin—and who had seen the remorseless anger of Genghis Khan when aroused—this seemed impossible.

"Who are you, to question the ways of God?" responded the king sternly. "He who divided in twain a river and brought forth water from a rock can quiet the quarrels of men, aye, though my blind eyes cannot see the road before us."

"And yet," pointed out the Cathayan, "there be two armed men—three for the captain of archers has come up the stair—at the gate, and my companion and I are weaponless."

"Come with me."

Prester John issued an order to one of the boys who ran ahead of them, and in the hall brought to the king a cuirass of steel bands sewn upon a leather tunic, a helmet, brightly polished, bearing for crest the steel image of a crouching lion. The other page hastened up with a cloak of red velvet and a long sword of iron with edges of keen steel.

Over these objects Prester John passed his hand with a quick sigh and ordered his retainers to arm Chepe Noyon.

"This is the armor and the sword of the king, my sire," he explained, "and it is known to my people. My son, if your words against Jamuka have been false, you will not live to take off this armor."

To Mingan it seemed that, though Chepe Noyon had told the truth, there was not much hope for the Tiger. But Chepe Noyon's teeth flashed under his mustache and he whirled the long brand above his head.

"Meanwhile," ordered the blind man, "do you, Cathayan, seek out the captive. Guard her from harm and bring her to my side."

Mingan watched the strange array go down the path from the castle door to the gate—the tall form of the blind man followed by the glittering figure of the Tiger, the two retainers and the mastiff bringing up the rear—and shook his head. Then, as he turned aside with Mukuli to the terraces, he caught his breath.

It was the brief space of full sunset, and in the flames of the western sky there stood out a single star. Before now Mingan had watched the evening star appear, yet he fancied it had never been so brilliant as now when it gleamed into the shadows of the garden of Prester John.

IX

The Fight on the Stair

In the half-light of sunset it startled the captain of the Turks more than a little to behold the approach of the blind man and his companion in strange armor. Peering at them, he took his stand in the path inside the closed portal of the wall, the two negroes on either side of him.

"Stand and advance not," he challenged.

But Prester John went forward until he reached the bar of the gate and felt that the door was closed. "Open!" he commanded sternly. "I am the king."

The Turk shook his head. "What king? Jamuka commands in the city, and by his order none shall leave the castle, nor shall the gate be opened until he comes." He thrust the blind man's hand from the bar. "Harken to yonder outcry below, graybeard, and flee to your hall. The Mongol dogs are crossing the river, and Jamuka will abandon the city streets, drawing hither his men to defend the stair. Nay, the angel of death walks below us—listen to his voice!"

Faintly below them a rush of sound came up from the valley—a buzzing that grew into a roaring burst of men's voices, clashing weapons, and screaming of horses. The Turk put his ear to the gate.

"Jamuka will be here in the space of an arrow flight—"

"And will find your body if you open not the gate," Chepe Noyon's voice menaced him as he turned angrily.

"Ho, this should be the minstrel! With a goodly array of children and dogs and prating graybeards—"

The Turk leered and, as he spoke, drew his scimitar and cut at the warrior. Chepe Noyon parried with his sword and sprang aside to strike down one of the mutes who rushed at him with javelin upraised. Before he could face the other warder the captain of archers was on him, slashing at throat and legs.

The Tiger knocked the scimitar aside and thrust with his heavy blade, through the beard of his adversary over the coat of mail, and, wrenching free his weapon, was aware of the other foeman who circled, dagger in hand, to strike him. Then Prester John loosed the mastiff that he held by the collar with a swift word of command.

The great dog rose from the ground, leaping against the chest of the mute and knocking him from his feet. Chepe Noyon stunned the fallen man with a blow of his sword, caught at the bar, and drew open the gate.

Over his head came a flutter of wings and a shrill voice that cried out of the air: "Prester John goes forth—pray, ye who are faithful—Prester John goes forth!"

It was the parrot, attracted by the clash and gleam of steel, crying one of the phrases that it had learned from the servants of the castle.

Chepe Noyon strode out to the edge of the steps with the king and halted with an exclamation. By the *caravanserai* fires were springing up, revealing masses of horsemen moving through the streets of Tangut toward the upper end of the valley. On each side of the lake barriers were being erected across the side-alleys by throngs of Kerait warriors. Fighting was in progress in the plaza. Halfway up the stair, with a score of warriors at his heels, a man who wore the skin and head of a bear was climbing toward them.

"Jamuka is on the steps, O king," he explained quickly, "and his men with him. We cannot go down—unless even now you have trust in the scheming dog."

Prester John bent his head.

"God's will be done. Nay, the guard at the gate was proof that Jamuka tricked me, who am unworthy of my high place. Let us defend the stair against him, for one of us must live to reach the Mongols and make peace."

"Go back, then, O king, into the castle!"

"Not so. This is my place."

Prester John leaned a moment on the shepherd's crook that he carried for a staff, his lips moving in prayer. The two boys collected the javelins and took their stand beside the warrior who watched Jamuka win to the last flight of steps and start up the steep ascent, his men panting after him. Then Chepe Noyon lifted his head and smiled. He took off the heavy helmet and flung it clanging down the steps, among the Turks.

"Tear off your mask, Jamuka," he called. "This time you cannot hide your face."

Mingan's actions on leaving the castle hall were peculiar to say the least. He whistled up Mukuli and began to run with the brown dog around the buildings in widening circles, urging his four-footed ally to seek out something. If the king had heard Burta's voice last night, the Gipsy must have been within ear-shot of the castle.

Near the flock of sheep the dog stopped, nosed around, and set off barking into the wood. Mingan followed, running hard to keep up, but using his eyes nevertheless in the failing light.

Burta would be guarded by some of Jamuka's men, and the Cathayan was not the one to fall into an ambush blindly. It was impossible, however, to silence Mukuli. Now, as he went, his long legs carrying him swiftly, Mingan was aware of a ponderous shadow that lumbered after him, and of a spotted form that slipped through the brush at his side.

The dog's barking had brought the bear and the leopard on the same quest. A chill chased up the man's spine, for he had not even a stick in his hand. It was nearly dark among the trees, and the Cathayan had no great faith in the gentleness of Prester John's pets.

He emerged into a lighter clearing and approached the pond where the kiosk stood. Mukuli headed directly toward the bridge, but half-across stopped with a growl. From the garden house came a man tall as he was broad—a burly, turbaned servant with a drawn dagger. As Mingan set foot on the narrow bridge, the Turk walked toward him rapidly, angrily motioning him away.

For a moment the two faced each other. Then, as Mingan did not give ground, the Turk lifted his knife and took a step forward. Experience had taught Mingan the danger of moving backward over uneven ground, and he poised on his toes, ready to grapple with his heavier opponent. He felt certain that Burta was in the kiosk, and he owed his life to the Gipsy.

Suddenly, watching his adversary's face, he saw the protruding eyes widen, heard the whistle of indrawn breath. He was aware of two eyes on one side that glowed green, and on the other side a shuffling form that rose up on its hind legs with a snort. Mingan knew that the leopard and the bear were looking on, but the Turk was startled. For an instant his attention wavered, and Mingan sprang at him, thrusting low, and striking the man's knees with his shoulder. The big slave was knocked back against the low parapet of the bridge, lost his balance, and fell into the pond, splashing through the water lilies and losing his dagger as he did so.

When he gained his feet—the pond was shallow—he beheld the green eyes blazing down at him from the bridge, and the long tail of the leopard twitching excitedly down from the other side. The slave quailed and turned toward the shore. But there in the last of the twilight, he was confronted by what seemed a fat man watching him closely. When the man-shape dropped to four feet and growled, the slave yelled aloud and went splashing back, to flee from the far side of the pond.

Meanwhile, Mingan had found Burta lying in the kiosk. He picked her up, carrying her easily in his arms back over the bridge and along the path that led to the castle gate. She was in a heavy sleep, induced by opium or hashish, probably administered by the hand of the guard following her cry of the night before.

As he neared the entrance to the wall, Mingan heard the clashing of weapons and the low voices of men. In the open gate stood the blind king, arms outstretched. In front of him the Tiger was fighting desperately, giving back when he was hurt, ringing himself with the slashes of the long sword. Several men-at-arms engaged him while others held torches. On the blood-stained landing were the bodies of the two boys and the mastiff. And from the open muzzle of a bear's head peered the face of Jamuka, wet with sweat and twisted with rage and impatience.

Mingan stooped to lay Burta on the ground and ran to the side of his companion. But from the stair below the struggling men came a shout of triumph:

"Hai, ahatou! Mongku-hai, Mongku-ho!"

Mingan knew that voice.

The Turks redoubled their efforts; a poleax smote Chepe Noyon on his mailed chest. The Tiger fell heavily, lying where he had fallen.

"Through the gate! Close it!" cried Jamuka thrusting forward.

As he ran to enter the portal, there confronted him the tall form of Prester John, hands uplifted, the shepherd's crook barring the way. With a snarl of rage, the Master of Plotting whipped out his scimitar and passed it into the body of the blind man. In a frenzy, Jamuka hacked again and again at the falling form of the king until Mingan turned his eyes away.

He heard the men-at-arms tumbling through the portal into the safety of the wall. Mingan looked and saw them trampling over the two bodies in the path, and heard the gate creak as Jamuka sought to close it after them.

Then a figure in rusted and blood-stained armor rose above the steps and leaped into the gap between door and gate post. A torch thrust into the eyes of the nearest Turks, and a great ax swung wide at them. It was a figure topped by flaming red hair, grimed and slashed almost beyond knowing, but nevertheless Subotai, the Buffalo, the sword-bearer of Genghis Khan. Behind the giant climbed into view other warriors, panting and grinning with triumph.

"Ho, foxes," laughed the Buffalo. "We have run you to earth."

The man-at-arms who held the poleax that had struck down Chepe Noyon lifted his weapon and stepped toward Subotai, who did not raise his ax. Instead, the right arm of the Buffalo snapped forward with a flick of the wrist. His broad-ax flew forward, striking the Jelair in the face and cracking open his forehead.

By now the oncoming Mongols were crowding through the door. Jamuka turned as if for flight, thought better of it, and cast down his sword. He motioned his score of men to do the same. The Master of Plotting actually smiled and took his stand over the dead Prester John. Bewildered by the calm of his foe, Subotai scowled and motioned back his men. He peered into the surrounding shadows distrustfully. Behind him voices called out: "*Temou*, 'way for Genghis Khan!"

The ranks of the Mongols opened and the chieftain came through the gate.

He was helmetless, and his black eyes gleamed in the torchlight; his gaunt cheeks showed that for days he had not left the saddle. Mingan saw that, although now leader of a hundred thousand riders, he wore the same stained armor of rude iron plates, hacked to pieces in many places. He looked around unhurriedly—he could move quickly enough when necessary, as those watching him knew. For that reason a silence fell on the men at the gate of Prester John.

So quiet were they that the roar of conflict welled up distinctly from the town beneath. It was quite dark now, and Mingan, a stone's throw from the group under the torches, was invisible. Chepe Noyon, in his strange armor, lay face down among other dead.

"Have you seen aught of the Tiger and Mingan?" Genghis Khan asked Jamuka. "The two palladins rode hither seeking Burta, and here they should be."

Out of the corner of his eye the Master of Plotting glanced at the body of Chepe Noyon that lay without semblance of life. Mingan, he believed, was long since dead of hunger and madness in the Gobi sand.

"Nay, my cousin," he made answer, trying to read the face of the Mongol. "Your heroes have not crossed my path."

Jamuka's life hung by a hair, and before anyone else could speak, he made a last attempt at trickery. It was as bold as it was clever. With his foot he turned over the body of the blind king so that Genghis Khan could look down at the hacked breast and bloodied features.

"Here, O my Khan, have I slain your greatest enemy, Prester John the Christian. It was he who plotted against you without cessation, who hunted you from place to place like a ferret. Of his skull I will fashion you a drinking-cup set with diamonds and covered with gold.

"I yield myself captive to you."

Stooping, he plucked some blades of grass and set them between his teeth in token of submission.

"By Allah," Jamuka continued, "I fought against you, obeying the command of this king. But when he took the maiden Burta, to hold as hostage, my heart turned from him, and forcing my way into his walls I slew him. At your feet I place my life. I have spoken."

"And falsely."

Mingan appeared, walking toward them out of the darkness, the Gipsy girl in his arms. In a few words he related how he had found Burta under guard of one of Jamuka's slaves. As he held the girl, her head fell back from his elbow and her tresses hung to the earth; she seemed without life. Mingan himself did not know whether she breathed or not, so heavily had she been drugged.

For a second the deep-set eyes of Genghis Khan searched the face of the woman, and the fingers of his right hand closed into a knotted ball. He looked inquiringly at Jamuka, who had started back in dismay.

The Turk was too wise to deny Mingan's charge.

"All this is true," he admitted. "At the command of Prester John was it done. To him the blame, to me the fault that I obeyed him. Now I would serve you."

On the ground near his feet a man stirred. Iron armor clinked, and Chepe Noyon raised himself on an elbow arduously. The first thing that became clear to the Tiger's hazy sight was the thin face of Jamuka. The next was the body of Prester John.

"Ha, Jamuka! Brave Jamuka—Podu in his sleep, and now a blind man slain by your hand! Dogs could not have sired you—dogs are faithful, and you betrayed the blind who trusted you! A sword—give me a sword. Ho, Mingan, are you near me? Help me to go up against this snake—"

The eyes of Genghis Khan glowed, and he held back the wounded man who was struggling to rise. Peering up, Chepe Noyon recognized him and sank back.

"A boon, O my Khan. Never have I asked a boon until this time. Let me finish my quarrel with Jamuka, but first do you cry a truce that the lives of the Keraits in the city below be spared. They were deceived by this Thing that walked out of a dunghill. They are no foes of yours. O my Khan, this that was Prester John is slain, and I ask of you what he came forth to beg—"

"The Keraits withstand me with weapons in their hands. Let them die so!"

The mask of anger did not fall from the grim countenance of the Master of the Horde. Motioning the half-frantic Tiger to silence, he strode among the Jelairs to confront Jamuka.

To do this it was necessary for him to step over the blind man, and Mingan saw him glance downward a single time, a little contemptuously. A weakling, this, the glance related plainly, as so many words—was this graybeard who could not save even his own life the Prester John of Asia? In this way, Genghis Khan greeted and said farewell to the friend of his father, for thereafter he thought no more of him, save to consent to Chepe

Noyon's request that the body be buried under the altar of the cross in the castle.

"Jamuka, my cousin," his deep voice proclaimed, "you are like the partridge that hides in the brush—like the horned owl that strikes at night. From afar my falcons have looked down upon your work of blood. I am not blind. I followed the tracks of the riders who raided the Mongol *ordu* during the snow season, and I saw that after a long time they led back to the Jelair lands. I looked for the branding marks on the ponies that rushed into my camp at Podu's feast, and they were Jelair marks. The Turkish wrestler who would have slain me with a dagger was your servant—as I knew when I advanced to meet him."

He put his right hand on the Turk's shoulder, gravely.

"You would have slain me. When you failed, you won over the Keraits by deceit so that you could overcome me and sit in my place. You have been faithless to one master; how could you be faithful to me?"

"I—" began Jamuka and said no more.

He stooped for the sword he had dropped and felt the hand of the Mongol slip under his chin. He was lifted from his feet, thrust higher, until the small of his back was on the shoulder of Genghis Khan, and legs, head, and arms dangled helplessly.

Once more the throng of men divided as the Mongol, walking heavily, moved through them to the head of the steep, granite stair. The arms of the chief tightened around Jamuka's head. A quick tensing of muscles, a heave of the powerful body, and Jamuka flew out into the air, seen for a second in the torchlight before he dropped a hundred feet upon the stone steps, his neck broken before the hands of Genghis Khan released him.

The Master of the Horde stood quietly on the landing, his broad figure outlined against the glow that was rising from the town beneath where thatched roofs were beginning to flare up. The followers of the slain Jamuka quivered as if a cold wind had struck them. Then all at once they caught up their discarded weapons and turned to run despairingly into the darkness, whither Subotai and his warriors pursued them.

Genghis Khan however returned to where Burta lay, and put his hand over her heart. He started, feeling that she lived. Brushing back the tangle of hair from her eyes, he saw that she was conscious and that she knew him.

The mask-like immobility of the man softened a little, and for the first time Mingan saw his eyes shining with exultant happiness. Burta saw it too—indeed she had been watching, fearfully, for just that.

"Temujin," she whispered, "you have come and you have not altered. You are Temujin, even though they call you conqueror and Great Khan."

Genghis Khan remained silent, only signing to his followers to carry the girl down to the ranks of his men. Out of sheer despair the Tiger gave utterance to his plea once again, seeing that the anger of the chief had lessened. Genghis Khan looked at his two palladins with something like satisfaction.

"Aye, Chepe Noyon, you have done well. Go down to my *tuman* and command that their swords be sheathed and their bowstrings loosed. If the Keraits will submit to my rule and aid me with horses and men, I will number them among mine."

So the Tiger departed down the steps, and in time the tumult died. Then Genghis Khan gave order to Subotai and Mingan to bear the body of the dead king into the castle and see that it was honored.

The wasted form of the blind man was placed gently on the table before the altar. New candles were lit in the candelabra, and the living took up places in nearby chairs. They talked together, soft-voiced for the reason of the emptiness of the great hall and the whispering of the wind against the hangings, until the Tiger rejoined them. He moved wearily, but the knowledge that the truce had been struck fired him with satisfaction.

As the three palladins greeted one the other, Chepe Noyon held up his hand, calling for silence. From the high windows of the hall came, above the rustle of the night wind, the flutter of wings and a crying voice that grew fainter until it passed from their hearing: "Prester John goes forth—pray ye who are faithful—Prester John goes forth from the castle."

X
Mingan's Ride

No song of birds is heard in the vines on the walls; only the wind whistles through the long night, where ghosts of the dead wander in the gloom.

The fading moon twinkles on the falling snow; the fosses of the wall are frozen with blood and bodies with beards stiffened by ice. Each arrow is spent, every bowstring broken—the strength of the war-horse is lost.

Thus is the city of Cathay.

—Song of a Chinese minstrel

The whisper began in the east, at the Wall of Cathay, and crept out across the Mongolian steppe. Spring came early, that momentous year the tenth of the twelfth century of Our Lord. And, traveling with the harbingers of spring, mounted couriers rode west and south with the message that began at the Great Wall.

The riders went to the tundras at the edge of the frozen regions where snow hemmed in the dark camps in wet ravines; sleds drawn by reindeer moved out upon the snow to the settlements of Subotai's people, and other riders passed swiftly south over wet, wind-whipped prairies, stopping only for a change of horses at the *ordus* of the tribes.

And wherever the pony-couriers had passed there sounded the clang of hammers in the huts of the smiths, the murmur of subdued talk in the winter-tents of the warriors, the shrill outcry of herd boys sent to round up horses.

Like a giant awaking from a long sleep, the steppe threw off its inertia of the winter and became a living thing. For the first time in its history the Mongolian steppe was under the rule of one man, and there was peace throughout it—except at the Wall.

So, too, when the pony-couriers—the messengers arranged by Genghis Khan for just such an event as this—had left the post-stations in the Gobi, long caravans of camels forged into motion over the high prairies and the sandy bottoms. They were going east.

Spring had come, and with it the message of war.

Around their fires the nomad Gipsies and the desert-men nodded wisely. They had known the tidings before the couriers of the khan rode past. How? Well, that was their affair. They laughed and gambled with open hand, fighting among themselves, counting the horses, the gold, and jade they would bring back as spoil from Cathay. How would they overcome the Wall, the barrier that had not been broken down since it was built hundreds of years before? Well, that was Genghis Khan's affair.

Beyond the Gobi the couriers rode. They covered a hundred and fifty miles a day through the fertile valleys of the west. They clattered into Tangut, still drowsy under its mantle of winter, its castle—uninhabited except by birds and an aged bear that limped out of its retreat to sniff the mild air—looming black against the blue sky, massive and forbidding as the tomb that it was.

Over more valleys, through populous settlements of hunters and herders of the streams that were now freshets racing down from the mountains, the couriers followed their course until they came to the Roof of the World. Here, by order of the conqueror, broad roads had been opened up to the vicinity of the Horde itself. It lay encamped by a lake that reflected the mighty buttresses of mountains, where messages were delivered to the palace tent of Genghis Khan.

Chung-hi was now the Dragon Emperor. He had sent an army out from the Wall of Cathay to the land of the Three Rivers, hoping to strike a blow at the home of Genghis Khan while the Horde and its master was absent.

Mukuli was in winter camp, and the old Tatar—left in command of some fifty thousand riders—had not been caught napping. He had drawn the invaders out into the open plain, had defeated them, and pressed the pursuit until he now held the districts of Cathay as far as the river Hoang-ho and the Wall. Aware that the gage of battle had been flung down between the Dragon and Genghis Khan, the Manchus, kindred of the Tatars, had marched with their bowmen around the gulf of Liao-tung to join Mukuli. The old warrior, pleased by the mistake of Chung-hi, was now at the head of more than a hundred thousand men. He plundered the towns on the far side of the Wall, seizing arms, captives, and supplies, asking only that Genghis Khan come with the Horde and break down the Wall for him. Mukuli was too wise to try that himself.

"The Dragon has stretched a claw over the Wall and has had it nipped," laughed Chepe Noyon. "Chung-hi must be a fool. *Ohai!* The Buffalo has been given the gold tablet of an *orkhon* and sent out of Tangut with the center of the Horde. Genghis Khan is making ready the rest of the Horde at Tangut and sends for me to take the standard of the Keraits. A hundred and twenty times a thousand riders will follow me. And what will you do?"

"I am summoned to the palace tent, to the Khan," replied Mingan.

"The Cathayans are your people," mused the Tiger, who seldom waxed thoughtful. "What will you do?"

"I do not know."

"Well, you must go with me, and we may not stop to drink by the wayside. These times are good times. Ten years ago we were youths and mock-heroes—appointed to rank when Genghis had no more than his shadow to his name and needed palladins to make a showing at Podu's tents. Now, elder chiefs dismount to hold our horses. We have cup-bearers a score and slaves a hundred to rise up when we clap our hands. Women—"

"Talk less than you. Come, if we must!"

"These times are good times, but dull," assented the Tiger, who was attired in the choicest silks of India. He was heavier in his tread, but restless as ever—more arrogant with the power that had come to him, yet devoted to his first friends, Mingan and Subotai. "I have never seen the courts of Cathay, Mingan. Have they really palaces high as hills and chairs of pure gold, and women with eyes like black opals?"

Mingan stroked his beard, frowning.

"Be not so sure that you will see the courts of Cathay that lie beyond the Wall. First you must win through the Wall, and that no army has done."

The summons had reached them a week late, for the two palladins had been hunting in the mountain passes.

Mingan had been well content these last years. He had gone with the Horde when Genghis Khan led his power—strengthened by the Keraits—against the peoples of the Roof of the World, as far as the bleak mountains that offered only rock-strewn sides that vanished up among the clouds,* and as far to the west as the fortified cities of the Turks. Mingan liked the experiences of new lands, listening to the talk of philosophers and astrologers.

The fellowship of the three palladins had continued unbroken, although now, with their duties as commanders, they were seldom together. As they assembled their followers and rode down the passes toward Tangut, Mingan was thoughtful.

"The successes of Genghis," he observed, "are due to two things. His campaigns have been on level land where horsemen can maneuver readily, and he is the finest leader of men in Asia. Lesser chiefs have attached themselves to him for their own advantage. Yet the horsemen of the Horde cannot out-maneuver the walled cities of Cathay, and Chung-hi's forces have machines to throw stones and fire and great javelins. As against the three hundred thousand of the Horde, Chung-hi has a million."

"You are middle-aged and foolish," scoffed the Tiger. "Mountains are as bad for horses as walls, yet Genghis built bridges of chains and tree trunks across these gorges and roads around the steep slopes. I will wager with you a hundred milk-white Arab barbs against gold to the weight of a man that I ride my horse through the Wall."

*The new empire of the Mongols extended to what is now Tibet, and to Russian Turkestan.

"You will not do that. Ah, it is in my mind to turn the heart of Genghis from this war."

"As well try to stem one of yonder freshets. But do you take my wager?"

"Very well."

It was a clear, star-lit night when Mingan answered for himself to the mounted patrols outside Tangut, entering the familiar lines of the camp across the river from the city. He picked his way through the horse herds, sniffing the warm odors of the felt tents, the taint of dung-smoke in the air, and the smell of leather and the reek of the camels that muttered dismally somewhere out of sight.

There were miles of tents, and standards that Mingan had never seen before, as well as black, shapeless masses standing in line. Carts, they were, loaded with supplies. Beside these were innumerable oxen, their muzzles thrust placidly into dried grass and barley on the ground.

All at once, as if he saw the Horde with new eyes, Mingan became aware of its power. And now—it faced Cathay.

Horses thudded softly past him, turning into the tent lanes, as he made out the yak-tail standard planted in front of the largest pavilion. As Mingan dismounted to enter the palace tent, he raised his eyes and beheld against the horizon glow the castle of Prester John.

It was now, he thought, the tomb of the blind king who had kept faith with his God. What if Prester John had not withstood Jamuka. He might be alive, and Mingan dead at the hands of the Turks. He wondered if there was a destiny that shaped men's fortunes, and if the stars foretold destiny.

The hour was late, but lights still burned in the palace tent. Genghis Khan was laying on the summit of a mighty dais; his women were seated on the step, tending the candles and giving food and drink to the assembled officers. Burta, her head against the knee of the chieftain, looked at him and smiled.

"*Mende sun tabe tiniger buis ta!* Are you quite hail and well, my companion?" Genghis Khan greeted his friend. "Talk to me, O teller of tales. I would sleep until the dawn hour."

Chepe Noyon and the higher officers made their adieus, to seek their commands before the Horde should move eastward at daybreak. Some of the candles guttered out, while the guards of the pavilion leaned on their spears to take rest as they might. The captains, sword-bearers, the masters of the herds, and others who remained under the dais put their heads on their arms and slept at once, while Mingan's voice repeated the familiar tales of hunting and the far-off places of Cathay that Genghis Khan liked to hear of.

Once when a gust of air stirred the banners overhead, brushing the tresses of Burta who also listened to Mingan, chin on hand, the Khan started up.

"Did the soul of Yesukai, my father, speak? Surely then there came a messenger from the sky-world of the elder heroes while I slept. I will follow the path of vengeance, for that Yesukai died of Cathayan poison."

"O my lord," Burta's soft voice made response, "it was Mingan."

She watched the eyes of the chieftain close. On the morrow Genghis Khan would leave her and only the gods knew when he would return. She loosed the gold chaplet from her forehead so that her dark hair fell around her face and Mingan could not see that she was sorrowful.

The teller of tales ceased his recital. The clink and thud of a mailed regiment passed the pavilion, answering the hoarse shout of the captain of the guard. Genghis Khan stirred and slept again. But his mouth was set in a hard line, furrows in his sloping forehead. Mingan, searching his face, knew that Temujin, the boy of the horse herd was long dead, and Genghis Khan had replaced him, a leader and a slayer of men.

The Horde did not sleep. And Genghis Khan was Master of the Horde; he had made it. Mingan started up as if out of a long slumber, a drowsiness of fifteen years. He touched Burta's knee and put into her hand the gold tablet of *palladin* that he took from his girdle.

"O mother of princes, to you I say farewell. When the Khan wakens give this tablet to him, saying that Mingan, the friend of Temujin, is no longer at his side; but Ye Liu Chutsai Mingan of Liao-tung rides to join his people and share their fortunes."

His lips barely moved in a low whisper.

"My sword and sword-belt are without the palace tent. I will leave them there. To Chepe Noyon and Subotai give greetings and my farewell. If ever I have served you, remember it for two hours, until the Horde arises for the march. Two hours must I have to win clear. Then forget the name of Mingan. *Kai*—be it so."

Not daring to remonstrate or answer, she nodded reluctantly. Over their heads the shoulders of the chief stirred as he raised himself on his hands, his eyes alert. He was wide awake and he had heard the message of the *orkhon*.

Mingan stood up.

"I cannot ride against my people. I must range myself with them, now that the Khan wars with Cathay."

He slipped down the dais steps and out the door, scarcely noticing the salute of the captain of the guard. Genghis Khan reached down and touched Burta's shoulder:

"Give it to me—the tablet!"

Stifling a scream, her fingers pressing her lips, the queen handed him the square of gold, and his throat snarled as he felt of it. Quietly, so as not to awaken the sleepers, he made his way to the tent entrance. The officer on guard strode toward him watchfully; then, seeing who it was, he fell on his knees.

"Gur-khan," the chief ordered brusquely, "seek out Mingan's brand from the pile. Take it, follow the hero to his tents, and be as his shadow until he quits the last line of our patrols and then—" his voice sank to whispered gutturals. "Fear not for your post; I will take command of the guard."

When the man had left to carry out his errand, the chief remained standing by the tent, looking up at the stars incuriously. He did not bother his head about portents or the working of destiny. He had his own way of dealing with men. Mingan had faltered, had become like a lame horse that must be loosed from harness.

Only Genghis Khan was sad.

Mingan handed his helmet and mail to his cup-bearer, and divested himself of his long mantle. He glanced around his tent at the bronze astronomical instruments, the carved ivory objects, the neatly piled manuscripts that he had collected in the last years. Then with a sigh he took down a hunting spear from the tent wall, a sheepskin cloak and saddle bags filled with food from the hand of another servant, and made his way to the picket-line of his horses.

Selecting the gray stallion, now a little aged and stiff of limb, and a long-striding mare, Mingan ordered a saddle for the gray. He tested girths and breast-strap before mounting, and then led the mare by her halter.

An hour later he passed out of the tent lines, a little uneasy, for it seemed to him that another rider followed. If he should be halted and questioned, the danger would be grave. He was leaving the Horde in time of war without permission and soon Burta would deliver her message, he assured himself.

If there was a man on earth that Mingan hated, it was Chung-hi, the new emperor. Yet no man more than the Prince of Liao-tung knew the menace that now confronted Cathay. Inbred in him was the sense of loyalty to the reigning dynasty. He had sworn to the dead emperor that he would be faithful to that dynasty, as had his fathers for countless generations. Mingan could not go to them with a clear face if he did not keep his oath.

To do so, he must first try to reach the Wall before Mukuli and Subotai should attack it. Then he must present himself at the Dragon Throne and abide by what followed. What? Mingan looked up at the stars searchingly, for the first time in his life wondering whether the planets were truly the messengers of destiny—

"Draw rein and stand. What is this led horse? Where do you come from and by whose order?"

Unseen by him, several horsemen had been waiting in the deep shadow under some willows by the river road. Mingan was confronted by a suspicious lieutenant, the commander of a patrol who did not know him by sight. From force of habit he felt his girdle for the gold tablet, then realized that he no longer had an insignia of rank.

While he pondered, a horse trotted up behind him and an authoritative voice spoke:

"I am gur-khan of the imperial guard. This man goes forth by permission of the Khan."

The newcomer exhibited the baton of a captain in the half-light of approaching dawn. The patrol was satisfied. Then, without ado, the gur-khan handed Mingan his own sword, belting it into place. Gathering up his reins, he lifted his hand.

"May the way be open before you." He gave the customary salutation at parting. "Keep your distance from the path of the Horde, *orkhon*."

"May it be well with you," Mingan answered mechanically.

Urging his horse forward, he struck into a trot. He was on the first leg of a seventeen hundred mile ride to the Gobi and across the heart of the desert—to the Wall.

XI

Distance Proves the Horse's Strength

Distance proves the horse's strength and time the heart of man.

—Chinese proverb

The gong in the tower over the Taitung or Western Gate of the Great Wall of Cathay struck the first hour of the day with an echoing clang. The commander of a thousand opened his almond eyes, yawned, spat, and stood up, pretending not to look to see if the nearest commander of ten had noticed that he had been asleep. Satisfied, the officer who had charge of the gate put on his wide-brimmed and tasseled hat, straightened the quilted coat on his broad belly, and tightened the belt from which hung the heavy, two-handed sword that dragged on the ground. After first pouring a sparing libation to Kwan-ti, god of war, he drank eagerly from a goblet of elderberry wine.

It was hot under the tower roof. Sweat, even at this hour of sunrise, trickled down the plump back of the commander of a thousand, and the wide, dusty road that wound into the plain of the west was whitish-yellow as the well-kept hands of the stout officer. For this was the month of the feast of Hao, when the sun was like a red ball in the midsummer sky.

Yet this month, Chung-hi, the Son of the Dragon, was not coming to hunt in the western plain. Instead, herds of cattle, horses, and men were pressing into the gates of the Wall to escape the Mongols, who, in the estimation of the worthy officer, were uncouth barbarians.

He saw that the forces guarding the towers had been doubled. On the summit of the wall, eight paces wide and as high, blue-smocked soldiers were chattering over the morning rice pots.

A double line of spearmen was forming at the road inside the ponderous gates. A score of crossbowmen had laid down their weapons in readiness to lift down the three iron bars that had held shut the gate during the night. The officer yawned and almost forgot the customary morning kowtow toward the Great Court. He blinked and scanned the sky—no smoke rising above the trees by the highway to the west; no hostile cavalry in sight. Only the herds of cattle, somewhat larger than usual, the tattered herders, and a dust-stained beggar with a long beard who limped forward, leaning on a staff, trying to push his way through the crowded cattle.

All was quiet. He gave the order to open the gate.

One after the other, the three bars came down. The lock was turned with a lever, and the weaponless archers laid hold of handles on the twin doors. Slowly, with a reluctant creak, the portals swung open.

The sun rose.

Dust eddied up as the cattle started into motion. The foremost steers passed under him, lowering their horns and grunting. The dust thickened, and the outcries of the drivers grew louder. The commander of a thousand leaned against the framework of a catapult and fanned himself pleasantly.

"Worthy officer," observed a calm voice at his elbow, "it were well to close the gate. There are Mongols between the foothills of the Kinghan and here. In the night I heard the passing of their horses."

The fat man was disturbed to learn that the beggar with the beard had climbed the steps to the tower summit without being heard. So he became angry.

"Ignorant and worthless!" he reproved. "You do not know that there are watch-pillars every two *li* between here and the hills. By day a warning smoke would be in the sky if the enemies of the Dragon were near—and a flare by night. I see nothing. Get you gone—I have no rice or water—"

So he said, observing the browned and cracked skin of the wanderer, the bloodshot eyes that glared with the glare of the dead. To show his superiority he quoted a proverb: "The blind man sees a ghost at night."

Somewhat to his surprise the tattered stranger responded with a proverb, speaking with the cultured inflection of a courtier.

"If you never climb a tree you will never see beyond the horizon. You, commander, can see the sky for five *li*. The Mongols can ride fifteen *li* between sunset and sunrise, and, surrounding one of your watch-towers, they can keep the summit clear of defenders with their arrows while they batter in the gate. Look to yourself!"

"Who are you, uncle?" said the officer a little uncertainly.

"I am Ye Lui Kutsai Mingan, prince of the district of Liao-tung."

"The Prince of Liao-tung was carried off by devils in the reign of the late emperor. You are a crazy man. It is true that the crazy man hopes the heavens will fall; the poor man hopes for a riot."

With an effort Mingan restrained his impatience. He was suffering. The gray stallion had died under him before he reached the sands on his long ride. He had bartered the mare and his sword for a camel, had crossed the desert, exchanged his worn-out Bactrian for a swift-footed pony, and had foundered the animal three days ago. Thereafter, begging food of evenings, he had limped along the highway, fearing that the van of Subotai's army had caught up with him, although he had seen nothing of them. But in the last day no Chinese market carts had passed him.

Still, he was at the Wall in time—if only the officer in charge would close the gate! There were men enough on the broad summit to hold it indefinitely—a hundred every arrow-shot along the parapet—squatting over their morning rice. Mingan did not like the looks of the rusty spears, or the chickens kept for dinner by some of the men-at-arms, or the cotton sun-shelters erected on spears, or the women camp-followers who strolled from group to group. His tongue was swollen in his throat from thirst, and his fingers quivered with weariness. His glance went from the Wall to the highway, and he uttered a soft exclamation.

From around the nearest turn, two miles distant, a tiny puff of dust appeared, rolling toward the wall as if blown by the wind. Mingan's eyes narrowed and he thought that black specks showed through the yellow dust.

"Look!" he cried.

The commander of a thousand looked, and his peace of mind was disturbed. He peered at the sky. No trace of warning smoke against the sheer blue. The dust was travelling too swiftly for carts or horse-sedans.

Clang! He struck the heavy gong with the bronze hammer three times—the signal to close and bar the Western Gate and take stations on the wall.

The dust was spreading out, fan-wise, on either side of the highway, as if a river in flood were surging around the turn in the road. It was little more than a mile away and already the black dots that were riders could be seen on the horses. Mongols they must be to maintain such a furious pace. But it was the sheerest folly for a sea of horsemen to dash against the rock barrier of the wall.

And then something happened below them.

As if taking alarm at the sight behind them, the cattle herders began to drive their beasts forward furiously, shouting, waving their high straw hats, beating the steers on the outer fringe of the herds. A solid mass of horned cattle was driving through the gate. The soldiers who were shoving at the massive doors of teak and iron found that the pressure of the cattle made it impossible to budge the opened gates.

They tried to turn back the stream of frantic beasts, but the herds followed the leaders blindly. Mingan, studying the herders, became convinced that they were Mongols in disguise, and the cattle were captured herds, sent to the gate purposely.

"Shoot down the beasts from the wall," he cried to the officer, who had begun to quiver in anxiety.

By the time archers lined the wall and began to direct their shafts into the bellowing masses, the Mongol attack was within a quarter of a mile. The first few riders carried smoking torches, and when these encountered the rearmost of the cattle, the beasts scattered to the sides of the road, away from the fire and smoke.

A regiment of cross-bowmen had taken station on or near the tower, and their quarrels whizzed down at the oncoming horsemen. Meanwhile, the rush of beasts through the gate had thinned out sufficiently for the laboring soldiers to move the doors forward slightly. Seeing this, one of the Mongol herders ran forward and cast himself in the path of the swinging mass of wood and iron. His body was caught and wedged between the lower edge and the earth. A dull snapping of bones was heard, and the gate ceased to move.

Mingan saw a rider, the first of the Horde, dash through the portal. He was struck from his saddle by a crossbow bolt. Another suffered the same fate. Two companies of Chinese spearmen ran forward to form inside the gate, but their ranks were broken by the rush of horses which jammed through the opening, forced forward by the weight of the column behind.

The cross-bowmen on the tower had barely loaded and wound their weapons a second time. For a mile on the western side of the Wall, groups of mounted Mongols wheeled, discharging a cloud of arrows at the summit. Shaft after shaft was released without pause, keeping the defenders engaged at a distance from the gate-tower, while the stream of horsemen passed through along the highway, wedging back the half-shut portals.

"I, unworthy," quietly spoke the officer at Mingan's side, "must now face my ancestors."

His limbs no longer trembled as, ordering the nearest commander of a hundred to hold the tower as long as possible, he turned and went down the steps with a firm tread. Pressing through the disorganized spearmen, he swung up his sword and cast himself among the ponies of the Mongols, disappearing from view almost at once.

The war shout of the Mongols rose over the clamor on the wall. A chief in resplendent attire came into view. He looked up curiously at the overhanging bulk of the arch that was no longer a barrier, and ordered the mailed swordsmen that followed him to dismount and storm the tower steps from the rear.

Mingan, already down from the wall and out of the fighting, recognized Chepe Noyon and reflected that he owed the Tiger a wager of a hundred weight of gold. He wondered, as he caught a riderless horse and threw himself into its saddle, if he were not dreaming—as in the past. No one molested the ragged, weaponless creature, and soon he was free of the throngs of fugitive soldiers and coolies. Looking back, Mingan saw that the dragon standard had been cast down from the tower, while horsemen were riding up the steps, forming a column at the summit to clear the top of defenders.

The battle of the Taitung Gate had only begun, but Mingan had seen enough to know.

The Great Wall of China had fallen.

He urged his pony into a trot and faced toward the city of Taitung to complete the last stages of his journey. He would carry the news of the disaster to the emperor.

XII
The Prophecy of the Stars

The court, however, had kept away from the western border. It was, in that never-to-be-forgotten feast of Hao, at the capital, Yen-king, which in time would come to be called Pekin. And, with the court, the Emperor Chung-hi was shut up in the palace grounds.

On the day that Mingan rode into the streets of Yen-king and crossed the bridge to the palace sector of the city, he was told that Chung-hi and his officials were listening to a new play in the Garden of Delightful Hours.

Mingan stabled his horse—he had exchanged the tired animal at a village on the highway for another beast—in one of the alleys of the fortune-tellers' quarter, under the rising ground on which the palace stood.

Mingan climbed the steps toward the main entrance and looked down when he reached the gate. Yen-king, vast as a kingdom within walls, was intent on the festival. Streamers adorned the barges and junks on the gray river; processions wound through the main thoroughfares; the smoke of incense sprinkled alleys and pagoda alike.

He won past the sentries at the entrance, saying only that he was a fortune-teller. His beard and tattered garments bore out his pretense. Astrologers and trainers of canaries and dogs often came up to pray for attention from the nobles, and—this was a feast day.

"Good sirs," he bowed to the idle soldiers, "I read the stars. Let me within, to prophesy!"

His experience with the keeper of the Western Gate had taught him the uselessness of proclaiming his name and rank. As quickly as possible, without attracting attention, he moved through the walks where he had played as a boy. The sun was very hot, and few people were about. But beyond the dwellings of the queen and the imperial concubines, he found a group of slaves dressed in purple silk. They were loitering in front of the arch that gave entrance to the Garden of Delightful Hours—a new pleasure spot, an artificial hill, built, as Mingan learned later, so that the emperor could take his ease where the summer breeze could be felt.

"I have tidings from the western wall," he announced eagerly. "The barbarians have passed the wall. Let me in to the Presence."

The leader of the slaves looked up from his task of feeding a peacock. He wrinkled his nose.

"The Son of Heaven may not be disturbed. Until evening he sits before the stage of the actors."

"Dolt!" Mingan's teeth gritted behind his beard. "I have ridden from Taitung, and before that from beyond the sandy desert itself."

"Perhaps you have come also from the ten courts of purgatory," gibed the feeder of peacocks.

He extended his hand suddenly to finger Mingan's pouch and girdle for coins, fruitlessly.

"Assuredly you will be shortened by a head if you cry out like this in the hearing of the court."

The others laughed and fell to jostling the stranger. Mingan planted his feet and smiled at them.

"Honorable keepers of an exalted post, if you will not admit me, send word within that the Wall has fallen."

Laughter greeted his remark, and, with a new inspiration, the prince joined in: "You are merry, good sirs, and I would like to abide with you. But I am one of the actors in the play, and the time for my appearance on the stage is almost at hand. I must seek my companions and paint my face."

The leader of the slaves grimaced cunningly.

"A blind cat can smell a dead rat! The players are all within—aye, even the one that takes the part of a barbarian Tatar, a most evil person whom you somewhat resemble."

Surveying Mingan's remnants of Mongol dress, however, he pursed his lips thoughtfully.

"Are you another—"

"Tatar," nodded Mingan. "And if the emperor is kept waiting you will all sleep this night in the city of old age—the burial ground. Ha—do you misdoubt me? Did I not take the part of a rider from the steppe, with news? Aye, mark you well—now I am a courtier of Liao-tung."

He stood erect with folded arms and spoke a few words in the dialect of the educated classes. Observing the effect on the attendants, he changed swiftly to Mongol gutturals.

The slaves were convinced. No one, they thought, but an actor of merit could assume such varied roles. Mingan passed up the steps to the highest terrace of the garden.

It was of vast extent. Here and there among the rose-beds groups of palace handmaidens sat, and guards rested in the shade. In the center, under a circle of canopies, the emperor and his courtiers listened to the declamation of the players on a bare stage in front of a clump of cypresses. Mingan surveyed the scene, frowning.

He could not penetrate the ranks of nobility, nor, if he did so, would he be permitted to speak to Chung-hi. He must devise some way to catch the emperor's attention.

Suddenly he smiled to himself and, circling the groups of people, sought out the clump of trees that stood at the edge of the terrace. Behind them was a drop of a dozen feet. On a lawn below sat a half-dozen actors—jugglers, flame-swallowers, and the like. Mingan judged that the players of the piece were all on stage, to which a bamboo ladder gave access from the lawn below. It led through the cypresses to the back of the stage.

Mingan descended hastily to the idle performers and, paying no attention to their stares, appropriated a pair of the shoes customarily worn by actors. When he had done this, he daubed his cheeks and forehead with red and gilt paint.

"What is this?" one of the mountebanks spoke up. "The Tatar of the play is already on the stage—"

"But I am not," smiled Mingan. He took advantage of the other's hesitation to step to the ladder and climb the rungs. The tinkle of the orchestra became clearer, in tune with the drone of someone's voice.

Pushing aside the branches of the screening trees, Mingan strode out on the stage. Only one actor was within view of the audience—a man, dressed as a woman of the court, who was reciting some verses that were apparently of an amusing nature. The rest of the company, hidden behind branches of the cypresses that served as wings to the stage, hissed at Mingan angrily. The "woman," surprised, ceased speaking.

Mingan stepped to the front center. The music—a wailing of reed-pipes, fiddles, and drums—went on because, according to custom, the orchestra was made up of blind men. Schooled in the manners of the stage, it was easy for the prince to invent a verse in accord with the music—

"Out of the sandy steppes I have come—like a wild goose flying before the storm."

Then came his introduction, as usage prescribed.

"I am a poor prince of Cathay, taken prisoner by the barbarians in my youth and forced to leave my beloved books for the pursuits of a warrior on the plain. From the ward of the barbarians I have learned many things not written in the books of the sages, and now in the hour of my empire's danger, I have come hither in the hope that I may take my place in the ranks of Cathay."

The other actor was staring at him in blank dismay, and the watchers under the canopies stirred with curiosity. Mingan's appearance had broken up the play most effectively, but he had the interest of the court, and that was what he wanted. The music changed to a harsher note, and the prince followed it out. Stamping one high-booted foot, he looked around as if searching for something he did not see.

"Unhappily, I find the Lord of Ten Thousand Years—" he looked directly at Chung-hi, who was seated in a chair raised above the others—"intent on other things than war. Where are the forty banners of the provinces with their mailed hosts? Where are the standards of the sun, and the wind, and *lui kung*, the thunder? Alas, I do not see them. Is it possible that the emperor has not been informed by his servants of the danger that confronts him?"

He leaped down among the musicians, who, finally aware that something was amiss, ceased playing as Mingan advanced across the intervening space to the chair of Chung-hi, where he made the triple obeisance.

Chung-hi, grosser of body, more arrogant of face, gripped the carved arms of his throne-chair, frowning. Mingan, abandoning the false tones of an actor, added gravely—

"The Mongols have broken through the wall and are besieging Taitung."

"What mockery is this?" demanded the emperor wrathfully.

After fifteen years he did not recognize in the sun-burned and bearded plainsman the Prince of Liao-tung.

"Sire, it is truth." He pointed out over the flower hedges of the garden.

"From the stage I saw the warning smoke of distant watch-towers, and, thereafter, your mailed cavalry of Liao-tung bannermen forming in front of its barracks under the palace hill."

Here and there officials rose; some whispered to attendants who moved out to the edge of the Garden of Delightful Hours, to look down on the city. Returning, their startled faces confirmed Mingan's tidings.

"By the first Dragon of the sky," cried Chung-hi, "what man are you?"

It crossed Mingan's mind that fifteen years before this same Chung-hi had sought to slay him by stealth, fearing the omen of the stars that the dynasty of Cathay was nearing its end, while that of the Prince of Liao-tung was ascendant. If he took a false name and claimed merit for his warning, Mingan might be rewarded well. Certainly, the men who stared at him now believed him dead. But his pride!

"I am Ye Lui Kutsai Mingan, last prince of the north, of Liao-tung. The tale that I repeated on the stage was true; by that device only was I able, sire, to gain a hearing."

Superstitious dread seized on the emperor. Mingan's sudden return to Cathay—his miraculous advent on the stage, in spite of the cordons of guards about the palace—his knowledge of what was still unknown in the city, Chung-hi feared that this was a spirit sent back by the demons that had carried Mingan off. And, Chung-hi had driven the prince into exile.

"A lie!"

He peered at the tall figure in front of him.

Now there came to the emperor's side a massive form in white, with age-wrinkled brow. It was the Servant of Mercy, the executioner of the court, who had once failed in the task of ridding Chung-hi of Mingan. The Servant of Mercy had a good memory, and seldom had he failed so signally.

And Mingan, recognizing him, drew back a pace, then smiled.

"Have you forgotten, Son of the Dragon, the night that you sought to slay me and I fled from the palace in my hunting-chariot? Then here is one who can vouch for me."

The man in white looked long into the face of the prince, and his eyes gleamed. Stooping, he whispered into the ear of Chung-hi, and withdrew, moving quietly as an animal. What he had said was: "This man is the one that was to be strangled fifteen years ago."

Whatever Chung-hi's faults, stupidity was not one of them. Assured that Mingan had come to him from the Horde, he was suspicious on the instant. Pretending incredulity, he shook his head.

"You are no more than a clever soothsayer, seeking our attention in this manner. What else do you seek?"

"To serve with my regiments of Liao-tung, O Lord of Limitless Life! To use my poor wisdom in the service of Cathay."

This was Mingan's right as a prince of the royal line, and if Chung-hi admitted his identity it could not be denied him. But Chung-hi realized that to give Mingan command of the strongest branch of the army would be to raise him to popularity—and power. He had a vivid recollection of how the prince had made him lose face before his father, and—he shook his head again.

"As I thought. Either you are a hobgoblin out of the steppe or you are a lying mountebank. Your tale is false as the voice of the grave bird crying at night among the tombs."

Chung-hi shivered a little, thinking of those others he had slain to clear his path of strong men. He signed to a group of spearmen.

"Take this presumptuous one under ward and place him in the dungeon of offenders against the Throne, under the palace."

Mingan bent his head. The voice was that of Chung-hi, his cousin and his enemy, but the gilt-chair and the dragon-robe were those of the emperor of Cathay. It was possible for him to prove his identity, but even so, a command from the Son of the Dragon would make it necessary for him to commit suicide or be beheaded. To disobey a command from the Throne was impossible for one of his upbringing. And yet—only after an inward conflict was he able to submit to his fate.

Later, when he had his hearing before the Board of Justice, he would have an opening for speech and liberty.

"Yet, sire," he cried, "heed me in one thing; for if I am a soothsayer, I am a true prophet. The Mongols are stronger than you think. *Do not divide your armies or send them against the Horde in open country.* Muster your strength in Yen-king and keep behind the great walls until losses compel Genghis Khan to withdraw."

He glanced eagerly at the perturbed general of Yen-king, a stout eunuch brave in the finery of his rank, and at the aged scholar who was president of the Board of Imperial Strategy.

"Now," a quizzical smile lighted his dark face, "my role is ended—"

Chung-hi hastily shook his sleeve by way of dismissal to the prisoner. At the same time he confided in the nearest officials that the fortune-teller must be a little mad—or a Mongol spy. Had not he, Chung-hi, a million awaiting his command in the warrior levies? Had he not been thinking of war with the Mongols? It would be a new diversion, better than the play—that was all.

"True—true," echoed the courtiers. "*Wan sui*—live for ten thousand years!"

Perhaps in this feast of Hao, the guests on high, the dead heroes of Cathay grieved, knowing all things of the past and future, even to the portents of the stars—for in that summer Cathay the unchanging, changed.

Their altars—the tablets of the ancestors—were neglected during the next months, although the shrines of Kwan-ti, god of war, lacked not for worshippers, and the very rivers were red with blood.

Chung-hi had intended to summon Mingan to question him in private, but events in the kingdom kept his mind occupied with other things. So it was months before the door of the dark cell opened for Mingan to come out. In that time the prince—being a political prisoner—heard little of what passed in the world above, save a word or two—that Genghis Khan had been wounded by an arrow at Taitung, that the imperial armies had been divided into four commands of two hundred thousand each—three to advance beyond the Hoang-ho to drive back the Horde, and one to hold the capital.

There was wondering and unrest among the northern regiments when they heard of the return of one who called himself their prince; then in the tumult of war he was forgotten by all except his warriors of Liao-tung and one who never forgot.

The corridors of the underground prison had been deserted for at least a day when Mingan, lying on the damp stones, heard steps in the semidarkness. His door was unlocked, and a man's hands fumbled with his fetters. Presently these fell off, and Mingan saw that his visitor was tall and clad altogether in white silk.

"Servant of Mercy," he said calmly, "if you have come, then my hour is at hand."

The executioner helped him to his feet, took the end of his girdle in one hand, and led him into the corridor, up winding steps to a hall where the air was sweeter. Flickering candles stung Mingan's eyes, long accustomed to the gloom. Waiting until his prisoner could endure the light, the Servant of Mercy conducted him out a postern door, across a small court, up other steps into the anterooms of the audience hall of the emperor.

Mingan was aware of two things: It was night, the stars were glittering in the cool air of early autumn, and the approaches of the palace were deserted. He wondered if Chung-hi wished his coming kept a secret.

Then he heard the measured intonation of temple gongs in the city beneath. Some important event was taking place.

The white-haired executioner folded his arms, his eyes closed. This bearing of a servant did not hide an impulse of strong feeling in the man.

"Your hour, Prince of Liao-tung, is at hand. If you harken to the voices of your ancestors—and I think you will—you will sit for the first time in the seat of honor. I, unworthy servant of the Dynasty, will choose the knife."

Mingan remembered the first visit of the strangler when he was still a youth. He had slipped out of his bed and laughed at the man. But he was hearing the voice of the executioner as a human being for the first time, and the message puzzled him.

"Was that why you brought me from the cell? At whose command? Speak openly. After five thousand hours of looking into darkness and silence I am old and am not disturbed."

In fact, Mingan's face was filled with tiny new lines, and his eyes, slow moving, were those of a man indifferent to all things.

"No one commanded your release, my lord. I came because it was not fitting that one of noble lineage should starve like a kite in a cage, and because there was no one else to sit in state in this palace. And this night someone must sit in the hall of audience."

"Chung-hi."

"Chung-hi and his courtiers are fled out of the kingdom to the south. There is no one in the palace save you and I and some old slaves and boys."

Mingan started.

"What of the garrison?"

"Chung-hi has taken it to guard his person."

In few words the executioner explained that of the three armies sent against the Mongols one had gained a doubtful success, at the same time that the two others were overwhelmingly defeated by two portions of the Horde under Mukuli and Genghis Khan. Then the Horde had united, scattered the remaining command of the Cathayans, passed the Hoang-ho, and had entered the outer walls of the city, which were weakly manned by levies of citizens. The inner wall had opened its gates to the conquerors, who were now seeking for the palace.

"But the palace itself could be defended!"

"Alas, sir, the slaves have plundered it and, having hidden their spoil safely, have turned their coats—so that they shall not be known for attendants of the Dragon—and sought safety."

Now, looking out into the corridors, Mingan was aware of stealthy shapes that flitted from shadow to shadow, snatching where gold or silver glittered in the light of candles that still burned in their places. He questioned the executioner further—surely someone must be in command here.

The Servant of Mercy shook his head. The Master of Slaves, left in charge of the palace, had carried off the handmaidens, to offer them as slaves to the Mongols. In this way he hoped to ensure his safety.

Mingan reflected, and when he looked up again, it was with a purpose formed.

"Conduct me to the dressing-rooms where court-garments are kept. It is not fitting that the palace should be found empty by the conquerors—like a thieves' nest."

Within the imperial wardrobes he allowed the Servant of Mercy to cleanse his face and hands and comb his beard. Then he dismissed the man and himself found and put on the dragon-robe of ceremony, the plush cap with the peacock feather of rank, and, folding his arms, made his way slowly down to the audience hall which was now quite empty.

Empty, that is, except for the figure that lay extended on the step leading to the chair of the governor of the city. The Servant of Mercy had taken advantage of the interval to cut his throat here, as if to suggest to Mingan what seat he should occupy.

With a gesture of acknowledgment, the prince stepped over the body of the faithful servant and sat down in the lacquered chair, leaning his head back against the silk tapestry that covered the wall. His eyes traveled down the vast extent of the tiled floor, empty as a tomb, and he mused upon the fate that had humbled Cathay.

Presently, bethinking himself of the farewell message custom prescribed, he took from his girdle the writing implements that were a part of the dress and traced on the lapel of the garment these words—

"Striving always to keep faith, I have labored against fate."

A patter of slippered feet, a panting and moaning, and into the hall ran a whining thing that, seeing Mingan sitting in state, cast itself at his feet, clutching with trembling fingers the hem of his robe. It was the master of the palace slaves, his fine purple coat turned inside out so that the gray lining might be unnoticed in the shadows of the corridors—all the bland composure with which he had once barred Mingan from the imperial gardens quite vanished.

"Excellency—majesty," he panted. "Exalted governor, guard me from the sharp-fanged dog that follows. I am a loyal servant, none more so—"

But with the words he shivered and from his wide sleeve fell strings of pearls, shimmering in the candle-light, and loose rubies and sapphires wrenched from their settings, plundered from the chambers of Chung-hi. What stifled his plea, however, was recognition of Mingan—not the governor of Yen-king, but the wandering actor whom the slave had struck.

Seeing the grave eyes that looked at him reprovingly from the thinned face, the master of the slaves scrambled to his feet, caught up some of the jewels, and fled away up the hall, seeking a door by which he might leave it. A burly figure in deerskins entered by the door through which the slave had come, a Mongol gur-khan armed with a heavy spear.

Sighting the fugitive slipping along the wall, the warrior grunted with satisfaction, planted his feet, and cast the spear. It passed through the master of the slaves, pinning him against the tapestry. Then, noticing Mingan, the Mongol called over his shoulder—

"Lord, here is one in authority who has not fled but awaits you."

Genghis Khan entered, cast a glance about the hall, and walked over to the chair where Mingan sat. His clumsy walk—he was better accustomed to a saddle than his feet—and uncouth fur garments made him as out of place as a bear in the dwelling of a man.

Resting the end of his scabbard on the step where the executioner lay, he leaned on the wide hand-guard and studied the man in the chair until his brows drew down and he growled—

"Mingan!"

"Aye." The Cathayan prince stood up. "I am in command of the palace and city that you have conquered."

The opinion, evidently, that the conqueror entertained of the manner in which the city had been defended was too contemptuous for words. He spat toward the south.

"Thither went your dog of an emperor. Mingan, you are chief of the northern people. Why do you serve the dynasty of Cathay? Are you Chung-hi's man?"

"Aye, Genghis Khan. My fathers have been faithful to the Dynasty, and I am not otherwise. To the utmost I strove to hinder your victory. Know that and do with me as you will."

The eyes of the chieftain gleamed with sudden feeling, and, strangely enough, with satisfaction rather than anger.

"One who served another so will serve me well," he exclaimed.

Mingan pondered and shook his head a little.

"You have conquered an empire in the saddle; you cannot govern it so. You know naught of Cathay save to trample it under the hoofs of your horse; I cannot stand by and see such a thing."

Saying this, he fully expected the Khan to draw his sword, but the conqueror still leaned on it thoughtfully. Presently he nodded in agreement.

"*Kai*—I am a wild boar of the steppe. They call me the man-slayer, and it is a good name. Certain things I cannot do, and must, at a time like this, call upon a wise man, a *magus* such as Prester John. He, being dead, can no longer aid me."

Whereupon, having spoken many words—a thing most unusual in him—the conqueror signed to the gur-khan, gave him some orders in a low tone, and beckoned to Mingan.

"Go with this man to the place whither he will lead you. There await my command and, when it comes, decide what you will do. Take this, as a token to protect you, in your Cathayan dress."

He held out the gold tablet, token of a Mongol hero, and raised his hand, dismissing Mingan.

When the two had left the audience hall, Genghis Khan turned over with his foot the jewels scattered on the step. He glanced casually at the dying slave who, propped upright against the wall, gripped the shaft of the spear with both hands. He remembered now that the work of the past months was ended and, to his satisfaction, that he was hungry. So he felt in his pockets and drew out some shreds of meat and dried milk-curds and began to munch.

Presently, catching sight of the official's chair vacated by Mingan, his lips widened in a smile and he chuckled noiselessly.

Meanwhile, Mingan and his guide passed out of the city through the cordon of Mongol guards. Amid lines of sleeping camels, a pavilion tent glowed with light. About it slumbering warriors, seated on the ground with the reins of their ponies in hand, looked up at their approach, but seeing the gur-khan, slept again. Stooping under the entrance flap, Mingan found Chepe Noyon and the Buffalo busily engaged in refreshing themselves at a well-laden table—at least Subotai was stuffing himself. The Tiger sipped the rare white wine of Yen-king and picked at the strings of a gold lute taken from some Cathayan palace.

The two palladins started up at sight of their friend, and Mingan waited to learn how they would receive him.

"Mingan!" cried Chepe Noyon, the first to recognize him in his state dress. "What mummer's garb do you wear now? *Hai*—your coming has saved us a mighty labor. We were ordered by the Khan to search Yen-king and find you within a day and night if we had to turn up the earth of the graves or the mud of the river."

For the first time he noticed the white streaks in the hair of his friend and the lines about Mingan's eyes. "Ah, they say Chung-hi bedded you down in darkness. The swine! A captive we took at the river, a captain of the Liao-tung regiment, told us that his prince had appeared in Cathay and had been quartered in a dungeon. His comrades of the north were disgruntled at this treatment of you, and they soon left Chung-hi for their homes, therefore. But enough of this—here are the three palladins united, and our goblets are dry."

Subotai, his mild eyes shining with pleasure, patted Mingan on the head and shoulders and quaffed a beaker of wine with an open throat. In Mingan's heart was a glow that came not from the wine. He was glad to be with the palladins, to stand in a wind-swept tent, listening to the sounds of the camp.

"Truly," he said gravely, "I am no longer your equal; Subotai is commander of a division and you are chief of the Keraits."

Subotai merely grunted, but Chepe Noyon laughed.

"Is it not honor enough, Mingan, that we used your trick to overcome the Cathayans who were numerous as fleas on a nation of dogs?"

"My trick?"

"Aye, so. But I forgot you were in gyves and fetters at the time. Why, the trick of the horse race. Genghis Khan gave to the Buffalo and me barely two *tumans*. Then he sent us against the strongest of the Cathayan armies, so that we were beaten and forced to flee with naught but our shadows. So, he matched his weakest division against the strongest of the emperor, willing to lose that while he and old Mukuli with the main power of the Horde bit into the weaker armies of Cathay like camels chewing a nose-cord. Thus it was that you matched ponies against the Gipsies and won."

Now Subotai folded his arms and stretched his mighty legs in front of him.

"A thought has come to me, O my friends." He paused to gather together words to express his idea. "Genghis Khan has tried each of us in turn. The Tiger he raised to a high place in the world. He knew that Mingan's heart was divided like a broken goblet when the Horde turned against Cathay. He was aware of the hero's flight, but stayed it not, wishing to test him—knowing that the Cathayans would meet him with dishonor. And now—what has the Khan in store for Mingan?"

A guard entered, conducting one of the councilors of the Mongols and a tall Cathayan in quilted armor, weapon-less, with the emblem of Liao-tung sewn on his shoulder, and a helmet bearing a captain's crest. At sight of Mingan, the Northerner threw himself on his knees, pressed his head against the ground, and joyfully craved permission to speak.

"Live for a hundred years, lord of the hills and forests. I, an unworthy captive, serving as interpreter, bear tidings from Yen-king that the grandees of Cathay, the nobles and councilors are assembling at the palace to salute the new governor chosen by Genghis Khan. Attend, O Bright One, prince of our race, for the northern provinces have need of your wisdom."

At this the Mongol stepped forward and confronted Mingan.

"By order of Genghis Khan—chief of chiefs, lord of the men of the earth—you, Ye Lui Kutsai Mingan, are appointed governor of Cathay under the Khan. Do you accept or refuse?"

Mingan started. He looked down at his countryman of Liao-tung. Then his voice failed him, and he could only nod assent. Chepe Noyon gave a delighted shout and announced that he would compose a new verse for his "Lament of the Doleful Officer"; Subotai threw his goblet crashing on the ground, seized the bowl of wine, and set it down empty.

As Mingan, followed by the two who had come to seek him, went forth from the tent, he heard the voice of the Tiger raised in song:

"From the gate in the north he sallied forth,
Riding with loosened rein,
To weal or woe, where the four winds blow.
Now he is home again.
What could he do?—'Twas Heaven's whim!
What could he say, a poor fellow like him?"

The House of the Strongest

He was Ermecin, the strong man. But that had not always been his name.

When he was a boy, he had raced with the other Buriat youths—and a Mongol horse race is no brief gallop along leveled land. And when he did not win, which was seldom, the Ermecin-to-be took from the winning youth by force the horse that was victor in the race.

In so doing the boy anticipated the practice of shrewd Chinese *tao-tai* (governors).

Yet when Ermecin lived, two hundred years ago, the sinister authority of the Chinese, the "men of the hat and girdle," had not spread over the upper Mongolian plain where the fertile edge of the Gobi touches the green slopes of the Syansk.

This was the land of the free Buriats. They were hunters and herders, these Tatars, and the stranger was welcome within their tents. The youths wrestled and fought and vied with bow and arrow.

Ermecin was the strongest of the youths. Somewhere among his fathers had been a Chukchee, of the fisherfolk from the North. And in Ermecin appeared the flat, high shoulders, the massive, swinging arms, and the small, quick eyes of this ancestor.

Among the Buriat men was a *batyr*, a proved warrior. He had fought in the wars of Muscovy. Once in an inn during a horse festival, he drew his sword on Ermecin. The boy, now nearly at his full growth, twisted the weapon from the warrior and broke the man's neck with his hands.

The sword Ermecin kept. It was a heavy affair, a foot broad at the head. Its hilt had space for two hands. But the Buriat youth could swing it, whistling about his head, with one hand.

With the bow he was more deadly, for that was his natural weapon. He could keep a bowstring of reindeer gut twanging in the air like a minstrel's fiddle-string, while he buried a half-dozen shafts in the splintering trunk of a sapling.

After Ermecin had killed the *batyr,* men looked at him before they spoke. They began to chuckle when he threw visiting wrestlers crashing to the earth in the bouts at the horse festival.

It was noticeable that when Ermecin returned one day afoot to the yurts of the Buriats where the camp was clustered by the clear water of Ubsa Nor, no one laughed at him. Now a Mongol likes to make fun of a comrade, and to walk back horseless from a hunting venture, is a predicament that invites fun-making.

Ermecin had gone after bear in the Syansk gullies among the peaks to the North. His closest friend had accompanied him.

One of the small savage bears had attacked the other Buriat, frightening the lad's horse, which threw him to earth. The bear had killed the hunter and made off. When Ermecin reached the spot, he cut the throat of his own horse without hesitation.

This was so the spirit of the horse could accompany the soul of his friend on the long journey through the sky where walking would be weary work. Ermecin hunted out rabbits and an antelope, hanging up their flesh as offerings to the spirits who flocked out of the sky to the spot where the soul of a man went from the body.

Concerning all this Ermecin said nothing. He was little given to words anyway; but the gossips of the yurts invested him with a stain of blood, because the two had gone hunting together and only one returned.

Over this Ermecin brooded. When there came to Ubsa Nor a caravan of Torgut brigands and many horses were stolen, he led the enraged Buriats in the battle that followed.

From it he gained many horses. Those who had seen him, his long mustaches flying in the wind, his shoulders hunched and his sword hacking through flesh, did not raise a voice against his possession of the bulk of the spoil taken from the slain enemies.

"He is Ermecin," they said, "the strong man. He is the strongest of us all. Hereafter what he wills to take he will take."

There was but one soul in the land between the Syansk and the Gobi that would not feel fear at the anger of Ermecin. And that was Cherla.

She had sprung from a line of chiefs, and at one time a Manchu noble had been among her ancestors. Her back was straight as a horse's leg, her long hair dark as a horse's mane. She walked with pride among the Buriats, for she had been told that she was of the white-boned folk—the leaders of men. While Ermecin and the mass of the other Buriat hunters were, she believed, black-boned men, commoners.

Cherla had a smile like the flash of sunlight on a running brook. When her eyes softened, they were dark flowers. When she ran to gather in her father's cattle, the strength of her young body and its grace enchanted the eyes of men who watched her—and many did.

So was Cherla running, or rather skipping, one noon where the heat of the sun was softened by a grove of ash. Ermecin saw her and whirled his horse across her path. When she halted, eyes flashing, he laid one hand beneath her chin.

He could feel the pulse beat in the round throat under his fingers. The girl's eyes burned into his, unafraid. Twice she struck him in the face, but he did not move or speak.

That night Ermecin drove up to her father's yurt a herd of horses. The horses he gave to Cherla's father; the girl herself he took from the ring of her frightened sisters.

There had been no consulting of the match-makeress, no ceremony of the gifts of the night. Only one herder of Ermecin's rode before them and stuck into the right-hand wall of his master's tent the white-adorned arrow, and placed before the yurt itself the trunk of a young birch as a symbol of the fruit of the marriage.

But Ermecin had sent out couriers that afternoon, and the Buriats gathered when he prepared a great feast of slaughtered sheep and horses, of richly brewed *kumiss*. Long into the night they ate and drank, and the father and brothers of Cherla were among the most drunk.

When Ermecin thrust his great body through the tent entrance after the feast, Cherla did not give him the *nimeleu qatvarkin*, the greeting from wife to husband. She sat erect on the bearskins, the headband about her smooth forehead and the silver ornaments in her tresses seeming to mock the ice of disdain in her face.

"You are a beast," she said. "You have black bones."

And the disdain did not pass from her eyes until death came to the yurt.

Cherla was not long in the yurt, for she ran away. Angry tears were in her eyes when she ran to the tents of her father and asked him to kill the beast Ermecin.

But when the master of many herds, the strongest of the Buriats, rode up to the tent where Cherla had taken shelter and dismounted without a weapon in his hand, no man drew sword or knife. Ermecin glanced at them all in turn and lifted Cherla in his arms. He flung the girl over the peak of his saddle and leaped behind her.

He rode home as if the foul fiend itself were after his horse. Not once did she cry out from the pain of the jolting or the bruising of the saddle-horn where it tore the skin from her soft flesh.

Ermecin flung her down in his yurt entrance and pointed at the fire.

"My woman," he said, and his deep voice was not hasty or loud, "I have paid the price of a girl. The birch has been planted in front of my house. I want to have sons so that the fire of my hearth will not go out."

He pointed in turn to the weapons, the bows and spears on the felt wall of the tent, to the *kumiss* cask, and the cooking-dishes, to the woolen cloths from which garments were made, and the furs that covered the floor. He told her, as if he was talking to a refractory colt, the things she must do for him. (Ermecin, in common with many Tatars, was gentle with horses, and used his voice in training them.)

"You are no better than a big beast," she said, her chin lifted. "I will never cease to hate you."

With a peculiar curiosity in his deep-set eyes Ermecin watched the slight form of his wife as she turned to prepare meat and mare's milk for the evening meal.

"Good," he muttered to himself at length; "she has mettle. She will bear me a rare son."

So Cherla was diligent in the care of the yurt, even while her pride was like a veil between them. Ermecin rode by day and sometimes by night over his lands, caring for his growing herds. But more often he was away fighting, or drunk at the festivals.

Among the Buriats, no male member of her family may look into the face of a woman that is married. Cherla sat alone in the tent, and when the match-makeresses gossiped to her about the mighty encounters of her husband her full lips pressed together and her eyes were cold.

Nor did she speak to Ermecin when he galloped up after two days in the saddle, to find a small hut built near his yurt and Cherla lying in pain among the old women who had clustered to a birth.

Custom forbade his going to the hut where Cherla was, but the old hags, after their kind, painted to him the suffering of his woman and said that the evil demon of sickness was within her.

Ermecin did not linger, but took two fresh horses from the group always kept near his yurt and spurred away toward the fastness of the Syansk where the clever witch-doctor Botogo had his hut.

Seventy miles he rode before dawn.

"We will take four fresh horses of your herd," he told Botogo, whose wrinkled face was intent and fearful. "And if you do not ride fast and send away the demon from Cherla, you will make magic for Erlik Khan in the place of the dead. Come!"

Alone among the Buriats, Ermecin did not respect the arts of the witch-doctor who could summon and dismiss the spirits of the sky. On the other hand Botogo was really afraid that his neck would be broken if Cherla should die. He made haste.

Seeing, when he came to the hut, that the woman was in no bad way, he regained much of his authoritative air.

"The demon," he admitted to Ermecin, "that has entered your woman is a *menkva*, a dark spirit of the secondary order."

Furthermore, he explained, to induce the demon to withdraw it would be necessary to offer it a horse to ride away on, furs to dress in, and boots to cover its feet. Ermecin at once ordered them to be prepared and given to the witch-doctor, who fell to his hideous incantations and the hubbub of brazen gongs that was indeed enough to cure or kill a very sick person.

"The *menkva* has a brother," he informed Ermecin after a space, "who is more powerful than he. Three horses and more furs will be needed—"

"That is easily done," growled the master of the yurt impatiently.

Botogo wished he had asked for more. He was still afraid, however. Even after a son had been born to the exultant Buriat and the witch-doctor had been sent away with many additional presents, Botogo nursed his enmity against Ermecin. He had been frightened, and to frighten some men is to make enemies of them.

No need for him to have been frightened. A Tatar is hospitable, and his guests are looked upon as an honor. Ermecin especially liked to have numbers of visitors in his tents. When a traveler would halt, to explain that some of his horses had been lost, the big Buriat would laugh: "What! Is that all, good sir? Dismount and drink, and before you have filled your belly I will have your horse here at the yurt. Look and see if I don't, now."

With that he would be off, on the first mount to hand. Being a skilled tracker and knowing the plain like a book, he would make good his promise, more often than not. If the stranger's horse should actually have disappeared, Ermecin would insist on giving another in its place.

"Will I have it said that a man was the loser by riding through my lands!" he would roar. "By the hide of Erlik Khan, I will not have it said! Come now, take your pick of this rotten herd, good sir. They are poor beasts at best."

Despite the fact that his sword was feared from the Syansk to the Gobi, numbers of poverty-ridden Buriats hung about the quarters of the strong man. They ate of his meat, and laughed with him when he chuckled at the antics of his six-month-old son, when the boy would be brought to the fire by Cherla at his request of an evening.

"Look," he cried once, "the son of Ermecin can stand. Now we will see!"

With the back of his hand the warrior tapped the child gently on the chest. It fell over backward, bumping its head hard on the earth. But without a whimper it rose dizzily and stood, its sturdy legs planted wide.

"What did I say?" bellowed the delighted father. "It will be a strong one, like me. It has its life from the old buck, my friends, not from the doe."

And he got himself royally drunk for two days, and slept for a third.

"Eh," he chuckled when he woke and rose from the skins in his corner, none the worse for the long bout, "that is a boy out of my loins. He will be like his father, ——eat me if he isn't. Come, good sirs, we are getting fat as men of the hat and girdle with all this stuffing and swilling. Let's mount for the Syansk and a good run after a stag. Or better still, a few good blows at the Torgut Mongols."

It was noticeable that few of the henchmen who surrounded Ermecin's fires followed his horse as he galloped off to the hills. They knew that meat was always to be had from his servants, and that when he returned after a scrimmage or so there would be spoil to be gambled for because Ermecin was almost invariably the victor in the clan combats. At the time of his marriage he was in the fullness of strength. He was able to ride in the saddle for two days and a night, eating only a little as he rode. The experience of middle age had begun to cool the headstrong temper of his youth.

He seemed to stay home only to play with his son or to look over his herds. His home was spoken of as the *armaci-ralin*, the "house of the strongest."

But never when he came home did Cherla say the *nimeleu qatvarkin*, the "Hail, my husband!"

Sitting by the fire in the fine garments of silk that she made, studded with silver, she would stare into the smoke, her fine eyes half-closed; and only when she nursed the boy did the light of happiness come into her eyes.

The boundary of the province of Cha-tsong Chien, *tao-tai* of the northwestern banners, should have ended before the lands of the Buriats began.

Cha-tsong Chien, being a Manchu, was arrogant; and because a Manchu is of the same blood as the Tatars, he was a hardy person. He had been colonel of a thousand in the Manchu army, and his counsel had resulted in the successful storming of the walled city of Lan-liang when his men had ripped up the houses and the women of a thousand merchants and sent the Mings themselves out of the world headlong, or, to be exact, shortened by a head.

As governor of the Gobi, Cha-tsong Chien pushed his boundaries into the fertile regions of the North, where Tatar horse herds and sheep made the game worthwhile. He encouraged wandering priests and mountebanks to bring him news of yurts within reach of his province where the plundering was good enough for an exalted person like Cha-tsong Chien.

There was little danger in this for Cha-tsong Chien, because the Tatar clans were so busy fighting each other that they could not unite to defend themselves. And reprisals across the Gobi against the soldiery of the Manchu were not to be thought of.

So Cha-tsong Chien was pleased one day in late spring after the freshets of the Tatar mountains had abated, when he heard of a horse festival of the rival clans the Torguts and Buriats near Ubsa Lake. He headed there at once, taking in his haste only a half-dozen bowmen and a lesser number of servants.

He knew that by playing his role of governor and setting one clan against the other he could exact a goodly tribute of horseflesh without danger of armed conflict. If he brought more men, the Tatars might take it into their thick heads to withdraw to their home yurts. So Cha-tsong Chien was riding toward Ubsa Nor when he met a solitary witch-doctor who saluted him servilely and fell into talk. This witch-doctor was Botogo, and he held the attention even of the exalted personage at his side when he related that the yurt and cattle of a wealthy Tatar were scarce a day's ride to the north, some distance from the Ubsa festival.

"O my honorable father and mother," said Botogo—*ex officio* the Manchu governor was a magistrate, and the witch-doctor addressed him with the requisite title—"the Tatar is a thief and a murderer, and the men of his clan live in fear of him. He has raped women from the tents of his neighbors. He has angered the good spirits of the air."

Cha-tsong Chien merely grunted and asked again the size of the Tatar's herds and the name of the man.

"On his lands are as many head of horses and cattle as at the Ubsa festival, O Exalted Son of Benevolence and Justice. His name is Ermecin."

Seeing a flash in the black eyes of his superior, the witch-doctor hastened to say—"Ermecin is at Ubsa Lake and by now is as drunk as a fish that lies on the land."

When, that night, Cha-tsong Chien drove the camels and travelers out of an inn, so his nostrils should not be polluted by the smell, he made much of Botogo and weighed silently in his mind the tales he had heard about the prowess of the strong warrior Ermecin against the veracity of Botogo, who said the Tatar was absent and drunk.

Dawn found Cha-tsong Chien riding fast with his men to the north, still silent, but wishing for a greater retinue. Then Botogo would have made excuses and left the cavalcade, but the *tao-tai* was no man's fool and kept him at his stirrup.

"If Ermecin and his riders are at the yurt, we will pay him out of our benevolence a visit of felicitation on the birth of his son."

Cha-tsong Chien knew the law of Tatar hospitality.

"And I will have heated mercury poured into your mouth to kill the devil of lies in your throat. If Ermecin is indeed at Ubsa, then your two claws will have cool silver poured into them—"

The round face of the governor broke into a smile. He liked his jest. And he smiled the more when he found the yurt of Ermecin deserted by all but a brace of herders and one or two hangers-on who fled at the first glimpse of the embroidered coat of Cha-tsong Chien. One herder was off like an arrow; the other died fighting.

Cha-tsong Chien walked into the yurt of Ermecin. A servant woman groveled, and he kicked her out and peered into the shadows where a comely girl nursed a six-month-old child.

He watched while Cherla covered her breast and rose to stand before him. Cha-tsong Chien was even taller than Ermecin, though not so massive in shoulder and arm.

"Welcome to the yurt of Ermecin, *tao-tai*," she said in blundering Manchu. "I am of the blood of your august fathers, and I can try to serve the guest fittingly. Will you be pleased to sit until Ermecin can be sent for?"

Cherla's heart was pounding under the embroidered silk of her tunic. She had often thought with reverence of the governor across the border. He was of the white-boned caste, and the splendors of his palace must be beyond telling.

But his moist eyes seemed to her like the eyes of a fish. Why had the soldiers of the governor struck down the herder? Cherla did not understand; she only knew that she was Ermecin's wife and must extend the hospitality of Ermecin's ill-suited tents to the august visitor.

The glance of Cha-tsong Chien ran around the weapons on the walls and came back to the woman as a group of his men clustered in the yurt entrance.

"Break those bows and spears," he commanded at length. "Fetch in the cattle and horses to the last one. Not until then can you have this woman for your sport. Make haste!"

Now as the men were tearing down the weapons from the felt sides of the tent one of them stepped upon the child, which began to cry. Indifferently, the soldier picked it up and tossed it to earth to silence it.

Cherla's heart stood still. But the son of Ermecin wriggled about on the furs where he had fallen and stood up, his fat legs planted wide.

"A strong boy!" exclaimed Cha-tsong Chien in surprise. "Aye, and there may be Manchu blood somewhere in his veins. We will take him with us."

With a scream Cherla cast herself over the boy, hugging him to her. Two bowmen tried to drag her away from the child. In her slender body was a surprising strength.

It was minutes before they had beaten her unconscious with the butts of their weapons. They tore the silver ornaments from her silk garment and in so doing ripped the tunic from her.

Cha-tsong Chien jerked them back angrily.

"Dogs—get you to the herds. We must be off at once. Give the child to a coolie to tie to his horse."

Botogo had spoken the truth, yet not quite all the truth. Ermecin was at the horse festival; but he was not drunk. In fact, drink never kept him off his feet, and just then he was watching the horse races with critical appreciation.

When the herder from his yurt galloped up on a steaming beast and shouted to Ermecin, the big Tatar became dead sober in that moment. In the next he was on his horse and off, over the plain.

The burning stacks of hay, the broken corrals, and the tumbled huts of his followers he took in with a glance. Passing by a group of curious and silent Buriats, he strode into his yurt, now empty of skins and ivory and ornaments and filled with broken weapons.

"Where is the son of Ermecin?" he asked his wife, scarcely noticing her torn clothes and the sweat on her disordered hair.

His deep voice was slow as if it had been dragged forth from his chest. His veined hands clasped and unclasped on his belt. Only his eyes glowed as if from a fire within.

"They have taken him away from you," she wailed. "They have taken him from me and put him on a horse while you were drunk at the festival. Oh, you are a beast, you are a beast!"

"They threw him on the ground," she cried, pointing to the spot. "But he did not die, because he is strong, strong. And they have taken him away from you, you—"

Ermecin had passed from the yurt. Cherla dragged herself to the entrance in time to see him go to the best of the horses that the Buriats had ridden up—the Buriats who had been his guests. As she watched the big, stooped figure gallop off alone after circling the yurt, there was a curious fire in her dark eyes. Her lips moved as if she was praying.

When the outpost that Cha-tsong Chien had stationed in the rear of his caravan of animals rode up to report a single horseman coming over the long slopes in the plain where the plain is like the waves of the sea, meeting the sand of the Gobi, Cha-tsong Chien smiled for the first time in some hours.

It was then nearly dusk. The one rider, so reasoned the *tao-tai*, could be disposed of by his bowmen. Then night would fall.

Their course across the northern corner of the Gobi would be undisturbed, and by dawn they would be beyond reach of any really formidable pursuit.

So he called in three of his bowmen, and then a fourth, from the herd. The two other bowmen and all the servants but one that carried Cha-tsong Chien's sword were needed to drive the uneasy animals.

The Tatar, Cha-tsong Chien mused, would rush up like an angered ox and would be stuck full of arrows in a trice.

The six men sat their horses with bowstrings taut and arrows fitted, while the pursuer galloped up over a rise and gave a shout at seeing them.

"Wait until he is close," ordered the *tao-tai*. "The light is bad."

Actually he was willing that one or two of his men should be shot down—he knew the skill of a Tatar archer—in order that the others should make sure of their kill. As for Cha-tsong Chien, he had a breastplate of Turkish steel under his robe. He had inherited it from his fathers and found it useful at times like this.

The rider headed toward them, and they saw a short, massive bow gripped in his left hand.

"Wait," counseled Cha-tsong Chien as his men stirred, "another spear's throw."

But then the rider swerved and began to circle the group at the full speed of his horse. As the herds with their guards had passed on, the plain about the Chinese was clear.

"Hai!" he shouted. *"Hai—hai!"*

With each cry he loosed an arrow. The shafts came as if expelled from a siege engine. One of the bowmen was knocked to earth, transfixed. The horse of another screamed and went to its knees.

The volley of arrows from the bowmen went wide, falling behind the bent figure that seemed to skim the ground on its shaggy pony. The Chinese bows were longer than the Tatar weapon, but their tension was less. Their shafts at that distance did not carry in a straight line, while they could scarcely see the darts of the Tatar that whirred in the air.

Cha-tsong Chien heard a thud, and saw the skull of a horse beside him shattered as a shaft hit.

"That is Ermecin!" cried his servant. "He is a champion. We must fly."

"Dog!" roared the aroused official, striking the man with the flat of his sword. "We are four and he is one—a Tatar."

Lifting his voice, Cha-tsong Chien bellowed for his men with the herd to leave the animals and ride up.

"Shoot down his horse!" he instructed his archers.

By an accident his followers made good his wish. The frightened servant turned his mount to flee. Ermecin halted his beast, took time to direct an arrow, and the coolie was knocked sprawling. But the moment's pause gave the Manchu bowmen their chance, and Ermecin's horse went down.

"We have him now," announced Cha-tsong Chien. "Let us await our comrades."

They waited long. Ermecin trotted off into the dusk in ungainly fashion. He was little used to being on his own feet. Presently he appeared again on another knoll, mounted. Following the herd, he had caught a stray horse and in doing so had met with one of the returning archers and killed him.

The other soldier and the servants remained hidden in the plain, perhaps not hearing the governor's shout, perhaps unwilling to ride into the danger that lurked in the deepening dusk.

Cha-tsong Chien felt a cold chill steal up the base of his stout neck at sight of the Tatar rider returning. But he made up his mind quickly.

"We must attack him," he said. "Come, a handful of gold to the one who lets out his life."

By keeping his distance and harassing the Chinese through the night, Ermecin would have fulfilled the wisdom of his experience. But at sight of them riding toward him, all the cool strategy life had taught him deserted him. Was Ermecin to turn his back on his foes?

So perhaps had Cha-tsong Chien reasoned as he kept prudently behind his men. Ermecin stood his ground. It was nearly dark.

Masterless groups of horses galloped by the band of Buriats, who followed cautiously by torchlight the trail of the herd that night.

"That is good," they said. "Ermecin has scattered the Chinese, and the herd seeks its home pastures. Aye, there are the cattle, going back."

Some left the torches to carry off beasts from the groups that straggled back. They preferred to steal in the dark because there was no telling when Ermecin might ride up to them. Had not the Chinese left the herd?

They halted at a place where two dead bowmen lay with a coolie stretched out a short distance away. From here they followed horse tracks for the distance of a bowshot.

"Ah, here was a fight for you, good sirs," they assured each other as they halted a second time.

A Manchu bowman, doubled up, was under their feet, an arrow projecting from his back. A few yards farther on they heard a groan. It came from another of the Chinese soldiers, his clothing torn, his hands dark with dried blood. The man's chest was cut nearly in two, and the air bubbled from his severed lungs as he struggled, dying, for breath.

Under him lay a Manchu body without a head. And near these two was the tall form of Cha-tsong Chien, the silk robe ripped from his mail, the steel hacked and bent. His sword was in his hand. He was quite dead, and the ground here was trampled as if two heavy bodies had churned it with their feet.

The broken halves of Ermecin's sword were here also, but of the Tatar warrior they saw no trace until they heard a thin cry in the night air. Others of their band who had investigated the plain reported that the Chinese coolies must have fled.

"Then that was a spirit of the sky crying to us," observed Botogo the witch-doctor, who was far from at ease. "They have snatched up Ermecin, for he is not here and he did not ride back to his yurt—"

Botogo spat on the form of the Manchu, and the others stared at him in awe.

Nevertheless Ermecin was there. When they followed the sound they had heard they found him on the ground, his body drooped forward, propped up on one elbow, his head and shoulder on the grass. His bare chest was agape with wounds, and he had bled out his life some time ago.

Under his kneeling form was the plaintive, struggling bundle of his child.

They took the boy back to Cherla, while fires were lighted about the *armaci-ralin*, the house of the strongest, and the Buriats flocked to eat roasted sheep and drink up the stores of *kumiss* beside the hut where Ermecin lay. Botogo was there in his role of master of ceremonies, for which he would be well paid.

Cherla sat in the yurt entrance, clad in a new dress, her tresses ordered. She was staring blankly into the fires.

"Only once did she speak," said the gossip crones to the men who surrounded the fires. "That was when the body of Ermecin was brought in to her. We have not heard her say it before. She said, '*nimeleu qatvarkin*—hail, to my husband.'"

Cherla, however, spoke again before the night was done. A gleam came into her dark eyes when the baby, hungry, began to pummel at her breasts with its sturdy fists.

"Ah, you, too, will be an *ermecin*, a strong man."

And in her voice was tenderness and a great pride.

The Road of the Giants

Chapter I
An Account of How Captain Billings Lost His Luggage

He who sets forth upon the road knows not what the road will bring; nor does he know the hour of his return.
—Mongol proverb

"God go with you, my excellent sir. Keep to the highroad, by all means, and don't fail to watch the verst-posts, my good gentleman. It's a matter of some twenty versts to Zaritzan, maybe thirty or forty."

The stranger who had stopped to eat a hasty supper at the frontier post on the highroad from Astrakan to Zaritzan sprang into the saddle of his pony and pulled the fur lapels of his greatcoat up around his ears. This made the soldier curious, for in the year of Our Lord 1771, in the beginning of February when the ice on the Volga was solid enough to support a coach and six, few travelers ventured alone along the frontier between Russia and the Tatar tribes.

"Take my advice, sir, and hire a troika with three fine horses that will pull you like the wind and a postillion to guide you over the way. Just beyond these windmills a woman and her baby were gobbled up by the cursed wolves. True, I assure you, by the holy pictures. If you lose your way you are done for, quite. Devil take me, sir, it's cold work standing here talking to you—Ah, my grateful thanks, well born!"

Captain Minard Billings, of Edinburgh and late of the high seas, tossed the Russian a silver shilling. It was one of his last, and he had not hired a sledge because the supper had nearly emptied his purse.

"Remember," the man called after him, "keep due north along the right bank of the Volga. On the other bank begins the great steppe where you would lose your way at the first turn. Then the men from over the river would rip you up like a fish and leave you in the snow. Mind my words—" his hoarse voice grew fainter—"if you see a Tatar from over the river, pistol him at once."

Passing the windmills at the end of the hamlet, Captain Billings smiled. A cheerful road this, he reflected.

It would have been better, of course, to have lain the night at the post and gone on by daylight. But Captain Billings had an appointment that evening at Zaritzan and he meant to keep it. There was a commission awaiting him at Zaritzan, and he meant to have it.

Captain Billings had been stranded at Astrakan, after completing a survey of the north coast of the Caspian for Governor Beketoff, of that town. Beketoff had been most polite, but being out of funds and likewise out of favor with the territorial ministry at St. Petersburg, Billings was not paid. Nightly he had played chess with the governor and sampled every vintage of wine the castle boasted.

The wine was not good, and Billings tired of putting Beketoff to bed every evening under the table. So he had borrowed a good pony from the governor, and—since he could not pay for a sledge—had entrusted his luggage to a detail of Cossacks under a *sotnik*, bound up the ice-coated Volga.

Now this luggage of Captain Billings was very valuable, to himself at least. It was the first time he had parted with it, even for a few days. It was a peculiar thing, that luggage. But the Cossacks traveled more slowly than he, and Billings had sent word ahead by courier that he would be at Zaritzan before midnight. He had a habit of keeping his promises.

From time to time as he rode, he tried to catch a glimpse of the gray sheet of the Volga, somewhere to his right. But the forest had set in again and the spruces made a corridor of the road that was merely a narrow track in the snow.

Already the sun was behind the pines, and a cold wind stirred up the fine snow into a dust that stung his face. He pulled down his sheepskin cap and fell to beating his arms across his chest. And he did not notice that the verst-posts were no longer to be seen. In fact, the trail he followed had narrowed down to the track of a single horse.

"My faith, it's cold as —— when the Devil's gone to mass," Captain Billings assured himself. "And not so much as a tavern to break the hedgerows."

His gray-greenish eyes, spaced wide, surveyed the shadows of the forest slowly. His high cheekbones were reddened by long exposure to the sun of the Caspian. Billings was of middle age with a back like a pikestaff and a swagger to his shoulders that concealed his lack of height.

Since boyhood—and a thankless one—he had grown up with weapons, lived by his wits. He wore no wig, and his yellow hair had been bleached by the sun to the color of tow. School had been, for him, the apprenticeship at the table of a master navigator, and the *salle d'armes* of a French swordsman, now unhappily dead during the vicissitudes of that changeful lady, Paris. He had not always found bread in plenty, but there had been no lack of fighting.

"A pox on these misbegotten Muscovite charts!"

He had noticed the absence of the verst-posts. These, however, had been covered for the most part by drifting snow. The moon had risen on his right, and by its light he scanned the lines of the map of the frontier. According to it he should have been at Zaritzan by now.

Instead, he was off the highroad. He could go back to the last post, or turn out into the river and wait for the sledge which should be along that night. But neither choice was to his liking. He tore up the worthless chart and plied his pony's flanks with the black Cossack whip he carried, resolved to follow the track of the horse in front of him so long as it led to the north.

As if in answer to his decision, the howl of a wolf came up the wind. Billings steadied the pony and settled himself in the saddle. He no longer needed the whip. His eyes narrowed against the cut of the wind, his glance thrusting into the shadows on either hand, to pick out the yellow gleam of eyes.

Drawing off a glove, his numbed fingers felt of the priming of the long pistols in the saddle holsters; the snow had dampened the powder.

Now the trees were thinning; curling wraiths of snow danced in the shifting moonlight as the wind came with a sweep across the dunes of the open. A moment later he drew in his horse. Beside the trail a figure appeared, standing over a dead pony.

"Zounds!" cried Billings under his breath. "Here's a merry go."

The other, in a long *kaftan* and a tall sheepskin hat too large for him, seemed to be no more than a boy, a swarthy boy with eyes like black jewels. He held a scimitar that dripped blood upon the white surface of the snow. Billings observed that the throat of the horse had been cut.

Promptly the lad, who might have been Gipsy or Tatar, sheathed his weapon and stood straight and quiet.

"*Koshkildui*, peace be with you, brother," said Captain Billings in Russian. "Get up behind me, young man."

The stripling took his time about answering.

"You are a *giaour*—an outlander," he observed slowly, in the southern dialect. "You are no man of Russia—I knew that by your first speech."

"Indeed!" Billings pulled at his yellow mustache. "Do you wish to follow your horse into the bellies of the wolves who are back yonder?"

"*Tchu*—I fear no wolves, uncle. You ride from Astrakan, and you have been at the palace of the excellency, Beketoff."

"The ——," thought Billings, reining in his uneasy horse, "this fellow is uncommonly particular about whom he joins company with!"

The rapscallion, however, had a certain bravado about him; might be a Gipsy, for all of his smooth, olive skin and large eyes. And he had certainly kept his sword ready to hand until spoken to.

"Uncle," went on the youth impassively, "if you were a Russian *boyar*, a noble, you wouldn't offer to take up a poor Gipsy behind you—now would you? Not when the wolves were afoot."

"Nephew, I am Captain Minard Billings, cartographer, and I am minded to leave you afoot."

"Cartographer—what is that?"

"A maker of maps."

In the moonlight a smile flashed over the face of the native. There was an elusive charm about the boy. Certainly, for all his respect, he did not speak in the manner of a serf or a suppliant son of Egypt.

Billings grunted.

"If you are satisfied, step out!"

With that he put spurs to the pony. The native promptly shed his heavy coat and ran beside, on the hard surface of the crust, clinging to a stirrup.

"How far is it to Zaritzan?" asked Billings.

"Two leagues, good uncle."

"The black pest on those Russians!"

At this the youth glanced up, startled. Billings had been thinking of the discarded chart.

"Is this the highroad, young man?"

"Nay, the road joined the riverbank, well back in the forest. But this track will lead you there."

Before long they heard a chorus of yelping howls in the distance. The wolf pack had reached the horse. The boy glanced up.

"My pony fell and came up lame. The wolves were near, so I cut its throat. Here we are in the forest again, and we must go swiftly."

With that he was up behind Billings, his breath warm on the traveler's neck. To keep his balance, the boy clung to the other's belt, reaching around to the clasp. Once the belt slipped and the native tightened it. He had drawn his scimitar and held it awkwardly in front of Billings.

"Pardon!" he cried.

The blade, slipping down, had cut the captain slightly across the upper leg. As if ashamed of the mishap he leaped down again, running beside the pony.

Although nothing more was heard of the wolves, they set a good pace until they passed an empty sentry box and, around a turn in the road, sighted the black bulk of a wall behind which rose the thatched roofs of houses, and a watch-tower.

"Zaritzan," panted the boy, pointing to a light that showed by the *stanitza* gate.

"Good!" Billings dismounted. "A bowl of hot porridge now, and some steaming brandy!"

"I cannot enter Zaritzan."

"Why not? Where would you go?"

The boy pointed to where the light—a lanthorn in the hand of a soldier, the same who had prudently deserted the sentry box—was moving toward them slowly.

"The wolves I fear are within the gate, uncle."

"Hum." Billings wondered what manner of man this was who preferred the black depths of the Volga forest to a town. "Hulloa—what are you about?"

The native had been whispering under his breath. His expressive eyes were serious. Now he seized the officer's fingers and lifted their hands in the air, toward the south and the other quarters of the compass. On the back of his wrist was a cut over which the blood had dried.

On Billings's fingers was the stain of blood from the slight wound over his knee.

"My lord," whispered the boy, "you have looked in the face of danger for my sake. This night you have saved my life, although you know not how. Now I have made us *andas*, brothers, as you first named me."

"And what foolery is that?" Billings pulled his hand away impatiently.

"When men become *andas*, my brother, both have one life; neither abandons the other, and each guards the life of his *anda*. Tonight I have bound the girdles and let flow the blood of both, and made strong our *anda*."

A Tatar! Billings remembered the boy had said he came from over the river. A native, Gipsy or Baskir or Tatar, would not go through this mummery of brotherhood without expecting some reward.

A second time the Tatar smiled.

"Give me your horse for this night and you will not lose it." His eyes flickered from the advancing sentry to Billings's face.

"Indeed, I will not. The wolves would make marrow paste of the mare."

"Not they, my lord. The mare will be under your hand within two days. Come, you have given me something already, Captain Beel-ing. Are we not *andas*?"

The boy stiffened, leaped boldly into the saddle, and was off pelting through the dead bushes.

"Pardon, my lord brother," he called back, laughing, over his shoulder.

Billings snatched at his belt and shrugged. Both his pistols were in the saddle holsters. His temper flared as he watched the mare and rider go flitting along the edge of the hemlocks down toward the shining lane that was the moon's reflection on the river.

It was rather curious, the ease with which the Tatar guided the tired horse away from shelter, riding as if he were one with the mare. There was no help for it. Horse and weapons were gone, and Billings felt the loss of both keenly.

"A witch," suggested the soldier, who had drawn close and was watching.

Billings reflected that the sentry at the last post had told him to shoot down any Tatar at sight.

"Oh, he bewitched me rarely," he muttered, disliking the idea of arriving in Zaritzan on foot, like a peasant.

"Of course," nodded the soldier, holding the lanthorn close to his visitor. "I saw it done. He did it with your hand, sir, like a regular Tatar werewolf, snatching where the blood runs."

The bearded sergeant was busy making the sign of the cross with his free hand. It was perplexing, after all, that the native had shown so little dread of the wolves.

"The Lord be merciful to us!" The sentry was staring at the cut in Billings's breeches. "See, there's where he sipped your blood. They usually take the back of the neck, just behind the ear."

When Billings looked up, the man was running toward the gate, stumbling over his musket in his haste. Dropping the firearm, he fumbled with the door to shut it. This was a trifle too much for Billings to stomach.

He sprang into the opening, wedged his boot against the door, and flung it back on the soldier.

"Hide of Beelzebub—so you would leave a Christian to the cold and the beasts, eh? A sergeant, too, on my word."

Muttering that he had orders to admit no strangers, the man changed countenance when Billings thrust his musket into his hand, wheeled him about, and requested that he announce to the *pristof*, Kichinskoi, that Captain Billings was here from Astrakan.

"At once—at once, your excellency. I assure you, captain, the witch robbed me of my senses. Enter, your honor. The Great Commissioner is expecting you, and gave word you were to go direct to his quarters."

But when Billings was not looking, the soldier backed away making the sign to ward off devils, with fingers crossed.

Billings paid no attention to him. He had just discovered that the purse attached to his belt for safekeeping had disappeared.

The moon by now was well overhead, and the whole of Zaritzan was outlined by the etching of shadow.

It was one of the forts just completed by order of the Czarina, Catherine the Second of Russia. These forts formed a chain along the western border of the great Tatar steppe.

An earthen rampart, surmounted by a palisade, was pierced for several cannon, all facing toward the river. The center of the place was a square of beaten clay, a drill ground in the corner of which, near the gate, stood wooden stocks, a knout hanging thereon by a rusty nail.

On one side of the enclosure ran a line of barracks and stables. Clustered against these as if for protection were the huts of traders, wine-sellers, and smiths. Behind these sheds a glow dimmed the moonlight, and loud voices broke the silence of the night. Groups of coated figures moved between the huts, swaggering out on the square.

Whenever the soldiers came near the gate side of the drill ground they hushed and walked more quickly. Here stood a rude church of logs, with a painting on the planks of the door and a weather-stained cross of silver gilt at the peak.

Beside the church and abreast the stocks was the two-storied bulk of the governor's house, its mica windows tinted with orange light, the watchtower built up from its roof. A deep voice within roared out a song of the steppe:

"Shen, shen, skivagen,
Seize your horse and spur again.
Ride, ride; speed and turn—
Burn, burn!"

As Zaritzan was on the river route of the Volga, and was the point on the steppe nearest the highway to Moscow, in this building the *pristof* Kichinskoi had his quarters—Kichinskoi, nominally Great Commissioner of the Tatars, was actually *surveillant* of the frontier for the Empress, an informant who had authority even over the military commanders, and whose word was law on the Volga.

Kichinskoi was in his office when Billings entered—a heavy man, with a smooth pale face and small features. He lay back on a sofa, one foot in a polished boot, on the table in front of him. He paid no attention to the captain after one swift glance, but went on talking to a timid-looking priest who sat on a stool close to the charcoal.

"Old wives' tales, I tell you, my dear *batko*. There will be no rising among the Torgut Tatars. I have talked with the Torgut Khan and told him a thing or two to put in his ear with the fleas. Pah! Didn't you see, Father Obé, that the Khan was afraid to answer me?"

"Yes, excellency, the Khan did not answer."

"Of course not."

Thrusting both hands deep into the pockets of a sable-lined overcoat, the *pristof* yawned and began to pick at his teeth.

"The Tatars are dogs. A little lashing, you know, goes a long way with them. Didn't they come to the steppe of their own accord several generations ago to beg for lands when they were driven out of China or some such thing? We need them, of course. The ministry wants horses and taxes, and the Torguts can give us both. And their Khan raised a levy of forty thousand cavalry in the war with the Sultan—killed a lot of infidels for the glory of God, and we got Azov. Isn't that true, priest?"

"True," muttered the small priest, with more assurance this time.

Kichinskoi took snuff from a gilt box. Without offering it to Billings, he closed the box and dusted off his chest with a silk kerchief.

"Dogs, or rather wolves," he resumed, "but we would fight them rather than lose them. I know what is whispered behind the doors of the ministry. Every house has its watchdog, Father Obé. You feed them bones—ha, yes! Our watchdogs are the Cos—"

He glanced toward the door whence came the noise of carousal and the mellow voice of the singer. While he seemed to pay no attention to Billings he was covertly scanning the visitor.

"I was going to say Tatars. Under my advice, they fight the Baskirs, Turks, and other accursed savages. Dog eat dog. You take my point. I have my hand on the lash, and they won't dare to rebel, whatever fools like Governor Beketoff may say—ha, Captain Billings, what does your friend the governor say now about those pagans over the river?"

He turned swiftly on his visitor. Billings had savored how he was being received in the first moment. Instead of standing, or trying to interrupt the self-satisfied official, he had seated himself on the stool opposite the priest, had thrown open his coat and taken out his pipe. After filling this, he took his time about answering, stooping instead to draw a coal from the brazier to light his pipe. "Beketoff," he responded calmly, "does not wag his tongue for the sake of hearing it go."

Kichinskoi brought his boot down from the table with a thump and frowned.

"Confound it, captain, you make yourself fiendishly at home, I must say. You're sitting down, I must call your attention to that. And am I smoking, pray?"

"No, you took snuff."

The priest cringed back into the shadows and raised his hands; Kichinskoi stared banefully into the emotionless, leather-like face of the adventurer. Billings's greenish eyes were frank and not at all cordial. Kichinskoi noted with some interest the smartly cut coat and the embroidered waistcoat of the captain.

Kichinskoi was a clever man, but—as is often the case—thought himself cleverer than he was. Already in the third rank of the nobility, he liked to be addressed as of the second. His weakness was vanity. He looked meaningly at Father Obé.

"Do you know, sir," the priest hastened to say, "that, Captain Billings, you are addressing the *pristof* himself? His excellency is commissioner over the Torguts, who are the Tatars along the Volga. Governor Beketoff has seen fit to send couriers to St. Petersburg—to high officials—charging that the Torguts are about to take up the sword against Christians. He asked you whether Beketoff still persists in that delusion.

"His excellency," he added in a whisper, "has denied to the Empress herself, the viceroy of the Church, that the Tatars would rebel."

"Then tell his excellency, Father Obé," said Billings quickly, "if he has brought me from Astrakan merely to repeat the confidences of Governor Beketoff, I shall make haste to return tomorrow morning."

Father Obé looked at Kichinskoi, who blinked like a disturbed owl. But, having studied the mapmaker, he changed his tactics.

"By the ashes of Sodom, my dear captain, you speak our Russian language well. *Foi de ma foi!* And my inform—I hear from Astrakan that you have completed a splendid chart of the Caspian shore for my friend Governor Beketoff, who did not pay you a kopeck. Also, you speak Tatar somewhat. I take it you are versed in—ah, astronomic science, and are—yes, a master hand at making a map."

Billings bowed without answering.

"Now unfortunately, Captain Billings, our Russian cartographers have given us poor charts of the Volga and the great plain to the east. *Vraiment, mon ami!* What do you think of those charts of the steppe?"

"Hum!" Billings smiled grimly.

"Exactly. I am commissioned by the Empress herself to prepare a map to present with my report."

"A map—of what?" Billings asked.

"Ah, you perceive the point. A map, my dear sir, of the great Tatar steppe." Kichinskoi drew a paper from the pile on his desk and read from it:

> *"It is desired an officer be commissioned to set out from the river Volga for the river Yaik, and from there to the Torgai. From this point he will journey to the Lake that is called Tengis, or Balkash, and he will complete a true and fine map of this territory.*
>
> *He is furthermore instructed to settle by astronomic observation the exact position of the Lake of Balkash, concerning which divers opinions are held. In all instances this officer is to conciliate the natives and confirm them in their favorable opinion of the Russian gov-*

ernment, to which they have recently submitted. By order of the Imperial Society of St. Petersburg."

"Practically the whole of the Tatar steppe," assented Billings. "Fifteen hundred miles—five thousand versts. First, plains down below sea level, then a desert—a blank place in your charts, ornamented by a picture of a tribesman sitting in front of his tent. And then—"

He hesitated. An old Armenian merchant at the Astrakan waterfront had sold him a map of the East. The traders of the caravan routes had a good knowledge of the terrain. And the Armenian had tales to tell.

"And then," prompted Kichinskoi, surprised at his visitor's knowledge.

"Mountains, *pristof*, shown on your maps by a pretty sketch of a lion emerging from a cave. But instead of lions—so I have heard—a race of men that are like animals. They bring women to sell as slaves in the bazaars of Tashkent and Bokhara to the south."

Kichinskoi frowned angrily.

"Tales—tales. My agents have provided against a revolt. Come now, my dear sir, you would be the—ah, *avant-coureur* upon the steppe that is still a blank space to us. Your name will be known by this map. Will you undertake it?"

He had spoken shrewdly.

"Your terms?" demanded Billings.

"Ah—four rubles a day while you are on your journey. Two hundred rubles when the map is approved by me."

"Four rubles—to hire horses and caravaneer's supplies?" Billings flushed.

"My dear captain! You have your own horse; and your outfit—planisphere, compass, and spirit level—is coming up the Volga under a Cossack *sotnik*. Besides, what will you do if you do not accept my offer?"

Indeed there would be nothing for Billings to do but return as best he could to Astrakan and walk the jetties. Kichinskoi had heard that the adventurer was penniless and so the *pristof* offered less than he had been instructed to pay for the making of the map. It is the way of the world's officials to drive a hard bargain with him whose purse is empty. Billings had reason to know this.

Some years before he had commanded a Russian sloop that made the voyage from St. Petersburg north along the White Sea, and thence along the edge of what was then called "The Frozen Ocean" to the mouths of the Yenesei, to establish a trading route for furs with the Mongol-Tatar tribes of the Arctic Circle.

The Russians bought, at very low prices, a huge amount of furs annually from the Tatar tribes—"sea otters," sables, ermine, black and red foxes. Billings knew that a large portion of the great fur trade passed through Zaritzan—the Torguts fetching the skins from the interior—and a goodly interest of the profits must stick to the fingers of Kichinskoi.

"I should return to Astrakan as soon as my luggage arrives," he responded thoughtfully. "And I should write to the ministry suggesting—as I have already done, you know—that the fur trade could be handled more cheaply through Orenburg or Astrakan than through Zaritzan. More cheaply, that is, where the officials are honest."

Again Father Obé looked troubled, but Kichinskoi managed to smile agreeably.

"On my oath, my dear fellow, I had forgotten your former services. But by the ashes of Sodom, the Empress must have her map. What are your terms?"

"Six rubles a day for the expenses of a small caravan. Five hundred rubles paid to me in advance. As much more when the map is delivered to you at Zaritzan. Also, your written promise that you will approve the chart. I want no retraction when the work is in your hands. It will be good, on the word of Minard Billings."

Kichinskoi inspected the well-kept fingers of a plump hand. His smile hid a sudden hatred for the adventurer. No one had dared to outface the *pristof* in that manner since he had come to Zaritzan. Billings, in reality, had no intention of writing to the ministry. But his shot had gone home.

"Oh, agreed, by all means," purred Kichinskoi. "—— my soul, should gentlemen quarrel over pennies? I will make up the sum out of my own pocket."

Even as he spoke he was planning to force harsher terms on the mapmaker. (Inasmuch as it was learned afterward that Kichinskoi had been furnished with sufficient funds to outfit Billings and pay him two thousand rubles to boot, it was literally true that what he surrendered to the mapmaker came out of his own pocket.)

Just then a house serf entered and informed the commissioner that his *matushna*—his lady—wished to see him. With a bow he excused himself and left Billings alone with the priest.

"That devil," remarked the maker of maps, "no, not Kichinskoi but the one we were talking about, across the river—you have seen him, Father Obé?"

The priest glanced involuntarily toward the door that had just closed. He had seen monks who refused to sanction the acts of Russian officials tortured in the prisons of Moscow. Even the Metropolitan of Moscow had been whipped by order of Catherine, herself a profligate woman. So he did not want to say anything that would interfere with the plans of the *pristof*.

"No," he responded. All at once a kind of flame came into his weak eyes. "But I have heard the talk of the heathen across the river. It is their high priest who is the archfiend. He has the face of an animal and is as tall as a tree. Our soldiers say he calls them, from the steppe. The *pristof*, Captain Billings, would save the souls of the heathen. We are sending the sons of the Tatars to our *kaleka*, our colleges, to instruct them in Christian knowledge."

"Do the sons stay in the *kaleka*?"

"You have the gift of foreknowledge. Nay, even today we heard that Alashan, the young son of the Torgut Khan, had escaped from Astrakan. A detachment of Cossacks pursued him in vain as far as Zaritzan."

Billings rose, having found out from the priest two things he wanted to know. The Tatars would be hostile to anyone attempting to chart their steppe on behalf of the Russian government. And the youth he had rescued on the post road was in all probability Alashan.

All at once he noticed that Father Obé was gasping and pointing at him. Following the direction of the trembling finger, Billings looked down. In place of his plain leather belt, he found that he was wearing beneath the overcoat a girdle of soft, red leather. Where the coat was parted he could see the clasp, a head of a wolf shaped in black iron.

"The sign of the fiend from over the river!" cried Father Obé.

In the dining-hall, to which the *pristof* ushered the mapmaker upon his return, the sight of Billings's belt produced instant silence. Dancers, Cossacks and women who had been flinging themselves about until the sweat flew from their faces and their hair came down—these stopped to stare and cross themselves.

Elegantly dressed under-officials attached to Kichinskoi's staff drew closer to inspect the emblem on the clasp; uncouth-looking Cossack captains drew back with scowls.

Captain Billings was sensitive, and was acutely conscious of the belt. He could not discard it—he had no other means of holding up his breeches.

Whispers came to his ears.

"The stranger has held commerce with those across the river."

"He had been tempted by the archfiend."

"No, a witch ran off with his horse and left him astraddle of the strap. I know that for a fact."

A giant of a man, bearded to the eyes although the front portion of his head was bald, joined Billings by the stove where the captain was warming his boots. As Kichinskoi had made no mention of meat and drink, the adventurer did not choose to remind the company that he was hungry. To eat in such a crowd was distasteful to him.

"To purgatory with Satan," growled the newcomer. Billings recognized the voice of the singer. "I am the *starshim*, Mitrassof, Colonel of the Volga Cossacks, and by the Heavens I know the different handiwork of witches and vampires. Vampires climb up behind horsemen. First they stupefy the traveler with a poisonous breath, then they suck the man's blood until he is half-drained and goes about for the rest of his life like an idiot or a cripple.

"A vampire takes the form of a child," nodded the *starshim*. "Always. Wasn't this one like a boy or girl, captain?"

"A stripling, and a rapscallion at that."

"Of course." Mitrassof pointed to the slit in the leg of Billings's trouser. "*Ai-a*, brother, you had it there. Don't you feel faint?"

"Somewhat—yes, devilishly faint."

There was no doubt about that, Billings having gone hungry since dawn.

"Well, that settles it. Within a week your limbs will begin to shrivel. Too bad, too bad. You should have dismounted at once and stuck your dagger in the ground and made the sign of the cross three times. A vampire can't stand that. He would have run down the dagger and into the ground."

"I have a better trick than that," spoke up another. "When a little girl vampire out on the Tatar steppe tried to seize my leg, I cut off her head with my saber—pouf, like that! Then when I reined in and rode back to see if she had changed into an animal, the body was gone. It was night, a moon like this, and I heard an old woman wailing in the thicket."

"True, true," nodded Mitrassof. "Vampires are more daring than witches, every time."

Kichinskoi's thin lips wore a skeptical smile. He was sitting on a couch fitted with a silk cover. Beside him was a plump German woman, his mistress. She wore an enormous round crinoline in the new fashion and made great play with a fan.

The woman with her airs contrasted grotesquely with the bare beams of hewn pine and the tiled stove. Kichinskoi sprawled at ease, receiving compliments from his entourage as a prince might.

Mitrassof's explanation had cleared the air for Billings. He was no longer bothered, and a hum of voices rose, drowning out the notes of a balalaika strumming somewhere in the shadows. Suddenly talk and music ceased.

A young lieutenant of Polish dragoons had entered, saluted Mitrassof, and come to a stand before the *pristof*. Billings noticed that the nerves of the assembly seemed not of the best and that everyone listened to hear what the newcomer had to say.

He had been out with a patrol across the river. He had to report that the Torgut chieftains were in council, and preparations were under way among the yurts for a movement of some kind. Cattle were being herded.

"Cattle?" Kichinskoi's brows went up.

"You come to me with a tale that children are herding Tatar cattle? What rot!"

The Pole flushed. He was a youngster in gallant attire in damask surtout and gilt spars, and obviously had thought he had done something well worthwhile.

"But it's at night, excellency. And the fires are going in all the family tents."

"Fires? You'll be assuring me next that the savages are eating breakfast."

"They are, excellency."

Kichinskoi snorted: the woman beside him hid her laugh behind a fan; the under-officials smirked in harmony. When the *pristof* set the tune it was up to them to dance attendance. Mitrassof alone became moody at the tidings of the Pole.

"But, excellency! That is no tale. Tatar outlaws have unsheathed the sword on the Volga. A band of them attacked and slew a Cossack *sotnik* approaching Zaritzan on the ice with a sled from Astrakan."

"Your mother blessed you with little sense, lieutenant. Come! A few robbers plunder a sled—you see a rising."

A crash startled the listeners. Mitrassof had flung upon the floor the glass of brandy he was holding. His beard was bristling.

"My men slain—by Torguts! Hey, there shall be an answer for that. I scent treachery." His scowling glance swept the room and fell upon Billings. "My soldiers were convoying your instruments and luggage."

"Then, sir, they were a cursed poor convoy."

Mishap upon mishap had fallen Billings's way in the last few hours. Except the clothes he stood in and his weapon, he was now stripped of the last of his worldly possessions. Now Captain Billings was no believer in that faithless jade, Fortune. Scratch bad luck, he would say, and you find somebody's ill-will. Somebody had planned to steal his belongings.

"You say that—you!" Mitrassof's temper flared. "You talked with one of the spawn of Satan, and gave up to him your horse so that he could escape us. Eh, I can see under a haystack like this one. A Tatar rider leaves you, gives you his tribal emblem to wear."

Now the boy, Alashan, or whoever he was, must have exchanged belts with the mapmaker in the darkness. Certainly Billings had known nothing of it. The death of his men had driven all metaphysical fancies from the Cossack's head, inflamed by drink.

"You have sold yourself to the Torguts, and you came here to spy upon the fortress."

Good-natured ordinarily, Mitrassof's savage, moody soul was violent when his feelings were roused. Billings could have answered that it was absurd that he should arrange for his baggage to be stolen, or to permit his own horse to be made away with voluntarily.

Instead he held his peace and glanced at Kichinskoi. It was up to the *pristof* to clear him. But Kichinskoi was frowning, his thin lips pinched together. He was not displeased at the quarrel, because the Cossack's words showed him how he might possibly humble Billings.

Suddenly the German woman, who had been whispering to the Pole, spoke up shrilly.

"A mounted patrol pursued the robbers, excellency, and the sergeant in command reports that the leader of the Tatars was riding the horse of Captain Billings. He saw the captain riding in Astrakan."

"Ha!" Suspicion leaped into Kichinskoi's gray eyes. He pondered the possibility that Billings could have been sent by Beketoff to stir up the Tatars to revolt. The suspicion died, to be replaced by a shrewd gleam of satisfaction.

Kichinskoi knew that he had sent for Billings himself, that both the captain and Beketoff were above such conspiracy; but he saw a way to gain a fresh hold, he thought, on the mapmaker.

Meanwhile Mitrassof was reasoning along other lines, or rather had ceased to reason at all.

"If you were a man and not a runt, I'd teach you a thing or two with a sword," he growled.

Instantly Billings's blade was out. Twice the flat of the heavy campaign rapier slapped the Cossack's red cheeks. It stung Mitrassof to blind fury.

"To one of us, death!" he gritted, sweeping out his saber.

There was no thought of seconds, no bothering about the code of duelists. The Pole, it is true, tried to herd the fluttering women out of the room. Kichinskoi, seeing that his sofa was well out of the combatants' way, leaned forward curiously. Hitherto no one in Zaritzan had cared to match strokes with the giant *ataman*. He might still have prevented the fight, but made no move to do so.

Billings was smiling, his teeth shining under the yellow mustache. A swift, sliding thrust severed a corner of the Cossack's black beard. It was a clever trick, appreciated by the watching soldiers; and it brought a wild glare into the widened eyes of the big Cossack.

"*Akh!*" he cried. "To one of us death!"

His saber flashed and fell, until the clashing of the two blades was merged into a single ringing grind. Billings stood close in, giving no ground, keeping the weapons engaged close to the hilts where the sweep of the saber was less potent.

Mitrassof was a slow thinker when his muscles were not in play, but he moved with alert swiftness. Springing back, he gained space for a full stroke and smote down at his adversary's head. The blow would have broken the other's blade like a wooden lath. Billings, however, was not there when the saber fell.

Consternation began to grow in the faces of the watching officers. Kichinskoi sprang up with a muttered command to stop the fight. The young Pole shook his head. It was too late.

But in the eyes of the woman on the sofa was a morbid eagerness. She was watching for the moment when one of the swordsmen would be pierced through or slashed into oblivion. So blinding was the play of weapons, she feared that she might miss the instant of the blow.

"Stop them!" cried Kichinskoi. "Or they are both lost!"

Both men were necessary to his plans.

Mitrassof was cutting at the smaller man's ribs. No longer could Billings step aside. The rapier darted at the Cossack's beard, and rasped the skin from the jaw bone.

Stung anew, the giant stepped forward, slashing without intermission. He walked across the room, literally bearing Billings down before him. Yet as he came forward the rapier caught once in his arm and again in his ribs.

Feeling his wounds, Mitrassof grinned, the blood running into his teeth and choking him. Billings halted, crouching, his sword upright; and for a second the two blades were locked. The faces of the two were not a yard apart.

A black arm caught at the chest of each man, and the priest Obé thrust himself between them, straining to push them apart.

"In the name of God, forbear!" he cried, keeping his grip with difficulty.

Billings wrenched free and stood ready to engage again.

The *pristof* hurried up.

"Quarreling in my presence," he exclaimed. "Colonel, captain, this won't do at all. Gentlemen—"

The panting Mitrassof paid as much attention to Kichinskoi as to a wandering fly. But the pale face of the priest kept in front of him.

"This is the command of the Church! Do you hear, Cossack?" There was the ring of authority in his thin voice.

Mitrassof became calmer and sheathed his saber. Scowling at Billings, he stared obediently at the priest, as a dog at its master.

"I will remember this in your favor," Kichinskoi was moved to say to Father Obé.

The priest seemed flurried by the condescension, blinked, and became once more his unobtrusive self.

When the gathering left the room, Billings noticed that Mitrassof remained behind. He returned to the door and saw that the Cossack was busied rubbing a mixture of gunpowder and earth on the cuts in his jaw and arm, moving stiffly to favor the side where his ribs had been slashed.

Also he had foraged for himself some cold mutton and bread. This he began to munch while he sought for a brandy bottle that still had some honor in it.

Noticing the adventurer, his beard bristled in a grin.

"Hey, that was a good bout," he observed, "you are the devil of a fellow to tackle."

Billings bowed stiffly, but yearned toward the cold meat. Suspecting this, Mitrassof poked the platter toward his guest. The duel had restored his good humor and cleared his head, and he ignored his hurts. They found brandy, and Billings relaxed.

"You're a swordsman yourself, colonel."

Lifting his glass, Mitrassof bowed.

"Not at all," he muttered politely. "You are my master with the blade. Aye, you would have let out my life before I could have cut you down. Health to you."

"Health to you!"

With a nod Billings responded to the toast and fell to attacking the mutton. He began to like Mitrassof. They talked long over the bottle, and the Cossack's song was not lacking. When dawn outlined the windows, the colonel conducted the visitor to his room.

Mitrassof insisted that Billings occupy his pallet. The big *ataman* went over to some skins in a corner, flung himself down like a dog, and was snoring almost at once.

Chapter II
Kichinskoi Writes

When smoke is in the sky, somebody has made a torch.
—Cossack proverb

The next day rumors sprang up from no one knows where along the Volga. It was whispered among the huts of the fishermen that the Devil himself had been seen walking along the opposite bank, as high as the stars and with eyes that flamed like two pine torches. And after his passing a star had been seen to glow with uncanny fire in the cast.

It was observed that the Cossacks in Mitrassof's command were moodier than usual, which might have meant either aching heads after a night of drinking, or a sense of foreboding in these half-wild men, who were blood kin to the Tatars.

Heedless of rumors or portents, the Great Commissioner Kichinskoi sat at his table penning a report to the Russian ministry. In it he gave the lie to his rival Beketoff's warnings concerning a revolt of the Tatars, and suggested that the eldest son of each family of *noyons*—the Torgut nobles—be taken hostage and brought up in Russian cities, "For these savages do seem to cherish great affection for the oldest boy in the family."

With even more zeal he composed a memorandum to the treasurer of the Empress, explaining that he had found a man who would undertake the perilous task of making a survey for a trade route across the steppe as far east within the countries of the tribes as Lake Balkash. A stranger would not be looked upon with suspicion by the Tatars, who were jealous of their rights and seemed to dislike all Russians, being under the influence of an arch-witch from Tibet, who was most likely a harmless mummer.

Kichinskoi then sent a servant to find Billings and bring him to the office. The man returned, declaring that the English captain had asked for a horse and gone off in the direction of the river. Billings had called back that he was about to look for the miscreant who had taken his luggage and horse.

"Ashes of Sodom!" muttered the *pristof*. "The fellow must love trouble." He thought for a moment. "Bring the *batko* to me."

When Father Obé entered, Kichinskoi bade him close the door and stand against it.

"As soon as Captain Billings returns, take him my compliments and this private word:

"Complaints have reached me that he is holding unauthorized intercourse with the Tatars, especially with one who is called Alashan, the son of the Khan. Alashan is an escaped hostage of the Russian government and the Holy Church. I have proof that Captain Billings aided Alashan to escape our hands. Captain Billings is also charged by worthy persons with possessing a talisman belonging to the pagan sorcerer of the Torguts. He is guilty of a brawl with the worthy *ataman*; in fact, even I cannot prevent his being taken to Moscow and tried unless he pledges himself to a course of conduct more becoming an employee of the Russian government. Hm—"

He considered.

"Tell him furthermore that I have proof under my hand that he is attempting to incite the Tatars to rebellion. Hint that Governor Beketoff, his patron, is in disfavor at court, whereas my star is rising. In short, *batko*, point out that if he chooses to escape jail he must show his zeal for the Empress by serving me, in the matter of the map, without any pay—no, without any money other than for his expenses."

Smilingly, Kichinskoi reflected that Billings would know better than to drive a bargain with him again.

Without a word Father Obé rose and left, after murmuring his assent. Whatever thoughts came into his narrow, secretive mind, he kept to himself. After all, there was the belt.

The message was never delivered.

Well pleased with the day's beginning, the *pristof* was even more delighted when his servant announced the arrival of a delegation from the Torguts.

"Ha—that does not smell of rebellion, on my word. Well, bring my sable coat, and the sword of ceremony. Is that cursed Cossack *ataman* sober enough to walk without staggering?"

"I think not, excellency."

"Well, order him to become so. Rub snow on his bald pate and scrape some of the filth off him. Hurry. See that the Tatars keep outside the fortress. By the way, who are they?"

"A hideous creature, your highness, and Alashan, the son of the Khan."

"I expected his father. Hm. Alashan!" Kichinskoi looked pleased. "Let me see, the seven infantry regiments of General Traubenberg, and several batteries of cannon—important things, those—are within four days' march, to the west. Then instruct the *ataman* to turn out the guard, with fixed bayonets. Mind the bayonets!"

Humming to himself, Kichinskoi summoned his valet and was attired in an officer's uniform, freshly polished boots, dress sword, and jeweled decoration at his throat. He took snuff liberally from the imported box until he saw Mitrassof walking stiffly across the parade ground toward him at the head of a squad of Cossacks.

Although a little pale, the big man was none the worse, apparently, for blood-letting or brandy. Kichinskoi allowed him to lead the way until they passed through the gate and saw the Torguts. Then the *pristof* stepped out in front.

The Torguts were unarmed.

"What is this?"

Kichinskoi pursed his lips and signed to the interpreter.

An old man stepped forward from the small group of Tatars and lifted his hand to his bronze, bossed helmet in greeting. Short, bowed legs supported a powerful body clad in a sleeveless fur tunic. His right arm moved with a rhythm of rippling muscles.

"I am Norbo, Master of the Horse Herds of the Torguts."

Kichinskoi was looking at the slender youth beside Norbo. Alashan was brave in finery of green nankeen and red silk, of furred *khalat* and fur-tipped cap. His fine, dark eyes were alight with some kind of inward merriment.

"Great Commissioner," went on Norbo bluntly, "I have been sent to ask whether it is true that the Empress has ordered our sons to be taken away to Russia. I await your word."

To gain time to think, Kichinskoi pretended displeasure and reminded Norbo that he should have lifted his hat at mention of the Empress.

According to Mongol custom, it was an unpardonable rudeness to bare the head during a conference of state. Norbo noticed that Kichinskoi's hat remained in place.

"Nay, I shall not do it," he retorted. "The Torguts are free-born. The Khan is no vassal of the Empress."

"The Khan! Your Khan will do what I tell him to. He is no more than a chained bear."

Norbo lowered his eyes and was silent, while Alashan smiled faintly, saying, "What is your word concerning the sons of the Torguts?"

Kichinskoi hesitated, for he had received as yet no authority from the ministry to act as he had suggested. He was thinking quickly, and thinking of a new decoration, prestige, influence at Court—if he guessed aright the secret plans of the great Catherine.

He made his decision and with it cast into the scales the lives of two hundred thousand human beings.

"This is my answer," he said, and ordered the Cossacks to seize Alashan. Mitrassof grew red and muttered that envoys were privileged.

"Bah!" whispered the *pristof*. "It is only an escaped student. I did not invite him here. Are you going to obey my order?"

"Am I going to obey an order?"

The colonel pulled at his mustache and looked up at the sky thoughtfully.

"When my Empress, the great Catherine, says '*Ataman*, there is work to be done, or a good blow to be struck'; why, then I tell my children and lead them, and, God willing, they die. That is right and as it should be. When the *batko* says to me, 'Colonel, that son of a pig, the Sultan, has been tearing down Christian churches again, or roasting worthy priests of the steppe,' I get my horse, turn out my barracks and polish up the frontier a bit. My turn will come. That is as it should be.

"But when you say to these Tatar chiefs, 'Come and hold council with me,' and then order them to be trussed up and carted off, that is a different thing entirely. Give that old bull yonder, who calls himself Norbo, a sword and, if it is your wish, I will stretch him out on the ground for you in a twinkling, although I am somewhat stiff this morning. But if you want to pluck the young envoy I'll send a man to call your Polish guards to do it. That's all I will do, by the holy Faith!"

Kichinskoi looked black, but there was no help for it. He fancied that the Tatar who had named himself the son of the Khan was laughing at him. No sooner had the Polish dragoons come up and secured Alashan than Mitrassof gave an order to his men and marched off.

To the surprise of all the Russians, Norbo and the other Tatars offered no resistance as Alashan was hurried to the gate.

"The son of the Khan is the first," explained Kichinskoi to Norbo. "Later the eldest boy of each family must come to us—"

Here, to the *pristof*'s chagrin, Norbo, followed by the other Torguts, turned on his heel and walked off without any leave taking. The Russian's last words had given him the answer he sought to his question, and, being a Tatar, he did not see the need of more words. So Kichinskoi was left without an audience, although he never felt more like making a speech in his life.

He was conscious of a shrewd exultation, a conviction of his own power. Had not the Tatars accepted his mandate without resistance? He felt sure that he, Kichinskoi, was playing at the regal game of empire and deciding the destiny of a people. And so he was.

It was near to the hour of sunset when Billings rode a steaming horse into the river gate of the fort and asked for Mitrassof. Learning that the *ataman* was out with the mounted patrols that kept watch on the western bank of the Volga, he turned over his pony to a serf from the stables and began to walk toward the commissioner's house.

He was thoughtful, because he had had his first glimpse of the Tatar steppe, the wide plain that began at the tip of the Caspian where it was below the level of the sea, and extended to the mountains that separated China from the western world. From dawn until dark he had seen not so much as a hillock in the white expanse of snow save where the native villages huddled in the hollows protected from the wind by clumps of willows or oaks.

Billings knew that like all desert areas the plain, now ice-coated, would be blazing hot in the summer months. Yet it was fertile, and the fine grazing was much coveted by the Torguts, who seemed indifferent to weather.

Reflecting upon the actions of Alashan, he saw now that the boy must have had urgent need of a horse the night before. And he believed—correctly, as he afterward discovered—that the exchange of belts formed part of the Tatar ritual of *anda*. He was rather skeptical, however, about the tie of brotherhood that the boy had knit between them.

As he passed the door of the church, Father Obé came out, locking it after him. Shivering, even in his heavy cassock, the priest hurried to join Billings.

"I tried to find the colonel, Father Obé," observed Billings seriously, "but I think you—as Kichinskoi's adviser—should hear my word. I have just come in from the plain. It's true as Holy Writ that the native clans are gathering. The cattle herds are being driven in from the villages to the center of each *urdus*—clan. Supplies are being packed into wagons. Yet I saw no signs of mobilization, nor any cannon.

"It is curious," he added.

"Some days ago," observed the priest, "one of my converts, a fisherman, told me that the anti-Christ across the river—the witch or fiend that wears a mask—had called together the Torgut council and urged the Khan to take up the torch and sword and lay to waste all the Russian hamlets from Astrakan to Orenburg."

"Hum. And the Khan?"

"Refused. But there is evil stirring, and you do wrong to wear the sign of the fiend."

Billings fingered the leather girdle and smiled.

"If someone will be so good as to give me another belt—" He shrugged. "I'm beginning to think the road across the steppe will not be without thorns. You wished to speak to me, Father Obé?"

"I have been told—" the priest began.

"What is that?"

The moon was coming up over the walls of Zaritzan. It outlined before the Englishman the shape of a prisoner in the stocks. A big Cossack was bent nearly double, his head and arms thrust through the holes of a heavy plank.

The lower part of the man's face was stained black and glistened in the faint radiance from the sky. Billings saw that he was in his shirt, his heavy *svitza*, or woolen coat, thrown on the ground under his nose. The fellow was shivering, his eyes fixed so that Billings suspected the lids were frozen.

"A sentry," the priest explained, "who let a prisoner slip through his fingers last night, when you, captain, reached Zaritzan. This afternoon his excellency the *pristof* condemned him to have his nostrils torn and to be locked in the stocks for twelve hours without a coat."

Bending closer, Billings recognized the Cossack who had first greeted him at the gate of the fort. Even if he had retained vitality enough to speak, the frozen blood that coated his lips would have rendered the soldier dumb.

Billings would have walked on, when his own words, spoken that last night came into his mind—

"You would leave a Christian to the cold and wolves."

Billings never wasted time in cogitation. He caught up the man's heavy sheepskin coat, flung it over his back, tying the sleeves under his throat and buttoning the lower part around his hips. The stiffened eyes turned toward him gratefully.

"Tell the commissioner about this, if you want to," he growled to Father Obé. "If he objects, present my compliments, and remind him that I do not happen to be his vassal."

Father Obé glanced at the mapmaker curiously.

"I shall say nothing, my son. The *pristof* gave me a message for you. You are a brave man, even if you hold commerce with the pagans. I—I shall let him deliver his message himself."

But Billings did not see Kichinskoi at dinner. Going from there to his room, or rather the one he shared with Mitrassof—for the castle was very crowded—he was surprised to find a sentry with a musket at the door. The door, too, was bolted on the outside. When Billings shot back the bolt and would have entered, the soldier motioned him back.

"I come from Colonel Mitrassof," Billings said, thinking the man was some guard of Mitrassof's.

Indeed, at the name of the officer the soldier fell back respectfully.

Yawning, Billings was preparing to take off his shoes and coat and throw himself on the cot, when he saw that it was already occupied. Alashan was surveying him with considerable amusement.

"Bless my eyes and blood!"

Captain Minard Billings seated himself on the three-legged stool by the bed. He sat very straight, muscular arms crossed, two fingers tugging at the end of a well-waxed mustache.

"You are the infernal scoundrel I've been looking for all day!"

"Where?"

"Across the river." This, Billings noticed, caused the boy to start. "Where is my pony?"

"Soon you will bestride her."

"Hum. And my luggage, pray? I have learned that the youth who rode my mare attacked the Cossacks who were with the sledge, and that Tatars shed Christian blood." The gray-green eyes of the mapmaker grew cold. "Look here my *bopobka*, my little elf, I have had my fill of mummery. Tell a plain tale, now, and no tricks."

"Nay, Captain Beel-ing—" Alashan could never compass the other's name—"I did not attack the Cossack guard."

The brown eyes of the youth were wide and clear. His small mouth was gentle and quick to speak. Scanning the boy's olive countenance, Billings wondered if there were not Persian blood in him. At any rate it seemed that Alashan, although Tatars were usually blunt and ill-schooled at deceit, could lie like a Baskir or Persian.

"My lord brother—" Alashan had read his thoughts—"you are my *anda*. My life for yours, and one pledge for the two of us. The tie was made fast when our girdles were exchanged. My tongue speaks no false words to you. Some things I may not tell as yet. Do but have patience."

"Patience!" Billings folded his arms. "Well, my prince brother, by our *anda*, let me know this one thing. What manner of a plot are you hatching against the *pristof*, out on the steppe?"

A change came over the boy's expressive face.

"Soon the Great Commissioner will be no more than a chained bear. But he himself has forged the chains."

"Riddles! What are you doing here?"

"I am a prisoner, and I wait."

"For what?"

"A scourging."

Alashan related how he had been seized and put into his present quarters—the other rooms of the house being occupied by clerks, officers, and friends of Kichinskoi. Billings reasoned that the *pristof* wished Alashan kept as near him as possible—a valuable hostage for the good conduct of Ubaka Khan. Also, Kichinskoi could report his capture of Alashan, by whatever means, after Beketoff's carelessness had permitted the escape of the boy from Astrakan.

"He has said he will lash me," went on the Torgut, the blood darkening his cheeks, "as a lesson to the Tatars who attacked the Cossacks. Nay, they were but boys; and the soldiers fired the first shot. So the Great Commissioner would lash the son of Ubaka, who is the grandson of Ayuka, who was Master of the Golden Horde, child of the royal race of Genghis Khan. *Kai*—it is so. But the knout will not be laid upon my back."

"I am not sure you do not deserve it, Alashan."

"Nay, you will protect me."

"I?"

"Aye, they will come when the night is half gone. It is nearly time."

"Indeed, I will do no such thing."

Billings shook his head decisively. Whether merited or not, the whipping of the boy was beyond his power to prevent.

"You will do it. Until dawn you will protect me."

Alashan laughed merrily, and Billings was surprised because he had never known a Tatar to laugh.

"And at dawn I will ride, free, from this house and these walls—aye, though there be a great, stupid yak with a musket outside your door, and three thousand like him within call. And you will go with me, as my lord brother should."

A sound of iron-heeled boots in the passage stiffened the boy's lips. All in a moment his eyes widened, and he grew whitish around the mouth.

"They are coming with the knout, Captain Beel-ing. Hurry, lock the door."

On the doors of the *pristof*'s house there were bolts on both sides for locking in prisoners or bolting out thieves as circumstances might require. Billings had already noticed this, but made no move to obey.

"You will not let them use the knout on me," persisted the stripling. "Look—"

For the first time Alashan removed the large velvet cap trimmed with fur. A flood of glossy, black hair descended upon the Tatar's slim shoulders and slipped down to the bed itself.

The olive cheeks that had been pale grew softly red. Billings knew that most of the Tatars wore a kind of long mane of hair; but this mass of curling locks belonged to a woman, and the face was that of a woman.

A rap resounded on the door. Billings glanced at the rusty bolt, and thrust out his boot against the lower edge of the door.

"Excellency," he heard a soldier say, "we will take away the Tatar prisoner, if you will have the kindness to open to us."

At the same time he felt that the heavy door was tried from without. It did not give.

"In a moment," he called over his shoulder. He looked at Alashan.

"Captain Beel-ing, I am not the son of the Khan. Do you think the Horde would give the son of a chief to another king? Nay, I am only a girl."

As she spoke she tore off the voluminous *khalat* that had been about her shoulders.

"In the name of mercy, you must believe me. My name is Nadesha, and when the order came for Alashan to go to Astrakan, I said I would go instead. I have Persian blood in me, I know the ways of the Russians, and I had wit enough to slip out of any noose they made for me."

"Agreed to that," whispered Billings. "Are you the daughter of the Khan Ubaka?"

"Nay, I am Nadesha, the child of Norbo, who is Master of the Herds. Word came to me to escape from Astrakan. God was kind. You aided me. So I made you my *anda*. Today I came with Norbo to see if that old buzzard Kichinskoi was really ordered to make slaves of the Torgut youths. It is so. You do not think I am a girl?"

Hereupon Nadesha, who had unbuttoned the cotton jacket she had worn under the *khalat*, began to jerk at the neck of her shirt with anxious fingers.

"You must not give me to the soldiers, who would strip me and take me to Kichinskoi when they find I am not Alashan—"

"Hold on! Enough!" Billings's ruddy cheeks grew redder. "I believe you."

"Excellency," came the summons from without. "Open the door and we will not trouble you more."

Billings searched the room with his glance. A collection of weapons belonging to Mitrassof had been removed when Nadesha was installed;

there was left only the bed, the stool, an ikon on the wall, and a miscellaneous mass of fine though soiled garments piled by the skins.

At his whispered order, Nadesha ran through this array of velvet and satin clothes, but no woman's attire was to be seen among the spoil of Mitrassof's forays. She looked at Billings, who frowned.

It was hard enough for him to be suspected of conspiring with the Tatars, without having to deal with a fair young witch. Witch! He could see Kichinskoi and Father Obé burning her, because her presence here certainly savored of magic, and it was more palatable for the official to claim that he had been bewitched than befooled.

Nadesha took matters into her own hands swiftly enough. She thrust her *khalat* into the pile of garments, took off her boots—too large for her bare feet—and shook down the masses of glossy hair over her shoulders. Then she kicked out the candle.

"Come in," she called pleasantly, no longer simulating the deeper voice of a boy.

A Cossack sergeant pushed open the door—Billings withdrawing his foot barely in time—and entered, followed by a soldier bearing a stained and smoky lanthorn.

"Come, Alashan," he growled, holding the dim light high in order to peer at the two occupants of the room.

Nadesha laughed and cracked her fingers. The lanthorn was moved over to her while the soldiers inspected her; then it was thrust about the bare room, finally coming to rest over Billings, who had not stirred.

"Where is the son of the Khan?" demanded the sergeant.

Receiving no answer, he looked under the bed upon which Nadesha kneeled, hugging her toes. Palpably, the room did not contain anyone else.

The sergeant went out. Voices ensued. The sentry came in, glanced around, peered at Nadesha, searched under the bed, and finally pushed his bayonet into the pile of clothes in the corner. He even lifted the skins on the floor.

Then he faced the sergeant and scratched his hair.

"I saw Alashan go in, but he is not here now."

The Cossack inspected the hole of a window.

"Large enough for a weasel," he muttered. He saluted Billings. "Excellency, have you seen Alashan, the Torgut?"

"No."

"When did this maiden come in?"

"She was here when I arrived."

This brought more bewilderment to the sheepish sentry. No one, he said, had been in the room when they put Alashan there, not six hours ago. Nor had anyone except Captain Billings entered since.

Very angry was the sergeant.

"If Alashan has escaped again, you'll be eaten by the crows, and I'll have my nostrils torn."

More than a little amused, Billings listened to the debate going on between the two. The *pristof* should be summoned. No, the *pristof* was asleep and he would consign to the strappado anyone who awakened him now. Well, then the officer in command of the watch. A fine thing, that—to put their heads in the noose before it was tied. Colonel Mitrassof? He was out with the patrols.

"Sergeant," observed Billings, leaning back against the wall with folded arms, "if you have finished with your questions, you might find time to reflect that an officer may sometimes desire to talk to a pretty woman undisturbed."

"Yes, excellency." The man drew himself up and saluted.

"Undisturbed."

"Pardon."

The Cossack prepared to leave, glaring about him suspiciously.

"Sergeant, for your own sake, make your report to Colonel Mitrassof and no other."

Billings listened and was sure the two remained outside his door. Although bewildered, the soldiers were not minded to release the prisoners—for Billings would now be watched. He was committed now to getting Nadesha out of this mess. Lighting the candle, he saw that the Tatar girl was curling up in the blankets, preparing to go to sleep.

"Not a bad idea," thought Billings, and sought the skins on the floor.

Although he dozed, one ear was conscious of the coming and going of feet outside the door. He had fastened the inner bolt. Presently the feet began to run through the passage; he was aware of shouts, the hoofbeats of a horse outside the house. A touch on his arm wakened him.

Nadesha had put on the *khalat* but without binding up her hair. He could see her only vaguely by the glow of sunrise through the window.

"Come, brother," she whispered.

Billings was alert at once, aroused by the tumult in the castle. Looking from the panes of mica in the window, he whistled softly.

Against the spreading crimson of sunrise in the east there rose numberless columns of smoke. The whole sky was full of these black pillars, so that the very dawn was the hue of blood. Listening to the outcry in the castle, he made out fragments: "The Tatars have risen . . . The world is burning up . . . Where are the Torguts? Their villages are burning."

Standing tip-toe beside him, Nadesha stared at the conflagration. She uttered a soft cry, of lament or joy, he did not know which. Tugging him after her, she drew back the bolt and pushed open the door.

The sentry faced her, dull with lack of sleep, his musket at the ready. Billings halted, but Nadesha knocked up the gun with a quick motion—she moved as swiftly as an animal—and drew from within her cloak a long pistol. Billings recognized it as his.

Thrusting the weapon into the soldier's beard, she backed him against the wall of the corridor.

"You little vixen!"

Billings caught at her, but she slipped away, running fleetly in her bare feet. The mapmaker dashed after her, leaving the sentry fingering his weapon and cursing, not daring to shoot for fear of hitting the officer.

Down the passageway they went, into an empty hall and through a door that gave upon a lighted chamber. This proved to be the office of Kichinskoi, and the *pristof* himself sat at the table.

He wore a purple dressing-gown, and his hair was tousled. He was alone. As Billings ran into the room, the door was swung shut behind him and, wheeling, he saw Nadesha standing against it, flushed with triumph, a pistol in each small fist.

With her bare feet planted wide, her tangled hair falling into her gleaming eyes, the girl was a veritable wildcat. Kichinskoi stared at her with surprised anger, until comprehension came to his alert mind.

"You are Alashan!"

"I am Nadesha, child of Norbo, Master of the Herds. Listen to my word, you, who would chain the Torguts like a bear—who would eat of the fat of the bear and wear his skin to keep you warm."

She gestured with a pistol, and Kichinskoi pressed back in his chair. Billings could see the *pristof*'s tongue moving spasmodically. Owing to the tumult in the castle, it would avail the man nothing to shout. Nor, by the discipline he enforced among those under his rule, was there a chance that anyone—except Mitrassof—would enter without permission.

Kichinskoi was cornered and he was helpless. Billings had an idea that in her present mood Nadesha would think nothing of pistoling them both.

"Blind!" the girl's cry went on. "You and your Empress would make slaves of the free-born. Fool! You did not see that we will not submit. Many there were who brought the truth for your hearing. You shut your ears. Now, have you seen the smoke in the sky?"

A nod from Kichinskoi, who was gathering his wits about him.

"The Torguts are burning their villages; the bear is throwing off its shackles. We are marching—now—to the east; we are riding to our homeland. The clan of the Torguts will go back to Lake Balkash and beyond to the river Ili, where you cannot follow. The Khan has chosen—yesterday after your word."

She cast a fleeting glance out of the window that was mellow with sunrise. Kichinskoi started.

"Impossible!" he muttered. "A year's journey, and—two hundred thousand souls." His eyes narrowed. "You would be attacked by your enemies, the Baskirs and the Black Kirghiz. Why, the snow—"

He almost laughed, feeling that the girl was deceiving him.

Nadesha smiled tauntingly.

"We have chosen, *pristof*. This is my word, from the council of the Torguts. If you send your soldiers to turn us back, there will be war, and a river of blood upon the snow from the Volga to Balkash. I have said it."

With the pistol still in her hand, she raised it to her forehead and then dropped it to her lips in mock salaam.

"I could slay you, my fine boar, but you are already dead. My lord Beketoff already is driving a racing sledge to St. Petersburg with a word for the ear of your Empress that will stretch you out under the snow."

Jumping up, Kichinskoi stared at her as if Nadesha had been truly a witch.

"You see, *pristof*," she said calmly, "I have learned a lot at your school." To Billings she added, "If you want your pistols, my little *anda*, come and get them."

With that she was gone through the door as swiftly as she had come. Billings guessed that the girl would not stay within the building. She must make for the stables and secure a horse—if she could—as her best chance of freedom, before Kichinskoi's men overtook her.

Knowing better than to try to pursue her, Billings ran out of the other door, through the dining-hall and the courtyard. Behind him Kichinskoi remained pale and rigid as if he had seen his death sentence written on the wall.

Billings found the gray light obscured by mists over the drill ground. Soldiers were running to stations, Cossacks who buckled belts and slid into overcoats as they ran. From the watch-tower a bugle blared. The men paid no heed to him, or to Nadesha.

As he had hoped, the captain sighted the long cloak and flying hair of the girl disappearing into the mist. She was looking back over her shoulder. Somewhat to his surprise, she was heading not toward the stables but to a gate through which horsemen were coming and going freely, men from the mounted patrols coming in and couriers going forth. The usual strict scrutiny was relaxed owing to the absence of both Mitrassof and Kichinskoi and the general disturbance caused by the conflagration.

In the shreds of mist Nadesha seemed like a floating wraith slipping over the snow. Just within the gate Billings sighted a large sleigh and recognized, by its gilded ornaments and pompons, that it was the one used by Kichinskoi himself.

Beside it the young Polish lieutenant sat his horse restlessly. Into the sleigh was climbing the plump woman who was Kichinskoi's mistress. Her maid, lugging bandboxes and shawls was trying to get in beside her. Not ten feet away stood the stocks, and from the frozen body of the imprisoned Cossack, two blind eyes stared at the tumult around the sleigh. The man had died in the night.

In response to Nadesha's call, three horsemen emerged from the dense shadows of the wall. They wore ragged sheepskin *svitzas* and nondescript black felt hats.

Billings, however, perceived that they were no peasants. He recognized the harsh features and immense shoulders of Norbo, Master of the Herds. Another was a youth of about Nadesha's age. The three evidently knew exactly what was expected of them.

Norbo spurred up to the Pole, who drew a pistol from a saddle holster, but not quickly enough to avoid a sweep of the club in Norbo's hand. The pistol was knocked into the snow, the Pole himself caught up, whirled from his mount, and flung to earth.

Meanwhile the other two had frightened off the two grooms with a flourish of bared sabers. Nadesha, as usual, had not been idle. Seizing the maid by the shoulders, the girl pulled her back, screaming like a wounded parrot. The bandboxes flew about, and the horses attached to the sleigh began to rear.

The German woman had risen, and the forward jerk of the sleigh tumbled her back. Nadesha wormed into the vehicle and fell to rolling the frightened fugitive out of it. Norbo rode up impatiently and put an end to this by leaning over and pulling the woman bodily out of rugs and sleigh. Nadesha screamed something up at the Tatar, who turned and looked at Billings.

The captain had come to a halt. One of the Tatars, the young boy, spurred toward him. Billings drew his sword.

"Alashan!" cried Nadesha, her voice shrill with fear.

Men were running toward them. The Pole, having rolled out from under the horses' feet, was shouting for aid.

The boy who had been called Alashan did not stop. He swung his saber slowly as he galloped. From the direction of the barracks came a ruddy flash and the roar of a musket.

Then Billings heard boots thudding in the snow behind him. He could not turn, for Alashan was almost on him. Something struck against the base of his neck, and a great crackling filled his ears. A red sea formed in front of his eyes. He felt a hand catch his arm; then all was darkness.

Above the roaring in his head persisted the shrill squawking of the fat woman who had been thrown in the snow.

Chapter III
Fight at Ukim Pass

> *Only for a moment can you say, "I am the slayer, he the slain." The shrill joy-cries of the women at your wedding change to lamentation at your death bed.*
>
> —Native proverb

In the year of the Tiger, by the Mongol calendar, Alashan was seventeen years of age. This was one year older than Nadesha. But the girl of Norbo, born of a Persian mother, grew swiftly to womanhood.

Alashan was still a boy, intent on sports and leader of a gang of Torgut rascals who tended the horse herds, racing the best of the beasts almost into the ground in their pastimes.

These other boys of the Torgut nobles were brawnier than Alashan.

True, he could ride with a fiery eagerness that won him races; yet in the goat *tamasha* he could not hold his own, although he rode until his lungs labored and his heart rose in his throat. The goat *tamasha*, in which each rider tries to capture and keep from the others a live goat, is a furious test of an hour or more during which clubs and cracked heads are often the lot of the contenders.

"You are worse than a hair on the eyeball," Nadesha had assured him spitefully after one defeat. "How do you ever expect to be a man and kill an enemy when you can't even keep a goat in your hand?"

Life, for the Tatar youths in the age when the great clans were still intact, was an ordeal. In the stag-hunts they had to follow the grown men, often from sunrise to sunrise, without eating and without pause except to rest the horses. The wild-swine hunts by torch and moonlight, where thickets coated the valleys, were less arduous but more hurtful. Many an overbold stripling had the calves of his leg ripped apart by angry tuskers, and some were hamstrung.

Alashan's body was more delicate, his eyes deeper than usual. He was much given to hanging around the councils of the older men, even listening for hours to the whisperings of the lama—the priest from Tibet—who was very willing to inculcate superstition and fear into the mind of the future Khan.

So it was from a two-fold fear that Ubaka, his father, had sent Nadesha in his place, disguised as a boy, to Astrakan. He was afraid the Russians might influence the "queer" mind of his son against him.

"Nadesha is more of a man than Alashan," he had said bitterly to Norbo, who, being too blunt to lie, said nothing.

The Khan was a broad man, less muscular than Norbo, more ponderous, with the strength of a bull. He was not clever, and care sat upon him heavily.

"Listen, Alashan," he had said to the boy, "to the words spoken by the All-Conquering, the mighty monarch, Genghis, who when he christened our clan, spoke in this fashion: 'You shall be called the Giants;* from birth your sons will have a sword in their hands, and they will die so; there will be no peace for you that is not won by blood and suffering. In the stars it is written you will be free men, until the hour of your passing; you are the Giants."

**Torguts.*

It was the longest speech Alashan had ever heard his silent father make. It lingered in his mind like the after-note of a bell.

"When you have proved yourself a man in the face of your enemies," the Khan added, "then you shall ride on my left side. Not now."

Often while he sat by the hearth in the wooden palace of his father on the steppe near Zaritzan, Alashan thought upon these words. So far, he reasoned, the words of Genghis Khan had proved true. The Torguts had migrated westward from China to keep their freedom. For a hundred and fifty years they had fought the battles of the Russians so that they might hold the steppe upon which their herds grazed.

For a hundred and fifty years the sword had been in their hands. What now? Alashan, while Ubaka was absent on the last campaign against the Turks and Nadesha away in Astrakan, listened to the talk of the women on the other side of the fireplace.

He heard that the levies of cattle and money paid by the Torguts to the Empress were to be increased. He himself had seen the forts going up around the territory of the Torguts.

When Ubaka rode home at the head of his men, Alashan waited in vain for a word of praise or reward from the Russians, and his anger grew. Ubaka became more silent.

One day Ubaka told Norbo to send for Nadesha, and called the Torgut council together. After long talk that the boy did not hear, a rumor sprang up on the steppe.

"We are going to the home of our fathers," the elder Torguts said.

Loosang Lama, the priest from Tibet, was consulted, and approved the plan for reasons of his own. The omens were taken from burned sheep's bones and found to be favorable for the undertaking.

Alashan was glad and hopeful. Although the weeks of preparation made the labor of the boys heavy, he looked forward to the setting out as a Moslem boy might await his first travel to Mecca. He mingled again with his cronies. They stole horses, on a dark night, from the hostile Baskirs—no easy feat, that. They dipped *kumiss* by stealth out of the big jars by the fire of their various tents and were blindly drunk for a while.

Then, to ease their spirits, they attacked a Cossack *sotnik* one moonlit night on the Volga. Nadesha put this idea into Alashan's head.

The girl had returned from Astrakan on a fine pony and with a brace of pistols that roused Alashan's immediate envy. She did not show the weapons to anyone else, confiding in the boy that they were "borrowed."

So was the horse, Nadesha admitted, but she let Alashan ride it on his foray. She said there was something valuable on the sledge, and she dared him to take it.

To the Tatar boys the chance of seizing a sledge bearing plunder was a fine thing. To tackle Cossacks was a big order; but on the following day they would be riding away from the Volga, and without doubt they would all earn for themselves the name of warrior.

Despite Alashan's craft, they were seen by the Cossack guard and fired upon before they could approach. Keeping to the shadows along the riverbank, they managed to remain out of sight until one of their number was drilled through the head by a chance bullet.

That let loose the devil in the boys, who until then had planned merely to try to run off with the sledge when the Cossacks halted to make camp. They rode their ponies out on the ice and sent arrows swiftly into the soldiers grouped by the sledge.

A musket is not so easily aimed as a bow in the moonlight. Two more boys were knocked from their horses and died soon after, but the three Cossacks lay writhing out their lives on the ice.

Without a shout of triumph, and without plundering the victims, the Tatar youths made off with the sledge and were seen climbing the riverbank by fishermen roused by the shots.

"You are no better than a child," the Khan said to his son when Alashan was brought before him the next day. "*Kai*, it is so. When I would keep secret our march, you rouse the Cossacks to fury, and our foes the Baskirs you would bring upon our heels. Go!"

Alashan would not confess that Nadesha had sent him upon the Cossacks. When he sought out the girl in the bustle of their village, he found her preparing to go to Zaritzan with her father, in his stead.

"But I am not afraid," he cried.

"That is not enough."

She made a face at him, and to add to this insult took his best *kaftan*, carefully slitting the inner lining to make a place for the two pistols.

"I am more of a man than you; the Khan said it."

Nothing could have made Alashan more utterly miserable. He sat by the cold hearth of the great log building that did duty as a palace. Nadesha was fairly safe, for even Kichinskoi, Alashan thought, would not lay hand on the son of the Khan.

Then came Norbo with tidings of Nadesha's seizure. Taking pity on the boy's anxiety, the Master of the Herds allowed him to share in the attempt to rescue the girl the next morning. Nadesha had found time to whisper to her father that she would manage to be near one of the gates just before sunrise, and they had counted on the alarm caused by the conflagration to aid their escape.

For Ubaka, as soon as he heard the decision of Kichinskoi to take the Torgut sons, had given the order to burn all the Torgut villages.

"Raise the *tugh*," he gave command after seeing that his abode was fired. "We will go to our homeland."

Smoke was already rising on every quarter of the steppe; the animals were restless. But when the yak-tailed standard was lifted and the trumpets sounded, the young boys yelped with joy. They were the first to move, driving off the cattle: then came the women, on horse, with other beasts dragging the heavy wagons on which stood the skin tents.

Children raced about in the snow. Dogs barked. The *jigits* outriding shouted to other bands that appeared beside them on the white sea of the steppe. Axles creaked and horses neighed. It all merged in one vast, joyous murmur.

"The Ili!" women cried to each other and nodded as they whipped up the cattle drawing the wagons.

Ubaka Khan, grandson of Ayuka, sat with the armed men on their horses, waiting to bring up the rear. With steady eyes he was looking into a sunrise that, seen through the smoke, was the hue of blood. This ruddy glow tinged the brown faces that passed the Khan; it dyed red the tossing horns of the cattle. Two hundred thousand humans had burned their homes and were mustering for a march in the dead of winter over one of the most barren regions of the earth.

Even the trampled snow was a crimson sea. Smoke hung above the moving shapes like a shroud—a pall that disgorged black cinders and ashes. Ubaka Khan had never seen such a sunrise.

Behind him there was the sound of a soft, chuckling laugh. He turned in his saddle to see the immense, emaciated form of Loosang Lama at his elbow. The man's countenance was hidden behind a lacquer mask, half-animal, half-human. A loose robe of the most vivid yellow hung slackly from a bare left shoulder, exposing the half of a wasted body, marked by knives and disease.

"It was your word, my Khan," whispered the priest, "that sent them forth. Do not forget."

Captain Minard Billings had been struck by the butt of a musket at the base of his skull, so that he lay long unconscious, heedless of his surroundings. When he opened his eyes—it hurt him to move them—nightmares were still racing through the back of his brain.

"Ferried across the Styx, by Jove! Lying in a cave with the shade of Hephaestus. Looking out on the procession of the lost and damned, at last."

He rolled his eyes to encompass the other side of the cavern-like abode.

"And that wench Circe sitting yonder with her court of beasts, poor gallants like me, egad! More of the beasts, horned and hoofed, laboring in front of the cave—brimstone in the very air."

At this muttering the figure of the woman rose and placed a cold, wet cloth behind his head and another over his eyes. Her hands were quick and tender, and smelled somewhat of cows. Billings subsided.

When he woke from a long sleep, he was shivering. It was colder than Hades had any right to be. When she rose from her corner to lay another sheepskin over him, Billings recognized that Circe was Nadesha, wrapped in a white *kaftan* made of the soft bellies of foxes. He saw too that Hephaestus was merely the grim and grotesque man who had led the rescue of Nadesha—Norbo, as he learned later.

The Master of the Herds was pounding at a steaming sword blade, on a small anvil. On a stone hearth between him and Billings a fire roared, filling the tent with smoke. Huddled as far as possible from the fire were a half-dozen odorous sheep. The tent, made of deer- and oxskins, was stretched over alder poles, the whole being mounted on a crude wagon drawn by ten brace of oxen.

Billings groaned and shut his eyes. This was no nightmare. He was stiff and weak, and shooting pains ran up into his skull, but his brain was cool. Nadesha surveyed him with all the insolence of ownership and made him drink some mixture in a bowl—mare's milk and wine, seasoned with sugar and pepper. He coughed and swore under his breath.

"So," she exclaimed angrily, "you let a milk-guzzling boy and a Russian yak stretch you full length in the dirt. Pah, I am ashamed that I took such pains with you, my fine captain."

"I did not expect an attack from the castle. Who knocked me down?"

"As I said, a Russian soldier. He ran out from Kichinskoi's door. When Alashan and Norbo had hauled you into the sledge beside me—and what a mess you made of Alashan's blue!—I heard the *pristof* himself call out for his men to take you prisoner. Alashan cut down the man who hit you, and we got away with only a little fighting because the mist was still heavy on the river, and the patrols thought it was Kichinskoi's fat woman in the sledge.

"*Kai*, you stupid milord, Kichinskoi would have made of you fine bait to drag across his trail. True, he hired you to make him a map, I have heard it said. But now his own bones will be summoned to the Empress's rack, and he would have said that you conspired with us and he caught you, and perhaps they would have pulled your joints apart instead."

It was significant that Nadesha thought of the Russian government in terms of the knout and the strappado and the rack.

"Was that why you carried me off, Nadesha?"

"Partly. I want you to do something for me, too. You must do it."

"Hum. Seems to me I'm always doing something for you, Nadesha. Where's my pony that you promised me? Confound it, you've got my sword now!"

He had just seen it, hanging, with the brace of pistols, on the tent wall over Nadesha's corner.

"You are my *anda*, Captain Beel-ing. I keep the weapons or they would be stolen. Here is your pony."

She pulled back a segment of the skin wall, a kind of adjustable window, and Billings saw his horse in a small herd driven beside the yurt by a Tatar rider.

"Here are your treasures."

Like a magpie with a cache to be exhibited but not touched, Nadesha flitted over to where she had made a temporary couch—Billings was occupying her own bed. Throwing aside the skins, she disclosed a number of bags that Billings recognized as those containing his personal kit, his spare stock of paper, powder, and tobacco. Also the sandalwood box in which he kept an astrolabe, spirit level, compass, globe, dividers, and rule—all his paraphernalia for observation and drafting. Nadesha had been using it as a pillow. Billings grunted with joy and then winced with pain because he had moved.

"What do you want me to do?" he muttered.

"You are a prisoner," she assured him. "This morning thirty Russians blundered into our line of march and were slain because the Cossacks are following and our men were frightened. Where we are going we can take no Christians. You would be left for the wolves if I did not take your part. Do you understand?"

Billings understood very well, but said nothing.

"I want you to make a map," declared the girl.

He waited.

"Is it true, my *anda*, what men said in Astrakan, that you can look at the sun and the stars and take your instruments in your hands as a lama takes his bones and prayer roll, and tell on what spot of the earth you stand? Eh?"

"It is true."

"Then you know *tenni-kazyk*, the polar star, and *jitti karaktchi*, the great bear, and all the others. You can tell what lies ahead and on each hand, just by looking at the sun and the stars."

"True."

"*Kai*—that is wonderful. Then you must draw a map of the road that we take. It was for that I brought you here."

"Where are you going?"

"To the lake that is Balkash, from which the river Ili flows."

Billings looked up in surprise. This, then, was the route that Kichinskoi had planned for him. The map was the one he was commissioned to make.

"Then make the map, and watch always if we are journeying truly toward Balkash. If our march turns aside, tell me of it. But do not speak to anyone else, or Ubaka Khan himself could not save your life."

Now the Armenian merchant of Astrakan had described to Billings the location of Balkash, which was known to the caravans, as the lake was large, a sort of landmark of Central Asia. The caravan routes from China to Russia passed along it, and, turning south, those to India and Tibet.

"I shall need accurate information brought in daily by riders who have been out to the north and south," he hazarded.

Nadesha clapped her hands.

"Verily, our line of march is wide, very wide, so that the horses can all graze under the snow, and fodder for the cattle can be had. The Torgut clans stretch to the north and south ten miles, and outriders go twenty more on each flank. Some hunters, questing for game, go much farther. Aye, they shall bring in reports to the Master of the Herds. I shall arrange it."

"And what is your part of the bargain—my *anda*?" he forced himself to ask.

"First promise you will make the map, and tell me if we turn away from the road to Balkash."

"So long as I am with your tribe, I will do it."

"Good. Then I can promise that when we reach Balkash you will be set free with horse, weapons, and goods and followers to take you where you wish." Seeing the man's face set stubbornly, she added: "Captain Beel-ing, you are in the heart of the Tatar Horde. If you escaped from this clan—the Wolf clan of Norbo—you would have to pass through a score of others on the steppe. Then you would fall into the hands of the Cossacks and be taken before Kichinskoi, who sent a soldier to strike you down before his gate."

Billings said nothing. He knew as well as Nadesha that the frightened *pristof* would leave no stone unturned to avert from himself the deadly anger of the Russian Court at the loss of the Torguts. A good case, as it happened, could be made out against him. Billings had no friends to use influence on his behalf. Mitrassof might speak a word for him—but Mitrassof was, if Nadesha's information proved correct, now in the field against the Torguts.

In common with Kichinskoi, Billings did not believe that the great tribe could escape beyond the reach of the Russian armies. By the time they were headed off and turned back to the Volga, Billings might be able to communicate with Mitrassof, if he stayed with the Torguts. He glanced around the dark tent odorous with smoke and sheep, and set his teeth, resolving at the first opportunity to seek word with the *ataman* rather than endure months of this prison on wheels. Meanwhile, he would work at his chart. It would give him something to occupy his mind.

"What makes you think," he asked, for this puzzled him, "that your Khan and his riders may turn aside from the road to Balkash?"

Nadesha glanced out of the opening at the entrance of the yurt. No one was at the front of the wagon. She had fancied she heard a slight movement nearby. Leaning her dark head close to the prone man, she whispered: "From here to the river Yaik, and from there across the steppe to the great river Torgai, we know well the way. Beyond there we have only the tales of our fathers and the wisdom of Loosang, who knows all things, who came from the temple of the lamas in the mountains to the south of our road. I have heard old riders of the steppe say that devils are in those mountains—devils with faces of beasts who fall upon the caravans and carry off women such as I."

A shadow crossed the girl's face.

"*Tchu*—I fear to go among the long, cold mountains. I want to go to the river Ili where the sun smiles on the hot grass."

Billings laughed at this child-like confidence, but Nadesha looked up with a start. She had heard the flap of the tent that served as window drop into place. The strip of skin was still moving. Darting to the entrance, she crawled out to spring to the ground and look about. She saw only the herd of horses and its driver.

On the other side of the yurt, his teeth set and his eyes savage, Alashan spurred away, plying his whip as if one of the thousand devils had climbed up behind him. Nadesha and the son of the Khan had been betrothed in childhood. The bride-payment had already been added to the herds of Norbo.

Unless one of the two fathers should declare Alashan unworthy of the bargain, the beautiful girl would belong to him. Now he had seen her black head pressed against the yellow mane of the *giaour*, the outlander. He had heard talk in the yurts that Nadesha had made the stranger her *anda*. He had come to ask the girl whether or not this were true. What he had seen would lead Alashan inevitably to fight Billings and if possible to kill him.

Now, when the chains of winter tightened upon the steppe, all life, human and animal, crept out of sight. The cold was intense, although the sky was clear and the sun's touch fell full on the deep blanket of snow that it could not soften.

In the fir belts, animal life kept together instinctively—elk, and the following wolf packs that ranged from forest to river. Even the rivers were motionless, ice coating their surfaces. Yet across this frozen world moved a black river. It was a stream of fur-clad humans, and as village after village was met with and the smoke of them left behind, the column grew to an army, the army to a horde.

The sound of it became a never-ending mutter, compounded of the groaning of hard-driven beasts, laboring wagons, and toiling men. And this muttering horde of men, going as no people had gone before, was unwonted. It broke, as one might say, the chains set about the steppe; it challenged the wilderness. Before it, as if in mute evidence of this, the elk herds, the wild swine, even the panthers fled out of its course.

But behind it the wolf packs began to gather, tearing to pieces the cattle and horses and sheep that fell by the way.

"A whole people has gone mad," men who had come to look at the moving columns from a distance said. "They will go to their graves like beds."

Others, Cossacks examining the trail of the Horde, pointed out the forbidding signs of hoof marks mingled with the tread of human feet and the black embers of fire in the isolated hamlets the clans had passed over.

These Cossacks of Mitrassof, as well as the Polish regiment, were closing in on the Torguts. The head of a viper, cut off from the body, still retains its poisonous fangs: Kichinskoi, in the last agonies of mortified conceit and dread, had ordered Mitrassof to take up the pursuit of the Horde and to cut to pieces any clan that refused to return with him to its residence on the Volga.

Shortly thereafter the doors of a prison cell closed on Kichinskoi, and before the end of that winter he died. But Mitrassof had his orders, and he carried them out. General Traubenberg also was moving across the Volga with a heavy force of infantry and artillery; but unlike the Cossack he took his time prudently, and when he did come up, it was upon the scene of the disaster at the Ukim.

Although the Horde made the distance from the Volga to the Yaik, three hundred and fifty-odd miles, in ten days, Mitrassof caught up with the rear guard of two clans on the near side of the Yaik.

Carrying out his instructions, he attacked the Yeka Zukor clan when it refused to surrender to him, and his veteran cavalry swept over the Tatars of that tribe. Disheartened, the other clan gave up and returned to the Volga.

This defeat caused the Horde, which had counted on a week at the Yaik to rest the beasts, to move forward again in spite of the loss of nearly half of their cattle from overdriving. Ubaka Khan had no means of knowing how near the main Russian army was to Mitrassof.

The Cossack colonel was a born leader of cavalry, and he saw his chance to deal a second blow. Ubaka was heading for the Torgai, more than a week's march. To gain the river he must cross the Mugojar Mountains, and for the space of some two hundred miles north and south there was only one suitable pass for a multitude. This was the Ukim Pass.

Mounting picked Polish cuirassiers—the armored ladies, of Tatar description—on camels and sending with them his own advance guard, Mitrassof gave orders to press ahead with all available speed, to gain the

Ukim, where a few hundred men could hold the gorge against as many thousands. Drawing reinforcements from a Cossack post on the Yaik and patching up his wounded as he went, Mitrassof came after his advance, circling the Horde.

And then the steppe called a halt. Snow set in, and a storm kept Cossack and Tatar alike in their tents.

The storm had driven the Torguts into shelter, and Billings was working at the outline of his map, sketching from a week's observation. He had stretched a square of scraped leather over a wooden frame and was laboring under a single candle, when Nadesha slipped in, shaking back the drift from her hood.

The yawning man-servant who stood guard over the weapons of Norbo and Nadesha blinked as the girl moved into the light and studied the parchment over Billings's shoulder.

"They are coming to slay you," she observed. "They say they will rip the skin from your body and put it upon a *tugh*."

She turned and gave a quick command to the Tatar, who stumbled out of the yurt, wide awake for once. Billings laid aside the dividers in his hand and looked from Nadesha to the sword and the brace of pistols hanging over her corner.

"Do not think of that, my *anda*," she smiled, following his eye. "The long pistols will go off twice—pang pang—and then you might draw your sword, the one that you cherish. They would pull down the tent and drag you out by your feet and trample you."

"Who are coming?"

"A crowd of fools who are beside themselves because they have been swallowing smoke and listening to the talk of Loosang. My father is away at the *sarga*—the council called by the Khan. The mob has had no toil today, so they have guzzled *kumiss* and their ears are open to evil. They want blood for the blood the Cossacks have shed, and Loosang has told them you are a spy. The lama has seen you making calculations with the needle that points always toward *tenni-kazyk*, the polar star."

Billings wiped dry the goose quill he was using as a pen. Then he covered up his map. Since the fighting on the other side of the Yaik, he had noticed that the Tatars no longer treated him with indifference. They had grown morose, and those who observed him walking among Norbo's henchmen spat and muttered to each other. Norbo himself was moodier than usual.

Men and beasts were hard-pressed. The Tatar boys had lashed the cattle and goaded the oxen to make them keep up, and each day thinned the herds. Occasionally he had seen bodies, twisted and frozen in the snow. The dogs no longer ran barking beside the wagons. They gathered in packs and fell upon the cattle that could not keep their legs.

Nadesha's eyes, half-veiled under long lashes, looked down into Billings's, and her full underlip thrust out disdainfully.

"Come, my gallant captain, are you thinking of the thousand men in Norbo's *urdus*, and the thousands that are like hungry wolves as far around you as you could run in a day and night?"

Even at night the Tatars kept fires burning at the limits of each *urdus*, and mounted patrols held the space between the clan camps. The storm might hide him, but he knew that no man would live long afoot in the icy wind and the snow flurries.

Billings picked up his sword from Nadesha's corner, tested the blade between his fingers, and smiled.

"Better this than the storm."

Nadesha glared, and her tongue had not been silenced in the least.

"Dog! Mud-puppy! Son of a sow! Have I brought you here when you ought to have had your neck broken with a rope? *Tchu!* Have I teased that old fool my father until my jaws cracked, just to have you turn into a—Put that blade down or you'll have your breath out of your body."

Seeing that her words were unheeded, Nadesha's tone changed.

"The men who are coming are common, black-boned louts. I can handle them until Norbo comes. I have sent the servant for him. *Kai*, if you do not believe me, watch! Oh, you are stupid!"

But no consideration would induce Billings to lay aside the sword. He had not recovered his strength, yet the feel of the hilt in his hand was a tonic. A murmur penetrated the tents, the sound of low voices, the clink of steel and the creaking of leather on wooden saddles. Horses seemed to be surrounding the yurt.

Billings listened indifferently. He heard the murmuring come close to the wagon, caught voices outside the tent entrance. After all, it was good to face these savages sword in hand and not skulk like a sick woman, behind a tent.

A hand swept aside the flap covering the entrance, a hand upon which jewels shimmered in the faint candle-light. A puff of snow sprinkled the floor. Other hands ripped open the whole front of the yurt, and Billings saw a score of men armed with spears and swords, their faces hidden in hoods coated white by the storm.

Nadesha sprang forward and tossed back the cape of the leader. An exclamation of surprise parted her lips as she saw a long, olive face with a trimmed beard and eyes as dark as her own.

"So," she cried, "Zebek Dortshi, chief of the council and *noyon* of the Red Camel clan of Irak, calls at the house of Norbo with armed men at his back! So, while Norbo is at the council, you have come by a dog's trail to his house."

The Persian Tatar motioned her back. Billings saw that his outer coat was velvet embroidered with gold, his belt set with turquoise and sapphires. He was a tall man, so that his eyes were on a level with Nadesha's waist.

"*Temou chu*, dwell in peace, maiden."

Zebek Dortshi pointed at Billings.

"We have come for that son of a witch. We have no thought of harm for the child of Norbo."

If the *noyon* was taken aback at seeing Nadesha in the wagon, he concealed it. But the girl had not looked to find a noble in the crowd. She knew that Zebek Dortshi was in Loosang's favor and, as head of the council, was second to the Khan in authority in the Horde.

"Shall I tell Norbo that you called for his prisoner without first asking the will of the Master of the Herds? He holds this officer for ransom."

Zebek Dortshi flushed, and Nadesha pressed her attack on his weak point.

"Does the *noyon* of the Red Camel clan steal like a Kurd? Or has he the command of the Khan to tear down the tent of Norbo?"

"I came from Loosang, spit-fire. He wishes the *giaour* slain."

"Oho—and has Loosang said aught to the Khan?"

She had him, but the crowd behind the noble was growing restive.

"That dog is a magician!" someone shouted. Others took up the refrain. "He has bewitched our cattle. Look, the yellow pig has a sword! Let us cut him open, sister, and to the Devil with gabbing about prisoners."

From this Zebek Dortshi took his cue. He opened his hands and shrugged.

"You see, Nadesha, this is not my affair—the men want the stranger's life."

Real scorn curled the lip of the girl.

"These are your men, my *noyon*. When you came wooing me you did not say that you were their servant."

"It is the will of Loosang, the lama of the *Tsong Khapa*."

"A beast in a mask!"

Nadesha stamped a booted foot, and a growl issued from the throng. The priest came from Tibet, wore the yellow robe and the black hat of a *chutuktu*, a disciple of the Dalai Lama, whose kingdom comprised the whole of Central Asia. The Tatars, knowing little of religion, respected the lama as a matter of course. They had a whole-hearted dread of the mysteries of the priests of the long, cold mountains.

"The time will come," the girl protested hotly, "when you will know that you have been sheep, following a jackal who wears a sheepskin. *Ai-a*, you are stupid sheep!"

Nadesha caught the gleam in the Persian's brown eyes and checked her words.

"This man is my *anda*. See, he wears my girdle."

Throwing open her *kaftan* she allowed them to see Billings's plain leather belt with the silver clasp wound around her waist.

"It is the law among the people of the tents—two pledged brothers have one life. If you slay the yellow-haired one, I will die with him. Neither brother abandons the other."

From the outskirts of the throng a figure hooded and cloaked pushed forward to a position close to the wagon tongue. The Tatars, intent on the astonishing confession of Nadesha, did not pay attention to the newcomer. They craned forward, each one anxious to see for himself the two belts.

Zebek Dortshi ran his fingers through his soft beard and his eyes narrowed. He was the most far-sighted of the leaders of the Tatars. He was ambitious, a reckless leader of horsemen in battle, admired for his wildness by these riders of the steppe.

A match with Nadesha had long been in his mind. He coveted the warm fairness of the maiden. She would, out of all the Horde, be a fitting match for the chief of the Red Camel clan. She had wit, fire; she was no sluggard, to be hugged and forgotten.

And now she had named as her pledged brother a foreigner, a Christian and impecunious prisoner. Zebek Dortshi knew there must be a reason for this. He thought she loved the Englishman. Speculatively the *noyon* glanced at Billings, who stood quietly, resting the tip of the rapier on the floor of the yurt. What kind of metal was in this man?

"You are a child, Nadesha." Zebek Dortshi's brow cleared. "And a child at play. Only between men is the *anda* tie knit, among the people of the tents."

"*Kai*, is it so? Then watch if this be play!"

She drew from her belt a curved dagger and flourished it in his beard.

Among the followers of the *noyon* there was hesitation. All knew that Norbo would take immediate and bloody revenge for any injury to his child. They knew, likewise, that if they rushed the prisoner, Nadesha would probably be severely hurt, if not killed. She might even kill herself—there was no telling what a woman would do.

Just then, while they muttered and fingered their weapons, Billings took matters into his own hands. He had had enough of talk—wrangling that he barely understood.

"Come," he said to Zebek Dortshi in broken Tatar, "and taste a sword. You are dogs, that bark at a girl and run off from a weapon."

Zebek Dortshi decided there was good metal in the prisoner. But the words released the floodgates of Tatar fury. Men clambered past the Persian, thrusting against one another, shouting hoarsely. Billings caught Nadesha's arm as she would have hurled herself against the invaders. He whirled her back of him to the floor.

The first man to gain his feet within the yurt held no weapon. As he stepped under the candle on the tent-pole, he threw back his hood and faced about.

"Alashan!" cried Zebek Dortshi, and shouted to his men to hold off.

The boy's thin face was strained and his eyes glowed. He leaned down to twist the dagger from Nadesha's hand.

"I will deal with this man," he said passionately to Zebek Dortshi. "Call away these dogs and be gone."

Although he was half a head shorter than the tall *noyon*, his anger made the Persian shrink back a little.

"I am the son of Ubaka Khan," he went on, "and I will attend to this one whom Nadesha calls *anda*. I will face him fairly and kill him with my own hand. Tatars, this is a vow. You will see it fulfilled, aye, and soon. Now, get to your horses before Norbo's men cut your hearts out."

Flinging down the dagger, he clenched his fists, looking up from face to face as if marking those who were present. Zebek Dortshi trembled with fury, and was pulled back by his men, who had heard horsemen who were entering the camp.

"Norbo—Norbo!" cried the girl. "It is Nadesha!"

As the Master of the Herds strode forward alone, the men of Zebek Dortshi gave back, puffing their hoods down as if not eager to be recognized. Norbo climbed slowly to the floor of his yurt and looked about him in silence.

"The Khan of the Red Camels has come to pay his respects to me," said Nadesha quickly. "With a score of armed men he came, to take the one that is my prisoner, the *giaour*. He entered the yurt and Alashan stayed him."

Norbo's seamed face was emotionless. One of the older Tatars, of hereditary rank, he had not prospered in Russia, and the more versatile khan of Irak had been raised above him.

"*Noyon*," he observed at last, in a rumbling voice, "you have a stick in your hand."

It is an unpardonable offense for a guest to enter the tent of a Mongol with a club or weapon of any kind in his grasp. Zebek Dortshi was thoroughly angry, but he was discreet. Chewing at his beard, he sheathed his sword and bent his head very low, mockingly.

"Take heed, O master of the house, lest one day your seat in the council be vacant."

As Norbo said nothing more, the man of Irak beckoned to Alashan.

"Come, puppy—they growl at us."

But the boy raised his hand in greeting to Norbo.

"May the road be open before you, Master of the Herds. I go!"

When the old khan had saluted Alashan, the boy left with Zebek Dortshi, without glancing at Nadesha, who looked at him long and curiously as if seeing him for the first time.

"Faith," muttered Billings, "the old chap treats me like a scab on the arm and the boy has promised to kill me, but I rather think they saved my life."

That night they ate heartily, for Norbo announced that Ubaka Khan had ordered most of the remaining sheep and cattle to be slaughtered, as the beasts were dying fast. While the snow endured the Torguts were to feast, against the beginning of the march. Nadesha disappeared into her corner when the bowls of cabbage and mutton and of fermented mare's milk were removed, leaving Norbo squatting by the fire, fingering an empty pipe.

Lying on his back, Billings studied the play of shadows on the wall of the tent, but when he started to pull the heavy skins over him, as the chill crept in over the floor, he hesitated. Finally he rose and offered Norbo tobacco from the pouch that he had cherished.

The Tatar grunted, sifted the black Russian tobacco in his gnarled fingers, and filled his pipe without a word. After Billings had warmed his feet and hands at the flames and was returning to his bed, the Khan spoke.

"Keep that stick in your hand, *giaour*, and sleep upon it. There are dogs about. You may need to use it."

Until then Billings had wondered how long he would be permitted to retain his sword, for he knew Norbo must have noticed that he still had it. Following the old man's advice, he thrust the blade in its scabbard well down among the skins and rolled himself up for the night.

Turning over presently on his elbow at a sound from the hearth, he found that Norbo had secured the sketch that was the beginning of his map and had turned it to the light. The scalp-locked head of the Tatar was nodding over it.

"Well, he knows good work when he sees it," thought Billings drowsily.

In reality Norbo had fallen asleep sitting up and was utterly indifferent to the map. Through the closed flap of the yurt there came the clang of a brazen basin—the gong that marked the hours for the camp. It was answered by the distant blast of a horn. Norbo raised his head inquiringly, but the trumpet was that of the lamas.

Presently the Tatar began to snore, with a sighing sound like the sucking of the wind in and out of the tent. From Nadesha's corner a murmur merged with the note of the storm. The girl was crying softly, her arm pressed against her mouth so that she should not arouse the two men.

Throughout the ten days of feasting while the snow lasted, Alashan kept to himself. When clear, frosty weather set in, he waited impatiently until the wind died down and the drifting of the dunes over the steppe ceased.

The dawn trumpet of the thirteenth day filled him with a glow of eagerness. He was to ride with the advance guard of the Horde that would make forced marches to the Ukim Pass. They would try to gain the upper gorge before the Cossacks; if the Cossacks were there first, there would be fighting anyway. This was what Alashan longed for.

He would show his hardihood in battle, and Ubaka Khan, his father, would declare him a man, with all a *noyon*'s estate. Then and not until then could he challenge Billings, the tow-headed Christian officer, to a combat with swords. The captain, Alashan knew, would refuse to match weapons with a boy. In imagination, when he could not sleep, the son of the Khan pictured his curved sword biting into the stalwart neck of the stranger.

What tormented him was the favor shown by Nadesha to Billings. When Alashan thought of her looking at Billings and smiling at the quick, Russian words of the stranger—words that he did not hear—his heart pounded and his teeth drew back from his lips.

So he urged his camel up with the scouts of his company. His father had placed him with the captain of two hundred musket men, mounted on picked Bactrians. Zebek Dortshi commanded five hundred other musket men, veterans of the war with the Turks, and the Persian had gone ahead somewhere to the right of Alashan's detachment.

Behind the two camel corps rode a regiment of mounted infantry, followed by the nucleus of the Khan's heavy cavalry. These were soon lost to sight in the rear.

Outriders informed the Tatar captain that the Russians were pressing forward rapidly from the north.

"It is a race for the rocks of the Ukim, my young kinglet," he confided to Alashan. "Aye, the power of the gods of the high places must aid us. If the Cossacks and the armored ladies reach the Ukim first they can hold the gorge until tribes hostile to us come up the Torgai from the south and reinforce them from behind. Aye, the Muscovite regiments are marching after us with cannon and can join battle within a week if we do not force the pass."

"Then we will be the first," shouted the boy. "Come, we must ride during this night."

"And kill our camels?" grumbled the captain. "Do you want your father, the Khan, to come up and find us standing like trees in the snow? *Tchu*, my foolish bearlet, he would have me flayed alive on a wooden ass for that, I assure you."

Nevertheless, the Tatar set such a pace that Alashan was stiff from exhaustion and cold by the breaking of the fifth day, when they sighted the heights of the Ukim against the gate of the rising sun.

By then they had lost all touch with Zebek Dortshi, who seemed to have vanished into the hollows of the steppe. Alashan fretted himself by trying to make his beast race ahead of the others, and a dozen times he fingered over the priming of the heavy pistol he had at his belt.

His young eyes were keen, and before noon he made out that mounted men were moving within the black sides of the gorge. He saw that the Ukim Pass was like the neck of a squat bottle. Only at the summit of the pass were the sides of the gorge precipitous; along the main slope, a wilderness of rock, shot through with outcroppings of pillar-like basalt, stood on either hand amid a scum of bare tamarisks.

Alashan's first thought was that Zebek Dortshi had beaten him in the race to the Ukim, and he gritted his teeth. The cavalry on the slope below the pass were mounted on camels and seemed to be awaiting their approach.

"The gods are kind!" he cried suddenly. "It was well I made gifts of gold and Russian money to the priest Loosang. Those are the Poles. I see the sun on their breastpieces and their long lances."

The Tatar chewed his mustache and squinted. Four—six hundred men in the pass, he reckoned. Why, by the white horse of Kaidu, had they not gone higher where they would have the cliff on either flank?

"Their beasts are tired. Aye, some Cossacks on horses are with them. The Cossack cavalry must be close at hand, and these fellows ahead have counted us. They wait on the slope instead of the gorge because they expect aid before the sun is much higher."

A murmur of assent from the Tatars close by greeted these words. Their own mounts were stumbling and groaning; they did not relish facing the heavy sabers of the Cossacks. Out of the corners of their bleared eyes they looked at Alashan. What would the son of the Khan do?

"Come, my brothers of the tents," shrilled Alashan. "We will strike the ranks of our foes like a thunderbolt; they will fall beneath our sword-strokes. Their camels have gone farther than ours this day—they barely can stand. Let us ride them down!"

Instinctively he exhorted his men. His brain was in a whirl. Never had Alashan ridden into the shock of battle; his limbs quivered, and his lips twitched. His eyes were glued on the horsemen above and ahead of him who sat waiting in ranks like sitting wolves.

The Tatar captain glanced around hoping to make out some trace of Zebek Dortshi's command. There were no other tracks to be seen in the snow; but his keen eye caught a light in the weather-hardened faces of his men. Fatigue had vanished.

"Let us ride after the boy," they said, one to another. "He is a falcon of the eagle's line. He is not afraid of the Cossacks. They are many—we will go from this spot up into the gate in the sky, over the mountains of Natagai where the *tengeri* ride on the wind. That is good."

Only the eyes of the captain were troubled. When the opposing groups halted, at the distance of a bowshot, to revile each other and pick out an opening for attack, Alashan's blood began to hum in his ears.

If only the thing would begin! The sweat was running down his legs; he feared every moment his camel would bolt, or he would disgrace himself in some way.

His men were shouting guttural challenges at the splendid-looking Poles, calling them hired women and blood-sucking insects, and steel-bedizened jezebels. The round-faced Poles did not understand, but the Cossacks flung back fitting answers.

"Ho, gutter-bred thieves—mud-puppies—sneaking sons of dogs—turncoat infidels who run from a good, Christian sword—"

Crash! A burst of musketry from the Russian ranks emptied some of the Tatar mounts and sent the hot blood into Alashan's burning eyes. He did not notice that the answering volley of his men went wild for the most part, that the Tatars followed their *noyon* up the slope in scattered formation, while the disciplined Poles kept well together.

He felt his teeth chatter together, saw his companion, the old captain, shoot an arrow into the beard of a short Cossack, only to be struck from his horse by a back-handed blow from a huge soldier whose open coat trailed after him like a cloak as he cast himself into the Tatars, hewing forward and back and roaring even after arrows stuck out from his ribs and arms.

The giant was finally brought down by the fall of his pony, and sat down in the snow with his head bent while his shaking hands fumbled for the ikon under his shirt.

The snapping of pistols sounded far off. Alashan came out of his stupor with a jerk, and was mad with rage on the instant. Tugging at the nose cord of his beast, he almost ran into a boyish-looking Pole who cast a lance at him. Alashan pulled the trigger of his pistol and saw the other's surprised face staring at him out of a cloud of smoke.

Without waiting to see if the Pole fell off his camel, the son of the Khan sprang down and secured a more agile mount, a riderless pony. The red mist was still before his eyes as he dashed here and there, striking and parrying.

Meanwhile the fight had dissolved into group combats, in which the Tatars were outnumbered and cut down rapidly, being unable to inflict serious damage on the armored Poles. Only the natural agility of the steppe riders and the deadly use they made of their short bows kept up the semblance of a struggle.

Half of them had their wish, and went to the land of Natagai, which is in the sky, behind the flaming gate of the northern lights.

Alashan halted, perforce, seeing no foes before him. He had come through the ranks of the Russians. A louder crackling of muskets caused him to stare to either side.

From behind boulders and tamarisk thickets Tatars were firing down on the Russians. They were advancing coolly down the slopes of the gorge on foot, kneeling to fire.

Alashan blinked and wondered if he were dreaming. Then he made out the brilliant figure of Zebek Dortshi sitting his horse on a summit nearby. When he shouted orders to his lieutenants, the *noyon* took a pipe from between his lips. Presently he raised his voice to call to the remnant of Alashan's men, bidding them withdraw a short distance and form again. The red cleared from Alashan's eyes. He felt the sweat, now cold on his limbs. Another was giving orders to his men.

The death of the Tatar captain had left Alashan in command of the camel corps, or what remained of it. He knew Zebek Dortshi must have seen him, and yet the *noyon* paid no attention to the boy, who was cut off from his own following.

Anger quickened Alashan's pulse; and he wheeled his horse, heading back toward his men. He went for them direct, on a course that took him through the scattered groups of Poles and Cossacks, who had been thrown into confusion by the fire of the Tatars in their rear.

This uncertainty saved Alashan his life. While some Russians were turning, to try to gallop up into the safety of the gorge, between the lines of Zebek Dortshi's musket men, others were still facing the Tatars below them.

Alashan cut off the head of a Polish lance aimed at his ribs, and broke his sword in the man's back as he passed. Dodging here and there, he edged through the Cossacks, who would have given more heed to the unarmed boy if they had known that here was the son of the Khan.

Reaching his followers, who greeted him with an exultant shout, Alashan led them up the slope again. But the fight at the mouth of the Ukim was about over. The camels of the Russians were giving out, and stretched themselves groaning on the frozen earth while their riders were cut down by Zebek Dortshi's men, now mounted again. The Cossacks tried to rush the rock nests and the tamarisk, and most of them were picked off by bullets and arrows.

Seeing that only a handful of Poles remained, standing back to back using their light lances as spears, Alashan left these and rode up to Zebek Dortshi triumphantly. The Persian Tatar was still on the summit, looking out over the plain. Alashan noticed by the tracks in the snow that the *noyon* had brought up his men quietly, on foot, into the thickets, coming in from either flank. The camels had been herded some distance in the rear of the rocks until it was time to mount.

A suspicion came to Alashan that the *noyon* had been among the thickets for some time, that Zebek Dortshi had been the first on the scene, arriving from the south, his approach concealed by the foothills of the Ukim.

"Where were you, *ahatou*—brother?" observed Zebek Dortshi indifferently. "I could not see you at first. Why, in the name of a thousand devils, did you try to ride through the whole Muscovite strength? If it had not been for the fire of my men you would have been hunted like a hare!"

It occurred to Alashan that if Zebek Dortshi had noticed his feat, the *noyon* must have caught sight of him before then. If so, why had not Zebek Dortshi called to him, or sent men to protect the son of the Khan? But Alashan was too pleased with his first battle to wonder about things. He had reined his horse through four hundred foes! He had killed his man more than once and broken his sword into the bargain!

Moreover he was sure blood was mingling with the cold sweat on one shoulder, and a piece had been slashed out of his boot. He gazed at that boot proudly. Then he gave a cry.

"There are men on the plain. They are fighting."

Zebek Dortshi looked at him sidewise and rubbed the gold-inlaid hilt of his sword.

"*Chu*, my gamecock, did you not see that the main force of the Cossacks had come up below us, and the heavy cavalry of the Khan, your father, close on their heels?"

He considered Alashan for a moment.

"Here, take my horse. It is a Turkoman and fresh. Bear the tidings to your father that I hold the gate of the Ukim. You will see more fighting down there—"

Waiting for no more, Alashan was off like the wind on a lean pony whose silver-inlaid saddle was covered with a fine silk cloth. In this way did Zebek Dortshi gain credit for giving the son of the Khan his horse during a battle. And the *noyon* remained alone in possession of the coveted gorge of the Ukim.

Alashan passed groups of Tatars moving slowly over the plain, binding up their wounds and looking at weapons they had captured. These were the horsemen of the Bear clan, heavily armed and wearing chain mail over their leather tunics. Their heads were covered with pointed steel caps and their black faces were scarred. They were the heavy cavalry of the Horde, the pride of Ubaka Khan.

From one of them, a commander of a hundred who was known to him, Alashan learned that they had come up in time to engage Mitrassof before the Russians could reach the shelter of the Ukim.

Mitrassof's need of haste had brought his men up in scattered detachments; the weight of the Polish dragoons had exhausted their horses.

"They fell like ripe wheat," grunted the Tatar. "The Cossacks were a sword of another edge. They were too few. You see some of their bodies here. The heads of others who were late in coming we cut off back there."

Listening, Alashan heard firing off to his right, to the north. Edging over that way, he found the lighter regiments of the Khan riding down the fragments of Mitrassof's command. More riders were coming up from the Horde constantly.

"Hai," laughed the boy, "they did not live long to boast about the Yaik."

The battle on the plain was about over. But some distance off he heard the clashing of weapons. A vibrant voice floated out, seemingly from the steppe itself. Alashan reined his horse toward the sound. He arrived at the edge of a gully where the stony, dried riverbed was littered with corpses. Several blue tops of Cossack hats were to be seen in the center of a ring of mounted Tatars who pressed them back toward the bank of the ravine.

Alashan heard the voice again, wild and exultant.

"Shen, shen, skivagen,
Swing the steel, swing again!
Ride, ride, to our play,
Slay, slay!"

Shadows, gathering in the gully, concealed the outlines of the fighters, but Alashan watched the flicker of swords, heard the moans of men who had fallen underfoot, and listened to the deep voice of Mitrassof making mock of his enemies. The Tatars drew back at last, and someone called for a bow.

Mitrassof was alone, half-standing, half-lying against the snow on the bank, his hat fallen off, his big head lowering on his shoulders. Alashan spurred down the slope of the ravine. A bow twanged, and after a moment the Tatars rushed in to seize spoil from the body.

"Peace, dogs," cried the boy. "This is the *starshim*, the chief of the Cossacks. Let him have honor."

Unheeding, they tore away belt, sword, gold-chased scabbard, rings, and the gold chain from which hung the ikon. Alashan lashed them with words, and, as they were moving away, one turned back and laid the chain with its cross on the body of the Cossack.

Then the others stopped, and presently all the spoil was returned to the body, which at Alashan's direction was picked up to be carried before Ubaka Khan.

The Khan was not found until his tent was pitched that night and he rode in, during a tumult of nakers and trumpets, to throw off his steel cap and sit by the fire. Alashan waited until Ubaka had inspected silently the body of his enemy.

After that Ubaka called for food, and the boy stood until his father had eased his hunger. The Khan had not eaten for two days. Alashan was quivering with desire to pour out his story of the fight at the gorge. He wanted, too, to point out that Zebek Dortshi had been first at the Ukim but had waited until Alashan attacked before entering the battle.

Ubaka sat gazing into the fire, his knotted hands resting on his massive knees. He lifted his head and looked at his son.

"I have been to the gorge of the Ukim. I have heard the tale of the skirmish. Zebek Dortshi, who is a leader among a thousand, I have rewarded with foxskins and inlaid daggers, with pieces of red leather and saddles sewn with pearls that we took from the Cossack camp. He did well."

Alashan's heart sank, and he waited for a word concerning himself. Ubaka was pleased with the daring exhibited by the boy, but his hoarse voice was gruff with displeasure.

"My son, a soldier can be reckless and as foolish as a *kulan*, a wild ass.

But a leader of men must think wisely when the swordstrokes begin. You are not yet a man arrived at man's estate."

Alashan, too, began to study the fire.

"The time is not, when my *noyons* will lift their hands to their eyes and say that you are a true son of the Khan—a falcon of the eagle line. I have spoken. Go!"

In the tent of Norbo, Nadesha came to Billings bringing the news of Mitrassof's death, and the capture of the Ukim. With the words of the girl went the last hope of rescue for the Englishman.

Billings thought this over far into the night, and fell to work on his map with new vigor, noting in the location of the Ukim.

Chapter IV
The Wood Ashes That Turned into a Tree

It was an evening early in spring, and the odor of wet marshland was in the air when Nadesha slipped past the tents of the Wolf clan and made her way toward the one spot of the camp that was forbidden her. This was the yurt of Loosang.

Ever since she had been a child—not so long ago—the girl of Norbo had longed to see inside this solitary wagon tent that was fashioned of purple cloth instead of the usual felt or hides and stood on a brightly painted cart. From its depths she often had watched the lama emerge clad sometimes in yellow, sometimes in purple with a scarlet scarf and the cube-like black hat that stretched his naturally great stature to more than the length of two Tatar spears. She had listened with awe to the note of the lama's trumpet that could be heard half an hour's ride away. Sometimes she fancied the eyes of the priest had dwelt on her.

But this night Nadesha planned to gain entrance to the yurt. She would match her wits against the lama's, and try to learn what the servant of the Dalai Lama had in store for the Horde. For now the Torguts had left behind the part of the steppe known to them and were nearing the edge of the unknown spaces where Loosang must guide. In a bag she held the last of the heavy Russian money, copper and silver, that still remained in their household. Now that the ground was soft underfoot, at the edge of the high steppe of the Kangar, all superfluous weight was being cast from the loads of the Horde.

And Loosang had declared that this money, useless now to the Tatars, was welcome in his yurt, useful in his ceremonial. He pointed out that by the favor of Bon and the gods of which he was priest, the Tatars had overthrown the Cossacks at the Ukim and passed the terrible Torgai safely on a floating bridge of bundles of giant reed.

On her way to the lama's wagon, Nadesha wheedled more copper coins here and there in the groups that clustered together on the wet ground.

The yurt of Loosang stood alone at the end of a red clay gully, and within fifty paces of it Nadesha was set upon by savage dogs that ripped her skirt and would have tasted her blood if a huge voice had not called them back from the tent.

Nadesha advanced, laid her bundle on the wooden platform, and kneeled against the wagon tongue until from the corners of her eyes she saw that the bundle had disappeared. Still she waited.

"What do you wish, daughter of Norbo?"

"I am cold, *chutuktu*, and there is a fire within. I have brought you a great deal of money."

As she spoke Nadesha shivered, because she half-believed the dogs would be set upon her, and the dark gorge was not a pleasant place.

"Have you a message from the Khan or your father?"

"Would a *noyon* send speech by a woman?"

"Wait, then."

It was quite dark before Loosang opened the flap of his tent. The girl's quick ears had caught the clink of coins. She wondered what Loosang did with the Russian money. He did not carry it along with him in the wagon, which would have been burdened by the extra weight. The Tatars were sure of that. They believed the coins disappeared during the ritual of the lama. Nadesha wondered.

When she climbed through the opening she gave an exclamation of surprise. A small fire glowed on some stones with a reddish hue. From it came a sweetish odor from some dried roots. Behind the fire sat what seemed to be a painted statue, draped in a yellow cassock, with waistcoat of cloth of gold, and purple apron. A high hat gleamed with lacquer work above a mask-like face.

Nadesha knew that still greater emotion was expected of her, and she pressed her face to the floor, clasping her hands behind her black coils of hair. Loosang's eyes scanned the slender shoulders of the girl, noting her supple arms and the smooth skin of her neck.

"You did not come hither to sit by a fire," he said slowly. "I have been expecting you. Sit by my side and speak when you are ready."

There were cushions near the lama, and Nadesha felt very comfortable. Her cheeks had fallen in a little from hunger and her eyes were overbright. She had put on a chaplet of pearls and a silk coat and washed her skin in oil and rose water.

"If I wished it," Loosang observed, "you would not leave the tent on your feet, and the dogs would soon make of you a thing of knitted bones. Two moons ago you went against my will when you saved the *giaour* his life. Why did you do that?"

"I am holding the captive for a price."

"It must be a big price. The day after Zebek Dortshi attacked the *giaour* you sent your father to Ubaka Khan. Norbo asked the Khan to declare to the Horde that the life of your captive must be spared. What is the price?"

"Protection for me."

"From whom?"

"From the gods, and especially Bon."

For some time Loosang gazed into the fire, occasionally placing upon it another root or stick of incense wood. When he spoke his high voice was tinged with suspicion.

"What makes you seek my protection, daughter of Norbo?"

Nadesha was aware that she was being studied covertly. She cradled her chin in her hands and pouted mischievously.

"*Kai!* Are not the gods greater than the Khan, who is a man?"

"Truly. Ubaka Khan has caused much suffering among his people. Seventy thousand souls have gone out, like candles in the wind, since the march began. In each family one lies sick. The wolves and the vultures follow the trail of the Horde. Many more will die."

"Of course." Nadesha nodded confidentially.

"Food and fodder are at an end. The clans hunt and pillage as they can. The men of the Khan's own cavalry are murmuring." Loosang knew that Nadesha was shrewd; he had watched the girl and found her to his liking. "So you think the day will soon be at hand when you must seek aid of the gods?"

"Aye," the girl answered. "The day will come, within this moon that is now new. Then the Horde will cross the Kangar Desert; at the end of the desert they will turn to you to lead the way. Whither?"

Loosang felt a sting of suspicion. But the girl at his side was open-eyed, and her brow was without guile. Still, he answered craftily.

"Whatever will happen is the will of the gods. For nine days I shall sleep, and my dreams will search out the far places of the spirit world so that I may know what is ordained." Loosang thought for a moment. "If the *giaour* is not given into my hands by Ubaka Khan at the end of the sleep, evil will come against the Horde. Aye, for one thing—" his hand caught the girl's wrist—"Alashan will be slain by your prisoner."

Nadesha tossed her head.

"My thoughts are not for the son of the Khan."

"Nor for the lion-haired *giaour*."

Here Nadesha took refuge in a smile. Instead of finding out things from the lama, the secrets of her heart were being probed. When the Persian Tatar smiled it warmed the blood of men, for her lips were a lure.

"True, my lama."

No more. But the smile and the words kindled the imagination of the priest.

"Nor do you love the Persian khan, Zebek Dortshi, daughter of Norbo."

"Again, most true. Though Zebek Dortshi will fly higher and faster than Alashan. A moon ago at the Ukim the *noyon* schemed so cleverly that the son of the Khan was within a sword's edge of being slain. Is it not so?"

Suspicion having passed from the mind of Loosang, he did not deny this. Nadesha half-caught her breath, for Alashan had told her about the act of Zebek Dortshi at the gorge and her wit had penetrated its motive.

"It is you, little dove," he whispered almost to himself, "who will look down upon a kingdom at your feet, and your petal-fingers shall play with jewels."

His long hand went out and touched Nadesha's forehead. It was as if a snake had crawled across her face, but she did not move. Only when the hand crept down to her throat and lingered on the vein of blood that was like a pulse, she spoke.

"I could love one greater than the *giaour*. At the end of this moon I will deliver my prisoner to you."

"*Takil-tebihou*—the bargain is struck."

"Then where is my kingdom?" Throwing back her head, the girl laughed softly at the surprise of the priest.

To play on the fancy of Nadesha, Loosang described to her the temple of Bon that stood at the edge of the Kangar upon a wide river that flowed down from the mountains of Tibet—the house of Bon, where the face of the great god peered out from the cliff itself, and monks, both men and women, passed their lives at the palace of the god.

They who gave up their souls to Bon, the Destroyer of earthly things, would taste paradise. In the place of their worship were paintings as old as the memory of man. The floors were jade, covered with silken rugs from Bokhara. The masters of the monks were warriors who wore gold and scarlet and carried standards as tall as the trees. Jewels were in their saddles, for they were servants of the Dalai Lama, who was the living Buddha, reborn during three times three thousand years.

And the master of the lamasery—

"I am *chutuktu*, abbot, of that lamasery which is at Sonkor, on the edge of the Kangar. And I have been lama of the Black Kirghiz, the greatest of the Tatar tribes of Asia."

So spoke Loosang, his breath warm against the hair of the girl. He had the gift of making others see clearly what he painted with words.

"When I ride back to Sonkor the *sakyas* will carry candles before me on the terraces. A *chutuktu* is a prince, for the Dalai Lama is a king. I shall go back—" just for a second he hesitated—"when my work here is done."

This time it was Nadesha who leaned forward to feed the fire. A startling thought had come to her, and she wished to hide her face. If the lama should guess what was in her mind, she would not see the light of the next sunrise, nor would the Master of the Herds know what fate had befallen his daughter, for Nadesha had come secretly to the yurt of Loosang.

Even as she bent down she was seized in an iron grasp and pulled back so that she lay across the knees of the priest. The face of Loosang had changed, as if he had put on one of his masks. His small eyes burned.

But it was passion and not suspicion that had stung him to seize the girl. So Nadesha saw in a flash. Yet his touch upon her neck and shoulder brought the color flooding into her cheeks. She twisted in his grasp, whipping out a knife from her *khalat*.

Before Loosang could move, she had placed the point of the curved dagger against his throat and pressed it in a little. The lama snarled angrily as his head, perforce, bent back. Then the knife was withdrawn and he saw Nadesha sitting beside him quietly, the dagger secreted again.

"You are a fool and a child!" he ejaculated, the harsh Tibetan accent creeping into his words. "No one has drawn steel against me, who cannot be hurt by steel."

The girl reflected that he seemed unwilling to put the matter to a test.

"No one has laid hand on me before this," she responded calmly. "Now it is in my mind that you lied to me about the kingdom of Sonkor where the Kirghiz are—"

"Lied? I?" Loosang, for the first time, was answering blindly the thrusts of the Tatar. He laughed shrilly. "Nay, your own eyes will see it. I will take you there."

"That is part of the bargain."

"Good. It shall be done, and sooner than you think."

For his part, the lama had tasted a little of the beauty of Nadesha. Now he meant to possess her. In this he could be patient. As for Nadesha, she had had a vision of a great doom preparing for the clans, for the Wolf clan and her father and the Khan. It was no more than a vision as yet, a mingling of the power of Loosang, the power of the Black Kirghiz, and the wiles of Zebek Dortshi. She felt as if she stood at the edge of a pit that was being dug.

But there was nothing that she could say to Norbo. There was only one thing to do—to be taken to Sonkor and there to learn what truth was in her fears. So, to this end, she prepared to play her part. She even thought of the curious disappearance of the money that had been brought to Loosang.

Her own bag was visible in a corner of the yurt, but the store of coins that had passed into the hands of the lama was not to be seen. Evidently he had disposed of them in some way.

Meanwhile the lama had bent his head to one side as if listening.

"I hear the voices of the council, the *sarga* of the Torguts, that is assembled in the tents of Ubaka Khan," he said. "They are cattle, those ancient ones of the Horde who bend the head to Natagai."

"True," assented Nadesha, wondering what he was leading up to.

She had known the council was in session to debate a message received from General Traubenberg, who was pursuing the Horde. The Russian offered pardon to all clans that would turn back with him to the Volga. So this night the issue must be decided, whether to press on to the Ili or retrace their steps to the Volga.

Seeing the hunger written in the thin cheeks of the girl, Loosang handed her a bowl of sweetmeats.

"The Khan is still as great as the lama," he observed dryly. "He is a yak, but the herd follows its leader. So—I hear his words:

"'My brothers of the tents, we are knit together as flesh with bone. Where one clan goes, all must ride. Or we shall be dust before the wind. Who would be a slave?'"

Loosang mimicked the slow, heavy tones of the Khan and threw his voice so that it seemed to come from the tent top. The girl ceased eating and waited anxiously.

"Ubaka is saying that at the end of the road ahead lies the valley of the Ili where are the graves of their fathers. There the gate in the sky can be seen, and the souls of the old Torguts may look down upon them."

"And what is the will of the council?" asked Nadesha, nibbling again at a date.

"Wait! And you will hear with your own ears."

Loosang motioned her back into the shadows behind him. Nadesha heard a small bell tinkle over her head several times. Soon came a footfall outside and a voice familiar to her.

"Norbo, Master of the Herds, is here to speak with the *chutuktu*. The *sarga* seeks the wisdom of the priest."

It occurred to her for the first time that Loosang had a watcher posted outside the tent in the shadow of the side of the gorge and that this man warned Loosang by ringing the bell of the approach of others. She smiled at the way her father clipped his words. Norbo had no love for Loosang, who opposed the old traditions of the Tatars cherished during the long stay in Russia.

Loosang, the priest, made a sign for Nadesha to remain quiet, where she could not be seen.

Norbo sat just within the yurt entrance facing the fire.

"Ubaka, our Khan," began Norbo bluntly, "has spoken in council. He says rightly that we should seek the skies of our old home. So does Zebek Dortshi say. But many of the *noyons* are wavering. So the vote was to send for your word."

Plainly the old chief did not relish his mission. The lines in his leathern face were deep as he scowled at Loosang through the heavy smoke.

As Loosang kept silence, Norbo repeated surlily.

"To press on, or turn our horses' heads? What is your word? For my part I follow Ubaka to the Ili with my clan."

The hand of the priest scattered more roots thickly in the fire.

"Look!" he croaked suddenly.

The glow of the flames died and a swirl of gray smoke swept up. Out of the smoke a stunted tree took form. Nadesha could even see branches in the semi-darkness.

She caught her breath and looked again. The tree was standing there, upright in the coils of smoke. Then a flicker of fire crept up, blazed, and the likeness of the tree was gone.

Norbo glanced up at the ceiling, then at Loosang, and bit his mustache.

"Go!" ordered the priest. "Say to the council you have seen an omen."

"What means the omen, *chutuktu*?"

"This. Out of fire and smoke will grow up the rooftree of the Torguts. The clans must go to their own land. I will show them the way."

Norbo's shrewd eyes snapped.

"*Ai-a*, that was the word of the mighty Genghis. It is a good word."

When he was gone, Loosang rose and stretched, chuckling to himself.

"You have heard, my little owlet. The lion asks counsel of the leopard. The lion thought he was strong and swift, but the steppe is wide. Oh, the steppe has a voice and a lure. It is like a fair woman. Men give their lives up to it. Now the lion limps, for he is lame—lame."

While speaking he walked slowly to the side of the hearth by the open flap, tossing upon the embers some brown powder he had taken from his robe. Again a thick smoke came up to the tent top where there was not the customary air vent. Nadesha choked.

Suddenly she sprang up with a cry. The fumes were strangling her. She started to run past the fire, holding her sleeve against her mouth, but Loosang thrust the girl back. Wavering, she sank down to the floor, her eyes closed, her lungs laboring. The lama, standing in the fresher air, coughed, and presently stepped outside, drawing shut the flap behind him.

Still muttering to himself, he hastened to the gully behind the yurt where his two disciples had been busied during the greater part of the evening. They had built up a shrine of stones, in which were stuck sticks bearing shreds of rags. It was customary with Loosang to mark in this fashion the places where his yurt had stood.

Now when he came to the pile of rocks the lama placed therein the bag of money Nadesha had given him and watched while the two men covered it up with more stones.

"For him who travels in the desert," he laughed quietly, "a landmark."

Chapter V

Loosang Sleeps

Rain was falling thinly as the Master of the Herds rode to find the quarters of his clan. The sky was broken—a cloudy dawn.

Norbo's powerful arms swung against his hips. Dried blood had stiffened one side of him, where shoulder and hip had been cut open by an enemy's sword. He had not eaten for two nights and a day, but tied to the peak of his wooden saddle was a hind quarter of an antelope, given to Norbo by a hunting party that he had met coming in from the marshes.

The old chieftain rode with his head raised. He was looking for the fires in the sky* that he had heard were to be seen above the valley of the Ili.

Very tired was Norbo, and he felt he would like to ride up into the gate where the souls of the elder heroes would come to meet him and all would have horses' meat and drink. He had been near to the gate that night, for the Baskir tribesmen had attacked the rear of the Horde in force.

Picking its way among huddles of soaked men and women, who lay sometimes half-submerged in water, the pony by instinct sought out its own clan. Norbo remembered a dawn last winter when he had passed by such silent groups, among them the body of his sister. The Tatars had frozen when fuel for the fires had given out.

"By the mane of my grandsire," he growled under his breath, "there is one who lies at ease."

His eye had lighted on the yurt of Loosang. Nearly all of the Torguts' wagons had fallen to pieces or been broken up for firewood; Loosang's was intact. The lama had given out word that he was about to sleep, in a trance, for nine days. During the nine days no one was to come within a spear's cast of his yurt.

Two disciples of the lama, armed, kept watch by the carved and painted wagon.

Norbo saw that a flag of yellow silk flapped above the wagon shaft. It was a prayer flag, and it had been hoisted when Loosang went into the trance.

His own yurt, together with that of the Khan, having been split up to be made into fresh spear hafts, Norbo's camp consisted only of a felt tent before which a half-dozen ponies stood obediently. He dismounted stiffly and splashed through a puddle, to peer into the entrance.

---

*The northern lights.

"Nadesha," he summoned, "I have meat; cook it. The clan must go forward within an hour."

Instead of the girl, Billings crawled out of the tent. His cheeks were pinched but shaven clear. After drinking from a bowl that had stood outside during the night, he offered it to the *noyon* without result and then emptied it over his head.

"Nadesha has not been here for a day and a night, uncle," he drawled.

Then, after shaking the water from his hair and rubbing it from his eyes, he set to work with flint, steel, and a pinch of powder to ignite some dry leaves and twigs he had kept dry in his blanket.

This done, the two men gave all their attention to nourishing the flame, first with broken pine branches, gathered during the last day's march against the possibility of food to be cooked, and then with damp birch sticks culled from a nearby thicket.

As the crackling grew, the smoke thickened, and the odor of sizzling meat spread in the air, men came to stand and look at the two. Norbo, who was gulping down his portion half-scorched, motioned them to come and partake of the meat.

"A plague on these savages," muttered Billings, cutting himself off a piece and roasting it on his long knife. "Raw or seasoned, 'tis all the same to them, and as for salt—"

With a sigh he contemplated his ragged garments, neatly sewn in a dozen places, and glanced over the plain of high grass, muddy and treacherous as a bog.

"Who among you has seen Nadesha the last day and night?"

Their faces, black with exposure to the sun, smoke, and grime, were expressionless. They had not seen the girl. Her pony, though, was missing from Norbo's herd.

"She chose her horse, yet took no weapons," Norbo grunted, frowning.

By noon he had no word of Nadesha. It was strange that the girl could have gone off from the clan in the center of the Horde without being seen. Billings, too, was thoughtful. He remembered that Nadesha had, when he last saw her, warned him to keep near to Norbo until this moon should be at an end. A blare of powerful horns caused him to glance up. The yurt of Loosang was approaching, rolling over the uneven ground, escorted by the two young priests, both armed. The yellow flag snapped and fluttered.

Billings watched it pass and kept his horse standing after Norbo's cavalcade had passed on. He was allowed to do pretty much as he chose in these days of mutual suffering. Riding alone, Billings had espied Alashan.

"Dwell in peace, brother," he smiled as the boy came up. "I have a word for you.

Alashan glanced at him coldly, but reined in and the two rode on in silence after the joggling cart.

"Nadesha," observed Billings, "has vanished. She is no longer in the Horde."

"And you?" The boy gritted his teeth.

"I am her *anda*. You are her betrothed. Good. This is a dark matter. I smell treachery, and so I would speak to you, as her brother."

Alashan became grave.

"You speak fairly. Do not forget that I have sworn to lift my sword against yours, until one of us dies."

"Meanwhile, Nadesha. The daughter of Norbo has been to talk with Loosang, not once, but several times. Now she is gone and the lama is not to be seen. No other Tatar, I think, would harm Nadesha. That is my word."

"What says Norbo?"

"Naught. But he is troubled."

"Then I will have speech with these snakes, and learn what evil Loosang has put upon Nadesha."

When Alashan spurred up to the sacred yurt, Billings was close behind. As the boy came within a spear's throw of the wagon, one of the disciples wheeled his horse.

"Back, Tatar! Away from the dwelling place of the lama whose spirit is with the living Buddha in the sacred city."

Alashan, however, kept on; and, his pony being the heavier, the *gylong*, the young novice, staggered aside, his loose lips shedding a venomous flood of curses. A second disciple, portly, and uncomfortable in the rain, faced Alashan from under the shelter of a purple canopy, held by two servants.

"Rascal unsanctified!" he bawled, taking care that his voice should carry to groups of herdsmen who had halted to watch the scene from a distance. "Ubaka Khan will set thee on a stake for this—"

Recognizing Alashan, the novice blinked, and his fat cheeks twitched.

"Is Loosang within?" demanded the boy calmly.

"The *chutuktu*'s body lies in the tent. In Sonkor, where he was abbot—"

"Stand aside. I would speak with the lama."

Such presumption made the pseudo-priest gape. His eyes grew round. All at once his stout body quivered. Snatching the umbrella from his attendant, be struck at the boy, who took the blow on his arm and reached out with his other hand. It closed on the crystal rosary the other wore, and he twisted it tight with no gentle touch. The mouth of the *gylong* opened wider and his eyes bulged.

"Harken," hissed the boy, "keep silence if you would not wear a noose instead of a rosary."

With a parting twist Alashan released the *gylong*. But the man was too startled to be reasoned with. As the boy jumped from his saddle to the wooden steps leading up to the front of the wagon, the fat fellow began to bawl again, sounding indeed very much like a cow.

As the son of the Khan raised the covering over the entrance, Billings saw the other *gylong* slip up the steps. The disciple had drawn a knife from the wide sleeve of a cassock. Billings had anticipated amusement, but matters were growing serious. He reined his horse up to the platform and caught the wrist of the *gylong*. A heave of the shoulders and the man was jerked back, to fall into a mud puddle.

Meanwhile the yelling of the fat disciple had brought the watching Tatars nearer. A glance showed Billings that they were from a clan unknown to him, and even in his rage the *gylong* had been careful not to mention the name of the son of the Khan.

The behavior of the two convinced Billings that Alashan had stirred up a hornet's nest. Drawing his sword, he swung from the saddle to the platform, shoving off the frightened servant who had been holding the reins. Alashan had disappeared within the yurt, and Billings was wondering what the boy had seen. But by now the herdsmen, convinced that something was very wrong, were beginning to run toward him. They shouted, brandishing knives and pikes.

Not so long ago Billings had encountered such a mob. He realized that Alashan had gone too far. With the fat priest crying them on, the Tatars would probably beat him to a pulp before they listened to any words from the boy.

Gathering up the reins in the hand that held his sword, he plied the whip that had been resting against the tent. Loosang's horses were well fed, and there were six of them. They lurched forward into the traces. Before the wagon could gain headway a pair of lean herdsmen leaped to the steps and lifted their pikes. Billings dropped the reins and was about to thrust with his sword, when he saw the two hesitate and lower their weapons.

"The wolf of Nadesha!" one of them cried.

They were looking at his belt. But Billings did not wish to be taken in hand, belt or no belt. He shouted to the herdsmen to give back and lashed out again with his whip. The horses broke into a trot and then to a jerky gallop. The two invaders dropped off.

Others, spurred on by the *gylong* who urged his horse frantically after the wagon, were running behind the yurt. A clamor of angry yells rose above the creaking of the axles and clattering of the wooden floor. The yellow flag whipped in the wind; the streamers snapped out from the eaves of the purple tent. Dogs barked.

Grinning, Billings plied the whip. It occurred to him that Loosang might emerge from within, and he kept a wary eye over his shoulder while he guided his imposing chariot along the muddy plain. He could make out two ample piles of skins, the beds of the disciples. Also a wine cask and an array of foodstuffs, all jolting about. A bell was ringing violently.

The tent bellied like a sail, and the front portions were torn loose from the floor pegs. From this aperture Alashan peered.

"By the mane of the white horse of Kaidu, what has happened?"

Taking in the situation, he smiled and beckoned Billings. As they had outdistanced the pursuers, the mapmaker brought his steeds down to a trot and tied the reins to a carved image of the sitting Buddha.

Behind a curtain stretched midway across the tent he saw a figure lying on a couch. It was clad in all Loosang's finery. Under the high, lacquered hat was the head of a panther.

As Billings looked, the eyes rolled in the head toward him, and the jaw of the beast turned a little. Overhead the bell began to toll again as the wagon crossed some rough ground. The flesh on Billings's back grew cold. In the strong odor of the tent there was a smell of something unclean.

"Look," said Alashan. Around the ridgepole were arranged other heads, some of familiar animals, some of ghastly and obscene shapes.

"A mask," muttered Billings. "What is beneath?"

"Nothing. Weights, hung under them, move these eyes of painted mica. The jawbone is loose. It is an effigy."

"To frighten those who might look in while Loosang is away."

"Aye. But here is no sign of Nadesha."

Abruptly the wagon slowed, lurched, and was still, tilted to one side. They were ditched. Looking out, Billings saw his pony and Alashan's horse. A spear's cast away was Norbo with his two servants and the pack animals.

Alashan walked to the horse of the Master of the Herds and Billings followed, while the Tatars stared in puzzled surprise. Luckily they were among a nest of dense thickets and no others were in view at the moment. But Billings knew that the mad flight of the sacred wagon across the plain had been seen by many, and that presently the fat *gylong* would catch up with them.

"My lord," the boy saluted the chieftain respectfully, "it is a lie that Loosang's body rests here while his spirit is abroad. Here is only a mask and garments. Loosang has gone from the Horde. Nadesha is not to be found. She has spoken with him. He is a master of evil, to my mind. I have read in his eyes that he lusts after her."

Unexpectedly the old woman-servant spoke up, seizing the stirrup of the noble, her master.

"My lord, chief of the *ulus*, it is said in the tents that the shape of the lama was seen on the night before last, riding like a demon as tall as a tree, and attended by his familiar in the form of a woman."

"Whither did they turn the heads of their horses?" asked Alashan.

"Who knows, my young lord? Up into the stars where the *tengeri* leap from mountain to mountain or down into the earth where—"

"Alashan," broke in Billings, "the fat priest called Loosang abbot of Sonkor. Is that truth?"

"Aye," assented the boy, "he comes from the lamasery that is nearest the steppe."

"Do you know where it lies?"

The boy shook his head, whereupon Billings showed him a strip of yellow paper he had taken from the wallet in his coat—the map of the Armenian, showing the caravan route from Constantinople to Tashkent. It was inaccurate and wildly picturesque as to distances. In the northeast corner was a picture of a tower and the legend "Sonkur." A mountain was drawn close by.

"It is in the air and in the water and the sand," muttered the old woman, "so the Kara Kirghiz say—the Black Kirghiz tribesmen."

With his sword's point Billings traced an equilateral triangle in the mud; then he glanced at the sun, reflecting dimly from the gray haze. With a last look at his map he replaced it carefully in his coat and thought for a moment.

"Sonkor lies in that quarter—" he pointed with his sword—"two days' and one night's hard riding."

Everyone except Norbo drew back hastily from the triangle in the mud, and all surveyed Billings expectantly. This was surely magic! Billings, with the knowledge that the *gylongs* would arrive very soon in the thicket, had done some rapid thinking.

The map—unreliable as to distances—told him that the temple of Sonkor lay near mountains, at the edge of the river Chu, which flowed from the mountains of Tibet far to the southeast. So the old woman had proclaimed—near the heights, the sand, and the water.

A single rider moves more swiftly than an army; Loosang would have left the Horde before they reached the point nearest to Sonkor. At the end of nine days he must be back again; so he could not give more than four days to each half of his journey, because even a Tatar *jigit* would need some hours' rest and a change of horses at Sonkor. Admitting that Loosang was travelling over the lower sides of his equilateral triangle, and the Horde had journeyed along the northern side for a day and a half, it was easy to see that Sonkor lay about two days and some hours and to the south by southeast.

Billings was sure of this when he observed that the route he had figured for Loosang and Nadesha skirted the edge of the Kangar. No one would willingly cross the Kangar.

"That will lead me through the desert," reflected Alashan.

"Will you follow Loosang?"

"Aye." Alashan turned to his horse.

Then Norbo spoke for the first time.

"You have not asked permission of your father, the Khan, to leave the Horde."

Nadesha was greatly loved of Norbo. All three knew that if she had gone with Loosang to the place of the lamas it would be only by the rarest of good fortune that she would regain the Horde. Loosang, if he desired the girl, would not bring her back to the protection of her father and Ubaka Khan.

Yet the Master of the Herds, who could not leave his post, reminded

Alashan that he was the son of the Khan and might not leave the Horde unbidden.

"Peace be with you, uncle," said Alashan moodily. "Let Zebek Dortshi and the others say that I have left the clan during suffering and hunger. Tell them so yourself, if you will."

He flung himself into the saddle.

"Give me goatskins for water, and another horse, Norbo! Give them to me. I shall follow Nadesha's trail until I find her." His dark cheeks flushed. "By the white horse of Natagai, my father will not call me a man! I go my own road."

The cracks in Norbo's worn face deepened and he pulled at his gray mustache. Billings, who had secured his own pony, now mounted and spoke, before the Master of the Herds.

"Alashan—" he listened for the splash of approaching hoofs—"I have told you one true word. And I have shown you where Sonkor lies. I can lead you to the temple with my maps. I will go with you."

The boy's eyes were hostile.

"Nay, I will find Nadesha without aid from you."

"Perhaps. But two swords are better than one. You are betrothed to Nadesha. I am her brother. We are together in this thing."

"*Kai*, be it so." Norbo nodded. "The son of the Khan must not go without a man to protect his back. Better a hundred of my clan—"

"Not so," barked Alashan. "They would take the word to my father at once and I would be bound and beaten." He looked long at Billings. "If you are my companion in this thing, you are nonetheless my enemy when it is over—if we both live. Is that agreed?"

Under his mustache Billings smiled.

"*Kai*—be it so."

There was no time for more. The man-servant who had been watching from the thicket reported the approach of riders led by the priests. Norbo quickly thrust the reins of his own horse into Alashan's hand, and gave the remaining riding pony to Billings.

"Come back to the Horde," he growled at Alashan, "or I am dishonored." To Billings he added coldly—"Protect the prince."

As they put spurs to their horses, drawing the two spare mounts with them, Billings was still smiling. Here was a chance at liberty. With a horse—two horses and a weapon—he could reach Sonkor and, by the aid of his maps, work south to Tashkent, where in time he could find a caravan going west to Samarkand and the Caspian.

In time, it could be done. He had promised to complete the map for Nadesha only so long as he should be with the Horde. Plying whip and spur, the thicket was soon left behind and they merged among the groups of tired riders who, half-asleep, splashed through the mud.

Behind them two furious *gylongs* righted the sacred wagon and searched fruitlessly the myriad tracks around the thicket. They shot questions and threats at Norbo in the same breath. But the old Tatar had retired into his habitual silence.

When the priests rode off he began to walk through the marsh with the ungainly gait of one whose stiff limbs are better schooled to the belly of a horse. Followed by the two servants and the pack animals, he trudged along, his eyes raised, from habit, to the gray expanse of sky in the east.

But not in two days and one night, or in twenty days, could Captain Billings have found the temple of Sonkor whither Loosang had gone with Nadesha. Before the sun had gone down for the first time, he had lost his direction and a cloudy night concealed the stars.

They kept the wind, the hot wind that had sprung up during the day, at their backs. They rode in silence, Billings in the lead. Progress was slow—deep sandy dunes to be met with for the most part, and serried clay gullies that turned them aside constantly.

Billings fancied that they were ascending. His ears strained for a sound, but the darkness was like a heated curtain. The croaking of frogs, the trilling of birds—all this had been left behind them with the marshland. Nor was there any moisture in the air. The steppe of the Kangar, the Hunger Steppe, was a blind labyrinth of dunes and gullies.

"Halt and unsaddle the horses," ordered Alashan, when the night was about half done and the air was becoming a little chill. "Eat and sleep."

Surprised, Billings reined in. The boy was already working at the saddle girths and made no response to Billings's questions. When the maker of maps climbed down, Alashan spoke curtly.

"We are wandering, first on one hand, then the other. I have been watching that rock for an hour."

He pointed behind them, but only after straining his eyes a long time did Billings make out a bulk that was darker than the sky and the sand, an outcropping of basalt or sandstone shaped like a pillar.

"You are merely keeping your back to the wind," pointed out the Tatar angrily. "The wind changes."

Billings heard the boy's jaws crunch on a portion of the dried meat he had carried between saddle and saddle cloth to keep it warm and soft enough to eat.

"Nay—your map was a picture; this is a desert. How will you find the right direction in the morning?"

Billings was engaged with his scanty rations of decaying cheese and tough meat. They had been able to buy some provisions from another clan, and had filled their goatskins at a pool before leaving the Horde.

The mapmaker was accustomed to laying a stick of wood along the course to be followed the next day when he made camp. But now he was aware that Alashan was right: he had been wandering from the true direction, and one quarter was like another. Moreover there had been no time at their departure to retrieve the compass from the packs containing his instruments.

"The sun will show us the way, Alashan."

"And if there be no sun?"

"Then we will see."

Morning dawned gray and cloudy. The wind had failed. The horses had found a scrub thicket of tamarisk and were feeding there, near a stagnant pool of yellow water. When Billings would have filled a half-empty goatskin here, Alashan pulled him back.

"That is death. Come, it is time—time."

They mounted, Billings stiffly, Alashan with a spring. The boy glanced over his shoulder.

"Which way?"

Surveying the sea of dunes, Billings noted the position of the purple finger of basalt. Away from this he turned his horse's head, and Alashan followed without comment. The boy rode like one possessed, pointing out the strips of clay that offered firmer footing than the sand on the tops of the ridges. He changed from horse to horse without halting.

At first Billings glanced at the boy, expecting him to halt, to eat. But Alashan pulled some of the dried meat from under a saddle and went on.

Billings removed his tattered coat and tied it behind his saddle, and then his waistcoat followed suit. He felt little relief. Then he tried chewing some of the meat, but that increased his thirst. Presently Alashan pulled down into the soft bottom of a gully. A line of tracks were visible.

"Two camels with riders," muttered Alashan.

He took the lead, following the tracks. They led slightly across the course Billings had been on. Before long other traces joined the camel tracks. Alashan studied them, dismounting in order to see the better.

"What can you say of this, my *giaour* captain?"

Utilizing the pause to fill his pipe, Billings shook his head good-humoredly.

"Nothing, except that they be horses."

"Horses of the Black Kirghiz. They are shod with yaks' hide, fastened by wooden plugs that leave traces in the sand."

"Hm," said Billings.

He had heard Nadesha say that the Kara Kirghiz were mountaineers, the most powerful tribe of Central Asia. Also, they were occasionally in league with the Baskirs from the steppe, the most bitter foes of the Torguts.

Alashan's green eyes were triumphant at the knowledge that he had divested the older man of leadership. Not Billings's fault, for the maker of maps had been unable to bring his compass and the sky had been clouded.

"There is another trail!" he exclaimed, pointing ahead.

This proved to be other horses, again two. Before an hour had passed a fourth trail turned into the main track. Billings reflected and turned to the boy.

"The Kara Kirghiz live in the hills to the south and east, the Hindu Kush. Four pairs, or at least three, are riding swiftly back through the desert. Do you see the meaning in that?"

For answer Alashan's lip curled. It meant that each man of the Black Kirghiz had a spare horse—and so was equipped for fast travel. It meant, too, that four riders outside their own lands were meeting at a rendezvous in the heart of the Kangar.

"The Black Kirghiz are dogs and thieves. They have sent men to spy on the Horde. They are returning with news of what they have seen."

"*Kai*—it is so." Billings nodded. "But what was their meeting place in this purgatory of God?"

The boy was indifferent. Nor did he take the precaution of riding below the ridges they had been following. Billings, however, was interested in the question of a landmark. How could four riders have met—or at least turned into a common path—within six miles? He studied the horizon and presently touched Alashan's leg with his stirrup.

Ahead of them was smoke, rising from a clump of dead trees. Alashan declared that tents were visible in the thickets under the gnarled willows.

He would have gone ahead, into the encampment, thinking only of finding his way at once to Sonkor and Nadesha, but Billings persuaded him to circle the spot, keeping behind the sand ridges.

"If they watch, it would be toward the north," he explained, and the boy reluctantly consented.

They found the place to be a village, some wretched shepherds' huts and a herdsman's tent, by a pool of muddy water. The peasants were away in the willow clumps along the dried riverbed in which the pool stood. The women and children ran and hid at their approach.

But on a bench outside a clay hut, Alashan found a Baskir man, dead drunk. A dromedary knelt by the desert rider, and under his sprawling feet was a sack of varied spoil.

"The Baskir fell in with the mountain men by chance," observed Alashan. "They gave him a skinful of drink to loosen his tongue and find out what he knew. Then they rode away to the south, as the traces show, in haste—because they did not lift his plunder. We will do so."

He sorted over the contents of the bag and found a soiled Cossack *svitza*, together with a fine red sash and green silk neckcloth. Rummaging further, he drew out a greasy lambskin cap. These things he gave to Billings.

"When we are outside the village you must put them on, my comrade," he pointed out. "The Baskir son of a dog has been robbing the dead in the path of the Horde."

He stared moodily at the snoring raider, and proceeded to strip him of *khalat*, pantaloons, leather leg wraps, and turban. When it was too dark to follow the tracks of the Kirghiz they halted and gathered some of the dried tamarisk branches for a fire, lighting it in a deep hollow screened by bushes. While the flame was bright, Alashan trimmed Billings's beard with his knife and shaved off the long hair back of the forehead. Then the maker of maps stripped to his shirt and boots and pulled on the rough nankeen breeches, the silk sash, and the heavy *svitza*.

The garments were rich in material and, though slashed and stained, were nearly new. Billings wrapped the green cloth about his neck and thrust the hat on the back of his head as he had seen Mitrassof do. He had the erect carriage of a soldier, and so the Cossack garments did not look amiss on him. Moreover the sun had burned his skin to the hue of leather.

Meanwhile Alashan had done likewise with the Baskir's outfit, screening his long black hair with the loose folds of the turban that came down to his shoulders. The boy's chin was lean, his nose thin and downcurved, so that he fitted into the part of a desert man.

Alashan looked up and his eyes narrowed. He had not known Billings would be so striking a figure in Cossack dress. "A real gallant," he told himself, and his eye fell on the belt with the wolf's head that Billings had cast carelessly into the sand.

"Would you part with that?" he cried.

"With what?" Billings glanced down and whistled reflectively.

If they were to go into Loosang's temple—and he had given up hope of overtaking the lama before then—he could not well wear the emblem of a Tatar clan. Alashan himself had suggested the disguises as necessary when he saw that the Kara Kirghiz were afoot.

"Look here, Alashan," he suggested, "why don't you keep the thing, under your girdle? Nadesha is your girl."

The boy flushed angrily. He would not receive a gift from Billings. The mapmaker could never understand the boy's nature. Nevertheless, he did not bury the wolf's head in the sand with his other worn-out garments but left it lying by the fire. In the morning he saw that it was gone, and judged that Alashan had it about him.

As they were lying down on their saddle cloths to sleep, Billings turned to the boy.

"Do you think Nadesha went with Loosang of her own will?"

Silence. Billings felt that he had said something harmful.

"Alashan, it looks as if the Kirghiz, whoever they are, were gathering around Sonkor. What does that mean?"

It was so long before the son of the Khan answered that Billings lay back and was settling his shoulders in the sand when a jackal snarled from beyond the hollow.

"The wild dogs are sitting on their haunches," said Alashan in a low voice. "The jackals have come from afar; the vultures are in the air."

"Here?"

"Nay, around the Horde."

Billings, as he pictured the road-weary clans crossing the desert steppe, a hundred and fifty miles in three days, thought this was more than likely.

Sonkor would not have been found by Billings alone for the reason that it was hidden from any searcher who should come over the steppe. Alone, the captain might have combed the plateau for months and seen only the occasional *aul* of a shepherd, or the basalt shafts that might have been tombstones of giants.

But Alashan followed the Kirghiz tracks with the nose of a ferret until hostile tribesmen, appearing ahead of them on the trail, forced them to turn aside. Then it was Billings who used an old trick of the explorers and ascended a height from which the ground in front of them could be surveyed as clearly as if drawn on a map.

"By Jove!" he said.

Even Alashan drew in his breath quickly. The red clay sloped away sharply in front, evidently to the edge of a precipice. Beyond and below this was a great, green valley topped on the farther side by mountains of immense extent. In the center of the valley they could see a sluggish river winding, and on the nearer bank of the river a camp of more than a thousand tents, with ranks of camels and horse herds grazing near the water.

"The Chu," Billings decided.

"And the camp of the Black Kirghiz," assented Alashan gravely.

They looked for signs of the horsemen they had seen along the trail, but the riders had vanished. It was late afternoon, and darkness would set in before they could pick up the tracks again and follow them down to the river.

Alashan pointed out the high, black hats on some of the soldiers in the nearest tents, the stacked arms, and the standards topped by huge elk antlers. He judged there were at least eight thousand of the tribesmen. The distance was too great for Billings to see these particulars, but it struck him that the number of horses was more than that.

"True," agreed Alashan after a pause; "the Kirghiz have been raiding. No Kirghiz women are in the camp. The horses have been lifted from the Baskirs, when most of the Moslem tribesmen were riding against us."

"Then it is well we did not follow the riders down to the Chu," Billings pointed out. "You wear the garb of a Baskir."

Alashan seemed indifferent. He was squinting into the distance, trying to read the answer to the question as to what brought the power of the Kirghiz so near the steppe. His face was drawn. From the *aul* where they had obtained their disguise they had wandered for two days, being forced to camp at night in order to keep the trail in view. It had been a test of endurance, and both were still fit. They had drawn on their reserve strength, Billings more than the Tatar, and their eyes were overbright, their hands restless.

"What are the Kirghiz doing here?" asked the mapmaker.

The tents seemed to him to be arrayed in a sort of semicircle, facing the height on which they stood.

Said Alashan, bitterly: "The wild dogs are sitting on their haunches, waiting; the jackals have come from afar. The Kirghiz live by raiding down from the mountains, but this is greater than a raid. They ride to a slaying."

"Hope it's not us," thought Billings. "I am going to look at the edge of that precipice," he added aloud. "That sandstone rock might be a watch-tower."

They had not much fear of being seen from below because numberless masses of sandstone made the summit of the slope jagged, as if it were a crenellated battlement. Billings climbed from his saddle and slipped down the slope, holding to the points of the rocks. He was careful not to dislodge any of the soft fragments of stone. Coming to the edge, he ducked down and, lying on his belly, stared over the brink. He was looking at Sonkor.

The precipice was nearly sheer, a wall of red and purple stone, beneath which stood a black temple. It was black from the top of its twin towers to the crude wall of flat rocks that surrounded its courtyard. Its lines were curiously deceptive.

"The walls slope in markedly, and so do the towers," he thought. "Let me see, two, five, seven rows of windows. Arrow slits, rather. Must be seven stories high. The slope inward must make it look gigantic from the Chu."

The peculiar black appearance was due to the stone used—granite and basalt, evidently brought by boat from the upper gorges of the Chu. (Billings was observing for the first time some of the devices used by the Tibetan lamas to make their temples formidable, in looks as well as strength. In Lhassa there were monastery halls with pillars of chenars that did not grow within a thousand miles.)

He saw too that more tents of the Kirghiz were clustered just outside the courtyard wall and that the court and the roofs of the temple were quite deserted.

Returning to Alashan, he reported what he had seen. The boy was all for searching out a way down the cliff. Billings nodded, but their exhausted horses stood with heads close to the ground, and legs quivering.

"Done for," Billings reflected. "Food's gone. Sunset—dark in half an hour." He glanced at Alashan. "Can we enter the Kirghiz camp? It surrounds the temple on three sides, and on the other side is the cliff."

"Nadesha is there, in the lamasery."

"True. And Loosang is there. Alashan, tonight is the sixth of his nine nights away from the Horde. It is in my mind that tomorrow he must mount again to ride to the northwest. If we are to reach Nadesha before he goes it must be this night."

"True." Alashan gnawed his lip. "In the dark we can slip through the camp, keeping away from the watch-fires. Within the lamasery we would find the going harder. No one is allowed within the temple gate except the guests of the lamas, and they are watched by armed guards—"

"I saw no guards."

"They watch from the embrasures. If the sons of the devil are all within the temple it means they are preparing a ceremonial for the night. If so the doors of the lamasery will be closed."

Billings tethered his horse reflectively to a dead oak and shrugged. Even the moon had been obscured for three nights, as if to make their efforts useless. To get down the cliff in the dark would be hard work. For a pseudo-Baskir and a Cossack bravo to penetrate into the temple of Bon would be a problem. To find Nadesha and speak with her under the nose of Loosang would be a miracle—if, indeed, Nadesha had actually reached Sonkor.

But Alashan was convinced that she was there. So far the instinct of the boy of the steppe had proved true.

"Have you a plan?" Billings asked the son of the Khan.

Alashan laughed, for the first time since the mapmaker had known him.

"I have no plan, captain. But I feel that a way will be opened. Look, there are vultures in the sky over the camp; and the sunset is red—the gate in the sky is red. There will be blood under our feet this night. *Kai*—I know it."

"He's a fool of a pagan, and a savage," thought Billings. "But, may the black pest take me, I can't let him go down into that cesspool of Satan alone. I'll stand by him until Nadesha is found, or the boy gets his throat slit; then I'll look after myself."

A brazen thunder shook their eardrums. It seemed as if the very clouds overhead had trumpeted down a challenge. Billings swore and clutched at his sword hilt. Alashan glanced up from narrowed eyes.

Again came the note of the trumpets, repeated three times, fainter and more mellow. An echo came back from the mountains across the river.

By a common impulse the man and the boy turned and ran back toward the summit of the slope leading to the cliff. Looking over the rise cautiously, they beheld four black figures below them on the edge of the cliff. Four bronze trumpets, longer than the tall musicians, were leveled out across the valley.

Then the horns were lowered over the precipice and the three notes repeated. This done, the four lamas turned to one side, in single file, and disappeared among the nest of rocks that Billings had called a pulpit.

Billings chuckled under his breath. He could see thousands of ant-like figures running out of the Kirghiz tents to stare up at the cliff.

"The way is opened," whispered Alashan. "There must be a passage down to the temple from the spot."

They crept after the four from boulder to boulder until they came to a sandstone ridge halved by a wide crack. Alashan pointed to the print of feet in the dust here. Entering the shadow between the rocks, they left daylight behind them at once.

Shelving downward, the path turned aside into what seemed solid rock. But here Billings saw the gleam of a candle far down and ahead of them. Quickening their pace, they hurried on and at the next turn made out the trumpeters, in single file, the leader with the candle.

The immense horns delayed the progress of the lamas so that Billings and Alashan kept up with them easily. The cleft had changed to a kind of wide tunnel, twisting and irregular. Only in the steepest descents were steps cut into the soft stone. Limestone, Billings believed, and judged that water had cut this channel down into the valley of the Chu hundreds of years ago, when the river was still eating its way down to its present course.

More than once they passed along the floor of a lofty cavern, their steps muffled by the inch-deep carpet of white, powdered rock. And once they edged warily across a natural bridge over such a cavern, almost losing sight of the candle as they did so.

The air grew much warmer. They were forced to stoop now, to work down a low passage. Billings judged that the air here was heated by the rays of the afternoon sun on the cliff outside, and that they must be close to the entrance. Nor was he wrong.

"——," he muttered.

He had seen the lama in the lead pause at a heavy, wooden door, and knock. The portal swung open. Stooping, the four trailed out with their horns. The door swung shut. Billings and the boy were in total darkness. Both knew that they could not find their way back. True, they had flint and steel and some powder, but there was nothing in the cavern to ignite.

They made their way down to the door, knocking their heads more than once. Feeling the stout boards cautiously and pressing against them, Billings decided the portal was barred on the outside. Wiping the sweat out of his eyes, he considered.

"Alashan," he whispered, "the lamas have stationed a guard at this end of the passage. The men with the horns did not open the door themselves. There was a sentry on the other side. Good. We will knock and get ourselves admitted to the presence of Bon before the guard goes elsewhere."

He did so, rather hastily. It had occurred to him suddenly that the lama on watch might have gone away after the others, being posted at the door to let them in. But it was likely, if anything unusual was in the wind that evening, that a man would be stationed to watch the door.

A step sounded on the other side of the barrier. Billings knocked again, loudly, as if he had a right to enter. One of the bars was taken down. Then silence.

Plainly the man on the other side was puzzled. Billings rapped a third time, impatiently.

"Stand back," he ordered Alashan softly. "Be ready."

The other bar came down. The door swung toward them, concealing them in its shadow. A shaven head, wrinkled and bare as a snake's, was thrust into the passage.

A flash, followed by the sound of metal striking bone. Alashan had brought down the back of his sword viciously on the priest's pate. The man sprawled forward, coughing, writhed; and Alashan struck again, this time with the edge. Then he caught the long, cassocked form and tugged it well into the passage. Billings was not prepared for this.

"*Tchou*, my cousin," Alashan hissed, "would you tie a viper with silk, or play with an adder in the dark? Besides, he is not dead. You do not know these devils. Look!"

He lifted the head of the guard, pulling back the lips from the teeth. Billings saw that they were sharpened to points. He glanced out of the passage. No one else was visible.

A lamp glimmered in a basin of oil beside the doorway. They could make out that the room outside the passage was very lofty, that its walls were the white limestone itself. In the center of the chamber directly in front of them was what appeared to be a broad column of black lacquer.

After Alashan had closed the door and replaced the bars, leaving the unconscious lama in the passage, they searched the walls for another exit. A second door stood opposite the first, and this also was locked on the outside.

Billings listened at the crack and made out a dull murmur some distance away. It was the camp of the Kirghiz. He knocked tentatively, but this time there was no response.

"Stop." Alashan caught his arm. "If we are seen coming from here, it will be the end of everything."

He pointed up over his head. They could see the front of the lacquer column now. The candle, behind it, framed in blackness a score of arms projecting from the sides.

"A spider," muttered Billings.

"Bon," said Alashan softly, "the Destroyer."

The entangled arms ended in hands, each gripping some weapon or object. In one was a child, in swaddling cloths. Snakes and varied beasts kept the child—in lacquer—company. On the breast of Bon, who squatted on a square pedestal, was a tiny woman, her legs and arms clutching the broad body of the god.

They could see clearly, because a round window in the rock wall directly in front of the face of Bon admitted the last, ruddy light of sunset. The face itself was like a Buddha, cold and expressionless.

"Pfagh!" grunted Billings.

He could understand now that the lamas had availed themselves of a large cavern just inside the cliff wall for a tabernacle for the figure of the god. The opening in the cliff let in light during the day, and permitted worshipers from the plain to see the face of Bon. If illumined from within, the effect must be striking.

Even as they watched, the last gleams departed from the glittering crown of Bon. They looked at each other curiously. To break down the door would be to bring the lamasery swarming about them. To return to the height by way of the tunnel was impossible.

There remained the aperture in the cliff. But the rock wall was sheer. So the two intruders sat down and listened to the faint sounds from the camp. They knew that in time someone would come into the chamber of Bon from the temple to relieve the guard at the tunnel door. Then they might slip out. Looking up once restlessly, the mapmaker drew in his breath.

The countenance of the god was shining with a soft, green light. It was a reflection of some kind.

"The moon is up," explained Alashan calmly.

Suddenly Billings chuckled and sprang to his feet.

"I know how we can look from the hole in the cliff. Help me up this pedestal."

When Alashan had boosted him up to the footstool of the image, Billings began to climb the front of the giant god, pulling himself up by the arms that stuck out in every direction, and the limbs of the clinging woman. Now the highest pair of arms were folded, hands crossed, just under the chin of Bon, so that Billings was furnished a perch within a yard of the round opening. Alashan joined him. The statue being fashioned of solid wood under the lacquer work, they were secure.

The ceremonial had begun. They looked out directly over the roof of the lamasery, between the two towers. Billings fancied that the door from the cavern led out upon the roof itself. The moon was rising somewhere to the left, over the valley, but its half-light was eclipsed by the smoking glare of lines of torches in the courtyard of the lamasery. Here the lamas were standing in rows, forming a lane out of the court, through the Kirghiz camp, down the slope toward the Chu.

"When the moon is full, these devils drag out their idols to the river for all to see," muttered Alashan. "It is at this time expeditions set out from the land of the *Tsong Khapa*. See, the Black Kirghiz are watching."

Already a line of *sakyas*—neophytes—carrying lighted pastels were moving out of the courtyard. Next was led a black horse, bearing the state robes of the abbot of Sonkor, horsemen in yellow cassocks, with painted spears. Behind a boy carrying a basin of glowing coals were thin Tibetans with the standards of Sonkor—long poles, wrapped around with rags.

"A tawdry manner of finery," thought Billings. "Hulloa!"

Following the standards and other rows of disciples came a cart filled with women wearing lotus flowers and carrying the blossoms in their hands. Seated among these women was a small figure wearing a red *khalat* and a cloth of silver cap.

Billings glanced at Alashan. The boy had recognized Nadesha in her Persian dress as she turned her face.

"There is Nadesha, the daughter of Norbo," he said calmly. "But Loosang I do not see."

Indeed, the cart bearing small, painted images of various gods that came after the women had no human occupant. Billings reflected that here was Nadesha's country of a thousand devils—the land where men wore the faces of beasts. For the lamas carrying the four trumpets of Sonkor were masked as usual.

But Nadesha herself was here—apparently of her own will—and riding in the cart with the women attendants of the temple. Billings wondered if she had left the hard lot of the Horde for this estate. He knew that Alashan, who loved Nadesha fiercely, did not believe this. He himself suspected that Nadesha was up to one of her games, a trick that bade fair to be her last, because it was Loosang she tricked and the lama had her in his power.

"Climb down," whispered Alashan curtly.

Not until he had quit the circle of subdued light did Billings hear the sound of the opening door that had aroused the boy. It was too late to gain the ground. They waited, poised on the fat belly of Bon, the Destroyer. Three men entered the outer door.

Loosang was the leader. The two others were bearded tribesmen, wearing heavy black lambs' wool hats and with girdles literally stuffed with weapons—good ones. For all their swagger, they eyed the great form of Bon sidewise, and Billings was grateful for the deep shadow that covered the front of the god.

As if puzzled by the absence of the guard, Loosang inspected the inner door, the candle, and walked around the image of Bon. Then, satisfied that no one was to be found in the rock chamber, he squatted down facing the tribesmen.

So long did the *chutuktu* wait before speaking that one, a red-haired giant, looked up.

"Where is that Russian money, you fox?"

"In the tents of the Horde, Nuralin Khan."

They spoke freely, believing themselves alone, and in Tatar, the common speech of the steppe. Billings did not understand it all, but learned later from Alashan what had passed. Afterward Billings decided that Loosang had taken pains to stow this cache away for himself where no one would find it.

"*Hai*, it shall be ours, Loosang, my owl. And the horses and camels of the Horde—tens of thousands of them, you say. And their weapons, bought of the Muscovites, captured from the Turks; good pieces, you swear. If you have lied, I'll make you dine off your cassock."

He leered at the lama, blinking. Nuralin Khan had kissed the jug that night. Then he began to stroke his unkempt beard with a hand on which the very hairs were red.

"All that is very well, my *chutuktu*. But you claim half the spoil. That is too much even for a devil like you."

"If it is too much, then you and your dogs can search out the Horde on the open steppe. Attack them there if you will, and see if you will raise their hides or not." Loosang spoke coldly.

The other Kirghiz, a stunted man with a pinched mouth and evil eyes, snarled at this.

"You have sworn an oath, Loosang. You have pledged your word to lead the Horde to the place where we will wait, in the hills. If the Torguts go the other way, over the plain to Balkash, then you will have no profit. Nay, our paths lie together in this. Keep faith with us, or we will bring our cannon to knock down the walls of Sonkor—"

"Fool, spawn of a lizard! Will you go against the word of him who is master of Lhassa?"

The elder Kirghiz fell silent. But Nuralin Khan, swaying as he sat, continued his grumbling.

"You will sit safe in your yurt, Loosang, while we face the arrows and the flintlocks of the Torguts. Ubaka Khan is an ox. He will take a lot of killing."

"And I—" Loosang's lips drew back"—have arranged that Ubaka will not be at the head of the Horde when you strike it. There is another khan in the Horde who will see to that."

This impressed the two chieftains. They looked at each other and asked the name of the lama's confederate. But Loosang was not telling all he knew.

"How many riders have you, Nuralin Khan?"

"A thousand and another thousand tents.* More will join us at the appointed place."

"You were foolish to plunder the Baskirs. With those wolves hanging on the flanks of the Horde, your task would be easier."

"And there would be more to share the Russian money in the Torgut tents, the leather and furs and weapons and horseflesh. As it is, a half is too much for you."

"A half of my share goes to Lhassa. The Dalai Lama is pleased to be angry with the Torguts because they favor the old beliefs and turn their eyes to Natagai, in the skies."

"So they must die, eh? Well, it is all one to us, provided you keep faith." Nuralin Khan considered. "Ubaka has been driving his men and beasts too hard. My *jigits* are in from the Kangar and they say the Horde is weak—weak."

Loosang stuck out his long neck, as if pleased. The Baskirs, he explained, had done that; the Russians under Traubenberg had not followed the Horde beyond Orenburg. So the Moslem clan had pursued the Torguts on its own account. Ubaka had thought the Russian army was on the march, and the Baskirs its advance.

When he might have rested in the fertile lands before the Kangar, Ubaka had set out again on his journey.

"How was that?" demanded the old Kirghiz.

"I persuaded him through the khan who is my friend. After the crossing of the Kangar his riders will be like foundered horses. They will go down before your swords like wheat under the wind. Not more than a hundred times a thousand souls are still living in the Horde. Mustering even old men with spears and young boys with arrows, they will have only fifteen times a thousand to ride against you. I will arrange that they suspect nothing, that the clans travel far apart, the fighting men mixed with the sick and the animals. You must have your full strength drawn up at the place agreed on."

The small eyes of Nuralin Khan twinkled. He stretched massive arms, one at a time, and yawned.

"The old women and the men will be slain; the younger women who are yet alive—"

"Half to me."

*About fifteen thousand men.

"Aye," leered the older Kirghiz, "silver and gold may be had for the Tatar youths in the slave market at Bokhara."

"It is all one to me," drawled Nuralin Khan. "By the Lotus, you councilors of the pit can slay many men with words. But my sword must do the work, you foxes."

Quickly he lifted his head. Alashan had been breathing rapidly during the conversation that revealed the treachery of Loosang. Just then his scabbard had slipped down from his knee to the full length of its strap and clanked against the lacquer image.

Nuralin Khan sprang to his feet. The moonlight had been growing stronger; by it he could make out, cradled in the long arms of Bon, a shapeless mass.

"*Tchou!* Look—it moves!"

The rat-faced chief, perhaps remembering that they had been speaking none too reverently of the sacred gods, ran to the outer door. Nuralin Khan followed more slowly, glancing back over his shoulder.

Loosang stood his ground, frowning.

Meanwhile Alashan acted. He leaped bodily for the lama, but landed heavily within the shadow in front of the image, plunged down on his hands with the shock of the fall. This was enough for Nuralin Khan, who fled through the door.

Perceiving that he was deserted, and, sensing danger, Loosang slipped out of the door, closing it after him before Alashan could reach him. The bars outside the portal were dropped into place, and Loosang's high voice lifted in a warning shout.

"Come, Alashan." Billings joined the boy, who stood trembling with anger, sword in hand. "Pick up your hat."

He unbarred the door into the passage, signed for Alashan to help, and carried the still unconscious guard back to the spot where the boy had jumped down.

"Loosang did not see you. I watched. Pray that some tribesmen come in with the priests."

He quenched the lamp and drew the Tatar back with him into the passage, closing the door nearly, but not quite. Almost immediately the outer portal swung open and a dozen armed lamas appeared, Loosang among them.

The torches that the newcomers carried soon revealed the prostrate figure under the pedestal of Bon. After scanning the chamber and finding nothing else amiss, they advanced to stare at the guard. They turned him over, noticing the bruise on his shaven skull.

Then Loosang looked up at the giant Bon as if puzzled. He had seen a man drop, in the shadow. Here was a man with a bruise on his head. Palpably this servant of the temple had been playing the spy, and—of all places—in the arms of the Destroyer. Loosang was not satisfied.

With a cry, one of the Tibetans pointed out the deep sword-cut across the side of the wounded man. They pressed closer, lowering the torches to see better. Some tribesmen edged inside the door in the wake of Nuralin, who had sobered rapidly. This moment Billings chose to slip out of the door opening from the passage and move along the wall with Alashan. They were concealed by the shadow cast by the ring of priests.

"The passage!" shouted Loosang, noticing the door. "Whoever has entered has gone back that way."

Although the most degenerate of men, the lamas were not lacking in zeal, daring, or intelligence. They rushed into the passage for the most part. Others bore out the body of the guard and started to clear the staring Kirghiz out of the temple.

Billings and Alashan had joined the tribesmen during the confusion. The mapmaker had pinned his trust to human curiosity; but this same trait was now confusing the Kirghiz—who had been drinking—to wonder how a Cossack and a Baskir were in their company.

Once outside the door, however, Billings gave them no time to grow more suspicious, but made off down the first stairway to hand. It led through the refectory of the temple, out into the courtyard. Coming from within the temple, they were not challenged.

They pushed through groups of the lamas, went out into the camp, and turned aside among the lines of camels where there were no fires. Alashan wanted to go down toward the river to find Nadesha.

"Listen, my captain," he said briefly. "What we have heard must come to the ears of Ubaka Khan, my father. We have not yet learned the place where the Kirghiz will lie in wait for the Horde. We must know that. Nadesha will find out. Then we will take her with us and steal horses from the cordon."

They came to the wagons standing by the riverbank. Most of the women of the temple had mingled with the crowd of soldiers and were laughing and singing about the nearby fires where feasting was going on in honor of the festival.

Nadesha however still sat on the edge of the temple cart, a lotus flower between her lips, her dark eyes, rimmed with *kohl*, surveying the crowd that kept at a respectful distance. For Loosang, mounted, and wearing his yellow robe of office, was beside her, a half-dozen armed lamas close behind him. Around the wagon eddied groups of tribesmen, thin Turkomans, squat, turbaned Chatagais, quarrelsomely drunk.

"The vultures are flying together," whispered the boy bitterly. "They would not attack the Horde in fair battle. They seek a corpse to pick bare with their beaks."

Billings nudged the youth to silence. It was all-important that they speak with Nadesha before Loosang and the women withdrew into the lamasery, where no tribesmen would be welcome. Just then Nuralin Khan swaggered up, having recovered from his scare at the temple. He advanced close to Nadesha, hands on hips.

"By the belly of Bon, here is a wanton to make glad the eye of a chief. A round face and a bright eye, a form fair and melting."

Nadesha smiled at him, and the Kirghiz sought to take her hand.

"Peace, Nuralin Khan," shrilled Loosang. "She is a Tatar who has claimed the protection of the god."

"Tatar or Persian—all one to me," mumbled the other.

And Billings, seeing his chance, thrust Alashan back. Pushing the Cossack hat over one eye and lifting the green neckcloth to cover his mouth, he lurched forward, clapped Nuralin Khan on the back and leaned heavily against the wagon, his head almost upon Nadesha's knee.

Nuralin Khan looked around, his hand on a pistol, but seeing only a besotted Cossack he spat and returned to his quarrel with the lama. Loosang glanced keenly at Billings, but the red-haired chieftain was between them.

Meanwhile Billings kept muttering to himself. The girl at first glanced contemptuously at him, then her eyes widened and she leaned forward, apparently to watch what was going on between the others.

"Captain Beel-ing," she whispered in Russian.

"Alashan is with me," returned Billings. "How can you leave the wagon and join us?"

"I cannot. The men of Loosang have orders to seize me if I put foot down from the cart of the women."

Nadesha smiled, gratified that two men had risked their lives for her. She could not keep her eyes from seeking out Alashan in the shadows.

"Ai-a!" Her mobile face clouded. "Why did you disobey my word and leave the Horde? I planned for you to show them the right road when Loosang tries to lead them where death waits."

"We will all go back together, Nadesha. That is—you and Alashan."

Billings broke off to curse a staring Chatagai and thrust the man away. The mountaineer laid hand on knife and eclipsed Billings's curse with a vitriolic insult. Billings drew his sword and the tribesman edged back, muttering.

"Harken, Captain Beel-ing," cried the girl. "I have found out that for which I came hither. Loosang plots with the Kir—"

"I know. Alashan seeks to learn the place of ambush."

"The ford of the river Kara-su. Remember, and go. Rejoin the Horde."

"Alashan will not go without you," said Billings, and repeated, "The Kara-su."

"Kai!" The girl's eyes glowed with pride. "He must go to his clan. Loosang will ride there, too. He must leave me in Sonkor. Tell Alashan that I will escape before long."

But Billings knew there was little chance of that. Nadesha, it seemed, had tricked Loosang. To do so, she had thrown her own life into the hazard. He had not realized before how much he liked Nadesha.

She threw off the hand of the Kirghiz and pretended to turn her shoulder to him.

"Alashan must ride with the news," she whispered to Billings. "Then Ubaka in truth will call him a man, and the Horde will know him for a son of the Khan—"

Breaking off swiftly, she lifted her chin.

"I am the woman of Loosang, the *chutuktu*. Go, Cossack, and wallow with your pigs of Christians!"

Billings had been too intent on her tidings to heed the silence that had fallen about them. Now he saw that Nuralin Khan had drawn back, that the Chatagai was whispering to Loosang, and that all eyes were on his naked sword. Too wise to try to leave the cart, Billings coughed and rolled his head stupidly, aping a drunken son of the steppe. The lama, head thrust forward, surveyed him.

"You ride far from your steppe, Cossack," he observed in Russian.

Billings blinked as if beholding the abbot for the first time.

"Aye, *batko*, father—I followed a thieving Baskir and lost my way on the Kangar."

He mumbled his words, but Loosang pricked up his ears. Billings's Russian was far from perfect.

"A Cossack—lost his way on the steppe! That is a lie!"

"I kissed the jug once too often, father."

"A Cossack—with a Frankish rapier!"

His long, straight blade had excited the curiosity of the angered Chatagai, who had pointed it out to Loosang. All the Cossack sabers were curved, after the lines of the Moslem scimitar. Billings was reluctant to open his mouth again, but there was no help for it.

"I had it from a merchant in Zaritzan. Devil take you, priest! If you want to sample the blade, set a tribesman against me; come, do!"

The other tribesmen pressed closer, and Nuralin Khan laid one huge hand on a long pistol stock. He had guessed the meaning of Billings's words.

"I will shoot the heart out of the dog," he proclaimed, lifting the weapon.

"Peace!" The lama held up his hand. "That sword I have seen before. *Ekh*—here is the *giaour*, the Christian prisoner of the Tatars!"

Nuralin Khan craned forward, interested. A thin smile spread the lips of the lama.

"Aye, this is the brother of Nadesha, who would make a map from the sun, to guide the Horde."

His vindictive delight showed how much Billings's seizure meant to the priest.

"Now my way is clear," he was whispering to Nuralin Khan.

"Loosang, *chutuktu*," broke in Nadesha, "I have kept my promise. I have delivered the *giaour* to you, in your hands. Now I claim protection of the gods."

Her brown eyes flashed warningly at Billings, as if to tell him that she would yet find a way out. But the maker of maps was eyeing Nuralin Khan's pistol. Words, he knew, could not help matters now. A few swordstrokes and it would be all over, one way or the other. He set his back against the cart and waited. Loosang bent toward the girl.

"Harlot!" he said. "The spy has spoken with you."

And he struck Nadesha on the lips. As he did so a figure in a soiled *khalat* and loose turban slipped between the Chatagai and Nuralin Khan.

Alashan decided matters in his own way. With the dagger clutched in his left hand he stabbed Loosang, the knife striking into the ribs of the lama. A squeal of pain came from the tall man's teeth.

A flurry in the throng, a general cry of rage. Alashan leaped to the cart as men rushed at him. He threw the dagger into their faces, caught Nadesha up in both arms, sprang off the opposite side of the wagon. Here, in comparative darkness, there were no bystanders.

"To the river!" shouted Billings.

He parried the stroke the Chatagai aimed at his head, thrust the man through the throat. Freeing his blade, he slashed wide at another face, and jumped to the cart.

Nuralin Khan's pistol blazed; and the powder blast stung his hand. Billings turned and ran after Alashan and Nadesha. The boy had set Nadesha on her feet, and the twain were running swiftly away from the torches, between the tents. A lane opened up ahead of them, and at the end of it gleamed the surface of the Chu.

The thudding of feet behind him told Billings that pursuit was close. He halted and swung about, crouching. A spear whistled over his shoulder, and his blade clashed against the scimitar of a Kirghiz.

The man staggered from a thrust in the stomach, and another who followed at his heels drew back before the glitter of steel.

Billings turned and dashed off, looking about for a horse. Instead he saw a group of armed men at the end of the tents, and Alashan and Nadesha struggling furiously against overpowering force.

"Captain Billings!" shouted the boy, his voice breaking. "Leave us. Ride to the Horde—warn my father—"

There was a sharp snap as his sword broke. Nadesha was still making play with her dagger. But Billings saw at once that they were as good as captives. Indeed, as he changed his course and darted between two tents he heard Alashan singing his death chant defiantly.

After all, Alashan had taken his own way in dealing with Loosang. For once luck favored Billings and he found himself among a nest of felt tents—the quarters of some noble. Tripping over the ropes, he dodged about, catching glimpses of running men and turning away from the glare of torches.

In front of him he sighted the river, a dense thicket of reeds lining its bank. This however was the goal toward which his pursuers were headed. A group of them were plunging close behind him, but momentarily he was in shadow, and they had lost the scent.

Billings halted, looked about, and flung himself on the ground, crawling under the side of a pavilion. Small chance, he thought, for him on the water, so bright was the moon. As he expected, the large tent was vacant, the occupants—if there had been any within just then—having run out at the noise of the pursuit.

It was a large tent, belonging to a person of importance, and a filigreed, bronze lamp hung from the top of the pole. Garments, skins, weapons were scattered about. Billings tore off his Cossack coat and cap, selected the first fur-edged *khalat* his hand touched, and donned a huge, black lambskin hat that came down over his ears.

Only a moment remained before the lamas would begin investigating the tents. Billings ducked out as he had come and began to walk quickly back toward the temple.

"They'll be harrying the river and the outskirts of the blessed encampment," he reasoned. "It won't do to leave for a while."

Suddenly perceiving that his sword was still bare in his hand, the blade smirched with blood, he thrust it under the *khalat* and swaggered on slowly, pausing when lights went past and avoiding the campfires.

"This won't do, either," he reflected. "The Kirghiz will be looking for a Cossack, to be sure, but the eyes of those devils of lamas—I can't chance that."

As a matter of fact the tribesmen he passed paid no attention to him. He saw nothing more of Alashan or Nadesha. The tumult had quieted down, but he noticed that the number of torches flickering among the reeds had increased and that armed and mounted lamas were patrolling every main avenue of the camp. It would be only a matter of time before they recognized him if he remained where he was.

Heading back to where he and Alashan had passed among the herds, he came to a fire, a mere bed of embers, over which a cauldron smoked with an appetizing odor. Several sleepy horse guards were lying about. These Billings joined. One muttered.

"*Temou chu!* Dwell in peace."

"*Ahatou*—brother," responded the mapmaker, dipping his hand into the cauldron. He was aware, all at once, that he was giddy from hunger. There were still portions of mutton in the pot, and of these he ate ravenously. From time to time Kirghiz came to the horse lines, saddled animals, and rode off.

"A very wizard of a *giaour* is afoot. We must take him," one said in reply to a lazy question from the men around the fire. "No doubt he was drowned in the river. May the black plague take the lamas."

Another who sauntered up from the direction of the temple did not even seek out a horse, but squatted down to light his pipe from the embers.

"They have the Tatar buck and his fiend of a girl up at the temple," he observed, yawning.

"Have they been tortured yet?" one asked.

"Nay; Loosang has sworn that the princeling and the woman shall be taken by the lamas to our ambush on the Kara-su, so that their eyes shall see the death of their clan."

The moon, by now, was low to the west, and Billings judged by the mist over the river and the feel of chill in the air that the night was well advanced. His companions, all but one who smoked and spat into the fire at regular intervals, were snoring. The camp was dark except for the towers of Sonkor upon which the moon still struck, over the trees.

It was time for Billings to move. Leisurely he rose, went to the pile from which he had seen Kirghiz taking saddles, selected one, and moved toward the line of horses. From the corners of his eyes he watched the dark bulk that was the wakeful horse guard. The man's pipe glowed on tranquilly.

Evidently Billings's stay at the fire had disarmed any suspicion. Nevertheless he was uneasy until he had secured what he sought from the piles of gear by the cordon—saddle bags, with a fair quantity of rice, dates, and dried meat. Then he flung the saddle on a large pony, praying that his choice might be a good one, adjusted the halter, and mounted.

"Peace be with you, brother," muttered the guard.

Guiding himself by the loom of the cliff on his left, he threaded his way through the camp. Once he passed a patrol coming in. Quickening his pace, he hastened to be out of sight of the camp before dawn should come.

His luck held good that night. A heavy mist rolled up from the river, and although Billings heard sentries calling more than once, he was not stopped. The memory of the fox-like faces of the lamas made him use his spurs.

"With daybreak," he reasoned, "they will follow any single track out of the camp. But I could swim my horse across the Chu, strike down south toward Tashkent, and be out of their reach in a few hours."

The river beckoned him to safety. Once in the caravan routes to Turkestan, he would be on his way back to Astrakan. This was what he had planned—except that Alashan and Nadesha were prisoners of Loosang instead of free. On the other hand, north of him was the Kangar, and he was in poor shape to cross the desert again. True, it would be skirting the eastern edge of it this time, but the country was strange to him and without Alashan he would be at a disadvantage. And soon the warrior monks doubtless would hit upon his track.

Alashan and Nadesha were dead, or as good as dead, he ruminated. Even if he should carry the word of the ambush to the Horde, it would not help them a whit. In fact if he reached the Horde he was not at all sure he would be believed.

He was very tired after the exertions of the night. The pleading eyes of Nadesha would not be dismissed from his mind. What was it the girl had said—when two are brothers neither abandons the other?

"Plague take it!" muttered Captain Billings. He jerked his horse's head to the left and trotted into the gullies that led up the slope to the north, toward the Kangar.

"We'll have a return match with Loosang, and it will be a good one."

As if to echo his words, from behind and below him came the blast of the morning trumpet call of Sonkor.

Chapter VI
The Ambush

> *The prudent man crosses the river at the ford; the shrewd merchant when his path leads into the mountains turns aside and seeks a valley.*
>
> *The foolish one swims his horse across the river, and spurs from peak to peak.*
>
> *Yet when death comes to the twain, it often happens that the wise man lies in a grave forgotten in the valley while over his head on the mountain summit stands the gold-adorned tomb of him who was unwise.*
>
> —Proverb

Fortune, Captain Minard Billings was fond of saying, was very much like a wild horse; it would never wait when you came after it with a halter. But for all that, luck had served him well in many a tight place. And this, perhaps, was because he never waited for fortune to knock at his door.

So it was at the Kara-su, the Black River. This was the stream that marked the boundary between the hills of the Kirghiz and the clay waste of the Kangar. Before it reached the water, his pony died. By his calculation he was yet a long day's ride from the Torguts, who, he judged, were moving eastward across the Kangar.

The trail he had been following north and east led down through the foothills to a ford—the river at that season in spring was in flood—and here he fell in with some Tajiks fleeing down the stream. They told him that they had seen the dust of the Horde moving toward the Kara-su from the steppe.

Billings drank his fill, washed, crossed the river, and walked briskly toward the steppe. A little more than a mile out, where the familiar gullies began, a camel rider appeared followed by a party of horsemen.

Without more than a curious glance at Billings they pressed ahead; their sweat-darkened beasts had scented the river. Then the sun glimmered on the points of lances and the long barrels of flintlocks. Through the dust, ahorse and afoot, threading the gullies came the Red Camel clan—red, in truth, with the baked dust that coated them. Invisible on either hand, Billings heard the *hoa-hoa* of men driving animals, the scuffle of hoofs, and once the eager cry of a child.

The Horde had sighted the river. Yet the cracked faces of the marchers showed no animation; their eyes were half-closed in a ceaseless squint; some slept in the saddle. They moved steadily on, and the loads they carried were the same with which they had entered the Kangar, a hundred and fifty miles back, four days ago. Billings was enveloped in a sea of moving things.

In order to stop the Horde he must find Norbo. Scrambling up a hillock, he caught sight of Zebek Dortshi in the center of the clan, brilliant in his crimson and velvet.

Billings knew that the Horde was far out of its true course—far to the south. (He suspected that the fact Zebek Dortshi was leading accounted for this.) And on the other side of the river death was lying in wait.

The quick-eyed chieftain noticed Billings's Cossack dress and urged his horse over toward the hillock. Behind Zebek Dortshi came a group of riders, Ubaka in the center. The Khan seemed weary; dried blood caked the corners of his mouth, and his woolen coat was thrown back exposing his knotted, bare chest. Norbo was not to be seen, among the riders who were all *noyons* of the council.

Billings, although Zebek Dortshi was the last man he wished to meet, hastened down toward them and raised his hand. His message could wait no longer.

"I have word for the Khan," he shouted in Russian.

Zebek Dortshi's brown eyes flickered as he recognized Billings, and he spurred his horse to keep between the mapmaker and the other Torguts.

"What is your message?" he asked.

But Billings moved aside and caught the eye of Ubaka. The Khan reined in with a frown.

"Where is my son?" he demanded.

The other khans pressed up close to Billings, staring at him and talking together in guttural whispers. They were restless, and he suspected that there had been dissension in the council. He wondered how much Norbo had confessed to Ubaka. Lifting his hand to his forehead in greeting, he spoke.

"May the way be open before you, Ubaka Khan. I have a message from Alashan, from Sonkor."

They were silent at this, all eyes intent. Zebek Dortshi gnawed his mustache and moved his horse nearer to the Englishman, who was now surrounded by a solid ring of riders.

"*Hai!* You have gone far and fast. Where is your horse?"

The chief of the Red Camel clan looked around at the others as if to warn them that he discredited Billings.

"Dead, on the other side of the Kara-su."

"The Kara-su! Is that near?"

It was Ubaka Khan who spoke, his deep voice ringing with amazement. Billings reflected that Zebek Dortshi seemed to know where they were, while the Khan did not.

"A mile behind me. Those hills—" Billings turned and pointed to the wooded heights two miles away—"are on the farther bank. I passed through them yesterday. Some shepherds on the river told me the Horde was coming this way. So I waited to give you the word of Alashan."

"Where is my son, that he will not face his father?"

"A prisoner. Nadesha likewise."

The Tatars waited quietly. Even the Khan showed no emotion. Alashan, his son, had left the Horde without permission from his father, and so, in the eyes of the Tatars, both were disgraced accordingly.

Billings pointed to where some armed riders of the Wolf clan were coming along the trail, Norbo among them.

"The Master of the Herds," he said, "can tell you why Alashan left the Horde and why he is in danger."

Now old Norbo was a faithful servant of Ubaka Khan; but he had never learned to shape his words like a courtier. He spoke what was in his mind, when he had to do so. And so he did now. Dismounting, he pressed the stirrup of Ubaka Khan to his forehead and, drawing back, raised a scarred hand to his head and lips.

"Speak," said the Khan.

"Lord, your son saw vultures gathering in the sky. Nadesha, too, had seen. She left me without asking my will and rode to Sonkor. Alashan and this prisoner followed, to learn what was to be found out at the temple of the lamas. He could not go to his father for permission, because he suspected treachery in those about the Khan."

"Treachery!" Zebek Dortshi laughed aloud, twisting the while the curls of his beard with deft fingers. "Aye, it is in my mind that treachery is afoot. Hear my word, O Khan!"

Knowing his listeners, the Persian Tatar paused, until sure that he would be understood. He was a skilful orator.

"Hear my word, Ubaka Khan," he repeated, and he did not give the other the title of Ruler of the Horde. "Is it reasonable to think that those suckling brats, Alashan and Nadesha, would have tried to ride to Sonkor? Captain Billings is the sworn enemy of your son. Would they be comrades, all in a day? Not so."

Smiling, he shook his head.

"Not so. And what word could this *giaour* bring from Sonkor that is not known to Loosang, the all-wise? Bethink you, Khan, did not Loosang warn you against this stranger from beyond the Volga? *Tchu!* He did!"

Then Zebek Dortshi frowned as if scornful of such tricks as Billings might play.

"This is what has happened, members of the *sarga*. The *giaour* has fought with Alashan, perhaps slain him. Aye, to avert the anger of Ubaka Khan the *giaour* has tried to flee. He failed. Then he has made lies, so that his crime shall be overlooked.

"Loosang, the lama, is all-wise. He foretold that evil would come of the stranger. Cut off the fellow's tongue, pierce his eyes, and let us, by the sacred Kandjur, ride on to the water. I have spoken."

"And well—you have said well," cried several of the younger chieftains.

"Speak, *giaour*," snarled Ubaka Khan.

Billings had been waiting for this chance.

"The Khan of the Red Camels lies," he said bluntly. "And here is the proof that the treachery was not of my doing."

He pointed behind him, to where the endless stream of riders was moving through the dust toward the gray glimmer that was the Kara-su.

"The Horde has been led out of its path in the time that I was not with the clans. There lies the Kara-su, the Black Stream. Beyond you can see the mountains, the foothills of the Kara-bagh that mark the territory of the Black Kirghiz. Lake Balkash lies back on your left, and it is far—far. Tell me, who guided you hither?"

All eyes turned toward Zebek Dortshi. But just then was heard the sound of blaring horns and creaking axles. Through the dust came the painted yurt of the priests. On the trail abreast the gathering of horsemen it paused. Once more the *gylongs* sounded their horns and waited, in the attitude of heralds.

Loosang appeared in the entrance of his tent house. He wore a purple cassock, and his thin face was ghastly, so that the skin seemed yellow parchment stretched over bones.

"The sleep of nine days has ended," he proclaimed in his high voice. All of the khans except Ubaka—who ranked with the lama—Norbo, and the chieftain of the Bear clan, dismounted and bent to the girdle.

"My spirit, Tatars, has been in the holy places. It has been in the mountains of the *Tsong Khapa*. I have a message for the Torguts. It is this. Continue your journey; drink in peace of the water you see in front of you; camp on the farther bank of the river. Have no fear but I will lead you to Balkash and the valley of the Ili."

A murmur of approval greeted this. The khans stood erect, looked eagerly toward the gleam of water. Zebek Dortshi, well pleased, took snuff.

"By Jove," thought Billings, "the old conjurer can ride. No wonder Zebek Dortshi was sure of his ground—after he had been speaking with the confounded lama."

To the Tatars—those who acknowledged the Dalai Lama—the pallor of the *chutuktu* was ample proof of the long trance to which he had subjected himself.

Norbo, knowing that Billings was a skilled geographer and that Nadesha had set great store by the Englishman's map, drew forth the chart of the steppe that Billings had made. He showed it to Ubaka, and the mapmaker explained their position, pointing out how the Horde had left the route to Balkash.

With a word Loosang dismissed it.

"Here are marks upon paper; there is a river and water."

The Tatars shouted approval and glared at Billings. But Ubaka, who had been silent, lifted his head with a roar.

"Quiet, dogs! *Giaour*, have you a token that you have been to Sonkor? For if you have, then this river is verily the Kara-su!"

They snarled, and Zebek Dortshi laid his hand openly on his sword hilt.

"A token?" Billings's eyes blazed. "By my faith, I have one. It is the message from your boy, Alashan."

"A boy," mocked Zebek Dortshi fiercely, "who rides after a girl. Men of the *sarga*, will you listen to the word of a dishonored Tatar—"

"—who may die at the hand of your enemies for sending this word," barked Billings. "Alashan warns you that Nuralin Khan and ten thousand Black Kirghiz are in ambush across that river."

"A lie!"

"Easily proved, my khan. Send patrols into the mountains; and if they come out unhurt I will break my sword and let you cut off my skin, Zebek Dortshi. The Kirghiz were at my heels the last three days." He swung around to face Ubaka. "They hold your son and Nadesha. The lamas hold them. Loosang has betrayed the Horde to Nuralin Khan."

Stirred by this, the Tatars mounted instinctively, and each man felt for his weapons. Ubaka's broad face darkened. His slow brain grappled with the problem while his great hands clenched.

"Proof!" snarled Zebek Dortshi, ignoring the suggestion to explore the land across the river.

"I will give it. Loosang at Sonkor offered the horses and women of the Horde to Nuralin Khan. I heard it, and Alashan too."

"Mad are you," said the Khan of the Red Camels, his brow clearing. "For it is known that Loosang has been within that tent—" he pointed at the purple from which the streamers hung, limp and stained—"for nine days."

"Not so. Alashan stabbed him in the chest when the lama struck Nadesha. Bid Loosang open his cassock and you will see the mark of the wound, fresh and scarce healed."

Loosang alone had remained calm. To Billings's surprise the lama slipped the long garment off his shoulders, and opened a heavy, quilted vest as thick as a man's fist. Over his ribs they could all see the dark red slit in the flesh made by a knife. Billings realized that the quilt had kept the dagger from reaching a vital spot under the ribs. Loosang laid a yellow finger on the seal tranquilly.

"It is true—true—" his high voice broke the silence—"that Alashan stabbed me. True, that the boy was hot with anger because Nadesha, his betrothed, had sought the protection of the gods. Seven days ago, when my body lay in this yurt, the boy and the *giaour* entered my wagon by force. Many Tatars saw it."

"True!" echoed the *gylongs* and more than one chieftain.

"Then Alashan stabbed me and fled. You, Norbo, know of that. You saw him fly from the sacred yurt."

The old Master of the Herds was speechless, confused by the swift wit of the priest. There was a cry of anger as he failed to deny the charge. Loosang raised his eyes to the sky.

"But my spirit, Tatars, was with the holy ones, at the knees of Bon. So, though my body was cut open, I live. Many times you have seen me cut myself with knives in the rites of Bon, and no harm came to me."

"Alashan!" A groan broke from the cracked lips of Ubaka. Suddenly his broad face grew purple. "By Natagai—by the shades of our ancient heroes in the sky—by the lights of heaven, you are lying, priest. You are a snake and your tongue poison. I believe the word of my son. Get back from the river, you dogs! Halt the clans! Am I Khan or a worm that lives in dung?"

Zebek Dortshi drew his sword, glancing around him.

"Let the *sarga* give its decision," he cried. "Is the council the servant of a mad ox?"

Ubaka rose in his stirrups with a bellow, but Norbo and the chieftain of the Bear clan grasped the reins of his horse. It was too late for sword-strokes. Loosang had turned the scales in favor of the Persian. Zebek Dortshi had wheeled his horse and called for the chieftains to follow him to the river.

Sight of the green fields and the shade under the dense forest across the Kara-su were too much for the thirst-tormented Torguts. First one then another put spurs to his horse. The dust rose in clouds.

Riders, who had been awaiting the end of the council, made off full pelt along the clay gullies. Shouts rose and were repeated along the columns of tired Torguts.

"To the river!"

But the yurt of Loosang did not move. A twisted, evil face was thrust close to Billings.

"Nadesha and Alashan," whispered Loosang, "are in the hands of a band of my followers, who will let them see the slaying of the Horde. Then my trumpets will sound and the head of the boy will be cut off. But you will be taken again to Bon—again to the arms of the god, to Bon, the Destroyer. I wait for that hour."

With that the priest was gone into his wagon.

A mass of cattle—the last survivors of the herds—came plunging along, joining in the general rush toward water. Billings, the Khan, Norbo, and two others who had remained were forced to mingle with the throng.

The clay gullies ended about a quarter of a mile from the edge of the flooded Kara-su. Here the ground sloped down evenly to the river. But on the other side there was a scant two hundred yards of lush grass before the forest set in.

Billings scanned the thick screen of alders that merged into the hemlocks, dense overhead yet clear around the trunks, good cover for an ambush. The hills, as if designed for this event, were rolling, a score of valleys opening into the strip of grassland by the river.

Almost as soon as it began on the farther bank, the trail vanished under the thickets. He could see no sign of men or weapons in the forest—nothing more than the crows that circled overhead erratically.

Norbo, too, noticed the birds.

"My time has come. This dawn when I looked into the sky I felt that I would be called."

Ubaka rode with his head sunk on his bare chest. He seemed not to hear.

"The Horde," he said between his teeth, "that was my grandfather's and his father's, even to the great Genghis—the Horde has no longer a Khan."

The thought that his son had deserted him took all the strength from his body. But the mind of the mapmaker was alert. When they reached the top of the slope leading to the water he saw the muskets of the Bear clan, slung over the men's shoulders, like a thicket. The heavy cavalry had kept together, even in the confusion.

"By Jove," he muttered, "I'll make Loosang wait a good while."

The sight of the orderly muskets of the Bear clansmen had roused him and set his wits to work. There was yet time, and something must be done. Only half of the Red Camel riders had crossed the ford. But others were spreading along the bank of the flooded river, looking for places to cross. Every moment brought more Tatars down from the steppe.

Billings could act only by forcing Ubaka Khan to act. And the chieftain had sunk into a kind of stupor. So Billings set his teeth and stooped down to pick up two fistfuls of gravel. The Khan and the men with him had dismounted.

Without warning, Billings threw the dirt into the face of Ubaka. It was perhaps the worst insult he could have hit upon. The Khan started and raised his knotted hands quivering above his head. His eyes grew red. The next instant, however, his head sank again and the clenched fists beat his bare chest instead of striking down the mapmaker.

"Aye," he muttered, "it is fitting that that dirt should be cast upon my beard."

Throwing his sheepskin cap on the ground, Ubaka Khan tore at the long scalp lock that fell over his shoulders.

"The *sarga* has turned its back upon me. When I spoke men laughed. It is the end."

The face of old Norbo writhed in silent anguish at this display of emotion. A Tatar never, of his own will, reveals pain. Billings was amazed by the result of his effort. It shocked him to see passing Tatars laugh at the old man. To them the dirt upon Ubaka's beard and the hair of his chest was only a proof that Zebek Dortshi was now the leader of the Horde.

Then Billings was filled with a cold rage. It was monstrous to watch a whole army, women and children too, ride to death. His own fortunes he had ceased to think of. Fatigue and the exhaustion of the last ride from Sonkor eclipsed everything but the one idea—to rouse Ubaka Khan.

"So," he said bitterly in Russian, "you are a woman. You tear your hair and let men spit upon you. Truly they call you an ox. You let a butcher rip out your throat, and you have not courage enough to draw back. Pah!"

The red eyes of the chieftain were dazed.

"Alashan had my honor in his hand. I trusted him. I would have made him a man."

Norbo laid his hand on Billings's shoulder.

"Forbear, *giaour*."

"Let be, you old dog." The maker of maps shook off the hand. "Do you want Loosang to make Nadesha a temple harlot?"

Seeing Norbo start, Billings pointed to the heavy cavalry.

"Those men will help you hold back the Kirghiz. The Khan is as good as dead, but you and I are still on our feet."

"We can give no command without Ubaka Khan."

"Watch me."

Billings turned to Ubaka and asked bluntly for the signet ring that was the Khan's seal of office. Ubaka shook his head, but allowed the Master of the Herds to draw it off.

"Norbo, this is what we must do within an hour. The riders of the Bear clan are here. Keep them in position. Order the women and children of your own clan to the rear and the men here. What are these two others that kept with us?"

"The chief of the Leopard clan and the master of artillery. We have no artillery."

"Nuralin Khan has."

Billings thought a moment. He noticed for the first time that the ground upon which the Tatars were deploying formed a kind of half-moon, where the Kara-su curved in its course. They were, in fact, on the highest point of a promontory, faced on three sides by the forest and the hills across the river. All of this ground could be raked by cannon from the other bank.

It was a good ambush, that of Nuralin Khan.

"——," muttered Billings. "Norbo, send the chief of the Leopard clan to bring up his armed fighters to the top of this slope. Send the women and children and baggage back along the trail. Order the master of your guns to ride far back along your line of march. When he has reached the clans that have not seen the river and do not know what is happening here, tell him to instruct the khans to muster their able-bodied men and ride forward with them alone."

Norbo moved away stolidly with the ring, and presently Billings saw the two Tatars mount and ride off. From a servant who still attended Ubaka, Billings took a telescope and studied the ant-like figures of the Red Camel Tatars. That clan had crossed the river, and the men were moving up slowly into the thickets. Fires were being lit here and there. Saddles were taken from the horses, which were grazing eagerly. Some women were singing.

Boys were gathering brush from the edge of the alders and piling it on the fires. Below him the herd of cattle had reached the riverbank and were churning the water into mud. A hot sun blazed down on the grass—still fresh with the moisture of early summer. Crickets kept up a chorus that was dwarfed by the stamping of horses, the creak of leather, and the cries of children.

Norbo, who had been urging the mounted Tatars to charge their muskets and string their bows, returned and wiped the sweat from his eyes.

"Who can stem the course of a torrent?" he grunted. "The Horde will not hold back from the river."

The numbers of soldiers around them had increased; but as Norbo said, the momentum of the mass was too great to be easily halted. More came up from the rear, with only one thought—to gain the shade on the farther bank.

"Hark to the crows," muttered Norbo. "They do not lie—I know, I know. And there goes Zebek Dortshi's red coat into the pines."

"The Red Camel clan is lost," nodded Billings. "There is nothing more we can do.

Then Norbo raised his hand, and the Tatars looked up. From the forest across the river came the blast of a great horn. It echoed down the valley like a brazen gong. Under the screen of the pines a pistol barked. A second time, faintly, the horn sounded.

"The trumpet of the lamas!" cried Norbo. "*Ai-a*—men are in those hills."

All noises had ceased in the Tatar throng. Children looked up at the sky, expecting the sound to be repeated. Men paused in the act of unloading the pack animals.

In the silence Billings could hear the distant *hoa-hoa* of drivers coming up with camels from the desert trails. But Norbo and his men heard other sounds, drowned until then by the clamor of people around them. Horses neighed over in the hills; brush crackled faintly here and there.

"Men are in those hills," repeated Norbo earnestly, nodding his gray poll. "They are coming this way."

By now Billings could see that the men of the Red Camel clan were gathering into groups. Other clans who had been about to cross the river held back. The lines of riders coming over the steppe were at a standstill. The bronzed faces of the Tatars were intent; they seemed to be trying to smell the air.

The momentum of the marching Horde had ceased. No longer did the drivers back on the steppe cry, "*Hoa-hoa!*"

"Thank God for that horn," thought Billings, wondering how one of the lamas with Nuralin Khan had been so idiotic as to sound a blast before it was time. He judged that the Kirghiz lines had been placed well back in the hills, to allow as many of the clans as possible to cross the river before the attack was made.

He observed that boys were running here and there in the Red Camel gathering, saddling horses, and that the women were moving back toward the river. The men were fingering muskets and watching the line of alders into which more than one scout had plunged at the sound of the shot.

Then from the brush ran a bareheaded man, waving his arms. Through the telescope Billings saw that his *kaftan* was torn to shreds. A crackle of musket shots broke out at the back of the fugitive.

The crackling spread along the river, grew to a splitting roar, and smoke began to float up over the pines.

The outcry of the crows was no longer to be heard. The groups of Red Camel men were thinner all at once, for many seemed to sit and lie down. Here and there horses reared. A woman carrying a bundle fell and rolled over, kicking up her booted feet.

In the ford a herdboy slid off the back of a camel into the water and did not appear again. Wailing came to Billings's ears, and a curse sounded from nearby. For the most part, however, the Tatars, schooled to misfortune, were silent even under the sting of wounds.

"Look!" cried Norbo, pointing.

At intervals on the heights across the river whole trees fell over. The round, black mouths of cannon peered out at them. At once they flashed, one at a time, and were hidden in dense, white smoke. The balls thudded into the grass or ripped through the mounted Tatars. Some raised great spouts of sand.

Back in the valleys, a half-mile away across the river, the heads of mounted columns appeared. The patter of the muskets continued steadily.

A few feet beneath Billings a little Tatar girl, her head bound in a clean, white kerchief, was standing hugging a doll. It was one of the household images that every Tatar yurt possesses. Billings saw the child start and look at her plaything blankly.

Red drops showed on the face of the felt doll. Then the girl began to whimper. All at once she screamed and tried to run back up the bank. Her feet failed her, but Billings picked her up.

She had been shot through the chest, over the heart. Knowing that there was nothing he could do to save her life, he laid the child in a hollow in the bank and mechanically picked up the doll to put in her lap.

She continued to whimper more loudly, but could no longer move.

"Loosang will pay for that," Billings promised himself, turning away.

As he was swinging into the saddle of a passing horse he halted, surprised.

Ubaka Khan was again in the saddle. The old Khan had cast off his coat and was bare to the waist. His brown body, heavylimbed as a bear's, was erect as he stood in his short stirrups to see the better. He had grown taller in the last moments, and his glance was hard and quick.

"Khans of the Torguts," his tremendous voice roared out, "ride to me."

The officers were already doing so. Ubaka glanced around and began to swing his naked sword over his head in a flashing circle of steel.

"Where is the *tugh*? Fetch the standard to me, you curs! Assemble your men, you sheep. Line the ridge with your horsemen."

"Aye," shouted one.

"Tell us what to do, father!" implored another.

"Where is Ubaka Khan—Ubaka Khan?"

Cries were heard in all quarters.

All those on the nearer bank could see the great bulk of the chief under the circle of steel that never stopped swinging.

"Llai-hai-hai!" roared Ubaka, seeing the standard approaching. "The Kirghiz have been building a *lopazik*.* We will tear it down. Where are my riders? Let me see their steel! Good, good, you sons of dogs."

Norbo threw back his head and bayed. The shouting was taken up along the line that began to fall in at the summit of the knoll. Norbo hurried off to put himself at the head of his clan.

"Where is Zebek Dortshi?" barked Ubaka. "I will put a blade down his lying throat."

"Master of the Horde," spoke up a man on foot who had been one of the first to run back through the ford, "I went with Zebek Dortshi into the forest. Few were with him. He met a lama and two Kirghiz khans and spoke with them, while his followers were cut down. Then we heard the trumpet blown, and the Kirghiz were angry. One of them shot at Zebek Dortshi. I ran away—because I saw that he had betrayed us, O Khan."

The man eyed Ubaka's broad blade fearfully.

*A platform in a tree from which to shoot game.

"Lord, Zebek Dortshi, when he knew that he was to be slain, put his back against a tree and smote down several who came against him."

"The jackal died like a lion," grunted the Khan. Suddenly he knocked the fugitive sprawling with the flat of his sword.

"Let no Tatar run from an enemy this day. My son spoke a true word. By the name of Natagai, Alashan sent us a true warning. He is the son of my loins. We will charge the Kirghiz."

The old man was drunk with pride and fury. But Billings laid his hand on the arm of the Khan. He pointed to where masses of the black hats were deploying from the valleys along a three-mile front, facing them. And on the ridge itself the Tatar horsemen were suffering from the heavy musket fire. Soon the cannon would be shotted for a second discharge.

"You would be an ox in truth," he said angrily, "to move forward into this trap. Let the Kirghiz cross the river, and hold this ridge meanwhile. They have fifteen thousand musket men and lancers, and you have not two thousand armed men here. Look at those cannon!"

The eyes of the Khan glowed red. Then he quieted and gazed long across the river, where the unfortunate clan was being cut down. He paid no further attention to Billings.

Nor did the massacre of the Red Camel clan and the plight of the Tatars on the farther bank hold his gaze, which sought out only his fighting men. He tugged at his mustache while the bullets began to whistle over the heads of those who were listening for his orders.

"For that word," he said under his breath, "you are a free man, Captain Billings. *Kai*—it is so."

Whereupon Ubaka Khan did a thing that amazed Billings. He ordered all the Tatar cavalry to retreat at once to the steppe.

If the stout shade of Starshim Mitrassof could have looked down from the everlasting quarters of the faithful Cossacks in the sky and seen what had come to pass on the steppe, no doubt the colonel would have slapped his ribs and chuckled with glee.

It was not a battle such as European marshals fought. It was the final, desperate struggle of a multitude for life, against a pack that lusted to take life and with life, spoil. For the Kirghiz had achieved the first slaying; they had reddened their swords in the bodies of the doomed clan of Zebek Dortshi, and Nuralin Khan himself had stripped the body of Zebek Dortshi, who had once been the hero of the Horde.

And the Black Kirghiz, like wolves, delayed to torture briefly the bodies of the older Tatars, with the children—to violate the younger women who had been caught on the Kara-su, or to snarl over booty loose under their hands. Then they moved forward into the steppe, and behind them came the jackals, the nimble tribesmen of the Kara-bagh, Tajiks, Sarts, and robbers generally who had held off until then to see which side would win the opening skirmish.

Retreating at once into the plain, Ubaka Khan, if he had been leading European troops, would have thrown his regiments into disorder, turned soldiers into fugitives, and laid his supply train open to attack.

But he had no supply train; every man carried what food there was under his saddle. And every Tatar knew how to handle himself in a feigned rout. Two miles back on the waste of clay, what had seemed a disordered mob of men became a gathering of armed clans, dust-grimed and grim, and with weapons ready.

Also, they were beyond range of the Kirghiz cannon and out of the net that had been thrown around the bend in the Kara-su. The delay of the Kirghiz in crossing the river had enabled Ubaka Khan to form into clans some eight thousand riders to oppose nearly twice that number of pursuers.

Windless clouds of dust revealed that camels, cattle, women, and children were seeking concealment in the loess gullies or riding to distant springs or climbing to mesas where they could rest and watch the smoke puffs that marked the line of battle. Strings of riders were hastening to the menaced quarter of the Horde.

"They are like bees when you break into the hive," said Billings to himself. "Or beavers, coming to a hole in the dam. But the charges of those black hats must cut them up before they have formed."

The rattle of muskets began again, and the dust stayed in the air. Billings began to perceive that the Tatars were not holding their ground, nor were they being cut to pieces as he feared. The clans fought separately, drawing the Kirghiz on and turning upon them fiercely with arrows and sabers.

The flintlocks of the Tatars, except those belonging to the Bear clan and the veteran infantry of the Turkish war, were handed to striplings younger than Alashan and to grandfathers whose hands trembled but whose sight was keen.

These held the tops of clay buttes and the sides of dried watercourses, taking cover behind the scrub that covered the breast of the Kangar. Here and there in the groups he saw young girls with bows. They had small, sharp knives thrust through their belts to use on themselves if the Kirghiz should take them.

No one paid any attention to him. As a precaution he had discarded his Cossack hat and coat. He sought for the yurt of Loosang until he sighted it standing apart as usual. There were no disciples in evidence this time.

Drawing his sword, Billings made his way through the curtains. He saw the bed of Loosang and on it a tall figure with a hideous face.

"Turned into an image again, by gad," he muttered, gazing down into the mask. "Can't be too sure, though, on my word!"

So he thrust his blade into the effigy of clothes and wool and found that it was, in fact, not Loosang. The lama had disappeared. Sheathing his sword, Billings wandered to a height where he could make use of his telescope. He wanted to find Norbo or Ubaka.

All he could see were countless bands of horsemen, visible when they topped some rise in the plain, and separating into couples above whom steel flashed in the sun when they came together. Here and there men were sitting on the ground, looking for all the world like shrubs. Stricken horses were stretched in front of him as far as the horizon. Already clouds of vultures were gathering against the blue curtain of the sky.

The sun scorched the back of his neck, and the hot sand under him warmed his blood. Captain Billings nodded once or twice and surrendered to drowsiness, having been without sleep for two days and nights.

A horse, galloping over him, awakened Billings. He found he was shivering; a cold breath was upon the surface of the steppe, indicating that the middle of the night was passed.

Instead of the sun, a huge, orange moon shone down on the carpet of white sand, etching sharply the shadows of the bushes.

Billings staggered to his feet and looked around. The horse had halted in a hollow behind him, where the red glow of a fire revealed a ring of faces. The wind brought to his nostrils the smell of burning flesh. This set every fiber of him to clamoring for food.

Reconnoitering the fire cautiously, Billings made out that the men were Tatars of the Wolf clan, by their belts. They had cut up the hind quarters of a horse and were roasting the meat over the embers, hardly scorching it before they thrust it into their mouths and gulped it down.

This time Billings did not hesitate to follow their example. He swallowed as much of the smoked meat as he could hold down and asked for water. One of the men pointed behind him; and Billings followed a horse track down a gully, at the end of which in the shadows was a pool of black water.

The sand around the pool was trampled, and Billings had to step over the bodies of the dead. He drank until his thirst was satisfied. Judging that dawn was at hand, he moved out on the steppe toward the nearest height to have a look at his surroundings with the first light. He wanted to get a horse and to find Norbo. He had thrown in his lot with the Horde, and meant to see the thing through.

"It would be a dog trick to ride off the field now," he admitted. "Besides, the show isn't over yet. Hulloa!"

The chills chased up his back. He had been stepping out on the surface of the mound when what seemed to be a dead man perched against a boulder extended a hand that gripped his leg.

"Look," said a Tatar's voice, "before you."

Billings looked and made out several tribesmen squatting in a circle. In the center of the ring was a man on his back. It was Norbo, almost under the mapmaker's feet.

"May the way be open before you, Norbo," observed he cheerfully; but then realized that the Master of the Herds was wounded. His chest was wet with a dark liquid that shone in the moonlight; the air wheezed in his throat, so that he could not speak. Only his eyes moved toward Billings.

Gently as the maker of maps tried to pull the hands of Norbo from his chest, he could not force the Tatar's fingers from the wound, to examine it. So he sat down to wait until Norbo should speak or day should come. Presently the labored breath of the wounded man was still.

"The gate in the sky," cried Norbo. "The gate—it is open!"

Surprised, Billings looked up. Crimson was streaking the sky in the east, and the wind was freshening. A moment later Norbo died.

He had not lived to reach the Ili, but death had brought to his eyes a vision that he had sought during the years of his life. As if the first streaks of dawn had been a signal, muskets cracked and the fighting was resumed on the steppe.

It was impossible to learn how the battle was tending. The wind stirred up the dust devils, and before full light a canopy of sand in the air obscured

the sun, while whirling pillars reached up into the gray vault of the sky. Billings wrapped his green neckcloth about his nose and mouth. Over his head he could hear the constant flapping of great wings.

The heat grew more oppressive.

"This is certainly Hades," thought Billings, "and if Alashan and Nadesha have been slain I shall no doubt meet with them."

Whistling to himself, he began to work his way back toward the river, determined to find out what had become of his friends. A horse was sorely needed, yet the poor beasts he met with riderless were foundered.

However, joining a party of Bear clansmen who were engaging a similar number of Kirghiz, he used his sword with such effect that the captain of the Tatars pointed out a fresh horse, and stopped long enough to answer Billings's question as to the battle.

"The jackals have left the pack," he said grimly, meaning that the outlaw tribes had deserted the Kirghiz, so Billings judged that the Tatars were more than holding their own.

He glanced curiously at the Cossack dress of the mapmaker.

"By the Heavens, good sir, you know how to use a sword. Come with us and you shall see Ubaka Khan himself, who is seeking out Nuralin Khan. We will duck that head-of-flame in the waters of the Kara-su where he set a trap for us."

Following the *noyon*, Billings came out of a gully into a mob of horsemen, Tatar and Kirghiz, without semblance of rank, hacking and stabbing at each other, the whole mass moving down the slope toward the river.

The charge of the tribesmen had reached the nucleus of soldiers that Nuralin Khan had formed about him during the night, and the Kirghiz had given ground before the whirling attack of the Tatars. On the steep clay slope the momentum of the horses could not be checked. Billings's beast was caught in the current and in a trice he was at the edge of the river.

In front of him the Kirghiz were swimming their horses across or crowding for the ford. The thirst-tormented animals lingered to drink of the muddy and blood-stained water. Neither side had pistols or muskets in use, so a pause ensued in which Billings made out the figure of Nuralin Khan, hatless, on the farther bank.

"Stop, dog, skulker, slayer of prisoners—" Ubaka Khan had heard from captives of Loosang's act in bringing Alashan and Nadesha to the river to be killed—"stand and await the ox!"

The eyes of the old Khan were sunk in his head, and blood dripped from his mouth. Billings could not understand how the man kept going, naked to the waist as he was in the heat that sapped human strength. Followed by lines of Torguts, Ubaka plunged his horse into the river and swam it across.

Nuralin Khan looked about him, saw his followers hanging back at the edge of the thickets, and remained where he was. To flee would be dangerous. If he could cut down Ubaka it would take the sting out of the Torgut attack, and he could then hold the line of the river.

As Ubaka trotted toward him, Nuralin raised his red head and cast a lance. The old Torgut was watchful and slipped to one side in the saddle, allowing the shaft to flash past his ribs. The belt of Nuralin Khan was still filled with an assortment of weapons; for an instant he hesitated which to draw.

And now a strange thing happened. Ubaka's sword was in its scabbard. Seeing this, the red-headed khan took his time. He drew out a long pistol, cocked it, sighted, and pulled the trigger. Ubaka was not ten feet away. The onlookers heard the click of steel striking flint, but there was no report. The plunge across the ford had dampened the priming in the weapon.

Quickly Nuralin Khan dropped the useless firearm, and his hands darted to knife and sword hilt. At the same time the Torgut chief reached forward and caught the wrists of his foe, pinning them down.

"Slayer of my son," he said slowly, "taste what ye have stored up for others."

With the words, he leaned toward the Kirghiz, putting the whole of his strength into his grip. The face of Nuralin Khan grew redder slowly. Once he spat into the eyes of Ubaka. But the old Torgut had no need to see what was to be done. The muscles behind each shoulder blade stood out in cords down to his belt. His head sank as his shoulders stiffened.

Billings saw the hands of Nuralin Khan wrenched loose from the weapon hilts. The Kirghiz was bent back over the high crupper of his saddle until his fingers quivered and his teeth gritted as the wooden edge cut into the small of his back.

Meanwhile he had succeeded in freeing his feet from the stirrups. Maddened by pain, he twisted to win free, failed, and struck his pony in the neck with a spurred heel. The horse started forward. And Ubaka changed his grip.

One of his vise-like hands thrust under the beard of the Kirghiz giant;

the other fastened behind the head. As the pony slipped out from under the Kirghiz and the man fell back, Ubaka gave a wrench.

Billings heard two sharp snapping sounds. One of Ubaka's stirrups had broken under the strain, and the neck of Nuralin Khan had broken.

The Torgut let the body of his enemy fall to earth and looked at it a while, breathing heavily. Without drawing a weapon the Khan of the Torguts had slain an experienced fighter, heavily armed and desperate.

To escape the rush of the Torguts, the Kirghiz who had been awaiting the fate of their leader fled into the forest. As his men came up, Ubaka halted them.

"Find Loosang," he commanded.

This suited Billings exactly, and he followed the others up the mountain slope along a track beaten down by the Kirghiz. Regardless of the fighting still going on to the right and left, the Tatars pressed on. The head of Ubaka Khan nodded as he rode, and the Khan from weariness slept in the saddle. But he was alert at any noise nearby.

A sulking Tajik pointed out the way that Loosang had taken, up one of the gorges, and before long they sighted the blue robe of a priest fluttering into the bushes ahead of them. With a cry the Tatars spurred on.

The bushes gave upon a clearing surrounded on all sides by pines, from which the whole of the Kara-su could be seen far below them. Here the *gylong* was cornered, but he was not Loosang.

No one paid any attention to him at first. In her bedraggled garments of the temple, Nadesha faced them, a knife in her small fist and her brown eyes glowing with hatred, until she caught sight of their Tatar dress and the big bulk of Ubaka Khan.

On the ground at her feet lay Alashan. One arm was thrown across his eyes as if to shield them from the sun. His right hand gripped the length of a lama's long trumpet midway between mouthpiece and flare.

Beside him was stretched the lifeless body of a *gylong*. The grass of the clearing was trampled and crushed as if many feet had stood upon it and moved about.

Without a word Ubaka Khan thrust aside those in front of him and dismounted, bending over the form of his son. Nadesha fell on her knees and attempted to free Alashan's hand from the horn.

"See, my lord," she said, "with this trumpet Alashan slew the *gylong* who lies here. Then they struck at him with swords so that he fell."

"Tell your story," ordered Ubaka.

"You have heard the tale of Captain Beel-ing, my lord." She looked at the mapmaker and then down at the boy. "You know that we were brought here, captives. The lama, Loosang, would not entrust me to any but his own men. They told us we would see the Tatar clans surprised at the fords of the Kara-su. Alashan said no word to me of what he meant to do."

She pointed down at the river.

"Here we were stationed, under guard of the lamas. When the first clan of the Horde crossed the river, the men from Sonkor began to watch eagerly through the trees. Those who had Alashan between them also watched. One he pushed aside and from the other he wrested this horn, which sounds a great blast. He blew it, once loudly, then again, before they cut him down."

"Ha!"

"It made the priests very much afraid, because they believed that Nuralin Khan would ride upon them and kill them for permitting the warning to be given. So they ran away into the bushes; but Nuralin Khan did not come because the fighting began almost at once. I waited here, keeping the sun from Alashan, who is sorely hurt."

Then for the first time Ubaka Khan's hand felt of the chest of the boy, and his fingers were thrust into the cuts to learn how deep they might be. Under the rude touch Alashan writhed and opened his eyes.

"Build you a horse litter," the Khan commanded his followers, "and see that he is taken to my tent. Tell the women to dress his wounds, for they are deep and half the blood is out of his body. But he will not die, for he is strong—strong."

Ubaka rose, and he held his chin high. Then the Tatar nobles spoke the words for which he was listening.

"The boy is a man in all things," they said, one after the other. "He is wise, because he saw the trick that we did not see . . . Alone he went among our enemies . . . They could not kill him . . . he is a khan.

"Ahatou—Alashan!" they repeated.

Even as they spoke, a blue-clad figure crept from among the Tatars and began kissing the boots of Ubaka Khan. It was the *gylong*, and his face was quivering with a fearful eagerness.

"Oh mighty Khan, ruler of unexampled benevolence—fortunate father of such a son—spare my life! You follow Loosang, and I saw where he went. It was that way!"

The priest pointed into the pines. Ubaka looked at him a moment in silence. Suddenly he stooped, caught up the bronze horn in one hand. Lifting it above his head, the Khan brought down the heavy end on the crown of the *gylong*.

The skull of the traitor was crushed inward. Ubaka hurled the trumpet into the bushes and strode toward his horse. The sight of his son had driven all thought of Loosang for the moment from his mind.

"The men have called him Khan," he repeated to himself. "So, he shall ride with me."

Down below them the firing had died out at last, and the Tatars were in possession of the river. But Billings had not forgotten the lama. He had noted carefully the direction the *gylong* had pointed out, and now turned to see how Alashan was faring. To his surprise the eyes of the boy were fastened on him. He beckoned Billings nearer.

"My father has called me a man," he whispered. "I give you thanks and honor for your ride to the Horde with the word of peril. And when my wounds are healed you and I will cross swords until one of us lies on the ground. I have sworn it."

His glance strayed to Nadesha.

Billings started to laugh and then grew thoughtful. He explained to the boy that, although he liked Nadesha immensely, he did not woo her, and that Nadesha herself loved only the son of the Khan. But Alashan shook his head.

"She has made you her *anda*, and henceforth her life must belong to one of us only. The swords will point the way."

By now the litter of boughs was finished, and Alashan was placed on it. The movement rendered him unconscious. As the Tatars were slinging the litter between two ponies, Billings, who had been standing in a brown study, glanced at the boy, but, perceiving that he was beyond reach of words, turned to Nadesha.

"I am not going to fight Alashan," he said in Russian, "after all this. There is a way out. I am leaving the Horde. Ubaka has said that I am no longer a prisoner." He pointed to the unconscious boy. "See, the son of the Khan wears your girdle, Nadesha."

For an instant her brown eyes dwelled on his, and she held out a slim hand.

"May the way be open before you, my brother."

But even as she spoke, she hurried after the litter, scolding the men for shaking the boughs and urging them to ride carefully. Billings thought briefly of his belongings—if they still existed—somewhere in the Horde, and of horses, supplies, necessary for his hazardous trip back along the road of the Torguts.

Ubaka, however, was out of sight, and there was something Billings planned to do that would not wait.

An hour later Billings had reached the edge of a ravine where the boles of the great hemlocks were close together and their branches formed a roof that made the light dim. For some time he had followed a faint track that had now lost itself among the rocks. Down the steep bottom of the gorge a stream rushed and roared in a series of falls.

Scanning his surroundings carefully, Billings strained his ears for any sound that might lead him to what he sought. The only movement he detected was that of some kind of a panther on a ledge under him. He could see the hide through a nest of rocks, and once he looked into its muzzle, raised toward him.

For a while he studied what he could see of the thing, and then smiled broadly.

"Gad, 'twill bear closer scrutiny!"

He tightened his sash and drew his rapier, laying the scabbard aside. Sliding, and lowering himself over the boulders, he made his way down to the ledge beside the fall of the stream.

He was within arm's reach before the hide slipped off the back of the false panther, and Loosang rose to his feet, pulling off his mask as he did so. For a moment the two regarded each other.

The lama was half-naked, the scars prominent on his tall frame. Over his waist hung an apron of skin, but his hands were empty.

"I have no weapon," he said slowly. "Come, Captain Billings, we have no quarrel, you and I. You are a *giaour*—I, a priest. We are wiser than the Tatars. Instead of fighting, we can share wealth together."

As Billings did not answer, he went on quickly.

"You do not believe me. But it is so. I have taken gold and silver coins enough from the Tatars to make you a rich landowner with serfs."

"I do not doubt it. But now we are going to fight—you and I—with our hands, if you have no weapon."

Loosang's lined face puckered. Billings never took his eyes from the lama's.

"Captain Billings, you are not a fool—although some would call you so. Each week, on the road of the Horde, I buried a large bag of Russian money—an official's salary, each time—under the stones of the shrines that were built where my yurt stood. I can retrace the course of the Tatars."

The lama broke off, his lips tightening. He had forgotten, as he spoke, the map that Billings had made. His hands fell to his sides.

"You see I am telling the truth. And you have seen the power of the Sonkor lamasery." Sweat glistened on his bald forehead, but his eyes were bold. "If I return there, safe, I can turn the tables on my enemies. It would be worth a fortune to you—and escort back to Russia."

"I don't think you have any second to serve in this duel," interrupted Billings coldly, "unless you wish to call in your friend the Devil. And we can dispense with a surgeon."

For the first time Loosang laughed.

"*Ekh*, after all you are a fool. Do you not know yet that steel cannot hurt a lama? What will you fight me with? That sword—"

With the words, Loosang cast himself at Billings. His hand darted under his apron and flew up again. In each fist was clasped a long knife. Lifting these over his head, he leaped.

And Billings, leaning forward, thrust his sword through the body of Loosang under the heart.

As he made the thrust he drew to one side, catching the lama's right wrist in his left and avoiding the downward sweep of the other arm. For a space he held the form of the priest passive, while Loosang squealed between set teeth. Then he drew out his blade, pushing the body clear of it, over the ledge into the rush of the falls.

He caught only one glimpse of brown limbs flashing down through green water. But presently over his head he heard men calling, and the scrape of boots on the rocks.

Billings's position on the side of the stream was bad if he was to be attacked, so he climbed up the slope as best he could and came out within a detachment of riders who clustered about his empty scabbard.

They were tribesmen, unknown to him. There were a round dozen of them, and he judged they had been raiding because they had with them several led horses, one a beautiful Kochlani mare; the other two beasts were loaded with skins, silver ornaments, and a large scimitar, splendidly etched with gold.

One of them, their leader apparently, held gingerly what seemed to be a roll of paper. Billings surveyed them until the headman dismounted and knelt, holding up the roll of paper.

"Billings, lord," he said in guttural Tatar, "we are ten and two men of the Yeka Zukor clan that was overcome in Russia and led back to the Volga. Our hearts inclined toward our kin. So Ubaka Khan this day commanded us to seek you out and serve you, under pain of having our limbs pulled from our bodies by horses. We will go back with you to the Volga."

He laid down the object he held in his hands, with a good deal of relief.

"Here, lord, is the map you made of our road. Here—" he pointed—"is a sword of honor from Ubaka, and a horse, and other things. Also your magic things for looking at the stars. We are ready. Say the word and mount and go."

Billings laughed.

"Mount—and come."

Halfway down the mountain they halted to look out over the plain. The long lines had formed again among the clans; the dust rose over the camel caravans. He could see the sun reflected on the muskets as the riders took up their journey to the east and the valley of the Ili. He could almost hear the *hoa-hoa* of the drivers, the shuffling of the cattle, and the creaking of the wagons.

So it happened that Captain Billings watched the passing of the Torguts along the road that led to the Ili. No other *giaour* set eyes on them again. But it is written in the annals of Keun-lung that those of the clans that survived the journey gained lands and peace in the valley of the Ili.

After sheathing his sword Billings rode on toward the setting sun. But the Tatar at his side had seen blood stains on the steel blade.

"Has my lord slain an enemy in the gorge?" he asked with interest.

Billings smiled.

"I cut off the head of a snake."

Azadi's Jest

They were torturing the Cossack *ataman*. They had him down in the garden, over the blue water, and two of them held his arms stretched out.

"He has not groaned yet," one whispered, "but soon he will talk."

The man who was being tortured stiffened his muscles and waited. Sweat glistened on his shaven skull except where his scalp lock hung to his shoulders. He had wide shoulders, and a fierce, sunburned face from which blue eyes gleamed. He was saying to himself that he would not talk.

"Give him the diadem," said a voice from the carpet under the trees.

The eyes of the Cossack *ataman* turned from side to side. Some men were busy over a charcoal brazier, fanning it to red-hot heat. Smoke rose and vanished into the sunlight. A slave in a leather apron brought an iron ring ornamented with iron flowers. Lifting it in his hands, he set it on the Cossack's bare head. The touch of the iron was cool and pleasant.

Then one of the soldiers at the brazier rose with something held in a pair of tongs. Swiftly he lifted the tongs and dropped something small and round and hard among the flowers of the iron diadem. It fell into a hollow and rested there, almost touching the skin of the Cossack's forehead.

For a moment they all watched the tense face of the young Cossack. Just a trace of smoke came up from the iron diadem, over his forehead. The skin of his head darkened with a rush of blood that clouded the whites of his eyes.

He did not say anything but he moved suddenly, with violent strength. The two soldiers who had been clinging to his arms fell away, and when he struck the one with the tongs, that one went down like a horse shot in the head. Then the Cossack tore the iron ring from his head, hurling it, with its red-hot ball no larger than a pearl, into the water at the garden's edge.

Before he could move again, half a dozen Turks were on him, gripping the massive arms in the loose sleeves, and the legs in their baggy leather breeches. He caught at a sword hilt and jerked the weapon from a janissary's scabbard. But they held his arm fast and wrenched the sword away from him. So he stood still, panting.

There were a score of janissaries and slaves around him, and all about the garden was the *serai* of the Sultan. It had three courtyards, with guards at the gates. The way out led through all three of the courtyards. And beyond the last gate was the outer court of the janissaries—beyond that the streets of Constantinople, filled with Turks and other Moslems. Around the city stood a triple wall, closed except for the Golden Gate with its seven towers. Well the Cossack *ataman* knew that he could not escape from this torture.

"Give him the necklace," said the voice from the carpet.

It was Sultan Ibrahim himself, Lord of Kings, Exalted Head of the Ottoman Empire, Guardian of Mecca and Jerusalem, Master of Aleppo, Damascus, Cairo and Babylon, of Africa and Asia and the White Sea and the Black; also conqueror of Greece and Wallachia, Supreme Ruler of the Seven Climates, in the service of Allah. He lay back on his cushions in the shade, sucking sweet mastic. He was Sultan of the Turks, although the unbelievers of Europe in that year, 1644, called him the Grand Seignior. That day he had kicked the Russian ambassador out of his council chamber, and he meant to bastinado the ambassador of France. But now he wanted to see this great dog of a Cossack panting and quivering on the earth at his feet.

"Nay!" the Cossack cried out for the first time, hoarsely. "I will speak."

The young Sultan looked up idly. It would make no difference, of course. Afterward the torturers would play with this infidel captive. Sultan Ibrahim knew a thing or two about torture—he had grown up in the harem among women. Hunting was his obsession—he would send his whole army to ring in the deer, the foxes, and leopards of the countryside, to drive the beasts to where he could shoot one after another with his gun. Between hunts he liked to practice with his gun, sitting here in the shade at the edge of the blue Bosporus, shooting at the people who ventured too near in boats . . .

A *bimbashi* of the divan stepped forward, always keeping his face toward the Sultan, the chosen of Allah. "Then speak!" said the *bimbashi*. "Where marches the army of the Cossacks? What is its strength? What brings it out of the steppes? What plan have the dog-souls, thy comrades?"

Beside him a secretary of the divan stood with quill and paper to write down the answers—for this Cossack *ataman*, whose name was Sokol, knew the Turkish speech.

The captive smiled. "Write, thou," he said slowly. "The army of the Cossacks marches in the night. Its strength is the strength of a rushing wind. It comes, the army of the Cossacks, to drive this spayed dog, thy master, from his hole—"

From the hand of the secretary the paper fell. "Yah, Allah!" cried the Turkish officer. But the Sultan rose, quivering. A white ermine kaftan hung from his shoulders and two silver-hilted swords were girded to his sides. Yet he drew a curved knife that flashed in the sun.

As a snake strikes, his arm darted at the throat of the *ataman*. And checked in mid-stroke. For the Sultan Ibrahim had a quick wit. Aye, he had the cunning of a ferret. He had seen the gleam of triumph in the cold blue eyes of his captive. And he knew that this chieftain of the steppes had almost won himself an easy death by a boy's trick.

"Nay," he said softly, "thy time is not yet." He sheathed the curved dagger, and considered. "Sokol, thou shalt taste the mercy of the Ottoman. Thou shalt go back to thy cell. Thou shalt have the richest food and wine that is craved by Christians. Wilt thou have a young, sweet-smelling slave girl to anoint thy wound and distract thee? Only ask!" He smiled pleasantly. "Then tomorrow, at this same hour, thou shalt appear again in my presence. To dance, Cossack, to dance. Thou shalt have the skin stripped from thy body, a little at a time, to be stuffed with straw and sent back to thy comrades. But thy body will be set free, to dance in the streets of my city without its skin."

Well did the Sultan know that when a man is nerved to meet an end swiftly, death comes unheeded. But when he has had hours of ease to think about what is to come, then courage oozes out of him.

The *ataman* Sokol held his head high, but his eyes were bleak. "Then give me beer and tobacco and a pipe," he responded moodily.

"Thou shalt have them," Ibrahim promised, making a sign to the secretary. "And what woman? We have all kinds at our command—golden-haired Circassian maids, ox-eyed Greeks—aye, noble Frankish ladies, fiery Spaniards who once were Christians. Now they are slaves and have learned the niceties of love."

Sokol laughed. "We Cossacks have a mistress," he said. "She whose embrace is strongest, whose kiss lasts forever. Aye, the dark-haired maiden who brings night with her. That is our mistress, Sultan. We call her Lady Death."

"Then thou wilt not have a woman?" persisted the Sultan. It pleased his jaded fancy to send a captive Christian noblewoman in to this captive warrior who was to be flayed alive on the morrow.

Sokol shook his head. He suspected a trick.

After that they took him away. They led him to a cell in the sea tower of the *serai* where he could look out over the blue water, where he could think about the next day when his wet skin would be stuffed with straw and the bleeding core of him would gibber and shriek in the dusts of the streets.

That afternoon Azadi had played one of her tricks. She was eighteen years of age and she made trouble persistently for the eunuchs and the slave women guards of the Sultan's harem. Because Azadi was a Tatar maid who had been brought a captive from the land of the Khan as a child.

So she had grown up in the harem without any occupation, or hope of any other life. Veiled and surrounded by guards, she was buried in that swarming prison of women, in the wing of the palace with barred window embrasures, courtyards without doors, and gardens where the walls were patrolled by armed eunuchs.

Azadi did not feel sorry for herself. By now she had forgotten her people of the steppes. She gorged herself on sweet things; she had a pet white cat that she combed diligently and scented with musk; she had a tiled room to herself in that honeycomb of galleries and dark chambers, and she had written her name over its bare, whitewashed walls. She had taught herself to write her name, and nothing more.

If she had been one of the girls in the Apartment of the Virgins, she would have been watched constantly by an old slave woman who slept at her feet. If she had been one of the hundreds of *hazaki*—concubines chosen for their beauty and sent to the harem of the Grand Seignior—she would have been given away before now, probably, to some Turk who merited a favor at the hand of the Sultan. If she had happened to catch the eye and fancy of Ibrahim himself, she would have been exalted to the rank of the chosen concubines who could never be touched by another man. She might even have joined the Mothers of Sons.

But the eye of the Sultan had not fallen upon Azadi as yet, in spite of her slender shape that was like a sturdy young cypress. She had high cheekbones and drowsy gray eyes that softened when she sang love songs to the sleepy white cat. And she had a temper that was like a sheathed dagger of steel.

She had need of it. They fed her in the harem, and the *hazaki* gave her at times their discarded garments. Yet the small, intimate things that become a woman's treasures Azadi had to garner by her wit, and save thereafter from the thieving blacks. Her only protection was her anger—the eunuchs learned that it did not pay to molest her.

That day she had heard how an infidel devil was to be tortured in the garden outside the Gate of the Birds. Azadi wondered if this captive would have a face like a demon and claws instead of fingers. She knew that, overlooking the garden, there was a screened gallery above the Gate of the Birds. And she persuaded two other girls to steal off during the bath hour, to slip into this unoccupied gallery and watch the torture of the infidel devil.

If they had been discovered there, they would have been beaten by the black eunuchs. So they sat without a sound, all eyes and ears. When Sokol, the *ataman*, was led off, they crept away, running to their rooms.

Azadi did not go to the courtyard of younger women for the evening meal. She lay among her cushions, shivering, and the white cat whined plaintively, unheeded. After a while the girl took the hand mirror from the locked chest of her belongings. It was a polished silver mirror that had caught her fancy and she had stolen it long ago. To Azadi's surprise, her face had changed. She shut her eyes, and before the eyes of her mind appeared the bare, dark head of the Cossack who did not, after all, have a face like a demon. It seemed to be in the room, looking right at her. And Azadi thought this must be a spell.

She knew the power of spells cast by night birds that flew overhead, and by clever old women who made images of people and tortured them. Painfully, she waited for the spell to leave her. But it did not.

Until suddenly the Tatar girl threw up her head, and drew out her best garments—a vest embroidered with silver thread, blue satin trousers, and a round *papakh* that perched like a dragoon's cap on the side of her tousled hair. Deftly she combed her long, dark tresses and touched her chin and throat with rose water.

Now the spell was relaxing, and she felt better—since she had made up her mind to see this strange captive again. Her gray eyes shone as she drew the thin veil across her cheeks and struck her hands together imperiously.

"I go to the *Kislar Agha*!" she announced to the black who appeared in the open door. When he hesitated—for the *Kislar Agha* was the Commander of Women, head of the entire seraglio—she brushed past him impatiently.

To the Agha, sitting by his water pipe, she explained more. The Sultan, she whispered, had expressed a wish, in the hearing of a certain lovely Circassian who was then very high in the imperial favor, that a girl be sent to talk to the prisoner. The Circassian had commanded her, Azadi, to go—but secretly. Then, afterward, she would tell the Circassian what the prisoner had said, and the tale might please the Sultan.

Knowing Azadi, the Agha was suspicious. "But the Favored of Allah," he pointed out, "desired a Christian lady to go."

Azadi shrugged a slender shoulder. Outwardly she seemed not at all pleased by her mission. "Perhaps," she suggested, "an infidel lady could not talk to this dog of the steppes. O my Agha, why was it commanded that I should go to the room of this devil who wreathes himself in smoke?"

The Commander of Women could think of no reason why Azadi should go, unless she had been sent by the Circassian favorite. So, reluctantly, he gave permission that she should be escorted to the cell; but at the same time he determined to question the Circassian.

At the entrance of the tower room Azadi stopped, her heart throbbing. Here was the young Cossack, with his back against the wall, his booted feet on the table. In one hand he held a long clay pipe; with the other he caressed a jug of honey mead. "*Yah paikou!*" he growled. "Get out, wanton."

A warm contentment crept through the girl. How beautiful he was—how splendid in his strength! Timidly she lowered her veil, and the blood rushed into her throat and cheeks when she bared her face. For a moment the blue eyes of the Cossack fastened upon the clear, gray eyes of the girl. And Azadi felt herself drawn toward him as if toward a fire from which she could not escape.

She sat down suddenly on the stone floor, no longer daring to look at him. Sokol sipped his beer, but his pipe went out. The guard leaning on a spear in the doorway looked at them curiously.

After a while Azadi mustered courage to rise and to fill the Cossack's goblet with beer from the jug. The Cossack's long arm reached out and he drank. There was a dark sear where his forehead had been burned.

Azadi ventured to dampen her clean girdle cloth from the silver rose-water jar that she always carried. Then, before he could prevent, she laid the cloth against his forehead. But she wanted to hear his voice again. "Eh, say," she asked softly, "what name hath my lord?"

"Sokol it is."

"What means that—Sokol?"

"A falcon. You see, little slave, I soar high—I fly far."

Yes, she thought, he was like that. An eagle, a chained eagle. The pride in his dark eyes could not be killed by pain. She wanted his voice to go on.

"Who was my lord's mother, and his father?"

The Cossack grinned, pulling at the tufted end of his mustache. "My mother's the Volga, my father's the steppe. Aye, child, the steppe where Satan pastures his steeds. When they rush past in the night, sparks fly from their hoofs that beat thunder out of the earth. Then there is a storm—eh, such a storm!"

He stroked her head, and put his arm around her, drawing her against his shoulder. Azadi sighed with content. When he kissed her ear and then her throat, she closed her eyes. "What manner of girl art thou?" he wondered.

"I know not," she said simply. And then, eagerly, "Thy slave—I am thy slave. If harm comes to thee, I shall suffer." She knew that now, beyond doubt. "Listen, Lord Sokol! Now I must go. But if—if they offer thee a new torment, take it. Do not fear."

Surprised, he stared after her, as she adjusted her veil and slipped away with a backward glance that caressed him.

That night the Sultan sat late with some officers in the kiosk outside the Gate of the Birds. There were lanterns hung in the kiosk, although the outer garden was dark. Mute servitors came and went with trays.

But no one saw the dark figure of the girl that crept closer to the marble fretwork of the kiosk, listening there until it rose to run forward and fling itself down, trembling hands clasping the Sultan's bare feet.

Startled, Ibrahim looked first to make certain that she had no weapon; then he raised her head to see if he knew her.

Azadi, half dazed by her own presumption, seized the instant to cry out before they could send her off to a lashing. "Hear, O Lord of Islam, a message. This slave hath been with the Kozaki giaour."

In surprise, Ibrahim considered her. "Eh, then say," he urged. "What message is this?"

Carefully Azadi had thought it out, praying that she would have courage enough to say it all to the Sultan.

"O Commander of the Faith—" she forgot the long list of his titles and hurried on desperately, "I have found out that the Cossack is a magician. Tomorrow he will not feel pain. Aye, he will laugh at the flayers and mock thy beard. Yet he is afraid—"

"Thou art Tatar born?"

"Aye, so."

The Sultan knew that Tatars understood many secrets of magic; their conjurers had often caused him trouble. "He is afraid of dogs," Azadi hastened on. "The Favored of Allah may defeat his magic with dogs. Let the accursed unbeliever be taken out and put in front of the hunting pack—"

"Who sent thee to say this?"

"Allah be witness, no one." Azadi's sincerity was beyond doubt. "I have just come from his cell, to give this warning to the Exalted of Allah. The Cossack will run—any man must run from the hounds; then may the Dispenser of Mercy hunt him down like a wild boar—"

"Be silent, thou."

Azadi lay passive while the Sultan pondered. If there was one thing Ibrahim craved above all others, it was hunting. Especially when he was out of humor. That day the Cossack had defied him, and Ibrahim felt that it would be pleasant to watch the man fleeing before the dogs—the Cossack could not mock him then.

He clapped his hands and gave an order to the mute who appeared. "Wake the Master of the Horse. Have him here. And do thou—" he turned to an officer—"order the Agha of the janissaries to lead out his men to the forest. Clear the wood beyond the hunting lodge, and post the ring of riders, as with a boar. And thou—" he glanced down curiously at Azadi, fearful that she would beg a reward—"thou hast leave to go."

Without a word the girl backed to the entrance, lifted hand to forehead, lips, and breast, and turned away into the darkness.

She had taken only a few paces when a hand gripped her shoulder, and an angry voice hissed: "She-devil—shameless one! No command was given thee to go to the Cossack. What hast thou done?"

Azadi recognized the voice of the *Kislar Agha*, and shivered with the dread that she would be locked up for her presumption. She must not be locked up because it was necessary, now, for her to escape from the palace.

"A trick!" She forced a giggle, and added triumphantly, "It was all a jest of mine. Let me go free and I will say nothing of it. I want to go away from all of you, to my own people."

"Thou wilt go now, this night, and keep a rein on thy tongue?"

"If thou wilt give me gold enough to buy a horse," assented the girl.

"Then, by Allah, it shall be so."

He went himself with Azadi to her room and watched her do up a bundle into which she thrust some of the treasures of her chest. Over her garments she drew a plain dark veil-dress. She bent down to stroke the sleeping cat, and followed the *Kislar Agha* silently into the darkness.

By then it was early morning and the palace slept—except for the few sentries, who did not cast a second glance at the *Kislar Agha*, followed by a woman in serving dress carrying a bundle.

At the last courtyard, the *Kislar Agha* turned aside to a postern door, unlocking it with a key from his girdle. When he peered out he saw no human being except a beggar curled up against the wall.

Azadi stepped into the street warily. Thrusting his hand into his wallet, the officer drew out a fistful of coins. Azadi gripped them tight. Then, picking up her bundle, she ran into the street toward a mosque, outlined against the stars by its lofty minarets. But the *Kislar Agha* touched the beggar on the shoulder. "Thou, Hassan—follow her, and send word to me at the noon prayer."

The tattered form that had appeared to be a blind beggar rose and vanished after Azadi, into the night.

At the noon hour Azadi was riding beyond the walls of Constantinople toward a wood.

When bands of the Sultan's riders appeared in the distance, driving the peasants away from the wood, she urged her horse down into a gully and followed the course of a stream toward the nearest trees, praying that she would not be seen. She had not thought that the Sultan's cavalry would clear the fields near the hunting lodge hours before Ibrahim's coming. Still, it gave her hope that the Sultan was really going to hunt, as he had said the night before.

When she entered the wood at last she sighed thankfully and began to make her way toward the lodge that had been pointed out to her from the city wall. She searched until she found a knoll overlooking the path that led out into the meadows, toward the hunting lodge, a long musket shot away. She knew it must be the lodge because already mounted soldiers and grooms were busied there. Hidden by brush, she could sit on the knoll and watch, while the horse pulled leaves from the bushes and chewed them.

Azadi studied the horse dubiously, wondering if he were really as strong and swift as the dealer from whom she bought him hastily at sunrise had sworn on the Koran that he was, beyond any doubt. He was big enough, but his bones showed strangely through his skin, and he seemed to stand always on three legs except when he lowered his head and wheezed.

Getting a clean cloth from her bundle, Azadi knelt upon it, arranging some of her trinket charms on its edge, and facing toward the southeast.

"*Yah Allah,*" she prayed, "O God, grant that this horse be swift as the wind. And grant that he will come this way, along the path."

Then, when the afternoon was near its end, she heard the yelping hounds. Men crowded around the distant lodge. They formed in a long line, facing the meadow and the wood.

In front of them appeared the hunting dogs held on leashes—a score of them. Then the Sultan rode up on a white horse, his lofty turban with the three nodding plumes rising above the nobles who followed him. Everything was in readiness, as often before when a giant boar had been loosed, to race toward the wood.

But now a man was led out before the horsemen, the Cossack *ataman*, bareheaded, in his shirt sleeves. Across the meadow came the sharp beat of kettle-drums. For an instant Sokol looked around. He began to run toward the wood, following the path, slowly at first.

Halfway to the nearest trees he quickened his pace. And Azadi started down the knoll toward the path, dragging the horse after her. Hastening through the brush, she tugged at the rein. She sprang down into the path, and cried out in dismay.

Between the trees on the other side of the trail appeared three men. One was the *Kislar Agha* on a great black horse, a drawn scimitar in his hand; another was the dealer from whom she had bought the horse, and the third the beggar of the palace gate.

"Little fool," said the *Kislar Agha* pleasantly. "So this was thy trick—to plot against thy Sultan?" He reined the charger at her swiftly. "Now, instead of gold, thou shalt taste steel—"

Azadi shrank back. Behind her the bony horse wheezed. The curved blade of the scimitar glittered in the sunlight. But the *Kislar Agha* turned his head, surprised. From far off came the baying of hounds on a scent. And down the path bounded a tall figure, clearing rocks, sweeping through the brush. The Cossack was panting and running as a man only runs from the pursuit of beasts.

"Allah!" muttered the *Kislar Agha*, reining aside watchfully to give the fleeing man room.

Pain swept through Azadi. Here she was, with a horse, and the Cossack was free, as she had planned. But now he could not escape—

"Uuh-aaul," Sokol howled like a wolf as he reached them. Abreast the *Kislar Agha*, he checked in his tracks, flinging up his arms, the loose sleeves fluttering.

And the great black horse reared, snorting. As he did so, Sokol ran at the *Kislar Agha*, who swung up his scimitar and slashed down. But the Cossack leaped under the blade, the hilt striking his shoulder. His arms closed around the waist of the *Kislar Agha*, dragging him back from the saddle as the black horse came down on all four feet. The two men rolled on the ground, the sword falling from the hand of the *Kislar Agha*. And the Cossack pounced on it.

The *Kislar Agha* scrambled to his feet, snatching a curved knife from his girdle. Savagely he struck with the knife. As he did so, he screamed.

Whistling in the air, the scimitar in the Cossack's hand slashed into the *Kislar Agha*'s head. There was a sound like that of an axe hitting rotten wood, and the Agha went down.

The two other Moslems had been running at the Cossack. When he turned, with a sweep of the bloodied sword, they sprang away and vanished into the brush. But the Cossack was after the black horse of the *Kislar Agha*. In five seconds he had thrust the sword through his belt, had caught the saddle horn of the rearing charger, and was in the saddle.

Azadi cried out joyously. She clapped her hands, and tore the veil from her face, her gray eyes shining. "It happened—oh, it happened. I did it. Now go—go like the wind!"

The Cossack stared at her.

"Go quickly!" she cried again. The hounds bayed near at hand.

Sokol tightened the rein, and the great black horse circled. He swung down from the saddle and caught up Azadi in his long arm. Gripping her across his knees, he turned the frantic horse and drove in the sharp stirrup edges. Horse and man and maid swept away, down the trail as the leading hounds raced up, to halt with a tumult of yelping where the scent ended at the dead body of a man.

At the heels of the hounds came the Sultan, and behind him a cavalcade of his officers straining for a sight of the fugitive who was to be torn by the dogs. Instead they came upon Ibrahim halted by the body of the *Kislar Agha*. They did not see the horse dealer or the spy because those two worthies were creeping away, with the fear of torture strong upon them.

The hounds ran in circles, crashing through the brush and returning always to the slain Commander of the Women. No one dared speak until the Sultan spoke, and Ibrahim clutched his beard, staring from the bloodied earth to the raw-boned wreck of a horse with the broken saddle that grazed calmly upon the bushes before him.

"Was the *Kislar Agha* mad," he said uncertainly, "to ride hither on such a thing as that?"

He shivered, because the Cossack had vanished into air above the body of the palace official, who should not have been in this wood, and who would never have come, in any case, upon a lame cart horse. "Aye," he muttered, "that Cossack was a magician. He cast his power upon the dogs and escaped. By the beard of the Prophet, there is a woman of my *serai* who will be cut from her skin this night!"

But the Sipahi Agha, who had dismounted and cast about the ground, salaamed at the Sultan's stirrup. "Lord," he said, "the sword of the *Kislar Agha* is missing. And yonder lie the fresh tracks of a speeding horse. Surely the infidel devil slew thy servant and fled on his horse. Give permission that I follow with a regiment. May my head fall if I do not bring him back."

"Go, then." The Sultan ground his teeth and headed back at a gallop toward his harem.

But he did not set eyes again upon the girl Azadi, nor was anyone found who knew what had become of her. She had vanished like the Cossack. And when, three days later, the Sultan heard that the Sipahi Agha lay dead with most of his regiment, he only nodded moodily. It was clear, beyond doubt, that magic had done this.

"It was written," he said, "and no man may alter what is written."

When the red ball of the sun went down behind the dark treetops, Sokol dismounted from his wearied horse. He still held Azadi in his arms, and now he turned her face up to the sky. He kissed her on the lips and he laughed.

"*Ohai*, the Cossack rides in the night, and who can follow him?"

Azadi pressed her dark head against his shoulder, dreading the moment when she would be set down and left alone here in the silent forest.

"But whither," she cried, "where will you go?"

"To the black water. Aye, to the sea." Again he laughed. "Harken, little Azadi, to what thy Sultan sought to hear. At the end of this forest is the sea, and on the sea a city of the Sultan. I know it well, because they took me captive there, when I came to find the way for my *kounaks*—my men. They follow me, my men—four regiments of the sons of devils, Azadi, in their long boats. Tomorrow, or the day after, they will be there to raid the Sultan's city. And when they see me with such a horse and sword, they will say, 'That is our *ataman*—he has been playing with the Turks.'"

Suddenly the girl threw slender arms about his shoulders, pressing herself against him. It seemed to her that she would die if he set her down and rode away to this city on the sea.

"The spell!" she cried, in pain. "This spell thou hast laid upon me I cannot break. I—I wanted to bring a horse, so that you could ride away from the dogs. But you never looked at my steed."

"That peddler's nag!"

She nodded, tears dampening her flushed cheeks.

"Nay, little Azadi," Sokol said slowly, "I have no skill at conjuring. The power of magic is in thee. For now that I have looked once into thine eyes I cannot let thee go from my arms."

A deep breath of amazement escaped the girl. A quiver of delight ran through her body, and she smiled up at him.

"Then look!" she cried softly. "Quickly, before the light is gone. Wilt thou take me to the sea? Now, look again. To thy land, with thee? Nay—I said only to look, beloved of my heart."

The Net

Kam knew that the long night of winter was nearly over. He knew it by the wisdom of his six years. His wolf dog no longer burrowed so deep in the snow of twilights, and the ice of the river was cracking.

For Father Yenesei was rising out of his long sleep, throwing off the white coverlet of ice and snow. At his headquarters in the Syansk Mountains far to the south, the snow was melting and the black water was rushing down with the ice floes toward the bend in the Yenesei where the hills of Mongolia meet the plain of Siberia—still called Muscovy in that year of the late seventeenth century—where was the hut of Kam.

Well did little Kam know the moods of Father Yenesei. Kam himself had no father; he lived with old Ostak, the blind fisherman at the bend of the river.

During the past winter the boy had played with the treasures of Ostak, a walrus head on which the skin was wrinkled like the skin of a dried apple, a bit of carved ivory, a silver talisman, cast up from the wreck of some trader's vessel, and a long iron whaling spear.

For Ostak, in the time before the light went from his eyes, had been a man of the North, a killer of animals on the edge of the White Sea, a man largely thewed and savage of temper. Kam played on the skin of a polar bear. Kam was no longer a child. He played at killing the walrus head with the spear.

"*Tchai!*" he cried. "Soon I will run upon the walrus herds. I have already speared a salmon in the river. You know it, Uncle Ostak."

"Aye," the old Buriat murmured, "you are a rare young buck. You are the eyes of Ostak, just as your sister Aina is my hand."

It was Kam's task to lead the blind fisher to the skiff, to find him his nets, to carry the cleaned fish to the village some miles away. His hours of work were long, for Ostak moved slowly and toiled painfully. The need of work and of guiding the blind had made Kam alert and shrewd for his age.

When the ice would be gone, and the labors of the day done, Kam would play with his wolf dog on the bank of Father Yenesei, watching the reflection of the pines in the water of the round bay by which the hut was built. He would count the ships passing up or down, traders' luggers, the sailing skiffs that bore black-robed priests from Muscovy, who wore strange, square hats and gave presents—sometimes.

But on this warm day in the Month of the Fox, when the silver sun of the past months was turning to gold and the snow was damp under foot, the only vessel within Kam's range of vision was an ice-bound lugger a mile upstream, and he was watching the approach of three men with a dog sledge.

Kam knew the three. They were Muscovites, distinguished personages who owned the sailing ship that had been winter-bound in the upper reaches of the river by an early freezing of Father Yenesei.

Frequently Kam had seen them in the Buriat village nearby. Their presence had added zest to the dull winter for him. From the inn door he had listened while they sang gigantic songs and kicked on the floor. At times they played with an assortment of small colored pictures upon a table and emptied mugs of vodka at a great rate.

They brought wonderful, painted dolls and bead work, with colored cloths to exchange at the inn for food and vodka. When they danced with the Buriat women to the two-stringed fiddles, the sweat flew from their faces and the floor shook under their boots, so high did they jump.

In short they were demigods, capital fellows, regular *batyrs*, or heroes. Kam scrutinized their approach to his hut with emotion, and his black eyes opened wide at the guttural oaths that announced the trio had missed their way in heading back to the lugger from the village.

"Give us a drink to warm our gullets, uncle," they shouted at Ostak, who was feeding fish fins to his dogs.

Kam was lost in admiration. The faces of the demigods were red as the crimson of the northern lights at the time when the merry dancers* were leaping in the air above the horizon. Their breath was as fragrant as wine. So it was, in fact. Their beards were like horses' manes compared to the long white mustache of Ostak that was like the fangs of a walrus.

---

*The colored flames that are often seen in the arc of the northern lights.

"Kam," grunted Ostak as if he had observed the men, "go and bid your sister draw *tarasun* from the cask and give these to drink."

"Nay," responded the boy eagerly. "Aina is down at the ice, the hole in the ice, spear-fishing."

"Draw the *tarasun* yourself. Give to each of these strangers for they thirst. I cannot see their number."

The leader of the three emptied the bowl of fermented mare's milk at a gulp.

"So, you are blind, uncle. Well," he laughed, tossing the bowl to Kam, "you will behold the angels in Heaven, so don't weep about it. Come along, Fedor and Lak—take your Finnish name—Lakumainen."

He waved good-bye to the impassive Ostak and whipped up the dogs that drew the sledge slowly over the heavy snow. When they could not start the sledge, instead of giving it a push, he kicked the dogs until, snarling, they got underway.

Kam was surprised that a demigod should beat dogs. Ostak, despite his surly moods, always cared for his few wolf-breeds.

When Fedor, the smaller of the two Russians, and the gigantic Finn trailed after the sledge, Kam brought up the rear. Having given the exalted strangers to drink, he felt that he had earned the privilege of following them awhile.

"Lift up your heels, my lads," sang out the leader of the sailors. "We've got this food to stow away and the ice may break loose any day now. You'll have to step a measure, then, because Father Yenesei isn't any smooth maiden to handle, you know."

Nevertheless he did not head directly for the distant vessel, but circled to go by the hole in the ice where Aina stood with her spear. Several salmon, already frozen, lay by her.

Fedor and the Finn followed, accompanied by Kam, who tried to swagger or rather lurch as they did.

Aina did not look up; she had already scanned them carefully. She was a slender Buriat, with a tiny mouth and sharp, black eyes with curving lids. In her foxskins and horsehide boots she looked much like a boy, except for the moonlike roundness of her cheeks.

"*Hai*, little seal," called out Stolkei, leader of the sailors, "give's a fish-kish. Pretty little Aina, a kiss."

He tossed a silver coin on the ice after long fumbling with his leather mitt in the flat-looking wallet at his belt. Signing to the Finn to stow the salmon on the sledge, he essayed a bear-like clutch at the girl, who slipped away around the water hole.

"Nay," she said, "begone!"

Stolkei tried to follow the alert girl around the black gap in the ice, failed, and began to mutter—

"*Hai, hai*, Aina, my lass!"

Shaking his head, he moved off again while Lak beat the dogs into motion. Kam paused to stare admiringly at the torn, cloth cap of the Russian skipper, the soiled, embroidered blue shirt that showed where he had flung open his bearskin *svitza*. Stolkei was roaring a song that had come into his head:

"Hai, hai, *Aina, lass,*
Is wild, is furious wild!
Hai, hai, Aina lass—
Don't get wild, my child!"

Lak, grinning, tried to take up the song. Only Fedor was silent, and cast a long glance over his shoulder at the watching girl.

Kam, pleased, began to dance around his sister, repeating "Don't get wild, my child!" until she boxed his ears roundly.

"Ow," he cried. "I like the song. I like those masters of the river. I wish we had them for uncles instead of old Ostak."

"Be quiet!" She added reflectively—"They won't ever pass through the dog-world in *kanun-kotan*, the sky-heaven, if they thrash their dogs like that."

Both children had spent many an evening in the dark listening to old Ostak telling of the sky-worlds. Even Kam knew that *sunyesun*, the soul, was caught up by the nets that came down from the sky, and thus left the body of a man.

Although he looked hard he had never seen the nets, nor the cloud people, the people of ancient times who lowered the nets and caught up the souls of men. But the sky-world was plainly to be seen, or rather its gate might be seen. Almost every clear night it stood there, the great arch of soft white flame in the northern sky.

Through this arch the soul must pass, riding a horse if the animal slain on the grave of the dead man was fat and strong; or leading it, if the horse were thin and weak. The soul must have a warm suit of clothes laid on the grave, for it was very cold in the *kanun-kotan*.

And the soul must pass through the sky-worlds of dogs, and those of the reindeer and the horse, and other beasts. And if the man in life had mistreated a dog or reindeer or horse, he would be bitten or hurt on his long journey through the *kanun-kotan*.

Also, if he brought with him anything that had been stolen on earth, the thing would be claimed by the *sunyesun* of its owner in the sky.

Kam thought to himself that when his time came he would ride regally through all the sky-worlds on a pony. All his garments would be of the richest sable and fox. All the beasts in each world would let him pass friendlily, and his wolf dog would be there to bark a greeting.

Everything that went with Kam in the net that came down from the *kanun-kotan* for him would be quite certainly and unquestionably his own, so no angry soul would take the coat off his back or the spear from his hand. Then he would be welcomed triumphantly by the One-Being-on-High, and have plenty of fat meat to set his teeth in and a walrus head to roll from star to star.

But Aina of the brooding eyes and soft voice would shiver when he mentioned this.

"*Ai-a*," she would sigh, for the flood of life was strong in her, "I hope when the net comes down for me it will be in the hands of our father and mother. I hope no angry soul will send the net for you, either. We must take care and be gentle with Ostak, for his time is near."

Until he was six years of age, it had puzzled Kam how Ostak would find his way in the *kanun-kotan*, since he could not see. Aina said it would be managed. And now Kam saw that it, indeed, would be simple. The horse, having good eyes, would see to choose the way and Ostak would tell him where to go, just as the fisher told Kam where to guide him.

The next day the sun was brighter. The ice began to move sluggishly toward the north, leaving strips of black water visible. Although walking to shore was now hard work, Stolkei announced that he would go back to the village a last time for some snuff.

Before setting out he ordered Fedor and the Finn to let go the rusty anchor to avoid drifting, and to mend the lug sails.

When the anchor was down the two watched until Stolkei was out of sight. Fedor looked long from a black speck on the still unbroken ice of the bay by Ostak's hut to the broad face of the Finn.

"Lak," he muttered, and coughed.

"Lak," he began again, "you and I are chums, ain't we?"

A smile on Fedor's thin, red face disclosed black teeth. He closed one red-veined eye.

"That girl of Ostak's—she's alone over there."

Looking at the speck on the ice, Lak nodded. His thoughts had been running in that direction since he woke up at noon.

"It'll be a long stretch down the Yenesei, with the ice ahead of us and behind. We won't be ashore again for a pretty spell, Lak. Look here, that Buriat girl is as sleek as a fox."

The big sailor rubbed the back of his hand across his mouth.

"Those —— Buriats at the village—" he was beginning.

"They won't know, Lak—why should they? Look here, Ostak's blind. There's no other soul along the bay, there. She'll think we want more salmon. I'll manage her." Fedor chuckled. "I'll say we'll clap her in the hatch in the ice if she doesn't come along to the ship. I'll manage her, if you'll carry her to the ship."

"What about the master?"

"The —— take the master—as he will, someday. Papa Stolkei has an eye for a girl, I tell you. Anyway, lad, he can't do anything. As for the Buriats, they are oxen! What do they care for Uncle Ostak? They know we have muskets, and they won't want a hole in their pelts just because of Ostak's brat."

The Finn's heavy face had not changed.

"If I carry her to the ship, I keep her awhile. You agree to that, Master Fedor?"

The turkey-faced sailor scowled. Then his brow cleared and he held out his hand.

"Agreed. Why, you're my chum, Lak."

For once Ostak's fingers were not busied at the making of nets, and Kam was not playing with the treasures on the bearskin. The boy stared up, puzzled, at Stolkei, who was sitting on the guest's side of the fire in the hut, his coat open, drinking *tarasun*.

"I'll open your mouth for you, Uncle Ostak," the Russian was saying. "I'll let you talk terms. You can name the *kalym*, the first payment, yourself. How much—eh? Spit it out!"

But Ostak shook his head, his eyes closed.

"Nay, master. The girl is not a woman yet, for going with you."

"*Tchai*, Uncle Ostak," Stolkei smiled, "you are blind enough. Aina is pretty as a fox. If she stays here some stripling from the village will come to open your mouth to talk of marriage."

"Nay. The girl is my hand, to work with. When the ice is on the river I cannot catch the fish. Soon little Kam will be able to use the spear, but not now."

Ostak spoke harshly. The foster children he had taken in had found their way into his heart, after a fashion. Irritable as he was with them, Ostak saw that they had the best of the food, that skins were brought for their garments, even silk and beads and iron ornaments for Aina.

"Well, you are a fool." Stolkei was angered. "You are a doddering old *Anakhay*—a one-eyed evildoer to children. I tell you I will pay a price, a good price. The girl will see Russia—"

"She would not live," again Ostak shook his head. "She is shy and quiet. She is her own land. Go your way, master."

Stolkei grew red with anger and would have thrown the empty *tarasun* bowl at the fisherman, when Ostak said quietly.

"There is a net spread around your vessel. If you do evil here, it will come upon you. I see!"

Perturbed a little, Stolkei was staring at the wrinkled face of the blind man when both heard a scream from the river. Recognizing the voice of Aina, the fisherman felt his way out of the hut, followed by Stolkei.

Ostak clutched the arm of the other.

"What has happened to Aina? Where is she?"

What Stolkei saw was this: Beside the hole in the ice a small figure in furs was facing big Lak, a two-pronged fish spear in its hands. The Finn sprang at Aina and jumped back as the spear drove into his shoulder. Then he brushed the weapon aside, caught up the girl, wrapped a neck-cloth about her face, and flung her over his shoulder.

They moved off along the shore toward the lugger. Fedor followed.

By the hole in the ice Stolkei saw that there remained only the dead fish, the spear, and the foxskin cap that had fallen from the head of Aina.

"What has happened?" he repeated slowly. A cunning light came into his black eyes and he pulled at his beard. "Eh? Why, pray to the mercy of God, Ostak. The ice about the hole has cracked. Aina has fallen in."

"*Ai-a*," moaned the old man. "And the river is moving under the ice! Run to the hole, master. I cannot see to go. Run swiftly!"

Stolkei put a hand over his mouth to keep from laughing. He started off at a lumbering trot.

"I go, uncle." Bethinking himself, he paused. "But, nay. The girl has gone under. The ice is moving in the bay, I tell you. Never will you see Aina again, old man."

It was true that here and there after the passage of the giant Finn with his burden, the white sheet over the bay revealed gray lines, wherein the black water soon appeared.

"Shame upon your head, old sinner," was the skipper's parting shot. "That you should make the girl go spear-fishing on breaking ice. Do not tell them of this in the village or they will set the dogs on you. *Tchai!*"

He hurried around the shore of the bay after the others. Ostak remained as if petrified. Then he began wringing his hands on his chest and moaning to himself. When this ceased he stood as if listening for a long time, his heavy shoulders hunched, his fingers closing and unclosing.

"Kam," he growled. "Kam. Did you see what happened on the ice?"

From under the floor planks of the hut crawled out a frightened Kam. He came to Ostak, whimpering. He told him what he had seen.

"Why did Aina cry out, Uncle Ostak?" he asked at the end. "Is she sick and are the lords taking her to their ship to make her well?"

But Ostak, seizing his hand, was making him hurry down toward the river. Near the fishing hole the blind man halted and told Kam to go out and bring him the spear. When this was in his hand, Ostak felt of the points.

Then he touched them again and held his finger to his nose.

"Blood," he muttered. "It was even as Kam said."

"Then Aina is very sick?" the boy demanded.

"How is the ice between shore and the ship?" demanded Ostak harshly.

When the boy told him, he shook his head, muttering. Where the three men were having trouble to cross, Ostak and Kam could not go.

The blind man took a step toward the path leading to the village. Then, still shaking his head, he turned and went back, led by Kam, slowly to the hut.

"Aye, Kam," he was saying. "The sister of your flesh is very sick. She will not come back to us. Her *sunyesun* will leave her body this night. It will be so."

"Then we must take her dress of silk, to clothe her, Uncle Ostak, and we must kill one of the wolf dogs, asking pardon of it, so it can pull her sledge to the *kanun-kotan*—"

"Nay, we cannot cross Father Yenesei when he is rising from his sleep. *Ai-a,* if only you were a boy full grown and could throw a spear!"

The boy began to weep.

There was no food that night for him or the dogs. Remembering the frozen salmon on the ice he went down and got them, but Ostak would not take his knife, nor kindle the fire.

"What do you see in the sky, Kam?" he asked toward morning.

"The gate of the *kanun-kotan,* Uncle Ostak. It is the white gate only. There are no fires climbing up to the stars."

"Soon there will be," muttered the blind man. "But they are not fires. They are the souls of the cloud people, of the people of ancient times. They are dancing and making merry—some of them. The white lights are the *sunyesun* unburied."

"Thus will we see the soul of Aina?"

"Aye, you will see it. The red lights are those who have died in violence. The blue are those enchanted. And the purple lights are the souls of those who wrought evil on the earth. They are dancing—aye, jumping up and down in pain, for it will be cold for them in the sky-world between the stars and they will not see the face of the One-Being-on-High. They will be carried off in the net of the angry souls—"

He bent his head as if listening. Kam huddled closer to him.

"Father Yenesei is angry," murmured Ostak. "I hear it."

But Kam heard nothing. Certainly the boy and the blind man, in the hut two miles from the lugger, could not have heard the splash in the river or the startled oath of the one of the three sailors who was awake.

There was no other sound but the splash. Aina, stealing out of the hold where the others slept, saw the figure of the watcher on deck—Fedor—and sprang over the side of the lugger.

The feet of the girl did not meet ice. She pitched into the water that numbed her with its cold as if a hundred daggers had pierced her flesh. The daggers reached to her brain and her feeble swimming ceased.

Fedor watched for awhile; then, reassured, he went below to empty the vodka bottle that his companions had left unfinished.

The next day, clouds hid the sun and the wind ceased entirely. During the darkness the moving ice cakes had vanished, leaving a mirror of clear black water on all sides of the lugger. Except along the banks where a fringe of ice blurred the reflection of the pines, the channel of the upper Yenesei was clear.

"The last of the ice can't rightly be gone yet," pointed out Stolkei. "Here, you dog of a Finn, help me up with the anchor, for we had best be out of here while the channel is clear."

The bearded face of the skipper was bruised, and blood had dried in a gash under one eye. Lak had drawn a knife on him in the quarrel of the night before over the girl. The Finn's mouth was bruised and his shoulder stiff where Aina's spear had ripped the skin.

They worked at the rusted anchor chain by fits and starts. Over their shoulders they cast glances at the spot in the snow that was the hut of Ostak. Through his telescope, as they drifted down the river, Stolkei could see the fisherman busied about his skiff on the shore.

"You see he does not think of us," he pointed out to Lak. "I tell you I planted a few words in his ear. He thinks he is to blame for—for the girl. He will hold his tongue, I tell you."

Lak did not look at the skipper. Fedor, kicked out of a drunken slumber, remembered what he had seen in the night.

"Aye, chums," he grinned, "the wench is frozen solid by now under our keel. She went down like a plummet—splash, like that! The ice was gone when she jumped."

"A true word." Stolkei heartened himself. "And look—the ice is out of the bay. A good thing for us, because some dog of a Buriat would have found the spear and the blood stains, maybe. It's all wiped out, now; the girl's dead. Come now, Lak, you ain't afraid of a blind man who doesn't even think you killed his girl?"

Lak's thick lips twisted.

"Fedor—he did it. She got loose from him."

The thin Russian moved uneasily and spat.

"Well, wasn't it Papa Stolkei who spoke first and tried to buy her?"

With a laugh Stolkei turned to the tiller, ordering them to bend the sails.

"We'll be under way before the —— can spit in ——. The channel's clear. I've loaded the muskets—not that we'll need them. If Lak wants to dream of water spooks, let him, I say."

Still they made little progress that day for the sails flapped against the mast, and the rudder of patched-up wood—the lugger's rudder had been damaged by the ice—swung in its chains idly. When they dropped anchor that evening they were a bare two miles downstream, abreast the bay where the black square of Ostak's hut loomed, a few cables' lengths away.

Even the current of the river seemed to have lost its force. The pine tops rose immovably against the sunset, and there was not a whisper of wind anywhere.

All these things little Kam reported faithfully to Ostak. The blind fisherman knew well the meaning of the signs. Up the river the outgoing ice had jammed, holding back the floes behind it.

The water, rushing down from the freshets fed by melting snow, was heading up against the packed ice. During the hours of quiet on the lower river the ice was gathering above.

Soon, with the wind or a twist of the pent-up current, the jam would be broken and tons of ice, rushing behind a solid wall of water, would sweep down the breast of Father Yenesei. Not until then would the winter garment of Father Yenesei be thrown off, and the upper river be safe for vessels.

That was why the lugger was still the only craft to be seen, even by the sharp eyes of Kam. The skiffs of the fishermen, the sloops of the traders, all awaited the passing of the ice jam, drawn up on the banks, or anchored well into safe bays.

So near was the lugger that the creaking of the yards or rattle of the rudder chains could be heard on shore, mingled with a snatch of song or laugh as the men drank vodka before sleep.

Kam thought he recognized one of the songs. He remembered the words:

Hai, hai, *Aina lass*
Don't get wild, my child.

The keen ears of Ostak heard the song, where he worked with fat and tallow, greasing the bottom of his ramshackle skiff and the wooden oarlocks. He worked the harder, for the darkness was no hindrance to him, and his wasted sinews swelled strongly under the toil.

Lak only did not sleep on the lugger. He snarled at Stolkei's voice that sang the song. When the two others were snoring in the hold he paced the narrow space between them, listening to the night sounds on the water.

Once he thought he heard the dip of oars, but the sound did not come again. Again, when the creaking of the yards ceased, he fancied that another creaking went on, down by the water at the stern.

Lak listened for a long time and was sure of a tapping, a straining, and gnawing somewhere outside the ship. Then came a loud creak. A Finn is deeply superstitious, and Lak crossed himself before going on deck to look around.

But the lugger's deck was deserted. The gray sheet of water was undisturbed about the ship. Only the man's heavy footfall sounded. Uneasy at a curious murmur from the river, Lak went down to the hold again where his companions lay. So he did not see the dark shape of a skiff move out from under the shadow of the lugger's stem.

He was nodding, seated on his bunk, staring at a lantern, when the murmur about the vessel's sides became a ripple. The shadows in the hold moved up and down. The yards knocked against the mast.

In an instant Lak was up, head and shoulders out of the hatch. Wind struck his cheek. He could see the outlines of the banks under the gray lantern of dawn.

Lak jumped up and kicked Fedor. He grasped the shoulder of Stolkei.

"Wind," he yelled. "The river is rising!"

With a grunt Fedor turned over in his bunk. But Stolkei stumbled erect, and climbed on deck.

The two stared at the moving tops of the pines, and the ripples where the current eddied down the river. The eddies wavered back and forth curiously. Early daylight showed isolated cakes of ice wandering here and there.

"It is bad," said Lak. "There is something coming upon the river."

Stolkei nodded and the two fell to work at the anchor. Suddenly they looked at each other. Upstream, beyond the bend in the river there grew a murmur that rose to a roar.

"Ice!" yelled Stolkei. "An ice jam has broken." He glanced about swiftly. "We can make the bay here."

Lak was already at the sail ropes, and the skipper jumped to the tiller swearing thankfully because there was wind. A short run to larboard—

The lugger began to move down the river. Stolkei put over the helm. The vessel did not change its course. They were passing the bay.

Behind them a white line appeared around the bend. They could hear the crackling roar of grinding ice. Stolkei worked at the tiller frantically. But the lugger only turned slowly as it gathered speed. It was now drifting before the wind, stern first.

"You fool!" roared the Finn. "What are you doing?"

"She won't mind the helm. The rudder—"

Stolkei swung around to stare with distended eyes over the stern. Lak wrested the tiller from his grip. The two men struggled for it, snarling and maddened by fear. The movements of the tiller served in no way to check the course of the lugger downstream, faster each moment as the wall of water, surmounted by the ice field, drew nearer.

A segment of ice struck the quarter. The lugger was swinging violently, as the flood struck it. Lak had knocked Stolkei down, and when the white flood came over the stern the Russian was carried overside, struggling to hold his feet. Lak was torn from the tiller and swept against a mast.

He clung there, gripping the wood with his great arms. He saw the ice pack grinding against the sides of the ship. The foremast went down, and with it the yard above Lak. Enveloped by the sail, the Finn fought against it, only to feel himself carried off on a block of ice.

For a moment he clung to the edge of the cake, numbed. Then the circling block struck another, catching the body of the man in the impact; the arms of the Finn went up, and blood rushed from his mouth.

Out of the hatch the head of Fedor was stuck, and his screams reached the shore before the lugger, filling rapidly now, settled down under the breast of Father Yenesei.

As much of this as he could see Kam related to Ostak where the two stood on the hillside above the reach of the flood.

"Why did not the ship come into the bay, Uncle Ostak?" the boy asked. "Was it caught in a net from the sky?"

"Aye," said Ostak, "it was caught."

So Kam watched that night when the merry dancers came out and the flames rose into the northern sky. He noticed particularly that the purple lights were very bright and he fancied that the three lords from the ship must be dancing very hard to keep out the cold on their long journey without horses or dogs in the *kanun-kotan*.

When he went into the hut, he found Ostak had added another thing to the ornaments of the hut. There was a rudder, patched up with bits of wood, from a ship, standing by the spear and the walrus head. Kam played with it until he was too sleepy to play anymore.

It was not until years later, when Ostak had departed to the sky-world and Kam was a boy full-grown and master of the hut, that he thought to look at the marks on the rudder, the marks of a knife, where by great labor the rudder had been severed from the rudder post.

The Book of the Tiger

The Warrior

Foreword by Harold Lamb

"The Book of the Tiger" is four hundred years old. It was written by Babar, conqueror of India, the first of the dynasty known to us as the great Moghuls. The Book is his own story of his life's adventures.

From these original Turki manuscript and copies, two English men of letters, Dr. John Leyden and Mr. W. Erskine, made a remarkable translation a hundred years ago. In completing this translation—a work of years—all copies of the original manuscript were compared, with the help of a Persian scholar, and the result left no doubt of its accuracy.*

"The Book of the Tiger"—the memoirs of Babar—was held in veneration by the people of India during the Moghul era. It was acknowledged by European scholars to be a classic worthy to be placed beside the confessions of Rousseau, or Cellini; yet until now it has remained little known in America.

Babar himself is a more familiar figure, closely resembling Henry of Navarre. He had the same high courage and grim humor, and his achievements were greater. His autobiography, written early in the sixteenth century, gives us word for word the adventures of one of the most famous—and certainly the most likable—warrior kings of Asia. It has been said of Babar that he lacked the stately and suspicion-fired artificiality of Asia's monarchs. He told the very human truth about himself and all that happened to him.

And the real story that appeals to us today is that of Babar the man, his

---

*The transcriber wishes to acknowledge his complete indebtedness to the translation of Dr. Leyden and Mr. Erskine, from which the following narrative is taken—also to the excellent commentary of Dr. Stanley Lane-Poole, entitled "Babar."

gay equanimity in misfortune, his love of danger—and no soldier of fortune faced death in as many forms as this Tiger of India.

He was not called the Tiger at first. His given name was Zahir ed-din; but when his Moghul uncles came out of the desert to view him in his cradle, they were unable to pronounce his Turki name, and dubbed him Babar, the Tiger. After a while everyone called him that.

He was a great-grandson of Timur-i-lang* and a descendant of that other scourge of Asia, Genghis Khan. The name Moghul is merely a European corruption of Mongol. The Tiger had all the restless energy of the nomad Mongol, and the fire and courage of the Chatagai Turk of the mountains of Central Asia—not at all the same thing as the Osmanli Turk of Constantinople.

He lived at first under the eaves of the world—just under the roof of the world. A very breeding place of mountains, where the Thian Shan, the Celestial Mountains of China, and the Hindu Kush and the Mustagh ranges of Tibet show their snow peaks on the skyline. Two hundred miles to the east lay a gray inlet of the Gobi Desert; to the west, the fertile valleys and great cities of Turkestan; to the north, the wide Mongol steppes. He was a prince of Tartary, one of the scions of Tamerlane, but this mountain kingdom of Ferghana was all the country his father had been able to hold together by the sword.

Now all Asia was at that time ruled by despots. There was no law of succession, except the rule of the reigning monarch. When a ruler died the throne was seized by whoever could take it. There was truth in the proverb, "Only a hand fit to hold a sword may grasp a scepter." The heir selected by the late monarch almost always had to fight for his claim.

Nor was there, as in Europe, a landed nobility. "Spoils to the victor!" Land, mountain castles, valley cities—all were prizes to be fought for. And Central Asia, then as now, was a very furnace of feuds.

Into this cockpit the boy king was plunged—his first act, to leap into the saddle and ride for the castle of his native city. Many of his father's nobles rallied to him. They were hard-riding, hard-fighting men, experts with the sword and bow. Every noble had a following of men-at-arms, gentlemen of good blood and sporting instincts.

In that age and place every mountain man bore weapons and used them. Only the townspeople in the valleys were peaceable folk—comparatively.

*Tamerlane.

And these Moghul gentlemen of fortune were cultured chaps, by sixteenth-century standards. They could quote the poems of Sadi and Hafiz, and any amount of the Koran. They knew the constellations and the omens of the stars; they liked to loaf in the courtyards and well gardens of the great observatories and mosques that Tamerlane had left them.

After a night devoted to horse-stealing they might be found sitting in the sun against a wall on a splendid carpet, listening to the exhortations of some *kwajah*, or learned man. They slept under tents in the snow of the heights, or plundered palaces in the Mother of Cities—tall and stout-limbed men, bearded as Allah intended a man should be. They guarded their summer pastures in the uplands, or rode like fiends over the desert floor to avenge a wrong or steal a city. The time of their death, they believed, was written, and life was a joyous thing. They could enjoy the flowers of a garden after a raid. And more often than not their horses went clad in mail, a helmet instead of a turban on the head of the rider.

Babar himself disliked heavy armor and was usually to be found in the thick of a fight without any protection except a light steel cap. The Moghuls had a few cumbersome firelocks that were used with crossbows in siege work; the mace and spear were often carried by the warriors; but the powerful Turkish bow and the tempered scimitar were the favorite weapons. Nearly always the fighting was from the saddle.

And the wars were not like the wars of Europe in 1500. Europe itself was no more than a name to these Moghul gentlemen—Vasco de Gama was still on the high seas seeking India. Standing armies were unknown. A prince or chieftain assembled his nobles and followers, and as many more as he could persuade to join him—mounted his horse and raced fifty miles or so to surprise an enemy in camp or mountain eyrie. The dash ended in a flashing of curved blades and a flurry of arrows—a thudding of hoofs and the affair was lost or won.

If a castle held out against the first surprise, a siege rarely followed—you cannot batter down the walls of a tower on a precipice without artillery. The vanquished fled, each man for himself, and thought it no disgrace. A day or a year or a generation later, they would manage to get back their own. A prince unfortunate enough to be taken captive could anticipate that his skull would be made into a drinking cup, or his eyes would feel the fire pencil. Yesterday or today, the quality of mercy is little esteemed in the hills of Central Asia.

As in all Asia, a monarch's worst enemies were most often his own relatives. "Kingship knows no kinship," it was said, and this was so. Babar in this respect was utterly different from the rulers of his century, in that he was perfectly willing to risk his own life for sheer delight in conflict, and he was always merciful to his own blood relations—a circumstance that moved his officers and men to vigorous protest more than once.

When he became king of Ferghana, at eleven years, his uncles and cousins promptly came forward to take what they could grasp of his little country.

His younger brother Jahangir was a weakling, a tool of his enemies. Unwarlike and intriguing, Jahangir played John to Babar's Richard Coeur de Lion.

His two nearest uncles were the Moghuls of the north, Mahmud Khan and Ahmed Khan, the Slayer. Babar speaks of them as the big and little khan—true Mongols of the steppes, kindly and hospitable, but avaricious. They intended the boy no personal harm, but it never entered their heads that he could hold his own against the veteran chieftains of Central Asai, and it seemed good to them to take the fertile valleys of Ferghana before others did.

Other uncles and cousins held the great central city of Samarkand—the rightful seat of the scions of Tamerlane, and the ancient cities of Heart, Merv, and Balk, in Khorassan to the far southwest. In these cities were the valley people, the Persians (Tajiks, Sarts), and Arab merchants—the craftsmen and the mullahs, the beggars and learned men. Caravans from India and far Cathay plodded toward these cities—the heart of Muhammadan Asia. The rulers were the dominant Moghul families, the military caste, sons of Tamerlane.

Of all the Moghuls, Babar had the best claim to Samarkand, the Rome of Central Asia—Samarkand, the golden, with its towering walls ten thousand paces in circuit, its imperial Blue Palace, and mysterious Echoing Mosque, its pomegranate and apple gardens, its pleasant canals and screened pleasure kiosks where the sons of ancient kings had reveled. In Samarkand, founded by Alexander, and given grandeur by Tamerlane, was the observatory of Ulugh Beg. It was a kind of earthly paradise.

And the youthful tiger set his heart on becoming king of Samarkand.

So the boy wandered in the hills with his band of followers who served him for his father's sake and tried to keep from him his birthright. He never gave up hope. He learned to use his weapons in battle—he became one of the finest swordsmen of his day—and the *kwajahs* schooled him in science and literature when the little band halted in some hospitable but poverty-ridden hill village to rest the horses. He grew to be exceptionally handsome—a straight-standing, fearless youth, reverent and more than generous, ready to fly a falcon or dispute the merits of a song with his officers, or to ride a hundred miles in a day to storm a tempting castle.

But here is his story in his own words.

Chapter I
The King Dies

In the month of Ramazan, in the year of 1494 and in the twelfth year of my age, I became King of Ferghana.

The country of Ferghana is a small one, on the extreme edge of the habitable world. It lies within the mountains, and on the other side of these mountains is Cathay.

Ferghana abounds in fruits and grains and is surrounded on all sides by hills except on the west, toward the valley and city of Samarkand.

Omar Sheikh Mirza, my father, had a rightful claim to the great city of Samarkand, and had several times led an army against it, only to be defeated and driven back, desponding.

My father was of shortish build, with a bushy beard, and very fat. He used to wear his tunic extremely tight, so that he was wont to contract his belly when he tied the strings; when he let himself out again the strings often burst. He was a middling good shot with the bow and had uncommon strength in his fists. He never hit a man without knocking him down.

He was a pleasant companion, and played a good deal of backgammon. Though he had a turn for poetry, he did not write, but read insatiably; his whole soul was kindly, and brave withal.

In the thirty-ninth year of his age a singular thing happened. My father was particularly fond of pigeons and used to teach them to do tricks in the air. His favorite pigeon-house was built on the edge of a steep precipice. On a day when he was within it, he fell from the cliff with his pigeons and house and took flight from this world.

When the fatal accident befell my father, I was in one of the garden palaces of Andijan.

Andijan is the stronghold of Ferghana—a pleasant city abounding in melons and grapes. Its citadel is near the outer wall, and separated from the rest of the town by a broad moat.

Only a few servants were with me when word was brought that my father had passed to the mercy of God. Although I was older than my brother Jahangir Mirza by two years, my father had many enemies among the neighboring princes of our family, and I did not know how many of his nobles and officers would be faithful to me.

I immediately mounted my horse and set out to secure the citadel, taking with me such followers as were at hand. As soon as I had entered one of the town gates, an old nobleman who had served my father seized my horse's bridle and led me toward an open terrace far from the citadel.

An idea had entered this officer's head that the nobles of Andijan might decide to give up both the country and me into the hands of my enemies. So he was all for riding away toward the hills, where I could join the Khans, my Moghul uncles.

But when the officers who were in the citadel heard of my movements they sent a learned *kwajah*, who had served my father from infancy, to dispel my fears. He rode swiftly and overtook us at the terrace and made me turn, leading me to the citadel where I alighted and faced the Begs* and officers, who greeted me with affection.

We talked together and decided to put the fortress with its ramparts and towers in shape to stand a siege. The next day other officers arrived to render allegiance.

Among them was Kasim Beg, one of the oldest leaders of the warriors, and Master of the Household. He was a brave man, distinguished by his use of the scimitar. His judgment was uncommonly good. Though he could neither read nor write, he had a quick and pleasant vein of wit.

Another was Kamber Ali, called the "Skinner"—a daring man. Once he had worked at the trade of skinner, but now he was a Beg. Dignity made him contrary-minded. He talked a great deal, and very idly—indeed, a great talker must often say foolish things, but Kamber Ali had a muddy brain.

A third was Ahmed Tambal, the Moghul, one of the best of the soldiers but a man of a restless mind.

All of them set to work with heart and soul to defend me in Andijan. And I gave to every Beg and officer some district or piece of land in Ferghana.

---

*Beg is a title of rank, corresponding to "knight." Amir may be rendered as "duke" or "earl." Mirza after a name signifies prince of a reigning family. Khan is the northern equivalent (among Moghuls and Uzbeks) of mirza, but most often means nothing but a trace of hereditary nobility.

Of all my nobles I had placed greatest trust in Hassan Yakub Beg, who was frank, good-tempered, and untiring. He was a man of courage, an excellent archer, and remarkable for his skill in games of polo and leap-frog. After the death of my father he became my minister—lord of Andijan and Master of the Household.

That year there came an ambassador from the sultan of Samarkand, bringing me gifts of almonds and pistachios, of gold and silver, and openly claiming kindred to Hassan Yakub. Secretly, the officer from Samarkand exerted himself to turn Hassan Yakub from his allegiance to me.

In the next few months Hassan Yakub's manners visibly changed; he began to quarrel with those who were most faithful to me, and to stir up disaffection among the men-at-arms. His object in reality was to depose me and make my younger brother, Jahangir Mirza, king in my place.*

When Hassan Yakub's behavior was past bearing, I talked with Kasim Beg and others and decided to put an end to his treason by dismissing him. As soon as I reached this decision I went to the citadel where he had his quarters. But he had mounted and gone hunting, and when word reached him of what was taking place he posted off for Samarkand, to my enemies. The officers in his interest were taken prisoners, and I allowed most of them to go off to Samarkand.

My former Master of the Household was not quite done with me. On the road to Samarkand he turned off to make an attempt to seize Akhsi—the city where my father's tomb had been placed. My officers took to horse at once to fall on him.

They had halted the second night and sent on an advance party to keep watch, when Hassan Yakub came down in the darkness upon the outpost. He surrounded their quarters with his followers and began to send flights of arrows against the house and the garden wall.

But the darkness was almost impenetrable, and he was wounded in the hind parts by a shaft shot by one of his own men, and was unable to join them when they drew off. So he fell a sacrifice to his own misdeed—he whom I had honored and trusted.

Another officer who took up the sword against me was Ibrahim Saru

*Babar has no word of reproach for his brother. Jahangir lacked his brother's impetuous courage, and allowed himself to become the tool of Babar's enemies more than once.

of the tribe of Minkaligh. He had been brought up from infancy in my mother's service and had attained the rank of Beg. Now he entered the fort of Asfera and read the public prayer for the king in the name of one of my enemies instead of mine.

In the spring after my father's death, I bade my followers mount and go with me to punish the revolt of Ibrahim Saru. For the first time I was about to lay siege to a stronghold, and to endeavor to direct my men aright in battle. No sooner had we come up and looked over the ground than the younger warriors in the wantonness of high spirits spurred toward the foot of the walk, climbed a rampart that the defenders had just built, and made their way into an outwork.

Seeing this advantage gained, the veteran officers pressed the attack. I had appointed Kasim Beg Master of the Household, as he had been during the life of my father, and this day he pushed on before the others and laid about him with his scimitar.

Tambal and others wielded their blades gallantly, but though Kasim Beg was an older man, he gained the prize of valor. Khoda-berdi, my tutor, was struck this day by an arrow from a crossbow and died. As my men had rushed into the assault without armor, several of them were slain and a great many wounded.

Ibrahim Saru had with him a crossbowman who shot astonishingly well, and struck down many of my followers. Huge stones were also cast down upon us by machines.

One of my men who had climbed up to the foot of the wall was hit by a stone. He came spinning down, heels over head, without lodging anywhere until he lighted, tumbling and rolling, at the bottom of the slope. Yet he had no hurt and mounted his horse at once.

We did not carry the fort in the first storm, and my officers set to work to build up frameworks of timber overlooking the walls, and to run beneath the gates. But all these contrivances were not needed. After forty days Ibrahim Saru made offers of complete submission and came out and presented himself before me with a scimitar suspended from his throat.

My father had tried in vain to win the great city of Samarkand. The rulers of Samarkand at this time had disgusted both high and low, soldiers and townspeople. Even the reverend *kwajahs* who had protected the poor, suffered hardships in their turn.

What added to the evil was that, as the reigning prince was tyrannical and debauched, his officers and servants all imitated him. Their warriors were drunken and unrestrained. When one of them had carried off a townsman's wife, the husband came and complained.

"You have had her for a good many years," he was told. "It is only fair that this man should have her for a day."

Another thing that disgusted honest men was that neither the shopkeepers nor soldiers themselves could leave their houses unguarded lest their children be carried off for slaves.

The people of Samarkand who a generation ago had lived in peace and ease, were stung to the soul and lifted up their hands in supplication for aid.

So it happened that the city was in disorder and tumult. A strong party of nobles proclaimed Sultan Ali Mirza, my cousin, king.

Almost at once, however, he was seized with some of his men in the citadel and condemned to be sent to the Gok-serai, and to have the fire-pencil put to his eyes.

The Gok-serai was one of the palaces Tamerlane built and is a place of both good and evil omen. For every prince of the race of Tamerlane mounts to the throne at this palace, and everyone who loses his life by aspiring to the throne loses it here.

Sultan Ali Mirza was accordingly carried to the Gok-serai and the fire-pencil applied to his eyes. But, whether it happened from intention or the surgeon's want of skill, no injury was done.

Pretending that he had been blinded and was in great pain, my young cousin made his way through the streets to take refuge in the sanctuary of Kwajah Yahia's house. In a few days he was able to make his escape from the city, with some men.

Kwajah Yahia, who was his friend, came to me with proposals of agreement between us. I went forward with my followers, and Sultan Ali advanced with his as far as the river Kohik. Each taking four or five men with him, we had an interview on horseback in the middle of the stream. It was settled that next summer he should move up with what forces he could muster from Bokhara and I was to come down with mine from the hills, to lay siege to Samarkand. We both had a just claim to the throne.

Accordingly in the next Ramazan I took to horse and ventured down into the long valley where the city lies.

My cousin did not show up, which was not a matter for great surprise, as he had more inclination to plan than to act. But fortune favored me in a singular way. We were moving down the river Kohik, which waters the valley, when we came suddenly upon a force of two or three hundred Moghul warriors. We took position around them, when they came forward and explained that they had been seeking me, to join my standard. In reality they had been off on a venture of their own—thanks to the general disorder—and my coming had surprised them.

With this reinforcement I laid siege to Samarkand.

For seven months my men camped in the cultivated fields outside the walls that were too strong to be assaulted. Hunger was the only weapon we could use, and in the end it opened the gates of the city to us. The Mirzas who had caused all the suffering in the city departed secretly with two or three hundred hungry and naked wretches, stealing away across the river. Word of their flight was sent to me at once, and we all mounted and rode toward the gates. The chief men of Samarkand and the young cavaliers who had looked anxiously for my arrival came out and greeted me.

So by the favor of God I gained the city and country of Samarkand.

But in the seven months the Mirzas had forged a weapon that later was turned against me. They had sent a galloper to beg aid of the Khan of the Uzbeks—the barbarians who lived in the northern deserts. At the time, I was not aware of this circumstance.

So great was my delight in entering the imperial city that I rode through the streets from the Shah's tomb to the grand mosque near the Iron Gate. I dismounted at the tomb of Tamerlane, and those of his descendants which are near the stone fort, as you go out at the gate.

We went to look at the observatory of Ulugh Beg the astronomer on the skirts of the hill of Kohik. Near this hill there is a pleasant spot, the Garden of the Plain, with a splendid edifice, the Forty Pillars. The pillars are all of stone, curiously wrought, some twisted, others fluted. In another garden is the China house, the walls of which are overlaid with porcelain.

Samarkand is a wonderfully elegant city surrounded by green meadows. As no enemy has ever stormed it, men have called it the Protected City. It was founded by Sikander.* I directed its walls to be paced around the ramparts and found that its circumference was ten thousand, six hundred paces.

For a few weeks I sat upon the throne of Samarkand. I showed favor to the lords of the city and gave rewards to my followers—Tambal the Moghul, above all others.

---

*Alexander the Great.

My men had taken a deal of booty on first entering the city, but since the city and the outlying districts had yielded voluntarily to me or Sultan Ali, it was impossible to give the country up to plundering. And how could a place be taxed that had been ruined by the Mirzas and sacked by my men?

Samarkand was so stripped of everything that we had to furnish its people with seed-corn to plant the next harvest. How could any contribution be laid upon the exhausted city?

On this account, there remained little to give my soldiers, and many of them began to think of home and desert by ones and twos. All the Moghuls who had joined me at the siege went off, and finally Tambal came to me, saying: "It would be well to give over Andijan and the hill kingdom to your brother, Jahangir."

This I could not do for two reasons. Had Tambal's request been made before the greater part of my men went off, I might have complied with a good grace. But who could bear with a tone of authority? Only about a thousand men, Begs and warriors, remained with me in Samarkand.

Another reason was that my uncle, Mahmud Khan of Tashkent, had expressed a desire to rule Ferghana. He had given me not a particle of aid while I was fighting to keep Andijan; now that I had conquered Samarkand, he asked for Andijan.

When I had explained this to Tambal he also went off and left me.*

Many of the officers joined him and collected all the men who had left me from disappointment. These deserters had been in fear of me until then, but now they went boldly with Tambal into my hill kingdom, and they were good soldiers.

Just at this time I was stricken by severe illness. Worry prevented me from nursing myself rightly, and my efforts to keep the remaining warriors with me brought on a relapse so that for four days I was speechless and the only nourishment I received was from having my tongue moistened occasionally with wet cotton.

This brought about the very thing I had feared. Those who were with me, Begs, cavaliers, and soldiers, began to think I was dying and to look out for themselves. Letters meanwhile had been coming in from my mother in Andijan saying that she was besieged by the rebels and if I did not has-

*It must be remembered that Babar was at this time only a boy of fourteen.

ten to her relief, matters would end badly. How could I ride to the hills when I was unable to command the men in the city?

At this crisis a servant of one of Tambal's officers came to Samarkand on some kind of an embassy. The Begs who still attended me very mistakenly brought him into the chamber where I lay and then gave him leave to depart.

In a few days I got somewhat better, but I had a little difficulty in speech. Riders came in from Andijan with earnest requests from my mother and grandmother and the officer I had left in command of the city, begging me to hasten at once to their assistance. I had not the heart to delay. After a reign of a hundred days in Samarkand I marched out of the city, toward Andijan.

Within a week a galloper came to me with word that the very Saturday I had left Samarkand the fortress of Andijan had been surrendered to the enemy.

What had happened was this: The servant who had been suffered to depart during the worst of my illness arrived in Tambal's camp and related all he had witnessed, that the king had lost his speech and was able to take no nourishment, other than having his tongue moistened with cotton. He was made to confirm all this on oath, before my governor who stood at one of the gates of the city.

Dismayed at the news, and lacking heart for further fighting, my officer surrendered the place, although he did not want of either men or weapons or food.

For the sake of Andijan I had lost Samarkand. For my cousin Sultan Ali Mirza had come up as soon as my back was turned. And now I found that I had lost the one without preserving the other.

I now became a prey to melancholy, for since I had been a ruling prince I had never been separated from my country and adherents. With Kasim Beg and two or three hundred who still clung to me, I went to the summer pastures in the hills, after failing repeatedly to win back any city of Ferghana. Kasim Beg, who was never disturbed by misfortune, went among the wild tribes and the wanderers of the hills and persuaded many to join me.

In the lifetime of my father I had been betrothed to Aisha Sultan Begum, a distant cousin. Her father having died, she came with a small following into the southern hills to join me. In the month of Shaban I married her.

In the first stage of my being a married man, though I had no small affection for her, yet from bashfulness, I went to visit her only once in ten or twenty days.

My affection afterward grew less, and my shyness increased, so that my mother the Khanum used to fall on me and scold me with great fury, sending me off like a criminal to see her once in a month or so.

My mother and my grandmother had been sent to me in exile, with the families of the officers who remained faithful. And some of my old men began to desert from Tambal and the rebels and make their way back to me. My falcons diverted me from my troubles. The goshawks seldom failed to bring down pheasants and quail; and we hunted fowl with two-headed arrows.

Yet, longing for conquest, I was not willing on account of one or two defeats to sit down and look idly around me. I had heard that the Reverend Kwajah Yahia at Samarkand was attached to me, and from time to time I sent persons to talk with him.

The Kwajah did not send me any message, but he went about forwarding my cause silently in Samarkand.

And then came tidings that Shaibani Khan and the Uzbek horde were invading the Moghul kingdoms.*

Chapter II
The Tiger Cub

Shaibani Khan had taken Bokhara and was marching on Samarkand. I went to the south of the city, beyond the hills. A week or two after my arrival news was brought that my cousin Sultan Ali Mirza had delivered up Samarkand to Shaibani Khan, the lord of the Uzbeks.

---

*The Uzbeks had been summoned to aid Samarkand some two years ago. Shaibani Khan was one of the most brilliant chieftains of Asia, and he needed no urging to come down from his deserts to the rich cities of the Moghuls.

The Uzbeks were Turks and Tatars, savage men and dour fighters. They were part of the tide that has always flowed down from the steppes of high Asia into the fertile valleys of the south.

Using England for example, the townspeople and valley farmers of Babar's lands were like the ancient Welsh—the Moghuls, the Saxons—the Uzbeks, the Normans.

It happened as follows: The mother of Ali was led by her stupidity and folly to send a message secretly to Shaibani Khan, proposing that if he would marry her, her son should surrender Samarkand into his hands.

Shaibani Khan, advancing as had been arranged with the princess, halted at the Garden of the Plain. About noon Sultan Ali, without informing any of his nobles or cavaliers and without holding any consultation, left the town, accompanied only by a few insignificant attendants, and went to Shaibani Khan at the Garden of the Plain.

Shaibani did not give him a very flattering reception; and, as soon as the ceremony of meeting was over, made him sit down lower than himself. My cousin's chief councilor, the Kwajah Yahia, on learning that Ali had gone out, was filled with alarm. But, seeing no remedy left, he also went out of the town and waited on the Uzbek, who received him without rising.

So, that weak and wretched woman, for the sake of getting herself a husband, gave the family and honor of her son to the winds.

Nor did Shaibani Khan heed her a bit, or value her even as much as his handmaids. Sultan Ali was dismayed by the situation in which he now found himself, and deeply regretted the step he had taken.

Perceiving this, several young cavaliers about him formed a plan for escaping with him; but he would not consent.

As the hour of fate was at hand, he could not shun it. He had quarters assigned him, near one of the Uzbek leaders. Three or four days afterward they put him to death in the meadow of Kulbeh. From his over-anxiety to preserve this transitory and mortal life, he had left a name of infamy behind him; and, from following the advice of a woman, struck himself from the list of those who have earned for themselves a glorious name.

After the murder of Ali, the Uzbek Khan banished Kwajah Yahia with his two sons. They were followed by a party of Uzbeks who martyred the Kwajah and both his sons.

Shaibani Khan denied all participation in the Kwajah's death, saying that it was the act of his men. This is only making the matter worse, according to the saying, "The excuse is worse than the fault."

I was without town or territory, without any spot to which I could go; I was only eighteen and had neither seen much action nor been improved by great experience; I had opposed to me an enemy like Shaibani Khan, a man of skill, of deep experience, and a man in the prime of life. No person came from Samarkand to give me any information though the townspeople were well disposed toward me, yet from dread of Shaibani Khan none of them dared to think of such a step.

At this time Shaibani Khan had gone out of the city a ways accompanied by three or four thousand Uzbeks and as many allies. My men, good and bad, amounted only to two hundred and forty.

Having consulted with all my Begs and officers, we were agreed that as Shaibani Khan had taken Samarkand so recently, the men of the place had probably formed no attachment to him, nor he to them. If anything ever was to be done, this was the crisis. Should we succeed in scaling the fort by surprise and making ourselves masters of it, the inhabitants of Samarkand would certainly declare in our favor; if they did not assist me, at least they would not fight for the Uzbeks.

At all events, after the city was once taken, whatever God's will might be, be it done!

Having come to these conclusions, we mounted and left the camp after noon prayers and rode rapidly the greater part of the night. At midnight we reached the bridge of the public park whence I detached forward seventy or eighty of my best men with instructions to fix their scaling ladders on the wall opposite the Lovers' Cave. After mounting by the ladders and entering the fort, they were to advance at once against the guard at the Firozeh Gate, to take possession of it, and then to let me know of their success by a messenger.

They accordingly went, scaled the walls opposite the Lovers' Cave, and entered the place without giving the least alarm. Thence they proceeded to the Firozeh Gate, where they found a merchant of Turkestan* serving under Shaibani Khan. They instantly fell upon him and put him and a number of his retainers to the sword, broke the lock of the gate with axes, and threw it open.

At that very moment I came up to the gate and instantly entered.

The citizens in general were fast asleep, but the shopkeepers, peeping out of their shops and discovering what had happened, offered up prayers of thanksgiving. In a time the rest of the citizens were informed of the event, when they manifested great joy, and most hearty congratulations passed on both sides between them and my followers. They pur-

*Turkestan here means the boundary of the Turks—the northern deserts where the Uzbeks came from. Modern Turkestan covers all Babar's kingdoms.

sued the Uzbeks in every street and corner with sticks and stones, hunting them down and killing them like mad dogs; they put to death about four or five hundred Uzbeks in this manner. The governor of the city was in Kwajah Yahia's house, but contrived to make his escape and rejoined Shaibani Khan.

On entering the gate I had instantly proceeded toward the college and the convent *serai*, and on reaching the latter I took my seat under the grand Tak, or arched hall. Till morning the tumult and war-shouts were heard on every side. Some of the chief people and shopkeepers came with much joy to bid me welcome, bringing such offerings of food ready dressed as they had at hand, and breathed out prayers for my success.

When it was morning, information was brought that the Uzbeks were in possession of the Iron Gate and were maintaining themselves in it. I immediately mounted my horse and galloped to the place, accompanied only by fifteen or twenty men; but the rabble of the town, who were prowling about in every land and corner, had driven the Uzbeks from the Iron Gate before I could come up.

Shaibani Khan, on learning what was passing, set out hurriedly, and about sunrise appeared before the Iron Gate with a hundred or a hundred and fifty horse. It was a noble opportunity; but I had a mere handful of men with me. The Khan, soon discovering that he could accomplish nothing, did not stop, but turned back and retired.

The men of rank and consequence now came and waited on me, offering their congratulations. For nearly a hundred and forty years Samarkand had been the capital of my family. A foreign robber—one knew not whence he came—had seized the kingdom, which dropped from our hands. Almighty God now restored my plundered and pillaged country to me.

At this time, Shaibani Kahn's wife and family with his heavy baggage arrived from Turkestan. He had remained until now near one of the suburbs; but, perceiving such a disposition in the inhabitants to come over spontaneously to my side, he marched off from his encampments toward Bokhara.

By divine favor, before the end of three months most of the fortified places around Samarkand had come under my allegiance. My affairs went prosperously everywhere. About this time I had a daughter by Aisha Sultan Begum, my first wife. She received the name of the Ornament of Women. This was my first child, and at the time I was just nineteen. In a month or forty days she departed to the mercy of God.

No sooner had I gained Samarkand than I repeatedly dispatched messengers to all the Khans and Sultans, Amirs and chiefs on every hand. Some of the neighboring princes, although men of experience, gave me all unceremonious refusal; others who had been guilty of injuries to my family remained inactive out of apprehension. The Khan, my elder uncle, sent four or five hundred men from the mountain country of Moghulistan; from my brother, Jahangir, the younger brother of Tambal brought a hundred men to my assistance.*

This winter my affairs prospered, while those of Shaibani Khan were at a low ebb. At the taking of Samarkand I had with me in all only two hundred and forty men. In five or six months they had so much increased that I could venture to engage so powerful a chief as Shaibani Khan in battle at Sir-i-pul, as shall be mentioned.

In the month of April I marched out of the city to meet Shaibani Khan, and fixed my headquarters at the New Garden for the purpose of collecting the troops and getting ready the necessaries of war.

Setting out from the New Garden, I proceeded by quick marches to Sir-i-pul—The Bridgehead—after passing which I halted and camped, strongly fortifying our camp with a palisade and ditch. Shaibani Khan moved forward from the opposite direction to meet us. There were about four miles between his camp and mine.

Every day parties of my men fell in with the enemy and skirmished with them. One warrior—who had a standard—behaved ill, ran off, and took refuge in the trench. There were persons who said the standard was Sidi Kara Beg's; and, in truth, Sidi Kara, though most valiant in speech, by no means made the same figure with his sword. One night Shaibani Khan attempted to surprise us, but we were so well defended by our ditch and *chevaux-de-frise* that he could achieve nothing. After raising the war-

*The boy king, Babar, had done what no other member of his numerous family dared to attempt: he had drawn the sword against the invading Uzbeks. But the Khan, his uncle, and the scheming Moghul chieftain Tambal—who had already settled themselves in Babar's hill cities to the north—would send him at first only a few hundred men. To Babar, who was accustomed to fighting his way with a handful of followers, a thousand warriors seemed an army large enough to challenge the Uzbeks, with whose fierce fighting qualities he was still unfamiliar. Babar's uncle and brother and Tambal were well satisfied to let him take the risks: they gathered the spoils.

shout on the edge of our ditch and giving us a few discharges of arrows, they drew off.

I now turned my whole attention to the approaching battle. Kamber Ali, the Skinner, assisted me. Two thousand men had arrived in Kesh and would have joined me in two days; fifteen hundred additional men who had been sent by the Khan, my uncle, would have come up next morning. Such was our situation when I precipitated matters and hurried on the battle.

The cause of my eagerness to engage was that the Eight Stars* were on that day exactly between the two armies; and if I had suffered that day to pass, they would have continued favorable to the enemy for fourteen days. This was all nonsense, and my haste was without the least excuse!

In the morning, after the warriors arrayed themselves in their armor and caparisoned and covered their horses with cloth of mail, we marched out and moved toward the enemy, having drawn up the army in order of battle, with right and left wing, center and advance. In the center were Kasim Beg and some of my inferior nobility and their adherents. In the advance was the Skinner with a number of my best-armed men and most faithful partisans.

We marched right forward to the enemy, and they appeared ready, drawn up to receive us.

"He who draws his sword with impatient haste, will afterward gnaw his fingers with regret!"

When the lines of the two armies approached each other, the extremity of their right wing turned my left flank and wheeled upon my rear. I changed my position to meet theirs. By this movement my advance, which contained most of my veteran warriors, was thrown to the right and scarcely any of them were left with me.†

In spite of this, we charged and beat off the forces that came to attack us in front, driving them back on their center. Several of his oldest officers

*Perhaps the Great Bear.

†This was Babar's first encounter with the dreaded Mongol "swoop." His left wing had been turned by the swift-riding and more numerous Uzbeks; and in facing his center about to meet this danger, he had opened a gap between his main forces and his right wing. The veteran Shaibani Khan attacked this gap from front and rear, and Babar had lost his first battle almost before he knew what was happening. But the young king never forgot this lesson and made use of the "swoop" himself thereafter.

represented to Shaibani Khan that it was necessary to retreat and that all was over. He, however, remained firm and held his ground.

The enemy's right, having meanwhile routed my left, now attacked me in the rear. My front was left defenseless. The enemy began to charge us in front and rear, pouring in showers of arrows. The Moghul forces that had joined me recently, instead of fighting, dismounted and betook themselves to plundering my people.

The Uzbeks made several onsets against the nucleus around me. They were worsted and driven back, they rallied again and charged. Surrounded and attacked on all sides, my men were driven from their ground. My advance guard was nowhere to be seen. Only ten or fifteen persons were now left with me. The river was near at hand. We made the best of our way to it and no sooner gained its banks than we plunged in, armed at all points, both horse and man.

For upward of a bowshot we were forced to swim our horses, loaded as they were. Yet they plunged through it. On getting out of the water on the south bank we cut off our horses' heavy furniture and threw it away. The wretches of Moghuls were most active in unhorsing and stripping stragglers—a number of excellent soldiers were unhorsed and put to death by them.

"Though the Moghul name were writ in gold, it is base—and false is the fruit of the Moghul seed!"*

Between the time of afternoon and evening prayers I reached one of the gates, and entered the citadel of Samarkand.

Many Begs of the highest rank, many fine soldiers and men of every description perished in this fight. The greater part of the rest fled and dispersed in every direction. Kamber Ali, the Skinner, the Moghul whom I had most distinguished by the highest marks of favor, at this time of need did not stand by me.

Next day I called together the remnant of my officers and held a general consultation. We came to a resolution to put the city in the best possible state of defense and to maintain ourselves in it, for life or for death. With Kasim Beg and my most trusted followers I formed a body of reserve.

---

*Babar's bitter invective against the race of his ancestors was wrung from him by repeated desertion and treachery on the part of the Moghul hardy nomads—true marauders. He was learning that he could only count on the warriors who followed him for his own sake.

I had a great tent pitched in the Astronomers' college in the center of the city, in which I established my headquarters. The other Begs and cavaliers I distributed at the different gates and around the ramparts.

After two or three days Shaibani Khan approached and took up his position at some distance from the city. The worthless rabble came out of every nook of Samarkand to the gate of the College, shouting aloud, "Glory to the Prophet!" and clamorously marched out for battle.

This ignorant mob that had never experienced the wound of arrow or saber nor witnessed the tumult of battle, plucked up courage and ventured to advance a considerable distance from the ramparts. When the experienced veterans remonstrated with them on such useless advances, they only answered with abuse.

One day Shaibani Khan made an attack near the Iron Gate. The rabble, who had become very courageous, had advanced most valiantly a great way from the city. I made a party of horse follow them to cover their retreat.

The whole of the Uzbeks, dismounting, fought on foot, swept back the city rabble, and drove them in through the Iron Gate. The fugitives, occupied only with their flight, had ceased to shoot arrows or to think of fighting for their ground. The warriors who were with me kept up a discharge from the top of the gateway, and this shower of arrows prevented the enemy from entering. Another day Shaibani Khan made an attack between the Iron Gate and that of the Sheik-Zadeh. As I was at that time with the reserve, I led them immediately to the quarter that was attacked, without attending to the Needlemakers' Gate. That same day I struck a pale white-colored horse an excellent shot with my crossbow; it fell dead the moment the arrow touched it.

But meanwhile the enemy had attacked so vigorously that they effected a footing close under the rampart. Being hotly engaged in repelling the enemy where I was, I had entertained no fear of danger on the other side, where they had prepared and brought with them twenty-five or twenty-six scaling ladders, each of them so broad that two or three men could mount abreast. The Uzbeks had placed in ambush seven or eight hundred chosen men opposite the Ironsmiths' and Needlemakers' Gates with these ladders, while they made a false attack on my side.

Our attention was entirely drawn off by this attack, and the Uzbeks in ambush no sooner saw the rampart opposite them empty of defenders than they rose and advanced swiftly, placing their scaling ladders all at once between the two gates.

As there was fighting on my side of the ramparts, the men in charge of this spot were not apprehensive of danger, and most of them were dispersed in the dwellings and markets. Only Koch Beg and three other cavaliers were on the wall. Nevertheless, these four boldly assailed the Uzbeks. Some of the enemy had already mounted the wall and others were in the act of scaling it when the four arrived on the spot, fell on them sword in hand, dealing out furious blows, and drove the assailants back over the wall. Koch Beg distinguished himself above all, and this was an exploit forever to be cited in his honor. Black Birlas too, who was almost alone at the Needlemakers' Gate, made a good stand. My men now came up from the houses, made a desperate charge, and the attempt was defeated.

It was now the season of the ripening of the grain, and nobody had brought in any new corn. All this time the rounds of the ramparts were regularly gone over, every night, sometimes by Kasim Beg, sometimes by myself. Setting out in the beginning of the night, it was morning before we completed our rounds.

Yet the siege had drawn out to great length, the inhabitants were reduced to extreme distress, and things came to such a pass that the poorer sort were forced to feed on dogs' flesh. The horses were obliged to be fed on the leaves of trees, and it was ascertained that the leaves of the mulberry answered best. Many men used the shavings of wood which they soaked in water and gave to their horses.

For three or four months Shaibani Khan did not attack the fortress, but approached every night, beating kettle-drums and shouting.

The ancients have said that, to defend a fortress, a head, two hands, and two feet are necessary. The head is a leader, the two hands are relieving forces to advance from outside, and the two feet are water and provisions within the fortress.

Although I had sent messengers to all the chiefs round about, no help came from any of them. Indeed, when I was at the height of my power I had received none, and had therefore no reason to expect it now.

Provisions coming from no quarter, and no reinforcements appearing on any hand, the soldiers and inhabitants began to lose all hope—went off by ones and twos—escaped from the city and deserted. Shaibani Khan, who knew our distress, came and encamped at the Lovers' Cave.

The famine had reached its extremity. Even men who were about my person and high in my confidence began to make their escape. There was no side to which I could look with hope. In these circumstances Shaibani Khan proposed terms. Had any stores remained within the place I would never have listened to him. Compelled, however, by necessity, we discussed capitulation.

About midnight I left the city secretly by the Sheikh-Zadeh Gate, accompanied by my mother. Two other ladies and my most trusted followers escaped with us. My eldest sister was intercepted and fell into the hands of Shaibani Khan.*

Entangled among the great branches of the canals during the hours of darkness, we lost our way; but by the time of early morning prayers we arrived at the hillock of Karbogh and the northern road. On the road I had a race with Kamber Ali and Kasim Beg. My horse got the lead. As I turned on my seat to see how far I had left them behind, my saddle-girth being slack, the saddle turned round and I came to the ground right on my head. Although I sprang up and mounted immediately, yet I did not recover the full possession of my faculties until the evening, and the world passed before my eyes like a dream.

The time of afternoon prayers was past before we reached the first hamlet to the northward, where we alighted and, having killed a horse, cut him up and dressed slices of his flesh. We stayed a little time to rest our horses, then mounted again and proceeded to Dizak.

Here we found nice fat flesh, bread of fine flour, well-baked sweet melons, and excellent grapes in great abundance—thus passing from an extreme of famine to plenty, and from calamity to peace.

In my whole life I never enjoyed myself so much. Enjoyment after suffering comes with increased relish and affords greater delight. This was the first time I had ever been delivered from the injuries of my enemy.

Chapter III
The Big Khan and the Little Khan

This winter many of my soldiers, principally because we could not go out on plundering parties, asked leave to go to Andijan.† Kasim Beg strongly

*In the Uzbek annals it is related that Babar's sister was part of the capitulation, that she was in love with the barbarian Shaibani Khan, and entered his harem. Characteristically, Babar has no word of reproach for his sister. Having done his utmost to defend Samarkand, he tried to put the disaster out of his mind, and even managed to enjoy a horse race in the Prince of Wales manner.

†The mountain capital, Babar's childhood home, now held by Tambal, the Moghul chieftain who kept Babar's brother with him and was waiting to cast his lot with the winning side.

advised me that, as these men were going that way, I should send some article of my dress as a present to Jahangir Mirza my brother. I accordingly sent him a cap of ermine. Kasim Beg then added: "What great harm would there be in sending some present to Tambal?"

Though I did not altogether approve of this, yet I sent Tambal a large sword which had been made in Samarkand. This was the very sword that afterward came down on my own head, as shall be mentioned.

I lived now at the house of one of the headmen of a hill village with a few lean and hungry followers. I was accustomed to walk on foot all about the neighborhood—generally barefoot, and when the habit of walking barefoot was formed I found we did not mind rocks or stones in the least. In one of these walks, between afternoon and evening prayers, we met a man who was going with a cow in a narrow road. I asked him the way.

"Keep your eye fixed on the cow," he answered, "and do not lose sight of her until you come to the beginning of a road, when you will know your ground."

Kwajah* Asidullah, who was with me, enjoyed the joke, observing: "What would become of us wise men if the cow were to lose her way?"

I now began to reflect that to ramble in this way from hill to hill without house and without home, without country and without resting place, could serve no good, and that it was better to go to Tashkent to the Khan, my uncle. Kasim Beg was very much opposed to this journey. He had once put to death three or four Moghuls as an example and punishment for marauding, and he had apprehension of going among their countrymen. Whatever remonstrances we could use were of no avail. He separated from me and moved off with his brothers and adherents, while I proceeded by the pass of Abburden and advanced toward Tashkent, to join the Khan.

Sultan Mahmud Khan, my uncle, was not a fighting man and was totally ignorant of the art of war. He had pretensions to taste, and wrote verses, though his odes, to be sure, were rather deficient. I had composed the following *rubai*, in a well-known measure:

No one remembers an unfortunate,
Who may not indulge his heart in happiness—
My heart is wearied in this lonely state.

I presented my *rubai* to the Khan and expressed to him my apprehension

*The title *Kwajah* is given to a man of learning or sanctity.

of the future but did not get such a frank or satisfactory answer as to remove my doubts.

Yet he was not unkind to me. When the army was led out, he placed me beside him in the salutation of the standard.

The ceremony was in this fashion: When the Moghul warriors had formed the *ivîm*, or circle, they blew the horns according to their custom. When the Khan alighted, they brought nine ox-tail standards and ranged them beside him. An officer fastened three long slips of white cloth beneath the tails of the standards. One corner of a cloth the Khan took, and, putting it beneath his feet, stood upon it. I did likewise with another slip, and the son of the Khan stood upon a third.

Then the Moghul who had tied the cloths made a speech in the Moghul tongue holding the shank bone of an ox in his hand, facing the standards and making signs toward them. The Khan and all his chiefs took mare's milk in their hands and sprinkled it toward the standards.

Upon this all the drums and trumpets struck up at once, and all the warriors raised the war-shout.

These ceremonies they repeated three times. After that they all leaped into the saddle, raised the war-shout, and put their horses to the gallop. This custom of the time of Genghis Khan has been preserved until now.*

From day to day we departed on great hunting matches, and once I managed to furnish a dinner that made all the officers and young men of the army merry.

While I remained at Tashkent at this time I endured great distress. I had no country or hopes of a country. When I went to my uncle the Khan's council I was attended sometimes by only one person, sometimes by two, yet I was fortunate in one respect, that this did not happen among strangers but with my own kinsmen.

At length I was worn out with this unsettled state, and became tired of living. I said to myself, rather than pass my life in such wretchedness it were better to take my way and retire into some corner where I might live unknown and undistinguished. Far better were it to flee away from the sight of man! I thought of going to Cathay, and resolved to shape my journey in that direction, as from my infancy I had always had a strong desire to visit Cathay. Now my kingship was gone; my mother was safe

*It must be remembered that the Moghuls (Mongols) were descendants of the warriors of Genghis Khan.

with her brother, the Khan—every obstacle to my journey was removed. Besides, it was twenty-five years since the Khan had seen my younger uncle, Ahmed, who dwelt in Moghulistan on the road to Cathay, and I had never seen him at all. It would be well if I went and visited him.

But I had about me a number of men who had attached themselves to me with very different hopes, and, supported by these hopes, had shared with me my wanderings. It was unpleasant to tell them of my wishes.

At this very crisis, a messenger came from my younger uncle, Ahmed Khan, bringing tidings that he was himself coming hither. A second messenger followed with word that he was close at hand. We advanced to meet him as far as some tombs, and, not knowing precisely the time the Little Khan would arrive, I had ridden out carelessly to see the country, when all at once I found myself face to face with him.

The younger Khan, Ahmed, surnamed The Slayer, came with but few followers; they might be more than one thousand and less than two. He was a stout, courageous man, powerful with the saber, and of all his weapons he relied most on it. He used to say that the mace, the javelin, the battle-ax, if they hit, could only be relied on for a single blow. His trusty, keen sword he never allowed to be away from him; it was always at his waist or in his hand. As he had grown up in a remote country, he had something of rudeness in his manner and harshness in his speech.

I immediately alighted and advanced to meet him; at the moment I dismounted the Khan knew me, and was greatly disturbed; for he had intended to alight somewhere and, having seated himself, to embrace me with great decorum; but I came too quick upon him. The moment I sprang from my horse I kneeled down and then embraced. He was a good deal agitated.

On the morrow the Little Khan, according to the custom of the Moghuls, presented me with a dress complete from head to foot, and one of his own horses, ready saddled. The dress consisted of a Moghul cap with gold thread, a long frock of satin of Cathay, a Cathayan cuirass with a whetstone, and a purse-pocket. All the younger Khan's men had dressed themselves out after the Moghul fashion, in satin embroidered with flowers, quivers and saddles of shagreen, and Moghul horses dressed up in singular style. When I rode back with him, tricked out in all the Moghul finery that has been mentioned, the men in Tashkent at first did not know me and asked what sultan that was.

As soon as the two Khans met, they sat down and talked about the past and told old stories until after midnight. They decided to march speedily against Tambal, who held my city of Andijan.

The inhabitants of the hill country, who were warmly attached to me, had longed for my arrival; partly from dread of my renegade officer Tambal, partly from the distance at which I had been, they had remained passive until now. No sooner, however, had I entered Ferghana, the country around Andijan, than all the wandering tribes poured in from the hills and the plains. All the fortified places except Andijan declared for me.

Tambal, without being in the least worried, lay with his forces facing the Khans. He had encamped and fortified his position with a trench. It came into my head to go on in advance of my uncles one night, to the vicinity of Andijan, to confer with the chief inhabitants about getting me, some way or other, into the fortress.

After Samarkand and Bokhara in the lowlands, Andijan is next in size. It has three gates. The citadel lies on the south of the city. Around the fortress, on the edge of the stone-lined moat, is a broad highway covered with pebbles. All round the city are the suburbs, which are only separated from the moat by this highway that runs along its banks.

To carry out this plan, I set out one evening and about midnight arrived within a league of Andijan. I sent forward Kamber Ali Beg and several cavaliers with instructions for one of them to make his way into the city and confer with the Kwajah and leading men. My party and I remained on horseback where they had left us.

It might have been about the end of the third watch of the night, and some of us were nodding, others fast asleep, when all at once saddle drums struck up, with warlike shouts and hubbub. My men, being off their guard and drowsy, were seized with panic and took to flight, no one trying to keep near another. I had not even time to rally them, but advanced toward the enemy. Three warriors accompanied me—all the rest had run off.

We had moved forward only a little way when the enemy, after loosing a flight of arrows, raised the war-shout and charged toward us. One cavalier, mounted on a white-faced horse, came near me. I let fly an arrow which hit the horse and he instantly fell dead. At this they pulled up their bridles a little.

My three companions said: "The night is dark, and there is no knowing the number of the enemy. We are only four men, and how can we hope to win? Let us follow our comrades!"

We galloped and overtook our men; we horsewhipped some, but could not make them stand. Again we four turned and gave the pursuers a few arrows. They halted a little, but when they saw we were only four, they came on once more.

In this way we covered our people, and held the enemy in check. They kept pursuing us until we reached a hillock, where one of my officers met us.

I said: "These people are few in number. Come—let us charge them."

When we turned and put our horses to speed, they stood still. And we discovered that they were Moghuls!

The affair had come about in this manner: Some Moghuls of Ayub Begchik's division had been unable to keep quiet and had gone prowling around Andijan on a pillaging party. On hearing the horses of my detachment, they came secretly on us. The watchword that night was *Tashkent*, and the countersign *Sairam*—or if *Sairam* were given as the word, the answer was to be *Tashkent*.

When they fell in with us, Kwajah Muhammad Ali was on my advance; and when the Moghuls came on calling out *"Tashkent! Tashkent!"* Kwajah Muhammad Ali, who was not too keen-witted, blundered out, *"Tashkent! Tashkent!"* The Moghuls, taking him for an enemy, set up the war-shout and let fly their arrows.

So, by a false alarm, we were scattered. My plan failed and I rode back from a fruitless journey.

But after a few days Tambal and his adherents became disheartened on learning that the people of Ferghana and the forts were siding with me. His men began to take themselves off to the hills and dry valleys. Immediately I mounted and marched against Andijan.

My inexperience made me guilty of a great oversight. Instead of occupying the bank of the river, which was naturally strong, we passed the river in the evening and camped beside the village of Rabat-i-Zourek in a level plain where we went to sleep without advance guard or videttes.

Just before the dawn, while our men were still enjoying their sleep, Kamber Ali galloped up, exclaiming—"The enemy are upon us—rouse up!"

Having cried out thus, he passed on. I had gone to sleep, as was my custom even in time of peace, without taking off my cloak, and instantly girt on my saber and quiver, and mounted my horse. My standard-bearer seized the standard, without having time to tie on the ox-tail or colors. So, taking the staff in his hand just as it was, he leaped on his horse and we advanced toward the point where the enemy were coming on. By the time I had moved forward a bowshot we fell in with skirmishers.

At this moment there might have been about ten men with me. Riding quickly up to them and loosing our arrows, we drove them back and followed. Pressing on, we pursued them for another bowshot when we fell in with the main body of the enemy.

Tambal was standing there, in front of his riders, with about a hundred men. He was speaking with another man in front of the line, saying, "Smite them—smite them!"

But his men were sidling in a hesitating way, as if saying: "Shall we flee? Let us flee!" Still, they were standing. There were now only three men with me. One arrow was on my notch and I shot it point-blank at Tambal's helmet. Again I felt in the quiver and brought out a green-tipped barbed arrow that my uncle the Khan had given me. Unwilling to throw it away, I returned it to the quiver and thus lost time enough for loosing two shafts. Then I put another arrow on the string and went forward, the other three lagging a little behind.

Two men came on to meet me, and the foremost was Tambal. There was a causeway between us. He mounted on one side of it just as I mounted on the other, and we met so that my right hand was toward my enemy and Tambal's right toward me. Except for the mail of his horse Tambal had all his accouterments. I had on my cuirass, and held my saber and bow. I drew up to my ear and sent my arrow at his head, when at the same instant an arrow struck me in the thigh and pierced through.

Tambal, rushing on, smote me such a blow on my steel cap with the heavy Samarkand sword I had given him that it stunned me. Though not a link of the cap was penetrated, my head was severely bruised.

I had neglected to clean my sword, so that it was rusty and I lost time drawing it. I was alone, solitary, in the midst of foes. It was no time for standing still, so I turned my bridle, receiving another saber stroke on my quiver. I had gone back seven or eight paces when the three retainers came up and joined me. Tambal attacked one of them.

They followed us about a bowshot toward the river. It was a large and deep stream, not fordable everywhere; but God directed us aright so that we came to a ford. As soon as we had crossed the river Dost Nasir's horse fell and we halted to remount him; then passed from hillock to hillock, through byways to our main camp. Tambal's forces slew many of my best men.

After two days I waited on the elder Khan. And on this visit he made over to the Little Khan all the towns that had rallied to me. As excuse, he gave the reason that since an enemy as formidable as Shaibani Khan had taken Samarkand and was daily increasing in power, it had been necessary to summon the Little Khan to our aid from a great distance. Since the younger Khan had no possessions in Ferghana, my uncle said it would be expedient to give him some.

Afterward, both Khans would proceed against Samarkand, which was to be conferred on me.

Probably all this talk was merely to beguile me, and in case of success against Shaibani Khan they would forget their promise. However, there was no help for it. Willing or not, I was obliged to appear content with the agreement.

On leaving, I mounted and went to visit the Little Khan. On the road Kamber Ali came up beside me and said: "Don't you understand? *They* are taking from you the country you have in hand. Depend upon it, you will not gain anything from them! Now you have some of the hill towns, and the wandering tribes are with you. Fortify your castles—send somebody to make peace with Tambal, who holds your brother. Drive out the Moghuls and then divide the country with your brother, if you will."

"It suits me better," I answered, "to be a vassal of the Khans who are kinsmen, than a king with Tambal at my elbow."

Seeing that I did not like his suggestion, he seemed to regret having made it, and drew off. Three or four days afterward, fearing evil consequences from his advice to me, he fled to Andijan.

I went on and met the Little Khan. He came out quickly beyond his tent ropes, and as I limped on a staff, being in considerable pain from the arrow wound in my thigh, he ran up and embraced me, saying—"Brother, you have borne yourself like a hero!"

Taking me by the arm, he led me into his tent, which was small and far from neat—much like a marauder's. Melons, grapes, and stable-trappings were lying scattered where he sat. He sent for his own surgeon to look at my wound. This Moghul was wonderfully skilled in surgery. If a man's brain had come out, I believe he could cure him; even when arteries were cut, he healed them. To the wound in my thigh he applied the skin of some dried fruits and did not insert a drain.

Chapter IV
The Trap

All this time the Khans were besieging Andijan with Tambal inside. But presently Tambal's brother, Sheikh Bayezid, who was in Akhsi, sent a confidential messenger inviting me to go over to that city. Akhsi was my father's city, and it is the stronghold of Ferghana. The river Sihun flows under its castle walls. The castle itself is on a high precipice, with steep ravines around. There is good hunting and hawking in the regions about, and the melons of Akhsi are the best in the world. From Andijan to Akhsi is a waste, abounding with stag.

The idea behind this invitation was to draw me away from the two Khans. Tambal and his brother knew that without me the Khans would have to withdraw from the country.

But to leave my uncles and join the renegades was a thing impossible to me. So I told the Khans of the message. They advised me to go by all means and try to seize Sheikh Bayezid one way or another.

Such trickery was not to my liking, especially as there would certainly be a treaty agreed on, and I could never bring myself to break my word. Nevertheless, I was anxious, somehow, to get into Akhsi—to have word with my brother and to see if I could win over Sheikh Bayezid to me.

I therefore sent a man to Akhsi to say that I was willing to come. When he again urged me I went.

Sheikh Bayezid seemed to be keeping faith. He came out of the gate to meet me, and led me to the citadel. Chambers had been prepared for me in the stone fort near the outskirts of the town which had been my father's palace. My few retainers were quartered throughout the streets in the town.

But during this time Tambal had sent hurriedly to Shaibani Khan, offering him allegiance. The Uzbeks, a messenger reported, were marching to join Tambal and Sheikh Bayezid.

As soon as my uncles heard this they were disturbed, and began to think of retiring hastily from Andijan to the north. The Little Khan was both just and pious, but the Moghul officers had oppressed my people of the countryside. I was not with them, and the townspeople began to drive the Moghul garrisons out of my forts.

I was now greatly worried. Although I had not the utmost confidence in the Khans, I did not like to abandon them. One morning Jahangir, who had fled from Tambal, came and joined me. I was in the bath when the Mirza, my brother, arrived at the stone fort, but went out as I was and embraced him.

Jahangir and Ibrahim Beg, one of my officers who had accompanied him, insisted that we must seize Sheikh Bayezid and take possession of

the intervening street, with Said Kasim and Dost Nasir covering the rear, I took the lead with Ibrahim Beg. We had no sooner emerged at the gateway than we saw Sheikh Bayezid with a quilted corselet over his vest and three or four warriors at his back, just riding into the town.

When he had been seized that morning, contrary to my wish, he—and these followers—had been left in charge of Jahangir's men, who had carried him off when they had been forced to retreat. They had once thought of putting him to death, but fortunately did not, setting him at liberty instead. He had just been released and was coming back to the town when I met him. Immediately I drew to the head the arrow on my notch and let him have it full.* It only grazed his neck, but it was a fine shot. He spurred through the gate, turning short to the right, and fled in a panic down a narrow lane. I pursued.

A Mirza who rode at my stirrup struck down a foot soldier with his mace. Another sprang aside from us and aimed an arrow at Ibrahim Beg, who balked him by shouting, *"Hai-Hai!"* and speeding on. But I was almost upon this archer when he let fly the arrow, which hit me under the arm. I had on a Kalmuck mail, and two of its plates were shivered by the shot. Then he fled. I sent an arrow after him. A foot soldier happened to be running along the rampart above, and the shaft pinned his headgear to the parapet. He grasped his turban cloth, twisted it around his arm, and ran off.

A man on horseback came careening down the lane up which Sheikh Bayezid had fled. As he passed I struck him with the point of my sword in the temples; he swerved as if about to fall from his horse, but caught the wall and made off, supporting himself by it.

Having scattered all the horse and foot at the gate, we reined in and took possession of it. There was now no fair chance of success, for they had two or three thousand well-armed men in the citadel, while I had only a hundred in the outer stone fort and at the gate. And, besides, about as long ago as milk takes to boil, Jahangir had been beaten and driven out, taking half my men with him.

Yet such was my inexperience that, posting myself in the gateway, I sent a galloper to Jahangir to bid him join me in another effort.

---

*Remember that Babar had pledged a truce with Sheikh Bayezid, and he was glad that his enemy had not been slain while he was a captive. But with Bayezid released and the whole trap revealed, Babar rejoiced heartily when they met face to face. Bayezid, it seems, was armed by them.

But, in truth, the business was over.

We hung on at the gate, waiting for the return of the messenger I had sent after the Mirza—Ibrahim complaining, fretfully because of his wound, that his horse was useless. Sulaiman, a servant, gave him his own mount—a fine trait of character in the man. The galloper did come back and told us that Jahangir had ridden off altogether, some time ago.

It was no season for tarrying, and we also set off. Indeed, my halting so long was very unwise. Only twenty or thirty men remained with me, and the moment we moved off a great band of the enemy came smartly after us. We had just cleared the drawbridge as they reached the town end.

Bandar Ali Beg, the son of Kasim Beg, called out to Ibrahim: "You are always boasting and bragging. Stop, and let us exchange a few sword cuts with these chaps."

Ibrahim, who was close to me, answered: "Come on, then. What hinders you?"

Senseless madcaps—to bandy rivalry at such a moment! It was no time for a trial of skill, or any delay whatever. We made off at our best, the enemy at our heels. They brought down man after man as they gained on us.

After a mile or so Ibrahim called out to me for assistance. I looked back and saw him engaged with a home-bred slave of Sheikh Bayezid. I turned my bridle to go when the two nearest men seized my rein and hurried me on, saying: "What hour is this for turning back?"

Within three miles the pursuers unhorsed the greater part of my men. Then for a while we lost them. A river lay before us, and up this we turned, eight in all—Dost Nasir, Mirza Kuli, Jan Kuli, the son of Kasim Beg, and three others. I myself was the eighth. A sort of trail leads upstream through broken ravines far from the beaten road. By this defile we kept on, until, leaving the river on our right, we struck into another narrow track.

It was about afternoon prayers when we emerged from the ravines upon a level plain. Here we saw a black mass far off in the plain. I put my men under cover and crept up a hillock to see what was moving toward us, when a number of riders galloped over the ridge behind us. We could not make out how many there might be, but took to our horses and fled.

The horsemen followed us. They soon appeared to be no more than twenty, and we were eight. Had we known their numbers when they first came up we should have given them warm work. But we thought they were an advance of a stronger party, and kept on. The truth is that the pursued are no match for the pursuers, even though numbers be in their favor.

"We must not go on in this way," Jan Kuli said, "or they will take us all. Do you and my foster-brother take a pair of the best horses apiece and gallop off together, keeping the spare mounts on your bridle. Perhaps you may escape."

The advice was good, but I could not leave my followers in the path of the enemy.

At length my party began to separate and drop behind. My own horse began to flag. Jan Kuli gave me his. I leaped down and mounted his horse, and he sprang into the saddle of mine. Just then the two rearmost of my men were dismounted by the enemy. Jan Kuli also fell behind; but it was no time to try to shield or help him.

We pushed our horses to their utmost speed, yet they gradually flagged and lost pace. Dost Nasir's horse was done up, and mine now began to stumble. The son of Kasim Beg jumped down and gave me his mount. He took mine and presently dropped behind. Another man turned aside to the heights, and I was alone with Mirza Kuli.

Our horses were too weak to gallop; we went on at a canter, but Kuli's horse began to move slower and slower.

"If I lose you," I said, "whither can I go? Come—be it life or death, we will meet it together."

I kept on turning from time to time to look back at him.

"My horse is altogether blown," he cried at last. "You cannot escape if you burden yourself with me. Push on and shift for yourself—you may still escape."

I was in a singularly unpleasant situation. Mirza Kuli also fell behind, and I was left alone.

Two of the pursuers were in sight. They gained on me as my horse began to flag. There was a hill a couple of miles off, when I came to a heap of stones. My horse was knocked up, I reflected, and the hill yet a long way off. What was to be done? I had still about twenty arrows left in my quiver. Should I dismount at this heap of stones and hold my ground as long as my arrows lasted? But it struck me again that perhaps I might yet be able to gain the hill, and if I did I might stick a few arrows in my belt and succeed in climbing it. I had great faith in my own nimbleness.

So I kept on. My horse was unable to make any speed, and my pursuers got within bowshot of me. I was sparing of my arrows, however, and did not shoot. They too were wary and drew no nearer, but kept on tracking me. About sunset I reached the hill, when they suddenly called out to me: "Where do you think of going, that you fly in this manner? Jahangir Mirza has been taken and brought in; Nasir Mirza has been seized."

These words alarmed me greatly, because if all three* of us fell into Tambal's hands we had everything to dread. I made no answer, but went on toward the hill.

When we had gone a little way farther, they called out to me again. This time they spoke more graciously, dismounting from their horses to address me. I paid no attention but continued on my way. Entering a gorge, I began to ascend it and kept on until about bedtime prayers, when I reached a large rock about the size of a house. I went behind it and found an ascent of steep ledges where the horse could not keep his footing.

They also dismounted and began to address me still more courteously and respectfully, debating with me, and saying: "What end can it serve to go on in this manner in a dark night, where there is no road? Where can you possibly go?"

Both of them with a solemn oath asserted—"Tambal wishes to place you on the throne."

"I put no trust," I replied, "in anything like that. To join him is impossible for me. If you really wish to do me an important service, you have a chance now that you may not have again. Point out to me a road by which I can rejoin the Khans, and I will show you kindness and favor beyond your utmost desire. If you will not do this, then return the way you came and leave me to fulfill my fate—even that will be no mean service."

"Would to God," they said, "we had never come, but since we have come, how can we desert you in this desolate plight? Since you will not accompany us, we shall follow you and serve you, go where you will."

"Swear then to me by the Holy Book," I asked, "that you are sincere in your offer." And they swore the heavy and awful oath.

The name of one was Baba Sairami, of the other Bander Ali.

The best thing to do, I decided, was to show some trust in them.

"An open road was once pointed out to me," I explained, "near this gorge. Proceed to it."

Though they had sworn to me, I could not manage to confide in them, so I made them go before, and followed them. After a couple of miles we reached a stream.

*If Babar and his two brothers fell into the hands of the renegade at the same time, they would have been turned over to Shaibani Khan.

"This is not the road by the open valley," I pointed out, "the one I spoke of."

"The road is still quite a way off." They hesitated before answering.

In truth we were on the valley road, and they were deceiving me and concealing that fact. We went on until midnight, when we came to another stream.

"We have not watched the way," they explained, "and have missed the valley road."

"What is to be done?" I asked.

"The road to Ghiva lies a little farther on," they said, "and it will take you the way you want to go."

We rode on accordingly until the end of the third watch of the night, when we reached the river of Karnan which comes down from the village of Ghiva.

"Stop here," Baba Sairami said, "while I go on, and I will come back after reconnoitering the road."

He did return after a short time and remarked—"A good many men are passing along the road; we cannot go this way."

This disturbed me. I was alone in the midst of an enemy's country, the morning was at hand, and I was far from the place to which I wished to go.

"Show me then," I said, "some spot where we can lie concealed during the day. When it is night we can get some feed for the horses and pass the river."

"Near here," they answered, "there is a hillock in which we may hide." And Bander Ali, who was the headman of Karnan, added, "Neither we nor the horses can hold out longer unless we get something to eat. I will go to Karnan and bring out whatever I can lay hand on."

So we passed on and took the path toward Karnan, stopping about two miles from the village whither Bander Ali went, and stayed a long time. The morning had dawned and there was no sign of our man. I began to be alarmed.

Just as it was full day, Bander Ali came cantering back bringing three loaves but no grain for the horses. Each of us taking a loaf under his arm, we went off without delay, reached the hillock where we wished to remain in hiding, and, having tied our horses in the low and marshy ground, we all mounted the knoll and sat keeping watch in different directions, and on each other.

Near midday we sighted Ahmed the Falconer riding with four horsemen from Ghiva to Akhsi. I thought of attracting the Falconer's attention and getting horses from him by fair words and promises. Our beasts were quite done, having been on the go for a day and a night without a grain of feed. But my heart misgave me, and I doubted whether I could trust the newcomers.

I talked it over with my two companions and came to an understanding that, as the Falconer and his men were likely to stay the night at Karnan, we should enter the town, carry off the five horses, and so make our escape to some place of safety.

Then at noon, as far off as a man could see, we noticed something that glittered on a horse. For some time we could not make out who it was. As he drew abreast our hillock I recognized him as a chieftain who had been in the last day's fighting. He had been at my side in Akhsi and, in the general scattering from the town, had headed in this direction. Now he seemed to be wandering and trying to conceal himself. Again I thought of calling out, when Bander Ali and Baba Sairami came and stood close to me.

"For the last two days," they said to me, "our horses have had neither grain nor fodder. Let us go down to the ravine behind the hillock and suffer them to graze."

To this I consented and we mounted, descending into the depression and letting the beasts crop what they could find.

About the time of afternoon prayers we observed a single horseman passing along the very height where we had been hiding. I knew him to be Kâdir Berdi, the headman of Ghiva village.

"Let us call Kâdir Berdi," I said to my companions.

We hailed him and he came down to us.

After greeting the headman, I asked him some questions and spoke him fair, trying to dispose him favorably toward me. I asked him to bring us a rope, grass hook, an ax, with other gear for crossing a river—also provender for the horses and ourselves, and, if possible, a fresh horse. We made an appointment to meet him at this spot, at bedtime prayers.

But evening prayers were no sooner over than a horseman appeared in the twilight, moving from Karnan toward Ghiva. We challenged him—all three of us.

He answered something we could not make out, and turned aside at once. In truth, this was the same chieftain we had sighted that noon. During the day he had moved from the place where he had been concealed to another lurking place, and in answering he had so changed his voice that I did not recognize it, though he had lived beside me for years. Had I only known him and kept him with me, it had been well for me.

The worst of it was that his passing made me uneasy. It looked as if he had been spying on us, and I dared not wait in the gully to keep the rendezvous we had made with Kâdir Berdi.

"There are many isolated gardens," Bander Ali said, "among the suburbs of Karnan, where no one will think of looking for us. Let us go thither and send back someone to lead Kâdir Berdi to us."

We mounted and rode slowly to the outskirts of Karnan. It was winter and excessively cold. My guardians brought me an old mantle of yearling lambskin, with wool on the inside and coarse woven cloth without, and this I put on. They also foraged and fetched me a dish of pottage of boiled millet flour, which I ate and found wonderfully good.

"Have you sent anybody to Kâdir Berdi?" I asked Bander Ali.

"Yes, I have," he responded at once.

These misbegotten, treacherous clowns had actually met Kâdir Berdi when one of them was off getting the pottage. Instead of bringing him to me, they had sent him to my enemy Tambal at Akhsi with word of my hiding place. Entering a house with stone walls, and kindling a fire, I closed my eyes for a moment in sleep. These crafty fellows pretended a vast anxiety to serve me.

"We must not stir from this spot," I heard them say, "until we have news of Kâdir Berdi." And after a while one of them added, "This stone house is too near the village. There is a place on the outskirts where we might lie safely hidden if we could reach it."

Evidently my choice of the dwelling did not satisfy them. About midnight we mounted our horses and went to a garden on the edge of the suburbs. The garden had a mud wall around it and a building of sorts with a terrace roof. Here Baba Sairami sat and kept a sharp lookout. And here we waited until the next noon.

Then Baba Sairami came down from the terrace and said—"Here comes Yusuf the Overseer."

I was seized with utter dismay and responded—"Find out if he comes because he knows I am here!"

Baba went out and after some talk returned.

"Yusuf the Overseer says," he explained, "that he met a foot soldier at the gate of Akhsi who told him that the king was in Karnan hiding in a garden on the outskirts. Without communicating this news to anyone, he had the man bound and guarded and hastened to you as swiftly as his horse could bring him. The Begs, your enemies, know nothing about you, as yet."

"What do you think of this?" I asked him.

"They are all your servants," he replied. "There is nothing left for you but to join them. Why do you doubt they will greet you as a king again?"

I did doubt, and greatly.

"After this last war and trickery, I can trust no strangers."

As I was speaking, Yusuf suddenly presented himself and fell on both knees, exclaiming: "Why should I conceal anything from you? Tambal Beg knows nothing at all. But Sheikh Bayezid Beg has discovered where you are, and has sent me hither!"

Although he was on his knees he spoke arrogantly, and his words alarmed me mightily. There is nothing in this world that stirs a man more painfully than the near approach of death.

"Tell me the truth!" I exclaimed. "Then, if matters are about to go against me finally, I may perform the last ablutions."*

Yusuf swore again and again, but I did not heed his oaths. Feeling very weak, I rose and went into a corner of the garden. I meditated, saying to myself, "Should a man live a hundred—nay, a thousand years, death comes to him in the end."

I resigned myself, accordingly, to die.

There was a stream in the garden, and at its edge I made my last ablutions and recited a prayer of two bowings, Then, giving myself up to meditation, I was about to ask God for His compassion, when irresistible sleep closed my eyes. I dreamed, and in the dream I saw the son of the murdered Kwajah Yahia with a great following, all on dappled gray horses, come to me and say: "Do not be troubled. The holy Kwajah has sent me to support you to your throne. Whenever you are in distress and danger, appeal to him and victory and triumph shall come to your side!"

I woke with an easy heart, at the very moment when Yusuf the Overseer and his companions were agreeing to seize and throttle me. After

*The purification before death—washing the hands, feet, and head. The young Babar, it seems, had determined to die fighting rather than be taken captive before Tambal. His invincible hopefulness had kept him watching until now for aid to turn up. To the two who betrayed him, the king was more valuable alive than dead—and they had a healthy respect for his sword.

listening to them talking about it a while, I opened my eyes and joined the discussion, saying—"All you say is very well, but I am curious to see which of you dares approach me first."

As I spoke, the tramp of a number of horses was heard outside the garden wall.

Yusuf the Overseer sprang up angrily.

"If we had bound you and taken you to Tambal, we would have prospered greatly by it. As it is, he has sent a large troop to seize you, and the noise you hear is the tramp of horses on your track."

At this plain statement, my face fell and I wracked my brains to decide what to do. At that very moment the horsemen, who had not managed to find the garden gate, began to make a breach in the crumbling wall. The mud bricks fell away and a rider jumped through, then another.

They were Mohammed Barlas and Babai Pargári, two of my most devoted followers, with fifteen or twenty others at their heels. When they had come near to my person, they threw themselves off their horses, and, bending the knee at a respectful distance, fell at my feet and overwhelmed me with marks of their affection. Amazed at what seemed to be an apparition—I was very weary and hungry—I felt that God had restored me to life.

"Seize Yusuf the Overseer," I cried to them at once, "and the wretched traitors who are with him, and bring them to me, bound hand and foot!"

Then turning to my rescuers, I said: "Whence came you? Who told you what was happening?"

With the loss of his homeland, and the defeat of his uncles, Babar's ten-year struggle for his heritage came to an end. Since he was Babar, and still alive, he did not give up the struggle for a kingdom. Having lost his own country, he set out to conquer a new land. And this second period of his life took him from his native hills to India, and gave us the story of the first of the great Moghuls.

The Book of the Tiger

The Emperor

Foreword by Harold Lamb

Four hundred years ago there lived a happy-go-lucky and gallant boy who was dubbed the "Tiger." He was born in the mountains of Central Asia, where the snow peaks of the Hindu Kush and the Roof of the World itself stand like sentinels against the skyline.

He was a Moghul, which is a European way of saying that he was a descendant of the great Mongols—Genghis Khan on one side, Tamerlane on the other. When he was eleven years of age his father died, leaving him the kingship of a small mountain country, Ferghana, and a fellowship of a few Moghul noblemen to serve him. Some of his nobles became devoted to the boy; others betrayed him for their own gain.

No one—least of all the Tiger himself—dreamed that he would one day conquer India. Or that he would be known to history as the first of the great Moghuls.

His days were spent in the saddle. In all his years he did not pass the festival of Ramazan twice in the same place. At seventeen he was already a veteran in warfare—in the warfare of the clans of Central Asia, than which there is nothing more merciless.

Ferghana, his native state, was wrested from him by his enemies. He won it back, only to see it grasped by his uncles who had helped to gain it, and they in turn were driven from it by barbarian invaders from the northern deserts.

Perhaps in all history there never was a prince more recklessly daring than the young Tiger. He was wounded a dozen times, twice in the head. Once his own followers believed him dying, and again he gave up all hope, made his last ablutions, and prepared to meet death, only to be preserved to life by the strange good fortune that dogged him in his darkest hours.

The Tiger was a remarkable swordsman. His strength, in full manhood, was such that he was known to pick up a man under each arm and run along the edge of a rampart, leaping the embrasures.

He had set his heart on gaining an empire. He was the heir of emperors. He meant to wrest his heritage from his enemies.

Samarkand, the golden city of Tamerlane, aroused his longing. Samarkand was at that time the rendezvous for the astronomers, the poets and savants of Asia—as Baghdad once had been, and as Cordova was in Europe. These Moghuls of his were born warriors, fond of making a pyramid of the heads of foemen after a battle, but they were scholarly gentlemen as well. Their knowledge of the exact sciences, of medicine, latitude and longitude—of music and letters would have astonished the contemporary barons of England and France.

The Tiger did make himself master of Samarkand, only to be driven out twice, the last time by the Khan of the northern barbarians, Shaibani. He never gave up hope. Hunted by his enemies, he gambled with his last stake, his life. It was one of the most remarkable feats in the annals of men.

Confronted by an army that outnumbered his own followers hopelessly, he rode out between the two lines and challenged any enemies who had courage to draw sword against him. Five foemen had the courage, and he killed or badly wounded all of the five, one after the other. It was sheer desperation, but his own retainers were fired by such an example and his foes correspondingly dismayed. Somewhat to the Tiger's surprise, whole tribes began to rally to him in his hills.

Besides his mother and his sot of a brother, Jahangir, he now had an unruly army to care for, and he reflected that his ancestors had once ruled the mountain city of Kabul, midway between Samarkand and India. So to Kabul he went with his tatterdemalions, and the Providence that watched over the Tiger guided him to the plunder of eight hundred suits of armor and the weapons he needed, on the way.

Beyond Kabul lay India, another world, and at that time a much harried world. Here were vast multitudes, and the treasures of centuries. It was divided then as now between Moslem and Hindu.

The Moslem portion was the empire centering around the Punjab, and Delhi was its chief city. Sultan Ibrahim, the lord of the Lodi Afghans, was king of Delhi, and a cruel sort of monarch at that, even for an Afghan. Even members of his own family turned against him, and one of them was to appeal to the Tiger for aid.

In the heart of India and throughout the Thur or desert country, the

Rajputs ruled the Land of Kings. They were chivalrous gentlemen, quarrelsome among themselves, with feuds that dated back to the sun and moon—magnificent swordsmen, Hindus all, and perfectly at unity when an invader was to be repelled.

Their feudal strongholds were almost impregnable—perched on masses of rock rising out of the plain—Chitore, the ruling city, the famous Rantambor, and Gwalior. Rana Sanga was then their overlord, being master of Chitore.

Until that day, cannon had been more ornamental than useful—huge pieces casting stones more often than balls, and depending more on the effect of one thunderous discharge—that might or might not do more damage to the artillerists than to the enemy—than any sustained fire. Foot soldiers were looked upon by Hindu and Moslem lords alike as a kind of inferior race, something in the way of camp-followers. Battles were fought by massed horsemen, and a charge driven home or broken, won or lost the issue.

A gorgeous pageant, India, in that age of Rajput glory, when horse and elephants were the servants of men and all men were of the blood of kings.

Down the Khyber Pass, into this array of multitudinous hosts, the Tiger was to advance with ten thousand hardy Moghuls and some Turks who had dreams of making artillery useful. He was aided by the strict discipline of the Mongols, by generalship that was the fruit of bitter experience, and by a determination never to turn back from this new land until he had conquered it.

He was to enter India without understanding the enervating heat and the fever that always took toll of his race, or the impossibility of returning again to the cool mountain kingdom of Kabul, in order to rule his new land from his old home—or the homesickness that thinned the ranks of his followers more than the fever.

Realizing these things, almost as the last battle was fought, the Tiger's will did not weaken. His empire gained; he would be emperor. The Providence that had aided him now took its toll, and sickness ended his days, in the prime of his life.

But the empire of the Moghuls was a thing achieved, and the foundation of modern India laid.

The Tiger has been in his tomb these four centuries, but his story has been written, and fortunately by himself. This indefatigable warrior who is known to history as Babar, the Tiger, had the gift of setting things down as they happened.

The *Babar-nameh*, or Story of the Tiger, has served as a literary masterpiece in Asia for four centuries. The most honored scholars and even reigning monarchs have copied it in different dialects of Persian and Turki. Because Babar told the truth about himself and told it clearly and well, the story is becoming a classic among Anglo-Saxons.*

Chapter I

The Lair of the Tiger

In the month of June† I set out from my homeland of Ferghana intending to pass through Khorassan, and halted at the summer pastures in the foothills. I here entered my twenty-third year and began to use the razor on my face.

The followers who still stood by me, great and small, were more than two hundred and less than three. Most of them were on foot, and shod with brogues, clubs in their hands and tattered cloaks over their shoulders. So poor were we that we had only two tents. My own I gave to my mother; and they pitched for me at every halting place a felt covering stretched over crosspoles, in which I took up my quarters. Though bound for the southern hills and a strange country, I was not without hope.

Jahangir Mirza was with me. Although it has been written, "Ten *dervishes* may sleep on one cloak, but two kings cannot rest in the same climate—" and although in the past there had been heart-burning and rivalry between my brother and myself, owing to our both desiring the throne—yet, at this time he had left his country to accompany me. He was my brother and dependent on me.

And messages began to arrive from the wandering Moghul tribes, that they desired to accompany the king.

So I left my encampment and marched against Kabul.‡ In three or four marches we reached the Pass of Ghur, and here we had news that Shirkeh

---

*The transcriber wishes to acknowledge his indebtedness to the translators of the *Babar-nameh*, Dr. Leyden and Mr. William Erskine, from whose excellent version written a hundred years ago the following narrative is taken—also to the valuable commentary of Dr. Stanley Lane-Poole.

†1504.

‡Babar went through the Kaluga Pass, little thinking that he, with his shepherds and marauders, was about to play a part similar to the great conquerors his ancestors, Genghis Khan and Tamerlane, who had gone through that pass—called the Iron Gate—before him.

Arghun, the officer in whom Mokím had greatest confidence, had taken post with an army to intercept any who might come by this route.

The instant I received this information, between midday and afternoon prayers, we set out and marched all night, ascending the hill pass. Until this time I had never seen the star Suhail. But on reaching the top of the pass, Suhail* appeared below to the south.

"That cannot be Suhail!" I said.

"It is, indeed," they answered, and one of the chieftains repeated this verse:

"O Suhail, how far dost thou shine, and where dost thou rise?
Thine eye is an omen of fortune to him who is lighted by thee."

The sun was a spear's length high when we reached the foot of the valley and alighted from our horses. The party we sent in advance to reconnoiter—a number of enterprising young warriors—fell in with Shirkeh and instantly attacked him. They kept harassing him until reinforcements came up and completely routed his following. Shirkeh himself was dismounted and made prisoner with eighty or a hundred of his best men. I spared his life, and theirs, and they entered into my service.

At this stage the Hazaras of the desert came through a pass in the east to join me.†

After a general council in which the siege of Kabul was decided upon, we marched forward. From day to day I sent messengers to Mokím, the usurper who held the city; they brought back sometimes excuses, sometimes pleasant answers. But his real object all the while was to gain time. When I took Shirkeh prisoner he had sent gallopers to his father and brother elsewhere, and he now delayed, hoping to have aid from them.

One day I ordered the whole host—main body, right wing, and left—after donning armor and clothing the horses in mail, to advance close up to the city walls. They were to display their arms and inflict some punishment on the town's garrison.

---

*Canopus—this star is not visible in the northern latitudes.

†The Hazaras were a people descended from a remnant of the horde of Genghis Khan, which passed near here. Babar was entering the hill passes of the Hindu Kush, the breeding ground of the fierce-fighting Afghan and Pathan tribes. In nearly every case these tribes flocked to give battle to Babar, but, after a beating, followed him cheerfully in the hope of more sword strokes and plunder. They poured out of the passes of the Hindu Kush a thousand strong. But it was no easy matter to keep them in hand.

Jahangir Mirza, with the right wing, marched toward the gardens of the suburbs. As there was a river in front of the main body, I proceeded by some tombs and took station on a rise facing high ground. The advance parties crossed the river and galloped insultingly close up to the Currier's Gate.

Only a few of Mokím's men had come out of the gates; these could not stand their ground, but fled and sought shelter in the city. A throng of townspeople had ventured beyond the walls to the outer slope of the citadel in order to watch events. As these ran for shelter a great dust arose and many were trampled and fell down.

Between the river and the nearest gate, on the heights and in the highroad, Mokím's men had dug pits in which pointed stakes had been fixed and the whole covered over with grass. Sultan Kuli Chenak and several other cavaliers fell into these pits when they pushed on too quickly.

On the right wing one or two of my warriors exchanged a few sword strokes with members of the garrison who had sallied out. But they soon fell back, as they had no orders to engage in an attack.

The men in the town were now both alarmed and dispirited. Mokím, through some of his chieftains, offered to submit to me and to surrender Kabul. Upon this, he was brought before me and tendered his allegiance. I did all I could to dispel his uneasiness and received him with kindness. It was agreed that the next day he should march out with all his followers and property and yield the fortress. I appointed Jahangir Mirza and another officer with some of my most trusty servants to guard Mokím's family as well as Mokím himself while he was leaving Kabul. So he set out with his train and departed in peace.

In the end of September, by the blessing of Almighty God, I gained possession of Kabul and Ghazni with all their provinces, without a battle or contest of any kind.

Kabul is surrounded on all sides by hills—the walls of the town extend up a hill. The skirts of the nearby heights are covered with gardens.

Here is both heat and cold. From Kabul you may go in a single day to a place where snow never falls, and in two hours you may reach a spot where snow is always found. In the summer nights you cannot sleep without a sheepskin coverlet. Though the snow falls very deep in winter, the cold is not intense.

The citadel itself is surprisingly high, overlooking the great lake and the lower meadows. These are very beautiful when the valleys are green. In the spring the brisk north wind blows incessantly—they call it the *badi-perwan*, the pleasant breeze. In the spring, too, the passes of the Hindu Kush to the north are closed, as in winter. The watercourses are in flood, and only for three or four months can the mountain tracks be used.

On the west lie the mountains of the Hazara and Nukdari tribes, to the south, Afghanistan,* to the east, the Khyber Pass, Peshawar, and some of the countries of Hind.† And Kabul is one of the two great markets between Hindustan and Persia. The goods and horses of Khorassan, Irak, Roum, and Chin‡ all come to Kabul.

And in Kabul are the tribes of all the mountains—Turks, Aimaks and Arabs, Tajiks and Afghans; in the bazaar a dozen tongues are spoken. The Afghans are great thieves and robbers, even in time of peace; they pray for war, and rarely had such an opportunity been offered them as now.

On every hand are rivers cold as ice, and pure, and gardens green, gay, and beautiful—with spreading plane trees that shelter agreeable spots. At the time when the shrubs are in flower, I do not know any place in the world to compare to it.

Inasmuch as it is shut in by natural ramparts, it is easy to defend and difficult to invade; yet, owing to its warlike tribes it is a country to be governed by the sword, not the pen. So many of the wandering clans had joined my standard that Kabul was unable to furnish them with necessary corn, horses, and money.

After mustering my army and questioning those officers who knew the country best, it was decided to make raids beyond the borders. Some advised that we should march against Khorassan; others, against Daman. It was at last agreed that we should eventually make a foray into Hindustan.

But in the next year my mother was seized with a slow fever, and blood was let without effect. A Khorassan physician attended her and gave her watermelons, but as her time was come, she died in six days and was received into the mercy of God. We carried her remains to the Garden of the New Year, and there Kasim and I committed them to earth.

During the period of mourning the tidings of the death of the Little Khan, my uncle, and of my grandmother, reached me. Our lamentation began anew, and great was our grief for the separation we suffered. After

*Babar refers to the mountains held by the Afghan tribes, due south of Kabul.

†Modern India.

‡Roum—modern Turkey—in Asia; Chin—modern China.

directing readings of the Koran and prayers to be offered up for the dead, we returned to our rule.

At this time there was such an earthquake that many ramparts of fortresses and many houses were shaken to the ground. Many people died when the houses fell upon them. One whole portion of a hillside broke off and slid the length of a bowshot, and a spring broke through, forming a well in the place where it had been. In other places the earth was so split that a person might have hid himself in the gaps.

A great cloud of dust rose from the tops of the mountains. Nur-alla, the lute player, happened to be entertaining me with the guitar at the time; he had also a lute with him. He caught up both instruments in his hands, but had so little control of himself that they knocked against each other.

Jahangir Mirza was at Tibah, in the upper veranda of a palace. The moment the earth began to quake he threw himself down and escaped without injury. One of his servants was on this same floor when the upper story fell on him. God preserved the man and he came to no harm.

That day there were thirty-three shocks, and for the space of a month the earth quivered two or three times every day and night. By great exertions my officers and warriors repaired the gaps in the walls of the fortress by the end of the month.*

Chapter II
The Terror of the Heights

In the month of June, tidings came from the Mirzas of Khorassan that Shaibani Khan had drawn the sword against them and was invading their country. So I set out for Khorassan to oppose the Uzbeks—mustering the great body of the army and pushing forward to the west in light array and with all speed.

How can any man refuse to give aid? How much better it is to go forward toward achievement and glory, even though life be lost. The wise have well called fame a second life!

On the journey, ambassadors came from Khorassan to urge me to join

*Delayed by the earthquake, Babar did not advance into Hindustan at this time, but thrashed the neighboring tribes to his heart's content. The Afghans and Hazaras began to have a healthy respect for the Tiger when he stormed their mountain sangars and erected pyramids of the heads of the slain. He also held his turbulent warriors in iron restraint. He still dreamed of driving Shaibani Khan from his homeland.

the Mirzas. What was to hinder me? I had marched eight hundred miles over the mountains with that very purpose.

The Mirzas had advanced as far as the river Murghab, and there I waited upon them. One of their kinsmen came out far to greet me; they were younger than he and ought to have come out farther to welcome me. Probably their delay was due to the last night's drinking-bout, and not to discourtesy.

It was agreed that they were to receive me formally at the Mirzas' Hall of Ceremony in the encampment—that I was to bow at once on entering and the elder prince was to advance to the edge of his dais to embrace me. As soon as I stepped into the Hall of Ceremony, I bowed and then advanced without stopping toward Badi'-ezzaman Mirza, who rose rather tardily to greet me. Kasim Beg, who was keenly alive to my honor—which he looked upon as his own—laid hold of my girdle and gave me a tug. I understood and advanced more slowly.

Although this was not a drinking-party, wine was put before us in gold and silver goblets with the meat. At that time I drank no wine. The entertainment was wonderfully elegant. On their trays was every sort of delicacy—fowl, goose, and assorted dishes.

Indeed the entertainments of Badi'-ezzaman were celebrated, and certainly this party was free, easy, and unconstrained. I likewise went to a feast of Mazafar Mirza. When the wine began to take effect, one of the Amirs began to dance, and he danced extremely well. The dance was one of his own invention.

These Mirzas had wasted—as I soon learned—three or four months in marching from Herat, in getting together their forces, before reaching the river. The princes were very good hosts, and skilled in arranging a pleasure party; they had a turn for conversation and wit; yet they had no knowledge at all of carrying on a campaign, or any warlike operations. They were perfect strangers to a battle or the hazards of a warrior's life.

When a strong detachment of Uzbek plunderers came within reach, all the princes met and everyone talked. But with all this ado they could not manage to order out a light force to drive in the enemy foragers. I asked permission to lead out my men. Fearful of their own reputation if they suffered me to do this, they would not let me move.

Nothing was accomplished. Shaibani Khan, who had captured the frontier city of Balkh, went into winter quarters unmolested. The Mirzas came on horseback to my quarters and urged me to stay out the winter with them in Herat.

Now in all the habitable world there is not another city so splendid as Herat. I was persuaded to stay for awhile.

At first the princes quartered me in the New Garden; but as I did not like the place, they gave me a poet's dwelling and there I remained for the twenty days of my visit in Herat. Every day I went to perform salutation before the elder prince as custom required; but they were more concerned with entertainment than with customs of Genghis Khan, which had always been faithfully observed by my family.

Once we were carried to the Tereb-khana, the Pleasure House, in the midst of a delightful garden. Every part of this little edifice was covered by paintings. Two carpets were placed in a balcony, and Mazafar Mirza and I sat on one—my brother and a sultan on the other. At once the cup-bearers began to supply everyone with pure wine, which they quaffed as if it had been the water of life. The party waxed warm. They took a fancy to make me drink, but when I excused myself, they did not press me.

The people of Herat sing in a low and delicate fashion. There was a singer of Jahangir Mirza's present, by name Mir Jan, who always sang in a loud harsh voice and out of tune. My brother, who was far gone, proposed that he should sing. He sang accordingly, but in a horribly disagreeable tone. The men of Khorassan pride themselves on good manners. Though they turned away their ears and frowned, no one ventured to stop Mir Jan out of respect for my brother.

Afterward we went to the new winter palace. By the time we reached it, Yúsuf, the foster-brother, being extremely drunk, rose and danced. He was a musical man, and danced well. The party began to be very merry and friendly. Mazafar Mirza pressed upon me a sword and a whitish Kipt-chak horse. Two of his slaves performed indecent, scurvy tricks while the company was heated with wine. The party did not break up until an un-timely hour.

During all the twenty days in Herat I rode out to see some new place, and a feast was always ready when we halted.

The winter was come and snow began to fall in the mountains that separated me from my dominion of Kabul. Both Kabul and Ghazni were prone to external violence and internal confusion—at the hands of the tribes. It was a month's journey by the short mountain road, even if this was passable. It did not seem good to me to winter so far from my kingdom, and as I could not make my hosts understand this, I summoned my men and left Herat.

At first I was obliged to march slowly, to give my followers who were scattered afield a chance to join me. So long did we tarry that before we left the foothills behind we saw the moon of Ramazan.

Snow fell incessantly. The farther we advanced, the deeper was the snow. At first it reached to the horses' knees; in two or three days it rose above the stirrups, and in many places the animals could not find footing. And still the snow fell.*

When we passed the last of the large villages—where we bought up all available grain—not only did the snow continue deep, but we began to be uncertain of the road.

I, and others, proposed going around by Kandahar in the south, where we could keep to the valleys. As it was winter, the shorter mountain road would be difficult and dangerous.

Kasim Beg, however, insisted that the southern road was far around, and this one direct. In the end we resolved to go ahead on the mountain track.

One Sultan Bishai was our guide. I do not know whether it was on account of old age, or his heart failing him, or the depth of the snow—but when he lost the road he never found it again.

As we had come this way on the urging of Kasim Beg, he and his sons were anxious to preserve their reputation for sagacity, and managed to discover a road, after dismounting and trampling down the snow. Next day the drifts were higher, and as the road was no longer to be found in spite of all exertions, we were brought to a stand.

There was nothing for it but to turn back to a place where firewood could be found in plenty. Here we sent our sixty or seventy chosen men to look for Hazaras or other tribesmen who might be wintering under the heights.

---

*Babar soon saw that the play-acting princes were not the sort that could oppose his enemy, Shaibani Khan. Nor could they bring themselves to let the young king, a veteran of ten years' warfare, strike a blow against the invader. Babar guessed shrewdly that if he did not head back at once to Kabul, he would have no kingdom left by spring. It was now mid-January, the road by which he had come was closed, and he set out to find a new route over the snowbound Hindu Kush.

At this place we halted three or four days, waiting the return of the men we had sent out. They came back, indeed, but without having found a proper guide. Putting our trust in God, and sending Sultan Bishai before us, therefore, we again advanced by the road where we had been checked.

In the days that followed we endured many hardships and difficulties—such suffering as I have not undergone at any other time. For a week we kept on, trampling down the snow, yet making no more than two or three miles a day. I helped at treading down the drifts. With ten or fifteen of my household, Kasim Beg and his sons and servants, we all dismounted and went at the labor.

At each step the man in advance sank to the chest, but still we went on trampling it down. The strength of the leading man soon became exhausted, and he gave way to another. The dozen who followed then pulled forward a horse without a rider; the horse sank to the stirrups, and was done up after advancing a bowshot. He was then pulled aside and another brought up. In this way our party broke the trail, while the rest—even our best men, many of them Begs—rode without dismounting along the track, hanging their heads. It was no time for worrying them with orders—if a man has pluck and endurance he will hasten to such work of his own accord.

Our trail led us in three or four days to a *khawal*, or cave, called Khawal-Koti, at the foot of the Zirrin Pass.*

That day the wind rose and the snow fell so heavily that we all expected to meet death together. When we reached the cave the storm was at its height. The drifts were so high, the path so narrow, only one person could move forward at a time. The horses, too, came on with difficulty over the beaten track, and the hours of daylight were at their shortest. We halted at the mouth of the cavern—the first of us who had reached the *khawal* before twilight ended.

When it was dark, about evening prayers, the men ceased coming in because they had halted wherever they happened to be. Many men waited for morning in the saddles.

The cave seemed to be small. I took a hoe, and after clearing and scraping the snow away, made a resting-place for myself at the mouth of the cave, about the size of a prayer carpet; I dug down in the snow as deep as

*The Zard Sang pass, over the Koh-I-Baba, reaching some 12,000 feet.

my breast but did not reach the ground. This hole gave me some shelter from the wind and I sat down in it.

My men urged me to go into the cavern but I would not. I felt that for me to be in warm shelter and comfort, while my other followers were out in the snow and the drift—for me to be sleeping at ease inside while my men were in distress—was not what I owed them. It would have been forsaking their fellowship in suffering. It was right that, whatever their troubles were, I should share with them. There is a proverb: "Death in the company of friends is a feast."

So I kept on sitting in the drift, in the hole I had dug out, until bedtime prayers when the snow fell so fast that, as I had been crouching on my feet all the time, I found four inches of snow on my head and shoulders. That night I caught a cold in my ear.

About that time a party, after exploring the depths of the cavern, came out and reported that the *khawal* was spacious enough to hold and shelter all our people. As soon as I learned this I shook off the snow that was on my head and ears and went into the cavern, sending out to call in everybody who could be found near at hand.

A comfortable place was available for fifty or sixty. Those who had any eatables—stewed meat, preserved flesh, or anything in readiness—brought them out. Thus we escaped from the terrible snow, cold, and drift into a wonderfully warm and safe place where we could refresh ourselves.

Next morning the snow had ceased falling. Moving out early, we trampled down the snow in the old way and opened up a road. So we came to the top of the pass. As the summer road winds up at this point to steep ascents, we did not attempt it, but pushed down into the lower valley. Before we reached the valley floor the day ended.

We halted as we were in the defiles, and the cold that night was dreadful. Many lost their hands and feet from the frost. Kepek lost his feet, Sewanduk Turkoman his hands, and Akhi his feet from the cold of that night. As soon as it was light again we moved down the ravine.

Although we knew we were off the road, yet, placing our faith in God, we descended along the precipices to the valley. It was evening prayers before we reached easier going in the valley. It was not in the memory of the oldest man that this pass had ever been descended when there was so much snow—or indeed that anyone had crossed it in midwinter. Although the depth of the snow had been a hardship, it was this very thing that brought us to our journey's end. If the snow had not been so heavy, how could we have crossed clefts and gullies where there was no road?* Our horses and camels must have fallen into the first crevasse.

It was bedtime prayers when we straggled into the village of Yeke Auleng. The people of the place had seen us as we descended the heights, and carried us into their houses, bringing out fat sheep for us, quantities of hay and grain for the horses, and plenty of wood and dried dung to kindle fires. For days we had had no fire.

To pass from the cold and snow into a village of warm houses, to find good bread and mutton as we did, is a joy that can be understood only by those who suffered such hardships.

We rested ourselves and the horses one day at Yeke Auleng and marched on. Word was brought in that the wandering Turkoman Hazaras had pitched their winter quarters with their families and flocks and goods on the line of my march. A body of them, posting themselves in a narrow defile, had checked my advance riders with arrows.

When I rode forward to investigate I saw that there was really no defile, but some of the Hazaras had gathered with their belongings in a gully on a steep knoll and were shooting arrows at our men. My followers who had tried to pass the height were falling back in confusion. I joined them and tried to encourage them, calling out—"Stand—stand!"

No one would heed me. They scattered to different places, and one of them shouted to me—"Arrows are flying near your head."

"Be you bold!" I assured him. "Many arrows have passed near my head."

And I added that retainers were kept to serve their master in time of need, not to look on while their master marched alone against the enemy. Although I had not put on my helmet, or horse's mail, or my armor, and had only my bow, I spurred on my horse.

*Babar's recklessness in crossing the Hindu Kush was rewarded. His determination to share the lot of his men, even at risk to his own life, earned their steadfast loyalty. Alone among Oriental monarchs of his age, he could raise armies of nobles, warriors, and wanderers by lifting his standard. His personal courage was almost unmatched. Once, when reduced to dire straits, he challenged an enemy chieftain to a mounted duel. The chieftain declined, but five of his champions accepted. Babar met them in turn, killing or disabling all of them. This incident, by the way, is not to be found in his memoirs.

When my men saw me making for the foe, they followed. Reaching the hill where the Hazaras stood, they began to make their way up, partly on horseback, partly on foot, without minding the arrows. As soon as the Hazaras saw that my men were in earnest, they did not venture to stand, but took to flight. Our people hunted them up the hills like deer. Such property as was abandoned, we took, with some of the sheep.

Keeping to the ridges of the hills, we drove off herds of the tribe's horses. When it all ended, fourteen or fifteen of the robber chieftains of the Hazaras had fallen into our hands. I had intended to put them to death; but Kasim Beg, happening to meet them, was filled with untimely compassion and let them go.

Chapter III
Rebellion at Kabul

While we were plundering the Hazaras, a messenger came up from Kabul. The flame of revolt had arisen in my city.

I had left Mohammed Hussain Mirza, my uncle-in-law, in charge as governor. With him was Khan Mirza, my cousin.

With the aid of the princess imperial, my grandmother, these twain had won over the Moghul warriors to them, after spreading a report that I, the king, had been seized in Khorassan and carried away to the Eagle Castle at Herat. Many of my people believed that I was dead, and the tribes were in tumult.

My own officers had behaved very well. They had put the citadel of Kabul in shape to resist a siege, and had withdrawn into it with the loyal forces. The rebels held the city and had attacked the citadel for twenty-six days.

Upon this I wrote the tidings of my arrival and sent the missive to my officers by a servant of Kasim Beg. To this man I explained the plan I would follow.

I was to circle to the north and descend by the Ghur Pass, marching on swiftly and taking the enemy by surprise in the rear. The signal of my coming was to be a fire kindled on the Minar Hill, and my officers were to answer my approach by a fire in the summit of the old kiosk in the citadel. When we attacked the rebels, they were to sally out. Such were the instructions I gave the servant of Kasim Beg.

Next morning we pressed on swiftly—those of us who were able to keep in the saddle. Mounting again before day, we descended the Pass of Ghur the following evening and halted in a valley where there was no snow and we could wash and rest the horses.

But as soon as we pushed on, the snow became deeper; near Minar Hill the cold became bitter. Here I sent two men to the Begs in the citadel, to let them know we were coming to keep our agreement and to order them to be on the alert. After surmounting Minar Hill we were forced to kindle fires to warm ourselves, or the frost would have made us powerless to move.

This was not the place where we were to kindle the beacon fire, but we were unable to stand the cold.

Dawn was near at hand when we set out up the slope toward the city, the snow reaching to the horses' thighs. The drifts were deep and such of our people as wandered from the track fared badly. Sinking in the snow and climbing out, we reached the gates of Kabul without being discovered, and at the appointed time.

Before then we had seen a fire blazing in the citadel, and knew that my officers were prepared. When we passed through the outskirts I sent the right wing of my forces to seize the Mulla Baba bridge. With the center and left I advanced through the caravanserais, into a deserted garden. We had gone forward as far as Mulla Baba's garden when my outriders brought back to me, wounded and unhorsed, a party that had pushed on ahead.

This detachment of four warriors had gone boldly to Khan Mirza's house, seeking my cousin, one of the leaders of the rebels. Without halting, they had run into the palace. The alarm had been given and all was uproar. Khan Mirza mounted his horse, galloped off, and escaped from the city.

My four men had been cut up by his followers, and were smarting from saber and arrow wounds. We had reached a dark alley where our horsemen were crowded together. Some of the enemy had come into the alley and made a stand, so that we could not go forward, or turn to go back.

I asked the men nearest me to dismount and open a way with their arrows, and at this the rebels were shaken and withdrew. We formed again in the saddle and waited—it seemed a long time—for the coming of my garrison from the citadel. Before they joined us the enemy had been driven from most of the streets. I made my way toward my cousin's palace, and fell in with the two men I had sent into the citadel, who were seeking the king. They led me into the garden from which Khan Mirza had fled.

Here, at the gate, Dost Sirpuli—a man to whom I had shown great favor in Kabul on account of his bravery—appeared with a naked sword in his hand and made at me. I had put on my quilted vest, but not my mail or helmet.

"Ho, Dost! Ho, Dost!" I called out, and spoke to him.

But the snow and the darkness confused him, or he was too bewildered by the fighting to know me, and came on without pausing, slashing at my bare arm. By the mercy of God, the blade turned and did not injure me. When my followers cried out at him, the man ran off.

Leaving this place, we sought Mohammed Hussain Mirza at the Little Garden where he lived. In a breach of the garden wall seven or eight archers had made a stand. I spurred my horse at them before my men came up, and they lacked the courage to keep to their post. One of them I reached and cut down. He went spinning off in such a way, I imagined his head had been severed from his body, and passed on.

As I came up to the door of Mohammed Hussain Mirza's house, a Moghul who had been in my service rose up from where he had been sitting. He fitted an arrow to his bow and aimed at me.

"That is the king!"

A cry arose on all sides, and he shifted his aim, loosed the arrow, and made off. The time for shooting had gone by and the rebel chieftains were fleeing, so what was gained by his one arrow?

The Mirza, my uncle-in-law, had hid himself away somewhere.

While search was being made for him, I ordered away one of the chieftains who had held the citadel, to pursue Khan Mirza. The townspeople and rabble of the city had taken to their clubs and were making a riot as usual. We sent out patrols to disperse them and drive them from the streets while I went to the residence of the princesses imperial, my grandmother and the wife of Mohammed Mirza.

I found them sitting together in the same house—one of the finest properties of Kabul that I had given my grandmother, who, nevertheless, had influenced my kindred to take up the sword against me. I had never failed in duty or service to the princesses and had cared for them when they came to me.

Now I alighted from my horse where I had always done, and went up to them, saluting them with accustomed respect. They were greatly alarmed, dismayed, and ashamed. I tried to overcome their uneasiness, but they could only talk incoherently, without making excuses or the proper inquiries after my health.*

All the while my uncle-in-law was hidden in their dressing chambers, where he had concealed himself in a roll of carpets. When I had written letters to the tribes, announcing my return and safety, I mounted my horse and rode to the citadel.

There Mohammed Hussain Mirza was brought before me. One of my officers had heard that he had taken fright and hidden himself in the apartments of the princess, and went to seek him, using impolite language in the women's palace. My uncle-in-law was unrolled from his rugs and carried to me in great fear.

I rose at his coming in and greeted him with my wonted respect. Had he been cut to pieces or tortured to death he would only have met with his just deserts; as he was kin to me I gave him his freedom and permission to set out for Khorassan.

In spite of all, this ungrateful coward went to my enemy, Shaibani Khan, and abused me—who had spared his life. It was not long before Shaibani Khan avenged me by putting him to death.

Meanwhile the party who had been searching for Khan Mirza, my cousin, found him among some hillocks outside the city and brought him before me a prisoner. He had lacked wit to flee or courage to fight. I was sitting at the time in a portico of the Hall of Audience, and said—"Come and embrace me."

He was so agitated he fell down twice while trying to come and make his obeisance. After we had saluted I seated him at my side. They brought in sherbet. I drank of it first in order to reassure him. After a few days I allowed him to depart to Khorassan. When Shaibani Khan overwhelmed the two princes of Khorassan and stormed Herat, Khan Mirza fled to me again and I received him as if nothing had come between us.

Indeed, by then the Uzbek Khan had sent most of my family to the

*"The Emperor without ceremony and quite cheerfully saluted his step-grandmother who had set up her own grandson as king in his stead. She was abashed and knew not what to say. Saying 'What right has one child to be angered because the motherly affection descends on another?' he laid his head on the lap of the imperial princess and tried to sleep. He acted thus to reassure her." (From the account of the chief conspirator's son.)

mercy of God, and in all our kingdoms there was no place for a son of Tamerlane.*

Indeed, at this time I held a council of all who adhered to me, and it was clear that the Uzbeks and Shaibani Khan had grasped forever the countries under the rule of my family for so long, and that, after ten years of struggle, I could not cope with the Uzbeks. My enemy was powerful, I was weak, and alone in Kabul.

So it was decided to journey to a country farther from the Uzbeks—to Hindustan.

In the end of this year when the sun was in Aquarius, my son was born. A few days afterward I gave him the name Humayun. I went to the king's garden and celebrated the festival of his birth. My people who were nobles and those who were not, great and small, brought their offerings. I never before saw so much white money piled up. It was a very splendid feast.

Until now no member of Tamerlane's family had assumed the title of Emperor. In this year I ordered that my people should address me as Emperor.

Chapter IV
Down in the Khyber

On a Friday in the autumn of 1525, when the sun was in the sign of the Archer, I set out on my march to invade Hindustan.

The reason for my decision to move out of my kingdom of Kabul was this—Kabul is a small country. Last year, with difficulty and by constant exertions the wandering tribes and the men who served me had been sheltered and provided for at Kabul. There was not sufficient grazing land for the flocks of sheep and herds of brood mares; nor had the tribes proper wintering places.

From the time when I conquered Kabul, twenty-two years ago, until now, I had always thought of mastering Hindustan. Sometimes by the misconduct of my nobles, sometimes by the opposition of my younger brothers, I was prevented from starting out, although I had raided three times into the Five Rivers. At length all obstacles were removed. There was no one, great or small, who uttered a word against my plan. I had already stormed

*Shaibani Khan, the Tiger's great adversary, was cut down in battle with the Persians soon after this. But the Uzbeks and now the Persians were too strongly entrenched in Babar's former kingdoms to be driven out—although the young king made one last effort to do so. Having failed to make himself king in Samarkand, he decided hopefully to conquer India—a country still unknown to him.

and taken the fort of Bajaur beyond my border, and now intended advancing along the Kabul river, through the Khyber Pass to Peshawar.

We set out and descended the passes to the river. We had always been accustomed to halt at Kerik Arik. I embarked on a raft with the companions who were near me. On coming abreast Kerik Arik, though we looked in every direction, not a trace of the camp nor of our horses was visible. Yet ten thousand men had been collected to follow my standard and must be somewhere not far off.

It came into my head that there was a shady, sheltered spot a little way down the river and the army had probably halted there. I went on to that place and reached it when the day was far spent. Still not even a camp-follower was to be seen. Without stopping, I went on all next day and night, only halting the raft while I took some sleep.

In the boat were many men who could make verses, and it was agreed that we should all compose verses out of hand to a certain measure, to pass the time. As we had been very merry, I repeated this made-up couplet:

"What can be done with a drunken sot like you?
Why should we listen to a sorry she-ass?"

Before this, whatever had come into my head in the way of rhyming, however bad or foolish, I had written down. No sooner had I composed these last lines than my heart was struck with regret at the unworthiness of it all. And from that time I gave up satirical and idle versification. I resolved to have nothing more to do with such unworthy writing and to break my pen.

About the time of early morning prayers we decided to land and await word from my men. And at sunrise the warriors began to appear coming in. They had been for two days in camp around Kerik Arik, although we had not observed them.

After two or three days' march I halted at Ali Masjid.* Owing to the narrowness of the pass at this place, I was always accustomed to take up my quarters on a nearby height; the army camped in the valley. As the hillock on which I pitched my tents overlooked the length of the pass, the blaze from the fires in the camp below was wonderfully brilliant and beautiful. Pleased by this, I had formed the custom of drinking wine whenever I halted on this ground.

*Midway down the Khyber gorge, where the British now have a fort.

Before sunrise I ate some hashish, and we marched on until we came to Peshawar, and then halted for another day while I went out to hunt the rhinoceros. We crossed the Black River in front of Peshawar and spread the hunting ring down the river. When we had gone a short way a man came after us with word that a rhinoceros had entered a little wood near the town. At once we turned and galloped toward the wood and cast a ring around it.

Instantly, when we raised the shout, the rhinoceros plunged out into the plain and took to flight. Humayun, my son, and those who had come with him from the northern hill districts, had never before seen a rhinoceros, and were greatly amused.

They followed it for nearly two miles, shot many arrows at it, and finally brought it down. This rhinoceros was poor sport, not making a good set at any rider.

I had often amused myself with wondering how an elephant and a rhinoceros would behave if brought face to face. When the beaters started up another rhinoceros near the wood, the elephant-keepers were ordered to bring out the elephants, so that one of them fell right in with the horned beast. But as soon as the elephant was started forward, the rhinoceros turned and fled.

The elephant was still a curiosity to most of my men. It is an immense animal, standing eight to ten feet, and of great sagacity. The Hindustanis call it *Hathi*, and capture it when young and wild, training it to understand what is said to it and to obey all commands.

In fighting, the elephant makes use of his two powerful tusks, with which he is able to tear up trees; the natives of Hindustan place great reliance on their elephants, and each division of their armies has a fixed number of the beasts—which are useful otherwise in carrying great quantities of baggage, in fording rivers, or drawing guns. Two or three elephants can draw a gun that it takes four hundred men to drag. I had few elephants and these were not used in battle; but the Hindustanis would without doubt send scores of them against my men.

The rhinoceros is another huge beast. It has a horn over its nose a span in length; out of one such horn I had a drinking vessel made and a dice box, and still some was left over. The hide of this beast is very thick. If a powerful bow be drawn to the armpit with all a man's strength, the arrow, if it pierces the hide at all, will enter only three fingers' breadth. Later in the expedition I frequently killed the rhinoceros with such a bow from horseback. In these hunts many men and horses were gored by the beasts' horns—once the horse of a young warrior named Maksud was tossed a full spear's length—whence he got the name of "Rhinoceros Maksud."

The tiger is better sport. Several years before on this same ground we heard a tiger howling where the road leaves the river. It soon sprang out of the underbrush. As soon as our horses heard the tiger's cry they became unmanageable and ran off, down gullies and over ravines. The tiger retreated again into the jungle.

I directed that a buffalo be brought and tied near the brush to lure him out, and before long he came forth again, howling. Arrows poured in on him—I also shot my arrow. One of the men near me rode up and struck him with a spear; the tiger twisted it and broke the point of the spear with his teeth and tossed it away. Wounded in many places, the beast crawled into a patch of brushwood. Another warrior dismounted and, drawing his sword, went into the brush. Just as the tiger sprang, my follower slashed him on the head, and another warrior pierced him in the loins. Still, he had strength enough to crawl to the river, where they killed him. After they had dragged him out of the water I ordered the skin to be taken.

That same day I lost my best hawk. Sheikham, the chief huntsman, had the charge of it. It took hawks and herons excellently. Two or three times before then it had flown away; this time it did not come back. It had pounced so unfailingly on its quarry that it made even a man with so little skill as I the best of fowlers.

I had never before been so far into the *germsil*, the countries of a hot climate, nor the land of Hindustan. Immediately on coming out of the hills I beheld a new world. The grass was different, the trees different, the birds of a strange plumage, and the manners and customs of the wandering tribes altogether of another sort. I was struck with astonishment, and indeed there was room for wonder.

While the army was being ferried over the river near Peshawar we had an inspection and listed the men by commands—as my son Humayun and the gifted leader Kwajah Kilan had only recently joined us with their men from the hills. Great and small, warriors and servants, the army amounted to twelve thousand Moghuls and allies.

As it had been a dry season in the Five Rivers, we moved through the foothills toward the southeast, to lay in a supply of corn. The Hindustanis had begun to gather ahead of us, and when my servants and men of all ranks were out searching for grain many of them were cut off. This was because my men were more intent on combing the countryside for prisoners than on bringing in the grain.

The day we halted I sat down with a few companions to drink arak. Mulla Muhammad of Parghar told us a great many stories. Said Kasim also liked his cup, and when once he started in became noisy from morning until night.

In the Afghan country Said Kasim and Dost Muhammad Bakir once had gone out of the camp, after drinking. Said Kasim was so drunk that two of his servants had to put him on a horse and hold him in the saddle until they got back to our lines.

But Dost Muhammad was so far gone that his companions were unable to get him on a horse. They poured a great quantity of water over him, without result. At this very moment a party of Afghans came in sight. Anim Terkhan, who was also very drunk, gravely gave it as his opinion that rather than leave Dost to fall into the hands of the enemy in that condition, it would be better to cut off his head and carry it away to safety.

Those who were more sober, however, contrived to cast Dost bodily over the horse, which they led along to camp.

In Hindustan I had formed the custom of going upon a boat to drink. Both the bow and stern of these boats were roofed over, giving a place for sitting. On one of these occasions, in a very pleasant spot I had some fourteen officers for companions, and we drank spirits until after noon prayers, and then we began eating *majaun*.* Those who were at the other end of the vessel did not know we were taking *majaun*, and kept on drinking spirits. About night prayers we left the vessel and mounted our horses, returning late to camp.

Two of my officers, thinking I had been taking nothing but spirits and imagining that they were doing me an agreeable service, brought me a pitcher of liquor, carrying it by turns on their horses.

"Here it is," they said. "Dark as the night is, we have brought a pitcher. We carried it by turns."

---

*A preparation of hemp, called sometimes hashish, after the Assassins of Persia, who were devotees of the drug. Only the mullahs, kwajahs, and exceedingly devout Muhammadans abstained from wine in this age. Babar drank no wine until middle age, but went to it with a vim when he began. He had a remarkable constitution and would appear in the saddle before daybreak after successive nights of drinking and drug-taking.

They were told we had no use for the pitcher, although they were extremely drunk and jovial when they brought it in. The drug-eaters and spirit-drinkers are very apt to take offense with each other.

"Don't spoil the party," I told them. "Whoever wishes to drink spirits, let him drink spirits; and let him that prefers *majaun* take *majaun*."

Some sat down to one, some to the other. But the spirit-drinkers soon began to make provoking remarks on *majaun* and hemp-eaters. There was much uproar and wrangling.

We resumed drinking spirits in the boat until bedtime prayers, when, being completely drunk, we mounted our horses. Taking torches in our hands, we came at full gallop from the riverside back to the camp, falling sometimes on one side of the horse, sometimes on the other. I was miserably drunk, and next morning when they told me I had galloped into the camp waving a lighted torch, I had not the slightest recollection of it.

But it was not now a fitting season for intoxication. I passed the river Jhilam by the ford. After sending word to the *ameers* of my garrison in Lahore to join me, I camped on the river Chenab, halting one day to rest my horses.*

At that time the whole empire of Hindustan from the Jhilam to the Ganges was in the hands of the Afghan dynasty. Their prince was Sultan Ibrahim, the son of Sultan Iskander. In his hands was the throne of Delhi.

His army in the field was said to number a hundred thousand men, and his elephants—including those of his *ameers*—were nearly a thousand. More than once he had driven in my allies when his elephants trampled them. Even the eastern kings of Jaunpur, whose forefathers had been cupbearers to a great race of sultans, had fallen into the power of the Afghans—although at that time some of the eastern *ameers* were in rebellion. The resources of Hindustan could raise an army of five hundred thousand men.

The kingdoms that depended on me were the tribal holdings under the Hindu Kush, and the mountain dominions of Kabul and Kandahar, but these countries could not furnish me with adequate grain and resources

*Babar's line of march was almost due southeast from Kabul. He skirted the border of modern Kasmir and the foothills of the Himalayas, crossing all of the five rivers of the Punjab. Sultan Ibrahim was assembling his host near Delhi and gave battle to the Tiger at Panipat, some fifty miles north of the city.

for a campaign—indeed to some of them I was then obliged to send assistance. My men and their followers of all descriptions numbered twelve thousand.

Yet, placing my trust in God and leaving behind me my ancient foes, the Uzbeks of Turkestan, I advanced to meet Sultan Ibrahim, lord of great hosts and emperor of wide domains. During the beginning of our march we had been troubled by ice and cold; now it rained incessantly and was so cold that many of the starving country people died.

South of the Sutlej River tidings reached us that Sultan Ibrahim, who lay this side of Delhi, was advancing, and that two strong detachments of his army were moving toward us. I sent men toward Ibrahim's camp, and others toward his advance force commanded by Hamid Khan, to find out what they were doing.

The next day, Humayun, who led the right wing, with Kwajah Kilan, set out with his lighter force to take Hamid Khan by surprise if possible. Humayun detached a hundred or a hundred and fifty picked warriors to go before him. On Monday this advance detachment sighted the enemy and hung upon their flanks until Humayun came up with his troops. No sooner were these seen than the enemy took to flight. Our warriors cut down one or two hundred of the Hindustanis—cut off the heads of some and brought the others alive into camp with seven or eight elephants.

Mirak Mughul Beg brought word of this victory of Humayun's to my camp. On the spot I ordered a complete dress of honor, a horse from my own stable, with a reward in money to be given to the bearer of the good news.

When Humayun reached the camp with his prisoners and waited on me, I ordered Ustad Ali, the chief of cannons, and the matchlock men to shoot all the prisoners as an example. This was my son's first expedition and the first service he had seen. It was a very good omen. At this same place the razor was first applied to Humayun's beard.*

The sun had entered Aries, while we moved on until we sighted the low banks of the Jumna, and held down the river for two marches. I crossed the Jumna by a ford and rode on a bit to inspect the country. We came upon a

*In the Turki MSS of the memoirs the following note appears at this place: "As my honored father mentions in commentaries the occasion of his first using the razor. In humble emulation of him I have noted down the same circumstance. I was then eighteen years of age. Now I, Muhammad Humayun, am transcribing a copy of these Memoirs from the manuscript in his late majesty's handwriting."

fountain from which a small stream flows—rather a pretty place. As one of my Begs praised it highly, I said, "Yours be it!" Sometimes, raising an awning in a boat, we drifted down the broad stream of the river, exploring the creeks and inlets.

One day we had tidings that six or seven thousand of the enemy horse had encamped across the river on a road leading toward us. Chin Timur Sultan, the son of my uncle, the Little Khan, and one of the most experienced of the Moghul officers, and the whole of the left wing, crossed the river and pressed on, taking the Hindustanis by surprise. The enemy fled, and seventy or more prisoners and six or eight elephants were brought back to me.

Here I arranged the whole army in order of battle, and reviewed it. Following the custom of Roumi (the Osmanli Turks), I ordered the wagons of the army to be linked up with twisted bulls' hides as well as chains. Between the guns were placed six or seven woven shields, and behind these the matchlock men stood. For five or six days we labored getting ready the breastwork and barriers. After every part was finished I called together all the *ameers* and men of experience and held a council.

We agreed that the city of Panipat would cover our right flank with its walls and houses; the wagons and cannon would protect our center, where the infantry would be placed. On the left and in various other places we dug ditches and threw up obstacles of tree-boughs. At the space of every bowshot an interval in the defenses was left, large enough for a hundred or more men to issue through.

The right wing was commanded by Humayun, with Kwajah Kilan. Many of our best officers were posted here. Chin Timur Sultan, the Moghul, had the right of the center. On the extremity of the two wings I had stationed picked Moghul mounted archers to form the *tulughma*, or swoop. As soon as the enemy approached near our lines, they were to fetch a wide circle and come upon the Hindustanis' rear.

At this council Dervis Muhammad Sarban said to me—"You have fortified our ground in such a way that the Sultan will not even think of attacking such a position."

"You judge him by the Khans and the Uzbeks," I answered. "It is true that when we fortified ourselves in Hissar the Uzbek Khans, who knew well the proper time to attack and saw that we meant to defend the place with our lives, retired and left us. But you must not judge the Hindustanis by the Uzbeks. They do not know when to go forward and when to retire."

Sultan Ibrahim, indeed, seemed to be a man of no experience. He was slothful in his movements; he marched without order, halted without reason, and engaged in battle without foresight. He had in his hands the accumulated treasures of his father and grandfather, in current coin ready for use. It is a custom of Hindustan in cases like this to hire soldiery. Had he exerted himself and parted with some of his treasure he might have had a hundred thousand more followers. Still, he had a great host and nearly a thousand elephants.

Many of my men were in terror. Fear is always harmful. Whatsoever Almighty God has decreed from all eternity cannot be changed—though, at the same time, I could not greatly blame them.

They had come two or three months' journey from their own country; we were about to engage in arms a strange nation that did not understand our language.

It happened as I had foretold.

For seven days we fortified ourselves in Panipat, and during that time a very few of my riders galloped up to the enemy camp and discharged their arrows without being set upon. Some Hindustani *ameers* who were serving with me persuaded me to send four or five thousand men to a night attack. This did not turn out well.

The detachments did not get off properly. The day dawned, yet they lingered near the enemy camp until it was broad day. Then the Hindustanis beat their kettle-drums, started out their elephants, and marched forth. Although this great force hung close upon our men, no one was killed. I sent Humayun with his division to cover their retreat. The parties of the night raid fell in with Humayun and returned safely. None of the enemy came near us.

The next night we had a false alarm. For nearly half an hour the call to arms and uproar kept up. The inexperienced warriors were confused and dismayed, but the lines quieted down at last.

By early morning prayers, when the light was strong enough to distinguish one thing from another, word was brought from our advance patrols that the Hindustani host was coming on, drawn up in battle order.

We, too, braced on helmets and armor and mounted.

When the first groups of the enemy were visible through the mist, they seemed to be moving in strength against the right wing. I detached the Master of Horse from the reserve, to reinforce the right.

Sultan Ibrahim's army, from our first glimpse of it, moved forward at a rapid pace without halting. When they came near enough to see my troops drawn up in order, behind defenses, they halted as if pondering: "Shall we stop, or not? Shall we go on, or not?"

The masses behind them pressed them on, but without the same speed as before. I sent gallopers at once to the flanking divisions, with orders to wheel around the Hindustanis' flanks and to attack immediately at the rear. The *tulughma* riders accordingly wheeled to the rear of the enemy and began to loose flights of arrows. Mahdi Kwajah, a very brave man, rode ahead of the left flankers. A body of foemen with one elephant advanced to meet him. The Kwajah held his ground, and my men, coming up behind him, forced the Hindustanis to draw back.

Hearing of this, I dispatched four officers with their men from the center to assist this left wing. The battle began to grow obstinate on the right. Thereupon I ordered detachments to advance through the gaps left in the breastworks and engage the enemy in the center, which had remained passive.

By now Ustad Ali, the Master of Cannon, was firing his *feringhi* pieces to good purpose, and the other cannoneers to the left were making effective play with their thunderers.

Meanwhile, the *tulughma* flankers had gained the rear of the enemy in strength and were hotly engaged with their bows. The Hindustanis made one or two very poor charges on the ditches and abatis in front of our right and left. My men plied them with arrows and drove them back on their center. Their wings being thus broken up and huddled with the main body, the enemy was in confusion, unable to set his masses in motion, forward or back.

The sun, which had mounted spear-high when the onset began, now was near to its height. Seeing the enemy disordered, I led forward my fresh and unbroken main body, and by the grace of Almighty God this great host of foemen was laid in the dust in half a day.

Ibrahim, the king of Delhi, was found under a heap of the slain, and five or six thousand of his men lay near him in the center of the field. Once the enemy fled in all quarters, we pursued with the mounted divisions, slaughtering and making prisoners. Fifteen or sixteen thousand Hindustanis had fallen that day. *Ameers* and Afghans began to come in, disarmed and prisoners. Elephants and their drivers streamed into my camp and were offered to me by their captors.

Having pursued them for some distance and supposing that Ibrahim had escaped with his life, I detached a strong party of my personal followers to pursue him as far as Agra. Then we passed through Ibrahim's camp, visiting his towering pavilions and quarters, and we pitched our camp on the river's side to rest our horses for a day before setting out for Delhi.

Being curious to see the beautiful buildings of which I had heard many times, I rode out to visit the tomb of a reverend *kwajah* nearby, the palace of Sultan Ala ed-din, and his minaret, and the royal tanks and gardens. After this I went back to the camp and entered a boat, where we drank spirits. I gave to two officers who were most deserving the governing of Delhi.

On Friday Moulana Mahmud made his way into Delhi to Friday prayers and read the *khutbeh*[*] in my name, distributing handfuls of money amongst the fakirs and beggars and returning to the camp.

A week later I entered the suburbs of Agra, whither Humayun had preceded me. Of their own free will the Hindu clans and families which had been shut up in this city presented to my son a tribute-offering of many jewels and precious stones.

Among these was one famous diamond which had been acquired by Sultan Ala ed-din. It is so valuable that a judge of diamonds valued it at half the daily expense of the whole world.[†] Its weight is about eight *miskals*. When I arrived Humayun presented it to me as a tribute-offering, and I gave it back to him as a gift.

I then entered Agra and took up my residence at Sultan Ibrahim's palace.

---

[*] *Khutbeh*, prayer for the health and long life of the reigning monarch. Ibrahim being slain and his head presented to Babar, the Tiger saw to it that the prayer was read in his name.

[†] This may have been the "Great Moghul" or Koh-i-nur diamond, or the "Ocean of Light." The Hindus who presented it to Humayun were the family of the slain Raja Bikramajit, and their act was not altogether under compulsion. They were not allies of Ibrahim's Afghan dynasty, and Humayun had placed a guard over them to protect them from inevitable plundering at the hands of the Moslem inhabitants of the city.

Chapter V
Dominion

At once I began to examine and distribute the treasure. I gave Humayun seventy *lakhs* from it, and a palace. To some of my lords I gave eight *lakhs*, to others less—on the allies, the Afghans, Hazaras, Arabs, and Baluchis, that were in the army I bestowed gifts. Every merchant, every man of letters, every person who had come with me into Hindustan, carried off presents, rejoicing in his good fortune.

All my relations and friends in my homeland had gifts sent to them, great and small, and to every person in Kabul I gave one silver coin as a gift.

When I came to Agra it was the hot season. Many of the inhabitants fled from terror, taking their grain with them; others hid it away, so that we could not find enough provender for ourselves or the horses. The peasantry of the countryside avoided my men, and the townspeople were hostile at first.

The villages had taken to thieving and robbery. The roads became impassable. It happened that the heat in this season was uncommon, and many men dropped down as if they had been struck by the *simun* wind, and died where they fell.

Although the country of Hindustan is populous and rich, it has few pleasures. The people have no good-fellowship, as in the northern hills—no kindness, no good horses, or meats or fruits such as our grapes or muskmelons. They have no cold water or good bread in the bazaars, no baths—not even a candle. Instead of a candle you have a gang of dirty fellows to follow you about with a kind of smoking lamp made of a wick in an iron vessel into which oil is poured.

The lower classes go about naked. They tie on a thing like a clout as a cover to their nakedness. In Hindustan even the time is altered, as they divide a day into sixty parts instead of twenty-four. They measure each part by the dripping of water from a hole in a cup, and when the cup is filled they beat upon a brass basin in such a manner that a man awakened from sleep in the night by the beating of the basin does not know what hour it is. I directed that they should likewise beat the number of the night watch.

Most of the natives of the country are pagans, who are called Hindus. The greater part of them believe in the doctrine of transmigration, and the son often works at the trade of the father. For every kind of work there is a certain guild, and the multitudes of craftsmen is a great convenience. In Agra alone I employed on a new palace six hundred and eighty persons each day.

Their buildings are purposeless and ugly; they lack pools or canals in the gardens, and during the rainy season the dwellings are far from staunch. At this time heavy rain falls ten or twenty times in a day; bows and their strings become quite useless; coats of mail rust and books mold. It is pleasant enough between rains, but in the dry season the north wind always blows and there is an excessive amount of dust in the air. It grows warm during the signs of the Bull and the Twins, but not so warm as to be unbearable—not nearly the heat of the northern deserts.

The heat had its effect on my men. Not a few of the Begs began to lose heart and complain of their suffering in Hindustan. Some made preparations to go back to the hills.

No one had behaved better or spoken more gallantly than Kwajah Kilan from the time we left Kabul; but a few days after the taking of Agra he was the most determined to go back.

As soon as I heard this murmuring among my men, I summoned all my Begs to a council, and spoke to them: "After great hardships and exposure to danger we have routed our enemy and conquered the kingdoms we now hold. Empire cannot be held without gathering the materials of war. To go back now to Kabul would be to retreat. What invisible foe compels us to give up the achievement of our lives?

"Let no one who calls himself my friend ever speak of retreat. But if there is any among you who cannot bring himself to stay, let him depart."

Nevertheless Kwajah Kilan was resolved to go, and it was arranged that he should have charge of the treasure I was sending to Kabul. He was heartily sick of Hindustan and at the time of going, wrote on the walls of a house in Delhi:

If safe and sound I pass the Sindh,
May the —— take me if I wish for Hind.

As some two or three thousand Afghan bowmen had come in to join me, and several of Sultan Ibrahim's officers had rendered allegiance to me, we had a great feast a few days after the end of Ramazan when the new moon first appeared. It was in the great hall of stone pillars under the dome of Sultan Ibrahim's dwelling palace. At this time I presented Humayun with a shawl of cloth of gold, a sword, and a Kiptchak horse with a gold-adorned saddle. To Chin Timur Sultan and to Mahdi Kwajah I gave a similar shawl, with a sword and dagger—to the other lords and officers I gave according to their rank and merits.

Yet the feast lacked something of the high spirits of our northern banquets. Rain fell heavily, and those who were seated outside the hall were thoroughly drenched.

From day to day I gave provinces and estates to those who had joined me, and sent them out forces to subdue the outlying chieftains.*

I had made up my mind to have running water in my new gardens of Agra, by building waterwheels at the river—and to lay out the gardens in better fashion. But the Jumna and the countryside was so ugly and detestable that I was disgusted. I was obliged to give up irrigating the countryside and to make the best of the palace gardens as they were.

First we sank a deep well and constructed baths at its edge, far below the surface of the ground. In every garden I sowed roses and narcissus and erected buildings out of white and red stone.

We were troubled by three things in Hindustan—heat, strong winds, and the dust in the air. The baths gave us relief from all three. Some of my veteran officers began to follow my example with their new estates—building regularly and not haphazard after the Hindustan fashion, which is merely to set up shelters of mud, branches, and wood, and palaces without plan or beauty.

My companions made their gardens and waterwheels after the manner of Lahore, and the men of Hind, who had never seen so much elegance, called our new countryside Kabul.

I had asked Ustad Ali, the Master of Cannon, to cast a large piece for the purpose of battering some of the citadels that had not submitted. After working diligently at the forges he sent word to me that everything was ready. Ustad Ali was devoted to his cannon. We went out to see him cast his gun.

Around the place where it was to be cast were eight forges with all needed tools in readiness. From each forge the men had made a channel that ran down to the mold in which the gun was to be cast.

On my arrival they opened the holes of all the different forges. The

*Babar gave his officers and the new Afghan nobles palaces and districts that were still unconquered. Naturally, they set out with considerable zeal to take possession.

metal flowed down the channels, a glowing liquid, and entered the mold. After some time the flowing of the melted metal from the forges ceased, one after another, before the mold was full.

There had been some oversight in the forges or the supply of metal. Ustad Ali was in terrible distress; he was like to throw himself into the glowing metal that was in the mold. To cheer him up I gave him a dress of honor and contrived to lessen his shame.

Two days after, when the mold was cooled, they opened it. Ustad Ali, in great delight, sent to tell me that the shot chamber of the great gun was without a flaw, and that they could easily cast the powder chamber. Having raised the finished chamber, he set men to polish it, while he began anew at the forges to fashion the powder chamber.

Three months later the great gun was finished—the powder chamber having been perfectly cast—and Ustad Ali made ready to fire it. We went to see how far it would throw the ball. About afternoon prayers the piece was discharged and carried one thousand six hundred paces. I bestowed on Ustad Ali a dagger, a complete dress, and a Kiptchak horse, to honor him.

When winter came on again, a strange thing happened, in this wise—the mother of Ibrahim, an ill-fated lady, had heard that I had eaten some things prepared by natives of Hindustan. A few of Ibrahim's cooks had been kept at the palace to prepare dishes of Hindustan for me. The lady sent a girl slave to Ahmed the taster with a bit of poison wrapped up in paper, and another slave to watch the first. Ahmed gave it to one of the Hindustani cooks with the promise of four houses if he would throw it into my food.

Fortunately the poison was not thrown into the pot, because the Hindustani cooks were closely watched at the fires, but he tossed it into the tray that was to be carried in. My graceless tasters were not watching, and he was able to cast it upon some thin slices of bread. In his haste, he spilt about half the poison. Then he put some fried meat in butter on the bread.

On Friday, when afternoon prayers were over, the dinner was served. I was not aware of any unpleasant flavor, but when I had eaten a little smoke-dried meat I felt nausea. When I knew that I could not check the nausea I left the table. My heart rose in me and I vomited.

I had never before done that, even after drinking heavily, and a vague suspicion crossed my mind. I ordered the cooks to be bound, and the meat to be given to a dog which was to be shut up immediately after. Next morning about the first watch the dog became sick, and his belly swelled. He would not get up even when he was poked with a stick. About noon he got up and recovered.

Two young men had also eaten of the meat, and one of them fell very sick. I ordered the cooks to be examined and at last all the details came to light.

On the next court day I directed all the grandees and the ministers to attend the *diwan* (council). The two guilty men and the two women were brought in and repeated all the plot. The taster was ordered to be cut into pieces. I commanded the cook to be flayed alive. One of the women was ordered to be trampled to death by an elephant, the other to be shot with a matchlock.

The lady* was deprived of her possessions and slaves and kept under guard. Someday her guilt will bring its retribution.

I had scoured myself inside with milk and the juice of the *makhtum* flower, and, thanks be to God, the illness had passed off. I did not realize until now that life was so sweet a thing. Whoever has ventured near the gates of death, knows the joy of life.

Chapter VI
The Land of Kings

At this time messengers began to come, close upon each other, from Mahdi Kwajah to relate that Rana Sanga and the Rajputs† were on the march.

*Babar does not mention by name either the princess or her grandson—a forbearance remarkable in an emperor of Asia, or Christian Europe in the early sixteenth century. The war-ridden provinces of Hindustan were discovering that he was an able ruler, and many were submitting to him. One whole Afghan army came in and surrendered. He rewarded the newcomers royally. Babar was always generous, and did not care to hoard up a treasure for himself. This allegiance of the fighting Afghan clans, and his splendid treatment of them, probably saved his throne in the coming struggle with the Rajputs.

†The Rajputs were the most warlike of the races of India. They were chivalrous warriors, and experienced, if impetuous soldiers. Rana Sanga was old in years and wisdom, with fifty sword and lance scars on his body, blind in one eye, with an arm cut off and one leg crippled. Seven Rajas and a hundred chieftains, eighty thousand horse, and five hundred elephants were at his back. He was in all things a foeman to delight Babar.

Of all the pagan princes Rana Sanga was the most powerful. He had won his conquests by his own valor and his sword. His original principality was Chitore. During the last wars he had seized such places as Rantambor and Marwar. He was the chief of all the Rajputs.

When I entered Hindustan, Rana Sanga, the pagan, had agreed with me that if I would march against Delhi he would advance from the other side against Agra. Yet when I defeated Ibrahim and took Delhi and Agra, the pagan did not move out of his forts.

At the edge of his country, yet near to Agra, was the city of Biana. The great cannon that Ustad Ali had fashioned was to batter down the walls of Biana. But when Rana Sanga marched with his army against Biana, the Khan of that place saw no remedy but to deliver up the fort to my troops.

I had sent Mahdi Kwajah to take command at Biana. In his messages he urged that a light force be hurried to his city in advance of my army. I sent the advance force, but it never reached the fort. The garrison of Biana had gone out toward the pagans with too little caution and had been routed.

When the affair began, Kittah Beg came galloping up without his armor and joined in. He had dismounted a pagan and was about to grasp him when the Hindu snatched a sword from a servant of the Beg and struck my officer in the shoulder, wounding him severely. Long after, Kittah Beg recovered, but was never entirely well. Whether from fear or to excuse themselves, all my people who came back from Biana bestowed unstinted praise on the courage and hardihood of the pagan army.

On a Monday in midwinter I began my march to the holy war against the heathen.

Of all the places before me, the water was best in the plains of Sikri, and thither I marched, in battle order, sending a galloper to Mahdi Kwajah with instructions to join me with the remnant of the Biana garrison. At the same time I sent out riders to watch the movements of the pagans.

The Hindus were marching toward us, and as soon as they had news of my advance detachment, which had pushed on incautiously ten or twelve miles from Sikri, four or five thousand of them fell upon my men, who stood their ground in spite of being outnumbered.

The moment I heard of this I detached a strong covering force under a veteran officer to cover their retreat. My men of the advance were badly cut up, lost a standard, and had to flee for two miles before they reached the covering division. Many good men and officers were slain.

From all quarters word began to come that the enemy were close at hand. We buckled on our armor, arrayed our horses in their mail, mounted, and rode out. After marching a mile or so we found that the enemy forces had drawn back.

As there was a large tank on our left, I camped in this place. We fortified guns and connected them with chains. Mustapha the Osmanli was very clever in arranging the cannon in the Turkish manner, but as Ustad Ali was jealous of him, I stationed him on the right with Humayun, keeping Ustad Ali with me. Where we had no guns the spade-men dug ditches.

And as we were greatly outnumbered, and my men disturbed by the bold charges of the pagans, I tried to make our position stronger by fashioning wooden barriers. I ordered things like tripods to be made of wood and fitted with wheels and chained together by ropes of twisted bull's hide. On these heavy tripods the matchlock men were to lay their pieces.

While my men were still alarmed and dispirited, a rascally fellow, Muhammad Sherif, the astrologer, began to add to their fears. Instead of helping me, he pointed out to everyone he met that Mars was in the west, and as we were going into battle from the east, we would assuredly be defeated.

Without listening to him, I went on fortifying the line and trying to get my men in a fit state to meet the enemy.

A day or two later, as I mounted to survey my position, I became moody during the ride. I reflected that I had put off the time of abstaining from my sins. Now that I had entered upon a holy war against infidels, I vowed to drink wine no more.

All my gold and silver drinking goblets I ordered broken up and given to the *dervishes* and the poor. I resolved to cease cutting my beard and allow it to grow. The wine that we had with us we poured out upon the ground. That night many of my *ameers* and warriors followed my example.

Meanwhile a general uneasiness prevailed in the camp. No one uttered a manly word. The *wazirs* who should have given good counsel and the *ameers* who were now masters of kingdoms alike did not utter a brave word. At last, when I observed this I called them together and spoke to them.

"Gentlemen and soldiers—every man that comes into the world must leave it. When we are gone, God alone survives, unchanged. Whosoever sits at the feast of life must drink the cup of death at the end. He who quarters himself at the inn of mortality must one day pass out of this house of sorrow—the world.

"It is better to die with honor than to live in shame. God has been good to us. If we die, death itself yields us immortal fame; if we live, we shall be the avengers of God. Let us swear by His great name that none of us will turn his face aside from the conflict until his soul is parted from his body."

Master and servant, great and small, swore the oath on the Koran. The effect of the oath was visible throughout the camp.

Yet at this moment danger threatened us. Districts and forts near and far fell into the hands of rebels and enemies. Another army of pagans blockaded Gwalior. Every day unpleasant news reached us, and the Hindustanis began to desert my army.

We let the fugitives go, but after a few days I decided that my men would be in better spirit if we advanced. I ordered forward my guns and the tripods, and the barricades, keeping the divisions of the army in battle array. The tripods had been placed on carriage wheels.

Ustad Ali was placed directly behind these machines, with the matchlock men, to keep communication between the real guns and the infantry behind him.

After the ranks were formed and every man in his place, I galloped along the line, speaking to each officer and giving each division instructions how to act.

The pagans were on the alert, and several parties of Rajputs drew out to observe us and advanced close up to us.

I did not intend to fight that day, and ordered the army to encamp, drawn up as it was, after moving two miles. At once we began to dig ditches and strengthen our barricades.

By way of taking an omen, I pushed on a few riders to skirmish with the enemy. They took a number of pagans and brought back their heads. This raised the spirits of my men.*

---

*Muhammadan warriors of this period were incurably anxious about the first omens of a battle. An initial success, however slight, was taken as assurance of victory. Babar knew this very well. And he needed all his vigilance during these trying days. Rana Sanga's army is recorded as numbering two hundred thousand. This is exaggerated, but the whole power of the Rajputs was in the field with ten thousand allies, followers of the dead Sultan Ibrahim. Babar had been deserted by his allies, and the odds of seven or eight to one were enough to awe even the fiery Moghuls. Never had an army been so confident of victory as the Rajputs. (The account of the battle in the memoirs is quoted from a rhetorical bombast of a certain Sheikh Zein, utterly different from the calm simplicity of Babar. In order to give any clear idea of the battle, it has been necessary to rewrite the version of the worthy sheikh, which begins after these paragraphs.)

Three days later we repeated the maneuver. We reached the ground we had selected and were pitching tents and working at the ditches when our outposts hurried in with news that the enemy was in sight. I mounted at once and gave orders that every man should go to his post and remain there, and the barriers around the guns be strengthened as much as possible.

On the field of Kanwaha near a hill our forces were mustered when the pagan standards appeared about the middle of the second watch in the morning. Few elephants were to be seen at first. The Hindus were all mounted and carried light spears, the riders being clad in finely wrought mail.

Immediately they launched an attack upon the extreme right wing, where Humayun held command. The charge of the mailed riders was sudden and earth-shaking.

Many of the most experienced *ameers* and the veteran Moghul warriors had been held in reserve behind the center. At once Chin Timur Sultan was sent at a gallop toward the right wing with a strong body of horse.

At the same time Mustapha Roumi began to fire the cannon between the center and right. He fired excellently well, and as the pagans had charged in close array the heavy balls shook them considerably.

Rana Sanga began to send divisions from his rear to succor his men at this point. Accordingly, three of my officers with half the remaining reserve were detached to aid Humayun. Dust began to rise and cover everything and the clangor was excessive.

So many pagans had pressed forward on our right that they were cut up by Mustapha's shots before they reached our line, and—though they hesitated not at all—their army became disordered and confused. At places they broke through our men, but they were pushed back by the charges of the reserve in a mass without form or order.

Meanwhile the pagans had made an even more desperate charge upon the left wing, and it was necessary to send the last of the reserve with all the Begs and my most trusted officer, Yunis Ali, to strengthen this wing. Already two or three hours had passed and the sun was at its height.

The Rajputs were undaunted. They were excellent swordsmen but their only maneuver was to charge, since they expected to sweep over the line of our shallow ditch and thin barricades.

They were unable to do this. Our matchlock men and infantry were not driven from their ground, and when this was apparent the two *tulughma*, the flanking parties that had been badly cut up in the first charges, were ordered to circle the pagan array, to the best of their ability.

Rustam Turkoman and many others penetrated as far as the rear of the Rajput masses, and used their bows with great effect. This could not be seen at the time, but the Moghul household troops and cavaliers of the center were beginning to chafe and to cry out that they wished to enter the fight.

Perceiving their excellent spirit, orders were given that the mounted divisions of the center, the mail-clad hosts of Moghuls, and the imperial standards should go forward. They advanced slowly through the gaps in the barricades and then put their horses to the gallop. As they were few and the Rajputs many, the infantry and matchlock men were also directed to go forward.

Until now Ustad Ali had been making play with his cannon, and an order was sent to him to drag his guns forward.

When my warriors on the flanks saw what was happening they also put their horses to the charge without instructions—for in the heat of the fight no messengers could be sent to those in command of the wings.

Although my divisions of the center were fresh, and although the Rajputs had been cut up by cannon fire, they did not fall into confusion or lose spirit, while such weight of numbers halted our men, and wearied them. The enemy spurred their horses forward desperately.*

They were swept away by the balls of the matchlock men, and went to their death by the way of the flashing scimitar. And still others pressed against us, although the sun was no longer to be seen, and dust and smoke deepened the twilight that fell on the field of Kanwaha.

The line of our standards did not waver; the mailed hosts of Moghuls did not break, and these last charges of the enemy were hopeless. A more

*Seldom, if ever, had a Rajput army been defeated by inferior numbers. Their terrible overthrow at Kanwaha was due to Babar's generalship and his maneuvering of the disciplined Moghuls. It marked, in Asia, the passing of the horseman as the supreme factor in battle—as Crecy and Agincourt had done in Europe. From the date of Kanwaha, February 1527, no Rana of a reigning house in Rajputana took the field against the Moghuls. Rana Sanga kept the field, it is true, and vowed never to enter his city of Chitore except as a victor, but he died soon after and his successors began the usual quarreling among themselves. The overthrow of the Rajput chivalry made Babar master of India and gave a central government to that much harried land, but the days of the Tiger were numbered and he did not long survive his victory.

gallant army than the Rajputs could not have been brought into the field, but it was an army no longer. So many Rajputs were slain that the others rode whither they could, without leaders or hope of life.

Rana Sanga was borne away severely wounded. Rawul Udai Singh and several princes, with as many chieftains of clans, had joined the host of the slain, and the roads from the field of battle were strewn with the wounded that died by the way. The throngs of the fleeing passed between the arrows of our *tulughma* flankers, and wherever a rider went he looked down upon lifeless nobles in all their splendid garments—now food for the crows and the kites.

So the last blows were given, and the heads of the gallant pagans made into a mound. Darkness closed in, and the striker and the smitten, the victor and the vanquished were no longer to be seen. Only the earth itself, and its fruit of the dead, was to be seen under the stars of the night that ensued.

Once the enemy were defeated we pursued them with great slaughter.* Their camp might be three miles distant from ours. On reaching it, I halted to inspect it, sending on some officers to harry the pagans and cut them off, so that they could not reassemble. Here I was guilty of neglect.

I should have gone on myself and not entrusted the pursuit to another. Nearly two miles beyond the enemy's camp I turned back, the day being spent, and reached my own about bedtime prayers.

The battle had been fought within sight of a hillock near our lines. On this mound I ordered a pyramid of the heads of the pagans to be raised. Immense numbers of the pagans had fallen, and we came upon bodies as far as Alwar and Mawat. At a council of my Begs it was decided not to go farther against the enemy, owing to want of water and the great heat of their desert country.

At this occasion, Muhammad Sherif, the astrologer, who had obstinately predicted defeat, came to congratulate me on my victory.

I poured out abuse on him. When I had relieved my heart by it—although he was self-conceited and an insufferable evil-speaker he was an old servant—I gave him a *lakh* as a present and ordered him to leave my dominion.

Indeed there was much to be done, in spite of the oppressive heat. Owing to the war with the pagans I had been unable to divide up the coun-

*Babar is speaking again.

try into districts or set to work building the tanks and wells; nor had the treasure been portioned off.

I had sent Humayun up to the hill district of Kabul. Every month brought some new rebellion, and I was troubled by fever and by the lack of wine. I had given it up because of repentance, but now I began to repent of giving it up.

God willing, I would have set out at once for the hills to join Humayun and Kwajah Kilan, the old general. How is it possible that the delights of the hills should ever pass from memory? Or that a man like me, who had made a vow of abstinence, should forget the delicious melons and the grape wines of my homeland?

Not long ago they brought me a single muskmelon from my home. While I was cutting it up I felt lonely as an exile. While eating it, I could not help shedding tears.

Although troubled by lack of sleep and thirst, I was unable to be out of the saddle for long, owing to the contests against the pagan lords who had retired to their strongholds without submitting to me.

Medini Rao, one of the chief followers of Rana Sanga, had shut himself up in the fastness of Chanderi with his Rajputs—a place that is desert and jungle and mountains in one. In the beginning of the next winter I set out against Chanderi.

The army was equipped and reviewed and we moved down the Jumna. After we had crossed the river, I sent Chin Timur Sultan on ahead with a strong body of six or seven thousand men.

We marched on, day after day, until in the district of Malwa the country became wild and pathless. Halting here, I sent on overseers and pioneers to level the road and to cut into the jungle growth on either side so the guns that were dragged by elephants and bullock teams could pass. Near a tank below Chanderi we encamped, and went ahead to survey the fortress.

It was a celebrated stronghold, built on a hill. The outer fortifications and the town lay halfway up the hill, the citadel at the summit. The main road—the only one by which cannon could be moved up—ran right under the outer walls of the town.

The country around was excellent, abounding in water and hunting places. And Chanderi itself is eye-filling. The houses were of stone, and beautiful. Instead of tiles, they were covered with flagstones. The citadel was hewn out of white stone. Nor did it lack water—beneath it a huge tank had been hollowed out of the rock. And a covered way led down to another large tank within the town.

Next morning I rode out and posted the different commands. Ustad Ali chose a level stretch of ground under the town wall to place his cannon. While some of the men dug emplacements for the big guns, others labored at making mantlets of hide and scaling ladders.

As Medini Rao was a man of authority and bravery, and one of the chief followers of Rana Sanga, I sent two officers to him to assure him of favor and forgiveness, and to offer him another stronghold for Chanderi. He was then in the citadel with some five thousand Rajputs.

Whether he mistrusted me, or put too much faith in the strength of his fort, I do not know, but the negotiations were broken off, and six days later we moved up to attack.

That same morning, just as we reached our ground, my chief minister brought me letters that had come in at dawn. The army of the east had been set upon by Afghan forces and routed; it had abandoned Lucknow and was falling back on Kanauj, which was no more than a couple of days' ride from Agra.

My minister was dismayed and alarmed and asked what was to be done.

"Confusion and doubt are useless," I assured him. "Except by God's will nothing happens. It is better to say nothing about the disaster in our rear, but to attack the fort at once and take it."

Now the pagans had drawn most of their men into the citadel, which was thus strongly garrisoned, and the outer wall of the town had few to defend it. My men entered the outer fort easily, and after a slight resistance the pagans who had held it fled to the citadel.

I gave orders that every man should push on to the assault of the citadel as soon as my standard was lifted and the kettle-drum beaten. Then I went to see Ustad Ali's cannon-play.

He fired off some of the larger battering pieces; but, his ground being level, the guns could not be elevated sufficiently. As the citadel works were hewn out of rock, the damage done was trifling. It was necessary, then, to storm the almost impregnable walls, and to do this without delay.

The weak point of the citadel was the covered run—the long tunnel of solid masonry that descended to the lower water tank. This point had been assigned to my own household troops.

When the signal was given the citadel was assailed on all sides, but our real effort was made in the covered way. Here the pagans had placed picked men, and stones and flaming pots and beams were cast down on my warriors. Through the smoke and the flames and the weapon-play they pressed on and up, until Shahem Nur Beg climbed out of the covered way where it joins the main wall.

Elsewhere we had gained a footing in two or three places, and now the pagans in the water-run fled back into the citadel and we had taken that part of the works. My men pushed ahead at once, and the inner walls of the citadel were stormed more easily.

Then a strange thing happened.*

After a short pause in the fighting the Rajputs rushed out, without clothing of any kind, sword in hand. They fell upon my men in desperation and put many to the sword. But the pagans, who seemed to be bereft of all reason, began to leap over the ramparts, falling to their death on the stones below.

The cause of this desperate sally was that they had given up the place for lost. They had put to death all their wives, women, and children. Resolving to perish, they had stripped themselves and rushed out. Their ungovernable desperation drove our people back along the ramparts.

Two or three hundred pagans had gone into Medini Rao's house, where numbers of them slew each other in the following manner. One person took his stand by the door, sword in hand, and the others crowded in and stretched out their necks, eager to die. In this way many went to —— and I gained this famous fort without raising my standard or beating my kettle-drum, or using the full strength of my arms.

I gave Chanderi to one of my shahs, leaving him three thousand Moghuls and Hindustanis for support, and hastened by forced marches toward Agra and the north.

Chapter VII
The Tiger Fights with Death

A good deal of mischief had been done in my absence. The remnant of my eastern forces had fallen back again from Kanauj and the rebels had

*This was the *johur*, the terrible sacrifice that accompanied the loss of a Rajput stronghold. Usually the inner wall of the citadel was fired, after the women had shut themselves up in it, and the men, clad in saffron garments, went out to slay and be slain. No one survived. In this case the swift attack of the Moghuls had hurried the ghastly preparations. Babar, who praised the bravery of the Rajputs at Kanwaha, has no praise for the *johur*.

stormed the fort of Shemsabad. We were delayed three or four days in crossing the broad Jumna, and when we neared Kanauj we learned that the Afghans had left the city and had recrossed the Ganges. They were drawn up on the east bank, believing that they would be able to keep my men from crossing. And they had collected all the boats for leagues up- and downstream on their bank.

I went and camped on the west bank of the Ganges, and my men went out and seized some of the enemy's boats which they brought in.

But the boats were too few to serve any useful purpose, and the river could not be forded here. I sent for an officer who was skilled at construction work, and ordered him to throw a bridge across the Ganges and to requisition everything in the way of materials that he needed.

The Afghans were amazed at our preparations to throw a bridge across the Ganges and treated the whole thing with contempt. Their contempt and laughter was not as great when Ustad Ali brought up a gun to test out the range, and began his fire.

For several days he played his gun remarkably well. The first day he discharged it eight times, the second sixteen, and the third and fourth day he kept up this rate of firing.

The gun he fired was that same great piece called the *Dig Ghazi*—Victorious Cannon—that had been used in the battle against Rana Sanga, whence it got this name. Another piece, larger than this, had been planted, but it burst at the first fire, killing eight or ten men.

The matchlock men as well were active with their pieces and struck down a number of warriors and horses, including two of the royal slaves. They manned a breastwork that had been thrown up on the bank above the place where the bridge was to be. Below the bridge a swivel had been planted on an island, and harassed the Afghans.

But my warriors were not content with the firing of the cannon. About evening prayers one day two sultans with about fifteen men crossed over in a boat without any incentive except foolhardiness, and returned without fighting, having accomplished nothing at all. I reprimanded them for having crossed.

Malik Kasim, the Moghul, ventured across once or twice in a boat and had very creditable skirmishes with bodies of the Afghans. Yet, at length, after driving back a strong party, they were carried away by overconfidence and pursued the fugitives up to the lines of the Afghan camp. The enemy sallied out in strength and attacked him, driving his men back to their boat.

They climbed in hurriedly and pushed off, but before they could get clear, an elephant came up and swamped the boat. In this manner Malik Kasim perished.

All this while the floats of the bridge were being pushed steadily toward the Afghan bank, and as soon as the bridge was nearly finished I moved forward some light troops to hold it. As the Afghans had retired beyond range of Ustad Ali's cannon, these light troops—infantry and Lahoris—crossed over and skirmished a bit. Two days later part of my household warriors—my best men—supported by foot musketeers, went over the bridge.

The Afghans lost no time in mounting for battle, horse and foot and elephants, and attacked my division. At one time they made headway against my left flank, but the men in the center and right stood firm and soon drove the enemy from the ground.

Two of my warriors hurried on too eagerly and rode some distance beyond the body where they belonged. One of them was cut off, dismounted, and taken on the spot; the other—man and horse—was wounded in several places. He fell, dying, and his horse, feeble and tottering, broke away and dropped dead when it reached its position in the party of my men.

That day seven or eight heads were brought in, and many of the enemy were wounded by arrows and matchlock balls. The fighting kept up sharply until afternoon prayers. And the whole night was spent in bringing back my scattered detachments across the bridge.

If that same evening I had moved forward my main forces, it is probable that most of the enemy would have fallen into my hands. But it came into my head that it would not do to trust fortune too far.* On Saturday our artillery moved over and at the next dawn all my men, horse and foot, crossed the Ganges.

About the beat of the morning drum our advance patrols brought in word that the enemy had gone off and fled in the night. I had crossed over

*The Tiger of ten years earlier would not have waited a day to cross. Constant fever, the pain of old wounds, and the effect of the Indian climate were beginning to tell on Babar. He longed to return to Kabul to rest, but saw clearly that his new empire must be ruled from Agra and not Kabul. Six months later he fought his last battle against the king of Bengal, and won it. After this the Moghuls held all central and northern India, and ruled it until India passed into the hand of the British Raj.

at early morning prayers, and had sent the camel train to ford the river lower down.

I commanded Chin Timur Sultan with a strong body of horse to gallop on after the Afghans. They pressed after the enemy without respite and without rest, until the Afghans had scattered, and much of their baggage and families and a few prisoners fell into our hands. So the Afghan rebellion was brought to an end.

A week later I reached Lucknow and surveyed it. Here I halted to settle the affairs of Oudh and the district and discovered on the banks of the river a well-known country called the Hunting Ground. When I had bathed in the river, either from the effect of the air or because some water got into my head, I became deaf in the right ear. After this I mounted and set forth on a hunting party.

The pain in my ear came and went and I took opium to ward off the cold rays of the full moon. Oppressive sickness followed the opium next morning, but in spite of it I went all over the palaces of the Rajas Mansing and Bikramajit. I had already visited the Rajput stronghold of Gwalior, but in the moonlight these two palaces were singularly beautiful. Lofty and splendid, and built of hewn stone, overlaid with white stucco—their domes covered with plates of gilded copper, the walls inlaid with painted tiles in the shapes of trees—they rise the height of twenty spears from the gardens. I took some peach flowers from the gardens and planted them in the palace grounds of Agra.

At this time, Rana Sanga having died in the forests to which he retreated after Kanwaha, messengers arrived from Raja Bikramajit, his second son, who was then in the nearly impregnable stronghold of Rantambor. He offered to render allegiance, and expressed the hope that an annuity of seventy *lakhs* would be granted him.

The bargain was concluded, and it was settled that he should give up Rantambor for another city, less strong. No sooner had he ranked himself among my subjects than he sent me the splendid crown-cap and golden girdle of Sultan Mahmud, which had been in the hands of Rana Sanga.

If the young prince stood by his terms, I agreed that by the blessing of God I would make him Rana in his father's place and settle him in Chitore, the chief city of the Rajputs.

At this very time a runner came from the hills with news that Humayun had got a son, by the daughter of Yadgar Taghai.

I wrote to Kabul, to Humayun and Kwajah Kilan that I had triumphed over the rebels in the east and west of Hindustan, as well as over the last of the pagans, and that in the next spring I would make an effort to return in person to Kabul:

> *To Humayun, whom I remember with longing to see him again—health. Thanks be to God, who has given you a child—*He *has also given to me comfort and an object to love.*
>
> *You who are seated on a throne ought to know that this is the season for you to expose yourself to danger and hardship and to exert your prowess in arms. Fail not to exert yourself, for indolence and ease suit but ill with royalty.*
>
> *Remember to act generously by your brothers. I have some quarrels to settle with you. In many of your letters you complain of separation from your friends in Hind. It is wrong for you to give way to such a complaint. There is a saying—"If you are fettered by circumstances, submit; if you govern circumstances, act boldly."*
>
> *There is no greater bondage than a king's, and it ill becomes him to complain of separation.*
>
> *To comply with my wishes you have indeed sent me letters, but you have certainly never read them over; if you had attempted to read them you would have found it impossible. I managed to decipher your last letter, with much difficulty. It is confused and crabbed, and you have used far-fetched words. You fail in writing because you try to display your knowledge. In future write unaffectedly, using plain words which cause less trouble to writer and reader.*
>
> *You are now about to set out on an expedition of importance to recover Balkh from the Uzbeks. Call your most experienced noblemen into council and guide yourself by their advice.*
>
> *If you value my approval, do not waste your time in private parties. Watch the discipline of your army and keep the hearts of your officers by courtesy of manner.*
>
> *I once more repeat my earnest wishes for your health. Written on Thursday the thirteenth of the first Rabi.*

For the first time since I entered Hind there was no need to take the field against the enemy. The condition of the Purab was still unsettled, and I sent word to the army in the east that if there was need of moving against the Bengalis I would, God willing, mount and join them without delay.

I had ordered the road from Agra to Kabul to be measured, and *minars* (towers) to be erected along the way, with post-stations for six horses every few miles.

And, in order fittingly to receive the ambassadors who had come to wait on me, and to reward my own followers, I gave a great feast in the garden at Agra. It was then the beginning of winter.

I sat in an open pavilion that had just been built and covered with damp *khas* grass for coolness. On my right and left sat the sultans and *ameers*, the noblemen and officers. The Red Hat* ambassadors were seated under an awning, fifty paces distant with my veteran commander Yunis Ali to attend upon them. On the other side the Uzbek and Hindu ambassadors were likewise stationed. Before the dinner was served all the khans, sultans, grandees, and officers came to present their congratulatory gifts of red and white and black money and other articles.

Woolen cloths were spread before me into which the gold and silver were thrown, as well as purses—heaped up, one upon another.

Before dining, while the presents were coming in, there were fights of furious camels and elephants in a cleared space within the garden. Then came ram fights and wrestling matches.

As the dinner was placed I began to give my presents of robes of honor and balls of pure gold and silver. A rich reward was given, deservedly, to the officer who had built the bridge over the Ganges.

And to the veterans who had come from Andijan, my homeland—who, without a country and without a home, had roamed with me in my wanderings through the hills—to all these veterans and tried men, I gave vests and rich dresses of honor, with gold and silver clothes.

While we were eating dinner the Hindustani jugglers were brought in, and exhibited their feats. One of their tricks is the following: They place one hand on the ground, then raise up their other hand and two feet, all the while spinning around three rings in hand and feet. And, clinging to a single wooden pole, they walk about on it, without fastenings to their feet.

One of the most remarkable feats is when a tumbler supports a long pole at his waist and another mounts the pole to perform his tricks. In another case, a young tumbler stands on the head of an older one while both

---

**Kizilbashas*, the Persians. In these imperial feasts Babar's adherents offered him large amounts of money, etc., as tribute, and received back in turn liberal gifts of horses, garments of honor, weapons, etc. Their estates were held as gifts from the crown—everything belonged to the emperor. The spoils of battle, elephants, and weapons were offered him, and he gave them back, or other presents as he might be inclined. This system of gifts and countergifts dates back to the early Mongol and Turki monarchs. It is very well illustrated by the great diamond that came into Humayun's hand at Agra. He presented it to his father as a tribute-offering, and Babar returned it to his son as a gift. Later Moghuls were not as generous as the Tiger.

exhibit their tricks. Many *pateras*, or dancing girls, were also brought in, and danced.

Toward evening a great quantity of gold, silver, and copper money was scattered. There was a precious hubbub and uproar. As night drew on I made the most distinguished guests sit down by me and talked with them until the end of the first watch.

It seemed as if Hindustan were at last reduced to quiet, and, God willing, I meant to set out for the hills without losing a moment's time. Just then came tidings that Sultan Mahmud and other chieftains had gathered together an army of a hundred thousand men to oppose me in the country beyond the Ganges.

I was suffering from fevers, and a Roumi administered to me a new remedy—boiling pepper dust and standing in the steam that rose from the earthen pot. Being then in the jungle country where wild elephants were found, near Chunar, we were setting out to hunt when a galloper brought tidings that Sultan Mahmud was not far away. I was obliged to leave the hunting and advance at once by long marches.

While riding along the bank of the river, I came, without knowing it, upon a steep precipice that had been hollowed out by the action of the current below. No sooner had I reached the edge than it gave way and began to tumble into the river. Instantly I threw myself, by a leap from the stirrups, toward the inner part that held firm. My horse fell in, and had I remained in the saddle I must have gone down with it.

That same day I swam across the Ganges for amusement. I counted my strokes and found out that I reached the other bank at thirty-three. I then took breath and swam back. Before this I had crossed, by swimming, every river I met with, except the Ganges.

By the favor of God, in one month's time we scattered the Bengalis. And before we could return, one night when the second watch was past, the clouds of the rainy season broke, and there was such a tempest and the wind rose so high that most of the tents were blown down.

I was writing in the middle of my pavilion, and so suddenly did the storm come on that I had not time to gather up my papers before the pavilion came down on my head. The top of the structure was blown to shreds and the books and sheets of paper were drenched, but were gathered together and placed between dry woolen cloths.

The storm abated in an hour and we contrived to get up a spare tent, lighted a candle, and with great difficulty kindled a fire, but did not sleep until morning, being occupied in trying to dry the sheets and papers.

As we had accomplished all I intended on the Bengali border, as the rains had set in, and as we had been for five or six months in the field so that men and beasts were worn out, I marched toward Oudh, sending notice to the outlying sultans and *ameers* that I should await them in Agra.

On the last night of the ride to Agra we made twenty miles and halted at a tomb before dawn; mounting early we advanced twenty-four miles by noon and at midnight reached the garden of Hasht Behist at Agra.

Next morning I went into the castle and a native of Balkh brought me a few melons he had kept for me. They were excellent.

That Sunday at midnight I met Maham Begum, the mother of Humayun, who had come from Kabul to join me. I was sitting in talk with her, asking about Humayun, when in came my son himself.

His presence opened our hearts like rosebuds and made our eyes shine. It was my custom to keep open table every day; so great was my joy that I gave feasts in his honor and showed him every mark of distinction.

He had hurried from Kabul without permission and without notifying me, yet such was the charm of his presence that we lived together for some time in the closest intimacy until Humayun took his leave of me and proceeded to Sambhal, his residence.

Either the climate or the water of the place did not agree with my son, for fever attacked him. I gave order to have him conveyed by boat to Delhi, and thence to Agra, so that a physician might attend him.

In spite of all remedies, he got no better. Instead, he became delirious.

At his bedside, Maham Begum said to me: "What cause is there for you to sorrow so? You are a ruler, and have other children, while I have none save Humayun."

"Others have I, yet none so dear to me as Humayun," I answered.

Then Mir Abdul Kasim, who was a person of great knowledge, explained to me that only one remedy could be applied in the case of such maladies. It was to make a sacrifice to God of something of great value in order to obtain from Him the restoration of the sufferer's health.

Thereupon, having reflected that nothing in the world was dearer to me than Humayun except my own life, I determined to offer myself in the hope that God would accept my sacrifice.

Kwajah Khalifa and other close friends came to me and said: "Humayun will recover his health! How can you speak so unwisely? It will suffice if you offer the most precious thing you possess of worldly goods. Offer as alms the great diamond that came to you after Ibrahim's defeat and which you gave to Humayun."

"But," I replied, "there is no treasure which can be compared to my son. I shall offer myself as his ransom. He is sorely stricken and his weakness has need of my strength."

Immediately I entered the room where Humayun was lying, and walked thrice around him, starting from his head and saying—"I take upon myself all that you suffer."

At the same instant I felt myself borne down and depressed, while he became quieter and stronger. It was not long until he arose in restored health, while I sank down in weakness. Feeling this coming upon me, I called the chief men of the empire, the grandees and the greatest nobles, and placing their hands in Humayun's—as a mark of investiture, I solemnly proclaimed him as my successor—*

*These were the last words the Tiger wrote, and were found in a fragment of his papers long afterward. In about a week he died, in what should have been the prime of his life, the age of forty-eight. He had spent thirty-six of these years in the field of war—in camp or saddle, and, weakened by old wounds and fever, he met his death without misgiving, a gallant gentleman. There have been other Moghuls of India, but not in all Asia a second Babar.

Sleeping Lion

It was midafternoon when Alai saw what she had been waiting to see.

Like a marionette, she sat with her face pressed against the lattice of her window, high up beneath the roof of the Treasury.

This window she chose because it overlooked the Green Mount. On the Green Mount grew every kind of tree. For Kublai Khan liked to have trees around him. Wherever he saw one he fancied, he ordered it taken up and brought to his palace.

Whatever Kublai Khan wished to do, that he did. For he was Lord of the Earth, ruling the world from the steppes of Russia to the island of Zipangu, and from the frozen tundras of the north to Ceylon, where the great ruby was. Kublai's wish was the law of the girl Alai.

She was registered in the books of the Treasury as Precious Pearl, aged sixteen years, a Tatar by birth. Her eyes gray, her long hair dark. The books did not say how slender was her throat, or how her lips curved with elfin laughter. Only that she was a candidate concubine of the third rank—one of the six chosen for their beauty from a Tatar tribe. Which meant that she must serve in the sleeping chamber of the great Khan with five other maids until the fortunate ones he favored were made imperial concubines.

These six girl candidates could not step beyond the gates of the Treasury, where the imperial women and riches were kept. So Alai watched daily from her lattice, observing all that went on in the palace grounds beneath.

Now, at midafternoon, before the beginning of the first night of the year of the Fire-Tiger, she saw the messenger ride into the inner gate. The Tatar guards bent their heads and took the reins of the big horse because he was the messenger of the Khan returning from Ceylon, whither he had been sent to buy the most precious thing in the world.

Other eyes than Alai's watched, as he paced across the courtyard of the silver water clock. Other minds wondered if he had succeeded in bringing that matchless ruby back with him to Cambalu.

Alai wanted to find out, for herself. She sighed when he passed the door of the Treasury and dismounted at the entrance of his own quarters across the courtyard. She thought he had a wide mouth and his eyes were hard for a man so young. Hard and clear as crystal. He rode with his stirrups long, for he was a man of the West, a far-wandering soul, Marco Polo by name. And he had a way of bringing back what he set out to get.

"Faith," his laugh echoed across the courtyard, "my bones are weary." Feeling inside one of his saddle bags, he drew out a knotted linen cloth, as a man with a shaven skull pushed through the guards around him and bowed low.

"Long life!" cried the shaven one. "Does the Lord Po-lo bring with him what Kublai, the Khan, desires?"

Holding the cloth by the knotted middle, Marco Polo beat the dust from his legs with the loose ends. "I brought a monkey from Ceylon," he responded, "and it is bald as thou art."

Still swinging the cloth, he turned into his door. The eyes of the shaven one peered after him. For Messer Marco had gone alone to far Ceylon, and no one in Cambalu could say if he had the giant ruby.

Alai slipped away from the lattice. Sitting before a bronze mirror, she pulled the gold and enamel flowers from her hair, and rubbed the pink powder from her cheeks. Over her embroidered tunic she drew a slave's gray coat.

She wanted something to carry in her hands, so she took up a tray with bowls of ginger and sugar paste, and cherries. To please the Lord Po-lo, she added a bowl of fresh rice wine.

After listening a moment at the entrance screen of her room, she slipped out when the corridor was empty. Lowering her head, and moving with the quick, short pace of a slave, she reached the gate of the Treasury where armed Tatars stood guard.

There she hesitated, her heart pounding under the loose robe. Beyond this gate no one would recognize her face. Beyond this gate the candidate concubines were forbidden to go. But Alai was determined to speak with the Lord Po-lo, and she went.

Messer Marco Polo sat in his counting room, his legs stretched under the carved table, looking at the knotted cloth between his hands.

For the months of a year he had traveled back from Ceylon by sailing junk, and river barge and horse post, always with that worn linen cloth under his hand or head. He had reached Cathay. He had succeeded.

And success—unlike the grotesque gods of Cathay—was Marco's god. From Venice he had crossed half the world, leaving the softness of his youth in the salt deserts and the snowbound roof of the world; he had come through the singing sands of the Gobi, where the magicians of Prester John raised storms, over the long road of Tartary. To wrest a fortune from the palace of Cathay, where the riches of the world were gathered.

Long had he labored to do this, that no man of the West had been able to do before him. Four languages had he learned, to be able to transact business for the great Khan. He had studied the old man's moods; taken notes on his journeys, so that he could please Kublai by relating all that his eyes had seen. So had he won Kublai's favor and trust. Now with a hairbrush he was writing upon silk paper the tidings of his success in Ceylon: *"I will tell you of the most precious thing in the world, that the King of the island had, the finest known to men."*

He undid one of the knots, and slipped the cloth back from what it held. As he did so, flame leaped from under his fingers. The late-afternoon sunlight struck into the giant ruby.

A moment Marco studied it, drinking in the hyacinth shape of this *hung pao shi*—this red precious stone. He put it on the balance that served to weigh his own collection of stones, and smiled. With all the weights in the scale against the ruby, the balance did not move.

"It is about a palm in length, and a man's wrist in thickness," he wrote. *"It is quite free from flaws. Its value is so great that a price for it in money could hardly be named. The ambassador of the great Khan offered the King of the island first the ransom of a city for it, but—"*

The sound was no more than the slipping of garments over tiles. Marco Polo glanced over his shoulder, through the open paper window, to the balcony. Nothing was there. But he thrust the ruby under a fold of the cloth and waited, listening.

In front of him the brocade curtain was drawn back timidly, and a girl entered. A girl who came toward him and knelt, to offer him a tray.

"Please," she whispered, "will my lord taste?"

Marco barely glanced at the sweetmeats and rice wine. "Look at me," he ordered. He had no woman among his servants. When she raised her head a pulse beat in her bare throat like a captive bird's.

"Why," he asked, considering her, "do you bring me all this?"

He knew the beauty of these Eastern girls. They could play upon a man's senses.

"Taste the wine, and you will know." She smiled pleadingly, and light glinted on the rice wine, as her hands trembled.

Messer Marco did not care to drink anything that his own body servants had not prepared—not in Cambalu, with the ruby of Ceylon under his hand. He wondered fleetingly where his servants had got to. And he leaned toward the girl, taking his hand from the cloth. "I am thinking," he said, "it is for no love of me that you are here. Who sent you?"

"This worthless slave saw the Lord Po-lo ride in at the Yen gate. Does he wish now to go to the presence of the great Khan?"

"Tonight," Marco answered idly. Tonight would be the beginning of the new year, of the Fire-Tiger year, and at such a time it was Kublai's custom to feast. Marco had ridden hard upon the post road, to be in time to lay the ruby before Kublai at that feast.

"Kublai is gone away, to hunt." Her eyes held his, and the color deepened in her cheeks.

"Far?" asked Marco, surprised.

"To Shang-tu—to the desert. Who knows where?"

"The devil!" Marco exclaimed, under his breath. He would have to await Kublai's return before giving up the ruby—he dared not trust it to anyone else until the Khan had seen it.

A thought cut like a knife into his brooding. The ruby was no longer on the table by his hand!

Something else was there, another stone—and the priceless red stone had vanished. So he thought, and turned to draw back the cloth. He fumbled with the cloth because a strange drowsiness filled him.

Then he stared. A ruby lay upon the table, but its outline had blurred. The unearthly fire had gone from it; and it was, he knew, only a smooth Balas ruby, flawed—worth no more than its weight in silver. Yet it lay in the place of the great ruby of Ceylon.

The girl, watching his face, set down her tray gently on the rushes at his feet, and drew back toward the curtain. Marco Polo saw her slipping away, and leaped through the curtain after her. Now his mind was clear, and he caught her roughly.

"Where," he whispered hoarsely, "is the red precious stone?"

She struggled against his hands, her eyes startled. "Where you left it," she cried, "there on the table."

"Nay, pretty harlot." His hands passed over her slim body, and pulled open the gray over-robe, although she strained away from him. "I wondered who had sent you—for what!"

Then he saw the dragon embroidered on the breast of her floss-silk tunic. The mark of a candidate concubine, who might not leave the inner palace of the great Khan. And he saw the fear in her eyes.

"Now let me go, Lord Po-lo," she pleaded. "Ai—I wanted to tell you the great Khan is far away, and now you have no friends in Cambalu. I brought the tray so that no one would take heed—"

The blood came and went in her throat, and her gray eyes were heavy with dread. Surely, he thought, she felt a fear for him. And, after all, she had not been within reach of the table. Certainly no one had come through the window behind him, lighted by the sunset glare, to take the ruby of Ceylon. It must be where he had placed it. He had been drowsy—a strange fancy had come to him, a fancy bred of the many moons he had watched over the priceless stone. He sighed, and relaxed his grasp. Instantly the girl slipped away from him, drawing the gray robe about her. Marco wondered what her name might be, and why she had dared to enter his quarters.

He went back through the curtain, intending to wrap the great ruby in its cloth again. And then he started. On the cloth as he had left it lay the Balas ruby, the travesty of the most precious thing in the world.

"The Devil," Marco Polo muttered, "has been at work."

Striding to the balcony beyond the window, he looked out into the sunset glow. No one was on the balcony or in the courtyard beneath him. Without moving, he waited to see if the girl would cross the courtyard, and he waited in vain. The sun dropped behind the trees of the Green Mount, and twilight leaped up at him.

It seemed, Messer Marco reflected, that he had been well tricked by a sweet wanton. Soon it would be known that he had bought the ruby of Ceylon at a terrifying price, and he had nothing to show for it but this flawed monstrosity. Worse, he could not explain how the ruby had been stolen.

It had been there, on the table under his hand, and it had changed into the false stone. And the only witness of his folly was a maiden from the Treasury of Kublai Khan, whose presence might not be mentioned.

Below him, he heard a silvery chime. That would be the silver ball dropping in the water clock, at the beginning of the first hour of the night. As he had done so often in these years of labor, Messer Marco looked past the gilded roof of the palace, to the black summit of the tower of the astrologers.

"Send Kao Hoshang to me," he ordered his servants, who had been rendered curious by his silence.

Alai had not crossed the courtyard. She was hurrying toward the nearest door when a man with a shaven skull looked at her twice and stopped her. A gold tablet glinted upon a chain at his throat.

"*Kai*, little flower," he said, "do you run after the sun?"

Impassive as a doll she stood, but she could not hide the flush that darkened her face.

"No slave art thou," he snarled. "Wait!"

His fingers twisted in her long sleeve, as careless steps came toward them. Two staff-bearers passed by, and then Alai dropped to her knees, trying to press her forehead against the floor. But the officer's hand restrained her.

A tall figure gleamed in heavy cloth of gold. A heavy head turned toward her curiously.

"May it please the Shadow of the Throne," whispered the man who held her, "here is a little night bird escaped from the Treasury."

The man in gold considered her. His fingers twisted through his black beard.

"Forgive," Alai breathed, "so that I may live. Alas, I wanted only to hear the voice of the barbarian lord whose eyes are kind."

"A pity." The Shadow of the Throne meditated. "If this is known, the Tatars will throw you from a tower, or perhaps ride their horses over you, little flower. You knew the punishment for setting foot beyond the Treasury."

"I am going back—"

"To the hands of the guards?" The man in gold bent over her. "Nay, that you may not do. For we have been seen talking here, and now must I know thy name."

"It is Alai," whispered the shaven skull, "surnamed Precious Pearl, a candidate concubine." He parted the folds of her gray robe. "Will the Shadow of the Throne look?"

Both men glanced curiously at the dragon embroidered on white floss silk—at the emblem of Kublai Khan. They could not remember a woman who had dared, before now, to venture from the inner palace. And it was the duty of the shaven skull to know such things.

"Yet," he of the gold robe whispered, "will I have pity on you, Alai. At the third hour of the night, at full starlight, come to my door beyond the lake. Come with your face hidden, and ask for Ahmed the Compassionate." He smiled. "I can protect one who pleases me."

"Aye, lord."

"And after the third hour of the night," the one called Ahmed added, "I will announce that the girl Alai was seen at the door of the Lord Po-lo."

When the men had gone on, Alai wandered out to the fountain veiled in twilight. She heard the silver ball fall in the water clock, sounding the first hour of the night. Since no one heeded a girl without covering for her hair, she could sit quietly on the marble walk by the water, and think.

Ahmed the Persian, she knew, could do what he said. The Minister of the Throne was also master of the Treasury; he had brought uncounted riches to the feet of the Tatar emperor. When he urged a matter upon Kublai, the great Khan always replied, "Do as you think right."

Wealth flowed into the coffers of the Minister as well as the Khan—for those who made a present to Kublai remembered to make a gift also to the Shadow of the Throne. Ivory of the elephant people of Mien, jade from the sandy rivers of Khoten, beaten gold from Hind. But the gift that pleased Ahmed most was a woman of new beauty.

Never, however, Alai reflected, had even Ahmed dared to think of possessing a woman who had entered the Khan's Treasury. At the step behind her, she looked up.

"*Hai*—Hoshang!" she called softly.

The stout astrologer who was padding by stopped. His gnome's head, reeking of wine, peered down.

"O magician," she begged, feeling at that moment helpless to do anything for herself, "you have skill to change the shapes of things. Can you make me invisible so that I may pass through gates unseen?"

"I can make a mountain invisible," he croaked.

"How?"

"By looking the other way," he snarled, and would have gone on, but she held to the skirt of his robe.

"Let me go with you, Master of Wisdom."

"Try your tricks on a greater fool," Hoshang reeled. "Nay, I go to the barbarian Po-lo, who counts his money with both hands." He spat.

Still she held fast to his robe.

"Why are you frightened?" Hoshang asked hoarsely. "This night unwonted things will happen. So the stars proclaim, at the appearance of the first moon of the new year. *Kai*—look!"

He pointed at the faint curve of silvery light above the last of the sunset glow. When she peered up at the new moon, he moved away noiselessly. But Alai followed.

She had seen Marco Polo within arm's reach. Hard he might be, as unbending bronze, sitting in his counting room, yet she thought he would be more kind than the mighty Ahmed, or the catlike astrologer.

As she left the fountain, the dripping water clock chimed twice.

Hearing the slap-slap of Hoshang's sandals, Marco Polo looked up.

"Long life," Hoshang kowtowed with a stagger. "May the great far-wandering lord live to see the sons of his sons—"

"Be still! Why were you so long in coming?"

"I stayed to speak," Hoshang admitted blandly, "to this girl."

Messer Marco moved impatiently, his dark eyes appraising the astrologer as if he were doubtful merchandise. He judged that Hoshang was a very skilled magician—at the Khan's feasts, he had watched Hoshang make a goblet filled with wine move along the table to the Khan's hand, without spilling the wine. A charlatan who could do that trick might also make a ruby disappear, and a false one take its place. "I've seen," he said, "a vanishing that could not be."

And he told Hoshang how the ruby had gone from beneath his fingers.

"That could be," the astrologer muttered. "Aye, that could be. You looked at something shining, something that moved?"

Messer Marco considered carefully. "Yes—at the wine in the bowl that girl held." He glanced thoughtfully at Alai, who had remained standing by the curtain. "And then at the ruby—the false ruby."

"And thou, ignoble one," Hoshang snarled at the girl, "what didst thou see?"

"Only Lord Po-lo," Alai answered. "And the fire of the setting sun."

"Aye, so. It was simply done, Lord Po-lo. Do not blame the girl. You frightened her, and ran after her. And, when you did that you left the great ruby of Ceylon uncovered on this table in this empty room."

"Nay," Marco shook his head, "I left the false ruby here. This one."

Hoshang nodded solemnly at the flawed Balas stone. "Aye, so you thought, Lord Po-lo—"

"I saw it."

"Aye, you saw it, when the glow of the sun was upon it, and its shape was a little blurred because drowsiness filled your mind. Nay, it was the thought of the thief, working into your mind. The thief who crouched on the balcony by the window, who came in and snatched the ruby of Ceylon, leaving this in its place—"

"Lies! How could another's thought come into my mind?"

"Oh, easily. Our children—" Hoshang's eyes gleamed suddenly—"play at that."

Drawing a deep breath, Marco rose. In the courtyard below sounded three silvery chimes. Alai started, shrinking back from the light.

"Tonight," Hoshang muttered, "is not as other nights. The Sant'ai stars of the great Bear are threefold bright, and a burning star fell. So is a prophecy made clear." He took a roll of silk paper from his sleeve. *"When He Who Sleeps shall awake,"* he read, *"the Mightiest of Men shall die."*

"And who," Marco asked, "is the mightiest of men?"

"Alas," sighed the astrologer, "we may not know, until it is revealed."

Marco Polo decided that the old astrologer must know of a plotting in the palace which would come to a head that night. Evidently Hoshang was disturbed, because he had been drinking.

"O soothsayer," Marco demanded, "if you are so wise, tell me who stole the ruby of Ceylon."

"It would be easier to find a fish escaped into the sea."

"Yet I can tell you what he is like." Messer Marco thought for a moment, while Hoshang listened skeptically. "He would be a man of power in Cambalu, to dare such a thing. He would be an officer of the palace, since he knew that I had been sent to Ceylon for the ruby. Aye—and he would have a collection of rare precious stones—because he'd crave the ruby for its own sake. He could not sell the Khan's ruby in Cathay."

"Kai!" Hoshang's eyes opened in surprise. The matter-of-fact logic of the West had no place in his tortuous mind.

"What officer of the Throne," Marco went on, "would answer to that description?"

Hoshang chuckled. "You, Lord Po-lo!"

For an instant the Venetian was taken aback. "There's more," he pointed out grimly. "Who would have a sorcerer to serve him—such as thou? And who could command a girl of the Treasury to beguile me—a girl such as this one? To amuse me while his thief stole in."

"Fool," said Alai, lifting her head. "Barbarian, blind as a buffalo tied to a well sweep! I came to warn you."

"Why?"

"I thought," she said quietly, "that I loved you. When first I came to Cambalu, I was lonely, and grieving. I watched from the lattice of my window—and you were unlike the men of Cathay. You feared no one, and you laughed merrily."

Messer Marco shook his head.

"I think Ahmed sent you," he remarked, "and I think Ahmed has the ruby of Ceylon."

He stretched his long arms, rising from the table. Thrusting aside the worthless Balas stone, he went to the wall where an old coat hung, a padded *khalat* that he put on at times when the room was cold. It was worn and ugly and covered with dust.

"The night air is cold," he said carelessly even while his fingers ran over tears in the lining of the coat that had been carefully sewn.

Hidden beneath those tears in the thick wool padding were pearls and sapphires enough to fill his two cupped hands. Marco had selected them with care, hiding them one by one until he had an emperor's ransom in this old coat that nobody heeded.

He had done so against the time when he might need to ride from Cathay. And now, he decided, that time had come. He had lost the ruby of Ceylon, and how could he explain that loss to Kublai, when the Khan returned?

When he slipped his arms into the sleeves, Alai came to his side.

"What will you do, Lord Po-lo?" she asked anxiously.

"I must see to some—merchandise."

"You are going away!" she cried. "You must not. If you leave Cambalu the Shadow of the Throne will say that you have taken the ruby with you."

Let him say that, Messer Marco thought, after I am gone. Brushing Alai aside, he went to the curtain, and paused as a babble of voices rose beyond it. His servants pushed in, chattering, but keeping well away from an officer with a shaven skull who wore a gold tablet at his throat. A dozen lantern-bearers and swordsmen followed him. Marco recognized the Great Quieter, who was Ahmed's torturer. T'ai wei, the Cathayans called him.

"Long life," said the T'ai wei amiably. "Alas that I must intrude upon the threshold of the Lord Po-lo. Yet it is reported that a candidate concubine has been seen outside the doors of the Treasury."

Messer Marco looked over his shoulders. Hoshang had vanished—probably out upon the balcony. But Alai stood by the table, and her eyes touched his once, fearfully.

"By what authority," he asked, "do you cross my threshold?"

The T'ai wei touched the gold tablet at his throat, and his eyes were insolent. "By the order—" and he kowtowed thrice—"of the Minister Ahmed."

"I think," Messer Marco said thoughtfully, "this is the second time you have stolen into my rooms. I think you are a thief, without a single honorable characteristic."

The face of the T'ai wei darkened, and his mouth remained open.

"The first time," Marco went on, "you left something behind you."

Swiftly the shaven man glanced toward the girl, and away. Alai, watching him, her hands clenched against her sides, saw him ponder. He had been disgraced before his attendants.

"Go quietly," Marco prodded him, "and the next time bring a little courage with you."

But the shaven man sidled away quickly, his attendants following, while Marco's servants made way for them.

"Whatever you may be," Marco said to the girl, "I'll not have Ahmed take you from my house. Unless," he added, "you wish it."

Silently she shook her head. "Now I have no place to go, Lord Po-lo. And within the half of an hour Ahmed will be here with his people."

"Time enough," said Messer Marco, knotting the scarf about his hips. "You'll come with me."

He caught up a curved blade of Zipangu steel and thrust it into his girdle, blowing out the candle as he did so. Then he caught up the slender girl, and carried her out to the balcony.

As he dropped to the stones of the pavement, a shadow detached itself from the wall. Marco turned, feeling for his sword, when the shadow whispered plaintively: "What are you doing, Lord Po-lo? They are watching us."

It was old Hoshang, quite sober now. Marco could see no one else near him.

"Faith," he said, "the bold trick is best. We'll walk out of here and see who follows us."

Taking Hoshang's arm, he strode toward the courtyard entrance, Alai following with lowered head. The slaves and light-bearers at the gate merely glanced up casually at them.

Clear of the inner palace, Marco turned to the right, toward the lake where white swans floated drowsily. He had gone a bowshot when, looking back over his shoulder, he saw a lantern following, and the figures of men about it. Another light hurried up to join the first.

"Alas," Hoshang moaned, "did not the stars foretell misfortune?"

"No!" the girl cried. "There is only one place for us now. Come quickly!"

Marco saw now what Alai meant to be

[Unfortunately, the text was printed without a linking segment in 1937, and the original has been lost. Readers will have to imagine for themselves how Marco Polo arrives at this concluding scene.—Ed.]

long in his skin, nor would he, Marco Polo, live another hour, unless—

"Hai!" he shouted. "The snake has come out of his hole, and is slain."

He thrust aside the T'ai wei, who was bending over Ahmed's gleaming body. And he pulled from Ahmed's girdle the rolled paper that the T'ai wei had been fumbling for. Glancing at it, he handed it to Kublai Khan.

The old Tatar put his hand to his mouth as he read, shaking his head slowly. "What is this thing? A sealed order in my Minister's hand, giving authority to enter the threshold of the Lord Po-lo and take the girl known as Precious Pearl?"

Alai touched his feet imploringly. And then from the wall Hoshang come forward, his lined face peaceful. He knelt before the Khan.

"Will the Son of Heaven hear the words of a dishonored old man? The Minister of your empire held you under the spell of his tongue, so that you became like one asleep. No one dared give evidence against him, while he lived. He took my granddaughter into his harem by force, and after her, her mother. My son, the husband, took his own life grieving. And I have waited to take vengeance on Ahmed. Have I not a right to speak?"

"Aye," Kublai nodded.

Gratefully, Hoshang sighed. "Now is the spirit of my son at peace. Much incense have I burned that this should be."

Kublai considered his astrologer. "You threw that knife?"

Bowing his head to the old Tatar's feet, Hoshang assented. "My poor hand dispatched the great Minister. For the stars foretold that when He Who Sleeps shall awake—and who could that be but the Son of Heaven?—the Mightiest of Men shall die. And who could that be but the wretch who abused his Power?" Hoshang nodded, his eyes elated, "No one can escape his fate."

Putting his hands to the breast of his robe, he drew out something that flashed crimson fire deeper than sunset. Marco Polo bent forward, with an exclamation.

"Here," said Hoshang, "is the red precious stone of Ceylon. I took it from the counting room of that foolish young barbarian Po-lo, before it should be stolen by Ahmed."

With an exclamation of delight Kublai took it in his hands, and seated himself to stare at it, turning it this way and that, to catch the light in its heart. He chuckled like a child with a new toy.

"Let the traitor Ahmed," he said to the Tatar captain, "be cut into seven pieces, and hung above the seven gates of Cambalu as a warning to others."

Alai had drawn closer to his knee. He smiled at the candidate concubine. "Precious Pearl," he said, stroking her dark hair, "you please me. But in the future do not try to manage the affairs of my palace."

"Nay, lord of my heart," she assented happily.

So Marco Polo left them in the jade house. With Hoshang and the Tatars who were bearing the body of Ahmed the Persian cut into seven parts, he retraced his steps down the Green Mount toward the palace, which he knew he could not leave now—however homesick he might be for Venice. And he reflected that, no matter how many years he might dwell in Cathay, he would never understand its people.

"How," he asked Hoshang suddenly, "did you steal the ruby?"

"Po-lo, I told you how."

Messer Marco pondered and laughed. "Kao Hoshang, you have no sons. And if you have no sons, how could you have a granddaughter?"

Hoshang bent his head and sighed. "Alas, that is a great mystery."

"Tell me why you slew Ahmed when you did."

"A dead enemy," the old astrologer nodded, "is better than a live one."

Appendix

Adventure magazine, in which many of the tales in this volume first appeared, maintained a letter column titled "The Camp-Fire." As a descriptor, "letter column" does not quite do this regular feature justice. *Adventure* was published two and sometimes three times a month, and as a result of this frequency and the interchange of ideas it fostered, "The Camp-Fire" was really more like an Internet bulletin board than a letter column found in today's quarterly or even monthly magazines. It featured letters from readers, editorial notes, and essays from writers. If a reader had a question or even a quibble with a story, he could write in and the odds were that the letter would not only be printed but that the story's author would draft a response.

Harold Lamb and other contributors frequently wrote lengthy letters that further explained some of the historical details which appeared in their stories. The relevant letters for this volume follow.

There were a total of 753 issues of *Adventure*, and no single library in the United States has a complete collection (few libraries have *any* copies of *Adventure*). With those facts in mind, perhaps you will excuse the inclusion of several additional Camp-Fire letters for which I do not have exact dates. Copies of them were passed on to me by pulp scholar Alfred Lybeck, and I have so far been unable to determine in which issues of *Adventure* they originally appeared, although there is no doubt in my mind as to their authenticity (due to typeface, Camp-Fire logo, comments from *Adventure* editor Arthur Sullivan Hoffman, Harold Lamb's distinctive writing style and knowledge base, etc.). Unlike the usual run of Lamb's letters, these were not pulled from issues containing his stories; rather, they were typed in response to reader queries. The subject of at least one of them would be considered politically incorrect today.

As with the other Bison Books editions of Lamb's work, the prefatory comments of *Adventure* editor Arthur Sullivan Hoffman also are printed here.

August 30, 1922: "The Road of the Giants"

Most of us aren't very wise in the history of ancient Asia—or the Asia of a few centuries ago, or even the Asia of today, so when Harold Lamb does the work of digging it out and handing it to us on a platter it tastes pretty good.

Berkeley, California

Our school histories, in fact all of our histories put together, do not give us much of an idea of Central Asia in the year 1771. It was that year and place, however, that saw the passing of the Giants.

Owing to this blank space in history—unwritten because no well-known battle took place therein, or any court cabal, or secret confessions of any lady in waiting—the writer will try to sketch the scene a little. The great empire of Genghis Khan had been broken up five hundred years ago. The wave of nomads, the Mongols from the steppe country of Central Asia, had settled back.

So the name of the mighty conqueror, Genghis Khan, was only a legend in the land; the grim figure of the lame Timur (called Tamerlane in European histories) had held its sway among the mountains of Central Asia, and rested now in the tomb.

Other nomads, the Chagatai Mongols—called by us the Moguls—had arisen in the mountains north of Afghanistan, had ruled India, with splendor and wisdom; but their descendants of the peacock throne were only effigies who watched the incoming of the Portuguese, French, and English. Warren Hastings is mentioned in our histories.

But India itself is separated from Central Asia by the Himalayas, and only Tibet had a hand in the passing of the Giants. Tibet—as we call it; the inhabitants term it Po, and the castle-temple at Lhassa the Po-tala—was the religious center of Central Asia, a kind of trans-mountain pope ruling over a hierarchy of priests, with spies, disciples, and a fine system of news collection by mounted couriers. The authority of the Dalai Lama or King-Priest extended from the Chinese side of the Gobi Desert (Pekin) to the outposts of the Russian armies on the Volga, and from Lhassa to the Arctic Circle.

In other words, the Dalai Lama had made himself spiritual master of a space about as large as the United States of America. This space—steppe land in the center, deserts and mountains on three sides, the frozen tundras of Siberia (then called Russian Tartary) to the north—was still held by the nomad tribes, the Tatars. They were not, however, the united Horde of Genghis Khan, but groups of separate tribes, herdsmen, with vague traditions of former battles.

Some were under Russian rule, others—in the Gobi region—were existing under the firm but benevolent hand of Ch'ien-lung, who was emperor of China at the time of China's greatest power. Some more of the Tatar clans were imbued with Muhammadanism, or were allies of the Dalai Lama. But they were—and are to this day—independent chaps. The Torguts especially—the clan called the Giants.

The Torguts, about 1620, during the brief empire of Galdan Khan in the mountains of Central Asia (the empire touched upon in the story "The Wolf-Chaser"), refused servitude and migrated west as far as the Russian border, on the Volga. There they built villages and remained, contented enough with fighting and cattle raising.

Meanwhile the various Muscovite states were absorbed into an expanding empire under the vigorous hand of Peter the Great and, after him, Catherine. The Torguts were threatened with taxation, and with seizure of their sons by the Russians. To escape servitude, a second time, they chose to migrate to their homeland at the headwaters of the River Ili, then unoccupied. Ch'ien-lung had extended them an invitation to do so.

And they did it. At the time no one thought it possible; the distance was three thousand miles, it was then the dead of winter on the snow-bound steppe. They had the disadvantage of covering the coldest region of the journey in a temperature around zero and crossing the two deserts and the Alai Bagh in midsummer. They also had their herds with all their possessions to transport.

Estimates as to the numbers of the Torguts vary somewhat. Palias calculates that 150,000 Torguts set out from the Volga; the annals of Ch'ien-lung mentions 40,000 to 50,000 tents (more than 200,000 persons). But it is known that only 70,000 survived to reach the Ili. In other words, seven out of about seventeen souls lived through the journey.

You see, they had to fight their way; the tribes along the route, and especially to the south, were hostile, the Moslems vindictive, the Cossacks gave them two stiff battles, and their own lamas were deceitful—anxious to betray them if anything was to be gained by it.

This journey of the Giants has been called "a colossal trek." So it was—the last of the great men-movements of the world.

As to the rate of progress made by the Tatars, I have set it down as it happened. Thirty to fifty miles a day at times under the conditions sounds like a tall order. Yet it was done. Also the 150 miles of the Hunger Steppe, or desert, was traversed in three days. This was necessary because the "yellow" water was found to be undrinkable.

How they managed for fodder for the herds on the snow steppe I do not know. Of course the beasts died off rapidly and it is rather a miracle that a portion of the herds endured for the first half of the journey. As for the camels, they got along well enough and the ponies, it seems, dug into the snow at times for grass underneath.

On their journey they carried off a European, who appears in the story. This man was eventually released and sent back with a quota of followers, reaching the Russian border safe, after earning the confidence of the Tatars. The character of Zebek Dortshi, chief of the Red Camel clan, is puzzling, first because I have not seen elsewhere any record of a Tatar noble who betrayed his clan and the name itself has not a Tatar sound. So I have set him down as being one of the ilkhan chiefs, a man with Persian blood in him.

The cult of the bonpas *among the Tibetan monks has a curious story. Magic originally had no part in the Buddhist ritual of the* tsong-kapa. *But the disciples of Buddhism who were establishing themselves in Tibet about 1100 AD found the native devil-worship too strong to wipe out. So the home-bred conjurers, the* mik-thru tse khen, *were enrolled in the priesthood of the Buddhists. Eventually the devil-worshipers became the prime movers among the mountain monks. So the originally humane doctrines of the Sakyas became a most degenerate thing. Today in Lhassa there is a quarter of the town devoted to the magicians.*

The Torguts are usually mentioned as "Kalmuks." The word Kalmuk is Turkish and means something like "remnant of a tree." It is a kind of nickname and today is applied to various native tribes in Turkestan and Mongolia. But the Tatar clan of the story called themselves Torgut, the Giants, and that is their rightful name.

July 20, 1923: "The Three Palladins"

Genghis Khan is almost unique among the conquerors of the world, because he came out of the desert. No armies were ready to his hand: no cities offered him the thews and sinews of war. He had had no schooling, of the book variety.

When he was fifteen or sixteen this chief was at the head of a tribe of forty thousand tents, about two hundred and fifty thousand souls, all told. He was surrounded by enemies. The northern Gobi Desert was—and is—much like our northwestern plains. A place of extremes of cold and heat, of a never-ending struggle for existence.

Out of these high prairies, just below the Arctic Circle, the Mongols rode to the conquest of China, and—as we know them today—the Himalayas, Afghanistan, Persia, and northern India. Eventually his followers overcame the Russians, the Magyars, and defeated the Hungarians and the knighthood of Germany in Silesia.

We have gained the idea that the Mongols were a great mass of barbarians that conquered their enemies by weight of numbers and a vague kind of ferocity. As a matter of fact the Mongol Horde numbered only a hundred and fifty thousand horsemen. It had no infantry. Sometimes, of course, it had allies.

Instead of having numbers on his side, Genghis Khan usually had the smaller army, and displayed strategic powers of the highest order.

It is rather amusing that our histories should try to teach us that the Mongols and Tatars were unthinking barbarians when our language uses the phrase "catching a Tatar" to imply a clever trick.

To rank Genghis Khan with Caesar and Alexander would raise quite a clamor of protest. Just by way of starting the debate—both the Roman and the Macedonian were generals of great empires that had been established before they were born, while the Mongol had only a tribe of herders and cattlemen to work with. Also Caesar and Alexander were products of a high civilization—both carefully schooled. Their conquests did not extend as far as those of the Mongols. (By the way, neither of them had to tackle the Great Wall of China.) The enemies they encountered were of a lower order of intelligence—always, in Caesar's case, usually in Alexander's. They did not find in their path such cities as Pekin, Samarkand, Bokhara, and Herat.

It usually happens that the feeling of the men of an army for their leader is the best possible indication of the leader's character. No man, the proverb runs, is a hero to his valet. Certainly no commander ever fooled his enlisted men.

While Caesar and Alexander were trusted and admired by the soldiers who followed them—Alexander particularly—both had to deal with mutinies at various times. Genghis Khan was beloved by his warriors. It is said that, in a battle, the Khan would give his horse to an injured man. One of his followers was frozen to death holding a fur windbreak over the sleeping king during a blizzard. In the annals of the Chinese—his enemies—appears the phrase that he led his armies like a god.

It looks as if Alexander were a greater strategist than the Mongol, but as a leader of men and as a conqueror Genghis Khan ranks ahead of him. And of Napoleon, too, for that matter. In comparing the achievements of men of other ages we have no standards except results. The empire of Napoleon fell to pieces before he died, and before that—there was Waterloo, you know. And then crossing the Alps is not quite the same as taking an army over the Himalayas.

The story of Genghis Khan is one of those things that grow on you in writing, and for the last year I seem to have gathered enough knowledge of the Mighty Manslayer to try to tell his story. As to that, it is a story that never will be told in full because the Mongols, unlike most nations, kept no annals. There are no "tombs" to be opened. So one has to proceed from Mongol myth—the few legends, anecdotes, that have come down to us—to the histories of the enemies of the Mongols. That is, to what the Persian, Arabic, Greek, Chinese, and Russian chroniclers have said about Genghis Khan.

No work for three years has been so full of interest in the doing! The tale is imaginative for the most part, but is based on events that actually took place. Prester John for instance—legendary as far as medieval Europe is concerned, but a real king in the annals of Asia.

The "pony express" of Genghis Khan in the Gobi is rather interesting for the reader who remembers the pony mail of the far West in the late sixties and seventies. I'm working up some information as far as possible on the relative speed made by the Mongol couriers. They covered more ground in a day than our express riders, but conditions were in their favor.

Mingan is one of the vague shadows of history—a prince of Cathay who acted as guide, councilor, and friend to Genghis Khan and his sons, and who, in fact, built up the wisest and most enduring part of the Mongol system of government. Ye Lui Kutsai Mingan is known to present-day historians as Yelui Chut-sai.

The Missing White Race

The missing white race of China. Now there's a subject that smacks loudly of adventure. Harold A. Lamb brings it up, and we know from his stories of Khlit the Cossack that Mr. Lamb is no stranger to the past of Asia. He and Major Quilty have been corresponding, and the following letter from Mr. Lamb is the result. Can any of you throw additional light? And if Dr. Beech is one of us I hope he'll tell us more about the strange people mentioned below.

New York City

Here's a point I'd like to pass along to the fellow members of Camp-Fire.

Major T. Frank Quilty, Constructing Quartermaster, Columbus Quartermaster Interior Storage Depot, Columbus, Ohio, is the man who asks the question. This is the question, quoted from his letter.

According to recent investigations, the Blond White Race, or Nordics (our race), now confined to Western Europe, at one time spread across Asia as far as the confines of China. The farthest Eastern subdivision was known as the Wu-Suns or Hiung-Nu in Central Asia, referred to in Chinese annals because of their blue eyes, as the Green-Eyed Devils.

Do you presume there is the slightest trace of the Nordic race left in these regions? Turkestan, according to Madison Grant (of the American Geographical Society), was at one time as blond as Sweden; the shores of the Caspian being, as regards race, as are now the shores of the Baltic. Bactria, "The Mother of Cities," has been, within historic times, a distinctively Nordic city.

A pretty big question, this. And the more you think of it the more interesting it gets. Did the white race at one time overrun Central Asia? And has it left traces which can be found today? Did the tribes of the great region from the headwaters of the Yenissei to the Indus, from the Caspian Sea to the western border of the desert of Gobi, have white forefathers?

Major Quilty says, in a second letter, that—whether Central Asia was ever dominantly Nordic—is open to debate. He adds that Bactria was found by Alexander to be inhabited by a distinctively Nordic people. And that there are—he believes—some Nordic traces still to be found in Afghanistan and in Turkestan—quite distinctively in the Mongolized Kirghizes.

Now, getting down to fundamentals, Madison Grant, who ought to know, explains that the Nordic race, unlike any other, has the long skull, light eyes, and, usually, blond hair. A tall race—that of (in ancient times) the Persians, Phrygians, Gauls, Goths, Franks, Saxons, Angles, Norse, and Normans.

It is the adventure race, as Major Quilty says, par excellence. *And it's interesting to picture to ourselves the ancestors of the Vikings and Celts sweeping across the highlands of Mid-Asia, driving the round-skulled, slant-eyed, and stocky races before them.*

Madison Grant says this actually happened, between 1200 and 600 BC. He mentions by way of proof the Aryan languages, Sanskrit and Old Persian, which were established in Northern India and Mesopotamia. Also the fact that remnants of an Aryan language have been found in Chinese Turkestan. (As to this, didn't the explorer Stein find, in the sand-buried cities near Khoten in Chinese Turkestan, traces of a language similar to Sanskrit?)

So much for language. Madison Grant, from the viewpoint of the scientist, adds: "Some traces of their (Nordic conquerors) blood have been found in the Pamirs and in Afghanistan. It may be that the stature of some of the Afghan hill tribes and of the Sikhs, and some of the facial characteristics of the latter, are derived from this source."

Language and history having given us, briefly—they probably have a lot more to say, if some one will print it out—their points, we'll ask the question of the explorers and adventurers.

Marco Polo says a lot about the mythical kingdom in Mid-Asia, of Prester John, the Christian. But this is no mention of an Aryan race. Marco Polo's story shows he saw, or heard of, an Asiatic people or tribe with an immensely wealthy and powerful ruler who may or may not have been a Christian.

Other medieval explorers speak of the "fair faces and tall bodies" of a semi-Tatar tribe situated about the eastern end of the Thian Shan Mountains—the Naimans, I believe. These were not the Kirghiz, mentioned by Grant.

Two other medieval priests who traveled across the caravan routes past the Pamirs and Chinese Turkestan (as it is now called)—Fra Rubruquis and Carpini—tell of handsome and tall tribes in the interior, but of no race which resembled Europeans. Naturally, the priests did no skull-measuring. Probably it would not have been a safe thing to try on the Central Asian tribesman of the sixteenth century!

In modern times C. A. Sheering, of the Indian Civil Service, in his trips along Tibet and the British borderland, ran across a tribe in the Southern Himalayas of the Khasia race, which, he states, "is certainly Aryan and connected with that branch of the great Aryan race which spread itself over the great Gangetic Valley." (In the Vedic times mentioned above by Grant.)

And then, out of a clear sky, comes this story of a modern missionary—Dr. Joseph Beech, president of the West China University at Chengtu, who was twenty years in China.

Dr. Beech says he saw "a tribe of good-sized men, who, for all I could see, were exactly like the Bohemians." (Note: Madison Grant states that the modern Bohemians are of the round-skulled races, like the Asiatic Tatars.)

Furthermore, he says:

My friends told me of another tribe which, as one Chinese put it, "are just like you." I was not able to visit this people. They live in the district of Sung Pan. It is ten days' journey, or about 300 miles northwest of Chengtu.

This tribe resembling Anglo-Saxons was described to me as consisting of large, furious men, whose bravery is considered somewhat of a marvel to the Chinese. "They never run away any more than you do," my Chinese friend told me. "They love to fight."

I was told the men often fight duels on horse-back which recall the duels of the Middle Ages. The duellists start the fight with a discharge of short blunderbusses—so heavy they rest them on a wooden cross attached to the saddle-bow. I judged they were made by native workmen, and rather inefficient weapons, hurling a handful of slugs.

The second stage of the duel is fought with stones, of which each has a bag. If the bags are exhausted without serious injury, the duellists draw nearer and throw spears tied to the ends of ropes so they can be pulled back and thrown again. Meanwhile the two horsemen are circling around and constantly getting closer.

In the final stage the antagonists ride up to each other and fight hip to hip with great swords, after the fashion of Richard the Lion-Hearted. The duel always goes to a decision, my Chinese friend told me.

(Has anyone ever seen a Central Asian tribesman with a "short blunderbuss," or short gun of any kind?)

Dr. Beech mentions a medieval castle that he saw on the border between China and the tribes country "which was totally unlike Chinese architecture."

Possibly the Chinese friends of Dr. Beech—the Chinese enjoy a good story and are prone to exaggeration—were describing one of the tribes of the mountain Kirghiz, who are good fighters and better horse-thieves. By the way, the Kirghiz tribes are not confined to the steppe around the western Thian Shan. Their auls *stretch north and east, well across the borders of Mongolia and into Siberia. E. H. Wilson, the naturalist, was ten years in the country around Chengtu and mentions no Aryan-looking tribes.*

Dr. Beech is now in this country. Perhaps someone in the Camp-Fire knows him, or his experiences, and can get word to us from him.

Perhaps some tribes of Aryan descent are to be found in the interior of China, between the Kuan Lung Mountains and the headwaters of the Yang-tie (the Sung Pan Ho and the Ta Ho rivers).

Mongolian Archery

A reader named Frank Huston, well informed in archery, asked a series of bow-related questions of a number of *Adventure* authors. Of Harold Lamb he asked "how the Mongolian archers compared with the English longbowmen, both as to range and accuracy." Here is Lamb's reply:*

New York City

I was greatly interested in your remarks on archery, British and Mongolian. As it happens, one of my tales, just in the process of completion, deals with the fortunes of an English archer among the Mongols in the early thirteenth century.

In reading the annals of the Mongols—or rather the histories of other nations that deal with the Mongols, for they left few written records of their own—I've gleaned only fragmentary ideas of the use of the bow by the Mongols. It was their favorite weapon, and was of vast importance in winning victories. They used—in the time of Genghis Khan—a heavier bow than the Chinese, the Persians, or Turks. Fighting invariably from horse back, they were able to outmaneuver and out-range their adversaries. More than once they dealt decisively with elephants; the quilted armor of the Chinese did not serve to stop their shafts; or linked mail of a single thickness.

I gathered that the Mongols were accurate to a considerable distance with their short, powerful bows; they had a habit of bringing down chosen warriors of the enemy with shots in the eye and throat. I remember one incident where a khan of the Tatar Horde sent as presents before battle a very heavy bow and silver arrow to his enemy, a Turk (for which read Persian or Kankali or Kurd, at pleasure), with the remark that such bows were very strong and such arrows shot a long way. The Turks could not handle the weapon.

History does not record the English archers ever opposing the Mongols in or around the Holy Land. It is most probably the case that an English yeoman with the longbow could send a shaft further and more

*This is my prefatory remark rather than Arthur Sullivan Hoffman's. The reader's letter was quite lengthy and dealt with bow matters addressed to other writers, so I have extracted only the relevant question. —HAJ

accurately than a Mongol (all Mongols were archers). It is doubtful if he could send shafts more swiftly from the bow, or work greater execution at close quarters. And as for comparing them mounted, a reasonably good archer of the Horde could set his horse to a gallop, discharge three arrows at a mark—such as a spear stuck upright in the plain—unstring his bow, use it as a whip, string it, and shoot another three shafts, behind his back after he passed the mark.

All of which brings us to the conclusion that at the butts the English yeomen would outshoot the Mongols; also that a regiment of the same English archers would have small chance of holding their own against an equal number of Mongols in open warfare. Remember when the Mongol Horde ran up against the Russians, Poles, Teutons, Huns (Hungarians) at the Danube?

Disputing Racial Theory

One of you wrote us a long letter, enclosing an article from the Dearborn *Independent*, but since, contrary to Camp-Fire custom, he did not wish his name printed with his letter, neither name nor letter is printed. However, I sent it to Harold Lamb of our writers' brigade, who as you know is an old crony of Genghis Khan, Prester John, Tamerlane, et al., and his reply makes plain the general drift of letter and article. He's always a good man to turn to for help, for he not only knows whereof he speaks but handles everything thoroughly—in this case, having omitted one point from his first letter, he was good enough to write a second.

Berkeley, California

I've discussed the J. S. letter with several men, from anthropological, archeological, and historical angles. A couple of these chaps are authorities, more or less. Here's the gist of what we threshed out:

1. S. has the merit of being sincere, and plainspoken.

2. The theory, that the yellow race is a product of black and white, is not proved in any way in the enclosed data, or elsewhere. In fact the contrary can easily be proved.

By the various tests (anthropologically speaking) the white man is fundamentally different from the black and is actually between the black and yellow. (Take one test, body structure: Black—long legs, short body; white, long legs, long body; yellow, long body, short legs.) Anthropologists deny that you can produce the yellow man by breeding black with white. Prove it by nature of hair, color of skin, shape of eye, skull formation, etc.

I know nothing about that, but it looks to me as if there is almost nothing behind this theory, and a well-organized trench system against it.

3. Take history. Dr. Legendre says that the Huns brought great num-

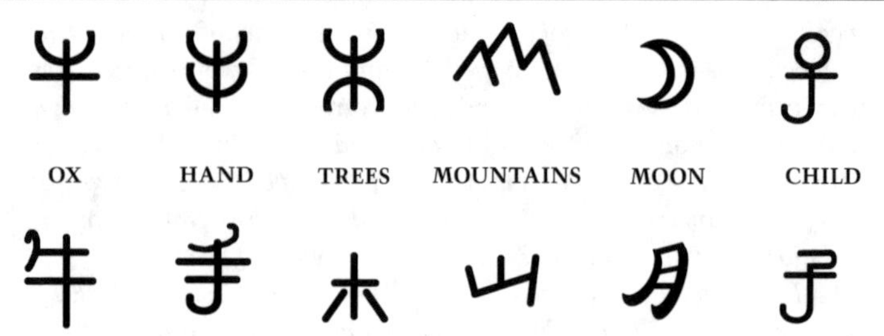

bers of conquered blacks—slaves—back to Central Asia and China. The evidences are against this. Where and when did the conquering Hunnish tribes ever have direct contact with the blacks? He assumes that the present yellow peoples of China are a product of a possible white Hun race, and a possible infusion of slave blacks. The Huns (Mans, Vandals, Mongols, etc.) never crossed the seas.

Legendre also draws in Babylonia, and Egypt, to explain Chinese ancient culture, arts, etc. There's been a lot of bunk poured out about ancient Egypt. DeLacouperie and others have taken pains to trace the source of early Chinese writing to Egypt. Early Chinese ideographs are nothing more or less than modified picture-writing.

I've seen enthusiastic "scientists" take just as many pains to identify early American picture-writing with the Chinese. There are resemblances. And you can easily find resemblances to the above ideographs in the pictures drawn by a five-year-old child, and Kipling's "Just So Stories."

Same with the "Babylonian" lions, griffons. The formula is this—"There were lions in Babylon and bone lions in China; ergo and therefore the grotesque stone lions of Chinese art were derived from Babylonian art." How? Well, the Persians took Babylonian art to themselves. Chinese trade caravans came into contact with Persia—and so on.

All this is hypothesis. So with the Chinese dragon.

Undoubtedly—and this has been ascertained by the explorations of Sir Marcus Aurel Stein, Sven Hedin, French missions, etc.—Chinese art owes much to Greek, and more to Aryan India. Just as the Buddhist-morality Chinese system of living owes much to Buddhist India and Tibet.

But, because certain beginnings of Chinese art can be traced to Greece and India, remotely, is no possible reason for denying that the early Chinese had a typical art and a typical culture.

(I have before me a series of reproductions of Persian, Arabic, and Turkish miniature paintings of the eleventh to seventeenth century. From the archives of the Bibliotheque Nationale. And the Persian and Turkish painters of the fourteenth century used Chinese technique.)

The point being that Legendre is "full of prunes, pink 'uns" when

PAGODA ROOF

TATAR TENT

he says that since these borrowings can be traced, there is no native Chinese art.

You can trace one of the most typical features of Chinese architecture to the Tatars. The drooping, curving roof lines.

But it's absurd to argue that because the Tatars had tents, the Chinese had no architecture. And what of the purely Chinese inventions—cross-bow, BC *400; gunpowder,* AD *900; paper, silk, astronomical instruments, clocks, etc.,* ad infin.?

I've never seen Legendre's book, and can't place him, except that his work seems to have appeared in L'Illustration *rather than in the* Revue des Missions Archeologique, *etc.*

Most of what he says is quite so, and has been said before. The present-day Chinese are *a conglomerate of different races, speaking different dialects, even separate languages. The origin of the earliest "Chinese" is uncertain, but is placed pretty definitely in the Gobi, west of Shansi, which was then a fertile land.*

And it's true that instead of being a pure-strain, awfully ancient and mysterious and cultured race, the Chinese have interbred with different conquering nations, have borrowed most of their culture and its ideas. But the net product is Chinese, not Aryan mixed with negro bastards.

It seems to me that Legendre is arguing like most Frenchmen, from theory to fact, instead of from proved fact to theory.

Take his point that the armies of Attila, Genghis Khan, and Tamerlane, etc., were not made up of yellow men, that is, of Chinese and Mongols only. Perfectly true, in a way. Take the horde of Genghis Khan. It was made up, eventually, of Kankalis, Kiptchaks, Ouighurs, Naimans—Ural-Altaic tribes, or Turko-Mongols. Also of Keraits, Mongols, and Tatars, and the ancestors of the present Manchurians, Koreans, and native Siberians. The Mongols were only one tribe of nomads that eventually won leadership over the others.

These tribes, the Turko-Mongols, as we call them, fathered in a very early day the American Indian, later the Huns, then another branch, the Mongols, the Moghuls who conquered India, the Manchus who conquered China. They were always hard boiled, remarkably interesting, and warriors par excellence.

Remnants of them are found, as Legendre points out, in Bulgaria, and the Balkans today, in the Finns and Kalmuks of Russia, as well as the Circassians of the Caucasus and the Caspian region.

The origin of these horse-riding nomads who came out of Central Asia and overran more than half of the earth is one of the nicest questions of modern research. To summarize hugely—the nomad Turko-Mongol is the descendant of the Scythian and the Scythian is "x" in the equation. Who was *he?*

Arthur Brodeur answered that question. The Scythian was the man who lived in Scythia, which is ancient Turkestan, BC 1000. *What kind of man was he? He called himself, collectively, the* Tokharoi *and other things, and he had a writing, which is now christened Tokharian, and resembles both Sanskrit and German. Branches of him spread into Kashmir and Tibet, and established civilizations.*

Was this Tokharian, as we may call him, a nomad out of Northern Europe? Or was he a highly cultured Aryan of Persian ancestry out of the Mesopotamia basin? He seems to have been Aryan, witness his writing, his weapons. But, little is known about the gentleman, though information is coming in yearly.

Hence the persistent rumors of "white" civilization in ancient Central Asia—the early Chinese references to "blue-eyed barbarians." Our legends of "White Huns," etc. And we hear that Genghis Khan had red hair, and that Kublai Khan looked like a "white" man. Throwbacks?

Well, we have traced this Aryan, horse-riding, Sanskrit-like writing and long-sword-fighting chap back to 1000 BC *and we aren't in the least sure how white he was then. Perhaps he was then more white than yellow and he certainly wasn't negro.*

But when his children, a couple of thousand years later, came out of Central Asia, our fathers in Europe didn't see any family resemblance at all—in fact called them devils. They were the Huns, the Alans, the Vandals, etc.

And when his grandchildren came out of Central Asia about twenty-three centuries later, our ancestors called them servants of Antichrist, and spawn of Gog and Magog, and "Tatars." And our ancestors ran away from them. And, though there were many Nestorian Christians among the Mongols and they seemed really eager to claim the European Christians as brothers of a sort, the Pope and all would have nothing to do with them. So our Tokharian's great-grandchildren became either Muhammadan or Buddhist.

Enough of this! But you can see why it's illogical to say, as Legendre hints, that Genghis Khan and his Mongols were "white" men, and, because of that, victorious conquerors. They were victorious because they were good fighters, and had remarkable leaders.

It's like Prester John. Our medieval ancestors believed from var-

ious tales that an enormously wealthy Christian monarch ruled in Central Asia, a white man.

The fact of it was that Wang Khan, one of the Keraits (Krits, hence "Christians"), ruled that part of Central Asia, that he was a Turko-Mongol who wandered about in barbaric splendor and some of his family were Nestorian Christians, and a large part of his people likewise.

So Genghis Khan was a Turko-Mongol nomad, whose ancestors probably were Aryan two thousand years before, who had red hair. He wasn't a white man in the sense that St. Louis of France, who lived about the same generation, was a white man. He was Genghis Khan, and a wonder at that.

To yawp that Genghis Khan was a white man, whose children were bastardized by negro captives, and produced the Mongols of today, is simply the bunk.

As an afterthought, on the Seller-Legendre, yellow race, descent of Mongols matter—the most important point was left out of my letter. The most important ethnological point, dating back a couple of thousand years. That is, the Mongol-Tatar tribes are not wholly of Turkish extraction. It follows, that they are not wholly of Indo-Scythian descent.

I have a lot of respect for the German, Professor Friedrich Hirth. This is what he says of the people between the Sea of Aral and Korea: "The Huns should be looked upon as a political and not a racial union. The Huns proper, as the dominant race (about 300 AD) were probably *of Turkish extraction. So were the Hiung-nu, their predecessors in the east." (Note the Hiung-nu—Wu-sun, Yue-chi, etc., are the chaps that had Aryan forefathers, maybe.) "But the Hiung-nu as a political power comprised ancestors of the races which we now separate from them as being of Mongol and Tungusic extraction."*

All of which simply means that the Huns who wandered over into Europe were part of a confederacy of Central Asia tribes that were variously descended—part Indo-Scythian, part Turkish, part aboriginal Siberian.

Now, glancing at a book written by d'Ohsson, who was an authority on the Mongols in his day, we find this: "There were three distinct races, Turks, Mongol-Tatars, and Tungusis, or Tchortes (Devils)."

This is encouraging, because it fits with what a lot of modern ethnologists say that there are three different races, the Turks of Central Asia, the Mongol-Manchu tribes north and west of China proper, and the Esquimaux tribes up under the Arctic circle.

Everyone disagrees heartily as to whether the American Indian is descended from the Esquimaux (as the Lap and Finn are) or from the Mongol-Tatar-Tungusi-Manchu layer, a little way south of the Arctic regions. I asked an ethnologist out here from whom the Mongol-Tatar-Manchu-Tungusi chaps were descended, and he said, "From the

Chinese, of course." No one knows where the Chinese came from. So there we are! Authorities say so many different things about the ancestry of the Central Asia people before 200–300 AD *that a modern story-teller like myself can't summarize their opinions.*

The legends of Central Asia, the Prester John mystery, the White Huns, the sand-buried ruins of the Gobi, the unknown Tokharoi and their language, the remnants of Alexander's Greeks, the Aryans tucked away in the mountains here and there, the red-haired conqueror, Genghis Khan, all these are intensely interesting to us today and we are just beginning to get at the facts behind them. It's the greatest treasure house of the world, and that's why men like Stein, Sven Hedin, Koslof, Hoernle, Andrews, Osborne, Huntington, etc., are devoting their lives to the exploration of Central Asia. The secrets hidden away there loom gigantic.

But as to the S.-Legendre (as quoted in the Dearborn Independent) *line of argument that there never was a yellow race, and that the armies of Genghis Khan conquered most of the world because they were white men, well, I pass the yellow race on to ethnologists. As to Genghis Khan, it's not often that a serious-minded fiction writer can say to a scientist, "You're drawing on your imagination, old chap."*

There was, among Genghis Khan's horde, a kind of affinity for Christians. Remember that after the generation of St. Thomas and St. Andrew, many early Christians penetrated Central Asia. They were Nestorians, mostly, and built churches all the way into Sinkiang in China. Among such tribes as the Keraits, the Christians were very numerous—hence the Prester John legend.

In the day of Genghis Khan these Nestorian Christians, the tribesmen of the Gobi region, had almost forgotten ritual and reading, but clung to the symbol of the Cross, and to semi-barbaric prayers. They were probably better Christians than most of us in America today.

Anyway, the Mongols were, literally, death to Muhammadans. But they dealt, for them, leniently with the semi-Christian Georgians of the Caucasus and really spared the Armenians. Marco Polo and the first Jesuits were kindly received at "Kambalu" Khan-Váligh—King's City, and Kublai Khan is said to have been half-Christian in his ideals. The Nestorian churches still existed. Hulagu, the Mongol prince who conquered Bagdad, wiped out the Assassins, etc., and protected the Christians in his province. (I've read a contemporary Muhammadan account that complains of how the "cursed Nazarenes" put on their best garments, men, women, and children, and paraded the streets openly, with songs, on the day that Hulagu issued his decree. Also, this Mongol threw open the Sepulcher to Christians. His wife was one. His successor, Abaka, was also.

At this time the Mongols in the Syria sector sent several letters to St. Louis, the Pope, etc., urging that the Franks and Mongols unite in driving the Moslems out of Syria and Egypt. But the Christians were too busy scrapping among themselves. And when the Mongol khans requested priests from Europe, two or three barefoot Jesuits were sent, brave men, but lacking authority, prestige, or presence. By degrees the Mongols in Asia were converted to Buddhism, in Persia, the Black Sea region, etc., to Muhammadanism.

So much for lost opportunity and the narrow-mindedness of our medieval European princes and Popes. We've sent enough missionaries since into all Asia and accomplished infinitely less than could have been accomplished then.

About the Author

Harold Lamb (1892–1962) was born in Alpine, New Jersey, the son of Eliza Rollinson and Frederick Lamb, a renowned stained-glass designer, painter, and writer. Lamb later described himself as having been born with damaged eyes, ears, and speech, adding that by adulthood these problems had mostly righted themselves. He was never very comfortable in crowds or cities, and found school "a torment." He had two main refuges when growing up—his grandfather's library and the outdoors. Lamb loved tennis and played the game well into his later years.

Lamb attended Columbia, where he first dug into the histories of Eastern civilizations, ever after his lifelong fascination. He served briefly in World War I as an infantryman but saw no action. In 1917 he married Ruth Barbour, and by all accounts their marriage was a long and happy one. They had two children, Frederick and Cary. Arthur Sullivan Hoffman, the chief editor of *Adventure* magazine, recognized Lamb's storytelling skills and encouraged him to write about the subjects he most loved. For the next twenty years or so, historical fiction set in the remote East flowed from Lamb's pen, and he quickly became one of *Adventure*'s most popular writers. Lamb did not stop with fiction, however, and soon began to draft biographies and screenplays. By the time the pulp magazine market dried up, Lamb was an established and recognized historian, and for the rest of his life he produced respected biographies and histories, earning numerous awards, including one from the Persian government for his two-volume history of the Crusades.

Lamb knew many languages: by his own account, French, Latin, ancient Persian, some Arabic, a smattering of Turkish, a bit of Manchu-Tatar, and medieval Ukrainian. He traveled throughout Asia, visiting most of the places he wrote about, and during World War II he was on covert assignment overseas for the U.S. government. He is remembered today both for his scholarly histories and for his swashbuckling tales of daring Cossacks and crusaders. "Life is good, after all," Lamb once wrote, "when a man can go where he wants to, and write about what he likes best."

Source Acknowledgments

The following stories were originally published in *Adventure* magazine: "The House of the Strongest," November 20, 1921; "The Gate in the Sky," February 20, 1922; "The Wolf-Chaser," April 30, 1922; "The Net," June 10, 1922; "The Road of the Giants," August 30, 1922; "The Three Palladins," July 30, 1923 (part 1), August 10, 1923 (part 2), and August 20, 1923 (part 3); "The Book of the Tiger: The Warrior," June 23, 1926; "The Book of the Tiger: The Emperor," July 8, 1926.

The following stories were originally published in *Collier's* magazine: "Azadi's Jest," November 11, 1933; "Sleeping Lion," November 27, 1937.